CRIMEU

Can You Dig It?

A Murderous Ink Press Anthology

****

Murderous Ink Press

CRIMEUCOPIA

Can You Dig It?

First published by Murderous Ink Press
Crowland, LINCOLNSHIRE, England
www.murderousinkpress.co.uk

Paperback Edition ISBN: 978-1-909498-74-7
eBook Edition ISBN: 978-1-909498-75-4

Acknowledgements

To those writers and artists who helped make this anthology what it is, I can only say a heartfelt Thank You!

And to Den, as always.

Contents

Let's Dance On, 'Til The Music's All Gone.... vii
Making Music, One Last Time — Wil A. Emerson 1
Music Keeps Me Sane — Robert Petyo 17
Handled In-House — Avram Lavinsky 23
Rachmaninov Forever — Dave Dempster 41
An Artful Death — John B. Elliott 49
The Songwriter — Jon Matthew Farber 63
The Girl Who Loved Beethoven — Wendy Harrison 71
Listener Favorites — Martin Zeigler 83
Finding the Groove — Ed Teja 95
Allan Longstreet's Blues — Victor Kreuiter 113
True Crime — Geoff Boswell 141
Sub Rosa — Diana Parrilla 151
Last Dance at the Discothèque — S. B. Watson 171
Bittersweet — Jay Andrew Connor 185
Dirty — Harris Coverley 217
The Usual Unusual Suspects 239

Let's Dance On,
'Til The Music's All Gone....

(An Editorial of Sorts)

We'd like to welcome you to the Crimeucopia *Palais de Dance—*

Where we hope you'll find somethin' given half a chance....

And while our house DJ starts stacking the decks, we open this Crimeucopia Roadshow with *Wil A. Emerson*, who hopefully isn't *Making Music One Last Time*, followed by *Robert Petyo*, telling us that *Music Keeps Me Sane.*

Meanwhile, although *Avram Lavinsky* says that everything will be *Handled In-House*, *Dave Dempster* returns, proclaiming *Rachmaninov Forever* (and please, no chanting *Dies Iraie* in the cheap seats, thank you.)

John B. Elliott allows Rochwal to almost have a night off, with a meal, a show, and *An Artful Death*, before *Jon Matthew Farber* recounts about Steven Hitt, *The Songwriter*. From there *Wendy Harrison* invites us to say 'Hello' to Zoe Tanner, and *The Girl Who Loved Beethoven*, leading *Martin Zeigler* to do a quick poll and update us on his *Listener Favorites.*

Ed Teja then puts the needle to the record, which is really the only way of *Finding the Groove*—and Canadian *Victor Kreuiter* gives us a rendition of *Allan Longstreet's Blues.*

DJ and Radio Jock, *Geoff Boswell*, hums along while he attempts to clear up some dark time *True Crime*, which opens the gateway sliding us down the slippery Noir slope that, according to *Diana Parilla*, is all parr for the *Sub Rosa* course.

S. B. Watson leads us to the edge as he offers us the *Last Dance at the Discothèque*, while *Jay Andrew Connor* goes 1980s retro Goth, and gives us a 7" Radio Edit version in the form of *Bittersweet*. And while he insists that all lyrics and band names are fictitious, they are, sadly, also indicative of his "disgustingly lowbrow tastes in music."

All of which allows *Harris Coverley* to get down and *Dirty*, before we spiral into *The Usual Unusual Suspects*, and have the runout groove trigger the lift and let it return the tonearm to its rest.

So, before you put another coin in the slot and press the buttons again, we hope you've found something that you immediately like, as well as something that takes you from your regular toe-tapping finger-popping comfort zone—and slips you, gently or otherwise, into a completely new one.

Because, no matter how many times you go round-an'a-round-an'a-round-an'a round, in the 5/12 time signature of our *Murderous Ink Press* motto:

You never know what you like until you flip your fiction wig and read it.

See you all at the runout…

Making Music, One Last Time

Wil A. Emerson

A rap on the door broke the late evening reverie.

"Nine at night. Why?" Hilary Fischer shook her head. She had no good reason to get up, a book propped in her hand, her portable night light curled around her neck. She paused. How long would he wait when he didn't hear her shuffle to the bolted door?

Her eyes shifted back to the book. A paperback with a bold, colorful front. A male and female braced back-to-back. Rippling muscles on his broad bare chest, dark wavy hair falling across his pensive coffee eyes. She with a mass of swirls and curls, a mix of submissive blond and vixen red. Green beguiling eyes, the same bright shade as Hilary's. Halfway through the tale of misery and woe, did Hilary want to lay the book aside?

Truth was, Hilary loved this genre. Melancholy romance, she tagged the series. Mismatches, derangement, forced marriages, unrequited love. One day she might meet the author and ask what prompted her to engage in such writing? Had she been heartbroken at an early age or were the pages just products of a wild, speculative imagination? Perhaps she thought she was an 'artist', too.

Hilary knew there were few true artists. Hollywood flashes in the pan. Their notions so off the left coast they should be dog paddling in mid-Pacific, as they mimicked the life of others. Well, who wouldn't try to be an *artist* if someone paid a lot of money and cleverly painted their faces to be free of zits and chicken pox scars? Only fools watched what was projected on gigantic screens. Exploiters, certainly. Artists, never.

The same with books or music. Wanna bes. No real talent. What about those hip-hop, do-wap, tweakers? Bitches, bangers and broom sticks. Shoot, kill, defile? Stamp your feet. Artists? Hardly worth a walk down the street. But wouldn't you know, the arenas were full of tongue-waggers, tickets in the hundreds of dollars, lines three blocks long. People who craved the gibberish spent their big dollars for these so-called stage gymnasts with their wonky instruments strapped to the sweating chests. Performers of a sort with short term attention. Artists, never.

Hilary turned a page. The lovers had come together again. Not in a tethered sense. Nor in the biblical spirit of uniting as one. The plot spinning to a possible conclusion the couple might overcome their differences. This was the part Hilary liked the most. At this point, if she were writing the book, she'd add a nine-millimeter weapon loaded with hollow-point bullets. Murder him, why not? Happy endings were a fallacy.

Rap, rap, rap. Louder, more energy behind the knock. Her reading light blinked. Almost as if the percussion on the wood door had interrupted the battery life. The digital band wrapped around her neck spurted. Momentary darkness startled her more than the feigned drumbeat at her door.

Only one way to get rid of a pest. She placed a book marker on her page and slipped out of bed. No need for a robe. The intruder was well accustomed to her loose tee shirt. Tonight, she wore a favorite and had no intention of covering it up.

With the chain still attached to the bolt, Hilary inched the door open.

"No surprise. But you know it's after nine. I don't socialize after nine."

"I didn't come to socialize, Hilary. I'm here to celebrate, make music. Your violin, my trumpet." Gregory Telemann smiled. His teeth white, a minor space between the incisors, his dark wavy hair falling across his left eye. He propped his arm on the frame of the door.

"I'm reading. That's celebration enough for me." Hilary gritted her teeth.

"It's our tenth, you know. And ten is a perfect number."

"Your hands are empty. Where's your trumpet case?"

"I'll show you my trumpet after I kiss the crest of your neck where you prop your violin. After I kiss and suck each luscious finger that holds those taut strings."

"Oh yes, our once-a-year romantic, sexual encounter. How could I forget?"

"Don't go nasty on me, Hilary. I really need to see you." He leaned his shoulder on the door. "I'm so lonesome. I cried myself to sleep last night."

"You didn't practice? We have a big performance coming up, you know."

"And you know, I have trouble before a performance. Can I just sit with you for a few minutes? If you play one piece, Vivaldi or Mozart. Yes, Mozart, Concerto number 3. It's magical in your hands. It will sooth my troubled soul."

"Are you begging, G.P.?"

Hilary released the chain and let him in. She called Gregory Telemann by the famous maestros' initials in her weakness moments. Only because the sound of Gregory's trumpet, in the horn section of the symphonic orchestra they performed in for the last ten years sounded blissful when they first met. As remarkable, spiritually fulfilling as the classical masterpieces once played by the great George Phillipe Telemann of whom Gregory was a far and distant relative. His music, his rendition of classicals, had captured young Hilary's attention, fostered the attraction between her and the introverted, minimalist guy. They spoke the same language when they had their instruments in their hands.

But Gregory didn't have his black leather bag with the brass handle which held his beloved trumpet with him. Which meant only one thing. Gregory needed, wanted, expected Hilary to play his god given 'trumpet'. That weird, awful, withered thing, useless through the years, which only offered minimal satisfaction on a rare day of sprouting. Gregory wanted Hilary to bend to her knees and do *it* for him. Gregory often confused wants and needs.

Yes, this could have been an anniversary event, their official tenth, but she had filed for a divorce the week after their ninth celebration.

The first year of marriage, she didn't mind giving him anything he wanted. Nor did she in the second year, but then the wick fluttered, by the third anniversary, the candle faded. Out—no light at all. It took six more years for Hilary to say enough is enough.

If Gregory had only shown a little more interest in her, it might have helped Hilary find him in the books she once liked to read. And he did practice his golden trumpet relentlessly, though, the music worthwhile if not perfection, but then he flopped on the bed at midnight too exhausted to even utter 'sweet dreams'.

Another setback came for both of them when he didn't get first chair as planned. He stopped washing, tending his clothes, paying the bills, eating out. He went to a few doctors who diagnosed him as a tense 'artist' with mild depression. He accepted the prescriptions to help him relax. Baclofen, his go-to when under stress, tense muscles and all that. Relaxed him, all of him, it did.

Hilary had a zombie in her apartment who only had enough energy to practice a trumpet. Yes, he did muster the strength to attend the required concerts and received the minimal paycheck as an orchestra member. After each performance, though, he sank into bed each night like a nutrition deprived mega-mouse. Long limbs, skinny torso, useless tail.

This wasn't the life or love of her dreams.

Hilary, knew she was the real artist in the family. She played first chair. She also earned the bigger salary, paid all the bills, arranged every meal, and cajoled her husband into functioning for the sacred orchestra. To the point she resented every single aspect of his being. Her only outlet in life was the two hours she took to soak in a tub, sip a glass of wine and read novels. Those fantasy books did not in any imaginable way mimic her life. Six days a week, she worked. On the seventh, no matter what day it turned out to be, because of the variety in performances, she tried to concentrate on Hilary. Tried.

Finally, she indulged herself and filed for divorce. In turn, with a heavy nudge to his back, Gregory moved out.

Hillary was happy to give up the child-man care. Nearly a year gone by and he was still living with his mother. Yes, they still saw each other at performances, traveled on the same buses for out-of-town gigs and sat for publicity photos when the management requested. Yet, Gregory to this moment, had not signed the defining, end of marriage, union termination papers.

However, since the break-up, Gregory turned up at least once a month, all charming and romantic. One frigging night, every month. Like clockwork. That little diddly thing sprung to life and its owner wanted it and him to be welcomed at Hilary's door. Rap, rap, rap.

What Gregory didn't know was Hilary had recently added another layer to her repertoire. She had met a drummer at a music store two months before and he played in a real rock and roll band. All too soon, she couldn't keep her hands off his stick. Plus, he had introduced her to the mystery genre. A whole new experience for her. Larry, being a huge fan of Josh Pachter, Jake Bates and Earl Staggs, encouraged Hilary to read her story after story of mysteries and murder. To her delight, most of the readings were conducted after an hour or two of extreme love making.

Larry, drummer boy, did suggest she read James Patterson on occasion, but cautioned high intrigue had left the author's muse. He told her that the lesser-known authors, the aforementioned writers, were better choices to broaden her awareness of criminal elements in the real world.

Too bad Larry Tutt was on a road gig this night and not with her. He'd most likely have taken his drum sticks to Gregory's soft shelled head and beat him to death.

As it were, on a lark, Hilary decided to let Gregory go forward with the seduction ritual and then just at the peak of his performance, she'd thrust out those old, parched divorce papers and demand his signature.

Pay to play.

If she could get him to agree to a permanent, binding split she might have a chance to make real music, day and night, with the wonder of her life. Mrs. Lawrence Tutt carried such a melodic tone and Hilary wanted very much to be married in every sense of the word.

Of course, her mother would have been almost as delighted as her daughter knowing her daughter had fallen for a drummer. Larry's last name being the same as Jerry Garcia's first drummer, the joyful woman would have showered Hilary and Larry with affection and a mountain of gifts. If only her mother had lived longer, Hilary would have all the platitudes and adulations she craved.

Yes, she'd long wanted daughter Hilary to follow in Jerry Garcia's footsteps. Play a Doug Irwin guitar and rock her way to fame and fortune. To the very top of the entertainment world. Maybe she could buy and rename one of Irwin's masterpiece guitars. Take a Wolf or Tiger in her hands and transform it. Danger Zone and Cheeta Pinkie, more suggestive of a female rocker, hit Berkley, California like thunder. Hillary could shake rooftops with her genius art, rock and roll masterpieces. Sad to know, her mother would never learn of Hilary's success, though.

Hilary tried so hard to please her mother, play the guitar, love its strings, to feel the music a timbered guitar could make, but her heart strings weren't there. Her grandmother, a strict European old gizzard of traditional and classical music, had given her a violin. 'Oma' expected Hilary to embrace every note, sound, tension, tempo of great music. After all, the Fischer family came from a long line of violinists. Oma's ancestors had filled the best European concert halls since the beginning of time. In Leipzig or Vienna, Johann Fischer and Dietrich Becker were still mentioned in casual musician speak. When teachers and performers gathered, they talked talk as if they were members of the Fischer and Becker families themselves. Hilary was indeed a Fischer and, thus so, had a natural talent for the violin. Oma started Hilary's lessons when she was only four and, thus, the voice of strings were imprinted in her veins.

Of course, she, also, had daily reminders of the greatness of her heritage. At that time, she lived with Oma nine months out of the year. The other months, broken up in days or an occasional full week, she was her unstable mother's daughter. Caroline didn't have a home, she stayed in hotels, someone's spare bedroom in a walk-up, a house with a swimming pool with dozens of 'friends' living together. But every year, around Christmas, her mother would visit Oma and stay a night or two in Oma's neat, uncluttered, warm house that smelled of fresh bread and sauerkraut. Stacks and stacks of music sheets were the only disarray in Oma's home.

Because of the distinct nature of the aromas young Hilary grew up with, she became unconsciously familiar with her grandmother's and her mother's differences. Her mother's sleeping quarters were full of what Oma called nefarious odors. Hilary learned in her early teens there was a vast difference between sauerkraut and marijuana.

Hilary's mother Caroline, named thus because of her grandmother Helga's love for German music, had nary a gift or liking for anything traditional, classic or German. When she turned sixteen, she ran away to shack up with a guy who played in a rock and roll band. Helga figured he was married but the law wasn't on her side when she tried to force daughter Caroline to return home. When Caroline turned eighteen, she changed her surname to Adams. It wasn't too many years later she called herself 'Mountain Girl' and continued to live the carefree live of a roadie who offered benefits.

Just about the time Hilary began to understand her mother's inherent nature, a cultural Joan of Arc who sought true freedom from societal restrictions, her beloved mother died in a car accident. The messy kind that people don't like to talk about in respectable quarters. Married man, exposed in a particular way, woman pressed underneath the steering wheel. No, the conversations and descriptions were hushed especially when Oma was explaining the situation to her granddaughter.

Hilary never connected in any meaningful way with Caroline 'Mountain Girl'. At one time, they might have laughed together. Instead, Hilary remained with Oma and stuck to playing beautiful, heartfelt, meaningful, classical music. A success in the making. True to her heritage. First chair violinist in a not-so-small Midwestern city's symphony orchestra. Perhaps Boston or New York in the future. Oma died with a smile on her face.

Hilary mingled within the circle of respectable, traditional musicians. As fate would have it, Gregory, her first love, turned out to be a big, lazy nerd, and Hilary's thoughts grew to sky-rocketing proportions on how to get out of the withering marriage. Like a painful ingrown toenail, Gregory hung around. All of nine years. Yes, finally, Hilary filed for divorce. But damn, Gregory wouldn't sign the final decree. Something had to be done.

Larry Tute, neither traditional or unconditionally respectable, was eager to make a new life for Hilary and made it clear he wanted permanency by throwing away the excess belongings of the hang-on husband. And because Larry shared his love for reading mysteries, it led Hilary to believe there might be other options for ending the marriage to Gregory.

So now sat Gregory in the soft, gray leather chair that he once called his own. "You know, Hilary, you gave me more than I deserved. You were the perfect wife."

"Oh, so that's what you've come to tell me tonight? To tell me I *was* the perfect wife. But Gregory, what am I now? Soon to be divorced. Long overdue, don't you think?" She eyed him suspiciously.

"We have wonderful memories together. Remember those first few nights. Delightful wouldn't you say?" He almost swooned.

Hilary chuckled, "Yes, I remember. Two virgins, twenty-two years old. Stumble, fumble, trying to get our act together. What fun." Then she gritted her teeth.

"But practice made perfect. And on every anniversary, we relived those glorious days when you…you know…you said you wanted to play my trumpet. That first time, your hands, your mouth…oh why, oh why can't we make it a perfect ten? I want you so bad, Hilary, I can hardly breathe." He leaned forward, tears in his eyes.

"Is that why you wore those light blue sports shorts, Gregory? So I couldn't miss the rise in your crotch? Let's get real, Gregory, I'm not the girl I used to be. And, definitely, you are not the man I want to spend the rest of my life with."

"I've changed, too, Hilary. You're right, I haven't been much of a husband. But I'm willing to try again. That's why I didn't sign the divorce papers. To prove I could change. I'll sign the papers tonight just to have you one more time. But only if you unfold your luscious lips and make it as if you are playing Mayler's 3rd symphony. Yes, I will scream with joy, sign those papers and walk away."

"Just that easy, huh?" Gregory had taken her by surprise. Wasn't she the one who wanted to bait him into signing? Why the turn-about? Was he being sincere?

"Let me think about it. Would you like a glass of wine?"

"That sounds so celebratory. Great idea." Gregory almost panted. He squirmed in the soft leather chair, adjusted himself and made sure he had easy access to his increasing organ. Marginal now, but a few more gestures from Hilary and he was sure he would rise to the occasion.

"Red or white," she asked.

"Whatever you're drinking."

White wine was her favorite, two glasses and she got lightheaded. Inhibitions lifted. A rarity for Hilary, but then he never could be sure which way Hilary might go. Truth, too, usually he was too tired after practice to remove those Grateful Dead tee shirts she constantly wore.

If orchestra members knew she dressed in loathsome Garcia rags at home, they would be mortified. Of course, it was a married couple's little secret, never to be shared with others. Of course, there were other secrets not to be shared, too. No embarrassments for either him or her.

"I decided to have a Stella Artois in a tall glass, of course," Hilary said on her return. "Brought one for you, too."

"Oh my, that's a surprise. Well, maybe I should join you." A profound change. Beer? Perhaps this was the beginning they both needed.

Hilary handed him the glass. "Cheers," she said. "Or maybe I should say 'Prost'. Oma always said that."

"Your grandmother drank beer?"

"Of course not. An aperitif occasionally. Prost means 'may it be beneficial'. A Latin phrase but it is fitting now, don't you think?"

She eyed the sport shorts again. Ole sly Gregory making a move? One way or the other, Hilary wasn't going to let this opportunity go to waste.

"Why don't we sit on the deck? It's a lovely night. Look at the stars. My great, great grandmother was an astronomer you know."

"Fischers have always been talented women. You are the most artistic, my dear. The notes you render, your lips perfectly formed for pleasure, makes a mortal man weak in his knees." Gregory sighed.

"You can't get it off your mind, can you? Maybe it was my mistake to make you a slave to one simple act. And only once a year at that." Hilary giggled.

The memory of the first time did have a degree of pleasure in it. If she wasn't careful, she might convince herself that she could enjoy it again. One last time? It had its appeal. Play Mahler's 3rd for him? How about Gregory playing some Wynton Marsalis. Any one of his Grammy award recordings. That would blast those yearnings into orbit. And then Hilary would end this evening with her own personal, perfect wifely concoction. Make a splash dear Gregory couldn't refuse.

"Hilary, I have something very important to tell you." Gregory propped his feet up on the deck railing and gazed at the sky. "I've decided I need order in my life again. And you are at the helm of it. Like I said, I wasn't the best husband."

"Okay, what's up your sleeve? What redemptive action could possibly be taken that would change my mind about a divorce?" She would toy with him a little longer. Yes, the moonlight was delightful, the beer was refreshing, and the stars were spectacular. But Gregory was still a dud, and she was one blow job away from final closure. Moving forward with a man who would never cease to disappoint her.

"I have a surprise. I'm weaning off the Baclofen and taking Viagra. Two tonight to get me started. Two hours ago. The doctor says I have about a four-hour window. That gives us plenty of time, don't you think?" He smiled and leaned closer. His eyes wide, he fluttered his eye lashes.

Evidently, Gregory was convinced he could charm Hilary into submission. The eye lash trick? Where or where did he get that from?

"Gregory, you sure have your ways. But a promise is a promise. I *will* means you *sign*." Hilary took another long sip of her beer.

Gregory gulped his drink, "You mean you're going ahead with this tenth-year celebration. A perfect ten, oh my, Hilary, I can feel the blossom. Shivers coming, it's on the rise. I'll sign to prove I can give you what you want. Then if the doctor's right we can do it again anyway you want. Of course, my first desire is always your lips. Do, re, me. I can feel the rhythm.

Hilary laughed. "You do say the sweetest things."

"Look, Hilary, it's working," he finished his beer and adjusted the opening of his shorts. "Let's do it right here. Under the stars. We've never done that before."

"We haven't, have we?" Hilary looked behind the small table at the end of the deck where she had placed a yoga mat. Where she laid with Larry Tutt and practiced the drummer's march. "I'm concerned we might be seen. Moonlight and all."

"Does it matter? But please, take off the Garcia tee shirt. I don't like his eyes staring at me. Intimidating, you know. He was such a ruthless stud."

"My mother adored him. I'll take it off and put it under my knees. But how about another beer. I'm very thirsty. It's better now than to break away later just to rehydrate." She smiled.

"Yes, yes. I can wait."

Hilary hurried to the kitchen, filled the glasses again and carried them to the deck. Gregory had arranged the chairs so they were facing each other.

She handed Gregory his glass, eyed the windows of the apartment that were a direct view, saw the shades drawn and removed her cotton tee-shirt. She folded it in a neat pile in front of Gregory's chair.

Gregory gazed at Hilary's lank body. Her breast not large, round small apples. Her hips were curved, her stomach had a fold, her thighs not quite slim but well within the margin of feminine. Who was he to complain about minor flaws? His chest had formed ripples, not all muscle, but his arms were firm after years of holding his trumpet. And his cheeks were big enough to hold an entire breast. That is, if he stayed awake long enough to do another verse. He gulped the beer, licked his lips and parted his legs.

Hilary grasped the medium appendage, it definitely was firm. More than she remembered. The Viagra or absence made the hard-on harder. With it in hand, Gregory squealed.

"Shhh, you'll wake the neighbors." She thumped the mid portion. "Ahhh," she murmured. The motion made Gregory squeal. Hilary's ordeal was almost over. One big swipe and he'd burst like a balloon.

Hilary rested back on her heels. "Are you satisfied, dear husband?"

"Spent," he said as he leaned back in the chair. "Drained of energy and senses."

How could he be? She had done the work so he could climax. Considering it was the nature of the beast, she didn't reply, but sat on the chair, in her half-naked state and gazed at the moon.

"A half-moon. I love sitting our here."

"If you're chilly, I could get you something to put on. I think I still have a couple of long sleeves shirts in the closet."

Wishful thinking, Hilary knew. Larry had carted Gregory's shirts to Goodwill the day after he slept over. She grabbed for the favored Jerry Garcia shirt on the floor. Hilary slipped Jerry over her head. "

This will do. Any plans for the rest of the evening." She took a small sip of her Stella Artois, just to get the lingering taste out of her mouth. She didn't want to ruin the pleasure of the newly acquired habit: delightful light beer. Larry loved it and she wasn't going to miss any chance to drink it again with him.

"I would love if you played one melody on your violin. Something soft and romantic. You have such a way with Tchaikovsky's music."

"Tortured soul that he was, I do love his Adante. It's not showy. It is filled with light and hope." She left out the part about darkness and shade. Why spoil Gregory's fantasy of continuing this false marriage.

"Perfect. My god, I think I've said 'perfect' a hundred times tonight. If not vocalized, then thought. The whole time your lips surrounded me, I was breathing 'perfect, perfect, perfect, perfect'. Oh my god, my penis is still perfectly hard." Gregory laughed.

"That it is, Gregory. Let's go inside and I'll play that 'perfect' piece. Then how about your favorite, fast 'perfect' late night meal. Then we might do a 'perfect' round of lip syncing in bed." Hilary giggled like a schoolgirl.

Gregory followed her, his hand cupped around his throbbing penis. "Viagra, perfect."

Hilary stood in the middle of the room, no music stand needed. She'd learned the notes when she was eleven years old. There hadn't been a week gone by that she hadn't used it as a refresher for rhythm and cadence. She could play the music and still think of other enjoyable moments like the murder mysteries she'd been reading with Larry.

"Oh my, Hilary. No wonder you are first chair. Excellent. And perfect," Gregory chuckled. "Shall I sit again and let you perform your magic." He paused, "I'm the witty one tonight, aren't I? It must be a side effect of the perfect blue pill."

"What a side effect to embrace," Hilary kissed his cheek, "Now 'perfect' husband, let's have that 'perfect' late night meal."

"You're not going to tell me it's creamy peanut butter on toast, are you." Gregory smiled.

Hilary was sure his knees would go weak. "That, indeed, is what we'll have. Then we're going to wrap ourselves in a perpetual hug and make music again. Look, you are sprouting like a husk of corn. Take that marvelous, perfect specimen and sit on the deck again. We'll enjoy out feast out there. Finish the Stella before it goes flat. I'll bring you another."

"I know where you like your peanut butter the best," he said with a broad grin. He cupped the Viagra induced organ and strutted back to the deck.

Hilary wasted little time with the dinner preparation. The necessary ingredients were on the first shelf of her cupboard. Jiffy smooth peanut butter, white bread. Even though Gregory hadn't mentioned the divorce document after her performance and not surprised by his lack of action, she wasn't going to deny him the pleasure of one last late evening meal.

The special powder, MSG one might call it, had been stored away just in case an opportunity arose to use it. It would enhance the effects of Gregory's euphoria. Saved from the year before, she sprinkled it between the two slices of bread. Like sugar, it disappeared into the creamy peanut butter.

Gregory chomped into the sandwich as if it were Russian caviar. Something Oma had introduced Hilary to when she was a teenager. Something she'd not eaten since she'd been paying off Gregory's debts.

"I'm in no hurry. Obviously, this chemical wonder is not going away," Gregory said, "truth be known, I took two of the blue capsules. This should last twice as long. We could sleep for a while and then play the second verse. Does that work for you, darling wife Hilary?"

"Perfect expectations," replied Hilary. She'd looked at her watch. Twenty minutes max and the Baclofen, in powder form and Gregory's previous drug of choice, would blend as the perfect elixir. Perfect, perfect, perfect. Time on Hilary's side.

Gregory finished his peanut butter sandwich and rested back in the chair. "I thank you from the bottom of my heart and the tip of this marvelous tool that is protruding out of my shorts." He laughed like a schoolboy.

Hilary closed her eyes, not to rest but to settle into a calm state of mind. The time issue, reaction, meshing of muscles and nerves, Gregory's wane could be momentary or could take thirty minutes. The miracle of chemistry was not a well-controlled art. Gregory finished his Stellar, then his head began to nod. The perfect time had arrived. She placed the divorce papers on the small table.

Gregory stood, "I do think, dear wife, I must go to bed. This rocket I've got will work if you would like to straddle it, but my mind is yearning for sleep. Off to bed, dear wife."

Gregory still had not added his signature to the document. Hilary knew he didn't have the core strength to terminate their union. It would reveal in his mother's eyes he was not the 'perfect' husband.

However, she had promised Larry Tutt she would spend her life beating his drum. She indeed could gain control of Larry's baton.

Gregory wobbled. His knees began to fold, then struggled to remain upright.

"Catch your breath," Hilary said. "Get centered. Three beers, dear husband."

She marveled at the effect. The Viagra still had a hold on this usually lame band member.

Gregory leaned against the railing, his knees folded again.

"Yes, G.P.," Hilary said, this had been the perfect ten. She placed her hands hard on his thin chest. And then she pushed him.

* * *

Gregory died with his hand cupped on an organ he could not play well. He'd tried one last time and failed.

The death was investigated, scrutinized per the laws of the state. Gregory had a history of abusing muscle relaxers, Baclofen the chosen drug. He had multiple sources of supply, a long paper trail.

The Viagra? A veil of tears from Hilary. They were attempting a reconciliation. How could she have known this would be his swan song? Their last musical night together.

Of course, his sudden death was reported in the Daily Centennial, in the features section. He was not a headliner like Wynton Marsalis and, thus, did not warrant the upper fold. He was a fourth chair trumpet player in a large Midwest town. Never would he have been first chair and, thus, the obituary was only four lines.

Sadly, it was noted Gregory did not like Jerry Garcia.

It didn't take long for Hilary and Larry to form a duo and went on to rock the music charts. They made a fortune with a funky mix of traditional rock and classical violin. Mozart would have applauded from his grave. Mountain Girl momma would have been proud, too. Oma might have died with a frown if she knew Hilary play popular music, but the whole world now listened to her beloved granddaughter, Hilary, play a mean violin.

Music Keeps Me Sane

Robert Petyo

I can't say exactly when the first punch was thrown, but I can pinpoint when the whole song got rolling. That would be when Screwdriver, sitting to my right just off top C on the piano, called me a baboon. Not that it bothered me. I don't think it was a racial thing, and that wouldn't have mattered anyway because I've been called a lot of names, and there ain't much these people can do or say that bugs me. All I care about is my music. The booze flows pretty easy in the club. People get a few drinks in them and they act up a little. No big deal. What else would you expect? I just shut it all out and focus on the piano. It's what keeps me sane in all this madness.

So they can call me a baboon if they want. Believe me, I been called a lot worse.

But my buddy Tommy Boy took offense. Tommy is one of the regulars. I call him Tommy Boy because he looks like a little kid. He's pushing fifty, but he looks like a kid. Big wide eyes. Nice caramel brown skin. Flawless. Not a wrinkle on his face. Me and Tommy Boy go way back. He does a dynamite version of *Bridge Over Troubled Waters* that brings tears to your eyes. He's good for three or four tunes a night, but that night he was kind of quiet. It was coming up on one o'clock and he hadn't asked to do a song yet. A real looker in a slinky dress did *Fever*, and a hairy stud with a leather jacket and rings in his ears did *Satisfaction* and *Honky Tonk Women*, but nothing from Tommy. A few times I had to turn around to make sure he was still there.

I figured he was down about Trish. She and Tommy were having a rough time. I figured we'd talk about it after hours. Tommy Boy always stayed after the bar closed to yak for a while and keep me company while I cooled down. We'd talk about his new grandkids. He'd brag and show me pictures. Tommy was an okay guy.

Anyway, the bar circles around me and my baby, although people get their drinks from the other bar that's against the wall. They sip their drinks at this bar, which sadly has its black marble chipped in quite a few spots. But they sit there to sip their drinks and hear me play while a few of them grab the mike and sing a song. I've been at Eighty-Eight Keys for eight years now, and it ain't the classy place it used to be. As the neighborhood went down, so did our customers. But one thing never changed. Whatever the type of crowd, all they want is a good time.

That's where I come in. I sit inside the marble circle and all I got is a small opening behind my stool. Sometimes I sit there for two hours before taking a break. Behind me on the last seat on the right is where Tommy sits. Fridays and Saturdays without fail. Once in a while he shows up during the week, but he's a weekend regular, and he's always alone. He never brings Trish. He's a computer programmer. He's got two kids and two grand kids. An okay guy. Good singer. Could have been somebody if he wanted to try my business, but he was too busy raising his kids.

Not like me. I left the wife and kids. They were holding me back.

Huh? Oh, sorry. Back to that night. How it works is this. The people sit at the bar that surrounds my baby and I play whatever they request, usually "oldies." Believe me, I don't get stumped often. I try to get everybody to sing along, and if anybody wants to do a solo, I give them the mike. I go all night. Only take two breaks. Because I like to play. I'm having fun. The people are having fun. I'm a piano man in a sing-along bar. What could be better?

Of course, I don't think I'll be playing at Eighty-Eight Keys anymore. Maybe nowhere else, either. At least not for a while.

What? Oh, sorry. Back to the night of the fight.

Like I said, this guy sitting just off top C calls me a baboon. He'd been drinking screwdrivers all night, getting louder with each one. He and his buddy, a big blond surfer type, were talking about how the Blacks were always looking for a free ride in this country. Of course, they didn't call them Blacks, but you know what I mean. I heard Screwdriver say that he wasn't going to pamper them just because some slave owner used to whip them hundreds of years ago. Surfer Dude said something about bringing back lynching. Said it would solve a lot of problems. I couldn't hear everything they said. Didn't care really. I just kept playing, hearing bits of their garbage when there was a break in the music, or if I needed a sip of water. Singing dries me out.

Huh? Oh, sorry. I'll stay on point. I knew they were chatting up some pretty sick stuff, but I kept playing. That's what I was there for.

I knew Tommy Boy heard them, too. He was a couple seats away from them, but I knew he heard. But stuff like that don't bother Tommy Boy. He says it just shows how ignorant bigots are.

That's why his reaction is hard for me to understand.

I had just finished *Crocodile Rock*, one of my favorites. The crowd really got into it. Even some of the tables in the back. I don't always get the back tables singing along, but that time I did. Anyway, I finish the song, and Screwdriver says, "What is he, a baboon?" I don't know his exact words, but it was something like that. Anyway, it didn't bother me. Like I said, I been called worse.

And I don't think it was a race thing. The guys were bigots. No doubt about that. But I think the baboon thing came from my feet. You see, I don't wear shoes when I play. I have white loafers but I kick them off when I sit down. I like the feel of the pedals on my bare feet. Can't do it any other way.

Anyhow, this guys says something and Tommy Boy starts shouting at him. "You apologize to my brother right now." Now, Tommy and me aren't brothers. I'm not Black. My Mama was a Puerto Rican and my Daddy was Syrian. That's where I get this skin. A lot of people think I am, but I'm not a Black guy. Brothers in music. That's what Tommy meant. At least, I think so. We were pretty close. Like I said, he spent some long nights with me. I know a lot about him and his wife. Their problems. I don't know, maybe we were kind of like brothers.

Huh? Oh, sorry. Back to the riot. Tommy Boy keeps hollering at him to apologize. Pretty soon Surfer Dude starts shouting, too. Other people try to shut them up, but they keep goin' at it, and pretty soon everybody joins in. See, we get a mixed crowd at Eighty-Eight Keys. About fifty fifty White and Black. But we never had no problems before. Everybody just wants to have fun. Now, I'm sitting there trying to figure out what to do. The shouting was getting out of control. All I could think of doin' was to play. So I go into *Shout*. I did it earlier in the night and I don't usually repeat myself unless I get a special request, but it was the first loud tune that popped into my head. And it usually got people singing along. So I started playing and singing, and a few people tried to join in, but by the second verse I knew everybody was watching the fight, or was in it.

Like I said, I don't know exactly when the first punch was thrown or who threw it. I was busy playing and most of the action was behind me. I heard punches. I heard a table flopping over. Some glasses smashed. But I kept playing. What else could I do? I went into *Great Balls of Fire*.

We only got one bouncer at Eighty-Eight Keys. Big bruiser named Roscoe. He's really a sweet pussycat, but he knows his job and knows what he's gotta do so he acts like the kinda guy you never want to mess with. We never have any trouble anyway, least not till that night. He usually keeps things under control. But this was worse than anything that ever happened.

The front window of the bar shattered. I was in the middle of a minor chord and froze for a sec. Somebody put a chair through the window. The sign was out, sputtering sparks across the sidewalk like an old drunk spittin' up. It musta snapped some other connections 'cause a few more lights went out. But my light stayed on, so I kept playin'.

I forgot was song I was in the middle of, so I changed up and started *Runaway*.

Out of the corner of my eye I see Roscoe dragging Screwdriver to the door. He had him in a major league headlock, and Screwdriver's feet flopped behind him like loose fire hoses. He almost got him to the door when the cops arrived.

Two White cops.

I knew that meant trouble.

The streetlights washed over them as they stood blocking the doorway. Big helmets and thick vests. Carrying clubs. I could see a few cars outside, too, lights flashin'. I tried to soothe things with a nice ballad. I started *What a Wonderful World.*

That was when somebody threw Tommy Boy over my bar. He slid head first across the piano, bashing his head into my tip jar. It shot off the edge and crashed to the floor. Crumpled bills flitted around like moths. Tommy Boy lay there with his feet and hands dangling off opposite ends of my baby.

I stopped playing, but only for a second. What else could I do? He kinda deadened the sound, but I kept pounding the keys. I really believed that my music was the only thing that would calm these people down.

Somebody climbed on top of Tommy Boy. I think it was Surfer Dude, but I can't be sure. He whacked Tommy good. Again and again. It threw my rhythm off and I had to change tunes. Tried another ballad. *Wonderful Tonight.* On a normal night that one gets some lovers up dancin'. But not last night. Too much goin' down.

My eyes were wet—with tears or sweat, I don't know. I kept playin' and watched as Surfer Dude, if that's who it was. Like I said, I'm not sure. Anyway, he clamps his hands on Tommy's throat. His head flops toward me and I see his eyes bulging out. His lips are moving like he's trying to take a breath. Or maybe he was trying to talk to me, to ask for help.

But what could I do? I'm just the piano player. Roscoe takes care of those kind of things. That's his job. So I kept playing.

I watched Tommy Boy. I could barely see him through my tears, but it was all I could do. The guy never let up. He kept banging Tommy's head down.

Just as I start playin' *New York, New York*, the shots start up. People start scattering. They dive under tables, the ones that are still standing. They try for the door, but the cops are still blocking it. There are more cops now, trying to settle people down. But they keep snagging people who try to get out. It was terrible. People screaming. The cops started clubbing people. I saw Slinky Looker twirl in the air, blood pumping out of her chest like water from a busted pipe.

But I keep playin'. I try to focus on my baby. Things'll calm down, I tell myself. As long as I keep playin', things'll calm down.

More cops. A few more shots. But finally, as I was finishing *Piano Man,* things start to calm down. The place was pretty much empty by that time. A lot of people got out, and cops chased 'em. People were crying. Some were still shouting. I went into *Imagine*, my personal favorite.

That's when I realized that Tommy Boy was still sprawled across my baby. Surfer Dude was gone, but Tommy was there. Not movin'. I swear to God I didn't know he was dead. Even when the cops grab my hands to stop me from playin', I didn't know. Do you think I woulda sat there and played if I knew he was dead? If I really thought that dude was killing him, do you think I woulda just sat there and played? What the hell was I supposed to do? I'm just one guy. I'm just a piano player for God's sake. That's all. I couldn't have saved him. That's your job. You cops were supposed to control things. Tell me. What was I supposed to do?

Handled In-House

Avram Lavinsky

Rochester, New York, 1989

Walking out of the frat house into the crisp spring air, Karl LeBlanc, best known as the bass player for Windegard, found his band's box truck missing and his own teal-blue Chevy Corsica crushed. He closed his eyes, certain that all the weed and the booze was playing tricks on him. When he opened them again, nothing had changed. The entire roof of his car had been crunched down to the level of the hood as if a Tyrannosaurus Rex had teethed on the sedan and then set it back down right where Karl had parked it. It was an '86, barely two years old, not even close to paid off, and now reduced to a crumpled pile of scrap metal and spare parts.

Stunned and disoriented, he staggered back to the frat and through the front door. The common area was a vast space. The mics, mic stands, and front-line speakers were gone, but the risers were still in place, as were the amplifiers and the drums. The place smelled like stale beer, tobacco, bong water, and sweat. Red plastic cups dotted every horizontal surface. Nelson, the drummer, was asleep on a couch, underneath a thin tapestry as a blanket.

Karl sat on the armrest and moaned. "Man, I knew we shouldn't have played here."

"Huh?" Nelson opened his eyes.

"We should have just stuck with what the production company booked. No more last-minute addons. No more booking through friends."

"What are you talking about?" Nelson's voice rasped painfully.

"They loved us. The place was packed. We got paid."

"Come take a look at my car. Then tell me about it."

A few minutes later, the two young men stood shoulder to shoulder, looking at the squashed-down roof of the Chevy.

Nelson pulled a pack of Winstons and a Bic lighter from the side pocket of his cargo shorts. "Yeah. I see what you mean." He lit up and took a long drag.

"How the hell could this happen?"

Nelson exhaled through his nose. "Yours is the only one… flattened?"

They both surveyed the parking lot. It was an expansive gravel rectangle between two large Victorian buildings, frat houses, both several stories tall with sharply pitched gable roofs and rusting fire escapes. No other cars were destroyed or defiled in any visible way.

"And," said Karl, "wasn't our truck right next to me?"

"The truck. Maybe Abel took it…took it to buy gas or get coffee or something."

Karl pressed two fingers to the bridge of his nose and shook his head as if trying to dislodge something jammed into his brain. "What do I do now?"

"We better find Vance," said Nelson. "I think he's in a room upstairs. One of the brothers is away or at his girlfriend's place or something."

The two bandmates returned to the common room of the frat house and climbed the stairs to the second level. The ceilings were not as high as those on the ground floor, but the hallways leading off in either direction were each punctuated with a dozen doors, and they could only assume the third floor would possess an equal number.

"How do we know which room?" asked Karl.

Nelson considered this, squinting and inhaling through what was left of his cigarette until the end glowed bright orange. He tilted his head back and exhaled. "Vance's feet."

"Vance's feet?"

"He wore those boots last night, right?"

Karl pictured Vance, the band's guitar player and singer, on stage the previous night. Always sensitive about his stature at five foot five, he'd worn boots with three-inch wooden heels. "Yeah. The snakeskin ones."

"The *fake* snakeskin ones." Nelson found a quarter-full red plastic cup on the floor and dropped his cigarette butt, which disappeared below the rim with a brief hiss. "His foot odor is always bad, but it's absolutely toxic when he wears those synthetic boots."

Nelson went to the nearest door, got down on his knees, and sniffed the crack at the base of the door, then methodically rose and went to the next one down the line.

Karl hesitated for a moment, then went to the first door on the opposite side of the hall. He stiffly worked himself into a sort of prostrate prayer position and inhaled, detecting only a faint odor of mildew in the sliver of air from the room beyond.

The two continued. Nelson made better time, completing his side of the hall while Karl was still sniffing his fourth room.

The room to that door suddenly swung open to reveal a pretty young woman, bleary-eyed and clothed only in an oversized men's T-shirt. Her jaw dropped, and she stared down at Karl with a look of utter disgust.

"Just looking for a friend," said Nelson, with a grin that might have passed for suave under better circumstances.

The young woman hustled away to the bathroom with her palms held outward in a gesture that clearly signaled *keep your distance*.

Nelson headed back to the stairs and across to the other side of the building, Karl in tow.

At the third door on that side, Karl, after sniffing deeply, nose to the floor, paused, detecting something rank.

A sound, the sniff of someone inside, echoed his own.

He sniffed harder and longer.

Another sniff in response within.

He sniffed a third time, very deeply.

Another echo. And a definite odor.

"Found something?" Nelson came over and nudged him aside with one hand.

Karl rose, swaying, lightheaded.

Nelson drew in a breath at the base of the door. "Aww. God!"

* * *

The coffee in all three decanters had largely evaporated leaving an inky substance that reminded Abel Glasse of black-tar heroin. He drifted to the register and asked the kid behind the counter if he would mind putting up another pot.

The kid didn't mind.

Abel had forgotten to wear his custom earplugs at the soundboard the night before, and the ringing in his head was only a decibel or two lower than the steady tapping of the dripping coffee. He tightened his bandana over the tangled mess of his hair.

The bells on the door of the convenience store made a harsh clacking sound rather than a jingling when the man entered. It jarred the sinus passages of Abel's skull.

The man looked around the store, checking all four corners of the ceiling, then hovered in the chips aisle, handling several bags as if deeply contemplating the ingredients. It was the set of his jaw that bothered Abel. Tweaker? Crack head? Hard to tell.

Abel drew a 24-ounce cup from the dispenser and slid the half-full decanter off the warmer. A single drip escaped from the machine, falling to the heated metal disk and sizzling for a few seconds before it evaporated. As he filled the cup, he snuck a peripheral glance over his shoulder.

The tweaker had angled himself away, and there was no mistaking the bulge at the back of his sweatshirt. Judging by the size, Abel guessed it was a revolver.

* * *

"Hey, guys!" Vance stood in the doorway, a cartoon grin plastered on his face. Behind him, a mirror lying flat across a tiny computer desk reflected a narrow band of light from the edges of a window shade. "Is it time already? Grab some breakfast and hit the road?"

Nelson, on his knees and still dangerously close to Vance's toxic feet, spun away awkwardly.

Karl risked standing his ground. "We have a situation."

Vance's cartoon grin grew impossibly wide. "A *situation*." He seemed to find the word hilarious.

Nelson rose and caught his breath. "We're serious. Did you even sleep last night?"

Vance swung his head to one side with an eye roll. "Sleep. So overrated."

"While you've been binging," said Nelson, "...and not sharing…someone seems to have crushed Karl's car."

"Crushed Karl's car?" Vance's eyes bulged. "Crushed Karl's car?" He repeated the words as if speaking some alliterative language of his own making.

"Yeah," said Nelson. "Crushed in the whole roof. And the truck is missing. Have you seen Abel?"

"Abel? No." He sniffed loudly. "Not today."

"We're so screwed," said Karl. "What the hell are we gonna do?"

"Well…" said Nelson, "probably find some yellow pages and look for body shops. Maybe call the cops."

"No! No, no, no, no, no." Vance's voice went deep like a radio announcer's. "Cops. Not happening."

* * *

Abel Glasse considered leaving the coffee behind and slipping out of the store.

Then the tweaker twisted around and locked eyes with him for a long second.

No. He decided to head to the register, hoping the tweaker would do the rational thing, wait until Abel paid and leave the store before robbing the place.

He pressed the lid onto his coffee and walked toward the counter at a leisurely pace, eyes low. From the horribly scratchy ceiling-mounted speakers, he could just make out the refrain of Creedence Clearwater Revival's "Bad Moon Rising."

The tweaker drifted closer. He took a university sweatshirt off a rack and inspected the label.

Abel placed his cup on the counter, sensing, if not feeling, the tweaker's breath behind him.

"Just the coffee?" said the oblivious pimply kid, ready to ring him up and sounding like he could use a cup himself.

"Yeah." Abel drew his wallet out of his hip pocket.

"I'll take that," said a reedy voice behind him. "And what's in the register too."

* * *

"If we don't get the cops to help," said Karl, "what do we do? We're supposed to play Binghamton tomorrow night. We have no vehicles."

"And no sound system," said Nelson.

"Come on," said Vance, the pasted smile looking even more strained. "The truck will show up. Abel's just screwing around."

"Abel doesn't strike me as the screwing-around type," said Nelson. "Everyone at WGP says he's the best."

Karl had to agree. Sound engineers from their management company, Will Grant Productions, were always good, but Abel Glasse took it to another level. He made great live recordings from the soundboard, and in the larger venues, the house engineers always seemed impressed with his knowledge and his esoteric patch patterns at the effects racks. "So where does that leave us?"

"If we don't want to deal with the city authorities," said Nelson, "we deal with the house authority."

Vance smiled even more vapidly and nodded.

Karl pressed three fingers to his forehead. "I'm sorry. What exactly are you talking about?"

Nelson attempted a Marlborough Man squint. "The frat president."

* * *

Detective Donna Weyland knew all three uniformed officers on scene. Norm Van Tyne, second year on the job, nice kid, unfortunately partnered up with Dwight Ahearn. Ahearn was one of those lazy throwbacks who would always believe that pure tokenism had led to Weyland making Major Crimes.

He greeted her with a thin smile. “Detective.”

“Gentlemen. Let’s block off the lot, assume the whole place is a crime scene for now.” She proceeded through the glass door into the store.

The officer with the cashier was Germain Cassel, better known as Cassy. He was unusually thin with a peanut-shaped head and thick Buddy Holly glasses. A good cop, he was easy-going but methodical and a heavy favorite to make sergeant. Seeing Weyland, he left the kid by the register and headed toward her.

“Hey, Cassy. You were first on scene?”

“Yeah. The kid behind the counter is Sam Oakley, freshman at the University, local kid, Dutchtown. He called it in. Dispatch had it as a 10-20, but our boy, Sam, says the suspect kidnapped a customer to hijack his truck. Got a good look at the perp and the truck but no plate.”

“Any surveillance cameras?”

“Broken since the kid started here.”

“Of course.” Weyland approached the cashier. “Hi, Sam. I’m Detective Weyland. You feeling up to answering a few more questions for me?”

“Yeah,” said the kid, “it doesn’t quite feel real. God, I hope that guy with the bandana’s okay.”

She took her pen and notepad from the inside pocket of her blazer. “Let’s start at the beginning.”

“The guy came in, just poked around a little, then pulled out a gun.”

“What kind of gun?”

“Kinda big. A revolver. Sorry, I’m not a gun guy.”

“You saw his face?”

“Oh yeah. He didn’t wear a mask or anything.”

“Could you describe him for me?”

“Average height, one seventy, I guess mid-twenties, fair skin, brownish scraggly hair.”

She copied down the description. “Anything unusual, scars, things like that?”

Sam shook his head.

“Do you remember what he was wearing?”

“He had on a grimy T-shirt that was worn real thin, couple holes too…but he stole a sweatshirt off the rack, one of the blue university ones.”

“Really.” She noted that as well. “And what happened after he pulled out the gun?”

“There was this customer at the register…with a yellow bandana tied over his hair. I was just about to ring him up when the guy pulled the gun. So the guy made the customer hand over his wallet. Then he made me hand over all the money in the register.”

“And then what?”

“Then he started going mental because it was only like eighty bucks total because we always drop cash in the safe when the register gets over a few hundred. He shouted at the customer, ‘What’s in the truck?’ The customer said it was some music gear, and he could take it all. The guy kept the gun in the customer’s back and walked him out. A minute later, the truck screeched away. God, I hope he doesn’t shoot him.”

“What about that truck? The patrol officer said you didn’t get a plate, but could you describe it?”

“It was a box truck, white. And it had a bumper sticker.”

“What kind of bumper sticker?”

“One with, like, weird lettering, but I’m pretty sure it said *Windegard*. Like that rock band. I saw the same logo on a flier on campus somewhere.”

Detective Weyland jotted down the band name and circled it.

* * *

“So,” said Karl, his mouth going dry, “we were just wondering if you could help us explain any of this cause we’re just not getting it.”

In his faded boxers, Eli Black, president of the Pi Omicron Tau fraternity, gave a stately nod from his perch at the edge of his loft bed made from stud lumber. He had the well-muscled but doughy body of a high school athlete recently transitioned to full-time partying.

Struggling with his role as spokesperson, Karl said, "We…um…thought about maybe calling the cops, but…"

Vance shook his head violently.

"Screw that," said Eli. "We can handle it." He grabbed a plastic sandwich bag and a pack of rolling papers from the exposed plywood by the corner of his mattress. "We'll check with the other fraternities. It's not like there's any magic to asking a few questions and figuring something out." He plucked a seed from a marijuana bud and began rolling a joint.

* * *

Detective Weyland had the uniforms search the parking lot while she called in the BOLO for the box truck, describing the Windegard bumper sticker but requesting that officers question any white trucks with any bumper stickers in case the perp covered it over with another, suspect armed and dangerous, possibly wearing a blue university sweatshirt.

The search of the lot turned up only a burnt spoon and two broken crack pipes, all unlikely to belong to the perp.

Weyland told them to bag it all anyway. "The harder we work, the luckier we get."

She surveyed the borders of the parking lot, emptying her mind, trying to let the scene speak to her. The lot had a subtle pitch to it. It slanted toward one side bordered by a deep gully overgrown with weeds and thickets. All kinds of evidence tended to work its way toward lower ground. Slowly, she walked to the lower edge, inspecting the asphalt for anything out of place. Then, she scanned the gully below from end to end. Something drew her eye back for a second look. Protruding from the tall sedges was a human hand.

* * *

The plan had made more sense while smoking Eli's excellent indica: split up so that they could cover all the fraternities. Karl had drawn Delta Alpha Kappa, the building across the parking lot.

He reached the frat house and pressed a doorbell button gunked up by many ancient layers of paint. He couldn't detect a ring. He tried again. Still no sound. There was a large brass knocker. He banged it three times.

The door swung open to reveal an imposing kid in a triple XL Buffalo Bills jersey with an astonishingly wide jaw and absolutely no neck. "What the hell?"

"Uh..."

"The damn door's not locked." The kid turned sideways.

Karl entered tentatively, eyes down, feeling the kid's leer all the while.

"Who you hear to see?"

"I...uh...the president of the house."

"*You're* a friend of Damon's?"

"No...see...my band played the frat across the lot last night, and someone destroyed my car, and our truck is missing with all our PA stuff."

"So you came here to accuse *us*?"

"No. No, I'm not–"

A bear-like voice behind Karl interrupted him. "Who's the scrub?"

Karl turned to see a guy built like a refrigerator in a Nike T-shirt with the sleeves torn off to show arm muscles like balloons.

"Nobody," said No Neck. He thinks he's cool cause he played music for the burnouts last night."

"What's he giving you a hard time about?"

"He says *we* wrecked his car and stole his stuff."

"No, no! I only said–"

"He wants Damon."

"Damon?" said Refrigerator Boy, stepping closer so that the two enormous bodies pinned Karl against the wall. "I think we can handle this situation ourselves."

* * *

"He's breathing!" Detective Weyland started to lose her grip under the unconscious man's shoulders.

Van Tyne jumped in and relieved her. Cassy shifted his grip from the ankles to the knees, and both officers crab walked up the steep incline to the lot.

Near the top, Weyland noticed a yellow bandana with fresh blood splatter. "We've got another crime scene. Careful where you step."

They set him down on a patch of grass along the asphalt. The face was bloodied.

She knelt by the man's side. "Sir, can you hear me?"

No response.

"Sir. We're here to help."

A dark pool of blood spread along the blades of grass by the man's head.

She pressed a palm hard against his bloody temple. "He's bleeding out. Probably pistol whipped. Somebody grab a bandage. Call EMS. Check him for other wounds."

Ahearn radioed dispatch.

Cassy ran his hands up and down the man's limbs and along his trunk. "I think it's just the head wound."

Van Tyne ran off and returned with a first aid kit. He passed Weyland a large gauze pad. She took the pad and pressed it to the wound. Van Tyne lifted the head and began wrapping the bandage tightly over the pad.

Another siren wailed in the distance.

* * *

"Guys." A voice across the room, not as deep as Refrigerator Boy's, but commanding all the same. A boy, shirtless in blue and yellow gym shorts, walked toward Karl and the two frat brothers. Though not a widebody like the other two, he had the taut, chiseled physique of a Greek god. His expression was dark.

"Damon," said No Neck. "Didn't see you there."

"Go get Panzer."

"Yeah. Panzer." No Neck bounded up the stairs two-at-a-time and disappeared.

Karl found himself staring hopelessly at the ceiling as the seconds dragged.

Then weightier footsteps crescendoed. The stairs creaked and groaned piteously as if they could give way at any moment.

Two enormous feet appeared on the landing. The boy had to bend sideways at the waist and duck his head to clear a section of ceiling as he descended. He had the biggest brow ridge Karl had ever seen.

No Neck followed, dwarfed by the new arrival.

Karl tried to speak, but his throat tightened and all he could manage was a few stuttering squeaks.

"Well," said the shirtless frat president, looking from Carl to No Neck, "I think our guest is a little tongue-tied. Someone else better go on and tell Panzer why he came to us."

No Neck stepped forward and pointed to Karl. "This weaselly little scrub accused us of wrecking his car."

* * *

Detective Weyland had never experienced a more disconcertingly chaotic sound than the inside of the music store. Different timbres, ranges, tempos, and keys started and stopped from every direction. A preteen girl played the power chords to "Smoke on the Water," the sound so distorted that the detective felt sure either the speakers in the amplifier or her own ear drums must be torn. Synthesized strings echoed from another room while further off, a drum fill repeated at odd intervals, and a loudspeaker overhead announced, *Percussion, line two. Percussion, line two.*

"I'm here about the stolen truck," she said to the aging hippy at the counter, shouting into his ear.

He nodded, but his furrowed brow suggested he didn't hear or understand.

"A patrol car identified a stolen truck pulling out of your parking lot."

"Right." He nodded more deeply, then lifted his phone receiver and pressed the leftmost button at the base. Loudspeakers overhead blasted his voice from all sides. *Pro Audio to the front desk. Pro Audio to the front desk.*

A bearded man with an impressive beer gut appeared at the other end of the store and waddled toward Wayland with a forlorn look. Reaching the front counter, he leaned into her to be heard. "You must be with the police."

"Detective Weyland, Rochester PD."

"I suppose we'll be S-O-L for the bass bins and the horns then. Too bad. Would have sold fast."

"Are you saying that the suspect in the stolen truck sold you equipment?"

"C'mon." He turned and motioned toward the back of the store. "I'll show you."

More thunderous drums and piercing guitar amps assaulted Weyland's ears as they walked the length of the store. The bearded man held open a thick padded door, and the two entered a room with square plexiglass windows. He closed the door behind them, and instantly the din outside became barely audible.

"These, right here." He stepped up to two enormous cube-shaped cabinets with a textured black plastic skin and recessed metal handles on the sides.

"Those are speakers?"

"Bass bins. Really good ones. A JBL twenty-four-inch speaker in each. Bought some horns from him too." He pointed to a pair of shorter cabinets with flaring black horns at the front. "Brand-new Yamaha diaphragms in 'em. He had some other stuff, microphones, a snake."

"A snake?"

"Not the reptile kind, a composite low-res audio cable, a nice fifty-foot, sixteen-channel one, but we haven't moved the last couple we picked up used, so I passed."

"Did he carry all this into the store?"

"Yeah. I think he used his own hand trucks."

"No one touches those speakers until I can have someone check the handles for prints." She took out her notebook. "Tell me what he looked like."

"Hard to say age. Maybe twenty-five to thirty-five. Kind of weathered looking. Fair-skinned. Five ten. Mousy-brown hair, a little disheveled."

"What was he wearing?"

"I do believe he had on one of those university sweatshirts, blue with yellow lettering."

* * *

Karl's breathing grew tight, and the volume of his own whimpering embarrassed him…until he realized it wasn't him whimpering.

The sound was coming from the mountainous Panzer kid, whose eyes had gone glassy. "I didn't mean to."

Damon, the frat president, reached up to rub his back consolingly as if comforting a colicky baby. "Go on. Get it out."

"It's just…" Panzer waffled for a few seconds, his Neanderthal brow ridge pressed into a series of deep furrows like the folds of skin on a breed of dog Karl had once seen. "Doors, they've always been my thing."

"Doors?" said Karl, utterly lost.

Damon exhaled. "Panzer rips doors off their hinges. It's his *thing*. There's…well there *was* a big steel door on the third-floor fire escape. Last night, he ripped it off the hinges and tossed it. Your car just happened to be parked where it landed. Panz, what do you say?"

"I'm sorry." He sniffled.

"Don't worry," said Damon, clapping Karl's shoulder. "His old man'll pay. He always does."

* * *

Karl watched through the soot-stained window as the wrecker rumbled out of the parking lot with his flattened Chevy in tow, fishtailing behind it. “Where the hell does that leave us?” He turned to his bandmates.

“The missing truck still makes no sense,” said Nelson. “Why would Abel disappear with half our equipment?”

“Our whole PA,” said Karl.

“It’s out of character,” said Nelson. “Abel’s always been a complete professional. We pay him too much money for crap like that.”

Vance drew the corners of his lips back in the same fake smile Karl had noticed earlier.

“Vance…” said Karl, “why do you keep making that face?”

“Uh…sorry?” The plastic smile morphed into a look of innocence mixed with complete attention.

“Your bullshitting face,” said Karl. “Upstairs earlier, you made that same face…right when we were talking about paying Abel.”

A moist sheen appeared on Vance’s forehead. “I…yeah…no clue what face that might be.”

“Abel gets paid every two weeks,” said Karl, “right?”

“That *is* his contract,” said Vance.

“You didn’t answer my question. You *have* been paying Abel every two weeks, right?”

“Well…I certainly try to be prompt with his pay, yeah.”

“Vance,” said Karl, slowing the cadence of his words, “I’m going to ask you a direct question, and I want you to answer it. Just the answer. Just the truth. When was the last time you paid Abel?”

Vance held his breath until his entire head and neck turned nearly beet-red. Finally he spit out a single word. “Never.”

“Never?” said Karl.

“I mean,” said Vance, “he was just so chill about it, and I *did* get him stoned.”

“You’ve got to be kidding me,” said Nelson, finally dropping any attempt at a Marlboro Man facial expression. “We’re making good money. You have the whole band fund if somebody pays us late.”

Vance’s sickly plastic smile returned.

"Oh, no," said Karl. "You put that up your nose too?"

"It'll all come back to us," said Vance, sounding glib and rehearsed. "I can work out the numbers. I'll skip my per diem."

"And Abel," said Nelson, "I suppose you think *he's* coming back to us?"

Since they had no way to make the Binghamton gig and since Abel was a Will Grant Productions employee, they decided to call the company office and give them the bad news. Vance dialed on the frat house phone while Karl and Nelson leaned in close.

Vance gave his name and got put on hold.

A few seconds later, all three stiffened at the gruff and angry voice that came through the line. "You fucking putz."

"Mr. Grant…"

* * *

"Mr. Grant," said Detective Weyland, holding her desk phone in place with one shoulder as she drew out her notebook, "I'm investigating a case in Monroe County that includes the theft of a truck that I believe your company may own or lease for one of your acts, a band called Windegard."

"I'm sorry that you wasted your time, detective," said the voice on the other end of the line. He had a Brooklyn accent with a hint of that Yiddish Jackie Mason inflection. "The truck's right here."

"It's right there?"

"Double parked right under my window."

"I don't understand. I found the driver unconscious in a ditch outside a roadside convenience store."

"Driver's right here listening. You're on speaker."

"Hello, detective." A quieter voice. "Abel Glasse here."

"Mr. Glasse, would you care to explain to me what's going on? If you're in New York City, that means somebody else got rolled at that convenience store robbery."

"Yeah…wow. Is that so?" Abel's feigned surprise was thick with sarcasm. "Maybe…I dunno…your perp tried to carjack the wrong guy and took a blow from the handle of his own gun."

Weyland considered for a few seconds. "Mr. Glasse, would you mind telling me, what are you wearing right now?"

"Jeans. And a new sweatshirt that I…uh…found. Good thing too. Somebody got blood all over my T-shirt."

"And you wore it when you stopped in at a music shop."

"Had to. Didn't think they would do business with me looking like Sweeny Todd."

"No, I suppose they wouldn't. Why did you sell off equipment from that truck?"

"The equipment owners stiffed him on a contract," said Grant. "He sold it to get what was owed him and get home. Got the receipts and cash laid out right here in front of us. We're going over the numbers right now."

"Because the owners stiffed him. Is that how you normally conduct business, Mr. Grant?"

"Sad to say, there is no *normal* in my business, but no, I don't like it either. I told the band that if they ever rip off one of my crew again, they'll never work another gig in the Northern Hemisphere. I told Abel if he pulls another stunt like this, I'll kick his ass, but as you're learning, he doesn't scare easy."

"You do realize that selling stolen goods is a crime."

"So is breach of contract," said Grant. "But you did say you work *major* crimes, didn't you, detective?" A long pause. "Are we all set here then?"

Weyland looked at the never-ending tower of case folders in her in-box tray and sighed. "We'll let you sort it all out in-house. Thank you for your time, gentlemen."

Rachmaninov Forever

Dave Dempster

Transfixed. Couldn't move. Couldn't hear anything else. As if everything stood still. His world would never be the same. The most wonderful sound. Deeply emotive. Profoundly tragic. Rachmaninov's Opus 18—the Second Piano Concerto.

Peter was only 6.

Peter's dad had excelled not only in banking. He had treated the Stock Exchange as a hobby. And a very successful hobby. Peter had grown up accustomed to the good things in life. An only child, he wanted for next to nothing. He came to believe, as his experience taught him, that he was *entitled* to continue to have everything his way.

The only obstacle in the otherwise idyllic landscape was discipline. Peter ran into it almost everywhere outside his home: school, music lessons, music college, even the part-time employment in a library. Most of all, though, discipline came in the persona of his mother.

She was hard on Peter, for as long as he could remember. It wasn't physical but mental constraint. He found her controlling behaviour hard to handle. She always insisted that he should "make more of yourself" rather than "just idling around playing or listening to music." How many times had he heard her favourite "DOESN'T PAY THE BILLS"?

* * *

Felt like the worst day of his life, that sombre day in October, as his father was lowered into the ground. But he knew it could only get worse. 14-year-old Peter had lost his protector. Now he had to fend for himself and fend off his mother.

So, when his dad died, Peter had reached a crossroads, a dangerous crossroads. Of course, it would go against his whole nature to simply resign and give in. To settle into some 9 to 5 sort of existence which conformed to his mother's ambition for him.

For Peter, any future life not dominated by music, and classical music in particular, would be unthinkable. He would continue with his piano lessons come what may, even if his teacher did have the annoying habit of rapping him over the knuckles with her pencil when his timing went astray. *How dare she*, he thought. Young Peter was already regarded as 'very promising' by The Associated Board of the Royal Schools of Music, when he passed his Grade 5 exam with distinction, at a prodigious age.

* * *

The crunch came when Peter's mother found love for a second time. Peter had just turned 18. It was quickly made perfectly plain that Peter had to move out. Thankfully, he could take his beloved Steinway with him. The grand piano had been a gift from his doting father years earlier. But on any level Peter's mother was cruel to her only child. She spelled out in unforgiving language that, as far as her new will was concerned, Peter no longer existed. In any case, on the few painful occasions in subsequent years when Peter could not avoid meeting up with his mother, it was clear that her new lifestyle had no room to leave money behind when her time came.

* * *

As it turned out, the next few years did bring Peter some limited success. He had graduated in music and had been able to establish a career as a piano teacher. His early promise had waned though. He was no longer concert pianist material. He had kept the wolf from the door, but only just. He had to endure kids with wealthy parents. Kids who had no real talent for music but kids to whom he dared not even speak harshly, for fear of it getting back to mum or dad. Peter couldn't risk losing their patronage.

Peter had fallen so far from his earlier days he felt he had to do something. How could he come by, not just some money, but a lot of money?

Marrying into money was quickly discounted. Peter had had quite a few late-night encounters, but no relationship had ever lasted beyond a fortnight. Every time, sometimes within hours, it became obvious that physical attraction gave way to demands on Peter's valued independence.

Nor was inheritance a solution. Peter had no surviving grandparents on either side of the family and there was only a distant uncle who had reputedly taken to drink, perhaps because he had little money in the first place.

The popular/rock scene had gone nowhere. Peter's teenage friend and lead guitarist, John, had always insisted on running the group *his* way. Their conflicting personalities ensured that the finale would be abrupt and ugly. Things finally came to a head at a gig, when they ended up wrestling with each other and rolling into the drum kit. Any hope of reaching the charts had gone. After that disaster, playing his trusty little portable electronic organ occasionally in upmarket restaurants and hotels was some consolation: a little much-needed cash and a supply of free booze, limited only by Peter's ability to continue sounding like a keyboard professional!

Trying gambling was a mug's game. Peter was bright enough to realise that casinos are in the business of winning and are always delighted to welcome new suckers. Even Lotto was unattractive—Peter had had little luck so far, why throw cash away on hopeless odds?

Crime was a more realistic prospect. It would have to be a near perfect crime. Being caught would be the finishing line for everything. Bank robbery would not work—dreaded dye packs made that self-defeating. Rather than falling further into depression, Peter turned on Rachmaninov, sank back into the couch, and visualised a favourite extract from *Brief Encounter*. He had seen the film so many times in his youth. Not for the romantic side, just for the music.

Peter found his small flat claustrophobic. When the sun came out in force, as occasionally as that was in Manchester, the heat became oppressive, even with open windows. Going for walks broke the tedium of staring at empty walls. Peter also enjoyed using his little Fujifilm camera to take what amounted to still life pictures of the natural environment outside—another way of combatting his loneliness.

* * *

Peter's salvation arrived unexpectedly one especially warm summer's afternoon. He found the sudden gust exhilarating soon after he left through the front door of the apartment complex. He enjoyed the feeling of lungs filling with crisp and unadulterated air. He had resolved to walk in a familiar direction. Towards Hale Barns, the most affluent area of Greater Manchester, and only a comfortable half-hour stroll away. Like another world. *What must it be like to live here*, daydreamed Peter.

Looking ahead, Peter could see the outline of the development where he knew only the very wealthy could afford to stay. Magnificently large houses, exuding opulence. Peter also knew that one of the lucky residents there was none other than Tanek Bukoski, aka 'The Spot Killer', due to his unrivalled skill in scoring from penalties. The star City midfielder was hot property. He had only recently turned down a multi-million-pound transfer deal with Real Madrid.

Peter had been there before but paused to bring out his camera, before taking another shot of the dream world in front of him. He wondered again about the apparent absence of anti-paparazzi equipment—surveillance devices are usually well-hidden, of course—but he was undeterred in moving closer.

That's when it happened.

Peter heard, in rapid succession, a loud male voice shouting, a very short scream from a female, and a metallic banging sound followed by the sound of sobbing. It lasted only a couple of seconds before what Peter then saw explained the episode.

A side gate, which must have led to some sort of courtyard, flew open and the head and upper torso of what looked like a teenage girl or young woman hit the deck. In the same motion, a muscular male right arm, bearing a large and distinctive tattoo, reached down to grab the victim's hair violently. In that moment, that split second, Peter instinctively snapped the scenario. When he looked again, nothing was there. Peter didn't stop to wonder if he had been hallucinating—he ran.

As his home came into view, Peter saw Tom. Tom was a pensioner. Life had not passed him by completely but equally life had not been kind to Tom. No-one in the complex knew Tom's second name—he was always just 'Tom'. He seemed to hang around the entrance area at all times of the day. His special interest was the weather. He would talk endlessly about it. Today's, yesterday's and tomorrow's. Not in any particular order but continuously without fail. Peter decided, on that day of all days, to apply the only practical remedy—a polite but firm withdrawal. After all, he had urgent work to consider.

* * *

First, Peter checked the photo excitedly. What a gem! Not a half second early, nor half a second late. Yes! Here was Peter's golden opportunity. Next, he rushed to check the internet. He was pleasantly taken aback at how quickly he was able to confirm that the tattoo was unmistakeably to be found on the right arm of 'The Spot Killer'! Research into the identity of the female victim took much longer but, again, serendipity smiled on Peter. It was the star's 14-year-old daughter, Sofia.

There it was. Peter would blackmail the star, who had physically abused his young daughter. He would threaten to go to the media. The star wouldn't even think of going to the Police—something like this would be leaked to the media for sure anyway. And the media would destroy the star if this got out, so there was a very good chance of criminal success.

Peter would not make the mistake of asking for too much. A mere £10,000 would do nicely. Ten grand might not seem a lot to most folk, but it was a godsend for Peter. Just what he needed to keep real poverty at bay. Besides, the star earned thousands every single week, so where's the great loss? If the star paid up, he might treat Sofia better, and if he didn't pay up, he *deserved* to be exposed. Peter didn't bear a shred of guilt. He was a modern version of Robin Hood. Crucially, he would only ask once. *Greed gives most criminals away*, reasoned Peter, and a second try would only increase the risk of being caught. So, Peter had to get the demand for money right first time, or this glorious chance would slip by.

Peter did not want to involve outside sources. That would only increase the risk of detection. His computer could manage all the necessary paperwork and copying. If any investigation reached as far as Peter's home computer, it would be game, set and match in any case. Peter had to make the demand message specific enough to have the desired effect. Brevity would add impact, but ambiguity had to be avoided at all costs. The demand for money was everything, concluded Peter, and he set about planning his next step.

After he uploaded the precious photo, Peter was nervous about the scanning and printing process—would some computer malfunction put paid to his efforts?—but the copy of the photo he would incorporate into the demand note was better than good enough. The accompanying text needed much more thought.

Eventually Peter composed the text, placed neatly below the embedded photo:

> PHOTO (you abusing Sofia) goes to MEDIA
> UNLESS
> PUT £10,000 used notes in bag under seat in bus shelter Watercress Street
> 3pm Monday 7 July
> YOU ALONE
> ONE CHANCE ONLY
> ANY TRICK/POLICE ?
> **MEDIA**

Even if all went well on the day Peter still had to guard against the star having a change of mind and trying to catch up with him. Used notes could be traced, of course, but a bank account transfer was far more visible. Peter intended to 'launder' the money in five instalments to reduce suspicion. After waiting patiently for six months he would begin to purchase Premium Bonds in £2,000 lots over an extended period. He could cash in at his leisure thereafter.

The bus shelter in Watercress Street was a suitably busy spot. Peter had an ideal vantage point across the street. Bench seating adjacent to a newsagent's. Arriving no later than 2.30pm, he would be able to see the star arriving from the expected direction. Peter had seen enough spy thrillers to be confident about spotting anyone lurking suspiciously in the area. He would only move in if he felt safe in picking up the bag.

Peter had signed up as a City fan to keep in close touch. The chosen date and time allowed the star sufficient time to get the money together and did not conflict with any team fixture or training session.

The final aspect was the most difficult. The envelope containing the demand note would be stamped 'Private and Confidential' emphatically, but how could Peter hand the envelope directly to the star? Attempting delivery in or around the Etihad Stadium was out of the question with far too many people around. There was no alternative. Fully disguised, using an old oversize coat which had belonged to his father, a cloth cap and dark glasses, Peter would go boldly to the star's side gate and try to manoeuvre the envelope into the courtyard. If challenged, he would pretend not to understand a word of English. He would just hand over the envelope, saying "gracias" continuously. If it worked for *Manuel* in '*Fawlty Towers*', why not?

* * *

When it came to it, delivery passed off without incident. Surprisingly, considering the excessive security measures surrounding stars and their homes, the envelope slipped effortlessly underneath the side gate. There was no interception. No siren. No searchlight.

Taking no chances, Peter feigned an abnormal gait for the first 50 metres of his retreat, before removing, and then carrying, his coat, hat and glasses the rest of the way home.

* * *

The big day arrived. Peter had doubts about a tallish man who seemed to be hanging around for no apparent reason near the drop site, but he was relieved when the man finally got into a car which had stopped to pick him up. Then, just before 3pm, a huge man appeared from the expected direction. As the man drew closer Peter could see that it was indeed the star. He looked even larger in real life. He behaved as instructed. The bag was placed correctly and the star duly left.

Peter waited a few minutes before crossing the road. His heart raced as he tentatively looked down into the bag. Had he been tricked? No! He glimpsed wads of lovely banknotes, swiftly lifted the bag up and walked off. After about 100 metres Peter was sure he was not being followed. Just like clockwork. A triumph!

As he neared home base, Tom began to emerge from the side of the building. Peter charged ahead, barging through the front door without giving Tom the chance. Fortunately, Peter had not used a disguise, which might have diverted even Tom from his weather obsession.

* * *

In the succeeding months Peter stuck to his plan. He only truly relaxed when the 5th and final Premium Bond instalment had been invested. They say that crime doesn't pay. Yeah, sure. What a clever boy he was! His father would have been so proud of his son's ingenuity.

* * *

Four years later, on a bleak November afternoon, there was knocking on Peter's door. *If that's the Jehovah's Witnesses brigade, I'll send them packing,* thought Peter. As the door opened, two men in dark suits stood there. The elder man spoke in a commanding voice.

"Are you Peter Bartholomew Balfour?"

"Yes"

"DCI George Smith and DS Noah Jones from City Detectives, Fraud Unit. We have a search warrant…"

An Artful Death

John B. Elliott

"I have an after-dinner show to go to—some son of a friend of an uncle's cousin is playing in it, which means I have to see *Seven Brides for Seven Brothers*."

"That's where they steal the women they want to marry, isn't it?"

"Something like that."

"Well, Rochwal, everyone has to do penance—better you than me."

"Unfortunately. Have you ever seen that musical?"

"I have better things to do."

"Like smoking cigarillos and drinking Wild Turkey?"

"Exactly. You know, art is really a form of magic—it isn't real and deludes us into thinking that what we see or hear or read is reality. That means, of course, that con men and politicians are also artists."

"And so are criminals since they want the illusion that someone else committed their crimes."

"Exactly. Everyone's guilty of delusion, Rochwal, which is why we need art to lead us back to reality."

"But you just said—"

"Have fun tonight."

The next morning, Daggett was at his desk trimming his fingernails when Rochwal arrived. He didn't look up. "Like the show?"

"It was canceled."

"I know."

"Someone in the cast was murdered."

"I know that, too."

"And I suppose you know—"

"Yes, Tamark Hightower was arrested for murdering the eighteen-year-old lead singer, Andreas Chambers, the biggest star not only of the musical but the whole high school so I've been told."

"Your rival, Inspector Higginsworth—"

"Is a fool."

"He's certain Tamark is the murderer."

"Well, that's another reason he's a fool."

"So, why do you think Tamark is innocent?"

"Because he didn't kill Andreas Chambers."

"Details, details. Except for that?"

"I've arrested Tamark several times. Murder isn't his style—he likes to beat people up."

"He went too far, this time. Even fists can kill someone."

"No, no, that's not the case—Andreas was knifed. I'm going to visit Tamark, why don't you come along? You should get to know him."

After surrendering their weapons and passing through a metal detector, Rochwal and Daggett sat down with Tamark Hightower.

"I didn't kill him, Mr. Daggett."

"I'm glad to see you, too."

"I'm sorry. I'm upset, that's all. How are you?"

"Keeping. And you?"

"I don't like being here, not for something I didn't do."

Tamark was a short man with olive skin and black hair he kept neatly trimmed. He didn't ply his face with indignation nor were his eyes welling with moisture, although Daggett imagined Tamark was angry if not wounded by the accusation.

"Why do they think you murdered Andreas?"

"I have no idea. It doesn't make sense."

"Did you know Andreas?"

"Of course, I did. I was going to give him a good talking to. Everyone at the Art School knows that. I was pissed."

"He's only a senior. Isn't that a little young for your anger?"

"He's eighteen and well-built and strong! That's why he's been bullying other kids for years."

"He bullied Jason? By the way, how is your son?"

"As quiet and withdrawn as always. No, he hasn't bullied him recently. Worse. He stole Jason's music score and presented it as his own senior project. Got an A, of course, and lots of applause."

"Jason's a junior, isn't he?"

"He's in tenth, but he wanted to start what he knew would be his senior project and really have it exceptional when it was needed. That's why I was going to beat the shit out of Andreas, even if he outweighs me. A guy like that should be stopped!"

"Didn't the school—"

"Andreas and his rich dad claimed it was his work and the vice principal swallowed it. If I had made a big donation to the school, maybe the vice principal would have listened to me."

"I want to talk to your son and anyone else worth talking to. Okay with you?"

"Yeah, but don't expect him to say much." As Daggett stood up, Tamark added: "I'm sorry Andreas got murdered, Mr. Daggett, real sorry. It's just one more pleasure taken away from me."

When Rochwal and Daggett returned to their car, Daggett said: "You were quiet in there, weren't you?"

"You were doing well enough, but isn't it possible Tamark has changed his style? He did say that Andreas' murder stole a pleasure from him, which to me, means he wanted to murder him."

"No, Rochwal, he's innocent. He's a postal employee and when he goes postal, he only uses his fists."

"Why does he call you Mr. Daggett?"

"I imagine he's allergic to law enforcement and that helps him think of me as a friend. Let's visit the art school."

On the way, Daggett swung by Hightower's house and talked with his son Jason, who was pretending to be sick so he wouldn't have to face other students asking if his dad was a murderer. His mother asked him to come into the living room, and she remained while Jason was being interviewed.

"Do you remember me?" Daggett asked.

"Yes."

"And Andreas, you knew him?"

"Yes."

"He stole your project?"

"Yes."

"Upsetting, wasn't it?"

"Yes."

"This is Inspector Rochwal. He's my partner."

A "Yes" was not forthcoming.

"Would you like some tea or coffee?" Mrs. Hightower asked to fill the void.

Daggett pondered. "I usually don't drink tea or coffee."

"I remember, but I don't have Wild Turkey. Something inferior?"

Glancing at Rochwal, Daggett replied. "Not today. Now Jason—"

"Did you arrest my dad?"

"No, that was someone else."

"You always did before."

"I didn't this time because your dad is innocent."

Mrs. Hightower shaded her eyes with her right hand as moisture came to them, and she sighed in relief.

"Could you tell us about your project," Rochwal asked.

"It's a miniature opera for three voices, alto, tenor and bass."

"Tell him the title," Mrs. Hightower prompted. When Jason didn't reply, she said: "*Trio of Triumph*."

"That's only the working title."

"But it has a story, not just the music and vocals?"

"Yes."

"How did Andreas get it in his hands?"

Jason was silent.

"Go on, dear, tell him," his mothered prompted.

"Sometimes, actually always, I take my project to school and work on it when I have free time. I left it on a table when I went to the restroom, and when I came back it was gone."

"Devastating, I'm sure," Rochwal suggested.

"I keep a master copy at home."

"Smart man!"

"I only lost what I had done that day at school and I could remember most of that."

"So how did you find out he was the one who stole it?"

"I didn't go to his senior project. I don't like him and he's always picked on me, but a friend told me about it."

"Had he bullied you recently?"

"A little, but he was really mean to a new guy, Jeffrey Winters. He's in dance. Called him a fag and all that."

"Could we see some of your score," Rochwal asked.

"He promises not to steal it," Daggett laughed.

After looking at the score, and having only a vague idea of music composition, Rochwal thanked Jason, and he and Daggett left for the art school. "You'll be able to check when they're performing the musical again," Daggett said gleefully, "so you won't miss it." He laughed boisterously.

When they arrived at the school, they talked first with the Vice Principal for Art, Roland Washington.

"Of course, we're upset about this, the whole school is. The principal called an assembly this morning to talk with the students, to dispel any rumors and assure them they are safe."

"How well did you know Andreas Chambers?"

"Very well. He's been with us many years. This school is both a junior and senior high."

"We understand he bullied several students," Rochwal stated.

"Oh, no, no. We don't tolerate bullying here. I'm sure that's ridiculous hearsay."

"He was stabbed several times according to the medical examiner," Rochwal persisted, "—passionate frenzy."

"He was? I didn't know." Roland chuckled. "A crime of passion that you think is related to bullying! Well, I hate to inform you, we have a very passionate student body, so you have nine hundred suspects! You'll find art-orientated students are also very exacting, and not particularly interested in anything but their own work."

Daggett took the lead: "Passionate or not, we understand Jeffrey Winters was bullied by Andreas."

"Jeffrey Winters? Let me think. Ah, yes, he's a dance student. I'll look into that. Better yet, you might mention it to Princella Gregorio, she's the Vice Principal of Academics, but she's also involved with counseling students if there are personal problems." He paused, then added: "She can also tell you about Andreas. She knew him quite well."

"Too well?"

"No, never." He laughed. "I wouldn't mind dating Princella myself, she's a beautiful lady. In fact, I did date her until she got interested in someone else." Roland shrugged. "But that's water under the bridge."

When they interviewed Princella Gregorio, Daggett noticed several books on music and a few unfinished scores on her desk, one of them framed. She saw his interest and said: "All our academic teachers and administrators have some connection to the arts. It's a requirement. I played the clarinet in college and did some composing—I still dabble."

"You knew Andreas well?"

"Yes. He's graduating, or would have graduated this year. The whole thing is shocking. I'm very upset."

She's pretty, thought Rochwal: smooth skin, oval face with pleasant features and, as they say, weight proportional to height. He noted a scar on her upper lip, perhaps from a childhood accident. When she spoke about Andreas her pain was evident, as expected for she would have followed his progress for six years. "What can you tell us about Jeffrey Winters?"

Her displeasure was apparent as she answered: "His dad called yesterday and told me he was withdrawing Jeffrey from school as Jeffrey is depressed and fearful because of the ill-treatment he received here, both physically and emotionally."

"Did he say who was mistreating his son?"

"Well, it wasn't Andreas, I know that for certain!" She paused and her mood changed to anger. "Mr. Winters accused Andreas Chambers of physically and emotionally abusing his son. That's total nonsense. He even went so far as to say Andreas demanded that Jeffrey, if you don't mind the exact words, suck his cock since he was a fag dancer. That's not like Andreas at all, he has no interest in male-to-male sexuality. Believe me, we have plenty of gay and lesbian students and there is never a conflict with them and their heterosexual peers."

"Was that the only allegation?" Daggett asked.

"Well, several other times Mr. Winters claimed that Andreas hit Jeffrey. We had the nurse examine Jeffrey after three of these complaints, and the nurse found no injury or anything to back the accusation. Sometimes parents have an ulterior motive in making complaints like this, such as having home-school for academics and have their child on campus only to attend art classes, but we are against that. We feel they should have the school community experience as well as their art."

Rochwal asked: "Can we have Mr. Winters' address? We need to talk with Jeffrey and his dad."

"Of course, but you won't find him home. Mr. Winters is a single parent, and he told me yesterday that not only was he going to put Jeffrey in counseling to counteract the abuse, he was going to leave today with Jeffrey on a bonding trip and would not be back for several weeks, then he'll enroll Jeffrey in another school." She wrote down the address and handed it to Rochwal.

"We'll drop by the Winters' house just in case they haven't left." Daggett smiled pleasantly. "Thanks for your time—we appreciate it."

On the way to the Winters' house, Daggett said. "Attractive lady, wasn't she?"

"I didn't notice."

"I bet! What I didn't notice was you asking about when the next performance of *Seven Brides for Seven Brothers* will be. You need culture, Rochwal."

"I'm sure I can live without it."

"Debatable."

When they found that Winters and his son weren't home and saw a low wattage table lamp lit in the living room, Daggett insisted a few margaritas and a light lunch at a Mexican restaurant was warranted, and ordered a Cadillac margarita as soon as they sat down. Rochwal, who limited his drinking to evening hours, asked: "So, this puts a hold on your effort to free Tamark. What now?"

"It only puts a hold on it if Winters is the murderer." He grinned. "I like things where the murderer is obvious, such as Mr. Winters disappearing right after Andreas was killed. It makes me think of alternatives."

"We have had cases where the murderer was obvious and you looked elsewhere, then later went back to the obvious perpetrator. Winters has motive, and I'm sure he's angry. I would be if I had a son attacked like that."

"Maybe, but I don't think he did it any more than Tamark. After we finish lunch, we'll visit Andreas' parents and see what they know."

Rochwal frowned but knew better than to argue, and despite Winters' anger at Andreas for abusing his son and his quick exit from town after the murder, they had to work with what they had, and at present, they didn't have Winters. Daggett continued: "It's a city homicide and our tenuous touch is only because Tamark is a postal employee. We can't issue a be on the lookout, you know that." After a Cheshire smile, he added: "Don't be so impatient."

No one was home at the Chambers' so they went back to the office. When they returned later in the day, they found Andreas' mother, an older sister and an uncle at the Chambers' house. The atmosphere was gloomy and the presence of his older sister and uncle was obviously supportive.

"My husband is in Chicago tonight for a meeting, but he'll be here tomorrow to help arrange the funeral."

"We'll hold back until after the funeral to talk with him. From what we know about Andreas, this must be an enormous loss for you."

She squinted as if to hold back tears and nodded her head at Daggett's words, then asked: "Why are you here? How can I help you?"

"We'd like to take a look at Andreas' room."

"I thought they caught the murderer," the uncle said.

"Yes, but there are certain things we need to know to make a better case against him. You wouldn't want him to get off on a lack of diligence on our part, would you?"

"But before the funeral?"

"The sooner the better. We never want to let something important inadvertently slip by."

"I think you should wait until after the memorial service," Andreas' sister piped up. "He's not even buried yet!"

"That's all right, Margaret, I want them to make the best case they can. Andreas was a wonderful son. He never hurt anyone, and I have no idea why this happened. Get what you need."

As Rochwal and Daggett searched Andreas' bedroom, either Margaret or the victim's uncle kept an eye on them. On the wall was a poster for Andreas' senior project, as well as photos of his performances during the six years he attended the School of the Arts. His work desk was neat and organized. "Take a look at this," Rochwal said and he opened a leather-bound diary to the first page. Daggett huffed a subdued laugh, then said "I'm more interested in these short segments of music scores tucked in a drawer. There must be twenty or so foot-long segments." He turned to the uncle who was keeping watch. "Do you have the score for his Senior Project?"

"I imagine it's here someplace, but I don't know about it. Andreas was into his next project, the musical, and when he's finished with something, he's finished with it. He was a very forward-looking person."

After searching further and not finding anything of interest, in particular the absent senior project, Daggett asked Mrs. Chambers if they could borrow the diary and the music scores. Though the uncle and Margaret looked annoyed, Mrs. Chambers quickly answered: "If this will help, of course you may."

Back in their car, Daggett looked at the diary Rochwal was interested in. "Not very subtle was he, Rochwal?"

"He even drew a pyramid on the first page, and the words, *e pluribus unum*, one of many. On the second page he wrote 'The future . . .' Evidently, he felt proud that he could scam other students."

"And beyond. The nice, couldn't-hurt-anybody Andreas Chambers was practicing a pyramid scheme even while he was still in high school. You've got names here, Rochwal, and dollar amounts."

"That will keep me busy. Why did you take the music scores?"

"A hunch. Let's go to dinner, and since it's coming on evening, you're permitted to have a drink with me."

"Thank you, Grand Master."

They both chuckled, and Daggett drove to a steak house.

When Rochwal entered the office the next morning, his partner had the scores he obtained at the Chambers' spread out on his desk and was mumbling to himself. Rochwal spoke first: "I did a little work last night on the diary. It's pretty certain Andreas burned several of his fellow students with his practice run of a Ponzi scheme. I visited a few, and the students I talked with were angry, but more than that, they were ashamed they were taken in."

"Well, that would be no problem for Andreas. Like most con men, it gives them a charge to dupe people and a bigger charge when the victim can't do anything about it. I imagine they get pleasure every single time they get an investor to hold on and keep the faith, their money is coming, just wait." Daggett interchanged two of the scores, then added: "Did you check the whereabouts on the night of the murder for those students who were burned by Andreas?"

"Of course, I did. Two of them were covered, but one, the student hurt most, I haven't been able to interview. I plan that for today."

"Don't bother, Rochwal. He's not the murderer."

"Basing that on?"

"My not so infallible intuition. I know who the murderer is, even his motivation, but unfortunately, I don't have proof. That's where you come in."

"I make an entrance?"

"Yes, in the play I've devised in a follow-up to *Seven Brides for Seven Brothers*. I visited Tamark's son last night and he identified these scores are from his project which was stolen by Andreas, but Jason noted they were all the same passage with only a slight alteration. That was to be expected in plagiarizing, but the alteration is so slight it really doesn't disguise the fact this is a section of music taken from Jason's project. In fact, this little bit of music is the same on all these sheets I brought from Andreas' room with the exception of two of the notes. Also, look down in the corner, each one is dated, usually at least a week apart, though sometimes more often and sometimes less."

"And that solves the murder?"

"Absolutely. These are codes for two lovers to meet secretly. One change of note is for time and the other designates a place." Daggett's Cheshire grin was enticing, and Rochwal knew he would soon be involved in a script written by his fellow inspector. "I hope you don't expect me to sing my part in this play you're producing."

Daggett laughed. "That would be amusing, but you won't have to stretch your vocal cords this time. It's someone else I hope will sing. Let me tell you my part in our little play, then I'll give you your instructions. I noticed on Princella Gregorio's desk a framed score which I believe is the same as these, except the date on it will be the first time she and Andreas got together for a sexual encounter. Andreas kept the others, either from pride or perhaps to use against her at a later date. They varied the times and meeting places for obvious reasons. I'll confront her, and I'm sure being exposed for having an affair with a student after all their clever planning will upset her. While I'm dealing with her, you'll be with the other vice principal."

Rochwal entered Roland Washington's office at the School of the

Arts at ten after ten that morning with instructions to observe Roland's reactions to everything that transpired. Rochwal told Roland he was working alone that morning as Daggett was reviewing new evidence. After a few minutes of chat about the school and its history, Rochwal received a phone call and gazed steadily at the vice principal as he made his replies.

"You found the murder weapon? My God, that's great! When was this?" Rochwal paused. "Last night? Here at the school? You should have called me!" He again paused. "Well, I don't like being left out of the loop, that's why!"

Even as he appeared to have a grievance with Daggett, Rochwal kept watch on Roland's reaction to the conversation, especially his concerned look when he heard the weapon had been found the night before. When he heard it was found at school, Roland jerked his hand below his desk as if to open a drawer, a look of fear on his face.

"You have prints on the weapon," Rochwal continued, "as well as traces of Andreas' blood on the blade? It's not Tamark Hightower, is it?" After he received an answer, he held his phone down by his chest and spoke directly to Roland: "This is good news, isn't it?"

Roland managed a weak sounding, "Yes."

"All we have to do is fingerprint everyone associated with the school. They're sending a team over now. We'll start with administrators and teachers to get them out of the way quickly."

Roland, nervous if not sick to his stomach, had his hand on a drawer handle and impulsively pulled it open. His face immediately filled with dismay. He sighed deeply, looked at Rochwal and began to close the drawer, but before he could do so, Princella rushed into the room.

"How could you do it?" she screamed as she literally flew over his desk and landed her fist in his face. Roland toppled backward, his hand still on the handle of the drawer which pulled out spilling the contents on the floor. Daggett walked casually through the door as Princella continued to hit Roland. "Now, now, Princella, you weren't exactly innocent in all this. Let the law take its course." He tugged on her arm to pull her up.

Rochwal put on gloves and slid the knife which had fallen out of the drawer into an evidence bag.

"We deserve another lunch," Daggett said. "This one's on me."

"As soon as we get the knife to the city detective in charge of the case."

Later that day, Daggett visited Tamark Hightower at the city jail. "You'll be out soon, Tamark."

"You found the person who murdered Andreas?"

"Yes, the Vice Principal of Art. He discovered the woman he wanted for himself was having an affair with Andreas. He was afraid that would continue after Andreas graduated, even going so far as marriage, and felt he had to stop it. My estimation of Andreas is that Princella Gregorio marrying him was pure fantasy on her part, though he would keep using her awhile."

"Why didn't he just expose her to the principal or the public? The parents?"

"If he had ratted on her, would he have a chance at wooing her? No, he had to eliminate his rival—that was the only way. His biggest mistake was in keeping the weapon, but it must have been a totem for him, a reminder of his power. Some would say token, but I think totem is more appropriate."

Tamark remained in thought for several seconds, then said: "If I were that vice principal, I would have just beaten Andreas up and told him to back off my girl."

"Yes, indeed you would have, but you should really stop solving every problem with your fists, Tamark. You'll always be the first suspect in a killing."

The Songwriter

Jon Matthew Farber

Zoltan was a problem. To be precise, an enormous problem, one that would alter my life's trajectory if not solved. But I should start by telling you about me; don't worry, I'll come back to Zoltan later.

I'm a songwriter. You may not know my name, and even if you did, you wouldn't recognize me on the street, but I guarantee you're familiar with my work. Top artists have recorded my songs, bestsellers, for decades now. I'm Steven Hitt, and yes, I've heard all the weak puns, about Hitt maker and Hitt record, and yes, that is my real name; I didn't change it eponymously (I'm a lyricist as well as composer, so I'm prone to use the occasional fancy word) for the publicity.

Some of you may actually even be able to attach my name to my music, if you're familiar with the Broadway smash based on a compilation of my early work. You know the one I'm talking about—*The Hitt Musical!*

Yes, the title is kitsch, and so is the story line, but with the royalty checks I'm getting, even larger now that it's also gone on tour, I'm not complaining.

Anyway, you may be wondering how I got into this. My early life gave no hints. I was an inner-city child, both parents heavily into drugs, and my life was no doubt destined to follow the same path. But then within a few months of each other, two major events occurred. First, my mother died prosaically, of an overdose. Not to be outdone, soon thereafter, my father chose a less popular method for passing on, but still part of the subculture, by being shot in a drug deal that went south.

So where did music come in after this start? As a newly anointed orphan, I was sent to live with my maternal grandmother out of town.

She was a lovely woman, but an ineffective parent (as could be seen by the way her daughter turned out), but at her house she had a piano, and I fell in love with it. We soon realized I had talent here, and after a few introductory lessons from her, I took off on my own, a teen-age prodigy, not just playing, but also writing, music. With my background, you might've figured I'd gravitate to hip-hop and rap, but you'd be wrong. My grandmother owned an extensive collection of popular music (vinyl, naturally), going back to the thirties, including all the major musicals; they became the sirens calling out to me to join them.

A little digression now about songwriters. An early superstar of pop music was Frank Sinatra, still known today, but back then his songwriters, such as Jimmy Van Heusen, Sammy Cahn, and Jules Styne, were also household names. The first big star singer-songwriter was probably in country music, Hank Williams, but it took the likes of Chuck Berry and Buddy Holly to get their feet in the door with mainstream pop. The floodgates finally burst apart when the Beatles came on the scene. Since then, all the superstars have pretty much been singer-songwriters, even if they can't really sing. Bob Dylan comes to mind here; he's an absolute genius composer as well as poet, but even his most ardent fans would have to agree he'd have struggled in the business if he'd had to depend on his voice alone. So why aren't I out there hitting the circuit and performing my own material? I can certainly carry a tune, but I have stage fright, and hate performing. Ergo, songwriting.

Anyway, there's still a role for me in the industry. Even singer-songwriters will glom onto outside material if it catches their eye. Consider Barry Manilow, who's written many hits for himself, but you know one of his biggest?—*I Write the Songs*—well he didn't write that one. And when you can write the way I could, well, let's just say I'm not hurting financially.

For example, you should see my place. On the ocean, and since I live alone, it's a 'modest' bungalow—just six bedrooms, five bathrooms, and a four-car garage. The obligatory swimming pool, for when the ocean's too frigid, is Olympic-sized. The interior of the house has even more impressive features. There's the bowling alley, the panic room with the entry/exit keypad and computerized communications center, and the home theater which seats forty people. There are even some rooms which serve as paeans to myself. Elvis had his jungle room, and I have my jingle room, where I keep my Clio awards for advertising, and publicity stills of the products they pushed. Again, you may not know the name behind the music, but you know the tunes—my sobriquet *The Conqueror Earworm* is well deserved—and the money I earn from them would blow you away. Of course, I have another room with my piano, where I do most of my composing, and where I keep my gold records and other awards for the 'serious' music I've created.

Backtracking now to just after I finished high school, I sold a few songs as album fillers and was on my way up. I had kept in touch with my best friend from the old days, JoJo (no last name here, for reasons that will become obvious) and flew out to my previous stomping grounds to visit him. He told me he was in sales, and he was also doing well: nice bling, expensive sneakers, and a well-furnished condo (although the building was slowly devolving towards being decrepit). We went for a walk as he gave me a tour of our old haunts. For reasons that weren't clear to me at first, he was carrying a baseball bat. We stopped in front of an apartment complex, and he suggested I wait outside while he took care of some business, said it wouldn't take long, and headed in.

Perhaps ten minutes later, he came tearing out of the building, bleeding from his ear, sans bat, yelling at me to follow him. As we dashed across the street, snaking around traffic, I heard police sirens. Down one alley and then another, it was apparent he was very familiar with the area, and we eventually zigzagged our way to a main street, after which we strolled into a café to settle down. He asked what I thought of the experience.

It was exhilarating, and at a primal level quite enjoyable. He told me I could work for him if I wished; I realized I was being recruited. I was young then, and tempted, but I knew I couldn't live my life constantly on the edge, especially if it involved physical confrontation. When it came to bodily violence, it wasn't just the possibility of receiving, but also even the act of bestowing, that dissuaded me; that wasn't part of my make-up. I then make a counter-offer to come with me, and I could get him started in the music industry, even if it was just as a gofer at the beginning.

In the end, we both stayed put, and I haven't gone back. He's been in and out of prison since then. For my part, I drew on the experience for the theme song to the movie "Prison is for Losers," which garnered me my first Oscar.

Anyway, back to the main narrative. After several highly successful years, having made my reputation, I also made it a requirement that if you wanted my song, I needed to be the producer, so I became well known for wearing two hats. Because of my second role, would-be songwriters were constantly sending me material to review, all of it eminently forgettable and at best suitable for using in my fireplace, until Zoltan Canosh showed up. This was around a quarter-century into my career, and, truth to tell, I was in a slump. Writers can get writer's block, and musicians can get musician's block. I could still handle lyrics, but the melodies were getting harder to come by. I used to compose in my piano room, but when that didn't work, I sometimes found that going into the panic room, shutting down the computers, and just sitting in the absolute silence helped. However, although my songs were still earning me money, they didn't have the panache and spark of yore, and weren't the megahits of days gone by. When I was shown Canosh's offering, however, and saw the potential, I knew I was onto something big. The material was raw of course, and needed a lot of work to bring it up to speed, but I polished the hell out of it, and by the time I finished, I had the song you now know as *I Thought Forever Meant Forever*, which won all the song of the year awards that year.

If I were an author, I would have simply bought a story from Canosh, used him as a ghostwriter, and published it under my own name. It doesn't work that way in the music biz, however, so we were credited as cowriters.

Another digression now, into songwriting partnerships. One model is having one person the tunesmith, and the other the lyricist. This is common, but the latter creator often winds up as a second banana. For example, can you name any of the people who wrote the librettos for a Mozart opera? Another model is that of a true partnership, both contributing at both ends. Lennon-McCartney is a good example here, at least early on; they would sit in a room together, and bounce around ideas and work out their next composition. By the end though, before the Beatles broke up, they were still stuck with using the name Lennon-McCartney, even if the song was purely McCartney (such as *Yesterday*) or Lennon (such as *Help*).

Anyway, back to Canosh and me. After this breakthrough, he gave me a few more songs, and it was obvious he wasn't a one-hit wonder. Given my waning abilities, I knew I needed to latch onto him while he was still bowled over by his success, and starstruck with me. We formed a partnership, Hitt-Canosh. There were two reasons my name came first. One is the obvious, that I was the established figure and he the shiny new object, a bauble which might lose its luster quickly. The second was more pragmatic. Reverse the order of the names, and say them, and what you get sounds like the punchline to a dirty joke. Try it.

We'll come back to the partnership later. The time has come, as you probably knew it eventually would, to talk about drugs. I'm sure this will come as a complete shock to you, but they're ubiquitous in the music scene. I personally don't indulge. I'm not a prude; heavy partying with alcohol, followed by passing out and waking with a monstrous hangover, is well within my skill set. However, given my family background, I've avoided harder stuff, although I keep my place well stocked, for friends and industry movers and shakers who I need to keep happy. However, Canosh took to it like a brat to candy, and it portended poorly for the partnership. You may have heard that being in an altered state of consciousness enhances creativity. My experience is that it almost never does, and it certainly didn't for Canosh. When he was high, he thought he was producing great stuff, but when he came back down, he would realize it was crap, and not even good crap at that. Fortunately, for a while he could still produce hits when straight, and when he did come up with a viable idea, he stayed off the drugs long enough to create something worthwhile.

Now, back to the partnership issue. After a few years in, I'd dried up completely, including lyrics, and Canosh was doing all the work; luckily, the partnership meant I was still getting shared credit for his work, and my reputation remained intact. However, as Canosh dove deeper and deeper into drugs, several things began to happen. The first was, he became more and more depressed. Drugs can of course worsen this, and the polypharmacy also led to his long-time girlfriend moving out, exacerbating his mood. Outside of home, it wasn't just me who noticed the downward spiral; his closest friends and even others in the studio could see it, and were worried. Second, he stopped writing. When he came over to collaborate, he would immediately pop some sort of pill, and most often wind up almost comatose, and unable to work, so we were relying on previously unpublished material, and the well would soon be dry. Third, he wanted to break up the partnership, and take sole credit for all the hits we'd had in the past several years, when he was essentially a solo act.

This last was a major threat to me. After I'm gone, I have a legacy I want to keep. I want my name to survive, and music is my way to accomplish this: Beethoven is still played today, Meredith Wilson lives on through revivals of *The Music Man,* and so on. The scandal that would erupt if word got out that he'd been solo writing our hits for several years would ruin my reputation, even that of *The Hitt Musical!* The music in that was entirely my own work, but it would be tarnished, people forever wondering if I'd cheated and used an unknown collaborator for this as well. Something needed to be done, but what? I didn't have an easy answer. In the absence of an outside miracle, this was going to take some concentrated thinking, free from distraction. I retired to my panic room, in the hopes that I might find inspiration there, to enable me to extricate myself from my dilemma.

* * *

The problem was subsequently resolved to my satisfaction, with the help of the police. With his heavy drug use, Canosh would often not show up for work at the studio when he was supposed to. However, after a week's worth of unexplained absences, with him also not returning calls and texts, people became worried enough to call the authorities. His house was situated a mile down the beach from mine. When the police arrived there, they found his clothes neatly folded on the sand, and above that an unsigned note stating he had had enough and was dedicating his life to the ocean he loved. The items were weighted down with a stone to keep them from blowing away. They concluded he had committed suicide by deliberately swimming out to sea as far as he could until exhaustion set in, eventuating in drowning. Not a method I would choose, but the police were comfortable with this explanation, and so was I.

It's now been three months since he vanished without reappearing, and that leaves me with two tasks. The first, as I am disinclined to retire just yet, is to find another collaborator. The second is to reboot the panic room to make it operational again, and to clean it up; I expect removing the stench of decay will be the hardest part.

The Girl Who Loved Beethoven

Wendy Harrison

He said his name was John Smith when he called to make the appointment. There had to be a million men actually named John Smith. The name was a cliché for a reason. I didn't like the odds that this one was legit, but I set a time to meet. I wasn't in a position to turn away business.

He knocked on the door to my office with my name, "Zoe Tanner, Private Investigator," painted on the opaque window. The office was large enough to hold an oversized, battered desk, with two chairs for clients and one where I sat. The décor was functional. File cabinets, a couple of lamps, and a MacBook Pro where I could access legitimate and not-so-legitimate sources for my work.

"Ms. Tanner? Zoe Tanner?"

I recognized him immediately. He was no John Smith. I stood and held out my hand. "A pleasure, Maestro."

He hesitated and then grinned, a smile too boyish for the graying hair and sturdy body, but charming anyway.

"I guess I should have come up with a more original name. Pleased to meet you, Ms. Tanner."

Handshakes tell a story. His was firm but not combative, a man who was sure of himself and didn't need to prove anything.

"Zoe, please."

"And I'm Maestro," he said, and his smile became a laugh. "But Nathan will do."

As he sat in front of my desk, I took a close look at my new client. Nathan Hancock was big news in Southview, our small Washington city. His daughter taught at the local high school and persuaded him to perform two concerts to raise money for her underfunded music program. The city went all out to welcome the famous conductor.

"How can I help, Nathan?"

It was the question I asked all my clients. Too often, they expected miracles from a private investigator. Sometimes, I turned them away because there were lines I wouldn't cross. So far, at least, no one had tried to hire me to kill someone for them, but it wouldn't surprise me if they did. After two tours in Afghanistan as an MP with the Army, I enjoyed the freedom to live by my own rules. My checkbook didn't always agree with my decisions, but I managed.

Nathan looked down at the scarred desktop. I could've told him he wouldn't find the answer to my question there. I waited.

"I've been very foolish." I waited some more. "I find myself in an embarrassing position."

I reassured him. "I've heard it all. Your secrets are safe with me, unless you're here to confess to a crime."

He met my eyes. "It depends on how you define crime."

This was getting interesting. "The usual way. A violation of the criminal laws."

"Then no crime. I find myself involved in a situation with a young woman." His eyes widened as he saw the expression on my face. "No. Good lord. Not that. A grown woman, in her 20s. Young by my standards. It was a poor decision on my part."

He told me he met Emma Murdock at a Portland jazz club earlier in the week, while his wife, Maria Meloni, was performing in New York.

He waited for my reaction, but I didn't recognize the name.

"Maria is one of the best known sopranos in the world." When I didn't apologize for my ignorance, he shrugged and kept talking.

"Emma's one of the bartenders at the club. She kept refilling my glass. In retrospect, I think she may have put something in my drink because I don't remember much of the rest of the evening."

Convenient memory loss? Floating an alibi? Just because he was a world-famous conductor didn't mean he wasn't a liar and a cheat.

He described waking the next morning, alone in his hotel room, tangled in the sheets and with a pounding headache.

"I thought it was over. But the next day, she was waiting for me on the steps of Symphony Hall when I arrived for rehearsal."

He paused. This was painful for him.

"She threw her arms around me and kissed me. I pushed her away, but she didn't care. Then she said, 'I love to listen to Beethoven,' and it came back to me. She kept chanting those words when we were…together. It was bizarre. I actually thought I might have dreamt the whole thing."

"Could be the effects of any drug she might have used."

He shrugged. "Doesn't matter. What matters is that she's threatening to ruin me. When I told her I was sorry but she needed to leave, she threatened to go to my wife and the press, to sell her story and destroy my life."

His concern puzzled me. He wouldn't be the first superstar to get caught with his pants down, so to speak. It was hard to believe a brief fling with a consenting adult would ruin him. It probably wouldn't do his marriage much good, but I couldn't see it ruining his long acclaimed career.

Before I could say anything, he added, "And she stole something from me. A special edition Gucci silk and cashmere scarf. It was a gift from Maria. Emma was wearing it when I saw her at Symphony Hall. I asked her to return it, but she refused."

"I can see this would be embarrassing, but really? Destroy your life?"

He looked down again. "It's the timing. I'm about to be appointed conductor of the Berlin Philharmonic. It's the best symphony orchestra in the world. Bad publicity like this would mean the loss of something I've worked for my whole life."

"What is it you want me to do?"

"Find her. Pay her off. Get my scarf back. That's it."

He agreed to my usual hourly rates, gave me a check for an impressive advance, and told me to offer her whatever it took. He gave me her description, blond and young and lovely, and the name of the bar where he met her, All That Jazz. I said I'd do my best, and Nathan left for rehearsal. I allowed myself a few minutes to think about what a bad idea this was. How could I get her to go away and make it stick?

The first step would be to find out as much as I could about the lovely Emma Murdock. I checked my usual data bases and social media sites. Emma was 25 years old, and she lived at the edge of downtown. No sign of family I could find. What I did find, though, was evidence of a bizarre obsession with Beethoven. Her social media posts were filled with collages she had created, all related to him, his music, his family, his life, his death. It wasn't surprising she had targeted Nathan. According to the classical music sites I looked at, he was the world's best Beethoven interpreter.

Was it a coincidence he happened to visit a jazz club where Beethoven's number one fan tended bar? Maybe they met somewhere else, some place he didn't want to admit. It wouldn't be the first time a client lied to me. Before I talked to her, I needed to be sure what the circumstances were of their relationship. Was it more than a one-night stand? Maybe Nathan had underestimated her obsessive behavior and tried to cut off what she would've seen as a serious connection.

I called the number on the card he gave me. I assumed it was his personal cellphone, so I was surprised when a woman answered.

"Maestro Nathan Hancock's office. Helen Bertin speaking."

"I'd like to speak to Nathan, please."

Pause. I thought maybe the call had dropped.

"Maestro Hancock isn't available. May I have your name?"

"Zoe Tanner."

"And the reason for your call?"

Who was this woman? She sounded like a jealous wife.

"It's personal. Please have him call me."

"I'm the Maestro's personal assistant. I can't pass on your message without knowing the subject of your call."

Was she kidding? Did Nathan have any idea his assistant was

controlling access to him? Please don't tell me she was sleeping with him too.

I had no time for this. "I suggest you tell him Zoe Tanner needs to talk to him. I promise you, if you don't, it will cost you your job."

"I'll give him your message, but I will let him know you threatened me."

"He'll probably congratulate me," I mumbled and hung up. If his wife was anything like his personal assistant, I was going to reconsider my disapproval of his seeking comfort elsewhere.

I didn't have much faith in my message reaching Nathan, so I decided I had enough information to track down the obsessive Emma.

All That Jazz was just like the Greenwich Village clubs my father used to talk about when he shared stories about growing up in New York. Dark, with scattered tables and a small stage. The perfect background for great music. My father had made a convert of me. I was the freaky kid who loved jazz while everyone else was into '80s glam metal. Motley Crue and Twisted Sister vs Miles Davis and John Coltrane. No contest.

I stood in the back for a few minutes and listened to a solo "Bye Bye Blackbird" being played on the piano. It was one of my dad's favorite pieces. I still missed him. What would he think of his ex-soldier daughter's career path? I smiled. He was a cop his whole adult life, died on the job at 52, and had no use for PIs. I hoped he would've made an exception for his daughter.

I got the attention of the bartender by holding up a twenty dollar bill.

"How can I help you, pretty lady?"

He must really want the twenty. At least he didn't call me a girl.

"Is Emma around?"

His tattooed hand reached for the bill, but I held onto it.

"Hasn't shown up. You a friend?"

"You might say that. When did you see her last?" I let the bill slip into his fingers.

"She was supposed to work tonight. Last night, too. She's not answering her phone, but Emma dances to her own fiddle. You dig?"

It sounded like Mr. Bartender spent too much time around old jazz players. He winked. "But you should know that if you're her friend."

"I sure do. That's Emma for you."

I wasn't making much progress. With luck, Emma was home and ignoring her phone. I had her address, and it wasn't far.

Southview was a wealthy community for the most part, but railroad tracks marked the boundary of a small, struggling, low-income neighborhood. The rundown house at Emma's address was on the wrong side of the tracks. I pulled up in front. Unmown grass threatened to bury a rusty car up on blocks. It was the sole lawn decoration.

I walked up the cement path and climbed the stairs to a small porch. When I knocked on the front door, it swung open. Not a good sign. I pulled my Glock from its back holster. I wasn't stupid. I had seen all those movies where you wanted to scream, "Don't do it," as the heroine went unarmed down into the dark basement.

"Emma?" I called her name as I made my way through the small living room. Above its well-used furniture, the walls were covered with pictures taped to the peeling paint. A quick glance showed they all had some connection to…of course…Beethoven. Creepy.

The galley kitchen was full of dirty dishes but no sign of life. Behind it were two doors off a tiny hallway. I knocked on the first, then turned the knob with the bottom of my shirt and pushed the door hard in case anyone waited behind it. I had a bad feeling about this. To my relief, it was an empty bathroom, and there was no one hiding behind the shower curtain. That left door number two.

I knocked and called her name. I wished I had brought gloves with me, but I used my shirt again and pushed the door open.

The bedroom was small, filled with a large bed, a small table next to it, and an old wooden dresser under the single window. The blond was sprawled across the bed on her back like a discarded Raggedy Ann doll, her head at an angle it wasn't designed for. I didn't have to check for a pulse to see she was dead. The bruising across her exposed neck explained how.

I knew I shouldn't disturb the crime scene, but it would be my one chance to search for the scarf and anything else that might affect my client. I wasn't planning on removing what I found, but I wanted as much information as I could get to earn my client's money.

It didn't take long to search the entire house. Emma had few possessions, none of them helpful unless you were into Beethoven memorabilia. I found a program from one of the Beethoven concerts Nathan had been doing this month. It must've taken every dime she had to afford the ticket. For the first time, I felt sorry for the disturbed young woman. In spite of her threats to Nathan, she didn't deserve a fate like this.

I started to close the last of the drawers I had opened. It was stuck on something. I yanked it toward me and saw a folded page from the *New York Times* sticking to the back.

The photo showed an elegant woman with upswept hair and large diamond earrings. "Maria Meloni, performing selected Italian arias." The date of the performance was a week ago. Could Emma have already reached out to Nathan's wife to tell her about his infidelity? And where was the scarf? It seemed unlikely she wouldn't have kept it here.

The questions had to wait. I hated to do it, but I had a call to make.

"Mackinnon."

"Sandy, it's me." Detective Sandy Mackinnon and I were an item, of sorts. He disapproved of my career choice. From time to time, we exchanged unpleasant words and parted. Fortunately, we always made up in a most enthusiastic way.

"I'm at 439 Second Avenue with Emma Murdock, deceased."

"Can I assume you aren't responsible for her current condition?"

"Funny. I suggest you get your butt over here with a CSI team. I'll wait out front. And don't insult me by telling me not to touch anything." It was too late, and I'm sure he knew it.

I sat on the porch steps waiting as instructed. Sandy arrived first, and I filled him in, leaving out the identity of my client and the reason I wanted to talk to the late Emma. PIs had confidentiality in Washington, like priests. Unlike priests, though, a process of law could compel me to talk. We both knew the law. Sandy had used it against me in the past. I hoped he wouldn't do it again. It hadn't done much for his sex life, or mine.

Sandy went inside, pulling on disposable gloves. He wasn't gone long. The cops he had called showed up and started stretching crime scene tape around the house.

"Don't leave town," he said as I stood.

"Not a chance."

When I got to my car, I turned and saw him watch me, exasperation written on his face. I could read his mind. I hoped he couldn't read mine.

My first duty was to my client. He had a concert in a few hours. I broke several speed limits on my way to Symphony Hall. I didn't bother trying to reach him by phone. The Gates of Hell weren't as closely guarded as Maestro Nathan Hancock was. I pictured Helen Bertin as a large nasty dog, who bared her teeth at anyone breaching the walls she constructed around him. A woman in her 50s at least, I guessed, single, with room for only one man in her life, one she could never have.

I wondered if Emma tried to get past the watchdog. According to Nathan, she hadn't had any trouble approaching him in front of the concert hall. Had she already failed to get him on the phone and decided face to face was her only alternative?

I found the side door at Symphony Hall for employees and performers. A security guard sat there, staring at his cellphone. I walked past him, nodded, and reached for the door handle.

"Hang on." The guard looked up at me. "You work here?"

I was realistic about my musical abilities and couldn't even pretend I was a performer. Instead, I flashed my PI badge, too quickly for him to read it.

"Maestro Hancock is expecting me. Got a call something went missing from his dressing room."

The overweight guard struggled to his feet. "I didn't hear nothin' about no theft. Not on my watch."

"You know these temperamental types. Probably put it down somewhere and doesn't remember. I'll be in and out in no time. Quick look around is all."

Before he could summon the energy to offer to help, I yanked the door open and stepped inside, letting it close behind me. I felt a little guilty. The guy was just trying to make a living, but so was I.

I wandered through the area behind the large stage until I found the dressing rooms. There was one with a big shiny star on it, so I knocked.

"Maestro? It's me. Zoe Tanner. Can I come in?" Without waiting for an answer, I opened the door and stepped inside. I had never been in a star's dressing room. It was huge, divided into a dressing area, a small kitchen, and a sizeable space with an overstuffed couch and several chairs. There was room left for a long table with piles of bound volumes of music.

A woman sat on the couch. I recognized her from the photo in Emma's apartment. Maria Meloni, diva, wife of the Maestro. She was younger and prettier than the picture. She needed to get a better publicist.

"Nathan? Someone here to see you." Her voice was calm, the tone pure. I suspected it wasn't the first time a strange woman had invaded her husband's dressing room.

The maestro came from a back room, his hands tying the bowtie on his tux. He stopped when he saw me. I could see the moment of panic as he tried to think of a way to explain who I was and why I was there.

I turned back to his wife. "Sorry to bother you, m'am. I was checking to make sure the Maestro had what he needed for tonight's performance." I summoned a broad smile. I hoped it didn't look as fake as it felt. "It'll be my head on a platter if everything isn't perfect."

Nathan was a quick thinker. I'll give him that.

"I do prefer the glass of water at the podium be only half full. Don't want to have any accidental spills in the middle of the third movement, now do we?"

"Of course not. Sorry to interrupt. Please don't hesitate to call me at the concierge number if you need anything else." I turned to his wife. "I'm a big fan, Ms. Meloni. Sorry again to bother you."

When I closed the door, I took a moment to breathe. The last thing I needed was to have Nathan's wife know he hired me to buy off a woman who was now on her way to the morgue. I hoped he'd take my hint and find a way to call me. I had a lot of questions for him. I hoped his answers would include a solid alibi for the time of Emma's death.

Nathan had a temporary office in the building next door to the symphony. The address was on the card he gave me. I'd rather get there ahead of Sandy and his team. It wouldn't take him long to link Beethoven girl to the famous Beethoven conductor. Although I didn't expect to find anything incriminating my client, there could be something useful there. I never crossed the line by hiding evidence, but knowledge is power, or so I'm told.

I didn't condone Nathan's getting involved with a much younger, and evidently unstable, woman, but I doubted he was capable of strangling her. He struck me as someone whose passion ran deep but only for the music he loved, not so much for the people around him. I could be wrong. Not every murderer looked like one.

I took the elevator to the Maestro's fourth floor office. Before I had a chance to rethink my plan, the elevator opened in front of a door with a temporary sign bearing his name.

When no one answered my knock, I used a credit card to open the simple lock. The flashlight in my phone showed me the light switch to the right of the door. There was a name plate on a desk in front of the inner office. The plate bore the name of Helen Bertin, Personal Assistant. I was in the right place.

In addition to a computer setup, her desk had a framed photo of Nathan in a tux with his arm draped around the shoulders of a young woman. The photo was signed, "For Helen, assistant extraordinaire, with gratitude, Maestro Nathan Murdock."

Two surprises. The formal signature suggested Helen wasn't more than an employee in spite of her obvious devotion to her boss. The second was that the Gorgon I expected to see was a woman younger than me and much more attractive. I wondered how many women in Nathan's life shared an obsession with him. And how much of this did his wife know and resent?

Questions for another time. I rummaged through the drawers of Helen's desk, not sure what I was looking for but certain I'd know if I found it. No luck. Across the room, I saw a closet. If I didn't find anything there, I'd try Nathan's inner office next.

There were several overcoats on hangars in the closet, alongside a half dozen white formal shirts. I started with the pockets of the coats. They were empty until I reached the last one. My hand touched fabric softer than anything I'd ever touched before. As I started to pull it out, the colors glowed. It had to be the Gucci scarf Nathan wanted me to retrieve. The one last seen around Emma's neck outside the Symphony when she confronted him.

I made a phone call and then started to push the scarf back into the coat pocket.

"What do you think you're doing?"

I turned to face Maria Meloni with the scarf still in my hand. "Just my job."

"Since when does a concierge's job include breaking and entering?" Her eyes dropped to the scarf. "I think you have something of mine."

"Actually, it belongs to my client."

"Who *are* you? That concierge bit didn't fool me."

"Worse. I'm a private investigator."

Before she could ask the obvious next question, the door behind her flew open. It was starting to feel like an Agatha Christie novel, where all the suspects gathered in one room. I wondered if I was supposed to be Hercule Poirot or Jane Marple.

The woman in the photo on the desk ran into the room.

"Ms. Bertin, I assume?"

She looked at the scarf.

"It was me." It didn't feel like the right moment for a grammar lesson.

"What was you?" Brilliant questions were my strong suit.

"I killed that girl. I'm the one who hid the scarf."

Right on cue, the Maestro walked in.

"Don't say another word," he told Helen. I realized he had been listening outside the door before making his grand entrance.

"I'll make sure you have the best lawyer. You can plead self-defense. You'll be fine. I promise."

His wife stepped between them.

"I know about the girl, Nathan." She sounded exhausted. "She called me. I went to see her this morning, but I was too late. She was dead. There's only one person who could've put that scarf in your coat pocket."

We all looked at Nathan.

No charming smile this time. "No one's going to believe that Maestro Nathan Hancock would have strangled that delusional young woman."

"Who said she was strangled?" I knew the answer to my own question. No one had.

Maria moved closer to Helen. "Time to call the police. I'm not covering for him anymore. And you're not either." She put her arms around the younger woman who began to weep.

The office door opened again. My favorite detective stood there, his phone to his ear.

"About time." I reached in my pocket and pressed the stop recording button on my phone. It looked like I had lost a client, but I was sure Sandy would find a way to make it up to me, maybe to the strains of Beethoven's Fifth.

Listener Favorites

Martin Zeigler

The final chord is barely over with, and already they are on their feet, slapping their hands and barking like seals. Here on the podium, still facing my orchestra, I barely detect the audience out the corner of my eye, but I would sense them even if I were deaf and blind. There's a certain offensive smell to their rising. And from all behind me I hear their incessant yelping of, "Encore, encore," to the point where I almost feel compelled to swing around and toss out fish.

Instead, I bid the orchestra to stand. Troopers, each and every one of them. I acknowledge them with a smile, but it means nothing. By all rights, I should not be expressing my appreciation at all but rather begging for forgiveness. *How many times must I put you through this?* I want to ask.

And now comes the time to face the music.

Baton in hand, I turn toward the concert hall, this chandeliered ark of bejeweled vermin, and take it all in at once, the fawning fauna all on their feet and furiously thwacking their forepaws. And when I step off the podium to take a bow, I work them into an even more frenzied pitch. Their mating cries of "Encore! Encore!" reach an ear-wrenching fortissimo, echoing from hidden corners of the concert hall I never knew existed. And just beneath me, in the second row, basking in the glow of the stage, a pink, pudgy-faced *turtleneckedus vulgaris* is standing with his megaphonic mitts to his mouth, bellowing up at me, "Bravo! Bravo! Bravo!"

My God, I wish he would stop. That they would all just shut their mouths and keep their oily hands by their side. Or better yet, now that they are standing, quietly slip into their coats and leave. Vanish. Shoo, go away.

Because it's not just the sycophantic shouts of "Encore!" and "Bravo!"

that gall me, although those are irritating enough. No, it's the standing I loathe most of all, the sudden rising to the feet as if everyone has just sat on tacks. Must every audience I get respond to every single piece I conduct with a goddamn standing ovation, even when they have all heard the piece a thousand times before?

Why, of course they must, for the simple reason they have all heard the piece a thousand times before.

Familiarity breeds contempt—in everyone, apparently, except the average concertgoer.

Why, I bet I could turn my back to them, lift my leg, and fart the Spring Concerto from Vivaldi's Four Seasons—selected this year, last year, the year before, and every year prior by Classic KWHATEVER listeners as the single best thing ever composed in the history of music—and they would be on their feet and belching hosannas before I finish blasting the first measure.

"Bravo! Bravo! Bravo!"

My attention turns once again to the spittle-spouting buffoon in the second row—what is it, seventh seat from the left?—with his bulbous face now blood-pressure red from enthusiasm, and I immediately want to make strategic use of the trombonist's mute.

Tonight, though, it's not spring, summer, fall, or winter that has concluded the program and still has everyone in the throes of overwrought adulation, but rather the equally predictable Beethoven's Fifth Symphony. Pardon me, Beethoven's *Immortal* Fifth Symphony, which, in KWHATEVER's annual listener poll, has come in at a close second every single year since radio was invented.

"Bravo!"

That's right. That's right. The pink, pudgy one knows what he likes.

There was a brief time, at the start of my career, when I seriously believed I had a say in the kinds of music this orchestra would perform. But I quickly learned, as symphony conductor, that I am little more than a monkey-suited marionette, tugged at by patrons, sponsors, endless foundations, commissions, councils for this and that, and endowments.

For instance, an early letter from a deep-pocketed contributor praised me at first for "giving the vital, contemporary stuff a shot" but then went on to suggest I balance things out by ditching the vital, contemporary stuff altogether.

"Stick to the classics," he wrote. "That's what draws the crowds. Haydn, Mozart, maybe a little Beethoven's Fifth to round out a concert or two."

What could I say in response?

Plenty, as it turned out, and in lengthy strings of as few syllables as possible. But the words out of my mouth were a bit more circumspect. "Thanks for setting me straight," was the gist of my response. "I have learned my lesson. I shall never err again."

So now, as I look out on this one-note crowd, I know what they expect of me at this very moment. That I exit the stage and return, exit the stage and return, exit the stage and return to their ever-rising crescendo of encores and bravos and plaudits, and that I finally relinquish and step up to the podium one more time. Or two. Or three. For that, in the end, is what they are really after—extra music for nothing.

I am tempted to point out that if it's more music they want, CD's are available in the lobby, for a price.

Instead, I exit the stage and return, exit the stage and return, exit the stage and return. And when I mount the podium and face the orchestra, the mollified multitude instantly turns quiet, save for the rustling of britches and bloomers as so many sweaty bottoms work themselves back into the seats. And save for one last abbreviated bravo from behind me in the second row.

And as I raise my baton, I can almost hear the hushed expectancy from every quarter. What will he play? What *will* he play?

What else is there, of course, but...Spring, from the Four Seasons? Any form will do, I'm sure, but I resist temptation and decide to stick with instruments.

* * *

By some recurring miracle which never ceases to amaze me, the concert comes to a close and I find myself once again ensconced in the blessedly silent dungeon of my dressing room.

As usual, I plummet into the couch, weary to the bone, head throbbing to beat the band, and yet afraid to shut my eyes for fear of seeing what I always see at the end of these never-ending nights—the dress circle, mezzanine, lower balcony, upper balcony, all crammed with row upon row of life-sized cutouts, their hands frozen in mid-clap, their faces in mid-encore.

It is an image that sounds ludicrous in the telling but one I fiercely try to avoid.

I have no say in the matter, though. It's as if my eyelids, too, were controlled by all those sponsors listed at the back of the concert programs.

And yet this time when my eyes fall shut, it's not a thousand rapturous faces I see, but only one.

A pink, pudgy one.

A pink, pudgy one a thousand times its original size, with a wide-open mouth so cavernous it obscures the entire concert hall and threatens to consume me in one astronomical bravo.

Thankfully, just as I am about to scream, "I want my old nightmare back!" a loud rap on the door comes to my rescue. I immediately open my eyes to a heaven on earth—a too-tiny, too-dark, too-cramped dressing room without a second row, seventh seat from the left in sight.

I hear another knock. This time the door swings open, and in swoops the manager of all things customer-related.

"Maestro, you did wonderfully!" she gushes.

She slaps her hands together—only once but quite loudly— and belts out her own rendition of, "Bravo!"

I level my eyes at her, silently daring her to say it again.

"Bravo! Bravo! Bravo!" she shouts.

Which I gladly accept, considering that she closes the door, locks it, and proceeds to remove her jacket and unbutton her shirt.

And as I do likewise with my tux, I say to her, "I need to ask a really, really big favor."

The wary tilt of her head and the skeptical arch to her brow lead me to assure her, "No, no, something else."

* * *

I allow her a minute or two to button up before showing her the door, with a peck on her cheek for her troubles.

Then, after a few preparations, including switching to jeans and a jacket, I step outside into the nighttime air and make my way toward the Norwood Apartments, which, as it turns out, are not that far from the concert hall.

Along the way, I spot my first chair, of all people, coming down the street. I figure he's out and about, celebrating the end of another concert by taking in the refreshing racket of the city. In any event, he's the last person I want to see.

But much to my relief—and encouragement, I might add—he passes me by without so much as a glance in my direction, indicating to me that my disguise is perfect.

At the Norwood, I wait in the shadows. And when someone emerges from the secure building, I slip inside before the door swings shut. I head to the elevator, aware of the overhead cameras but not fearing recognition in the least, thanks to that chance encounter with my ever reliable first chair.

Upstairs, I knock on the door to the proper apartment, and when the door guardedly inches open, I push my way past the tenant before he realizes what is happening.

Fortunately, when he does react—with words like, "What? Who? Who are you? What do you want?"—his delayed outrage is so anemic, the sound barely carries into the hallway.

Before he can give it another try, I rip off my fake mustache and pocket my thick glasses, revealing myself as a symphony conductor once again. And immediately the tenant's pink, pudgy face turns even pinker and pudgier with delight.

"Why, Maestro…why, Mister…why…" he begins.

"Maestro is fine."

It's late and he's still wearing the same turtleneck from the concert. Probably the same wrinkled trousers, too, although he just as likely could have culled them from his dirty laundry when he got home. And for all I know, maybe he went to the concert in those slippers coming apart at the heels.

"Oh my goodness!" he says. "I can't believe this. What a…what a sur…what a surp…what a surpri…"

Listening to him, I get the impression that all his words want to escape his mouth at once, like a panicked throng through a single exit.

"*Surprise* is the word you're aiming for," I offer helpfully. "But don't worry. You would have got there eventually."

"Yes, yes, yes, a surprise, this is indeed, indeed a surprise. But why the mustache? The glasses?"

I shrug modestly. "Autograph hunters. They're everywhere."

He quickly nods his understanding and adds, "But, Maestro, what places you bring—I mean, what brings you here of all places? And at this late hour?"

"Don't you know? You won the drawing."

"Drawing?"

"Your concert ticket stub was selected at random and you won first prize—a late night visit from me."

"I don't recall drawing a—I mean, entering a drawing."

"It was all explained on the back of the ticket. Don't you look at the back of your tickets?"

"Well, no."

"And why should you? As a devoted concertgoer, you probably read the program notes instead. Now how about giving that door of yours a little push?"

"By all means! I mean, by all means!" He is absolutely beside himself. And while both of him step forward to close the door to his apartment, I stand back and take in the rest of the place at a glance.

I should be astonished at what I see, bowled over, knocked to the carpet from utter amazement. But for some reason the sight before me is more or less what I've been expecting and comes as no sur…surp…surpri whatsoever.

Every inch of wall space—from the floor to the ceiling, from the living room to the dining room, and even along the hallway to the other rooms—has been usurped by shelves upon shelves upon shelves of compact disks. Not one wall molecule has been spared the cheap particleboard, and not a single iota of shelving has escaped the vertical plastic jewel case. Everywhere I turn, I see a veritable infinity of CD's, all of them cramped together like the thin, emaciated masses of humanity one encounters in those hysterical visions of overpopulation.

From where I'm standing, I can only guess at the contents. Endless music for nineteenth-century elevators, perhaps. Or maybe a million and one Beloved Masterpieces that arrived in the mail as a boxed set years ago, along with a thousand and one other forgettable trifles for "ordering now."

The pudgy prize-winner brushes up alongside me. He's closed the door and is back to himself again. "I bet you're wondering why there's no music playing," he says.

Well, no. What I'm really wondering, as I look around at all this deranged wallpapering, is when, exactly, did my fuchsia-colored host finally come to terms with being an irremediable dullard.

But in the interest of civility, I merely suggest, "Could it be because it's getting really, really late at night?"

He shakes his head vigorously. "No, no, no, Maestro, that's not it, no, not at all, and in fact I just finished listening to something before you knocked, but here's the thing: now that it's ended, I have to pick something else to listen to, and that's not as easy as you might think, as you probably know, being a music lover yourself, and so that's why it's so quiet, because I'm between choices right now, trying to decide what next, what next, what do I play next?"

"Well, then," I say, seizing the opportunity, "as long as you're in a deciding mood, maybe you can help me decide where to put this."

He eyes the small instrument case I pull out from under my jacket. "Oh, my! Please—right here, right here."

He sweeps an area clear on his dining room table, and I set down the case, snapping open its latches but keeping the top closed.

"I didn't know you were an instrument—I mean, played an instrument," he says.

"I don't. But one is never too old to learn something new."

"How true, how true," he says, wringing his hands, no doubt at the possibility of listening to a symphony conductor play something other than a baton.

He begins staring at me as if a deity had floated into his apartment and he is just now realizing it. He seems at a complete loss for words, a rather pleasant experience from my perspective until it occurs to me I better get cracking.

I nod my head a few times, as if recollecting something, and then wag a meaningful finger at him. "I remember you from tonight's concert," I say at last. "You shouted bravo."

"Oh, yes, yes, that was me, bravo, bravo! How could I help but shout it, shout it up to the rafters? That was a masterful performance, simply masterful, masterful."

"That's probably why you stood up."

"Oh, definitely, I did stand up. Your performance of the Fifth Symphony was worth an ovation, a standing, a standing ovation and nothing less."

"It's a wonder you didn't shout encore."

"I was tempted, but to me it was a bravo performance all the way."

"Don't you mean *bravura*?"

"Yes, *bravura*. Does one shout bravura? Maybe in the future I should shout bravura. What do you think? Would that be better? Which do you prefer?"

I shrug. "Bravura, bravo, encore. It's all of a piece when it comes to Beethoven's *Immortal* Fifth."

"Oh, Maestro, isn't that the truth?"

"Speaking of which, you wouldn't happen to have a recording of it lying around by any chance, would you?"

"You mean…Beethoven's Fifth, Fifth Symphony?"

"Yes, yes," I say, as I eagerly interlock my fingers in prayer. "You do have it, don't you?"

He begins to perspire, his face now taking on more of a crimson hue. "Oh, boy, this is going to be a challenge, a real challenge," he says.

"Why is that?"

He stretches his pudgy lips into a broad smile and extends his arms, turning his head to indicate the entirety of his domicile with its wall-to-wall shelves. "Explore to your heart, Maestro, to your hearts, to your heart's content," he says.

Deciding a pilgrimage to the far end of the living room would not be worth my while, I step in closer to the nearest set of shelves and let my eyes scan the contents. By the third row I get the point and drop back in a curious state of revulsion and vindication.

"Do you see now what I mean, Maestro, when I say it's a challenge, a challenge, a real challenge?" he says. "When one Fifth Symphony ends, which one do I play after that, do you see? And now you're asking me to pick one for yourself, and this will be very, very hard, Maestro, because the Fifth, I mean Beethoven's Fifth, is all I have and they're everywhere and in no particular order, and so the one I pick for you to listen to could be out here in the dining room or in my bedroom or in one of the closets or in the cupboard in the bathroom next to the toilet paper, do you see? I have everything, every recording ever made. Name a conductor, any conductor, past or present, and if they recorded the Fifth, you can bet I have it, and if they recorded the Fifth a hundred times, you can bet I have it a hundred times. I have amateur recordings, professional recordings, student recordings, recordings made from every single globe of the corner. And let's not forget transcriptions, I've got piano transcriptions, guitar transcriptions, organ transcriptions, brass, wind, vocal, and get this, Maestro, I even have an arrangement of Beethoven's Fifth Symphony for tugboat whistles."

"Imagine that!" I intone as I picture a fleet of torpedoed tugboats at the bottom of the harbor.

"And it says without going, Maestro, that I have your CD, as well, or, rather, that of your orchestra with you conducting, and in all honesty I have to say it's probably the single best rendition I own, but I'm guessing you're up for something different tonight, am I right?"

"Oh, you're absolutely right," I hasten to inform him. "So I suggest grabbing the first CD that isn't mine, and that'll be the one I'll listen to. Right this very minute. I can't wait."

He leans in toward a middle shelf, canting his neck at an impossible angle in order to read the labels, mumbling nonsense about acoustics and metronome markings. "Oh, you'll love this guy, he observes all the repeats."

"That's exactly what I want. Beethoven's Fifth with all the repeats."

But evidently he thinks there is something even better, and so he continues his search, methodically working his way to the right, stopping at the thirtieth CD, now at the forty-first, in his tireless progression toward the seventeen thousand four hundred and fifty-third.

"Ah, yes, this one," he rhapsodizes. "This one…this one…"

As pleasurable as this visit has been, I do not want to be here all night. Or, to put it another way, I do not want to be here a second longer. And so, with as robust a timbre as I can manage given how tired I've become just standing here, I tell him, "As long as you play it nice and loud, that's all I care about."

He turns to look at me, letting a finger reserve his spot. "You know, Maestro, that's exactly how I feel, but you can bet my neighbors won't like it, oh, no, they're always on about something. Classical music lovers, they're not, they'll be pounding on the horns—I mean, the wall—before the horns come in."

"To hell with them. Crank it up all the way."

He nods happily, realizing he is in the presence of not only a refined, cultured impresario but also an Everyman who has no qualms about saying things like, "To hell with them."

His back is to me now as he delicately plucks the disk from the jewel case and places it into the CD player's tray, all the while whistling the da-

da-da-dum from the opening bars. In the meantime, I don't whistle anything as I quietly back up along the carpet toward the dining room table.

"Be sure to turn it up all the way," I remind him as I open the instrument case and first pull out the gloves.

Though I'm unable to see his face, I can almost detect a rosy glow reflecting off the volume knob as he spins it as far as it will turn. "Are you ready, Maestro, are you? This was a really, really tough choice, but I think it will have you shouting bravo."

"Yes, I think I'm pretty close to being ready."

My choices are difficult, as well, but thank goodness they boil down to only two—the claw hammer or the ball peen.

* * *

On the way home, once again adorned in bushy mustache and thick spectacles, it occurs to me I have unfinished business.

Once my dear manager of things customer-related reads the newspaper article that is bound to appear one of these days—*Pink, Pudgy-Faced Man Found With Claw Hammer Buried In Skull*—she will notice his address and remember the favor she did for me—locating, in her customer database, the address of that occupant in the second row, seventh seat from the left.

Can she be trusted to keep that secret?

The answer to that, of course, is obvious. As is the answer to the question *ball peen or claw*, since I now have only the one left.

No, the question I really should be asking is: which recording would make the perfect accompaniment?

On the one hand I am free to choose anything I wish without any pressure whatsoever. Something avant-garde, perhaps. Or something dissonant. Or maybe even something vital and contemporary.

On the other hand, as much as I hate to admit it, perhaps there truly is something eternal about the old standards, the listener favorites, and especially that one weathered opus in particular.

After all, the days are getting longer and the flowers are in bloom.

Finding the Groove

Ed Teja

The first time Sandy came into The Backbeat, she was drawn in by the magnetic force of curiosity. The name, written in script on a small, dim sign, resonated inside her. After all, she was a bass player. She lived for backbeats, those deep bottom lines.

Only later could she acknowledge that the tug she felt involved more than that. Much more. It went deeper. It sank into the lowest registers, almost below hearing. Resonating. Filling a void.

Wandering aimlessly on that foggy night, the bar appeared like a doorway into a world that had faded. A world she had read about. A world of music she had listened to.

This hole-in-the-wall bar, stuck in a row of brick buildings on a back street of the Big Easy, gave off the soft vibe of old-school jazz.

Although she had braced herself for disappointment, expecting to find some retro place filled with rich people, walking in, laid-back jazz wrapped itself around her. A low, softly pulsing heartbeat meshed with hers. She turned her face toward the source—a thin, hollowed out older man held a monstrous standup bass, melded with it. His head was tipped at an angle toward the instrument; he could have been asleep except for the way his large fingers caressed the thick strings.

She drifted in past the bar's three tables, all full of murmuring drinkers, and sat at the bar. The bartender, a small man with a mustache that framed a smile, wearing a red vest over a white shirt, slipped up to smile his inquiry. She ordered a whisky.

He served her the drink, smiling at the way she sipped the alcohol and inhaled the atmosphere.

"The band…?" She let the question hang.

"Smooth Sam's trio," he said. "Sam on piano. Jerry on drums. Mickey on bass."

"This your place?" she asked.

"Name's Bill and yes. Partly, anyway."

The bar was as much a throwback as the music. It was an assault on the senses that took her to another time, to a time when the music didn't so much explode, the way her band's tunes did, but floated and sometimes soared, flying you to the moon and back again.

In here it was still the 1940s.

She sat at the bar and sipped whiskey and music until closing.

The next week, she came back.

As much as the vibe was right for a girl who wanted a break from her own time, from the constant hustle of living in a modern city, it was Mickey Monroe that drew her back week after week.

Night after night, Mickey Monroe, a tall, scrawny, ugly mick with an ancient string bass, stood on the tiny stage putting the bottom in Smooth Sam's trio. She would sit listening to him making love to his bass, working those throbbing strings, supporting the tunes in ways she'd never imagined—putting down a foundation that didn't come from music theory.

She became a Thursday regular, sitting at the bar, listening. The band was there Thursday, Friday, and Saturday, but on Friday and Saturday she played bass in a rock band that worked at a club across town.

Her band wasn't a bad band at all, but they lacked magic. They weren't going anywhere. They played the same music a thousand other bands were playing. Their take was personal, but not intimate.

And intimacy defined what she found in the jazz that Smooth Sam's Trio played—intimacy and a groove that seduced you.

She got to know The Backbeat's other regular customers. Most were older men who wore fancy clothes and gold necklaces, with a few women in low-cut dresses decorating the fringes. Men and women of various colors and races, and from the same circle.

One night, one of the men, a tall black man in an expensive suit, sent her a drink. She smiled her acknowledgement. He smiled back—a nice smile in a nice face.

"That is Calvin," Bill, the bartender, told her.

"He's always here."

Bill grinned. "The place is sort of his office."

"Office?"

"Calvin has businesses. This is one of them."

"Your partner. What else does he do?"

"Gambling, I think," Bill said. "Or involved in gambling somehow."

"Somehow?"

Bill winked and poured her drink. "Bartenders don't want to know shit like somehow."

"Not even if it involves their partners?"

"Especially then."

She liked that. Distance was good. Bass players, even bass players in rock bands, could focus on not giving a shit, too.

She turned her attention back to getting some inkling of the magic of a mysterious little ascending riff that Mickey was playing under Starlight. It was so simple, so fucking spot on for the transition to the diminished chord. Sam reached into the sky for those notes and the trio brought it to earth for the mortals listening.

Talking to the musicians during the breaks, she found she liked them, their immersion in what they were doing. But trying to put what he was doing on the bass into words brought an amused smile to Mickey's haggard face. A wan and pale smile, but a smile.

"It's the groove," he said. "Not some fucking theory. It ain't a word thing. Let me show you." Then he took her to the stage and let her hold the bass. She put her fingers on those thick strings, still warm from his hands. Those strings were probably the ones put on it in the factory years ago.

"Don't think. Feel what the instrument is telling you about the song," he said.

She tried. And failed. But she persisted. Thursday after Thursday, when the band took breaks, she got Mickey to show her some magic.

Then he would sneak off to shoot up while she burned the riff into her fingers and brain in an attempt to own its secrets.

And yes, the brilliant Mickey was a classic cliché, another throwback—the junkie jazzman. When he slipped away, hands trembling, Smooth Sam would sit at his piano and sip his drink. Jerry, the drummer, would look at her and shrug.

"Mickey was a giant once," Jerry said. "Played with the best."

"And now us," Sam said.

She understood. The trio was good, not great—a small-time jazz trio that played in a tiny and relatively unknown club. Sam owned a small construction company; Jerry worked for him.

Mickey was on disability for something or other.

Thursday after Thursday she came in to hear them. Coming early, she would meet Sam's battered station wagon when it pulled in behind the bar. She'd help him and Jerry haul in the equipment… drums, that huge bass. The equipment stayed on stage the next few nights, then on Saturday they took it home again.

She helped, but mostly she listened. She talked to Mickey about playing over changes. Again, that amused him. "That's all head stuff," he said. "Feel the groove and it just comes."

One night, Sam sent her out to his car to get his cigarettes. "In the glove compartment."

She took his keys and found them, a pack of Marlboros sitting right next to a Glock pistol. She picked it up, hefted it. Aimed it at a window and said: "Pow." Then she put it back.

"A gun?" she asked when she handed him the smokes.

He shrugged. "Jazz clubs ain't always the friendliest places. And construction sites often are no safer, especially when I'm carrying a payroll."

It made a certain amount of sense even if she couldn't picture Smooth Sam shooting a person.

Periodically, Calvin bought her drinks. Her interest in jazz seemed to amuse him. Eventually she got to know them, his friends. A core group, Danny and Ricky in particular.

They brought in different women and sometimes other men, younger versions of themselves. They would be there all night, talking, laughing, drinking. Except Ricky. Rickey didn't speak. He glowered, mostly.

And then there was a host of younger men, in shabbier clothes, who would come and go.

Some of them would slap Calvin on the back. "Hey, bro," they would say, and hand Danny a package. Discretely. Without fuss.

For Sandy, the gamblers and their women were just wallpaper—part of the club and therefore part of the music. Their chatter was like having another band there, improvising against the tunes Smooth Sam's trip played, their moods shifting as the band went from "Straight, No Chaser," to their favorite swing tune, "Seven Come Eleven."

She liked that they mostly ignored her—the out of place, tattooed, skinny girl with short hair, wearing a black tee shirt and jeans. She got comfortable among them, nestled between the notes and rhythms they all seemed to appreciate. The gamblers seemed to enjoy seeing her struggling with Mickey Monroe's bass, which dwarfed her. She liked struggling with the damn thing and, over time, it got easier.

One night, Mickey came in weak and weary. Under the weather. Or hard done by drugs. Whatever. During the last set, he was dragging… his playing was way off.

Calvin came over to pat Mickey on the back. "We need you on your game, baby," he said, slipping something into Mickey's palm. "It's Willa's birthday."

Willa was a girl Danny had brought in.

Mickey took the package with a strange look of thanks. Then he glanced at Sam. She couldn't see Mickey's face, but Sam raised his head and looked at Sandy.

Sam had busy eyebrows, a pair of lovely fuzzy creatures that danced across his wrinkled brow when he played. Those eyebrows were always looking ahead, tracking Sam's concentration, finding the next notes, the next chord or modification to one. Now they were sitting up and talking to her.

"Can you sit in for Mickey?" they asked.

Mickey must have heard those eyebrows. "Just for a couple of tunes," he said, looking pale. "While I get fixed up." He looked at Sam. "Maybe start with 'Bye Bye Blackbird' in one flat."

It was a tune he knew she knew.

She gasped, feeling like she was going on some crazy audition. When Mickey leaned the bass toward her, she grasped the neck and watched him stagger off toward the bathroom.

She grappled with that monstrous bass, holding it upright and, with Mickey gone, feeling alone, feeling like she had never played a note on the bass.

She gripped the thick neck and pressed a string. This was so different from banging out solid notes on her slender, rather battered Fender electric. Her eyes turned to the expectant crowd. They were new, too. Different.

When she was banging out rock and roll with her band, their sound shook the dancers. They created a sound and provided a pulsing beat that sent the dancers into a trance. Here gamblers with gold necklaces and fancy women watched, ears alert to hear what she would do, actually listening to her. These people were interested in the music.

Now they were waiting to hear what the tattooed white girl could do to tunes they knew intimately.

They all had the same question: Would she find the groove?

Jerry's brushes shuffled over the snare, clicking the skins in tempo with the tick-tick-tick of her heart.

How did he do that?

"Blackbird with a little kick-ass up-tempo shuffle," Jerry said, winking at her. "One, two, three."

He launched them and Mickey's bass followed, as if it didn't need her help, as if it remembered every direction it had gotten from Mickey's fingers over the years. She rode along, thumping those big, thick strings from D to G and then, with a short pause, introducing the opening chord from Sam's piano.

And she fell into it, losing track of the universe. Her brain melded with the shuffle, the compelling forward momentum that came with packing up all your cares and woes, here we go…

At the end of the tune, Sam grinned broadly and, instead of wrapping it up, right when they got to the spot where the tune would end, he smoothly riffed a few lines, changing keys deftly, and swept them right into the intro of a bittersweet blues.

Stormy Weather was the tune and in Sandy's head, Ivie Anderson stirred and stepped up to a mic to sing about how it was raining all the time.

"Sweet," Sam said.

She opened her eyes. The man's big brown eyes were focused on her. Pleasure radiated over her, warming her.

"Swing it a little more, Jerry, and we gonna take it up a couple of steps."

The world swallowed her up, and Sandy felt the piano working inside her, moving to Jerry's crisp brushes.

And then the song ended.

She inhaled sharply. Had she been holding her breath? It felt like it.

When the final string she had plucked stopped vibrating, she came awake from a deep sleep. The memories of playing faded like a soft dream.

What notes had she played? She had no idea. Everything was a glowing haze.

The crowd drowned her in applause.

"The white girl can put down a line," Calvin said, his face overflowing with appreciation.

She shivered from the playing, the intensity of the experience. Her clothing was damp in sweat. Then Mickey was there, appearing from nowhere, bathing her in that smile of his.

"That's how you do it," he said. "Be careful, you'll get hooked."

As Mickey resumed his rightful place on the bandstand, Calvin put a drink in her hand and led her to his table.

"You got the soul for it, baby," he told her.

She sat at the table for the rest of the night. While Smooth Sam continued their musical journey, taking them all through Chicago and New York, invoking Benny Goodman and Duke Ellington, Calvin's friends drank, and Danny started talking about bands she should play with, people they might introduce her to.

"He thinks big, Danny does," Calvin said.

"We got the big game next Thursday," Danny said.

"And?"

"It's an opportunity," he said. "We should celebrate. Maybe at a bigger club." Danny looked at Sandy. "Maybe a new band."

"We will be right here," Calvin said firmly. "We operate out of my place." He put his hand on her shoulder and whispered, "Never mind Danny's bullshit. He digs your playing is all. Thinks you want to be a star."

"Don't I?" she asked.

He shook his head. "You want to be a player."

"A player." That sounded good. Right.

Calvin touched her arm. "I see you, girl. You are there for the music and if people appreciate you, fine. But you don't control that. You care about the music inside, about letting it out."

Sitting there, with Calvin's arm around her, she thought he understood, but it was an outsider's understanding. The words, not the feeling.

With that came an awareness… Calvin and his friends occupied a separate world within the jazz world of The Backbeat.

That sense was bittersweet. As much as he clearly loved the music, the club, there was something about Calvin's world, his sense of life, that jarred when pressed against soft jazz. There was a friction he didn't see.

The next Thursday, Calvin had her sit with him again. He was attentive in ways that made her feel warm, just as the music did. The same, but different.

The world of the club's audience involved motion and interconnection with the outside. While they drank and listened to the intoxicating music, those faceless, forgettable people wordlessly brought their mysterious packages and left. She had no interest in the packages or the intruders. But Calvin saw that she noticed.

"They are just messengers from associates we do business with." He waved an arm to indicate Danny and a couple of other men.

Danny folded his hands. "Associates who should be working for us." His voice carried a minor chord of accusation that earned him a cold, hard look from Calvin. Sitting next to him, she felt the darkness and disapproval in that glance.

And so it went, week in and out. The groove of jazz and booze and packages, and underlying it, tension. Over time, living in the jazz world and having a foot in Calvin's world grated even more against her other world—the one where she played rock. Making the transition each weekend of getting herself into the mindset of blasting out rock became a chore.

The groove was there, but it was solid, unyielding, and predictable.

She quit the band and got a day job waiting tables. That let her go to the club every night the band played. That let her spend evenings sitting with Calvin, listening to the bass line pushing the tunes. She learned. And sometimes, she played.

Each night, when the band took a break, she would leave Calvin's side to study string magic with the chief wizard, Mickey Monroe. Calvin would sit back, feet stretched out, legs crossed, watching. Smiling.

One Saturday night, Mickey came in looking a little down, a little weak, like he was recovering from a flu bug. He struggled with trying to lift his bass onto the stage, and Calvin jumped up to help him.

Then, when Mickey was settled, Calvin whispered something to him, slipping something into his pocket.

A strange look came over Mickey's face, but he nodded.

"Gotcha, man."

At the break, as usual, she and Mickey talked, but he was distracted, his eyes wandering. His hands shook. "Would you take the next set for me?"

"The next set?" she gasped.

He nodded. "Sam wants to start off with Billy Boy—in C." Then he disappeared into the bathroom.

She looked over at Sam, who rubbed his long face and then nodded. "Sure, girl. You can do fine."

Then he sent a sad look down the hallway toward the bathroom that had swallowed Mickey.

When it was time, she stepped on that stage determined to do right by Mickey. She balanced that monstrous bass and slipped into the delicious trance that Jerry's drums evoked.

Some power draped over her like a shroud, like a hood over the head of a kidnapped person. The audience and the bar disappeared. Sandy's entire body came alive, vibrating with the notes from that bass. She was alone with the tune. Her fingers moved of their own accord, propping up Sam's weak left hand, responding to Jerry's delicate rhythms.

At the end of the set, Sam and Jerry applauded her. She gave them confused looks.

Were they teasing her? They didn't seem to be.

Still in the swing of things, still vibrating with the music, she saw Mickey at the bar. He seemed calm. Composed. A steady hand raised a glass in a toast.

She went by him, and he slipped off the bar stool.

"You found the groove, girl. Now you got to be real careful," he said.

"Careful?"

"There are cats who spend their entire lives searching for that groove. You fucking fell right into it." He shook his head. "I never seen anybody find it so natural like. But being in that groove is dangerous."

"Dangerous? It's incredible."

He nodded. "And seductive. If you don't watch it, one day you might find you done sank into it so deep you can't get out."

His eyes glistened. He was stoned, of course, but still.

"That's what got me," he said.

"Sure," she said. Mickey was rambling, not making sense. Who wouldn't want to live forever in that groove?

In that heady state, when the bar closed, it wasn't a surprise that she let Calvin take her home to his high-end apartment where he kissed her, caressed her, made crazy love to her.

They spent the weekend together… much of it in his bed.

Monday morning, when things looked different, or were supposed to, she opened her eyes and tried to examine the dream she found herself in.

"What was Danny saying about a big game?" she asked.

He shook his head. "A stupid basketball game that is on this Thursday night. It's a funny thing, too. A couple of the players got in a beef, actually had a fucking fistfight about who is best. A video of that fight went viral, and now we have fools losing their minds betting on it left and right. You'd think they were betting on those boys duking it out."

"And you take those bets?"

"My associates do."

"The ones who send packages to you at the club?"

He nodded. "Bookies send over my cut of the take."

"They cut you in on this because they love you?"

He smiled. "Absolutely. But they love me because Danny ensures their operations run safely and efficiently. And Danny works for me."

Protection.

"But you don't think it's as big a deal as Danny does?"

Calvin's face became serious. "True, that. Danny sees opportunities… sometimes he wants to go too far."

"Too far?"

"He wants it all. Sometimes he thinks too fucking big," Calvin said.

"Like making me a star."

"You are one. But Danny is greedy."

"So are you," she said.

"For some things," he said, pushing her back onto the bed, spreading her legs apart.

Later, over breakfast, she pointed at him. "You gave Mickey drugs."

"I helped him out," he said.

"You gave him heroin so he would let me play."

Calvin scowled. "I gave him a boost, is all, one he wanted. Needed. He was in no condition to play. You play as good as him and look a damn sight better. And it's my bar."

"Yours and Bill's."

"Mine," he said with a smile that didn't cheer her thoughts.

He put his hand on her and his eyes told her that he intended to make her his, too.

The clash was clear. Jazz seduced you and gave you the freedom to explore wherever you wanted to go. Calvin's seduction was different.

One night in bed together made him think he had a claim on her. While she had definitely enjoyed screwing the man, and had good thoughts about doing it again, this whole crime-syndicate boss man vibe didn't play well with her.

On top of that, he and Danny were on a collision course, and he accepted that as a normal thing. Colliding like that and not minding, contrasted harshly with the smooth, luxurious texture of the jazz she loved. So different from sitting in with players, finding the groove and letting your sounds make love to the piano and drums.

Going into The Backbeat, she had begun hearing the song of her life. Now it occurred to her that they'd reached the bridge—the place in a tune where you could change the mood and maybe the tempo. The bridge was where you set things up for the final verse.

"If Danny's ambitions bother you, will you get rid of him?"

He scratched his nose. "Maybe, after the big game. I want him around until it's safely tucked away." He kissed her. "Got to be careful he don't guess. Danny won't like being cut out, and he can be a dangerous man."

"What is going to happen on Thursday?"

He grinned. “I will sit in my fucking club, watching my money roll in, and listening to my girl play jazz.”

His girl.

“Me?”

“I want you on that fucking stage.”

“What about Mickey?”

He waved a hand. “It’s my bar,” he said. “Besides, he’d rather shoot up.”

Her musical ear caught the pitch of finality in his voice. He had his mind made up.

He made love to her again, and this time, noting his greed, she made a decision. Calvin’s certainty and the greed he and Danny shared more than Calvin would admit, were okay in the background. You could improvise over shit like that. But now he was putting it in her face, manipulating Mickey, double-crossing Danny, and generally interrupting the floating sensuality of the jazz.

She got up and dressed. “I’m heading home. I have some shit to do.”

“See you at the club tonight,” he said.

“Count on it.”

On the way home, in the shower and, as she got ready for the evening, ideas danced to the music in her head. Some moved in restless counterpoint to others.

What was important was the music. The bass propelled the tune.

With no sheet music to follow, no plan, she determined she needed to do what Mickey had taught her and let the changes, the tempo, and the mood dictate what and how she played. She had to learn to find the groove.

She got to the club early, right when Bill was opening up, turning on the air con, putting the chairs down. When Smooth Sam’s old station wagon pulled up out back, she helped him and Jerry unload the gear, haul in Mickey’s fucking monster of a bass.

“Calvin plans to get Mickey fucked up,” she told Sam.

Sam worked at a sorrowful look. “The man is struggling. That sure as hell won't help his dumb ass."

"I don't think we get to say much about it."

"Fucking gangsters. Why can't our fans be normal people?"

She laughed. "You should see the assholes rock bands play for."

He smiled. "Hell, I'd probably bitch if they hung me with a brand-new rope. I'm lucky. I got my construction company."

Calvin came in, clearly in a good mood, telling Bill he was buying a round. "Danny and Ricky are handling collections tonight. They'll be in later. Get out that brandy Danny likes."

"We have a fucking case," Bill said. "No one else drinks that shit."

"Good."

When Mickey came in, he was the poster boy for Calvin's plan. A wreck. Shaking, nervous, and absurdly grateful for the glassine packet or two the man slipped him.

"Take the night off, if you want," he said. "Sandy will take the gig."

Mickey looked crushed. "Well, maybe I'll just go spruce myself up a bit," he said.

Calvin touched his arm. "Cool, man. Take your time." The picture of concern.

The crowd filtered in, and Sam gave Sandy a grin. "I guess you are our bass player tonight. We got an arrangement of Camptown Races that swings. In D."

As guilty as she felt about displacing Mickey, he wasn't fit to play, and the moment they started, she slid into that welcoming groove, that trance that made her feel whole.

All too soon, Calvin led raucous applause that marked the end of the set. She inhaled.

"Where is Mickey? He should be at the bar."

"I'll check on the boy," Sam said, ambling back toward the bathrooms.

Danny and Ricky came in the front door, looking around nervously.

She'd never seen them act like that. Danny was carrying a gym bag. One stuffed to the gills. He went to the bar, went behind and opened a door, shoving the bag inside a low cabinet.

Calvin was on his phone. He jumped up. "What the fuck did you assholes do?" he shouted, giving Danny that withering glare.

"I told you this was our chance!" Danny said. There was anger mixed with fear in the man's voice.

Ricky lingered by the door. The frightened look on his face surprised her. She'd never seen him look anything but mean or bored before. He had a gun in his hand and waved it about nervously. Danny stumbled back toward Calvin.

"I know what you said, Cal, but look here, a man gets one chance at the big time. You just gotta take it when it comes."

"You dumb fuck!" Calvin roared.

"He's dead!"

The quiet voice came from behind and penetrated through all the shouting. She turned to see Sam standing, staring at her. Anguish distorted his face.

"Mickey?" She'd feared it, but hearing it…

"The man overdosed, I guess. Still got the needle in him." He glanced toward Calvin. "Unless someone gave him bad dope. Either way, the man is stone cold dead."

"You are sure?" she asked. Her pulse was thready and a trembling, a bad kind, rippled through her.

"I know dead, girl," he said, his voice sour. "I surely do know a dead man when I see one." He nodded toward the bar. "Let me buy you a drink, then we call the cops and get Mickey taken care of."

The argument at the table was getting louder. She faced the man and held out her hand. "Sam, right now I need a cigarette."

He pulled out a pack and held it out. "Didn't know you smoked. Never seen it."

She shook her head. "I'm improvising, Sam, and I need one from the pack in the car. The one in the glove compartment."

"Don't go nuts on me, Sandy."

"Keys," she said.

Sam sighed and pulled them out, dropping them in her hand. "Don't be stupid, girl."

"Stupid happened a long time ago, Sam. This is what follows stupid."

She started toward the door and then stopped and turned to face him.

"Hang your coat on the back of a chair, Sam. Anyone ever asks, I stole your keys when you weren't looking."

Not waiting for him to reply, she strode determinedly out to the car and unlocked it. The gun was where it should be, tucked in the glove compartment. The chamber was empty, but it had a full magazine.

She took a long breath and tried to hear the music. You couldn't put down a baseline without knowing what tune the band was going to play. At first, nothing came, but she strained to hear. The theme music for a moment like this could take on a number of flavors, but she knew that, for her, for her moment, it had to be a blues. A really melancholy blues that tore your heart out.

With the right arrangement, Stormy Weather worked fine.

"Sing it Ivie," she said, and she heard Duke Ellington's band building the intro, pausing, and then the girl cut loose inside her head.

Sandy stood in the lot behind the bar, hearing roars and shouts from inside, and focusing on letting the woman in her head sing. It infused her. When Ivie got to: "Can't go on, everything I had is gone, Stormy weather…" she raised the gun, pulled back the slide and put a round in the chamber. Then she headed into the bar.

A loud crack, possibly a shot, echoed from the building. Then another.

Sam and Jerry ran by her, heading out. "Don't go in there," Jerry said. "All hell is breaking loose."

"Perfect," she said.

Another series of shots, a rapid series of cracks like overly loud firecrackers tore at her ears; scattered answering shots followed them. People in pain screamed out a dissonant harmony.

Behind the bar, Bill lay face down, not moving. He had a shotgun in his hand and a pool of blood around his head.

Stepping into the main room, she stepped over the body of a woman. Two more women lay sprawled out, stopped in their tracks as they headed for the door… a door Ricky was sagging against with his gun hand drooping limply at his side.

He gave her a strange smile, gurgled and sank to the floor.

Danny faced Calvin, a gun in his hand. "I told you man!"

Calvin stood by his table with his hand pressed against his side. His other hand pressed down onto the table, holding him in an awkward, cockeyed stance. He gave Danny a "what the fuck?" look, then coughed, and fell forward onto the table, then the table toppled, and they fell to the ground.

Danny turned and saw her looking at him. A wild-eyed grin crossed his face. "It's mine now!" He raised his gun and fired a shot at the ceiling like some Mexican bandit in a bad movie. It was a bad movie.

"Mine now and I want you to play for me, Sandy," he said. "I want to hear some Jazz."

"Jazz," she said, raising her gun, firing three times.

The second and third shots were baroque ornamentation, unnecessary additions to the main theme. But that first shot made fireworks music that exploded Danny's head, splattering blood across the room.

She watched him fall. That was the end of this set.

A strange calmness came over her. She walked the room, checking on the unmoving people, ensuring they were dead. When she got to Calvin, he looked up at her through glazed eyes. Blood trickled from his mouth.

"That's my girl," he gurgled through blood. "Help me, baby."

She stared down at him. "You killed Mickey."

"I wanted to hear my girl play."

He thought he owned her; a single shot through his forehead fixed that.

She went to the stage. Mickey's bass had been hit by a bullet near one of the f-holes, splintering the wood.

"We will fix that," she said, then she dragged it out the back door.

Jerry and Sam were long gone, but she had the keys to the dusty station wagon sitting there. Wrestling the bass into the back, she went back into the bar and retrieved the bag Danny had put there. It was filled with money. Enough to fix a wounded bass. Enough to support a jazz player for a long time.

She remembered a guy who ran a music store and worked on instruments. The fucker did wonders with violins; a standup bass was like a big violin, right?

As she got behind the wheel, sirens began to fill the air with a new chorus: Whoop whoop! Blip Blip! Shrill, discordant.

There was no room in a tune like that for a backbeat, for a strong, mellow bass line, so she left them to this new band. Putting the car in gear, she drove away.

She'd have to get the bass, Mickey's bass to the repair guy. That was the priority. Then she would call Sam. There were possibilities now. They could form another group. They'd gelled.

As quickly as the idea came, she swept it aside. Sam had a business and a wife, shit like that. Jerry would stay with him.

No, she would keep Sam's wagon. She needed it to haul the bass and could send him some money.

She lit one of Sam's Marlboros and coughed, trying to smoke it while she thought.

When the bass was fixed, she could drive up to Chicago, where she'd heard the jazz scene was making something of a comeback. It was still small, always would be, but that was fine. She didn't need an audience, just a place where she could find other musicians and a stage for Mickey's bass, just somewhere she could go where she could find musicians and settle into that groove.

What Mickey said made sense now. She hadn't been careful. She'd let herself fall into the groove. Now the sides were too steep to climb out. All she could do now was keep her fingers on the strings and let her heart and soul move with the changes.

Allan Longstreet's Blues

Victor Kreuiter

When Laska arrived, there was a patrol car on the street and one in the driveway. An ambulance was pulled all the way up to the single-car garage, lights spinning, doors open, empty. The detective pulled just past the drive, parked and stepped out of his car. The neighborhood was bungalows and small ranches, all neat and tidy, all on small city lots … porch lights on, people huddled in driveways, standing on the sidewalk, peering at the police business. It was a Thursday evening, mid-September. A uniform was waiting on the porch, and when Laska got there he asked "You here first?"

The uniform shook his head. "Nah. I heard the call … got here after Washington." He pointed to the uniform inside. Laska looked inside. The uniform was standing. A woman was on a couch, head down and arms wrapped around herself.

"She find the body?" he asked.

The cop shrugged. "I guess so … Washington will know. I got here, checked the house and the yard, walked up and down the street …"

"See anything?"

The cop shook his head.

Laska leaned and looked inside again. "Know who she is?"

"A daughter, I think."

Laska pulled out a cell phone and dialed. His partner answered on the first ring: "I'm on my way," he said.

* * *

The morning paper reported that Allan Longstreet, 64 years old, was found dead in his northside home the previous evening. A photo ran next to the story and the caption mentioned he was a musician.

According to the brief article, his career encompassed everything a musician could aspire to: performer, producer, arranger, sideman, session man, songwriter, lyricist, vocalist, bandleader, teacher, coach, mentor, promoter. What the paper didn't say was that when found, he was face down, an ink pen shoved into his neck and a pool of blood below his chest.

* * *

Joe Laska knew nothing about music. With enough pressure from his wife, his mother, his sisters, he could be dragged onto the dance floor for a polka, once per wedding. Other than that, nothing. His partner was the opposite. Jason Darnell Bell was handed an alto saxophone at the start of fourth grade. It fell in love with him. In junior high he moved to tenor. It loved him, too. In high school he was picked for the all-city youth orchestra four straight years, alto *and* tenor. Could he have gone on with the music? Maybe, but the family business was police. Father, uncles, two aunts, cousins … all police. After high school it was to junior college for an associate's, then the academy. Years later, his wife, watching him come home too often carrying the job with him, provided him the perfect technique to wash away the stress after a shift in blue. She bought him a piano.

It loved him.

When Detective Jason Bell entered Allan Longstreet's home the night of the murder he walked into Longstreet's practice room, stood over the corpse, turned, walked back outside to his car, leaned on the hood and steadied himself. He was shaking and trying to steady his breathing.

He'd taken lessons from Longstreet in that room. In that room Longstreet nagged him about his sight reading, drilled him on the rudiments, coached him on theory, ran him through one exercise after another, then taught him how and when to improvise. Patrolman Jason Bell would, within a couple years of those lessons, be invited to played gigs with what Longstreet called "the serious amateurs." Usually filling in for someone, Bell found himself playing soul, some rock 'n' roll, some blues. Once a year, for years, he'd call Longstreet for a refresher; they'd get together, plonk around on a piano and spend more time talking than playing.

After Bell made detective, the practice at home slowed, gigs were usually declined and the visits with Longstreet became few and far between.

* * *

"Here's what I got so far," Bell said. It was Friday morning and he was sitting on the edge of his desk at precinct, Laska, next desk over. "Longstreet just finished a recording and it was scheduled for a Christmas release. He was going out on the road after the holidays and was putting a road band together. Word was, the hope was, this release would break him nationally. According to what I've got, he'd been auditioning and negotiating with musicians for a couple weeks. The guys on the recording—guys he'd worked with for years—some wanted too much money and weren't going on the road." Bell paused, stared at his notes then looked at Laska "Maybe there was some bad feelings about that. Think?"

Jason Bell and Joe Laska were salt and pepper, both of them squat, square-headed, close-cropped hair, thick in the chest, hands like hams. One black, one white. They'd paired up the year they became detectives.

Laska wiped his mouth, rubbed his chin. "So, we run down the musicians?" He knew he would not be in the driver's seat on this one.

"I say let's start at the studio," Bell said. "Select Studios, out on Manchester. Maybe get the big picture first." He watched Laska nod, then said "I called. They know we're coming."

Laska patted his desk. "Okay, boss," he said, then he stood up, hesitated. "You see the photos?"

Bell nodded, grim.

"Like he was reaching for something," Laska said.

"I know. Looked like it to me, too." Bell paused, bit a lip. "I was in that room, years ago. I remember it."

Laska watched Bell carefully, then said: "An ink pen?" He paused.

"You think an ink pen is premeditated?"

Bell squinted, ran a hand over his face and shrugged. "You see what was in his right hand?"

"Harmonicas, right? Lab guy pointed them out." Laska shrugged. "There was a couple scattered around him, too. You see that?"

Bell nodded. "Guitar picks, too. And the uniform said there was a small amplifier still on and humming." Bell watched Laska blink it in, then said: "You ever wonder what goes through a dying man's mind?"

* * *

Bernie Cohen, an animated little man, wore a suit and tie every day. He favored brown suits and brown shoes and the only indication he had a life outside Select Studios was the family portrait sitting on the desk in his office.

"I hate this," he said. Cohen looked mournful; it was not an act. "I can't tell you how long …" He stopped, shook his head. "I've known Allan Longstreet for thirty years. Forty, even. A delight to work with." He stopped, rubbed his brow. "Let me tell you something. Me and Allan, we used to do commercials … jingles … years ago. Lots of em, for furniture stores, grocery stores, automobile dealers, whatever." He lit up, remembering. "First thing I'd do, call Allan. He was *always* an hour early for the job. *Always*. I bet he wrote or rewrote half what we recorded." Cohen mugged, shrugged, looked down at his shoes, and when he raised his eyes up he wore a sad smile. "Allan made money here, I swear. Lots. Cash." Cohen puffed, looked around, pointed to his desk and sat there. The detectives found chairs.

"You got something to write on?" Cohen asked.

Laska pulled out a pad and pen, looked at Bell and nodded toward Cohen.

Cohen slumped, and started.

"This recording? Maybe eight or nine guys come in with him, total. Fifteen or sixteen tracks. I can check, if it matters. Tic Toc played drums on about half the tracks." He stopped, looked at Bell. "You play too, don't you." It was not a question. How did Cohen know?

"Used to," Bell said, "fairly regular. Weekends."

"You know Tic Toc?"

Bell nodded. "I do," he said, "by reputation. Drinks, right?"

Cohen nodded. "Drinking got him fired. Allan warned him again and again. Words were exchanged."

"It get ugly?"

Cohen shrugged. "Naah. Tic Toc came in lit up, Allan walked him to the door, the end."

"Tic Toc get paid?"

Cohen shrugged again. "Don't know. That's not on me." He tapped his desk for no reason. "Grayson Hayes played bass on about half, too. You know him?"

Bell nodded, rubbed his chin, lowered his brow. "Tall guy. Pencil thin moustache. Light skinned. That him?"

"That's him," Cohen said. "So … the other rhythm section was two kids … seemed like they were friends. Black kid on drums and a white kid on bass." Cohen stretched his neck and puffed up his cheeks, thinking. "They were students or something, I could tell. They were good. Clean cut, quiet, paying attention to what Allan wanted. They could do it, too. Whatever he wanted." Cohen paused, exhaled, tapped his lips with a finger. "Jimmy Kirkland on saxophone."

Bell smiled. "If Allan was playing, Jimmy was either playing or watching."

"That's right," Cohen said. He smiled. "That's right. Jimmy played tenor. Kerry Weigand played baritone."

Bell laughed out loud. It felt good. "I've met him." Bell shook his head. "Man, Allan loved a baritone, didn't he?"

Cohen's smile grew. "Allan loved a baritone." He paused and the smile faded. "Was a white guy on trombone. Just one track."

"You know him?"

"Never seen him before. Raymond Whitaker. Not much there, to tell you the truth." Cohen covered his mouth with a hand, inhaled and held it. "Billy Shaw on organ and piano, and then two guys on guitar.

Young guy, D'Marco Sanders, and an older white guy, Abe Keller." Cohen stopped, rubbed his hands together and thought. "He got fired, too." Another pause. "Allan kept telling him to back it off … keep it simple. Guy wouldn't follow direction."

"Did *that* get ugly?"

Cohen chewed on a lip. "I don't know. The guy had the sniffles, you know?" Cohen put his index finger under his nose and sniffed.

"Drugs?"

"Honestly, I don't know, but I suspected it the first time I met the guy."

"You ever see him before?"

Cohen nodded. "Yeah, sure. Over the years."

Bell shrugged, then, "Billy Shaw played keys? On everything? Allan didn't play any piano?"

"Allen played some piano, sure. Played organ, too. Played guitar, too." Cohen paused mid-thought, smiled, dropped his head and the smile faded, raised his head and the smile bloomed all over again. "Allan Longstreet was on his way," he said. "He was determined, you know. He had a plan and was working it."

Cohen stopped. Bell cocked his head, waiting for more. Laska looked up, made eye contact with Bell, looked back down.

"We'd always talk," Cohen said. "He'd stop by, or he'd be in here working for somebody, you know … session work. A couple years ago Allan told me it was time … he was getting older." Cohen squinted, remembering. "He was going to step it up, be a front man. He'd made up his mind. He said he needed to set up his retirement." Cohen stopped, raised his eyebrows and opened his eyes wide. "I agreed with him. Completely. He was taking everything he learned and he was gonna get himself some success. Some money. So that's what these sessions were all about … Allan as a front man. He put his mind to it, worked at it. Man, he could *blow*. He worked on that for the last couple years, serious about it. When Allan Longstreet did something, he *did* something. He was that way. Allan had a nice voice, too. He worked on that, too. I know he did. He had a vocal coach … him, at his age. So, this record, this thing … when he …"

Bell interrupted. "Blow? Blow what? Allan Longstreet picked up a horn?"

Cohen shook his head. "No, not a horn. Harmonica. Mouth organ. Mississippi saxophone. Man, when he set his mind …"

"Harmonica?" Bell interrupted again.

"Yeah," Cohen said. "Harmonica. He put his mind to it, I swear. Those recordings … you gotta hear 'em."

* * *

Tic Toc's girlfriend was lying. Laska and Bell could see it. She hemmed and hawed, licked her lips, tilted her head. "Last night? No, we was here all night, watching TV. We was in bed early. You know, Tic Toc had a few too many … *again*." She forced a laugh.

"You didn't go out for anything? Food, a drink, anything?"

Her name was Leslie Parks. Laska checked her out in advance. A nurse with no record and multiple unpaid parking tickets.

"Look, Leslie," Bell said, "we know Tic Toc was out last night, okay? We *know* that. He sat in at The Night Owl ... maybe eleven o'clock or thereabouts. What he did before and after, that's what we need to know."

Leslie went closemouthed, like she'd been insulted. She shook her head and glared at Bell. The room got chilly.

"Okay, here's the truth. I don't know where he was last night. He wasn't here, okay? I ain't got to be lying for him." She was working on getting wound up. "I'm sorry," she said, bitter. She dropped her eyes, blinked and looked up. "Look here, you're looking to find him? Well, tell him I'm looking to lose him. You find him, tell him Leslie Parks said that."

She stood up, taller than both detectives. Bell and Laska stepped back. "Tic Toc's name?" It was Laska asking, meek-like. "His real name?"

Leslie puffed out her cheeks, exhaled, put hands on hips. "Donald

Ernell Armstrong." She huffed. "So now tell me … what's the first thing you say to him when you find him? What did I tell you to say?"

* * *

Grayson Hayes, in his late fifties, lived alone. When he opened his apartment door he wasn't surprised to see two detectives. "Allan Longstreet," he said. He looked them both dead in the eyes, shook his head and invited them in.

"I knew Allan a long time," Hayes said. "Very talented. A generous person." He inhaled, held it, then sighed. "I'm sad," he said. He looked at the two detectives. "Who would want to kill Allan Longstreet?"

Bell's eyes opened wide. "Who said anything about murder?"

Laska kept his eyes on Hayes. Hayes backed up to his couch and sat, motioning for Bell to take the chair next to the door. "Don't try that on me," he said. "Hell, word was on the street before the ambulance left that man's house." He shook his head slowly. "Sorrowful," he said. "It's sorrowful."

"So, where were you last night?"

Hayes looked up, worked to keep the insult off his face. "Working."

"With who?"

"I wasn't playing," he said. Hayes glanced at Laska, back to Bell. "I work Monday, Tuesday, and Thursday nights—four to midnight—every week." He rose, stepped inside his small kitchen, opened a drawer and withdrew pad and pencil, sat back down and wrote. He tore off a sheet and handed it to Laska. "Check there," he said. The sheet held the name of an Asian grocer, an address and phone number. "Go ahead, call Mr. Yeng. He'll tell you I was there, four to midnight." Hayes rubbed his neck. "Mr. Yeng gives me a ride home, too, every Monday, Tuesday and Thursday night."

Laska handed the sheet to Bell, Bell looked and handed it back. "You in the studio when Tic Toc was fired?"

"I was," he said. "I wasn't surprised and it wasn't none of my business." Hayes twisted his neck, raised his eyes and set them on Bell. "I know you," he said. "We played together. You remember that?"

Bell did.

"You was good," Hayes said. "I remember. Years ago. You played well. Soul, right? With some female singer, right?"

Bell nodded. "Yeah, that was me."

Hayes nodded. "Okay, we got that straight." He didn't smile.

"What about Tic Toc?"

"I've played with Tic Toc many times," Hayes said. "Hundreds of times. He's a solid drummer. Steady. Easy to work with. But me and him, we're not close."

"You think Tic Toc could kill a man?"

Hayes held his head still, eyes down. He raised up both hands, palms out. "Look," he said, "I have no idea what Tic Toc does with his time." Hayes stood up, stared into his kitchen like he was trying to remember something. "No offense," he said., "but that's all I want to say." He turned to Laska. "Call that number on that paper. Ask for Mr. Yeng."

* * *

Jimmy Kirkland managed a small bar on the near north side. That's where he was the night Allan Longstreet was murdered.

"Awful," he said. "Heartbreaking." He shook his head.

They were sitting at a corner table in Most Likely, a bar with a reputation for good music, decent food and an older clientele that appreciated both—at an early hour. Most Likely closed at midnight on the dot, every night. The bandstand went silent at ten-thirty. Musicians *loved* the early night.

"You here last night?"

"I was," Kirkland said. "Ask around. It's okay."

"You play?"

"I did," he said, and smiled. "seven-thirty to ten-thirty. With Billy Shaw. Polly Woodard on bass."

"And after?"

"Straight home," he said. "Talked with my daughter—she's living with me." Kirkland rolled his neck. "We get an older crowd in here. Get to play standards. It's fun."

Bell and Laska let it get quiet.

"You did some sessions with Longstreet, recently. We heard there was problems in the studio. You know, personal issues. Like that." Bell watched Kirkland's nod slowly.

Kirkland took a deep breath, put a hand to his jaw.

"Tic Toc, I guess," he said. "But Allan has worked with Tic Toc before. He knew Tic Toc was gonna show up at least once all lit up. Tic Toc knew he did wrong. But he knew he'd get paid for work he did. That ain't the first time Allan Longstreet fired Tic Toc." Kirkland laughed.

"He fired a guitar player, too, right?"

Kirkland smiled, mirthless. "Guitar players. Man, for some of them guys, too much ain't enough."

"You know the guys?"

"Sure. D'Marco Sanders? Nice guy. Good. But he'll put in three passing chords between the four and the five, you know? Allan had to sit on him."

"You know the other guy?"

"Abe?" Kirkland said. "Another good player. One minute you think, 'man, this guy is spot-on,' and the next you're thinking, 'when's he gonna stop that racket?' And to be honest, I think Allan liked some of that racket, you know? But …"

Laska interrupted. "They have a fight? In the studio?"

Kirkland went blank, then he laughed. "Abe Keller wanted the road work."

"Was he hired for the road?"

"Don't know," Kirkland said. "Talk to Sal about that. Sal Molina."

* * *

Bell and Laska got a call from precinct. … somebody was asking for them. They headed back, walked in and saw a white guy, long hair, bearded. "You guys looking for me?"

The found an empty interrogation room and escorted Abe Keller in.

Bell started. "So how long have you known Allan Longstreet?"

Keller chewed on his lip. "Decades," he said. "Worked with him, on and off, for twenty-plus years."

"Wanna tell us where you were last night?"

"Sure," Keller said. "I had an NA meeting. A church basement in Skokie. After that, maybe 9:30 or so, I attended an AA meeting." He took a moment to check out both detectives. "I got baggage," he said.

"Anybody confirm that?" It was Laska.

Keller puffed out his cheeks. "No names or phone numbers. That's the point of those meetings, right? The NA was in Skokie. AA meeting was at a Catholic church in Niles."

Bell turned to Laska, watched him scribble, then turned back to Keller. "I need your address."

Keller shrugged. "I'm staying with a ladyfriend in Morton Grove. A friend, okay? No romance. I was waiting around to go out with Allan Longstreet. He told me he wanted me on the road with him."

"You were hired for the tour?"

"I was."

It got quiet. Keller looked sober and he acted somber.

"So how did you react when you found out. You know it was murder, right?"

Keller leaned forward, grimaced, sat back and shook his head. "Well, the thought crossed my mind." He paused. "You know, I've never been in Allan's home. Don't even know where he lived." He paused again, furrowed his brow, opened his mouth … then shut it.

Bell saw it. Laska saw it.

"Go on," Bell said.

Keller shook his head. "I have a drug problem," he said. "Alcohol, too, okay? It's not easy to trust myself."

"But you want to say something."

Keller sat perfectly still, eyes down. "Tic Toc," he said. He raised his eyes slowly and looked at both of them. "I'm just sayin', Tic Toc was *not* happy about losing that work."

"Tic Toc wasn't hired to travel?"

"Nope. The college kid was gonna go."

"And you think Tic Toc could murder someone?"

Keller, eyes down, shook his head again. "No. No, I don't. And I shouldn't have said anything like that. I'm sorry."

* * *

Late in the afternoon they found Raymond Whitaker in his office at Loyola.

"I know," he said. He appeared nervous. "I heard." Whitaker toyed with something on his desk then opened a drawer, pulled out a scheduler and handed it to Laska. "My Thursday evening seminar runs until eight." He blinked, looked at Laska as if he'd proven something, glanced at Bell then stared at his open office door. "If that's what you want to know," he said.

"Okay, after class, you did what?" Bell questioning.

"Straight home, watched the news, then to bed."

"Home is where?" Bell asked.

"Evanston," Whitaker said.

"Is there someone who can verify that?"

Whitaker huffed. "I'm divorced." He sat up straighter. "Am I being interrogated?"

"You are," Laska said. "We're investigating a homicide."

Whitaker craned his neck. "Me? You think *I* might have something to do with this?"

"Don't know." Laska paused. "You were in the studio with Allan Longstreet. If there's anything you could tell us about Allan, or the other musicians. Anything important."

Whitaker huffed again. "I barely knew Allan Longstreet. I *paid* to play that session. I bought the opportunity at a raffle, some raffle for our campus radio station." Whitaker squared his jaw as if he'd won a moral victory. "And honestly, the experience wasn't something I'd care to repeat."

"Can anybody vouch for where you were after your seminar last night?" Laska again.

Whitaker frowned, perturbed. “No,” he said. “I’m divorced. My children live far away.”

* * *

“What’re you thinking?”

Bell was driving, Laska paging through notes.

“I’m thinking I’m working tomorrow,” Laska said. “That what you want to hear?”

Bell nodded. “I guess. My wife is going to rap my knuckles, but I want to see these guys right away. Billy Shaw, the other guitar player, those college kids. I’m betting they’ll all be sleeping in on a Saturday morning. Let’s start early.”

They parked at precinct, went in and found Charlie Burns waiting for them.

Charlie Burns looked old, *was* old, and was determined to die on his feet in a crime lab. He held a photo and showed it to the detectives. They looked and shrugged. “We’ve seen it,” Laska said.

Burns nodded. “I know. The coroner told me Longstreet had those things in a death grip and that sounded like something. I keep looking at the photo, and so I go down to Evidence to look at those harmonicas.” He was eyes smiling. “You know harmonicas have different letters stamped on each one? Letters stamped in the metal?”

Bell nodded. “That shows what musical key the harmonica is in.”

Burns nodded. “Whatever. Doesn’t matter. I’m just saying those harmonicas had different letters.”

“So what’s it mean?” Laska asked.

Burns laughed loud. “Hell, that ain’t my job, detective.” He pointed at the photo. “Three letters,” he said. “Don’t know if they mean a thing, but those letters …”

Bell interrupted. “Come on, Charlie, give it up.”

“D, E, and A.” Burns said. “Held like that, in that order. You guys figure it out.”

* * *

It wasn’t the serious amateur musician who made the connection.

Laska wasn't asleep more than a half hour when he woke up with a start.

D. E. A.

Donald Ernell Armstrong.

* * *

Saturday morning, police were out looking for Armstrong.

At precinct, Bell and Laska were revisiting photos, lab results, fingerprints … everything. They reviewed their conversation with Angela Longstreet. Laska called Officer Washington—first on the scene—and they walked through the night again. Bell talked with Officer William Bartell—second on the scene. What had they missed?

Cops were sent to canvas the neighborhood, again. At 9 a.m. Billy Shaw walked in, escorted by a uniform. The uniform pointed to them and Shaw approached.

"You the guys wanting to talk to me?"

"Indeed we do," Bell said. "How'd you hear?"

Shaw walked to an empty desk, pulled a chair around and faced the detectives. "Jimmy Kirkland called."

Shaw looked edgy. Brittle. "You already know where I was Thursday night. So … I left Most Likely about eleven, made a few stops on the way home, bed by one. I can tell you where I stopped and who I talked to when I was there."

Bell and Laska were quiet.

"It wasn't me," Shaw said. "I was in. Allan hired me for the road. Keys, vocal, and music director." He paused. "Ask Sal Molina. He'll tell you."

Bell and Laska stayed quiet.

"Who in the world would want to hurt Allan Longstreet?" Shaw looked Bell in the eye, Laska in the eye, drummed his fingers on his knee.

Laska leaned forward, glancing at Bell, then concentrated on Shaw. "Let's run through Thursday night," he said.

Shaw walked them through his night. Three-plus hours at Most

Likely, leaving around 11 p.m. A stop at a club featuring jazz. A drink at a neighborhood tavern three blocks from his home. Then, "Wait," Shaw said, "I pumped some gas about midnight. Maybe just after. They got them cameras, don't they?" He gave them the address of the gas station.

Bell spoke. "So … Allan okay lately? No problems? Concerns? Everything okay with him?"

Shaw slumped. "Everything was coming together for Allan," he said. "He built it right." Shaw went tight-lipped. Anger? Did Laska see anger?

"This Molina," Laska asked, "you got contact info?"

Shaw pulled out his wallet, extracted a business card and handed it over. "Salvador signed us up just a couple days ago," he said. "First real rehearsal was day after Christmas."

Laska handed the card to Bell, Bell reviewed, handed it back and asked, "So who's going on the road?"

"Ask Molina," Shaw said. It came out harsh.

"You don't know?"

Shaw sighed and looked Bell directly in the eye. "Don't matter now," he said. "But according to Sal it was me, them college kids, and D'Marco."

Bell looked at Laska. Laska looked at Billy, then spoke. "Abe Keller? He going?"

"Not according to what I was told," Shaw said.

* * *

"You Kerry Weigand?"

Kerry Weigand nodded.

They'd found him at his day job, The Mint, a used record/CD store he owned and operated with his brother. They had three locations and the detectives had stopped by two others before they found him.

Weigand looked at a kid behind the cash register, pointed at the office and motioned for the detectives to follow. He sat. They sat.

He pulled a sheet of paper from the desktop, handed it to Bell and watched him read. "That's my Thursday night," he said. "Names and phone numbers."

Bell handed it to Laska. "Jimmy Kirkland call you, too?"

Weigand nodded.

"How much time did it take to put that together?" Bell pointed at the sheet in Laska's hands.

Weigand shook his head. "That ain't nice," he said. He returned a hard stare, looked at Laska and gave him the same. "Allan Longstreet is dead. That's all I know. That's too much for me, to be honest. But that sheet of paper is one-hundred percent accurate. Ask me anything else, go ahead, 'cause now you know where all I was Thursday night."

Bell accepted the attitude, then asked, "Guys got fired from the sessions? That right?"

Weigand shrugged. "Sessions … they're funny. Allan lets a guy go, could be any number of reasons. It ain't nothing to argue about. Everybody's in, then everybody's out. That's studio work."

"Tic Toc got fired."

Weigand nodded.

"This Abe—he get fired?"

Weigand shrugged again. "I know Abe for years. He's here for a while, then gone for a while. I think he goes down to Florida. The Gulf Coast. Works the tourist seasons, that's what he says."

"Drug problems?"

Weigand shook the question off. No answer.

"Volatile?"

"Abe?" Weigand thought about that. "I know him, but then I don't. He's in town, then he's gone. He's got a girlfriend, then he don't. Got a place, then he don't. He's that kind of guy."

"How long he been around this time?"

Weigand scratched an elbow. "Don't know," he said. "The sessions I played on—he was on two. Then I didn't see him again. Hadn't seen him for about a year." He paused. "Abe likes that rock blues stuff."

"This professor … trombone. Know him?"

Weigand shook his head. "Shouldn't have been there. Don't know why he was. Wanting to read a chart and lost because there wasn't none."

"He seem upset?"

Weigand's humorless smile almost turned into a joyless laugh. "Spent half his time telling me how educated he was and I let him go on. He got his real education when we started playing, asking 'What key? What key?' Allan wasn't happy about it. We had to stop so Allan could write out a simple chart for the guy, and that didn't help much either."

"Tic Toc?"

"Known him for years. Sober, he's the man on the throne. Drunk, he ain't half-bad, either."

"The college kids. You know them?"

Weigand rubbed his jaw. "Good players. More than I expected, really, but I don't know 'em."

"D'Marco Sanders?"

"Man, D'Marco's family. My cousin's boy. Likes jazz but it ain't easy to make a living playing jazz. D'Marco's good."

"Anybody else … anything you can think of? Allan have enemies? Gambling? Drugs? That sort of thing?"

Weigand shook his head. "No. Nothing like that. You gotta know that already."

* * *

Daniel Gaines lived with his parents, and although the arrival of two police detectives was expected, it was nonetheless disconcerting. The detectives were invited in and led to a sitting room. Both parents stayed.

"So," Bell said, "how'd you meet Allan Longstreet?"

Gaines, small, thin, glanced at his parents before answering. "Well, Gene and I work together often, as pick-up musicians. The invite came from Gene."

Gaines' mother leaned forward, looked at both detectives. "Daniel is a music major at Northwestern. Cello."

The boy looked embarrassed.

"And Gene is Eugene Duncan?"

Gaines said "Yes sir."

"Drummer?"

"Yes sir."

"You didn't know Allan Longstreet before the sessions?"

Gaines shook his head. "No. First time I met him was in the studio."

"You hit it off?"

The boy smiled. "I think so. A very nice man. Professional. Easy to understand. Patient." He looked at his folks again. "I was going on the road with him."

Laska was watching the parents. Mom a bit nervous. Dad watchful. "How you folks feel about your son going out on the road like that?"

Mom twisted her hands and dropped her gaze.

Dad looked at his son, turned to Laska and said, "I'm sorry to say this, but it's how I feel. He was throwing away his education." Eyes back to son again. "He's been first-chair cello for two years. He would give that up and play rock and roll in taverns?"

* * *

Eugene Duncan lived with his parents in Irving Park, in a big square two-story. His parents, too, stayed by his side.

"How long have you known Allan Longstreet?" Bell asked.

Duncan wore dreadlocks, sported dark-rimmed glasses. He wore blue jeans and a David Bowie t-shirt. He looked at his dad for support, then turned to Bell. "I met Allan maybe three years ago, right after high school. I got a call for a pick-up job and Allan was the music director. Three nights—a weekend at a convention or something, downtown."

"Since then?"

"Well, on occasion, I guess. He remembers me, always asks about school. I'm a music major. He told me to stick with it."

"There were evidently some arguments in the studio. You see 'em?"

A glance at his parents. "No sir. Nothing like that."

"Abe Keller? D'Marco Sanders? You work with them?"

Duncan nodded. "One long session, yes. With each. Abe's session went into the night." Pause. "We did five, six, seven songs with each of them."

"Tensions? Problems?"

"Well, Allan was boss. He was in charge."

"Anybody there difficult to work with?"

Duncan looked at his parents, dropped his head to think. "Uh … touchy, maybe. I don't know how to describe it."

"Drugs?"

The boy shrugged. "Uh …" He looked at his folks again. "I don't know. Didn't see any."

Laska cleared his throat and looked at Duncan's parents. "So your son was going on the road with Allan Longstreet for what? A month or more? You okay with that?"

Mom smiled. Dad looked at his son. "We were," he said. He looked at his son. "We made him promise to enjoy himself … then get back here and finish his degree."

His son smiled, nodded, dropped his head.

"I was happy for him," Duncan's father said. "He wants to play music. That's okay with me. He treats it professionally, so yeah, I told him to do the job and do it right."

* * *

Bell and Laska were on their way to D'Marco Sanders' apartment when they got the call. Tic Toc was in custody. "Keep him cooled off," Bell said. He listened, nodded, then said "Be there in a couple hours. If he asks for a lawyer, get him one."

* * *

D'Marco Sanders was tense. Sitting on the edge of a couch, legs tucked, back straight, hands clasped at his waist.

His Thursday night? Rehearsing with his church's praise orchestra.

Asked about the musicians he'd worked with on Allan Longstreet's recording sessions, his answers were short and noncommittal. "Look," he finally said, "those guys … Tic Toc, Grayson, Jimmy and Kerry, Billy Shaw … they're all older than me, okay? I'm scrambling for a spot …

you know, some recognition. This was a break for me." He stopped, looked around the room as if searching for something, then pushed himself back on the couch. "Do I think one of them guys did this? No. No way."

Bell let it get quiet, then let the quiet stretch before asking "Some money on the line here? Some recognition?"

Sanders nodded. "Sure," he said. "Good money, I'll say that. Good enough. Recognition? Yeah, maybe. My name is gonna be on that CD. Is that recognition?"

Laska stepped in. "What about the guys left out? How do they feel? Hard feelings?"

Sanders shrugged. "Horn players? Allan didn't have the money. They understood. Jimmy, Kerry, they know. They have jobs. They're cool."

"This trombone player …"

"No," Sanders said. "That was some charity thing. Something like that. That man never been in a studio in his life. He was struggling for what little he did. I'd bet money his playing ain't on the finished CD. His track was wiped, I'm sure. He didn't have it."

"So how …" Laska again; he paused. "So how is Allan Longstreet gonna do that material without horns? I mean …" Laska looked at Bell for help. "How's that work?"

D'Marco was shaking his head before Laska finished. "No. No, Allan's arrangements—he explained it to us. He'll do some of the horn lines on keyboards. We'll have two keyboards onstage every night, okay? Plus, Allan had that chromatic *down pat. Seriously* … it was gonna be *large*. He plays that big 16-hole chromatic. He'll be able to replicate the horn lines, no doubt. He and I, we talked about it. I was looking forward to starting rehearsals …" He stopped, blinked, looked at the detectives and his hands were visibly shaking. "This is awful. This is just awful."

* * *

Salvador Molina had been in the business for decades. He'd owned a bar, owned a studio, started a small label, then sold it. Managed artists, booked artists, hired and fired.

Longstreet had hired him to put together his upcoming road work. Molina mapped out a loop heading due south: Bloomington, St. Louis, Indianapolis, Memphis, Nashville, Knoxville, Louisville, Cincinnati and back. A mix of clubs and colleges. The band would get a week off after that warm-up, then head west for thirty-plus days on the road. If things went well, Molina was already sketching out an East coast swing mid-year.

They found him at home, a modest brick in Elmhurst.

"Should I have called you guys?" he asked.

Bell and Laska exchanged glances. Bell spoke. "Not unless you have something we need to know."

Molina shook his head, dropped his gaze down. "No. Sorry, I can't really think clear right now anyhow." He paused, looked at them both. "I talked with Angela Longstreet this morning. She's …" He let it hang.

Bell hesitated, glanced at Laska, then, "So let's talk about Allan for a minute, okay?" Molina got them into a small, neat living room. Eyes downcast, he wiped at his chin, raised his eyes and motioned he was ready to talk.

Bell started. "Anything unusual lately? Anything in his background that might lead to violence?"

Molina shook his head. "No. Come on, nothing like that, ever."

"How long have you known him?"

Molina shrugged. "Thirty years maybe? Longer? Done business with him on and off."

"And what did you do for him?"

"Booking agent, on and off. Handled some legal work for him and Bernie Cohen. Supplied him musicians if he couldn't find anybody short-notice. I've done all kinds of stuff." He paused, then "I have contacts in the industry—all over." He watched the detectives—questions in their eyes. "It's a funny business," he said. "It's all about people and trust. Who do you trust? I have connections and honestly, I guard them jealously. My reputation is based not only on what I can do, but what the people I vouch for can do. I trusted Allan completely, and he trusted me."

Laska looked to Bell; Bell nodded. "So who was going on the road with Allan Longstreet?"

Molina pursed his lips, puffed his cheeks, exhaled. "Okay, Billy Shaw, vocals and keyboards. He'd be music director."

Laska butted in. "Music director?"

Molina nodded. "Allan had turned himself into a front man. Worked at it. He was going to be out front, all night, every night. He wrote a lot of the material they'd be playing. What he didn't write, he arranged. He'd have his hands full being front man, okay? That's *selling*, okay? That's looking your audience right in the eyes and *selling*. So, the music director—that's Billy—he makes sure that any message—*any change during the show*—gets delivered to the rest of the band. The band doesn't watch Allan and Allan doesn't watch the band, okay? Allan watches *the crowd*. The music director—Billy—watches *Allan*. And the band watches Billy. That's how it works."

"So who's in the band?"

"Billy. D'Marco Sanders, guitar. Danny Gaines on bass and Gene Duncan drumming. That's it. With Allan, that's five pieces."

"No horns?"

"No. Horns on the recordings but no horns in the road band."

"Why college kids?"

Molina raised a hand and rubbed thumb and fingers. "Same reason as no horns on the road. Money," he said. "The determining factor in much of success can be money, just like in any other business. You take someone on the road, besides the pay there's three squares and a bed. It mounts up."

"Okay, this professor … Raymond …"

Molina waved it off. "Forget it. It was a gift. Somebody convinced Allan to allow someone to record with him—some fund raiser. Allan said 'okay.' But that guy—he was a tourist, nothing more."

"Abe Keller? He told us he was hired for the road."

Molina shook his head. "Never," he said. "Abe has baggage. Allan doesn't need that kind of baggage on the road."

"Keller told us he attends AA meetings. NA meetings, too."

Molina raised his eyebrows and lowered his chin. "I hope so," he said. He leaned over, reached into a pocket, came out with two coins and handed them to Bell. "Seven years," he said.

Bell examined the coins—one stamped NA, one with a triangle and a motto—then handed them to Laska.

"Abe says he went to an NA meeting and an AA meeting on Thursday night," Bell said. "One in Skokie and one in Niles. Sound right?"

Molina leaned over, indicated he wanted his coins back. "I went to an NA meeting in Skokie on Thursday night," he said. That's my regular meeting. Niles? I don't know. My AA meeting is in Park Ridge. I go Mondays."

Laska glanced at Bell, stood up over Molina, hands in his pockets. "Mr. Molina, was Abe Keller at that meeting in Skokie, Thursday night?"

Molina looked up at Laska, looked to Bell, then dropped his gaze and took a deep breath and exhaled slowly. "It's anonymous," he said. "That's one of the reasons it works."

* * *

Tic Toc jumped up when the detectives entered the interrogation room. "Come on! Man, this is …"

Bell held up a hand. "Let's clear this up right now," he said. "Will that work?"

Donald Ernell Armstrong walked to the wall, turned and leaned against it. "Listen, you can't do this …"

Laska pulled out a chair, motioned for Tic Toc to sit, then took a seat across from him. Bell sat, too.

When Tic Toc sat, Jason Bell leaned toward him, both arms on the table. "Whereabouts, Thursday night," he said. "That's all we need. That's all we're asking for."

"I was at my girlfriends," he said.

"Leslie Parks?"

Tic Toc raised up and pulled back. He shook his head. "Leslie is …"

"Leslie never saw you Thursday night," Bell said.

Tic Toc quieted, shaking his head. "My other girlfriend," he said. He blinked, looked away, leaned on the arm of the chair. "Leslie don't know," he said. "I got this other girl." He paused, swallowed, then turned to face the detectives head on. "I'm gonna be a daddy," he said. He smiled. "That's right, we're getting married. Wanna go there right now? She's at her mom's place. That's where I was."

Donald 'Tic Toc' Armstrong was released after Deborah Watts, his future mother-in-law, admitted he'd spent Thursday night at her home with her daughter, who, she said, "was foolish enough to get herself pregnant by a man like Donald Ernell Armstrong."

* * *

Sunday morning, early, Bell and Laska tapped on Raymond Whitaker's front door. He answered, holding the door close to his head. "Again?" he said.

Bell looked at Laska, then turned to Whitaker. "We can ask questions from your porch," he said, "or you can invite us in."

Whitaker frowned, opened the door, turned and led the detectives into his living room. "This is a bit much," he said. "I've already told you everything I know."

"Well," Bell said, "we need a bit more confirmation. You need to corroborate your whereabouts for Thursday night."

They heard footsteps, the detectives turned and watched a man stepped into the room from a hallway. "Ray and I were together," he said.

"Stop!" Whitaker grimaced, walked to a couch and sat, then dropped his head into his hands. "David, don't do this."

David Ackerman crossed the room to sit next to Whitaker. "I spent Thursday night here, with Raymond," he said. He paused, turned to Whitaker, then looked at the detectives. "My wife is out of town for a week," he said. He leaned forward slightly, hoping his point was taken. He waited, saw no change, then said. "Raymond and I are in a relationship."

Raymond Whitaker leaned back onto the couch, crossed his arms and looked at the detectives. "You could ruin this man's life," he said. "I'm asking that you not do that."

* * *

It was the serious amateur who woke up just before sunrise with a start. He slipped out of bed, walked into his study and powered up his computer. It didn't take him long to find what he was looking for.

D'Marco Sanders had said it and Bell had missed it.

Longstreet played a 16-note chromatic harmonica. A further search revealed those harmonicas were mostly available in the key of C. Bell remembered the crime scene photos showed only standard diatonic harps, three in Longstreet's hand, in what the coroner called a death grip. Others were scattered around. If he'd intentionally grabbed the D, E, and A, why? Did he choose specific harmonicas? What did that dying man have on his mind?

It took a night of restless sleep and a bolt of inspiration to wake Bell up.

Bell, the serious amateur, had to put himself in Allan Longstreet's shoes, and Allan Longstreet's shoes belonged to a man who based a significant part of his career on eighty-eight keys. Longstreet hadn't been *thinking harmonica* when he chose those particular harmonicas. He was thinking like the musician he was, and for Allan Longstreet, everything was birthed at the piano.

* * *

"Look," Bell said, "A standard harmonica needs to be transposed in order to play the blues and soul stuff Longstreet was playing."

Laska blanked. "I'm lost already," he said. "It's me, remember?"

"Okay," Bell said, "here's how it goes: a standard harmonica, a diatonic harmonica like the ones Longstreet held in his hand, that harmonica plays blues, soul, country, *anything*, in what's called the *second position*. It has to be *transposed*. It's not in the same key as the piano—that's *why* it has to be transposed. When the piano plays in the key of D, the standard harmonica—played in that second position—would be in the key of A. The letter stamped on that harmonica would be an A."

Laska shrugged. "So?"

"When a song is played—on piano—in the key of E, the harmonica would be in the key of B. The letter stamped on the harmonica would…"

"I'm lost," Laska said. "I'm trying …"

"B," Bell said, "and one more harmonica was in Longstreet's hand. It was in the key of A. That means the piano was playing in E."

Laska shrugged. "Man … sorry, I'm trying."

Bell paused, nodded, then sat back on his desk.

"Allan Longstreet doesn't play diatonic harmonicas in his band. D'Marco Sanders told us that. Longstreet plays the chromatic harmonica. I checked through the photos again this morning. I checked Evidence. There was no chromatic harmonica in that room. Don't know who those diatonic harmonicas belonged to—maybe Allan—but all we've been hearing is that Allan Longstreet spent some serious time investing in his ability to play chromatic. Hell, I'm sure he can play those diatonics with no trouble. And it was a good thing they were there, because he left us a message the only way he could. He used the letters stamped on those harmonicas—the keys. *But* … and this is the interesting thing … he was thinking like a piano player. A piano player would know those diatonic harps would need to be transposed, and a piano player of Longstreet's caliber would know what those transpositions would be. *And* … in this case, the D—E—A in his hand works out to A—B—E."

Bell watched Laska's eyebrows squirm, then heard him say "A … B … E. Abe. You sure about this? You *sure*?

Bell started nodding and kept nodding. He stood up, stretched, keeping his eyes on his partner. Laska rubbed his chin, nodding. He stood up, rolled his neck, padded his pockets, looked around the squad room, then reached over and slapped his partner's shoulder. "I'll get the car," he said.

* * *

Keller was gone.

It took five months to find him. He'd worked his way through his usual stops—Memphis, Charlotte, Jacksonville, Daytona Beach, Key West—then the trail went cold.

It was a DUI in Austin that did him in.

When he was walked off the plane that returned him to Chicago, Jason Bell and Joe Laska were waiting.

"Abe, good to see you," Bell said.

Keller had lost weight, lost the beard and cut the hair. He looked both detectives over before speaking. "I want an attorney," he said.

Bell looked at Laska. "Joe, this man wants an attorney."

Laska nodded, stepped to Keller, then watched as the U.S. marshal removed cuffs and handed the prisoner over to him. "Mr. Keller," Laska said, "you have an attorney waiting. She knows exactly what we know and she'll be happy to share it with you."

Laska thanked the marshal, then asked "We'll get the fingerprints?"

His reply? "I'm thinking they're already at your precinct."

Laska cuffed Keller, and the detectives guided their prisoner through the airport to a waiting car. Bell took the wheel and as they pulled from the curb Laska turned to face Abe Keller.

"You told us you'd never been to Longstreet's home," he said. "Remember?"

Keller looked out the window. No response.

"Your prints aren't on the guitar picks all over the floor in Allan's studio? Those aren't your prints? Those aren't your prints on that little amplifier? It was on, you know—buzzing—when police walked in."

No response. Keller looking out the window.

"Allan Longstreet left us a message, too," Bell said. Abe Keller swung his head, looked into the rearview and met Bell's eyes.

Laska turned back to face forward. "That's the surprise," he said. He looked out the window, took a deep breath and relaxed. Over his shoulder he said, "We got a surprise ending, Abe, and it's gonna give you the Allan Longstreet Blues. You play the blues, dontcha?"

True Crime

Geoff Boswell

I couldn't help it.

The sigh came out of me unbidden and my colleague of the day, a stranger called Jackie, here on overtime, asked 'what?'

I turned from the email I'd been reading on the screen and commented 'I just can't understand people these days. They make no sense'.

'You mean they're unintelligible, or they're stupid?' she enquired. I sighed again.

'Yes' I said without explanation. Jackie didn't need one. She did the same job as me, only at a different station usually.

'Is it a *He said She said?*", she wanted to know. I confirmed that it was, albeit without punctuation, grammar, capitalisation, or common sense. 'Just close it down' she advised, moments after I started closing it down. She continued, 'At least you didn't get a weirdo'.

I liked 'weirdos', they were more entertaining than infuriating, especially if you spent a long time on the Avaya Software, single online home system that gathered all the general public's 101 emails together, and presented them for idiots such as me and Jackie on just above minimum wage to handle. For handle, I mean make a log of, or an occurrence for, or a simple reply to, or (as many of us do) just read them, sigh, and put them back in the digital pile.

'What are you doing with it?' I asked her. She told me once more that it was a weirdo, and that he was Jasper Carrot's *nutter on the bus*. That showed her age. I knew what she meant, as it showed mine too. Also, I hadn't queried her assertion of a he. HR would be miffed with us both had they known. 'Nah, I'll close it' she decided.

'What number is it' I wanted to know, I needed a diversion. She told me, I scribbled it down, and I keyed it in, then made it '*read only contact*' and started to scan the incoming enquiry form. I was hooked.

We did spend well over ten minutes swapping Jasper Carrot anecdotes, thereafter, before I offered to make the tea. Again. Jackie was one of those people who you think you recognise, but don't know where from. I then went back to the weirdo.

The working day with Merthonshire Constabulary could be scintillating.

The following shift I found I was on my own, single crewed, I shouldn't be as I couldn't be trusted on me jack, being little more than a long time trainee. I couldn't get my head round another piece of software - called Niche - sufficiently enough to please anyone, including my supervisor, who only kept me on the books because I was marginally better than her. So, being single crewed, I had to lock the front office door, barring entry to the MOPs (members of the public) who may try to access me to ask about lost mobile phones, aggravating neighbours, their impounded car, or to report as a registered sex offender or firearms holder. Technically, you could be all of the foregoing. Or hand another knife in. Or tell me for the umpteenth time about the smell of dope coming from number 32. I loaded Avaya on the computer, as was required of me when I had no real work to do. You can guess what came soon after.

I sighed.

I closed the offending email down, as I had entered a fugue state known in the Force as '*couldn't be arsed*'. I stared at the screen for the length of time it took for the knocking at the closed front door to desist. I then fumbled around in my pockets for my current version of Gollum's Precious. It was that scrap of paper with an Avaya incident number scrawled on it in my inimitable script. It was inimitable in that few people ever wrote anything anymore. Why spend ten seconds writing a note when you can spend ten minutes trying to get your software to load, or your phone to work? I keyed it in, and much to my delight, but little surprise, it was still *new,* no-one had pulled it and handled it. I wasn't going to either, I just *read only contact*-ed it and reread the text I'd reread half a dozen times before.

I went and made myself tea and ate my lunch two hours early. It's what you do in a police station. Especially when you're on just above minimum wage. They pay peanuts, they get monkeys. I could even waltz around a (usually) empty station singing 'Oh, oop boopy doo, I wanna walk like you hoo hoo…' And so, having bought it to mind, I did just that.

'An ape like me hee hee, could learn to be, you hoo human too'. I felt singer Louie Prima turn in his Disney grave. I've already told you a working day in the Merthonshire Constabulary could be scintillating. A copper came in the back door to go on duty. There's a novelty. I sat back down at the desk wondering how much of my singing he'd heard in the car park. Car park: gravel patch at the rear of the station, generally frequented mostly by dandelions in summer and low level drug dealers in winter. And summer. All the time really. The drug dealer's name is Andy. You'll be riveted to know, we called him Andy Capp and he counted at least two of the PCSOs as customers.

The officer sauntered past my open door. 'Mornin'' he mumbled in time honoured police tradition. 'Wotcha cock' I replied just to insert a modicum of difference into his thought processes. It didn't work, but he did offer me tea, which I gratefully accepted prior to finishing the other tea I'd made myself not that long ago. His name was also Andy, but he was no relation, nor customer. This Andy was more prone to Benson & Hedges and Carlsberg, and his hobby was Benson & Hedges and Carlsberg. As he walked toward my desk carrying tea, I quickly got Avaya upon the screen, just for the look of the thing.

'Got anything?' he nodded at the screen.

'Weirdo,' I replied.

'Don't task me then,' he threatened.

'Wouldn't dream of it dear,' I countered. 'It might need investigating thoroughly'.

He snorted and went back to the car park for a fag with his own tea. Andy was also one of those people you thought you recognised, but couldn't quite place. Workdays, Merthonshire Constabulary, and all that.

Yes, the weirdo was still on the screen. I bet your dying to know, but you have to remember dear reader, I can't give it all away in the first few paragraphs. It's not how they do it on the telly in Inspector Morse, or Inspector Semaphore, come to that. Get over it, settle down, and I'll continue.

I'm sorry, I was a little harsh with you there. Perhaps I'm more Police-like than I give myself debit for. The weirdo then. If you read and reread the narrative, you'll eventfully cotton to the fact that you couldn't necessarily claim it was a *He*. They had given a surname, a rather foreign looking one at that, but for the first name it was just an initial. There was an address, but it was of the alleged incident, not for the reporting person (RP, or Source, or Weirdo). The date of birth had been given as 30-02-1800, which was singular but ultimately not original. No, I know I haven't said was the name was. Patience child. The email given was me@mail.com and the telephone number was 01234 567890. Again, highly unoriginal. But, if you are playing games, why give what looked like a proper address? Or was it?

Neither Jackie nor I had done a search on the address. Well, I knew I hadn't, so I loaded Niche (*oh gawd*) on screen, pulled out my *Dummies Guide To Niche* (some handwritten notes made in terror one supposed training day) and did the address search. The address existed. I used a map function, where a big red pin pulsed ominously over a suburban road some ten miles or so from here. Jackie, being a stranger to these parts, might not have known any differently. I wrote the address down on another scrap of paper. Why have one scrap of paper when you can have two? Coincidentally, as often happens in tales of this sort, Andy the copper came back in, coughing and with tea down his stab vest. As he sauntered past my doorway I called to him.

'Andy, you know where this is?' I held the paper so he could read it and choke at the same time.

'Bout ten mile from here,' he confirmed. 'Think it's-a housing estate. Dunno, What's going on there?'

I was just pondering on how to lie when he gave in and started to leave with a 'Look it up on a SatNav if yer going,' to me over his shoulder. He wasn't interested.

You see, unlike Andy (the copper not the dealer), I am not a warranted officer, and consequently there's a lot of things I can't do, shouldn't do, and could get fired for doing or not doing should anyone find out, or care. Going to a reported address being one of them, and not telling anyone else would be another. Well, not telling anyone *and* going, to be precise. The Merthonshire Constabulary held great store in precision. Mostly. It wished to be *seen* to do the right thing, even in preference to actually *doing* the right thing.

Merthonshire is a wonderful place. That, dear reader, is sarcasm. The only place I've lived in or visited enough to comment on, that would be rated as worse than Merthonshire, could be Cornwall. Or Newport in South Wales. No, it's got to be Cornwall. I make this point before telling you that, in the evening, the SatNav couldn't get a 'valid GPS signal'. There was no Wi-Fi, or hot spot for my mobile phone for me to make a call on. On 2G. This is the 21st century, but not in Merthonshire. Neither had I brought my carrier pigeon with me. I had, however, brought along my *Geographers A to Z of Merthonshire and Surrounding Districts,* which I bought recently in 1997. Heavens forbid, the torch app on my mobile actually worked. So I toddled off, some ten miles away, in a car that's seen better days, weeks, months, and decades. I had considered booking out a Force pool car, but considered that was taking the piss too far.

I lived in one of those surrounding districts previously mentioned, and so moved into the heart of the A-Z by means of driving along the A5862 in an easterly direction, obeying the laws of the road as set out in the current version of the Highway Code. I bombed along in other words, as the surrounding district I lived in was empty of civilisation, traffic, and traffic police.

With occasional referrals to the A-Z when personal knowledge failed, I found myself in a part of Merthonshire not often frequented by judges of architectural excellence or awards in town planning. The buildings meant you could have been in any town in the UK, including Newport, and not known which. You always knew you were in Cornwall. I'm still in the police so I can't really tell you many factual details (oh, for crying out loud, hadn't you got that yet?), but we'll call it Merthon Town (he typed, coughing).

I was looking for a suburb of Merthon called Pergetary, which sounds, when voiced, remarkably like *purgatory.* Go on, try it, you know you want to. Still, place-names in these shires are often biblical in origin or essence. (My favourite is *Kyrse* in Cornwall, which should be used in a horror movie by John Carpenter). My A-Z proved too old at this juncture, so I did the obvious thing. I swore at it, which helped as much as swearing at one's computer screen or TV ever does. Now, the sharpest of you will have noted that I am a one for scraps of paper. Therefore, my pockets were investigated thoroughly (I had done the online training through the College of Policing), and the fingertip search produced a range of pieces of paper, in miscellaneous sizes, and varying hues of white. One was the Avaya incident number, another the address I'd shown Andy, and one was an A4 folded map of the route I must have printed off back at the nick, shoved in my arse pocket, then promptly forgot about. Netherworld Avenue. Left, left again, into Judge Road, past the chip shop (frying tonight sign in the window), turn at the Damn & Blast pub, into Netherworld. Park near the gore with Sheol Street, get out, look for number 13 (good grief, really?).

Got it. I stand over the road near number 14's front door step, simply because 14 reminds me of Valentine's Day, and I'm sad. Look at the house. Typical semi, adjoining number 15. 15 looks dead, no lights on (its bloody dark by now and the street lights aren't working, which is no revelation), perhaps the residents of 15 are out. That would be a sensible strategic manoeuvre as number 13 looks like the party capital of Party Town (no, it's not in the *Geographers A to Z Of Merthonshire* etc.). Every light was on in every room, the music was, well, presumably deafening for those inside (The Rolling Stones), the heating was on because the steam was bellowing out of the boiler flue down the side alley to the rear of said property.

The Stones faded out, Black Sabbath came on. I decided on decisive action, which I couldn't decide on immediately, so walked to outside number 12's door. At that point, the front door to 14 opened and a woman stepped out, still putting her overcoat on.

'Evening,' I said as the only thing I could say, being as surprised by her exit as she was by my presence and nocturnal greeting.

'Oh my God,' she yelped, symbolically clutching her heart or at least an imaginary point of it central to her chest and just outside her body. I apologised—sorry to scare you—type of comment, making out I was just passing, coincidentally, as these things happen.

'Bit noisy over there, aren't they?' I asked of the neighbour still taking deep breaths and slapping at the heart approximated position on her now adorned coat. She additionally waved the air in front of her face before replying to me.

'Ain't the first time, nor the last. Still, council don't give a shit even if they says they do, and the Police, well, don't make me larf, they do fuck all anyway, they do.'

'No,' I muttered *soto voce*, as she stormed off down the street toward the Damn & Blast. I needn't have moderated my shame faced agreement as my voice was drowned out by the sound of Motorhead.

I had an idea that amounted to being hung for a sheep than a lamb. I went back to the car, dug out my work top complete with police staff epaulettes, and put it on again, I hadn't got out of the police kegs yet that day. Holding my pieces of paper for effect, I impersonated an Officer by nonchalantly strolling over to #13, and peered with feigned disinterest at the property in question. Let me be clear, both wearing the police staff kit outside of the office and pretending to have a warranted officer's powers and duties would both get me fired, again if it became known, and again if anyone cared.

The door had a plaque on it bearing the legend 'Sheol Cottage', which was either pretentious or egregious. I shrugged, getting tired at this time of the night, and rapped on the door. I stood waiting while Slade came on and Noddy Holder started shouting at me. I knocked again, and after a few moments—and more shouting from Noddy—the door opened. I adopted a semi-officious stance and peered down at my paperwork.

'Evenin' all,' I started with no irony, 'I'm looking for a B. El Ze Bubb of this address please.' I looked up whilst instructing the door opener to 'turn that bloody music down'. Jackie stood there, in a glittery dress, with a cocktail in her hand and still jiggling to the sounds. I was flabbergasted.

'Hallo colleague, got here then?' to which I stared mutely at her. 'He's here Andy,' she yelled over her shoulder and seconds later a party-goer remarkably resembling copper Andy—can of Carlsberg in one hand and a filter tip in the other—appeared, asking Jackie:

'Yer wot?'

She nods toward me, Andy looks over and starts to double up laughing.

He pulls Jackie to one side and says to me loudly (Noddy was still playing) 'You comin' in then?' Stunned, I merely grumbled a set of consonants vaguely sounded like *cmng*. I took one step over the threshold and froze. Something wasn't right. I'd obviously been set up but…

'Why?' I stepped back out. 'Why? I mean, a jokes a joke. But I don't understand.' Jackie stepped outside, followed by PC Andy, complete with drinks and smokes.

'Wasn't our idea mate,' he said, Jackie nodding in agreement. 'Ask your ex-wife'.

'Ex-wife?'

'Stacey,' Jackie clarified.

'Stacey' I repeated, 'Ex-wife, I know'.

'She says you owe her,' Jackie clarified.

'Gettin' you back, mate,' Andy shouted.

'But why you two?' I asked, suddenly fearing the answer.

'Well, she is my cousin,' called Jackie over the sound of Ian Hunter.

'And mine.' Andy confirmed.

At that moment, both the people who you think you recognise, but are not quite sure where, when, who, what, why or how, became apparent in all those elements.

'And you never recognised us, you twat.' Andy continued.

'No,' I said, chastened.

Jackie continued, 'And she said to tell you that although you think you look good in black, you look just like a wanker.'

'Right. The email?'

'Not difficult mate,' Andy began. 'Free email address and off you go. Just had to enter all the bits she said you'd be interested in, secrets, signs, potions, symbols, ghosts, Knights fuckin' Templars and witches.'

'I turn up on overtime,' Jackie breaks in, 'And feeds it to you. You went for it. Hook line and sinker.'

'And who you gonna tell? No-one mate. Coming out here at night, uniform, pretending to be on police business'.

'No,' I said, defeated. 'But B. El Ze Bubb, I never saw it. Thought he was foreign.'

'What?' said Andy frowning, then looking at Jackie. 'I didn't put that name in. Did you?'

She shakes her head. 'No, it was something like Hugh Jerkoff. Anyway that other name he's got, that's the bloke throwing the party.'

'What?' said Andy. 'What?' I repeated.

The sound of the music rose as the door reopened. A large red arm reached out and pulled Andy back in, then another came out dragging Jackie backwards into the party once more. A wall of heat thundered out the house as a tall, heavily muscled man in a red party costume grinned at me, the horns on his head glistened with sweat as he slammed the head of a pitchfork into the doorstep and asked: 'Will you join me?'

My reply, delivered at a speed to match my reversing pace was 'Will I hell as like!'

'Indeed,' he said disappointedly as he closed the door slowly.

I didn't need the A-Z to get home.

Technically, I was the last person to see ever see both Jackie, and Andy. In actuality, I was the last person to see Jackie and Andy alive, but not in the way my colleagues in Merthonshire CID concluded. You had to be stupid or unlucky to get done by Merthonshire Constabulary.

I still work at the station and I spend a fair bit of time thinking up ways to pay Stacey, my ex-wife back. I did give Andy Capp, the druggie, her address, along with fifty quid, so we'll see how that pans out to start with.

I still have to do the Avaya single online home 101 emails, and create Niche occurrences, or Storm logs from them. I don't tend to dwell on the weirdos any more. Not now I know they have little to do with Jasper Carrot. I occasionally entertain the voluntary Chaplain, who (sadly) hasn't a clue. I make the tea when he comes and ask about the nature of evil. He asks me about section 165a—Seized Vehicles—as he seems to have a devil of a time with the odd traffic related problem himself. Namely with car insurance, or the lack there of.

All pretty routine and run-of-the-mill, when all's said and done.

But then, the working day with the Merthonshire Constabulary is often quite scintillating.

-oOo-

True Crime: The Original Soundtrack

Cocteau Twins — Speak No Evil
AC/DC — Hells Bells
The Rolling Stones — Sympathy for the Devil
Black Sabbath — Evil Woman
Motorhead — Devils in My Head
Judie Tzuke — Demons
Slade — She Brings Out the Devil in Me
David Sylvian — The Devil's Own
Linda Gail Lewis — Diggin' My Way Out of Hell
Ian Hunter — Purgatory
Jump — Judgement Day
Nemesea — Beyond Evil
Bruford — Beelzebub.

Sub Rosa

Diana Parrilla

"Make the world wait."

Unknown faces before me, but my eyes were fixed on the glass partition separating the performance hall from the rest of the joint.

The thorned rose tattoo shimmered under the velvet-red lights of the jazz club. Or so it seemed. Small, decorating the back of her arm. But that wasn't what that man had noticed about her.

"Without you my heart freezes."

It wasn't her tattoos, nor her height or those endless legs, nor the cascading wave of hair falling over her updo, covering one eye to balance the shaved side of her head.

Scat portion.

"Please Miss Hidalgo, would you be so kind as to give me an autograph?"

I imagined that's what the stocky man was saying as he extended the Christmas calendar featuring Maria Rosa's photo. Her beautiful face loathed this. All of it. It wasn't her beauty or mystery that drew them in—it was her disgust. That expression of revulsion. Her weariness of being what she was, of being noticed at all.

I sang before my audience, and now came the high note, a G6.

She released the crooked "Welcome" sign, momentarily abandoning her statue-like pose in the club's photo spot to retrieve a pen from her clutch.

"I was a different color until you painted me your favorite."

Hand beneath the cardboard for signing, beyond the glass barrier. Satisfied faces within the windowed area.

Bang. It should've thundered, but it didn't. And it wasn't my singing that covered it up. A lipstick case protruded, tearing at the calendar cardboard. If it hadn't been for the 1858 Remington revolver muzzle it was screwed onto, I wouldn't have suspected it was acting as a modified suppressor, making that first shot—which struck the autograph-seeking man's forehead—sound more like a champagne cork popping.

Maria caught the man's body mid-free fall, embracing him with... love? No, she was already gripping his shirt collar, using him as a human shield against the other shots, these ones muffled by real suppressors, raining down on her as she sought cover behind the grand piano.

I don't know why I kept singing, but I did. I don't think it was about the show must go on—rather to give her privacy, believing that keeping the innocent audience oblivious to what was happening behind them was an act of protection. Though honestly, I think it was my shock that wouldn't let me stray from the only thing I knew how to do: sing, and dance. Oh, and let's not forget impersonating voices—I'd always been good at modulating my voice since childhood, no matter how high the pitch or what accent or timbre it needed.

Her gloved hands didn't quiver as she dropped the second armed man. Of the five men who occupied the entrance lounge, only three remained, and she had four bullets left. Her reflexes, at around forty years old, were like her—nothing you'd expect.

Another well-aimed shot, but the men retreated behind the cigarette vending machine, and her plump lips traced a curse word. One man's head peeked out—that was enough for her to take him down. Two bullets. Two men still standing.

The climax of my song arrived and I closed my eyes as usual, wishing this was all just a nightmare. But when I reopened them, only one man remained standing and she was taking cover on the other side of the vending machine. The empty click of the revolver was devastating, and when the last man standing rounded the machine, she used the empty revolver as a hammer, gripping it by the barrel to strike his jaw. The sound wasn't a musical note but the noise of bone giving way. The men's guns, Ruger Single-Six's, lay on the floor, surely empty. The poor piano had absorbed all their ammunition.

"I wasn't looking for you and I found you."

The man staggered, clutching his face as if trying to keep it in place, but quickly managed to recover. Too bad for him. Maria was already launching a kick to his lower abdomen, but he reacted, gripping her leg firmly, preparing to throw her backward. However, she clung to the lapel of his wool coat and, with a precise twist, landed a direct hit to his dislocated jaw with her fist, right where the sapphire ring adorned her hand.

The music was canned, predictable, while the stage stood empty but for me. Like a mechanical doll, I danced—just enough to keep the illusion of movement alive, tapping my feet as though I still had control. I could've synced with the gunshots outside, but instead, I stayed locked in my preordained routine, drifting on autopilot.

The man, a supposed officer by the gun he carried but not the ragged clothes, faltered. Maria sensed the distortion in his balance, and with a quick push, she unmoored him from whatever tenuous grip he had on the world. A swift sweep of her leg, and his body hit the floor. She didn't give him time to react. Her stiletto heel struck his nape, locking him into unconsciousness, ensuring he wouldn't rise again. He wasn't dead like the others, who lay with holes in their foreheads.

Maria retrieved her purse as though she were picking up an accessory. She reloaded her weapon, finishing the task. The job was complete, but not without blood—dark and thick. It splattered her face, staining her delicate skin a red more intense than the shade of her lipstick.

Applause.

I bowed, grateful for my audience's attention, and when I looked back to where the action had been taking place, there was no trace of the men, their bodies, the battered piano, or Maria.

I was the first one out while the audience, oblivious to everything, prepared to leave—it being the last show of the night, well into the early morning hours. Outside, everything was in order, no traces of blood or anything that could betray the chaos that I still believed I hadn't imagined.

Think, think. If Maria was bloody, she'd be in the bathroom cleaning up. That's where I went, to the ladies' room, didn't care about being a man, and found her at the mirror furthest from the door. Her perfectly manicured nails were working at something around her nose. I came at her with a casual comment, because somehow it seemed right.

"Lucky Mr. Venice wasn't here tonight. Might've had a bit of a situation."

"Who's that?" she asked, clearly toying with me. Who didn't know Russell Venice? The CEO of basically everything in our country. Realizing she might need to explain, she added, "That guy's so weird, I feel like I don't even know him, even though he spends more nights here than in his mansion."

"Yeah, his tastes do change. Maybe he's one of those people who gets bored easily. You know how it is when you're the big boss of a robotics and AI company that controls security and all digital commerce in the country. I guess you've seen it all—one day it's a blonde's company he wants, next day it's yours, then mine..."

I felt that was enough small talk. "Hey, what just happened?"

She sighed, cleaning blood from her nose that clung to it like the permanent ink of her tattoos. Then she yanked it right off.

"My God," I said, seeing her nose was nothing but a prosthetic. Not for beautification. It wasn't about enhancement. No, without it, she was something else entirely—more striking, more real, like a perfect statue lost in time, its form frozen in some forgotten era of idealized proportions.

"You're the only witness, you've seen it all, so this changes nothing, right?" she said.

"Why were those men after you? Who were they?"

"Cops or agents, whatever you want to call them, and they wanted something I have, something I took when I retired."

"Retired from what?"

"From my old job." Her indolence lingered, even after taking down a squad of armed men. Cryptic as ever.

"Coming to my place?" I tried my luck.

"The usual service? Today too?"

"Well, today I'd rather talk, not the usual, but I'll pay the same rate."

She lit a cigarette and blew smoke in my face. I coughed, always did.

"Aren't you afraid? After what you've seen. I could kill you, you've seen too much."

"No, I'm not afraid, I'm terrified," I admitted.

She took another drag. "And you like that, don't you? Everyone loves it. You feel fear, fear of losing something, and it gives you the false illusion that you have something, or maybe you just didn't know how to value it."

"How did you do that thing before?"

"This?" she said, lifting her hand, the ring gleaming like little pieces of the night. Not a scratch, not a mark—perfect, like it had been untouched by the mess she'd just waded through. "Looks like sapphire but it's just physical vapor deposition. Tungsten carbide. Hard, good for hitting. Extra help."

I swallowed. "And did they find it? What they were looking for?"

"Nah. They must've turned my place upside down and not found it, that's why they came here. My dressing room was a mess, had to clean it myself." Another drag. "But no, I won't go to your place today," she said curtly.

"Don't you trust me? Think I might be a spy trying to get information or something?"

"I don't know," she said, looking at me like she might kill me. "Are you?"

"Of course not. I'm just... me. Phillips."

"Of course you're not," she murmured, her eyes narrowing like she was sizing me up for a casket. "I already know that. I know everything about everyone who works here. I've investigated you all. That's why I know you can be useful to me. And that's also why I saw the attack coming."

She sighed then, long and slow, exhaling a cloud that swirled around her like some kind of ghost she'd just conjured. "Everything was fine until my face started showing up in those newspaper ads."

"It was inevitable, you know? You're too damn beautiful to stay hidden forever. And honestly, you're even better without the... disguise," I said, pointing to the bloody, melted piece of fake nose still dripping down the sink.

She flicked the ash off her cigarette. "They've found me," she muttered. "That's what's happening. I've got something they want, something I know what it opens. Took it as a little retirement gift when I left, thought I'd never need it. Told myself I wouldn't use it. Keep things quiet, relaxed, just me, no more of the mess. But now they're looking for it, and I have no choice but to find out what it opens myself." She took another drag, letting the smoke sit in her lungs before releasing it. "And you, well, you're in this now. Like it or not, you're helping me."

"Me? Playing spies? Hold on, this thing you took—assuming it's a key—where did it come from?"

That night, walking with Maria through the familiar dark alleys to my apartment, I kept my mouth shut about all that protective bullshit I used to spew in the early days. No more of the "It's late, shadows crawling with dangers, but don't worry—I'll keep you safe" routine.

I'd promised tonight would be different, but old habits die hard—her velvet clothes already decorated my floor, cash stacked neat in her hand. This time though, I eyed those garments like they might be rigged to blow. Or worse. Maybe they were packed with some high-tech armor I couldn't see.

She was elegantly disrobed, but that hand of hers burned hot when it caught me by surprise. Forced my chin up toward her—smooth as honey against my dark skin, but with steel underneath. Her other hand nursed a cigarette.

"You never smoke," she said, as if it were some kind of crime.

"Voice. Bad combination."

"Why do you keep paying me?"

"Same rate as always, right? Unless something's changed?" I wasn't angling for a discount on account of whatever mess I was getting pulled into. I couldn't tell if she was hinting that I could make something of this, like she thought she deserved a bigger payday.

"You're no spring chicken, and neither am I. But I'll give it to you, you're not bad at all."

Coming from Maria, that was practically a love sonnet. In the short months since she'd appeared at Jazzin Hot, I'd never gotten better.

"You could have your pick without paying," she said, breathing smoke away from my sweaty face this time. "You could always find something similar between cheaper sheets."

"Maybe. But those sheets don't come with you tangled up in them. And like every other person with working eyes in this city—hell, probably the whole damn country—you're what I want. That comes with a price tag. My crooner's salary doesn't stretch far, but I spend it where it matters. Call it selective taste."

"Yeah, mine doesn't stretch far either, that's why I take these... extra jobs." She brushed off my attempt at romance and clicked on the TV.

"Sir, our audience has a lot of questions, especially about why, since the founding of your company, you stood firm against an agreement with the government, claiming you didn't want to contribute to their alleged constant surveillance of the population with your tech brand, Venevolant. Now the deal is sealed, and not only will it be used in private companies, but also in the public sector. What's your take on that?"

Venice's ridiculous cow-lick filled the screen, another one of his endless interviews. Even dyed that sickly bovine green. Behind him stood the blonde—her features set in a subdued, almost melancholic expression, eyes distant as if she were looking at something far beyond the screen.

"Poor wife," I said absently, watching Edna Venice's poker face.

"Nothing poor about her, she's gorgeous."

Though I'd meant something else—the Jazzin Hot visits his wife surely knew about, along with others. My expression clearly didn't convince Maria, as she shot me a look and added, "What's wrong? Not into blondes?"

"Not my type, can't help it."

"Right, you're into mystery, like everyone else. But you know the problem with that? Once it's solved, everything vanishes." Like her cigarette smoke.

"Not for me. I'm persistent," I said, kissing her collarbone.

"Obsessive, I'd say."

I chuckled. "Maybe, but hey, we all have our flaws, right? Take you—hunted not just for your beauty but for other things, from what I can tell... and given your background, if you're a spy, I'm guessing not for our government, since the police were after you..."

"You're saying that just because of my name—sounds Latin, foreign, so you assume I'd work against this country?"

"I'm not criticizing. I owe this country nothing. We all do what we must to survive."

"Yeah, speaking of survival." She stubbed out her cigarette, grinding it into the ashtray like it had personally offended her, and poured whiskey like she owned the place. "Our little job."

"Ah, that," I said, watching her move with enviable confidence, even without the sheathing of expensive fabric. "Wouldn't it be simpler to give them the key and go back to our quiet lives?"

"Not possible. They'll kill me once they have it. Not want to, Phillips. Have to. They've forced my hand. So that's that—I won't give you more details, don't ask. All you need to know is this key opens Vault 169 at the top bank. Whose vault? Don't know... yet."

"Where'd you get it? You can tell me that much, right? Doesn't compromise me—unless you're a witch, because damn, I feel bewitched."

"You came pre-bewitched," she said with a mocking smile. "Got it on my last mission. Nobody asked me to take it—I was just there to collect intel from a government whistleblower, but when I reached the drop point, they were gone. I took the information they'd left, but found this key on the ground. Nobody told me to take it or turn it in. Nobody knew it existed. I just... kept it. Then, after I retired, I dug in and found out what it opens. I never thought I'd actually use it—I had no need. Besides, that would only draw the attention of the people I was trying to leave behind."

I stood, struck by the full force of her statuesque beauty. My skin, polished mahogany in my own mind, was plain—no freckles, no tattoos, unlike hers. "So, where's the key?"

She smiled. Not flirty—murderous. "You certainly don't need to know that."

"So." I took a step closer. "I'm stuck with metaphors and scraps of intel again, huh? Don't worry, I've gotten good at surviving on your crumbs."

Her silence answered for her. My saxophone-worn fingertips brushed her arm. "You're burned," I said softly. Her skin was impossibly warm—pyretic, like she burned hotter than the rest of us, even in the dead of winter. "And you want to set the rest of it aflame—your past, your enemies. That key... is a way out, isn't it? It's your freedom. Your shot at a life that doesn't feel like running through fire every day."

* * *

The neon Amaryllis sign might've inspired a new song—if the word 'Bank' beside it hadn't killed my muse dead.

"Welcome to Amaryllis Bank, how may I—Wait, what do my bespectacled eyes see? Maria darling, radiant as ever," said the receptionist, middle-aged and working the Sunday night shift—the day of rest.

"Adriel, remember the last time we met?" Maria twisted a curl that had escaped her updo, her finger twitching like it yearned for a cigarette it couldn't have.

"How could I forget, darling? That special rate—you said I'd pay the rest in kind if you ever needed a favor. Unforgettable. It's just that my wife came back from her sister's village, recovered against all odds, and now she's living with us again, so I haven't been able to—"

"Don't worry, dear. What matters now is that the time for that favor has come."

I maintained the prescribed distance she'd specified en route, but close enough to monitor their exchange.

"I need you to deactivate all security measures, just briefly. You know, all those hostile robots—we don't like hostility, do we?"

"Of course not, queen. I can handle that, but like I told you before, the lasers can't be turned off from here—no one can, only from the inside. Vault access needs both the key and voice recognition. And the cameras? They have heat sensors that can't be disabled, and they're linked straight to the police stations. Oh, and the guard at the booth will notice."

"Then bring him over! The more the merrier, right? Call him in—I'll handle him, hmm?" She tickled his beard as if she'd mapped his weaknesses. He giggled like a schoolboy. "After that, I need you to connect this device. You'll lose the camera feed because it'll redirect to me, just temporarily, okay? Virus is loaded in here." Her hand settled over his, concealing a miniature flash drive.

The man nodded, entranced, while summoning the night guard to reception. With everything robotized, security was supposedly maximized through minimal human interference, reducing human error to its lowest possible threshold. Or so the security system's architects believed.

Maria then produced her compact mirror, touching up makeup that, to my trained eye, barely altered her appearance. But instead of reflecting her weathered, hypnotic face, the mirror displayed the facility's live security feeds.

"You called, Adriel? Any problems here?" The guard stood

unnervingly tall, his face as elongated and rugged as a saiga antelope's muzzle.

"There is a problem," Maria said, her tone treacly—nothing like her true self. "Three's a crowd." A lascivious smile traced her lips as she situated her hand near his iliac crest. The man stiffened, his face flushed, too stunned to react, as she seamlessly disarmed him without a single hitch.

That was my cue. I slipped into the bank, making my way toward the vault's chamber. The map was burned into my mind, just like the memory of my last conversation with Maria—the one where I had told her I'd follow her anywhere. Whether it was a bank heist, the end of the world, or peeling chestnuts. Pathetic, really.

The last I heard from Maria—in person, not through the comm—was that dulcet voice threatening the guard, followed by a metallic thud: body meeting the artificially engineered lobby floor.

The cameras' vitrified optics offered only a sightless stare as I approached the private vault corridor, where laser beams burned retina-searing red. "Dance for me, contortionist," Maria's voice purred in my left ear.

I exhaled sharply. "Why do you know that? Tell me. I deserve that much."

"Simple enough," she said through the comm. "Circus kid. Mom's protégé. Contortionist, tightrope—until she found your better talent. Then the tiger incident, and you went solo, far from the big top." I clenched my jaw and hit play on the mini-cassette in my pocket. Zipped the compartment shut, silencing Maria's voice. Time to work. Time to dance.

"I was a different color until you painted me your favorite."

The rhythm flowed syncopated, marked by irregular pulses. Swing made the measures glide with oscillating movement, creating a sensation of balance and fluidity that beckoned dance. Strong and weak beats emphasized unpredictably, but always with a cadence that left you teetering between nervous breakdown and the most restful sleep of your life. Tension and release perfectly timed.

The saxophone's sibilant expiration—a torpid blues riff that invariably resonated within the medullary cavities of my bones. I drew in a breath, the arctic, metallic piquancy of the room's atmosphere assailing my nostrils. Then, I extricated myself from my compact form.

My spine, a lithe calamus, retroflexed, my digits grazing the gelid concrete substrate as my costal cage vaulted to an improbable degree. The initial laser, a carmine filament, bisected my visual field. I undulated beneath it, the music orchestrating my peregrinations. A flexed patella, drawn close to my sternum, served as the pivot for a restrained gyration. The subsequent beam, a fulvous streak, abraded the instep of my foot as I pirouetted.

Maria. Her entrance was less an arrival, more an intrusion. Her gaze, obsidian and sharp, fixed upon my still-contorting form, sending a frisson of pressure through my fatigued muscles.

A trombone's lugubrious glissando instigated a profound retroflection, my occiput nearing my calcanei, the lasers now a scintillating reticulation overhead. I maintained the posture, until the cymbal's abrupt clangor impelled me into an anteflexion, my trunk folding like a scroll.

She divested herself of her faux-leather integument—sliding from her shoulders like an ebony carapace. Beneath it, the full-body cryogenic suit revealed itself. The outer layer of the garment, as she had meticulously detailed earlier, was a dense polymer resembling vulcanized rubber, acting as a barrier against the supercooled fluid within. Its surface had a subtle sheen, interrupted by the robust stitching reinforcing its seams.

The bassline vibrated. It was a summons to stabilize myself, a momentary lull before the apogee. I rectified my posture, mimicking the punctuated eruptions of the clarion. A torsion of the trunk, a flexed malleolus, a subtle declination of the humerus—each minute rectification a response to the music's subtle requisitions. Panting laboriously, my gloved hands hit the reticulated floor, facing backward—toward Maria instead of the finish line.

Beneath her vest's impervious shell lay a series of insulated compartments, interconnected by a liquid nitrogen delivery system. The vest had a noticeable bulk due to these internal structures, but it still clung closely to her torso—a fact I, even in that moment, found myself oddly grateful for.

As the terminal, protracted note of the saxophone faded into my ears, the lasers shifted into a waning asterism as I pressed the "Lift Vault Chamber Security Lasers" button—never breaking eye contact with Maria as my encased palm made contact with the surface. The melody lingered, though.

"Make the world wait."

She didn't know it, but the song still echoed in my ears as she approached through the now laser-free corridor. More of a runway walk, really. Those lethal eyes fixed on me while she smoked. "Don't worry, Adriel disabled the fire detection system too."

I stood frozen as she drew closer, her hand grazing my face. "Well done," she said. I nodded, as if that praise was payment enough—and truthfully, it felt that way. She passed me her cigarette. Honestly, the reason I took a drag before extinguishing it, suppressing a rough cough afterward, escaped me—lost somewhere in my nerves.

Maria pressed a button on her suit at hip level, activating a digital readout that flashed: "Extreme Mode Engaged," followed by "Hypothermia Risk" blinking below. Without a word, she stepped into the vault chamber, facing the temperature-sensing cameras, while I waited in the doorway of the unlocked entrance—courtesy of our friend at reception.

The cameras broadcast a signal that only Maria could receive in its true form. Anyone monitoring—assuming she hadn't already dealt with them all—would see nothing but a looped feed of normal activity in the area.

She didn't flinch as she approached the cameras, her blood burning like paradise in hell. She accessed her cryogenic vest's liquid nitrogen reservoir through a nozzle. From her purse came a hairspray canister, modified to accept the nozzle, creating an improvised channel for the liquid nitrogen. She methodically sprayed this makeshift freeze spray from camera to camera. The extreme cold overwhelmed each sensor's heat detection capabilities, effectively blinding them to her body temperature.

She waited, watching as stress fractures from the rapid temperature change rendered them permanently disabled until repairs could be made.

"You can enter now. Quick—find vault 169 and figure out who owns it while I finish here," she instructed. Through the gaps between vaults, I watched her, following the arrow pointing to the 160s, her jaw crackling slightly from the cold as she disabled the remaining cameras.

169. I clicked the vault's voice panel. "Mr. Lewis, please state the words displayed on the screen into the intercom to disengage the lock and allow for key insertion."

A tiny metallic click—the sound of her suit succumbing to inertia—registered behind me.

Red crystal.

"Mr. Lewis," Maria said, tapping away at her handheld tablet. "James Lewis, the U.S. Secretary of State at the G7 summit." She tapped a few keys and played a brief news clip. His voice was higher-pitched than I expected.

"Come on, don't give me that look," Maria teased. "You hit G6 notes. I know you can modulate your voice to match his—and anyone's, for that matter."

I swallowed, trying to summon my inner impressionist.

"Red… Crystal," I intoned, attempting a faithful replication of our representative's vocal timbre.

"Access granted." The lock's tumblers yielded, relinquishing their hold and leaving the obsidian structure ready for the flat key to be introduced in the next phase.

Maria shed the vest clinging to her full suit, exposing her arm.

Maria's fingers brushed over the inked lines of the horned rose tattoo that wrapped around the back of her left arm.

"No, that can't be. Was it there all this time?" I was shocked. "How many times have I kissed that tattoo and never noticed?"

She just half-smiled. The ultra flat metallic implant lay concealed in plain sight, the key pressed flush against her skin. She retrieved a small, sleek device from the inner pocket of her jacket. It was a magnet, probably calibrated to work on the specific alloy of the implant. As her fingers steadied the device against the curve of her arm, the magnet's pull coaxed the implant free from the skin's adhesion.

Maria leaned in, applying a light mist from her improvised freeze spray to the area around the implant. The cold hiss of the liquid nitrogen mixed with the air as she aimed the nozzle at the edges of the key, allowing the freezing agent to help loosen the metal. The combination of the magnetic pull and the numbing cold caused the implant to lift slightly from her dermis.

Finally, she peeled the key free from her tattoo, tucking the flat key into her palm. The tracery of the rose remained intact, save for the almost imperceptible rubescent blemish at the implant's former locus.

"Key recognition in progress. Access granted." The door slid open automatically. Inside lay bags, some long enough to suggest morgue containment. Digital panels adhered to their surfaces.

Fearless as ever, Maria unzipped one of the larger bags.

"Christ!" The exclamation escaped me as I saw that distinctive green pompadour, attached to an intact but lifeless body, eyes open yet simultaneously seeing nothing and everything.

"Venice? What is this?" Maria touched the digital panel, activating its display.

"Synthetic Model vh3. Status: Failed. Identity Match Confirmed: Clare Scott. Officially declared deceased 16 years prior."

Maria unzipped another bag, revealing a second identical body. The same green hair spilled out, though longer this time—just like Venice had once worn it.

"They're Venice clones? Is that why he's so erratic? Where's the real one? And these bodies... they're synthetic... has he used his own tech to clone himself?"

I couldn't speak, my gaze fixed on a smaller central bag. When I touched the screen with my tactile gloves, it activated. "Original subject. Genetic reference."

"Think I found the real Venice," I managed, swallowing hard.

Maria opened the bag—bones and teeth. "They killed the original because he wouldn't cooperate with the government?"

"Possible. Doubt he did this to himself. They must be keeping his remains in case they lose the original genetic sample, but why so many failed models?"

Maria activated another bag's display. "Defective synthetic model vh2. Identity: unverified."

"Dead people... they're loading dead people's consciousness into their clones?" she murmured.

"Doesn't seem intentional, or it wouldn't say 'failed.' Maybe the robots aren't following their programming, instead showing some kind of independent personality? One that in some cases they've linked to deceased individuals?"

"And why was this key at the whistleblower's drop point? Never knew their identity—maybe someone tied to this operation, someone who made a copy of the evidence vault key." Maria pulled out a knife and severed one of the fingers. "And these bodies don't decompose?"

No blood emerged, only a stratified cavity beneath the synthetic flesh, its layers resembling stacked translucent gel films.

"Take out the earpiece," Maria said.

I touched my left ear. "Not that one. The other," she added.

"The other?" My hand moved toward my pocket.

"Tsk tsk, no weapons, FBI dog." The click of her tongue carried pure disdain as she leveled her revolver at me. Perspiration began to bead on my forehead.

"It's not what you think, Maria." I raised empty hands in surrender.

"It's exactly what I think, darling. Did you honestly believe I could know your entire childhood and miss the small detail of the FBI reaching out to you right after I joined your little club? They told you to get close, extract information. They suspected I was working for foreign intelligence within U.S. borders, that I possessed something capable of compromising them. They knew sending more thugs to handle it would fail, as it always does."

"I... they told me I'd be helping my country while earning extra compensation. I've had to make ends meet, just like you, since your retirement. But they never told me much—least of all about this. I'm no agent, just someone they saw in an advantageous position."

"Someone close to me... I know. But here's the thing—not only have you been useful to me, but now you're the one who executed this operation. The lasers, the voice impersonation—not exactly legal, and it's all recorded. As luck would have it, I have it all, while you were cooperating with a foreign spy. The FBI may have tasked you with gathering intelligence, but I seriously doubt they authorized betraying your country in the process." Derision poured from her laughter.

I bit my lower lip. "The cameras capturing my intrusion, the feed... it's in your modified compact mirror. I saw it."

"Observant. Quite the catch, indeed. Yes, it's there for monitoring, but I've been transmitting a real-time copy elsewhere. It's queued to be sent to the appropriate authorities in a scheduled email, unless I personally cancel it—something I couldn't do if anything were to happen to me, right?"

I let the earpiece drop from my right ear, a tiny piece of nanotechnology. I hadn't activated it, and now I never would.

"Sure, you could explain all this to the FBI. They might even believe you. But even with real proof... justifying what you've done? Well, they don't leave loose ends. You've seen that with Venice. It doesn't matter who you are, and now you know things they never told you—things you shouldn't know. If they find out... This serves you just as poorly as it does me. Let's be honest—you've got skills, but not agent training.

Without me, and with them on your tail, you wouldn't last long."

I scanned the space around me, options dwindling. Maria raised the synthetic finger she'd just severed with her free hand—the one not promising my death. "Like everything in life, one thing leads to another, one key leads to the next. Imagine what we could do with Venice's fingerprint, perfectly replicated. With this, we're just a few pieces short of planning our next heist. You in? Could be the next key we need to keep going."

"Keep going what? Living?"

"That key was hope for me, not liberation, Phillips. Hope that there's always something more. And when you run out of keys, you make new ones, like I just found our next." I couldn't decide which was more unnerving—that inert finger between hers or the loaded weapon she waved casually, unconcerned about accidental discharge. "You're in as deep as I am. Take it or leave it?"

A symphony, halted mid-play, still spiraled in circles through my mind. "I was a different color until you painted me your favorite."

She'd painted me in her colors, draped me under her flag of betrayal. And now, I was a traitor to my own country.

"Fine," I surrendered. "I'm in, Agent Sub Rosa."

With her fleshy lower lip drawn inward, she laughed without a sound. "Knew you knew more than you let on."

* * *

"Official pronouncements have confirmed the resignation of Secretary Lewis, citing imperative health considerations. The newly designated strategic consultant, Mr. Venice, was initially under consideration for the vacant post; however, scheduling conflicts preclude his presence at the approaching G7 summit. Consequently, in a surprising dénouement, his wife, Edna Venice, a highly qualified individual with extensive experience in international diplomacy, will accede to the position."

Maria lowered the TV volume, exhaling smoke into the already dense room. "The vault breach cost him dearly, it seems."

"Apparently, they still don't trust synthetic clones—sending the wife instead of Venice," I said, adding my own smoke with ease, no cough, as I helped obscure Maria's svelte, brazen figure perched atop my dresser beside me.

On screen, Edna Venice prowled triumphantly through interview spaces her husband once monopolized.

"Clearly picked the wrong femme fatale to chase, FBI dog," Maria said, her burning hand on my shoulder. "That one's got more power and secrets than I do."

"Nah," I replied, dropping my cigarette as I looked up from my spot on the cold floor, seeking relief from the heat swirling inside me. "Told you, my color's brunette."

Last Dance at the Discothèque

S. B. Watson

Part I—Carlos

Carlos stepped from the darkness between the corrugated-tin shacks. Dizzy's Discothèque sat low and shadowed along the side of the mountain, lit by one flickering bulb at the peak of its gable and a dim pot-light above the recessed back door. Carlos' electric-white suit glared, even in the dimness of Dizzy's dilapidated lighting, as he crossed the street.

A stocky doorman pushed off the door as Carlos approached. The overhead light rimed his flat, Quechuan features in upside-down shadows. He put a hand out and shook his head.

"We're full, brother," he said, in slurred Spanish.

The knife glinted in Carlos' hand, slamming into the doorman's throat. The fat body spasmed and twisted. Carlos gripped him by the collar, coiling his fist into the loose fabric of the man's suit and lifting the knife-blade to open the wound, draining the blood down the man's chest, careful not to let any blood land on his own, immaculate jacket.

Under the pot-light, the glimmer in the man's eyes faded. The pudgy body sagged. Carlos slid the blade out, turned, and dropped the body face-first into the dirt.

Two shadows separated from the shacks across the street, flitting into the light of the discothèque. They were similarly dressed, in old-style suits with wide lapels and flared pants. Both wore plastic-yellow carnations.

"Dump him by the shit-pits," Carlos said, stooping to wipe off the pocketknife on the doorman's butt as the men dragged the body away.

Carlos folded the knife and slipped it back inside his jacket as he straightened up, looking out across the city that sprawled below him. Dizzy's was higher up the mountain than most, so the view was good. *La Rinconada* made a dirty, dishwater-yellow constellation across the Peruvian mountainside, glimmering wetly in the night. Mercurial vapors drifted upwards across the city, rising from makeshift ore-smelting ovens, shifting like Spanish dancers in the city lights.

And above it all, high enough to escape the fetid pall of *La Rinconada*, the snow-capped peak of *Bella Durmiente*—Sleeping Beauty—loomed in the pristine moonlight. The mountain whose captive gold held the high-altitude mining city in its clutches.

After a few minutes, the two men returned, brushing their hands on their pants.

They gave Carlos a brief nod as they passed, and opened the heavy door. Energetic music spilled into the entryway, shuffling with a disco beat, then choked out to a muted rhythm as the door closed behind them.

Carlos waited a few minutes, then raised two fingers.

Two more shadows separated from the shacks across the street and crossed into the light. Both wore retro suits and the same yellow carnations. The suits were a bit tattered, but it wouldn't matter under the swirling lights of Dizzy's. They nodded as they passed.

Carlos stood alone under the pot light, counting the minutes, timing the next entries, watching his breath fog in the nearly-frozen air, listening to the faint rhythm. After five minutes, ten men had slipped inside.

Finally, a single shadow crossed the street. A slender man with a scarred face and only one ear, in a burnt-orange suit.

"Ready, Rico?" Carlos asked.

"Sure this'll work?"

Carlos shrugged. "We know he's here. Meeting a man with a yellow flower. Keep your eyes open. We'll get him." He pulled a yellow plastic carnation from his pocket as he talked, and pinned it to his lapel, then turned and opened the door.

The music swelled around him as he stepped into Dizzy's neon-darkness. Swirling lights flashed in pulsing waves, flickering across the milieu of dancers that filled the room from wall to wall, bodies snapping sensuously to the beat of the disco. The aroma of hot sweat, spilled beer, stale cigarettes, and musky perfumes all mixed into one overwhelming flood. Smoke filled the air, roiling beneath the revolving disco ball, rainbow-droplets scattering through its blue haze with epileptic energy. Naked arms curled in the purplish light. Bare legs shuffled to the beat, hips swayed, shoulders twisted.

Carlos pushed into the crowd. Rico was lost instantly in the darkness.

Above Carlos the ball swirled. Against one wall, on an elevated stage, Dizzy's DJ—known only as *La Pepita*, The Nugget—bobbed and side-stepped at his mixing board as he wove the music track into the next song. He wore a white suit too, frosted in rhinestones, and a tinsel-gold mask that covered his face.

Bodies pressed against Carlos, swaying to the beat that blared from the speakers around the room. Hands gripped him. Hips pressed against his, everyone moving in a swirling current, trying to pull him into the undertow of the music.

He made his way across the floor to the bar, a long counter lit beneath a strand of Christmas lights that flickered in rainbow colors.

The old bar-tender, Pablo, smiled at him, and said something. The words were lost under the volume of the music.

"Beer!" Carlos shouted.

Pablo shrugged and laughed, grabbing a bottle from an ice-chest beneath the counter.

Carlos slid onto the only empty barstool and leaned against the counter, eyes scanning the crowd, shadowy bodies moving with a collective purpose, dark under the kaleidoscope of disco lights. Even though the night was freezing outside, Carlos felt sweat beading on his forehead, dampening his collar.

For a moment he caught sight of a yellow carnation on the dance floor. Then it was gone, lost in the glittering mass.

El Buitre, The Vulture, was here. Somewhere. Looking for a man wearing a yellow flower. He was here, and they would find him. Carlos had never seen The Vulture before. Nobody in *Los Carroñeros* had. He ruled behind a screen of brutal anonymity. But all that would change. Tonight.

Carlos took the bottle from Pablo, and walked along the edges of the crowd. The music changed again, the beat slowing, a dippy guitar laying down a rhythm. The dance floor lost its communal pulse. Bodies slipped from the press, brushing into Carlos as he moved along the wall towards the restrooms.

Then the beat dropped. *La Pepita*'s golden mask began to bounce. The hook slammed into the music like a boxer's fist into a punching bag. The dance floor boogied.

Carlos didn't see the hit coming, just felt the wind knocked out of him as the man's shoulder drove into his chest. They careened towards the wall. Carlos dropped the beer bottle. It was lost in the darkness, all sound covered by the blasting music. They hit the wall and burst through the swinging door to the men's restroom, tumbling to the floor.

Part II—Chaska

Chaska pushed the man against the urinal, grinding her body against his, swaying her hips to the muted sound of the music outside, on the dance floor. His hands pulled her against him, hooked around the small of her back as he kissed her neck. She untucked his shirt, running one hand up the rough skin to his shoulder. The other hand followed his belt along his waist, inch by inch, wrapping around him.

The door slammed open beside them. Two struggling bodies plunged to the floor, filling the restroom with swirling neon lights and the suffocating beat of the music. Two men, well-built and tall, dressed in retro suits, wrestling in a grasping mess across the bathroom tiles, twisting and grunting into each other, elbows jabbing into stomachs, legs hooking, fingers gouging at eyes. The man on top was heavier, with rough, mallet-hands, which he slammed into the smaller, rat-faced man in the white suit with the yellow carnation.

The door swung closed behind them.

A knife sliced up between the two men. Mallet-Hands caught it in his fist, slammed his face into Yellow Carnation, who kneed him off and threw him into the wall.

Chaska's hand slid the rest of the way along her lover's belt and gripped the pistol tucked at his right hip.

Yellow Carnation kicked Mallet in the face, against the wall. The bigger man slumped back, blood streaming from his nose. Carnation rose to his knees, coiling back the final punch—the one that held the knife.

Chaska pulled the gun and shot the back of Carnation's head. The slicked-black hair jumped, red spray speckling the mildewy wall as he tumbled forward into Mallet's lap.

Without hesitation, Chaska turned and fired three shots into her lover's chest, throwing him back against the urinal. Writhing in pain, he slid to the ground, arms retracted against his chest, leaving the white-porcelain urinal smeared red. He was dead when he reached the floor.

Chaska turned back to the mallet-fisted man.

"Who are you?" Chaska asked, her Spanish curling musically from her tongue.

The man shrugged, and wiped the blood on his face with the back of his hand, smearing it down his chin. "Pacha," he said.

"Who is he?" She asked, nodding to the dead man in the white suit.

Pacha looked from the blood-smear on his hand to her. "Who are *you*?"

Chaska leveled the gun at Pacha and reached into the deep V of her loose dress. "Police," she said, pulling a badge and holding it up.

Ignoring the gun, Pacha struggled up, away from the growing pool of blood surrounding the white-suited man's head. "I didn't think police actually existed in *La Rinconada.*"

"There're a few of us."

Pacha looked up as he gained his footing. "Can I wash my hands?"

Chaska thought for a moment. "Sure." She lowered the gun.

Pacha moved to the sink. A reservoir of water hung above it, a ribbed plastic tube running down to the tap. He opened the stop and brushed the blood from his hands in the trickle of yellowy water.

Chaska stepped between the bodies, and stooped over the man in the white suit. "Who is he?" she repeated.

"Don't know." Pacha stopped the flow, and dried his hands on his pants.

"But you tried to kill him?"

"Why should I tell you?"

Chaska looked up, and lifted the gun barrel. "Because I have the gun."

"Alright, good reason. Yeah, I tried to kill him. He's wearing a yellow carnation."

Chaska frowned. "What's that signify?"

"He's *Los Carroñeros.*"

"So?"

In answer, Pacha pulled up his right sleeve, revealing a tattoo of a nude dancing women.

Chaska raised her eyebrows. "*Puta Reyes*?"

"*Si.* You walked into a gang war, lady. The top men of *Los Carroñeros* are here, wearing yellow carnations. Word leaked yesterday, from Vaquero."

"Why?"

"Rumor is they're trying to trap their own leader, The Vulture. We were sent to clean up any *Carroñeros* who came."

Chaska stood up, her dress fabric tightening across the curves of her body. "Pull up the toilet," she said.

Pacha raised his eyebrows. "What?"

Chaska waved the gun towards the stall. "Get the toilet out of there. Help me dump these bodies."

"I don't understand."

Chaska put the gun on the sink and began to drag her dead lover by his ankles. "*I* didn't walk into a gang war, Pacha. *You* did. That's why I'm here. Vaquero sent me too. Who do you think runs the police? I'm here to help snare *El Buitre*."

"Vaquero sent *you*?"

Chaska dropped the dead man's legs when she reached the stall, then moved back to the body of the man in the white suit. "Apparently, he called everybody. *Los Carroñeros* to pick off their leader. *Puta Reyes* to clean up the *Carroñeros*." She gestured towards the body at Pacha's feet. "And *Sendero Dorado* to finish the rest."

Pacha opened the stall and dragged the toilet from the hole in the floor. The opening dropped away, outside the building, to a slanted ramp cut into the mountainside leading down to the shit-pits. Chaska watched as he grabbed the *Sendero Dorado*'s ankles, and stuffed him through.

"You know Vaquero, then?" Pacha asked, as he took the man in the white suit from Chaska, and dragged him to the hole.

Chaska laughed. "Nobody knows him. He's a ghost, just like *El Buitre*." She took the gun from the sink, and tossed it out into the darkness. Pacha dragged the toilet back into place.

"Listen," Chaska said, picking up the purse she'd dropped by the urinal earlier. "You've walked into a death trap, Pacha. In twenty minutes, *Sendero Dorado* will start picking off *everyone* on that dance floor. Everyone I haven't cleared."

"How do they know you've cleared them?"

Chaska opened her purse. Inside was a mass of plastic green carnations. "Wear these," she said, grabbing a handful and stuffing them towards Pacha. "Give them to the other *Puta Reyes*."

Pacha hesitated.

"You want to live?" Chaska hissed.

The mallet-fists closed around the carnations.

"Twenty minutes," Chaska repeated. "Now go."

Pacha turned and slipped from the restroom.

Chaska waited a moment, then followed, the music swallowing her like a grooving ocean wave. She moved quickly through the darkness, through the pulsing mass on the dance floor, threading the rhythm and the swaying bodies.

She found who she was looking for at the far corner, standing in the shadows beside the bar, watching *La Pepita.*

"*Sendero Dorado*?" she asked.

The man looked down at her. He was big, tall, and fat, his face round like a Peruvian cherub, cheeks red and scuffed, the skin flaking from years of mercury poisoning.

"Juan is dead," she said. "He sent me. The *Puta Reyes* are here. They're wearing green carnations."

Part III—Pacha

Pacha watched Chaska slip through the crowd.

He pushed into the dance floor, but lost her halfway.

Above him, the disco ball spun, prismatic shafts slicing through the curling cigarette smoke. The beat snapped, shuffling incessantly, throbbing in his head. *La Pepita* stood above him, bright in the stage lights. The golden mask swung back and forth, watching the crowd, emotionlessly bobbing to the rhythm.

Pacha moved back to the shadows along the wall. A yellow carnation swayed into view beside him. His hand jabbed out, slamming the pocketknife he'd lifted from the man in the white suit into the dancer. Pacha saw the man's rhythm falter. He pulled the blade and walked away. At the wall he turned. The dance continued. Nobody cared about the body, somewhere underfoot.

Did she really expect him to trust her?

A *Puta Reyes* slipped up beside him. Said something. He saw the mouth move, but couldn't hear the words. He shrugged, and moved back into the crowd, dropping into the rhythm, circling towards a woman in a sherbet-orange dress. He'd seen her from the wall. She was easily noticeable. When he reached her, they began to dance. She pressed close, rubbing against his chest. He slid his arm around her back, gave her a kiss on her rough cheek, then put a carnation on the chest of her dress and danced away.

In five minutes, he'd planted half the green carnations on random dancers. He returned to the bar. Pablo slung him a beer. Pacha leaned against the counter and watched the woman in the orange dress. She swayed and swung to the music, sliding into the depths of the churning crowd. Then she disappeared.

Pacha drank the beer, and looked for the next. A tall man in a yellow blazer. This time Pacha saw it happen. Saw the big, fat man sidle up and slam his fist into Yellow Blazer's back, then slip away.

One by one, the green carnations were being taken out.

The dance floor was beginning to thin as bodies littered the ground. A few women scampered away, flitting through the spinning lights. Some men pulled the bodies to the side. Dancers flowed back into the space, slipping on blood.

Pacha felt the heat flush his brow.

The bitch tried to trick him.

He scanned the room. She was nowhere to be seen.

"Hey," he snapped at a *Puta Reyes* by the bar. The man shook his head, and leaned close. "*Sendero Dorado* are here, as well as *Los Carroñeros*."

The man's eyes turned wide. He said something.

"What?"

The man yelled.

Pacha chucked his beer bottle into the shadows. "Ah, fuck it," he snarled, turning and revealing the compact Uzi in the concealed holster at his side.

The other man's eyes got even wider. Pacha put a hand out and made a spraying motion towards the dance floor. Then made a 'five' sign. The man nodded and moved away.

Pacha watched the familiar faces of his *Puta Reyes* gradually emerge from the throng, wading through the people towards the edges of the room. The fat man was still out there, picking off green carnations.

After five minutes, Pacha pulled his Uzi, leveled it towards the dancers, and opened fire.

Part IV—*El Buitre*

The punctuated staccato of rapid-fire gunshots hammered above the music. From all sides, muzzle-blasts lit the crowd on the dance floor, like camera flash-bulbs. Bullets thudded into the mass of people, sprayed the walls, tore through the ceiling tiles, scattered the bottles behind the bar in glittering shards.

Shadows dropped to the floor, writhing beneath the panicked feet of the survivors. Bodies pushed and pressed. The mob split into currents that swept against the walls, blindly rushing for an escape. More gunfire broke from the corners of the room, and some from the dance floor as the surviving *Sendero Dorado* and *Los Carroñeros* returned fire. And above it all the music hammered on, covering the screams, muffling the stampede-footsteps of the fleeing victims. The disco ball spun, sowing prismatic light across the color-shifting room.

The last of the panicked dancers finally slipped away, through back entrances and side doors, leaking out of Dizzy's like water from a sieve. The gunshots crackled to an occasional report, then fell silent.

The music track ended. *La Pepita* was gone, so the music simply stopped. Only a backbeat continued, endlessly cycling.

Pablo opened the trapdoor behind the bar and climbed up, his calf-skin leather dress shoes crunching on the broken glass as he rose and cautiously surveyed the scene.

The door to the men's room groaned open on broken hinges. Chaska stepped from the room into the purple light. Her eyes met Pablo's. He smiled.

The backbeat thumped above the emptiness.

Pablo walked from the bar, taking a long-barreled revolver from below the cash register, and sauntered onto the dance floor. A few of the bodies still moved. Pacha—the muscular *Puta Reyes* Pablo had seen give the sign for the massacre—was struggling beneath the body of a fallen hooker. Pablo leaned over as he passed and blew his brains out. A few feet away a wiry man in a burnt-orange suite, with one ear, floundered in a pool of his own blood. Pablo considered shooting him, but it looked like he was dying anyway.

Pablo walked towards the empty DJ platform. A huge fat man, dress-shirt bulging against its buttons, slumped against the base of the stage. Five or six bullet holes oozed blood down his stomach, but he still breathed heavily, watching as Pablo approached. Pablo shot him in the temple as he climbed the stairs to the stage.

La Pepita was nowhere to be seen. Only the golden mask lay, glinting in the overhead light, at the edge of the stage. The digital DJ equipment flickered like a 1980s sci-fi prop. Pablo frowned, and started pushing buttons. Music started and stopped. Beats laid over the top of the backbeat. Below him, on the dance floor, Chaska moved towards the stage.

Finally, he found the right buttons, mainly through chance. An old Salsoul classic by Bebu Silvetti started up, sharp piano chords shattering the air, laying the hook, the beat filling in beneath it, then a heavy bass guitar, setting the jive.

Pablo looked up.

Chaska was dancing. Her lithe body swayed and snapped beneath the disco ball.

She'd done well.

It wasn't easy, ruling a gang through anonymity. A month ago, he discovered dissenters in *Los Carroñeros*. The normal solution was simple—have loyalists kill them, and their families. However, because Pablo ruled through a secret identity, *El Buitre*, that wasn't a viable option. Only Chaska knew his secret. And now, with the mysterious Vaquero hunting him as well…

So, Pablo tasked Chaska to spread rumors using her contacts as a police officer, but had her spread them under the guise of Vaquero's management. Rumors for *Los Carroñeros*, to lure the would-be traitors to the discothèque, rumors to betray the traitors to the *Puta Reyes*, and rumors to betray them all to the *Sendero Dorado*.

Truth be told, there was no guarantee any of it would work. The actual result was better than Pablo had expected.

He climbed down from the stage, feeling the beat infect his step. The disco ball lights sparkled like spring rain as he moved towards Chaska. She pressed against him, stepping to the music. Hips together, they danced in the roiling smoke, stepping between the bodies on the floor.

The music swelled. The beat was relentless. Chaska's dancing was smooth, snapping to the rhythm with sensuous fluidity. She brought her arms above her head, pressing her breasts against Pablo's chest, her deft footwork bringing them in a spin beneath the ball.

Then she slipped into the darkness, revealing the dark form standing a few feet away, draped in a thick leather duster, face shrouded beneath an old fedora, cigar glowing in bared teeth, holding a stubby revolver aimed at Pablo.

Pablo stood motionless. He'd left his gun at the DJ stand.

Beneath the fedora, the man smiled.

Part V—Vaquero

Earlier, Vaquero watched from the shadows as Carlos killed the doorman. He'd followed the *Carroñeros* into the dimly lit discothèque, and taken up a spot in the corner. He saw Pacha ambush Carlos, saw Chaska approach the *Sendero Dorado*, and saw the *Puta Reyes* as they moved into position. He'd seen it all, from the corner shadows, behind an unused refrigerator unit, only the smoldering light from his cigar hinting at his presence. The shootout, the panicked escape of the dancers… And finally, Chaska's dance with *El Buitre*, revealing his identity.

Just as they'd agreed.

Behind every kingpin was a woman. Unfortunately for Pablo, Chaska was a woman with a price, which Vaquero had paid.

Vaquero raised the revolver and fired into *El Buitre*. Three shots. Pablo stumbled, his feet staggering. It almost looked like he was still dancing. Then he coughed and blood burbled down his chest. His legs gave out beneath him, and he fell to the floor, sighing his last bloody breath.

Vaquero drew on his cigar, tasting the nutty tones of leather and oak, and turned as Chaska came to him.

Behind every kingpin was a woman.

He put his hand in her hair and bent her head back, pulling her into him. She smiled under the lights, opening her lips expectantly.

Vaquero lowered his mouth to hers, and felt the suction as they kissed.

* * *

Chaska felt the music in her bones, tingling in the tips of her fingers, electrifying her hair by the roots. She swayed, she spun, wild abandon swelling within her as Vaquero shot *El Buitre.*

This was her man. *This* was the one who would give her what she deserved, who could take her from this hell-hole city, tucked beneath *Bella Durmiente* with its cursed gold.

She moved into Vaquero as Pablo fell to the ground. Surrendered her body to his as he pressed her into him, pulling her head back to kiss. Closed her eyes as their lips met.

Then she felt the hard jab of the stubby revolver under her chin.

Chaska opened her eyes.

The disco ball spun. The music plunged endlessly onward. Vaquero was warm and strong against her. Then everything erupted into a bloody swirl of swimming colors, and the music stopped, and Vaquero vanished like a ghost, and everything faded to black.

Bittersweet

Jay Andrew Connor

I see you dancing
In the acid rain,
Feeling it burn,
And loving the pain.
With visions of Empires,
All turned to dust,
There's nothing left,
That can slake your lust.
Push the lever down…
(Down, down, down)
Just push the lever down…
(*Push the Lever Down—BeHellMoth*)

* * *

His name was actually James Horace Stephenson—at least when he had been at school. Horace… As a young kid at the start of the 1970s that had made him a real stone magnet, especially when the only option had been walking home at the end of the afternoon classes. Then a decade or so later, a London West End therapist had told him, "That's probably when your repressed multiple personalities had been born."

Thankfully the therapist had been talking to Horace at the time….

* * *

Thursday 16th April 1987

Record producer and *BeHellMoth*'s agent, Gary Miles, stood up, put his hands on the oak and leather desktop and leaned forward. "What *I* fucking *want,* is for you to stop pissing about, finish the final fucking album, or break up the band. Gene is already doing the screaming fits over composer rights and royalties—and you both need something in the bag, otherwise it's going to be a breach of a three album contract."

Band frontman, Switch Boy (nee James Horace Stephenson) stubbed his cigarette out in an ashtray on the coffee table in front of him, then angrily pushed himself further back on the couch—the leather of his biker jacket and trousers audibly rubbing against the leather upholstery.

"Let him! We agreed when we started out—no individual writing credits—All or nothing. He signed the agreement the same as I did. There's nothing to contest. Anyway, you can remind him who it was who forked out for Rhadamanthus. He'd have nothing without that Yammy DX—or the time I put in learning how to programme the thing." From a jacket pocket he pulled out a half crumpled packet of *Disque Bleu* along with a gold *Colibri* lighter, and lit another one up before continuing. "Anyway, the tosser can't even hold a note, let alone hold it together on stage. If it wasn't for me, he'd still be second guitar in that shitty little no hope punk outfit, The Dead Fish."

Gary sat back down and sighed. *And if you hadn't slept with him, or got him hooked on heroin….* But he left that thought unvoiced—remembering the framed gold disks on the wall behind him that *BeHellMoth*'s first and second album sales had generated. Hybrid Goth Metal, the music press had named it—and Stephenson (then aka Stevie Fabulous) had abandoned the electro-orientated Blitz Kids/New Romantics ship in favour of… Well, whatever the fuck it was, Gary was happy to ride the wonga tsunami, until, ultimately, *BeHellMoth* became financially spent. Which, going by Stephenson's attitude, wouldn't be long…

Gary Miles took a long breath, then, "I don't care what you might have already. I need at least eight—no, make that twelve new tracks—mixed down ready for cutting and pressing, by the end of May."

Stephenson sucked and shortened the French cigarette by a quarter inch, held the smoke in for several seconds, then exhaled, half whistling as he did so. "Call it June?"

"Okay, June it is. Hell, I don't fucking care if you get one of your roadies to give you some of the tapes they use to press up the bootlegs they sell to the punters post-concert. We could maybe even give PyraMax a double album—one studio, the other live. That way we can cut loose, and they have a sweetener in the deal."

Of course, PyraMax would pull 4 tracks and repackage them as two 12-inch singles, then just before Christmas, put all 4 onto a Limited Edition 12-inch coloured EP, or a picture disc version. Anything to exploit the *BeHellMoth* fan collector base.

Stephenson stubbed out the remains of his cigarette and got up off the couch. "Okay, end of June it is."

To Stephenson's departing back, Gary said, "I'll have the paperwork readied and couriered over to your studio tomorrow morning. And this time, please don't offer to suck his cock in lieu of a tip…"

Just before the office door closed behind him, Gary saw Stephenson making a *You Fucking Wanker* hand gesture with his fist as he turned to walk past the receptionist, then out into the Wardour Street afternoon sunshine.

* * *

I take total control,
Of your body, and your soul
You are mine…
…And I possess you.
(*Sub-Missive—The Carnacki Experiment*)

* * *

Stephenson had gone along Wardour Street, then over and down Boshwick Road, and from there he'd let habit guide him through the backstreets until he walked through the front door of *The Sync Hole*—a single room pub that stretched rectangularly away down the back, with a second entrance-cum-exit opening onto the parallel side street. On the floor above, on a Friday and Saturday night, was the Dark Room—for those who liked their gay sexual gratification totally 'no-strings anonymous.'

Stephenson scanned the room as he walked up to the bar. Only a double handful of hardened drinkers were dotted about the various tables—nothing remarkable for a Thursday afternoon. Shuggie, the day staff bartender, came up to serve him. "The usual is it, big man?"

Stephenson just nodded, and the barman opened an ice cold can of imported Jolt Cola, and poured it into a straight pint glass. 40 seconds later he put the shot glass of room temperature sake alongside it.

Leaning in towards Stephenson, he said in a low voice: "We've been raided three times this week, so if you're carrying, then you know where the toilets are. If you get my drift…" Then, as he started to walk away, he added, "Oh, and *kanpai*." A Japanese toast to Stephenson's seeming addiction to sake bombs.

He picked up the pint, took half a mouthful off the top, then dropped the shot glass into the high caffeine drink. He gave the pint glass a swirl, then chugged down half in several large gulps—desperate for some kind of rush, even if it was just caffeine from the drink.

From behind him, a voice said, "Yu-You're Switch, aren't you?"

He turned to look, and saw a young student—maybe 18 or 19—whichever it was, he didn't look street legal 21. "What's it to you?"

"I-I'm a fan. Have been since I first saw BeHellMoth at Croydon, before the release of Death Knell."

Stephenson glared. "That was five, maybe six years ago." He turned back to his drink. "Anyway, Croydon was shit." He took another slug of the sake bomb, then: "Now the Camden gigs, they were something different." He heard himself talking in the past tense, swore under his breath, and shook his head as the caffeine and sugar started into his system.

The young guy smiled shyly. "You had the new drum machine going through the KORG—"

Stephenson became defensive. "Well, there was no way we were going to risk taking the DX on tour. We're not fucking Genesis, for Christ's sake." He turned and took a proper look at the guy. Around 5ft

10, snow-white Billy Idol hair, pale complexion. The snug black jeans and studded leather jacket appeared secondhand Elephant and Castle, but the rings in his ears were way above the usual Kensington Market quality. Stephenson started to feel his senses perk up.

He leaned back against the bar. “Okay, so you know who I am, but who the hell are you?”

“I’m Michael,” then rapidly he added, “But everyone calls me Micky.”

“As in Finn?”

“What?” Obviously confused, he stumbled on. “No, as in Micky Coulshaw.”

Stephenson smiled inwardly. This was going to be easy. “Okay, as in Micky Coulshaw, you go and find us a nice, quiet, space at the back, while I get the drinks. What’ll you have?”

“Th-the same as you.” Then, to make sure he hadn’t overstepped, “If that’s okay with you?”

Stephenson brought his right hand up and firmly patted Michael’s cheek. “Just find us somewhere, and I’ll be along in a minute.”

Michael had almost ecstatically trotted off towards the back of the pub, and Stephenson couldn’t help himself from watching Michael’s arse, emphasised by the tight black denim. As he turned back to the bar, he found Shuggie already standing in front of him.

“You don’t hang around, do you, Jimmy. Two more sake specials?”

“Why not? If he’s drinking, then I’m sure you’ve already verified his age?”

“According to his provisional driving licence he’s old enough to drink.”

“And…?” The Sync Hole management had a strict policy in regard to the age of consent.

“If the licence is to be believed, then you’re in luck, big man. He was 21 at the start of last month.”

Stephenson felt a warm glow beginning within him. “In that case, then yes, two more it is.”

* * *

Hello stranger—
No, don't be afraid....
I always glow this bright
After midnight....
(*Thirteen O'Clock—Atom Beach Refugees*)

* * *

"You've reached Miskatonic Mansion Studios. Nobody wants to talk to you right now, so leave a message after the tone..."

"Hu-Hello? Switch? It's Micky... Are you there? It's been three days now... I wanted to tell you that I had a really great time. I-I've never been to a nightclub like that before. It was...different. And it was so good of you to let me suck you off. And paying for my taxi afterwards, you really shouldn't have.... But, what I really wanted to say was—"

"End of message. Thank you for calling. Goodbye."

* * *

The following Thursday, at a corner table in the back of The Sync Hole, Stephenson sat across from Micky. Gently swirling his pint glass, Stephenson said, "You've been pretty persistent, haven't you?"

Not making eye contact, just looking at his hands on the table, Micky started, "I..." Then his voice trailed off for a moment. "I thought we had something between us...."

"What? Just because I let you suck my cock at the end of a night out?"

"Well, I—"

"Do you have any idea how many groupies, or how many super fans, queue up after a gig? They do it because they all want a piece of me. Yeah, until the next roadshow pulls up for a night, then they can't wait to get themselves a piece of whoever that band's lead singer is."

"But I'm not like that—I never have been!"

"I told you before, I'm not looking for some one night, two night, goodnight relationship. Being with me isn't like any normal relationship." Stephenson took a swig from his pint glass, then, "We're going back on the road for a 3 month UK tour starting at the end of

September. You want to come along?"

Micky's emotions went from depressed to ecstatic in 2 seconds flat. "I'd give anything to be on tour with you! You mean it, don't you? You're not just teasing me?"

"Depends…."

"On what?"

"On whether you can be comfortable with being around other incessant fans—all looking to grab a piece of me for their own gratification. When we're on tour, I don't want to have to worry about you getting bratty and throwing a tantrum, just because one of the groupies tosses a jockstrap on stage, along with an offer to wank me off on the tour bus after the gig."

Micky felt himself dropping down into despair again. "I can handle that. It's all part of the lifestyle, right? On stage, or just after a gig… I ju-just want to be given a chance—to prove myself, and my commitment to making it work between us."

Stephenson picked up his pint and took another mouthful. Glass back on the table, he looked directly at Micky. "I've made mistakes in the past—believed people, only to find out they were just grasping for money after they'd become bored with the star-fucking."

"But I'm not like that, Switch!" He knew Stephenson's real name—*well, what ardent fan didn't?*—but he had always called the singer by his stage name. Somehow he felt it made it all the more personal between them. "Believe me!"

Stephenson inwardly smiled at Micky's emotional state. *Maybe this would turn out to be the one after all…*

Stephenson pursed his lips, as if thinking things over. Then, "Okay, so let's say we have a trial period—until after the next tour ends in December. If we still feel that things are good between us, then we can spend Christmas together. Maybe New Year in L.A?"

Across the table, Micky looked wide eyed. "Are you serious? I mean, you're not just saying that to, you know, brush me off or anything?"

"Yes, I'm serious. If you like, I can get our agent's legal team to put together an agreement if you want?"

"No! No, there's no need to do that.... Believe me, you're not going to regret this."

I know. Stephenson looked around the pub, then said, "Tell you what." He picked up his glass and downed the last of his sake bomb. Taking the now empty shot glass from between his teeth and putting it down beside his pint glass, he said, "How do you fancy coming back to the studio? We need to get a couple more songs finished and mixed for the next album."—Gary Miles had been on his back again about completing the 12 track deal—"And after that, we can get to know each other a lot better."

He'd thought Micky was going to wet himself with all the enthusiastic nodding.

Pushing his chair back, Stephenson said, "Okay, finish up. We'll go out the back way, and I'll get us a cab."

Micky had nearly choked on the shot glass, and it rattled as he put the almost empty pint back down on the table. Then, as he stood up, Stephenson had come around the table. He put his right hand into the hollow of Micky's back and pulled him in close. Then his left hand was at the back of Micky's head, pulling it even closer, and into an intimate, tongue-probing kiss. Stephenson felt the younger man's body relax against his, lips pressed hard against teeth—and quickly greeted with submission as Micky half opened his mouth to let Stephenson's tongue gain access. Stephenson's right hand slid down to fondle and cup Micky's buttocks, taking in the pleasure of feeling Micky half moan, half sigh, at the sensations Stephenson was creating.

Then Stephenson's left hand yanked at the back of Micky's jacket collar, pulling them apart—leaving Micky confused at the mixed signals Stephenson was giving him.

Lifting the front of Micky's t-shirt up, Stephenson made a little show of bending slightly and wiping his mouth dry. Letting go of the material, he said, "The exit's behind you. That's if you still want to come with me back to the house and studio."

Without waiting for a reply, Stephenson pushed past the young man, knowing full well that he would be behind Stephenson even before they had reached the back door leading out onto Clarkdale Street.

* * *

Curiosity!
You stand at the head of the stairs…
Curiosity!
But in the darkness you cannot see what's there.
Curiosity!
And then you feel your reluctance ebb.
Curiosity!
As slowly I draw you, into my web…
(*Down the Spiral Staircase—The Mutant Spiders*)

* * *

"Why the hell are you fucking around like this? You know as well as I do that PyraMax won't cut more than 21 minutes per side, even using a Neumann VMS. A 25 minute 'concept' track will need compression, and that's just going to screw up the sound."

Gene Franklin (aka Doktor Keys)—the 'other half' of *BeHellMoth*—was at the mixing desk, looking over the tape logs. "Gary said we're still short of two tracks when he called me this morning. I can go back over our early demos, do some rearranging—transfer them over to the TASCAM 16 track…"

"Then what?" Stephenson sounded like a petulant school kid being given detention.

"Then we can give PyraMax the third album, and get out of that shitbox contract. You should never have signed that in the first place…." It had always been a sore point between them. Gene had always wanted to go Indie throughout. But signing with the label had gained them overnight success—especially in light of the electro-poppy crap getting airplay since Giorgio Moroder got involved with *Sigue Sigue Sputnik* almost a year ago.

Stephenson pulled out a packet of *Disque Bleu* and lit one up, knowing full well that smoking in the control room was one of Gene's peeves. "That contract is the only thing keeping us in a lifestyle we never thought possible back in 1981." He waved his left hand around expressively, the cigarette briefly leaving smoke trails. "Anyway, we get this contract signed off, then I'm going solo."

Gene got up from behind the mixing desk. "Suits me just fine. I've already been asked if I was interested in putting together a Dead Fish retro box set—"

Stephenson's voice sounded sneery. "You haven't got enough for an A-side, let alone a whole 7-inch single."

Gene shook his head, opened the door and stepped out into the corridor. Turning back, he said, "There's over three hours of material. And none of which you had a hand in." As he pulled the door half closed, he added: "Just go and play with your new twink. I'll come back once the smoke has cleared and finish off the tracks." He'd then slammed the door closed and walked out the back of the mansion, into the Essex countryside night. Maybe, when he'd calmed down a little, he'd take the Ducati out for a ride. Somehow the motorbike always managed to put him in a good headspace….

* * *

I keep you warm and safe
In my tight embrace.
I lick your neck,
And enjoy the taste…
Ah, if only you knew
What all this leads to…
(*The Great Deceiver—Iron Lung*)

* * *

All 12 tracks had come in mid-way through July. Gary Miles knew they'd be late, which was why he'd negotiated an August deal with Frank Leander at PyraMax. Though he didn't tell Stephenson, he did tell Gene, just to keep the poor bastard's blood pressure down. To help, he'd also 'finally succumbed' to Gene's pleas to get him a new KORG

Opsix for the up-coming UK tour. And why not? The tour was one of those 'back to our roots' gigs—40 medium-to-small venues in just under 90 days. And, once he'd been sent the cover designs for *Creatures of the Night Worlds*, the double album he'd finally managed to sell PyraMax on, then maybe he'd take a short break before announcing the breakup of BeHellMoth, due to the age-old reason of 'creative differences,' naturally.

Gary took a sip of his now hand-warmed Hennessy XO, and settled back in his office chair. It had been a good run, but like everything else, you always have to move on to new things in the music business. He'd take Gene with him—clean now for over 5 years, no thanks to Jimmy Stephenson—and who seemed to be turning into some kind of Vince Clarke singer-songwriter....

The phone rang on his desk. He picked it up and pressed the button to take the call.

"Gary? It's Moira. I've just had the NME on the line wanting to know when we're going to be running the BeHellMoth tour campaign. I told them I'd get back once I'd spoken with you."

"Good girl. We'll probably go for a full page, running for 6 weeks prior—that should generate enough advanced ticket sales." He paused for another relaxing sip of brandy. "But before you agree a price, tell them that Sounds are offering a 20 percent reduction if we advertise with them."

Moira sounded a little surprised. "Are they? Can they afford to drop their price like that?"

Gary smiled. "Fuck knows, love. But it'll worry the shit out of the NME when it comes to giving us a costing."

* * *

The smell of oils and leather
Heady and exotic
Black souls in Angel suits
Walk under a bloated moon
This is a place of dark intent
So let the initiation begin...
(*Horn of Corruption—Beyond Eternity*)

* * *

It was 1am by the time they'd returned to Miskatonic Mansion and Micky was standing in the middle of Stephenson's massive bedroom. He didn't know what to make of the night out, or the new-found range of emotions he felt.

He had been with Stephenson for almost 16 hectic weeks—even staying over nights and weekends—as they had 'found out about each other' as Stephenson had called it. Yet, he'd always been hinting at something more, something he said he would reveal to Micky when the time was right. And tonight was supposed to have been right for that revelation.

Earlier, as Stephenson had finished putting in some work on his big concept piece, *The Nightcreeper Suite*, he'd turned to Micky, and held Micky's face with both his hands.

"Do you feel you can trust me?"

Micky tried to nod his head, but Stephenson had held it firm.

"Tell me that you do…Or not. I need to hear it."

"I… Yes, I trust you, Switch. Why? What's wrong? Is it something I've done? If so—"

Stephenson had let go, and smiled. "You've done nothing wrong. In fact you've been doing everything just right. So now I want to take our relationship to the next level. Come on, we're going to an exclusive club I know."

The taxi had taken them across town, then into the outskirts, and had dropped them outside what looked like a factory warehouse. Around the mesh fence, large halogen security lights added a cold starkness to the area, and Micky had started to feel the first twinge of apprehension. It became a little stronger when Stephenson had paused in front of a plain, unmarked steel door. He had turned to Micky, taken a swipe card from his back pocket, and with a glint in his eyes, said: "Are you ready for this?"

Bravado had taken control of Micky's mouth. "Yeah. Bring it on."

But in no way had he been ready for what had been on the other side.

Through the doorway had been a short, square platform, and the top step of a ten-foot-high metal spiral staircase that led down to what he'd supposed was a basement area.

The low lighting from the room below had been a slow moving mixture of blood reds and cloying purples, which had reminded Micky of the retro 60s Lava Lamps he'd seen in magazines. Through a slight haze of tobacco and cannabis smoke, mixed with sweeter spices and the musky humidity generated by a crowd of people, Micky had heard soft background music. It seemed to be nothing immediately identifiable—just a background rhythm that had sounded sort of African, then hints of Arabic, then possibly Aboriginal. Whatever had been in the mix, it had a universal tribal addiction that had Micky nodding his head fractionally, in time with the back beat. The atmosphere had started to buzz in his nose and catch a little at the back of his throat, making him wish he had something to hand to wash the dryness away, and as Stephenson had already started to descend, Micky had quickly followed behind.

Maybe it had been the smoke, combined with the twisting spiral, but halfway down Micky had to pause in order to stop his head spinning. As he'd looked out across the club floor, he'd seen a long bar over against the far wall, with tables set near, and two other walls taken up with more private booths. Over by the forth wall hung heavy stage curtains—closed, with the footlights turned off. Yet it had been the clientele milling around the bar and tables, and casually slipping in and out of the booths, which had made Micky stop and wonder what it was he was getting himself into. Yes, he'd seen one or two of the costumes before—though only in the occasional gay fetish porn he'd allowed himself from time to time, between studying for exams and finally graduating from university. But it had never been as integrated or as full on as it seemed to him then, in real life.

Parading around in the clearly lit area had been two men. They had been dressed in midnight black, full length, leather body suits, some pieces laced up with blood red cords, and brightly embellished with chrome buckles. He'd watched as they had walked lazily through the groups of tables and around the booths. One had been carrying a long bullwhip casually over his shoulder, the end snaking along the floor a little way behind him. The other held onto the end of a platted leather lead, attached to the back of a studded collar wrapped around the neck of a six and a half foot tall, broad shouldered bear. He was naked, save for what looked like a tight silk posing pouch—the straps up high on his hips—and underneath the masses of body hair, Micky had seen the solid outline of weight-trained muscles. He was securely blindfolded, and had been manoeuvred in and around the tables by flicks and swats from an expertly aimed riding crop to his buttocks.

Over near the bar, four men lounged in a circle of chairs, wearing leather outfits, all with their booted feet on the naked back of a fifth, on all fours, his wrists and ankles shackled and chained to the floor like a prisoner. The four had chatted, smoked and drank as if the fifth didn't exist at all.

Micky now knew why he had carried on down the spiral staircase, rather than going back up and away from the place. He had been attracted by it all. Deep down, inside himself, something had felt the urge to experience part of the obvious Master/slave, Dom/sub dynamic.

Stephenson had been even more effervescent as he'd stepped off the stairs. Without stopping, he'd grabbed Micky by the waistband of his jeans and physically pulled him along to the bar, seemingly oblivious to the stares and glares he was generating from everyone else around them. Even the bar staff had made a point of ignoring them, until Stephenson had slapped the bar loudly with the flat of his hand.

"Hey! What do we have to do to get some service around here!?"

Micky had been conscious of the atmosphere towards them, but had held his ground when one of the barmen came quickly over.

With an obvious forced smile, the barman had looked directly at Stephenson. "I'm going to have to ask you to leave, sir. This is not novices' night, and your friend—" He made the word sound slightly distasteful—"Is inappropriately attired. So I'm now asking you to leave under your own volition. Otherwise I'm going to have to ask security to remove you."

Stephenson had looked around, then said, "Come on, Micky. This isn't going to be the primer I hoped it would be." As he turned and took hold of Micky's waistband again, he said to the barman, "This looks more like vanilla leather night."

The barman remained emotionless. "There will be a car waiting for you at the entrance."

Stephenson had just sneered, then pulled Micky up the spiral staircase, and out into the cold night air.

As promised, the car had been waiting, and once Stephenson had swiped his membership card through the payment box, the driver had taken them back to Stephenson's mansion.

They'd ridden back in silence, Stephenson taking sips from a small hipflask, and Micky had sensed Stephenson's frustration at how things hadn't turned out the way he'd wanted.

And now he was in the middle of Stephenson's massive bedroom, waiting for Stephenson to come out of the en-suite bathroom and, hopefully, tell him what it was all about.

* * *

My smiles are warm, but my eyes are cold
You put ice in my heart,
Destined never to melt
And still I smile…
I am your Janus.
(*Janus—Midnight Bloodsuckers*)

* * *

Four months. Must be some kind of a milestone, Gene thought. He'd seen Stephenson and his present plaything arrive back at the house via the security cameras. There was a feed in the control room, so if anyone was working into the early hours, they would have an idea as to what was happening around the mansion perimeter—rather than being totally 'lost in the moment.'

And, going by his body language, Jimmy was not at all happy.

Behind him, the TASCAM had finished rewinding the last of the Dead Fish mix-downs, and Gene had put the full spool into a protective library case. From there it would go into the mansion's fire safe—and as part of his insurance, he'd changed the combination without telling Jimmy. *Don't want him 'accidentally' recording over the tracks, do we?* Tomorrow he'd get them couriered over to the engineer at Spotlight—get a couple of acetates cut for Gary. There had already been some interest in Europe, and Gary had said that an indie German label—*Außerirdische Mutationen*—was willing to press up a limited 500 run to gauge market potential.

He put the tape box down by the side of the engineer's chair, sat back down, and felt his shoulders sag. Fuck, he really needed to get away from Jimmy Stephenson… At least the up-coming tour would be their last together—saying they didn't break up halfway through it… Still, the next four months were going to be, quite literally, Hell….

* * *

Oh Great Anubis,
My protector,
Keep me safe from Death…
(*Temple of Night—Sludgewalker*)

* * *

In a low voice, Micky said, "I'm sorry about tonight."

Stephenson had come out of the bathroom, and Micky had immediately stepped up behind him, massaging the tops of Stephenson's shoulders in an attempt to dissipate the tension and anger inside the man.

Stephenson had slowly relaxed, then gently moved away. Without looking directly at Micky, he said, "What did you think of the club?"

"I, er…" Images flashed back in his memory…What would it be like to wear a collar and lead, just like the bear had done? What would it feel like to be restrained, hand and foot, helpless… The riding crop being repeatedly brought down against his arse…

In front of him he suddenly realised that Stephenson had turned around, and was looking at him curiously. He stepped in close to Micky, maintaining eye contact while rubbing the palm of his right hand against Micky's crotch—feeling the erection pressing against the other side of Micky's fly.

Stephenson smiled. "Did it make you feel good? Did it make you want to… experiment? Let your inner self submit to the thrill of it?" He moved in closer. "Answer me honestly, because your cock doesn't lie."

"I…"

Stephenson moved his head and gently started mouthing and biting Micky's earlobe while cupping Micky's crotch in the palm of his hand. "Do you trust me?"

A half whispered reply. "Yes, I trust you…"

"Do you really trust me?"

"Yes, I *really* trust you."

Stephenson had stepped away from Micky, then heading towards the built in wardrobe, he said, "Have you ever worn a leather harness?"

Micky had seen them being worn in some of the fetish videos he'd secretly watched while at Uni. They had seemed…attractive…though he'd never had the courage before to buy one.

Stephenson had pulled open a drawer, then turned around to Micky. In one hand was a maroon coloured jockstrap, and in the other was a leather chest harness in ox-blood red, with chrome studs and D-rings.

"If you really trust me, then put these on."

Micky wasn't sure, but it felt like Stephenson's voice had become calmer, slightly deeper, more commanding…

Stephenson had picked out several more items from the large drawer, and started heading for the en-suite bathroom. "You have less than five minutes. When I come back, I want you standing and wearing only those." There was a moment's pause, then, "If you know what's good for you." Then Stephenson had walked into the bathroom, closing the door behind him.

Micky had gone over to a bedroom chair, hurriedly stripped off, and folded his clothes neatly on the seat. Then he stepped into the jockstrap and pulled it up, feeling the elastication of the waistband and supporting straps, and the sensation of the material cupping his ballsack and cock. It reminded him of getting ready for rugby practice—the sweaty, musky, heady smell of a crowded changing room….

Seconds later the harness went over his head, cool straps resting on his shoulders, the chest band running just under his pectorals. He cinched the buckle in another hole, so that the strap was tight against his chest. Like the jockstrap, it felt…good.

From behind him he heard the bathroom door open, but as he started to turn round, the voice behind him said loudly, "Did I give you permission to look upon me?" Before he could answer, there had been a faint swish sound, followed by a sharp sting at the top of his legs, just below his arse. Seconds later the discomfort had turned into a warm, pleasant tingling.

Close to his ear, Micky heard, "Do you trust me, yes or no?"

"I…" The swish and the sharp sensation generated a "Yes!" And Micky knew he meant it.

Moments later he felt his arms being placed behind his back and a piece of silk rope being tied to each of his wrists, binding them together. Pressure on his shoulders put Micky down on his knees, the carpet pile cushioning the impact, and a hand to the back of his head pushed his chin onto his chest as Stephenson moved around to stand in front of him.

Only it wasn't Jimmy Stephenson—at least not the person he'd come to know and want to be with since the start of their relationship. Standing over him was what seemed like an ancient Egyptian interpretation of Anubis—or Seth. White kilt with gold embroidered finish, wide gold bracelets around the wrists were matched by gold snake amulets winding up his biceps. A gold Ankh hung from his neck by a wide red ribbon, but his face… He was wearing an all-black neoprene hood mask, that had been shaped with jackal ears and an extended snout, though without the bottom jaw, giving Stephenson's mouth room to speak clearly.

Stephenson took a step backward then, in the low, commanding voice, said, "Come to me, supplicant."

Micky had moved forward on his knees, feeling his stomach tighten with excitement—his erection held in check by the jockstrap. Several knee-step shuffles, and Stephenson had put the flat of his hand on the top of Micky's bowed head—"Enough!"—before taking a length of wide red silk from the kilt's waistband. Bending forward, he blindfolded Micky, then stood back up.

"Do you still trust me?"

Through the adrenaline and anticipation, Micky suddenly realised who it was who now held the power dynamic. Switch Boy had to hear him say 'Yes' before he could move on to the next stage. If Micky said 'No,' then the dynamic would collapse like a defective vacuum flask, and Stephenson would be thrown out of whatever Headspace roleplay he was now inhabiting.

Micky had taken a breath, then said, "Yes. I trust you, my Lord."

* * *

Something written in the water,
Reflecting fire from the skies
Mirages and fantasies take their turn
And they give to us our highs
Before they let us crash and burn....

(*Home to Roost—The Rayguns*)

* * *

"Have you seen Switch?"

Gene looked up from the MIDI keyboard he was using to programme the DX. "If you mean Jimmy, then no. He went out about an hour or so ago. Why?"

Micky had never felt comfortable around Gene. The guy always seemed to radiate unprovoked hostility towards him. "He said he would pick something I've written—include it on the tour, towards the end of the set."

"Really? He said that?"

Micky nodded his head.

"Well, take it from me, there's fat fucking chance of that happening this late in the day. We kick the tour off in less than three weeks. Everything's been rehearsed, timed, choreographed, and the running order's been set into the KORG. There's no way we can make any last minute changes just because you're his present fuck-buddy." Then, half under his breath, he added, "Which probably won't be for very much longer anyway…"

"What do you mean by that? He's told me that we're going to be together permanently—he's going to announce it right after the tour and when BeHellMoth break up."

"God, you really are a sad bastard, aren't you? Here," he opened his Filofax, flicked through and jotted some telephone numbers down on a scrap of paper torn off a clipboard cue sheet. "Try these."

Micky took the paper and looked at it silently.

Gene tried to soften the realisation. "The first is Martin. He's Jimmy's usual fallback fuck. The next down is Dimitri. Bet you didn't know that Jimmy dabbled in the occasional session of Urolagnia, did you. Third down is Adam. Jimmy uses him when he's feeling in a masochistic submissive mood."

"But he usually tops!"

"Why do you think he calls himself Switch Boy?" Gene half smiled. "Though 'Boy' is woefully out of date…" Gene turned back to the keyboard. "Anyway, you didn't really think you were going on tour with us, did you? All that fresh meat, Jimmy will be tossing them off the tour bus on a daily basis, and nightly come to that. It's what he does. He picks up star-fucker twinks, then eventually gets tired of them and moves on. The only reason why he and I are still together is purely contractual. That, and the fact I'm the technical wizard who knows what plugs into where, and why."

Realisation and anger had started to rise within Micky. "You're lying! You-you're just saying that because you couldn't have him!"

"Oh, I've had him. Repeatedly. Also he got me hooked on China white for a while, and tied me up with some financial legal string. But 6 years ago I went into rehab, cleaned myself up, improved my writing, and found myself a boyfriend who wants absolutely nothing to do with the music business. He loves me, and I love him. That's why Jimmy can't hold breaking up BeHellMoth over me anymore."

"But he said…."

"He'd say anything to get his cock up your arse." Gene's voice softened. "Don't tell me, he did the King Tut routine on you? Or was it King Arthur and Sir Lancelot? Michael, he lives in a mass of fantasy worlds, where everything revolves around him. At best he's a narcissist. At worst he's a sociopath."

"But… Los Angeles for the New Year… He-he promised…"

"Oh no," Gene slowly shook his head. "He won't be going anywhere near the US for quite a while."

"What? Why?"

"There's at least two court cases pending over there. Several of his old 'US tour conquests' are claiming he's given them HIV. You know, the Gay Plague—though rumours say you can get it from sharing dirty needles as well now." He looked at Michael starting to slump in the control room doorway. "You two didn't do it bareback, did you? There's been those adverts on TV recently—the ones with the gravestone…." Gene got up and stood in front of Michael. "I'd suggest while he's out, you pack whatever you have here, and go find somewhere safe for a while. And get yourself checked out to see if you're sick. You have anywhere to stay?"

"I…" His parents had thrown him out of the family home down in Dover when he had come out to them, and over the last 6 months he'd sort of burned his friendship bridges by being such an arrogant insufferable twat.

Gene went over to the Filofax again, flicked to some numbers at the back, wrote one down on another corner of the track log, and tore it off.

"Here," he handed the paper to Michael. "Tell them I sent you, and I'll pay for a month's food and board. They know where to call to confirm the arrangement."

Michael had looked at Gene, as if discovering the person for the first time. "You've done this before, haven't you."

"More times than you will ever want to know…"

* * *

I once bathed in fire,
And flew with dragons.
Now I look at you…
And all I see is dust.
I have no way to say Goodbye,
Except by sacrifice.
(*Bye-Bye—Alien Love Bandits*)

* * *

Joanne came back up the stairs and knocked on his room door. "Hey My-Key…?" She was the South African who rented the bedsit across the landing from Michael. She knocked again. "My-Key, I got a package for you. A courier just delivered it. He had a fancy bike for a courier. If the money's that good, I might try doing that kind of work. Anything's got to be better than working in a bar, right?"

Michael had reluctantly half opened the door, not wanting to let her see the state of his room. "Sorry. I'm not myself today." He held out a hand and she put the wrapped box into it. As he started to close the door, she said:

"No offence, My-Key, but it isn't good for you to be like this. You need to get some help…"

He'd muttered a "Thanks," and had started to close the door further when Joanne added:

"It might also be a good idea if you took a shower, or had a bath, because some of the other residents have started to comment down in the kitchen of a morning…."

"Yeah… Yeah, I'll do that…" And he'd finally closed the door on her.

He'd carried the box across the room and dropped down on the worn out sofa. No return address. Only his name, room number and street address, printed on a non-descript white sticky label. He gave it a shake, but didn't hear anything rattle from inside. Absently he gone at the wrapping tape with bitten fingernails—and then in frustration he'd picked up a discarded plastic takeaway fork and attacked it with that.

Beneath the wrapping, the box opened to reveal a plain brown Jiffy padded envelope, and something below it wrapped in cloth and bubble plastic.

He shook the envelope, and into his lap fell a white label cassette tape, the sort you used for sending demos to agents or record label A&R departments. He got up and went across to the room table and single wooden kitchen chair. On the table top was a secondhand boom box, surrounded by a haphazard scattering of other tapes—some commercial, some looking like obvious bootlegs.

He sat down, put the cardboard box on the table top, dropped the cassette into the player and pushed the Play button. Silence as the leader tape wound through, then tape hiss and hollowness as the AGC increased the volume until: "Do I have a thing with commitment? According to some £150-an-hour experts, it's down to my parents and childhood…But then isn't everything these days?"

Michael had immediately recognised Jimmy Stephenson's voice—despite it being a touch slurred. Either drunk, or off his face, or more likely both. The tape rolled on…

"That's also why I like star fucker fan boys and twinks…" there was the distinctive sound from his *Colibri* lighter as Jimmy flashed up another cigarette. "Like Dion DiMucci almost sang: 'I fuck 'em and forget 'em, 'cos to me they're all the same…' They believe everything I tell them. Lap it all up and then look for more. The whole 'I love you—I love you, too' shit. And they all fall for the 'You're the only one who—'"

"—who really understands me so well…" Michael had completed the sentence in a low voice, tears already starting to leak from the corners of his eyes.

He'd kept listening and gently crying until the silence of the end leader tape and, moments later, the silence-breaking *CLICK* of the auto-stop kicking in.

He'd ejected the cassette, emptied the contents of his metal waste bin onto the floor, and had then gone down and out into the back garden. Putting the bin on the iron patio table, Michael had pulled and tugged the tape from the cartridge, dumping it into the bin as he unravelled it. Moments later he'd found the bottle of barbecue lighter fluid from under the kitchen sink, liberally splashed it over the mass of recording tape, struck a match and dropped it in.

* * *

See now, Medusa,
Your bloodied reflection…
…You turned my heart to stone…
Push the lever down…
(Down, down, down)
Just push the lever down…
(*Push the Lever Down—BeHellMoth*)

* * *

When the flames had finally died, and the waste bin cooled down, Michael had gone over to one of the flowerbeds by the back fence, and tapped the ashes out into a space between some plants.

He'd walked back into the house, up the stairs, and into his room. He'd put the bin down by the door, then he'd laid down on the sofa and closed his eyes.

He had been such a fucking fool. He had found Switch Boy in a Soho gay bar that had a notorious dark room on its upper floor. The excitement of being with his hero had deafened him to the alarm bells… Now all he could feel was anger and hatred towards the bastard. He'd given Michael so many dreams and hopes—all now turned to ashes and soul-numbing shame…

He got up, went over to the table, and looked at the now wrapper-less box. The tape had been pretty raw sound quality. Maybe something recorded late at night, post-gig, back on the tour bus... Whatever, it didn't dispel the self-loathing he now felt for himself at being taken in so easily....

As he picked up the box he remembered the bubble and cloth wrapped object in the bottom of it. Opening the lid, he'd shaken the second package onto the table, and with it had come an oblong concert ticket.

Cautiously, he unwrapped the object, and there in the palm of his hand rested what looked like a cartoon revolver. Blue steel, with the smell of machine oil and cordite. A handmade two-shot .22 single action. Being south of the river he'd seen enough of them in the pubs and clubs since he'd moved into the bedsit. Cocking the hammer rotated the cylinder, bringing up the first cartridge. Pull the trigger, fire the bullet, then cock the hammer again, and fire the second bullet. A pair of cartridges had been taped to the barrel—tips filed flat, with a small hole drilled in the middle of each...

Laying the weapon down on the table he'd just stared at it, and the ticket—BeHellMoth Saturday 19th December, Bloxton Academy, NW5....

He half closed his eyes, and the pain that lived at the back of his skull made itself felt. He needed to think—put things into perspective. Memories of being with Switch surfaced, and Michael could hear his own whiney, pleading voice: "Take me with you. I just want to be with you. Take me...."

Michael had felt the tears start again...stripped back, the memories really were nothing more than painful embarrassments...all now meaningless....

Fingers had fished in the coin pocket of his jeans as he pulled out his last two mazzies, swallowing them down dry. Did he have some more stashed somewhere? He couldn't remember, or even think straight just then. He'd probably have to contact Denzel, see if he would sell him some more of the pills.

In under three minutes Michael Coulson was asleep on the bedsit sofa, facial muscles and hands twitching as he began walking in the realms of Mamu......

......Ten hours later, he was standing under the shower in the communal 1st floor bathroom. Joanne had been right. He had neglected his personal hygiene, his bedsit, his sense and purpose in life. He'd taken a pair of scissors to his scruffy beard before finally cleaning it off with a Bic. His hair needed sorting out as he was starting to look like some kind of hippy, for fuck's sake. Mel on the ground floor did cheap cuts on her days off from the salon. And he was due his DHSS gyro at the end of the week....

Of course, if he needed extra money on the quick, then he could always go on the game now and again. He was street legal, which always put some johns off, but he could pass for 16 or 17 under dim lighting.... With free condoms being supplied in gay bars now, he'd insist on his punters rubbering up—no exceptions, no matter how much extra was on offer....

In fact anything to help make ends meet, and pass the time until Saturday, December 19th....

* * *

I will make
Us *Whole*
Bod-dee
And *Soul*
Bind you with
Dark *Arts*
Never to be
A-part....
(*Osmosis—The Beltane Girls*)

* * *

—Testicles, testicles! One, two, three, four, testicles!

—Karl, stop fucking about and let's get this sound check over with, okay? I want to catch some sleep before we start the gig tonight.

—Okay, Gene. What's next? You want to run the opening light sequences?

—Might as well, but put your shades on, when those halogens come up they'll take out a retina.

……Number 344 bus to Waterloo, then the Northern Line to Camden Market. It would take about an hour, if there wasn't any delays, and Michael had spent nearly £2 on getting a One Day Travel Card. It was valid until 4am the following morning, after the pubs, clubs and venues had finally kicked everyone out. It meant he didn't have to piss about with ticket offices, or the bastards who worked behind the glass……

—*Anyone seen Jimmy? Anyone?*

—*Not for a while. Did he go back to the hotel with one of his pets? Hey, you wanna come up and see my mic stand upright?* (Laughter from several other roadies running cables to the mixing desk)

—*You're such a fucking riot, Karl. Why am I always the one left to sort everything out before a show? Jimmy's supposed to be the front man, for fuck's sake. If he turns up and starts bitching about it being the wrong fucking shade of green gel in the up-lighters, I'll slap the twat into the middle of next week.*

—*Sorry, Gene. Hey, as it's the last gig, you want us to do a Carrie on him and organise a bucket of fake blood from the overhead gantry?*

—*Karl, tempt me one more time and I swear to God I am going to say yes.*

—*Okay… What if we got a bucket or two of the real stuff in from a local abattoir?*

……The Friday Market down the Elephant & Castle had been worth the effort. Michael had been able to pick up a reasonably tidy black hoodie from *Secondhand-Me-Downs*, a stall in the covered market area. The skater kids were wearing them all the time now, so they were getting commonplace. This one even had a demon riding a board on the back of it. It didn't matter. All he wanted it for was the large pockets at the front. Somewhere he could keep his hands from being seen. If he timed it right, he would push in on the first wave of fans through the door—the rush usually meant the bouncers didn't have the time to do searches. Still, on the safe side, he would put the gun in the middle of his back—hold it there in the waistband of his jeans, so even if he got patted down, it would be missed. It was a gamble, and one he was prepared to take.

He looked at the clock. 18:15. The gig wasn't due to start until 8pm, and even then there would probably be 40 minutes or so for the support act. For the final gig it was going to be The Necrotic. They were shit, but then anything was when compared to BeHellMoth.

Black jeans, black t-shirt, black trainers and black hoodie. He'd keep the hood down on the bus to Waterloo mainline, and also on the Northern Line over to Camden. Once back up on street level he would throw the hood over his head, and hopefully find a group of other fans heading for the Bloxton Academy. There would be safety in numbers, though he didn't feel like chatting to anyone, either on the journey, or on the pilgrimage to the gig……

—I'm not joking Jimmy. No more crowd surfing. We can't afford the insurance, for one—not after the last time. The bitch says you took out two of her front teeth with one of your rings when you landed in front of her. Gary's still trying to settle out of court, but he's sure she wants her 15 minutes in the spotlight at Snaresbrook.

—It's the last night. They're all expecting it. Their only chance to touch a Rock God. I'm even wearing one of those fibreglass cricket boxes, just in case someone wants to take my balls as a souvenir.

—Jimmy, this is non-negotiable. This is a hard no *to diving into the audience.*

—You know what? Fuck you, Gene. This is going to be our last night performing together. After that you're on your fucking own!

—I just can't fucking wait!

(Over the In Ear Monitors, Karl says:)

—Okay, the stage is now reset for BeHellMoth. Floor mics are now live, and the video team are sync'd to the click track on the mobile studio outside. House lights off! Five, four, three, two, one—Light Desk

hit it! You two, on stage now!

......He had been ready for the wall of lights to flare at the opening. When the house lights had dropped, Michael—along with hundreds of other hardcore fans—had pulled out dark glasses, some even welding goggles. And even ten lines back, he had still felt the momentary burst of heat. Blackness again, followed by rhythmic heavy machine drumming—120bpm—and the jungle animal screams that formed the intro to *The Voodoo That You Do...*

Michael discreetly took the gun from his back and transferred it to one of the hoodie's wide pockets. He kept running his fingers over it, like a blind person reading braille, before curling his fingers back around the broom handle stock, his thumb resting on the hammer's spur.

—Go on, you fucking twat! Even though the stage mics were still live, Gene doubted that anyone had heard him over the almost deafening chanting of the audience. From his vantage point on the keyboards riser he had seen Jimmy—hair, face and bare chest slick with sweat, the leather gladiator style shoulder and arm protectors now removed and cast to the back of the stage as he arrogantly strode to the front and almost overloaded the mic with his heavy breathing.

—I'd like to say thank you for coming here to the Academy tonight (massive cheer from the audience) *and we're going to close our final set with a song from our first album* (the standard cue for Gene to raise his hands above his head and wiggle his fingers, even though this time he wasn't smiling) *So let's all* Push the Lever Down... (Jimmy turned and walked towards the back of the stage as the mixing desk kicked in the complex intro tape, and Gene got ready to pick up the live side with a power chord sequence.)

......It couldn't have worked out better. People around him were starting to jostle forward, eager to get up close one more time. Michael kept his distance, centre to the stage, and about 15 people deep……

— I see you dancing in the acid rain… You feel it burn, and you love the pain… All your empires now turned to dust, there's nothing left that can slake your lust! Push the lever down… (Jimmy holds the mic out, and the audience faithful chant: Down! Down! Down!) *Just push the lever down…*

……Typical. Switch fudging the lyrics as always. Michael had noticed it on the bootlegs he'd picked up from previous concerts. It didn't seem to alter the song much though…except that Doktor Keys had also seemed to shorten the middle bridge by a couple of minutes, because Switch had already turned and was walking to the back of the stage……

—Embrace the power, and savour the thrill… Load your weapon and shoot to kill—

Stephenson had turned to face the audience, then had rapidly run and launched himself off the edge of the stage as the audience surged forward to catch him.

……Michael raised the revolver from his hoodie, cocking the hammer with his thumb, then pointed and squeezed the trigger at Stephenson diving head first over the front rows—the sound of the shot being masked by the audience cheering and chanting:

Down! Down! Down!

The hollow point bullet smashed into Stephenson's left clavicle, breaking up on impact and sending fragments into Stephenson's lung and heart, stopping it almost instantly as the audience continued:

I push the lever down!

And Michael Coulson heard himself utter the final line: *And send us all to Hell…* before he re-cocked the revolver, put the warm barrel upwards into his mouth, and pulled the trigger a second time……

* * *

Wednesday 17th February 1988

Gary Miles leaned back in his office chair. “You do realise that PyraMax are positively gagging to get hold of the tapes of the Bloxton Academy gig, don’t you?”

Gene, dressed conservatively in unbuttoned fawn blazer, white t-shirt and blue jeans, sighed. “You can clearly hear the two shots—especially the second one where the poor guy tops himself. Hell,” he sat back trying to relax a little, “Even the roadies haven’t done any copies—just as well, as I’d be down on them like a ton of crap if they did.” Another small sigh, then, “The only stuff out and about is from a couple of fan boys who managed to smuggle a cassette recorder into the gig. Now the sound on that is absolute shite, so Frank Leander can whistle Dixie out of his arse—and you can tell him that from me. I made sure that the band personally rented that mobile studio, and purchased the recording tape before the tour—and all from our own funds. PyraMax can whinge all they want, but we....” Gene corrected himself, “But I own everything now that Jimmy’s gone We gave them three albums, and a tour as well to promote them.”

Gary decided to let it rest until later—though he knew Gene wouldn’t be ‘grieving’ for long. “And there’s no word as to why this guy did the whole murder-suicide thing?”

“Well, he was one of Jimmy’s more recent conquests, before Jimmy dropped him for some fresh twink.” Gene brushed a knuckle under his nose and sniffed self-consciously. “The day he left the mansion, I got him a place at the Rendall shelter. I think he found somewhere else for himself down Lambeth way after that.”

“You were always good to Jimmy’s castoffs…”

“Somebody had to be.” Gene got up off the sofa. “Is it okay if I get Moira to call me a cab, on expenses?” He patted the pockets of his jeans. “A wallet would clearly spoil the outline…”

Gary had already started to move onto his ‘next thing to do’ so said,

"Don't see why not." Then, as an afterthought, asked, "Given the state of the traffic, I'd've thought you would've come in on that swanky motorbike of your."

As Gene opened the door to leave, he said, "The Ducati? I sold that a few weeks before the last tour. I finally realised just how dangerous it was…"

But Gary was already reaching for the desk phone while searching for a number in his Filofax….

Gene had quietly closed the door behind him as he left.

Dirty

Harris Coverley

Aaron Lowden rolled the company car, a silver-grey 2015 Toyota Yaris, into the parking place seven places from the red-orange brick walk up to the main entrance, which was lit up in a diabetic yellow. Ever since he had pulled off the main road towards Hallow Brook's town centre he had been making mental notes: the amount of rubbish strewn across the green spaces; the width and frequency of cracks in the car park tarmac; the general feel of an abandoned internment camp somewhere just above the Arctic Circle.

Clicking off the mainstream rock station on the radio with a grunt, Lowden got out of the car and sniffed: he could smell the pollution of the motorway grinding on some hundred metres away and instinctively tried to cough it out.

Possibly not suitable for asthma sufferers, he thought.

He checked his watch: 8:28. He was later than he expected, but if they gave him any trouble he would punish them for it. They *all* got punished in the end.

Lowden got his short wheeled suitcase out of the boot and slammed it shut with vigour so as to appreciate the echo across the lot. As he went up to the entrance, he looked up at the name above the glass doors: RoadTel.

He had come across some bad names in the job before, but this irked him in particular as being especially bad. He had been to three others in the RoadTel chain, but he never could quite get over it. The structures themselves were sandy-coloured but fake, all three levels, small and grotty, built in the 1990s but already crumbling like a dried-out pastry cake.

Clacking the wheels over the edge of the dipped pavement, Lowden got off the road and through the doors. The reception area was smaller than he had expected, washed in cream with maroon-purple trimmings, the carpet rough and black, yet silvered by dirt and impurities. In the corner was a group of lounge chairs, two filled by travelling salesmen, their ties relaxed.

Lowden went up to the middle-aged woman behind the counter, shifting papers and whatever else about underneath in some needless busywork, and timidly asked, "Excuse me?"

The woman looked up, but she did not smiled, just looking at Lowden with cold eyes locked behind the lenses of her glasses like fish floating static in a tank.

"Hello," Lowden said quietly with projected nervousness. "I, erm, reserved a room, err, for tonight, erm-ah, James Henderson. Is it under that name?" He inflected hard to be sure that the question portrayed that he was a man of great uncertainty and low confidence in regards to basically everything—a man who needed support to remember even his own name.

Still unsmiling, the woman typed into her keyboard.

"I'm sorry," she said.

Can't spell Henderson, Lowden noted.

"Are you sure?" he asked as whinily as he could.

"Can you spell your name?"

How the hell can you not spell Henderson? he thought. *And even if you can't, you should lead with that rather than fuck around like you have done.*

"Yes, of course: erm, H-E-N…D-R—oh sorry! Let me start over…"

Letting a sigh out, the woman, whose name tag Lowden noted read *Judee*, stopped him to say, "Don't worry, it's come up now."

What the fuck are you up to woman? Lowden thought while maintaining his slight, polite smile. *Don't you fucking know how to work the fucking system?*

"Oh good…"

"Check in was for eight," the woman said with sternness, looking back into his eyes.

Bitch, he thought. *Fucking bitch.*

"Oh dear," he wittered. "You mean I can't have the room?"

"No it's okay," she said, finally smiling back at him. "It's 3B, on the first floor."

"Oh, very good, thank you…"

Why the fuck tell me that? Lowden thought. *Why try to scare me? Bullshit fucking power play jobsworth shit...*

Judee had him sign the registry, but as she was about to hand Lowden his room key, there was a banging noise from the back room and Judee turned around.

"Hold on one minute Mr Henderson," she said, and got out of her chair to investigate.

She opened the door and at what she saw barked, "You! You're late!"

There was a muffled response to which she replied, "I don't care…"

She looked back at a pathetic-looking Lowden before going into the dark room and pushing the door closed. There was a muted exchange from behind the frosted glass from which Lowden gleaned the odd word: "time", "out", "gone", "lazy", "useless", and few F-bombs.

After nearly a minute a red-faced Judee came through the door followed by a shorter, younger South Asian man of about twenty-five or so, with a sharp black crewcut and a chin of managed stubble, between which were olive eyes dull and sickly. He wore the same purple uniform shirt and black trousers as Judee, adorned with a gold name tag that read *Salim*.

"Salim will serve you," said Judee to Lowden. "My shift is over."

Lowden smiled and nodded to this, but inside him: *More bullshit waste of my time! Finish your task! What point are you proving?!*

Salim checked his form and the registry before giving Lowden his key. "Here's your key, enjoy your stay."

Lowden almost broke his façade as he looked into Salim's lax eyes, touching his cool clammy hand as it touched his with the key. He winced, but he kept smiling and thanked the young man, who responded with a silent, continued dull look.

Lowden went up the corridor to the lift, re-noting everything: a lack of help with the suitcase; inability to properly direct one to the room, in fact no chaperoning at all; argument between staff in earshot of customer; changing the staff in the middle of a transaction. It all looked pretty bad.

The room was easy enough to find, just on the right from the lift. It had plaster white walls, with a few holes crudely patched. The eiderdown cover on the bed was the same purple as the staff shirts, but the sheets beneath were at least well-laundered Lowden noted. The light was stale but provided adequate illumination. He checked the *en suite*: everything seemed clean, the toilet, the bath, the shower head, the other fixtures, the sink and its mirror—but he would put it all to the test.

He lay back on the bed for a few minutes, tired after his interaction, the act he put on, and before that the two hour car journey up from down South.

Lowden had been working as a consumer agent for the British Choice Foundation for six years now, and as far as they were concerned he was an effective, if stern, representative for consumer interests. Anyway, it was better than his old job as a civil engineer, and much more than that, it allowed him to indulge his hidden self as often as he wanted to.

As he stretched out he felt the TV remote on the side cabinet and it came to him:

Would she be on tonight? It was *a Thursday...*

He grabbed the remote and switched the TV on. The hard red light flashed to fluttering green, the screen turned blue then a cacophony of grey and white.

He played with the inputs until he came to the free view system, and then slowly and painfully scrolled up through the channels on the tacky and shallow-buttoned remote until at last, on the channel slot of 202, was what he was looking for.

The People's Free TV was an odd ragbag of a station. It aired programmes from only three in the afternoon until one in the morning, and much of it consisted of either hyper-local ultra-cheap shows that had somehow, through some producer's grace, been permitted to air on a national station, or one of a series of conspiracism-related talk shows and pseudo-documentaries. One of the latter was airing at that moment: *Opened Mind with Thomas Dupree*. Dupree was a greying fifty-something man in a pastel shirt who had once written a series of articles on the two Kennedy Assassinations for the *Daily Express* that had been roundly criticised by the press watchdog. His guest was a jam jar-bespectacled man by the name of Ernest Monk, who with obvious discomfort at being outside of whatever obscured hole he usually subsisted in, was expounding upon his theories with the help of fuzzy images projected on the back panel of the set: "…and if you look at the earlier pictures, you'll see that *these* chemtrails are different from *those* chemtrails…"

As Dupree nodded along and began to ask an inane question Lowden snapped, "Oh piss off…"

He muted the channel and scrolled through the infobox into the near future, where he finally found it: *MoshWire* at ten o'clock.

He breathed a sigh of relief, rubbed his thighs, and grinned. He checked his watch: 8:46.

There was time for a bit of work beforehand.

Lowden turned the TV off, gathered some toiletries from his case, and went to the *en suite* toilet and shower room. Careful not to touch too much of anything, he combed his hair, considered a shave of his three day beard before rejecting such a notion, and put some eye drops into his dry sockets. He looked into the mirror: there had once been a handsome-enough man staring back at him, but that person had long gone. At least his hair was still thick and his teeth not too yellowed. He then turned off the lights and went out down to the lift.

He went through the ground floor lobby, past the South Asian clerk dozing with his eyes still open, checked the back exits to the rear courtyard, and then went on into the bar-*cum*-canteen area. As with everywhere else, the walls were washed cream, but the floor was a nasty and deep lime green. To Lowden the place gave off the air of the dining hall on a stranded cruise liner moments before the evacuation order was to be given.

There was a smattering of salesmen, some fully suited up, others with their shirts open, their ties flopping. In a far corner a small group of office workers who had been attending some nearby conference were having a loud but amiable discussion about some *faux paus* one of them had committed earlier:

"You couldn't have bloody done that?!"

"No way bruv…!"

"I just didn't know that *that* was her!"

"Seriously?!"

They all laughed and took a big drink from their lagers.

Wankers, thought Lowden, and went up the bar.

The barman, wiping down the Stella Artois tap, could not have been more than nineteen, his chin flecked with a spaced-out archipelago of ginger hairs.

Poor fucker, Lowden lamented as he smiled. "Hi my man, can I please get a Jim Beam and coke?"

The barman stared at him as though he had attempted to communicate in Nicaraguan sign language.

Lowden continued smiling: "Jim Beam and coke, please?"

"Sorry?" the barman asked, leaning forward.

There was no music in the lounge, just a minor rumble of voices, and there was no reason why he could not have heard Lowden.

You little bastard! Lowden thought. *I'll fucking have you for this…*

Lowden's smile intensified into a grimace: "A Jim Beam and coke, PLEASE!"

The barman cracked into action. "Erm, erm, yes, yes sir, straight away…"

"Thank you."

About fucking time fruitcake, thought Lowden. *Can't get the staff these days? Too fucking right...*

After he received it Lowden sat at a table at the wall opposite to the office workers. He sipped his drink and found the coke flat, the whiskey weak, and even the ice cubes too warm. He put it down and drummed on the table, his fingers in a wave. He looked around, making his mental notes.

A moment later a thirty-something woman with Miami Beach blonde hair, red faux-leather jacket, and a black faux-leather skirt that started late and ended way too early over fish-netted thighs walked in from the lobby and looked about.

"Here we fucking go," Lowden said under his breath.

She walked up to the bar and the barman, in contrast how he had just served Lowden, swooned, smiled, eyes starried, paying close attention to every greasy word the woman uttered.

You poor, poor deluded fucker, Lowden thought.

At a lull in their conversation, the barman turned away and the woman looked over to Lowden.

He turned away, but it was too late. He was her first target of the night, in this hunting ground at least. She put on her most seductive stroll and swayed over, hips swinging, teeth gleaming, thin lips stretched like washing lines between flat blocks.

When she got to his side he could not ignore her.

She towered above him in the most garish of man-made fibres, her make-up laid on by the pallet.

"'Ello darlin'," she smiled, her tone betraying her Estuary origins.

Lowden rested his chin on his arched hands and smirked back: "Hi—*fuck off*."

The woman scowled. "No need to be rude sir..."

"Yes there is: *fuck off*."

The woman bit her lower and snarled, "Now look 'ere you twat, I'll—"

Lowden pulled a badge from his inner jacket pocket that shut her up.

"Okay, erm," she stuttered. "Erm, good evenin' sir, er, good night."

She spun around and walked straight out of the lounge, and then out of the complex itself.

A fake police badge was risky, but it always did the job. It was worn and faded, but that was purposeful—it added to its realism, its utility. The only problem was that it had the name "Gilbert Fields" on it, which made it basically useless unless he adopted that identity, but he was not foolish enough to go *full on* impersonating a police officer.

The young barman looked over to him and Lowden shrugged back.

As the lounge ebbed and flowed, Lowden switched to lager, downing two pints before realising it was almost ten.

Lowden took his glass back to the bar and said to the boy, who was about to serve a woman from the office group, "Don't do it son, it's a mug's game."

"Sorry?" asked the barman, the woman also looking at him.

Lowden tapped his nose. "*You'll* get what I mean…"

With that he turned and walked out.

Christ, he thought. *That shit's gone to my head.*

He got upstairs to his room and switched the TV on. The free view input had reset to the first channel, so he had to go through every channel again to get to People's Free TV.

"Fuck! Fuck!" he chanted clicking through, sitting on the end of the bed. "Fuck! Fuck! Fuck!"

At length he got to 202 and the screen became one of a grey-brown apocalypse. It was a music video: shot in brown-and-grey, a lead singer, a scrawny white woman with short dreads, a set of nose rings, and a prominent tattoo on the left side of her neck, wandered through a bleak landscape, almost screaming of a betrayal she could never possibly get over, punctuated with squealing interjections from the guitarist, a six foot black woman also with dreads but reaching to her knees, wearing night vision goggles.

Lowden could not quite work out what sub-genre it was: alt-metal? Extreme metal? Metalcore? Extreme sadcore? Whatever it was, it was not getting to him.

As the singer's death-agonies ceased and the terror-changs of guitar settled down, the video faded out and Lowden beheld that which he believed to be the most perfect and delectable creature in all of Creation.

Not yet twenty, Carrie Creepers (not her real name of course, which Lowden had been able to identify as Miranda Reid-Roberts) was petite with a heart-shaped face coated in a luminous arctic white foundation; a tiny button nose; big cobalt eyes edged with tar-like mascara and sable eye shadow; full black-painted lips with a gold ring pierced in the centre bottom. Her complex blonde and black-banded hair was roughly half-beehive, half-mohawk, the sides shaved. She was dressed, as always, like some gothic Japanese schoolgirl sex doll; her ample pallid breasts held back by a deep black V-neck that nearly reached her navel. Her naked, stubby but unblemished legs were crossed, ending in colossal platform boots. Her expression was of the upmost detached and cool neutrality. She sat upon the usual black sofa-bench, the wall behind adorned in tattered and peeling concert posters.

Lowden caught his breath. "My little black and white flower…*hello*!"

"That was 'Never Always' by The Geequins, requested by…"—she checked a little moleskin notepad by her side—"…Jess in Ashton-Under-Lyne."

It was all in her signature monotone, her eyes solid and disclosing nothing.

"Call in, tell us what you think."

There was a chime and Creepers clicked a button on the mini-console on the table in front of her: "*MoshWire*, you're on."

MoshWire was a strange show: someone, somewhere, had wanted a programme dedicated to the alternative heavy music of both the present and the past two-odd decades, but the production itself seemed to consist just of Creepers, who controlled all the calls herself on air, and the mostly silent guy behind the camera who Lowden believed was also the director and controlled the video and audio input. Creepers herself seemed to have been roped in without much enthusiasm, so she must have been making *some* money from it somehow. Maybe it was her only option: Lowden imagined having been thrown out of her home for being a no-good gothpunk, or for being in love with another woman (she *must* be bisexual, he was sure of it), or for smoking weed, or any number or combination of reasons, and struggling to survive until given this chance to exploit her sense of style and immense beauty. He wanted to bring her to his home and show her all the love she needed, give her all the love he could give her.

On the phone was man with a Brummie accent. "Yeah, erm, am I on?"

Creepers almost rolled her eyes. "Yeah, you're on *MoshWire*."

"Awh, cool, right, well, it was all right that…"

Lowden was seething: how could he talk about damn music when she was there?! He had the privilege of talking to her and he was wasting it on crap!

He had to rectify this. He leapt up and went over to his suitcase. He lifted up the covering flap and dug around in the pocket. He found both of them: burner phones, £6 each from the dodgy tech stall on the indoor market in his home town. He had to make each one count.

Lowden sat back down on the end of the bed and dialled. He did not need to check the number on the bottom of the screen.

The Brummie thanked Creepers for taking his call and she nodded.

She clicked him off and Lowden heard the beep on the phone. He muted the TV.

Her voice came through the speaker: "You're on *MoshWire*."

Lowden was immediately at half-mast.

"Hi, am I on *MoshWire*?" he grinned, knowing the reaction he would get.

This time Creepers really did roll her eyes.

"Yes, you're on *MoshWire*. What did you think of the video?"

Putting on a more southerly accent, Lowden said, "Honestly didn't care that much for it. What I'm more interested in is how that damp little pink pussyhole of yours is feeling right about now?"

Without a second thought Creepers leant over to the mini-console and clicked Lowden off, her countenance static.

He roared with laughter and grabbed his crotch. He licked his lips. He would wait a while until his next shot.

A couple more calls came through, one asking for some songs by Raw Machine to be played (she said maybe on the next show), another complaining that The Geequins had really gone downhill since they had changed drummer on their third album, with whom Creepers passively agreed.

All the while, Lowden worked himself up, rubbing his knees, continuing to lick his lips, the skin cracking as it dried between licks.

"Yeah…*fuck yeah*…"

Ignoring the light on the console, Creepers introduced the next song which was "Inner Knowledge" by Goody Badwife, another all-female group.

Lowden bit his lip—was it going to be female artists all night?

This video was colourful, but the music grinding: the lead singer, a tall blonde woman, was dressed in rags and scrambling through a junglescape, looking for something that ultimately was revealed to be a silver plate with her soul trapped in it (or so Lowden surmised). It continually cut during instrumental breakdowns to the full band in a jungle clearing, also dressed in rags, surrounded by crude wooden structures, all of which put Lowden in mind of those old Italian cannibal films.

The music petered out and the screen faded back to the *MoshWire* studio, Creepers looking stonily into the camera.

"That was Goody Badwife—a better effort than their last single I'd say."

The console beeped and Creepers clicked it: "*MoshWire*, you're on."

The caller from the East Midlands wanted to passionately defend The Geequins song from before, and as he and Creepers went back and forth, Lowden grabbed the second burner and began to work on a new voice. He settled on something more Welsh, and practiced a recollection of John Hurt's performance in *10 Rillington Place*: "It were Christie what done it—*it were Christie!*"

He briefly set back to his own voice. "Yeah, that'll do."

Lowden dialled and in seconds got though.

"You're on *MoshWire,*" Creepers sighed.

Lowden stroked the end of his erection and shuddered.

"Hello, am I on?" he asked in his heightened tone.

Creepers sighed again. "Yes you're on, did you like the last video? Or is this about the bloody Geequins?"

"Oh, the last video," Lowden wittered Welshly. "I couldn't help but think while watching it, with the band members palming around the jungle and that…"

"Yeah?" asked Creepers, curious as to where he was going.

"…yeah, I couldn't help but wonder how much of my cock I could get down your tight bitch throat before you choked to death?"

"*Your cock?*" she said, and even cracked a small smile before clicking him off.

Lowden dropped the phone and stood up, stomping around.

He was close, but not for himself close enough.

He was out of burners, but he looked at the phone on the side cabinet.

He went over and lifted the receiver.

"*Dial one for front desk, dial two for outside calls,*" vibrated the canned voice. "*All outside calls will be charged to your bill.*"

Lowden used burners because they were extremely difficult to trace, even though a private company or citizen as opposed to the police or national security doing so with the phone company's assistance would be engaging in an illegal act. He also used them because often enough the number would immediately be blocked on Creeper's console. He had sometimes had success with repeat calls on burners and landlines—no tech was perfect—but in the past month it had become more accurate in its sanctions.

Lowden breathed in and out. He was throbbing all over.

"Fuck it," he said, and dialled the number.

It rang five times while another caller was on, criticising the video while Creepers defended it half-heartedly, until he was put into a queue for another twenty seconds.

"Oh you don't know what you're talkin' about," the caller of indeterminate accent said.

"You certainly don't," said Creepers before clicking him off.

"Next caller." She clicked Lowden on. "You're on *Mosh Wire*."

Lowden used a quiet, slightly ailing voice: "Hello Carrie, how are you?"

"Fine," she said plainly. "Did you want to talk on the video?"

"No, that's all right, I have a request, if that's possible."

"Erm, requests are supposed to be made in advance…"

"Oh, I'm sorry…"

"Well, I can see what I can do—what did you want?"

"I was just wondering…"

Lowden faulted, but managed to get it out, every vein pounding. "I was just wondering, if you could possibly get the right one out and give the nip a bit of a suck?"

"What, sorry?"

Creepers leaned forward and Lowden got more of the cleavage he lusted for.

"Yeah, that's good," he said, far too much in his natural voice.

Creepers cocked her head. "This is *you*, isn't it?"

"Who's *me*?" asked Lowden, ridding of all pretence.

"The guy who's always calling with silly voices…I know it's you, you know."

"Yeah?" Lowden groaned. He had never had this extensive a conversation with her before.

"I know you wanna shag me," she said, offering up a grin. "A lotta guys *and* girls wanna do that."

"They couldn't do it like me baby."

"Yeah?" Creepers said, and brought her hands across her abdomen, just below her breasts. "And what can *you* do?"

"All kinds of stuff…"

"Like what? Make me give you head?"

"Oh, I'd do a special twist on that."

"Oh yeah?"

Lowden bit his lip again, coming close to tearing it open: "Yeah baby, I'd rip all your fucking teeth and tongue out so I could fuck your throat more easily."

Creepers did not let up with her smile, her foundation beginning to break at the edges. "*You sick bastard.*"

She then clicked him off.

Lowden immediately dropped the phone and switched the TV off.

He shook uncontrollably for a minute or so, before looking down: a hot darkness coated his crotch. He felt the slimy, viscid stain, and was marvellously disgusted with himself.

"*That was fucking great,*" he growled, drooling a little.

He put the phone back and changed his trousers and boxer shorts, shoving the used pairs into a plastic bag in his suitcase.

It was now nearly half past ten—it was time to do some work he thought or he would never get it done.

He made a series of notes on his pad: rude, inattentive staff; general feeling of malaise and depression; possible pollution problems; likely criminal activities being carried out in and around the area.

This specific RoadTel was not the *worst place* he had ever inspected, but it had to be in the *bottom ten*. He doubted nothing however could ever beat the SuperTraveller outside Reading wherein a pimp had chased another pimp through his room and out of the first storey window; the Master Inn where the addicts came into the dining room, took the coffee out of the machine and snorted it like cocaine in front of everyone; or the small theme park outside Nottingham called Magic Realm with the raw sewage in the pond by the children's play area and the raw chicken in the Caesar salad sandwich on rye from the café.

He put his pad back in the suitcase and got out the all-purpose blacklight. He closed the curtains and switched the lights off, before re-illuminating the room with the blacklight. He poured the light over the carpet and the walls, observing the various abysmal stains that the quick wipe overs of the staff had failed to fully remove.

Around the side of the bed was definitely the recent site of a puddle of semen. His own fresh semen had splodged next to it, but he was just decent enough not to level that at them.

"Jesus," he said, even himself repulsed. "Was this guy a fucking horse or something?"

Lowden briefly considered the logistics of bringing a horse into the RoadTel, getting it up to the first floor and so on, before shrugging it off. He checked under the bed to observe mountains of dust, before switching off the blacklight, turning the room light back on, and getting his pad back out to make more notes.

Now it was what dreaded the most: the *en suite* bathroom. They tended to be the worst part of any hotel room, and this was no different, perhaps one of the most gruesome he had ever seen. Virtually every surface was encrusted and smeared in semi-hidden filth. The blacklight illuminated entire continents of vileness, but what caught Lowden off-guard was a certain series of stains on the wall opposite the sink, between the toilet and the bathtub. The blacklight showed a set of spatters at roughly chest height, streaking down into wide lanes and collapsing into what had been a wide pool on the tiled floor. There were related stains on the toilet and the side of the bath.

Lowden had seen such stains before, but never in this quantity. It was blood—lots and lots of it. He went over it four times, and even checked a little guide he had on his phone to distinguish marks and grime, but it was unmistakable, and in this amount this *en suite* had to have been the site of someone's death.

He sat down on the bed and thought, *What the fuck am I going to do?*

Lowden went through it logically: this death was obviously *off-the-record*. The stains were no more than a week old, but he had heard of no murder or accidental death occurring anywhere in this motel, never mind in his room.

Therefore, this *had* to have been an undiscovered murder—but who was *responsible*? Such a bloody killing could not have been undertaken by a guest or an interloper without the staff being alerted. Even though the stains were obvious to his equipment, someone with some knowledge had had a fair go at the marks, and managed to get almost all of the blood off. This was no clumsy hit in the night—this was an *inside job*.

But *whom*?

The place was undermanned and that was how the management in this industry liked it. There was a small contingent of staff for him to speculate over, but Lowden had a hunch. He had to play it right, or it would explode in his face.

He sorted out the room, took some blacklight pictures of the stains, and made to go back downstairs to the lobby.

Before he did, he could not resist turning the TV back on and going back to People's Free TV for one last look.

The video playing was of a rap metal song, the cornrowed lead singer scream-flowing beneath an underpass somewhere in the urban blight of Southern California about oppression, war, and the structural racism inherent in every crack and crevice of Western civilisation.

"At least it's not all-female," Lowden consoled himself.

The song tapered off and Carrie Creepers was back, unruffled and unfazed as ever.

"That was the Bro-Yo-Brass with 'American't Do Dis'. Call in, tell us what you think, but I know you will anyway without my encouragement…coming up we've got Arlen, we've got Spasm Group, Monkeygruel…"

She was in Lowden's mind as gorgeous and as edible as the first night he had seen her some three months ago. He would have licked the screen if he had not had known from the blacklight that somebody else already had.

Lowden blew the VJ a kiss and switched the TV off. He had a mission to undertake.

After concealing another certain illegal item in his inner jacket pocket, he got down to the lobby and went up to the front desk.

It was nearly eleven and Salim was to be on duty until six in the morning.

Lowden eyed the young man.

Salim seemed to have gained a little energy from the strong coffee he was drinking. “Can I help you, sir?”

“Yes chief,” smiled Lowden. “I’m Henderson, in 3B.”

“Oh yes,” Salim said, before his eyes widened. “Yes…erm, is there a problem?”

“Why would there be a problem?”

Whatever he had been on had stopped him realising that he had given that certain room key to Lowden earlier, and his abnormal reaction now gave the consumer agent everything he needed to know.

“Erm, erm, is there a problem?” stumbled Salim, not looking at Lowden, but down, over to his left.

“There *might* be a problem,” said Lowden. “Why don’t we discuss it somewhere else?”

“I…I can’t leave the desk for more than a couple minutes.”

“Don’t fuck me around…”

“Why can’t we—”

“You *know* what this is about.”

Lowden could see it in Salim’s face—*he* knew that *he* knew, and the lad could not fathom it.

“Meet me outside, in the rear courtyard.”

“What? What if—?”

“Just come after me in two minutes…”

Lowden turned and left down the left of the desk, through the lower corridor, and out into the back courtyard, cold and forsaken.

After five minutes of standing in shadow, Salim came out and Lowden waved him over.

“You’re fuckin late,” Lowden said, hands in his pockets. “You don’t get a fucking option on being late now.”

“Look bro,” said Salim, unable to hide his nervousness. “I don’t know what you've found—"

Lowden cut him off: "Look *bro*: I'm a hotel inspector. British Choice. I've used the blacklight. Blood's all over the fuckin' shop. Unmistakable."

Salim breathed deeply. "How…why you think it was me?"

Lowden could not help but laugh: "You're *fucking bad* at this mate. Everything you've done so far you've incriminated yourself. Besides, I've got the evidence…they'll know, they'll find it all out."

Salim rubbed his face. "*Fuuuuuuccccckkkk…*"

"Yep," chirped Lowden. "Who was it anyway?"

Salim sighed. Lowden might as well have been a police officer with a loaded gun to the clerk's head at this rate.

"Nobody," said the clerk. "She was just some bitch—erm, some woman, acting up, not liking, er, what I got, what I had."

Lowden wagged his finger. "Naughty boy…what did you do with the body?"

"I tossed it…" began Salim, but he stopped himself and turned to Lowden. "Hey, why the fuck should I tell you owt? Why should I take this shit from you?"

He went to grab Lowden by the shoulders, but the agent pulled back and brought out his retractable nightstick, the club end gleaming in the nightlights.

"Don't fucking do that again," growled Lowden. "And don't get any ideas about doing to me what you did to that whore. Listen: I'm giving you an *out*. You give me something, and you get that room to yourself for another deep hard clean."

The logic worked on Salim and after cooling for a moment he asked Lowden what he wanted.

After some probing, Salim admitted there was about three grand and some gold items in the office safe, for which the day manager had been too lazy or distracted to arrange a pick up by the bank. The amount was not as much as Lowden wanted, but it would do under the circumstances.

The cameras on the ground floor had been inactive for weeks, but a robbery would still have to be faked with some violence.

"How we going to do that?" asked Salim.

"Like this," said Lowden, and punched the clerk square in the mouth with his free hand.

Salim staggered back, hissing blood.

"Fuckin' 'ell! he shouted, wiping his mouth. "You fuckin' bastard!"

"It's the only way," Lowden replied, rubbing his fingers. "You were in the office, two guys came in one, one chinned you, and then they forced you to open the safe."

Salim glared at him, but knew he was over a barrel.

He led Lowden back into the motel, up the corridor and into the back office. He opened up the safe, smearing some of his blood on the door at the agent's insistence.

Putting on his own gloves, Lowden handled the money and gold jewellery into a plastic bag.

"Right," Lowden said, tying it tight. "I'm gonna walk out the back, around the motel, come in through the side. In five minutes, you call the police, tell them like I said it happened."

Salim was glum, avoiding Lowden: "Right."

"Repeat it to me."

"What?"

"Fucking repeat it to me or everything goes to shit."

"Two guys."

"Yeah."

"Came in."

"Yep."

"Punched me."

"Right."

"Made me open the safe."

"Correct."

"All emptied out."

"Mmm-hmm."

"Ran straight out and left me."

"All good!"

Lowden slapped Salim on the shoulder. "Cheer up...it could be worse! I'd say start working on those descriptions…"

Lowden leaned out the door, saw the corridor was clear, and went right back up to his room to count his money.

Salim sat in the office swivel chair, sucking in the blood from his gums.

No one came to the desk, as he could see through a mirror on the back wall, through which he could also see his swelling lips, and with them a spot of red on his purple shirt.

Part of him, a lot of him in fact, wanted to cry. But that would not be manly he thought.

Five minutes passed, then ten, then fifteen.

Salim did not feel like moving.

It was close to midnight when the automatic doors alerted him to someone entering.

He got up and went to the desk.

"Are you okay?" asked the young woman there.

"Yeah," Salim said, unthinkingly. "I'm fine."

He looked at the woman: an obvious prostitute, and a bizarre one at that. She wore a long black leather coat, platform shoes, an oversized red beret over black and blonde hair. Most of her white foundation had been wiped away, but her lips and eyes were painted black still, a gold ring on the bottom lip.

She looked at him curiously. "Okay…"

"Do you have a room here?"

"No, it's a bit odd…"

"That lounge is closed for now," said Salim. "You'll have to come back tomorrow night."

"No, it's not that," she said.

The woman leaned forward, her coat parting to reveal her cleavage, and the clerk shuddered.

"It's just," she continued, "that maybe you've had someone a bit weird in here tonight?"

"Weird?" asked Salim.

At that moment an exceptionally tall and lanky man stormed in and came up to the desk. He was as pallid as she was, with a dense complex of neck tattoos that formed an all-encompassing sleeve.

"Is this him?" he asked the woman, staring at Salim with rage. "Is this the bastard?"

"No Kaye!" she said. "No, I'm sure it's not a Pa—an Asian guy."

"You sure?" he growled, not tasking his eyes off the exhausted clerk.

Salim looked at the two of them, and it came to him. He *knew* who they were looking for. It was a cosmic link, a text message of sorts from a higher power.

"Going out on a limb…" he began.

* * *

Lowden was not completely happy. He had counted £2,670 in paper money from the safe, well short of what Salim had promised. The gold items were next to worthless until he found a good fence—legitimate dealers would not touch it, or worse would try to turn him in.

He counted it two more times before re-wrapping it in the plastic bag and lying back on his bed. He had not heard any police sirens as of yet, but the whole country was in a sorry state—it might be another half an hour yet before they came to even a violent robbery.

Hands beneath his head, Lowden floated the idea of coming back in a few weeks and greasing Salim for a bit more. He had gathered that his surname was Mansoor—was that Punjabi? Gujarati? Anyway, they all had big families he reckoned; relatives to draw on, beg from, squeeze from.

"What the fuck is he gonna do?" Lowden asked aloud and giggled.

He turned the TV on hoping for just one more glimpse of that white chest, but *Mosh Wire* was long over, and People's Free TV had moved onto another conspiracy show broadcast from Missouri, one of the worst of the worst nutters they had on offer blaring away in a thunderous torrent about the World Economic Forum and the city council of San Diego wanting to turn all life on Earth trans, or at least gay.

Lowden watched for a minute, but felt tired.

He cut it off and was just removing his shoes when there was a knock at the door.

"Who the fuck…?"

He got up and went to it.

"Salim?" he asked the wood. "That better not be you."

"Hello?" came a woman's voice.

Lowden's heart fluttered and he flung the heavy door open.

It was like a dream: there she was, all in black, her cute little beret, her smiling face usually so aloof, stood in the middle of the corridor.

"Carrie!" he beamed, and made to grab her.

A huge hand came from the left side of the door and grabbed him by the throat. An inky giant of a man came from around the frame and pushed Lowden back into the room, Creepers following after and closing the door.

"Is this the cunt?!" the goliath asked, holding him by throat and by arm against the wall.

"Well I can't tell when he can't talk," said Creepers looking around, touching Lowden's artefacts.

The great man called Kaye ceased throttling Lowden and took him by the shoulders.

"What the fuck is this?!" Lowden shouted. He looked to Creepers. "Who is this bastard?!"

Kaye got Lowden in the stomach with side of his fist and he doubled over with a yelp.

"Don't you fuckin' look at her!" the giant shouted.

"It's him all right," Creepers said. "He's not as good at disguise as he thinks he is."

"How did you find me?" asked Lowden, looking away at the curtained window. He was helpless.

"We traced your call arsehole," Creepers said, delighted. "You *had* to call from a fucking landline for so long. We've been waiting for you to fuck up."

Lowden could not hide his frustration. "Bollocks!"

"If you say so," said Kaye and brought the side of his forearm into

Lowden's crotch.

"Ooofph!" cried Lowden and he fell to his knees.

"And Hallow Brook here is maybe a thirty minute drive from the studio."

"What do we do to him now?" asked Kaye, pulsing.

"We'll have to teach him a lesson," said Creepers, pondering. "Get him in here..."

As Kaye dragged Lowden across the rough carpet, he pleaded with Creepers. "Carrie please! I thought we had something!"

Creepers shook her head. "You're even more messed up than I could possibly have fucking imagined...*paste him!*"

Kaye dropped Lowden onto the *en suite* floor and kicked him in the ribs.

Lowden managed to rear up and grab Kaye's arm, but Kaye expertly twisted out of it and grabbed both of Lowden's arms. He pulled them fast across his chest, straining both of his shoulders.

Lowden screamed and fell back to the floor.

Kaye stomped on his chest before he stopped at Creepers's cry.

"Babe look at this!"

The giant turned around and saw the girl holding the plastic bag of money, open at the top exposing a thick wad of grey-purple notes.

"What is this?" asked Kaye, his foot on Lowden's hip. "Who the fuck are you?"

Lowden had a flash of inspiration. "I'm a police officer! I'm part of a sting! Check the badge in my inner pocket! The jacket's hung on the chair there!"

Creepers reached into Lowden's inner pocket and pulled out the fake badge.

"Shit Kaye!" she panicked. "I think he's telling the truth."

"Wait a minute..." said Kaye, and after kicking Lowden afresh to keep him down, he walked over to Creepers to take a look.

"Nah that's fake that," the thug said, examining it closely. "I've seen this shit before...besides..."

Kaye took Lowden's wallet off of the side cabinet and looked through his cards.

"Yeah, it's shit. That badge says Gilbert Fields and all these say Aaron Lowden, like the licence…and *other names*…he's a fuckin' con man!"

"Fuck me…"

Kaye held up the money at Lowden as the agent lifted his head up.

"These your fuckin' spoils are they?"

Lowden could not fight it any more.

"Fuck you," he managed to spit out with a little blood.

"*Ours* now you little bitch!" yelled Kaye, and he rushed back into the *en suite*, bringing his boot up across Lowden's chest and into his jaw. The solid tip of the sole brought two of Lowden's front teeth cracking out, flying upwards against the wall like vertical skipping stones, and tinkling down into the bathtub.

Lowden's blood sprayed out in two thin jets, over the toilet, the bath, and the wall between, as Kaye pounded down over and down, fist and foot, and at one point Creepers leaned in herself to scratch Lowden's cheeks and forehead with her long sparkling nails.

After what felt like hours of torture, Lowden lay on the *en suite* floor: his face swollen and bloodied; six teeth missing, five chipped; three cracked ribs, with a collapsed right lung; a broken left arm, along with four of its fingers; and a dislocated ankle, with his head gored, multiple bones bruised, and myriad sites of internal bleeding.

The place looked as though a new murder had been committed.

Lowden could see in his haze, nearly dropping into unconsciousness, but he could hear the lovers as they left:

"Goodbye student support loans!"

"Fuck that! Let's have a fuckin' party! Celebrate! We took the fuckin' creep down…"

"Christ I fucking love you baby!"

"And I fuckin' love you too bitch…"

As the room door was opened, Lowden was just able to raise his head and out came a tiny weak whisper: "Carrie…don't…go…I…I…"

He could not even finish his pathetic plea.

Lowden's head dropped down. He tried to breathe through his nose and brought fresh blood into his throat, which he coughed up with great protest from the rest of his body.

Nearly in a coma, occasionally moaning involuntarily, he was alone for a few minutes before he was disturbed.

He managed to open his eyes and saw a dark figure looming over him.

"Salim!" he croaked. It was hard to form words with so many missing and damaged teeth, along with a swollen and cut up tongue.

"You need…to stop them…they have…the money…"

Salim smiled down at him.

"I know, and I've got *you*," said the clerk.

He brought up his foot and kicked Lowden twice in his raw abdomen, the prostrate agent bellowing. Salim was not to know, but it was his kicks that finally ruptured Lowden's large intestine.

"*Motherfucker*," Salim muttered, cleared his nose and spat, hitting Lowden's chin, and left the agent to, at last, blackout.

*****

"Yeah, er, ambulance."

"Hello, what's your emergency?"

"Yeah, this is the RoadTel at Hallow Brook. A guest here has had the shit beaten out of him basically."

"Okay, is he conscious?"

"No, I don't think so…"

"Okay, is he breathing?"

"Yeah, he's breathing…"

"Sir…sir?"

"Erm, yeah, yeah?"

"Are you—are you laughing?"

"Erm…no…"

The Usual Unusual Suspects

Wil A. Emerson has been on the writing path for approximately 15 years. While not fresh out of college to write the Best Seller, she spent her early years as a Registered Nurse. Now on the fringe of being overlooked due to the inconvenient late start, she's successfully published in anthologies and has one novel under her belt. *Taking Rosie's Arm*, a Five Star, Thorndike publication, recounts the story of an elderly woman who befriends a troubled, but determined young girl. Writer, artist, traveler, cook: soup's on.

Wil's recent work is mainly mystery and women's fiction, and she has appeared in the following*Crimeucopia* anthologies: *Careless Love*, with her piece, *The Driver* — followed by the 'second installment' *The Road to Reconciliation* in *Crank It Up!*, and *Cracker Jacks and Granny Cases* in *Great Googly Moo!*

Also a struggling artist, her art can be viewed on her website. *www.wilemerson.com*

Robert Petyo is a Derringer award finalist whose stories have appeared in small press magazines and anthologies. He has appeared in several Crimeucopia collections, including *Boomshakalaking*, *Crank It Up*, and *A Load of Balls*.

Though he mainly writes crime fiction, he has published some mainstream and science fiction in small press magazines, and in the deep dark past he wrote three science fiction novels under three different names.

He can be reached on X or Facebook @RobertPetyo.

Avram Lavinsky is a recovering musician with one gold record on his living room wall and countless unsold ones in his attic. He has published a dozen short works in esteemed magazines and anthologies including *The Mysterious Bookshop Presents the Best Mystery Stories* *of the Year 2023*. He's also earned starred reviews from the nation's toughest critics, his three teenage sons, although not often.

Dave Dempster is a retired lawyer and aspiring writer, who was an enthusiastic chessplayer in a previous life. His *Thank God for the Nineteenth Hole* appears in *Crimeucopia—A Load Of Balls* and his *Where is the Truth?* in *Crimeucopia—What the Butler Didn't See*. His work can also be seen online in *Jonah, CafeLit, East of the Web, Neon Origami (2032-Time's Up)* and *Close To The Bone*.

John B. Elliott has worked as a typesetter, pressman, bartender, social worker, biologist and teacher. He has a passion for the natural world, especially deserts and mountains; has had play productions, notably one about Federico Garcia Lorca, and published fiction in, or upcoming in, *Calliope, Sonoran Horror, Open Ceilings, Lifespan Anthologies Loss and Older, and Crimeucopia*, as well as poetry in *The Comstock Review, Southwestern American Literature, Poetry Quarterly, Borderlands: Texas Poetry Review, Tanka Journal, The Fourth River*, and three anthologies.

Jon Matthew Farber is a retired pediatrician in northern Virginia. He is an avid chess and bridge player, with dozens of humorous articles on the latter game to his credit. A member of the Mystery Writers of America, he has published many short stories, including in *Ellery Queen Mystery Magazine* and, most recently, *The Third Black Beacon of Mystery*. He has also co-written (with Daniel Reinharth) the fair-play whodunit novel *Do Not Resuscitate*.
He first appeared (under the pseudonym John Bertram Fawet III) in *Crimeucopia—Let Me Tell You About...* with *The Last Gunfighter*.

Wendy Harrison is a retired prosecutor who turned to short mystery fiction during the pandemic. Her stories have been published in numerous anthologies including *Peace, Love & Crime, Autumn Noir, Crimeucopia (Tales from the Back Porch, One More Thing to Worry About, Totally Psycho Logical, Chicka-Chicka Boomba!*, and *A Load of Balls), The Big Fang, Gargoylicon*, and *Death of a Bad Neighbour, More*

Groovy Gumshoes, and *Celluloid Crimes,* as well as in *Shotgun Honey.* When Hurricane Ian destroyed her home in Florida, she moved to Washington State, as far from Florida as she could get.

Martin Zeigler writes short fiction, primarily mystery, science fiction, and horror. His stories have been published in a number of anthologies and journals, both in print and online.

Every so often (okay, twice), he has gathered these stories into a self-published collection. In 2015 he released *A Functional Man And Other Stories.* More recently, in 2020, a year we will all remember with fondness, he released *Hypochondria And Other Stories.*

Besides writing, Marty enjoys the things most people do. And besides those, he likes reading, taking long walks, and playing the piano.

Marty makes his home in the Pacific Northwest.

Ed Teja is a lifelong storyteller, as well as a martial artist, former Caribbean boat bum, blues musician, and magazine editor. His stories blend and crisscross crime and speculative fiction and the strange situations and people often come from his somewhat surreal life. Ed's *Crimeucopia* debut is in *Crank It Up!*

For more information and news, go to www.edteja.com

Victor Kreuiter lives, reads and writes in the Midwest USA. His stories have appeared in *Ellery Queen Mystery Magazine, Halfway Down The Stairs, Bewildering Stories, Tough, Frontier Tales, Del Sol SFF Review, Literally Stories*, and other online and print publications. His story, *Miller and Bell* — originally published in the August, 2022, issue of *Mystery Magazine* — was selected to appear in *The Mysterious Bookshop Presents the Best Mystery Stories of 2023.*

Geoff Boswell is a British writer, hailing originally from the West Midlands, now in exile in North Cornwall. He studied Creative Writing, Advanced Creative Writing; and Voices and Texts through the Open University and has been writing poetry since 1980 debuting under the auspices of Skate Press. He has been a lyricist and vocalist in a band, has written rituals (you'd better not ask), and sermons (ditto), technical specifications and such works, reports for community development purposes, short stories (which is why he's here), and has started a number of novels, just like many writers do. For five years he's devised, scripted, and presented music internet radio shows on both NCB Radio and Raiders Broadcast, his NCB Halloween shows being his forte. (Boo!). He is currently employed by Devon & Cornwall Police from where he gets ideas beyond his own imagination, but that's the British public for you.

Diana Parrilla is a versatile writer. With a degree in economics and mastery in Japanese, she shares her passion for anime and games on her YouTube channel and social networks, where she goes by the handle buffyta17. Her publications span various horror and speculative fiction genres.

S. B. Watson has been published in *Mystery Magazine*, *Mystery Tribune*, and *Punk Noir Magazine*. His Crimeucopia appearances so far have been in the historical *Through The Past Darkly* and *What The Butler Didn't See*. His story in *Crimeucopia — Great Googly Moo!* was a 2025 Shamus Award finalist.

John 'Jay' Andrew Connor has been writing and publishing under a menagerie of names and genres since the late 1970s — sometimes even professionally. He's worked at a variety of jobs, in various locations, and has also published small press, and semi-pro magazines in the past. Sadly, even though he's now on full time medication, he's at it again.
Parts 1 and 2 of his *Memindip Quartet — The Death and Life of an Unwilling Investigator* series, set in an 'alternative' North African city, in 1969, appear in *We'll Be Right Back—After This!* and *Great Googly Moo!*

Harris Coverley has more than a hundred and twenty short stories published or forthcoming in *Penumbra, A Darker Continent* (Belanger Books), *The Black Beacon Book of Horror* (Black Beacon Books), and *parABnormal Magazine*, amongst many other places. A Rhysling and Dwarf Stars Award nominee, he has also had over two hundred poems published in journals around the world. His *Ballbreaker* appears in *Crimeucopia — A Load of Balls*. He lives in Manchester, England.

Don't You Never Look Inside the Mojo Bag...

...'Cos it got the juju! An' that is hot stuff...

However, it's true to say that all the wordsmiths contained within the covers of this Crimeucopia, have been looking inside all sorts of Mojo bags, and are more than willing to recount what it is they've seen.

So sit back, relax, and let:

Anthony Kane Evans, Carlos Ramet, Tristan J. Deehan, Christopher Deliso, Tucker Struyk, Ed Teja, Gene Kendall, Hal Dygert, Ian Blackwell, L.C. Adams, Patrick Ambrose, Kamal Mouhoune, Rand Gaynor, Rob Loughran,
and ***Edward St. Boniface***

take you on guided tours around their worlds—going from Cosy Country to Noir Central, and back again, provided you booked a return ticket that is.

Because we hope that, whenever and wherever these authors take you, you'll find something that you immediately like, as well as something that takes you out of your GPS and Timezone monitored comfort zones—and puts you into a completely new one.

Because, in the Random Shuffle spirit of our Murderous Ink Press motto:

You never know what you like until you read it.

Paperback ISBN: 9781909498648 — eBook ISBN: 9781909498655

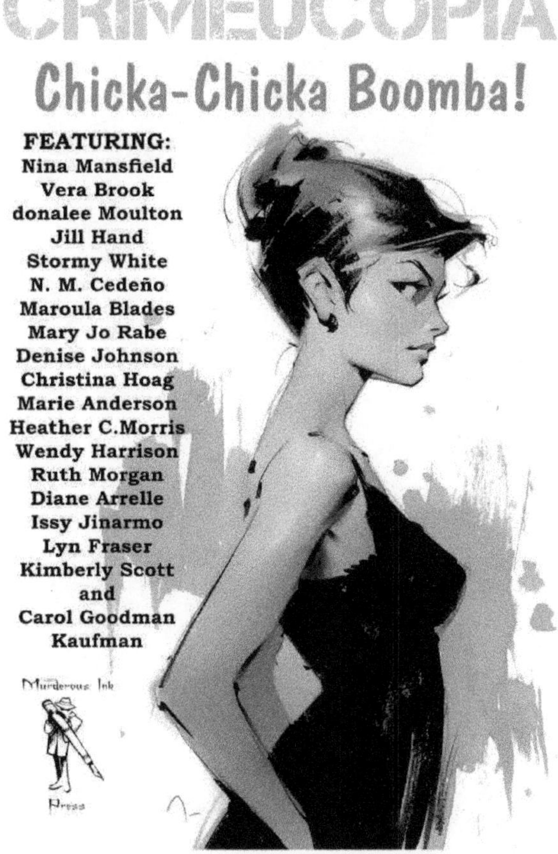

It would be hard to pinpoint exactly when Crimeucopia moved from being a 'scratch project title' and became a masthead—but it seemed to match our idea of presenting as wide a spectrum of Crime fiction genres as we could.

From there it was probably *Fate* which brought together the Aly Fell base artwork, and the 16 contributors who went on to become the initial Countesses of Crime, and appeared in Crimeucopia—The Lady Thrillers.

4 years down the proverbial publishing line, we felt it was time to celebrate the anniversary with another all-women anthology—and let these 19 Countesses of Crime tell it like it is, was, or could have been....

Because, in the eclectic, off-centred spirit of our Murderous Ink Press motto: You never know what you like until you read it.

Paperback Edition ISBN: 9781909498662 — eBook Edition ISBN: 9781909498679

This is the first of several 'Free 4 All' collections that was supposed to be themeless. However, with the number of submissions that came in, it seems that this could be called an *Angels & Devils* collection, mixing PI & Police alongside tales from the Devil's dining table. Mind you, that's not to say that all the PIs & Police are on the side of the Angels....

Also this time around has not only seen a move to a larger paperback format size, but also in regard to the length of the fiction as well. Followers of the somewhat bent and twisted Crimeucopia path will know that although we don't deal with Flash fiction as a rule, it is a rule that we have sometimes broken. And let's face it, if you cannot break your own rules now and again, whose rules can you break?

Oh, wait, isn't breaking the rules the foundation of the crime fiction genre?

Oh dear....

Paperback ISBN: 9781909498426 eBook ISBN: 9781909498433

www.ingramcontent.com/pod-product-compliance
Ingram Content Group UK Ltd.
Pitfield, Milton Keynes, MK11 3LW, UK
UKHW042052271225
466429UK00002B/29

9 781909 498747

The Spy in the Berlin Sky

Gary W. Ladd

The Spy in the Berlin Sky

The characters and events portrayed in this book are fictitious. Any similarity to real persons, living or dead, is coincidental and not intended by the author.

ISBN: 978-0-9980433-2-6 (digital)
ISBN: 978-0-9980433-3-3 (paperback)

Cover design by: Rafido

Printed in the United States of America

"When once you have tasted flight, you will forever walk the earth with your eyes turned skyward, for there you have been, and there you will always long to return."

- Leonardo DaVinci.

Contents

Chapter	*Page*
Prologue --	5
Chapter 1 --	8
Chapter 2 --	22
Chapter 3 --	34
Chapter 4 --	49
Chapter 5 --	60
Chapter 6 --	71
Chapter 7 --	82
Chapter 8 --	94
Chapter 9 --	114
Chapter 10 --	125
Chapter 11 --	136
Chapter 12 --	146
Chapter 13 --	155
Chapter 14 --	160
Chapter 15 --	168

Chapter	*Page*
Chapter 16 --	188
Chapter 17 --	203
Chapter 18 --	210
Chapter 19 --	233
Chapter 20 --	247
Chapter 21 --	265
Chapter 22 --	281
Chapter 23 --	294
Chapter 24 --	311
Chapter 25 --	327
Chapter 26 --	344
Chapter 27 --	361
Chapter 28 --	381
Chapter 29 --	394
Author's Note --	414
About the Author --	427

Prologue

Spring 1912: Gebsattelbrücke, Munich Germany

Hermann shifted his weight from foot to foot, trying to dodge the rainwater that fell in rivulets from the bridge overhead. "Damn storm," he grumbled. It was a damp, foggy evening, and he was soaked and impatient. He had arrived at the agreed-upon time, made his way under the bridge, and positioned himself in the prearranged location. Wedged under his arm was a soggy newspaper--a makeshift prop he'd brought to make himself appear inconspicuous. That ploy, Hermann now realized, made him look ridiculous. Who but a crazed street beggar would carry around a soggy lump of newsprint? He tossed what was left of the newspaper into the street and watched the runoff carry it into the gutter and down a storm drain. "Gunter, you little shit, where are you?"

Several minutes later, Hermann heard footfalls echoing against the sides of the tunnel-like structure that formed the bridge's central arch. Someone was approaching from the north, along the street under the bridge. He edged into the shadows, drew his knife, and stooped into a defensive crouch. Better not take chances, he reasoned—no telling who's out here at this hour.

A hunched, diminutive figure emerged from the fog and ambled in Hermann's direction. Hermann peered intently at the approaching figure. Most likely a man, he surmised, and whoever it was had Gunter's build and gait. He relaxed slightly, took a deep breath, and waited for the man's facial features to come into view.

Halfway under the bridge, the man paused, did a slow pirouette, and whispered, "Hermann, are you here? It's me, Gunter."

Hermann stood, slid his knife to its sheath, and stepped out of the shadows. "About damn time, Gunter. Where the hell have you been?"

"Don't be impatient, Hermann, it's still early. What have you planned for tonight's merriment?"

"We're meeting Bruno and the boys at Herr Schloper's Biergarten in an hour or so. Bruno's girlfriend is bringing her friends. We'll drink and dance and then go on a hayride. Do yourself a favor, Gunter. Take a bath and wipe the manure off your shoes. Girls won't dance with you if you smell like a farm boy."

"Don't lecture me, Hermann. You're a good friend, but you've misplaced your priorities. Nowadays, I often notice you chasing some maiden, hoping she'll let you cozy up to her. It's become an obsession, and it won't end well."

"Spare me your barnyard wisdom, farm boy. Are you going to help me or not?"

"I agreed to meet you here, didn't I? What do you want me to do?"

"The whole crew will be at the Biergarten tonight--Bruno, Rolf, Gerhard, Kurt, Otto, Friedrich, and Wilhelm. Plus, Bruno's girl will likely bring five or six friends. We need enough money to pay for beer and a hayride, but I've only got a few Pfennigs. I can't raise that kind of money in an hour--I was hoping you could help me with this predicament."

"Ok, Hermann, I'll fix this."

"How?"

"I've told you before: Don't ask--you don't want to know."

"Well, how can I help?"

"Just meet me behind Schloper's Biergarten in an hour."

◆◆◆

Hermann walked briskly through the Mariahilfplatz and then turned east on Schweigerstrasse toward Herr Schloper's Biergarten. It was time to meet Gunter, drink beer, and convince the girls to go on a hayride. While rounding the corner, he heard a muffled groan. He turned toward the sound and saw a man lying face down in the gutter on the opposite side of the street. When the man became aware of Hermann's presence, he raised his head, peered at him, and uttered something. Unable to comprehend the man's words, Hermann drew closer and leaned down to investigate.

"Help me! I've been robbed. Some scoundrel knocked me down, stabbed me, and stole my money."

Hermann surveyed the man's clothing and saw that blood was indeed leaking through a narrow gash in the fabric of his coat. Fearing for his safety, he stood, backed away from the injured man, and nervously surveyed his surroundings. Several dark alleys were nearby, one only a few yards away. The predator, Hermann reasoned, had probably staged his attack from that alley and could easily be lying in wait, preparing to pounce on him.

"Look, I'd like to help you, but chances are the swine who did this will attack me too. I don't want to be the next victim. I'll summon the police."

Before the man could reply, Hermann turned and fled. He ran along the

Schweigerstrasse until he reached the Biergarten. Then, he cautiously walked to the rear of the building and searched for Gunter.

"Now, who's late?" Gunter scoffed.

"I've got a good reason. I stumbled into a guy who'd been stabbed and robbed. He was lying on the street, bleeding. He looked like he was dying. I wanted to help him, but I was afraid the crook who robbed him would attack me, too. So, I said I'd call the police, and then I ran—I just left him lying in the gutter."

"Look, you shouldn't get involved. The police might think you did it. Besides, the guy probably deserved it."

"That's a rather callous perspective, don't you think?"

"Quit moralizing," Gunter said. "Here, I got what you wanted." Gunter handed Hermann a small leather pouch.

Hermann opened the pouch, looked inside, and gasped. The bag was filled with large-denomination banknotes.

"Gunter, there must be thousands of Marks here. Where did you get this?"

"As I said, don't ask. You don't want to know."

Chapter 1

Spring 1915: Somewhere over France

It was the third reconnaissance mission in as many days. Chances were that today's photographs wouldn't be any better than those from yesterday or the day before. It was midday, and the sky was cloudless, but the sun's rays barely penetrated the smoke rising from the trenches below. Hoping or praying for a reprieve was a waste of time. The air marshal insisted that they fly these missions because, in his words, "any pictures of artillery emplacements, even smoky ones, were better than no pictures."

Bruno Loezer flew two passes over a particularly dense concentration of Allied field artillery without a hitch. He'd dodged antiaircraft fire while holding the wings as steady as possible so that Hermann, his observer, could put his camera to good use. Now, on the third pass, his luck ran out.

Loezer leaned out of his cockpit and shouted, "Hermann, return to your position!" but the Albatros' prop wash swallowed his words, and his plea went unheeded. Loezer cursed, waved his arms repeatedly to no avail, and then banged his fist against the fuselage. Desperate now, he screamed at the top of his lungs. "Get in the cockpit, Hermann, there's a Gun Bus on our tail!"

Now alerted to the impending danger, Hermann glanced rearward past the Albatros' tail section and spied the reason for Bruno's concern. A Vickers F.B 5 "Gun Bus" was nose down, descending into their flight path, and closing fast. There was no time to lose. To free his hands, he stuck his camera's leather strap in his mouth and bit down, clamping it like a bit between his teeth. He grasped the wingtip, wrapped his leg around a strut, and levered his body onto the Albatros' lower wing. Then he got on his knees and slowly crawled toward the fuselage.

As he edged his way between the wing struts, he heard the unmistakable sound of gunfire. A hail of bullets rained down around him, ripping holes in the wings, splintering the struts, and puncturing the fuselage. Hermann froze, unsure whether the enemy pilot was targeting him or firing indiscriminately upon the Albatros. All became clear when the Vicker's pilot nosed alongside, aimed a pistol directly at Hermann, and pulled the trigger. Fortunately for Hermann, the shot went wild.

The Albatros rolled as Bruno banked away from the Vickers. Hermann held tight and watched as the wing he clutched rose above the horizon, and the Vickers dropped out of sight. Relieved to be out of the line of fire, he exhaled sharply, drew a deep breath, and cursed the enemy pilot. Taking advantage of this reprieve, he let go of the struts, slid down the sharply angled wing, and let his body crash against the fuselage. As he reached for his cockpit, the plane hit a downdraft, pitched violently, and launched him against the biplane's upper wing. The blow nearly knocked him unconscious, but somehow, as he floated weightlessly in the slipstream, he had the presence of mind to grab the rim of his cockpit and pull himself into the plane. The entire airframe shook as he fell into his seat.

Bruno bellowed, "Scheisse! About damn time!" and undertook more extreme evasive maneuvers. While the Albatros lurched and rolled, Hermann struggled to tie the camera to one of the cockpit's internal struts. He needed to protect the photographs. After all, those photos were why he and Bruno were here, surveilling the Allies' fortifications. Moreover, he'd just risked his life to take the pictures. Prior missions had taught him that it was practically impossible to photograph enemy positions from the rear cockpit of the Albatros because its lower wing obstructed his view of everything that passed under the plane. It had become necessary to improvise, and eventually, he'd devised an effective tactic: he would crawl out on the lower wing, loop his legs around a strut, and snap photographs while he hung over the wingtip. The tactic's margin for error was near zero, but its benefits far outweighed its risks. In his estimation, it was the only way to obtain high-quality reconnaissance photographs. His superiors had lauded his ingenuity, and among his airborne brethren, he had become known as "the flying trapezist."

Spring 1915: Temporary Luftschiffhafen, Southeastern Germany

The tent hangar's canvas roof rippled and flapped as it resisted the onslaught of a strong westerly wind. The hanger and five other hastily assembled structures stood in a pasture near the French border alongside a dirt road that served as an airstrip. Tonight, before the ground crew put the planes to bed, the hanger doubled as a mess hall for the German pilots and observers.

It had been a long day. Most of the men had flown multiple missions over Allied positions, and as daylight faded, they had returned to the aerodrome tired and hungry. Their reward for the day's efforts was sausages and potatoes—the same Abendessen, or evening meal, they had consumed the previous night and every other night for the last month.

"More schnapps, Hermann?" said Rolf, a squadron pilot and one of Hermann's friends.

"Ja, Rolf. I need something to wash down the sausages. Tonight's portion contained more sawdust than schweinfleisch."

"Here, drink up, and then tell us about your exploits. Did you entertain the enemy again today with your trapeze act? Will Hauptman Schmidt be pleased with your reconnaissance photos?"

"I've used this tactic only a few months, so it remains a work in progress. I am still experimenting. However, the smoke was less dense in some places today, so I think Hauptman Schmidt will be pleased with some of the pictures I took of the enemy's artillery placements."

"Bravo, Lieutenant Göring!"

"Thank you. Now let me ask you something, Rolf. What do you target when you shoot at enemy planes?"

"Odd question for an observer, Hermann. Engines and fuel tanks, if you must know."

"You don't aim for our adversaries—the pilots or observers?"

"Demolishing the enemy's weapons—their ability to wage war—is foremost. However, air battles take place in a dynamic environment. The shooter and target are moving, so a pilot's field of fire is never precise. Pilots and their crew are often collateral damage."

"That I understand. So, tell me this: When enemy pilots fire on you, what are *they* targeting?"

"I assume their tactics are similar, but it's not something I've given much thought. Why do you ask?"

"Because today, a French pilot tried to kill me."

"You mean he shot at your plane?"

"No, he tried to take my life. He came alongside, aimed his pistol directly at me, and fired. He targeted me, not the plane."

Other pilots, now lubricated with schnapps, overheard Rolf's and Hermann's conversation and voiced their opinions.

"Göring, you neophyte," remarked a seasoned veteran. "This is war! What did you expect?"

"Observers don't shoot people; they take pictures," Göring replied.

"But what you do isn't harmless, is it?" another flyer retorted. "What do you think Hauptman Schmidt does with your photographs?"

"This isn't the infantry, and we are not waging trench warfare," Göring countered. "We are the first men in history to battle in the skies. What we do is unprecedented, calling for a unique military etiquette. From what I have witnessed, German pilots obey an unspoken code of honor. What happened to me today violates that code."

There was a brief silence, followed by derisive snorts and chuckles. "So, Göring," one of the flyers said, "are you having trouble fathoming why your opponent failed to salute when he drew alongside your plane or applaud when he saw you hanging from the wing? Perhaps he didn't find your trapeze act entertaining." Loud guffaws ensued.

When the hanger quieted, Karl, another pilot, spoke. "Göring thought air duty would be safer than fighting in the trenches. I have it on good authority that he's disobeyed orders and failed to report to his infantry unit."

"My friend may be naive, but he has a point," remarked Gunter, coming to Göring's defense. Gunter was Göring's best friend and one of the squadron's most aggressive pilots. "What is unprecedented is this war's brutality. The Allies' savagery and inhumanity make it necessary that we change the way we fight. The German code of honor is outdated and must be replaced with a viciousness that equals or exceeds the Allies' corrupt tactics."

"There is some truth in what you say, Gunter," said Karl, "but you overlook the main reason for the Allies' savagery. Göring's encounter is rooted in the Allies' beliefs about Germans. They see us as warmongers and barbarians—a people no better than wild animals. They fear us and think we can't be tamed, so they hunt us for sport and seek to eliminate us from the face of the earth."

"You might be right, Karl," Göring conceded. But what is the solution? What should I do if this happens again?

"What choice do you have?" Karl scoffed. "Remain in your cockpit so you don't compromise Loezer's maneuverability, or bring your pistol and shoot the swine--preferably before they kill you!"

Spring 1915: Verdun Aerodrome, River Meuse, Northeastern France

During the evening squadron meeting, Robert Weber fought to keep his eyes open while Captain Aguillon reviewed the day's mission objectives and listened to the officer's situation reports. Weber and thirty-two other pilots and observers of the French Air Service, or FAS, had spent the day flying sorties over German airspace. Now, he sat inside a ramshackle barracks, drank coffee, and tried to stay awake during Aguillon's briefing.

The barracks Aguillon had chosen for the briefing had seen better days. Along with a few other dilapidated wooden structures, it was all that remained of an army base that Napoleon's forces had built on the banks of the Meuse River, east of Paris, over a hundred years ago. Because of the base's proximity to the German border, the FAS Air Service recognized its strategic value. After considerable political wrangling, it wrested the base from the Army and converted it into an Aerodrome.

Weber was not officially a member of the FAS, but he regularly flew as an observer with an experienced French pilot named Francoise Durand. Among the first students to study aeronautical engineering at MIT, Weber had traveled to France at the outset of WWI in search of advanced pilot training and combat experience. He attempted to enlist in the FAS but was rejected when the recruiter discovered he was an American citizen. Not to be deterred, Weber went to the Verdun Aerodrome and found work as an aircraft mechanic. Pilots soon recognized his skill and brought him their most challenging problems.

Durand, in particular, found Weber indispensable. Engine troubles had made his Nieuport 10 unreliable, and no mechanic could repair it. Weber had quickly fixed the 80hp Gnome engine and won Durand's respect and friendship. Soon after that, Durand invited Weber to fly with him, and throughout numerous reconnaissance missions, Weber had proved his worth as an observer.

Although Weber thrived in this role, he still longed to be a pilot. Durand had sympathized and, unbeknownst to Aguillon, had occasionally traded cockpits with Weber so that his friend could acquire some flight time and hone his skills as a pilot. Weber had been a natural and, with Durand's tutelage, had matured into a formidable combat pilot.

After the last pilot presented his situation report, the tone of the squadron meeting changed. Aguillon stood, scanned the room to make sure no one was sleeping, and then uncovered a tactical map that hung on the wall at the front of the room.

"Men, most of you have been gathering reconnaissance on troop movements or working as artillery spotters, but I have just received new orders from headquarters. Starting tomorrow, our squadron's mission priority will be to locate and photograph enemy air bases."

Before Aguillon could continue, Claude, one of the squadron's most outspoken pilots, interrupted. "But Captain, why pull us off air support? For the first time in months, our troops are on the offensive. Who cares where the Germans keep their planes? Searching for enemy air bases is a fool's errand."

Aguillon held his tongue, but his jaw tightened, and his face flushed.

When he spoke again, there was steel in his voice. “Claude, report to my quarters after this meeting.”

Now, all eyes in the room were on Claude. “Yes sir,” he replied sheepishly.

“As I was saying,” Aguillon continued, “you will find and photograph the enemy’s air bases. The Air Ministry is reporting an uptick in air attacks and related casualties, and the Germans appear to be fielding new aircraft and modifying their existing planes. To keep our edge, we need better intelligence. We can’t sit idly by and allow the Germans to develop air superiority.”

“But won’t this require extended flights deep into German territory?” asked one of the pilots.

“Possibly, but like us, the Germans must reach battle zones quickly and economically, minimizing flight distances and fuel consumption. I suspect many of their bases are just over the border, no more than twenty kilometers from our trenches. I have it on good authority that the Germans are building new, temporary aerodromes and stationing more of their aircraft near the front.”

“So, what exactly do you want us to do, Captain?” asked another pilot.

“Our objectives are to gather intelligence on the strength of the German air force, the placement of their planes, and the innovations they’ve made to their aircraft. Your mission is to locate and surveil as many enemy air bases as possible, including permanent and temporary installations. When you find a base, map its location and layout, count the number of planes stationed there, and take pictures of new or modified aircraft.”

As they returned to their barracks, Durand confessed to Weber that he had misgivings about Aguillon’s orders. “Look, I hate to be a pessimist, but does Aguillon realize what he’s asking? He wants us to waltz into a lion’s den, ask the beast to open his mouth so we can count his teeth, and then force his cubs to pose while we snap photos. We will be eaten alive.”

“I agree that the mission is dangerous, but it is not impossible,” Weber replied. “Our survival chances will increase if we catch the Germans by surprise. To use your analogy, we must sneak up on the lion while he sleeps.”

“And how do you propose we do that?”

Having reached the barracks, Durand went inside and sat on his cot. Weber followed but said nothing. Rather than sit, he paced the room, deep in thought. Finally, he faced Durand and spoke.

“I suggest we approach near nightfall or before dawn—after the

Germans have gone to bed or before they wake in the morning. Not only will we catch them off guard, but all their planes will be on the ground, available for us to observe and photograph."

"Very sly, Weber, but surely you aren't suggesting that we fly in the dark?"

"No, that would be foolish," Weber agreed. Dusk, perhaps, is too risky. If we're delayed, we'd have to fly back to base in the dark. Dawn, however, makes more sense. We wait for a night with a full moon and depart just before sunrise. If something unexpected happens, we won't have to fly blind in the darkness. It will only get brighter as the sun rises."

"Tell you what, Weber. I'll commit to an initial reconnaissance flight. I'll fly the plane, and you can look for enemy aerodromes. If you find one that we can reach from our base before sunrise, then I'll decide whether I am willing to take part in your predawn suicide mission."

Shortly after sunrise the following day, Durand gunned the Nieuport down the runway, took off into a cloudless sky, and climbed until the plane reached a high easterly altitude. After twenty kilometers past the German border, he banked north and began flying a series of expansive, ever-widening circles. Weber, meanwhile, kept an eye out for luftschiffhafen or enemy aerodromes. He spotted one on the plane's third rotation and signaled Durand. Durand nodded, reined in the throttle, and nudged the stick forward. The Nieuport's nose dipped below the horizon, and the plane descended several hundred meters. As the luftschiffhafen came into focus, Weber counted five large tents, all of which stood in a pasture next to a dirt farm road. Next to the tents were objects that Weber thought were planes. However, the Nieuport was still too distant from the German airbase for him to identify the aircraft.

Not wanting to reveal their position, Weber again signaled Durand, who banked hard to the south and then set a course for home. Thirty minutes later, they were on the ground, drinking beer in the Verdun Aerodrome's mess hall.

"Time to decide, Durand," quipped Weber. That luftschiffhafen is less than twenty minutes' flight time from here. There is a full moon tonight. I say we go tomorrow."

"All right, but you have to get us in and out of the lion's den before the beast awakens and bites us in the ass. This was your idea, so you fly the plane, and I'll count the lion's teeth. Make sure you have us back here in time for lunch—and there better not be a scratch on me or my plane. Can you do that?"

"Just be ready for a predawn take-off. And bring your sidearm. We must defend ourselves if we go down inside German territory."

"Weber, if you crash my plane in enemy territory, I'll shoot *you* with my sidearm."

It was pitch black inside the barracks when Weber rolled out of his bunk. He donned his uniform, strapped on his sidearm, and stumbled past the rows of cots filled with sleeping men. Once outside, he searched the night sky for clues that might foretell the morning's flight conditions. The sky was clear and filled with stars, and the moon was full on the horizon. There was a cool breeze blowing from the east. Encouraged by what he saw, Weber walked along the narrow gravel path to the hanger that housed Durand's plane. If his luck held, the mechanics he had bribed would have the Nieuport fueled, armed, and ready to fly.

One of the mechanics greeted Weber as he strode into the hanger. The Nieuport was front and center, ready to be rolled onto the runway. He smiled, clapped one of the mechanics on the back, and crawled into the pilot's cockpit. Several moments later, Durand walked into the hangar, looking like death warmed over.

Why did I let you talk me into this, Weber?"

"Come on, admit it, Durand. You're secretly thrilled by the prospect of flying a night mission. Besides, what could go wrong?"

"Do you want me to make you a list?"

"If I'd wanted my mother to come on this mission, I'd have invited her. Now, get in your cockpit. We're burning moonlight."

After Durand climbed into the plane, the mechanic and another ground crew member pushed the Nieuport out of the hanger and onto the tarmac. Weber flipped the ignition, the mechanic spun the prop, and the Gnome engine coughed and came to life. Weber pulled back on the throttle, let the engine rev, and then released the brakes and let the plane coast onto the runway. When he was in the take-off position, he looked ahead and tried to discern where the runway ended and the surrounding forest began, but the moonlight wasn't strong enough for him to see that far. Weber hesitated, unsettled by the ambiguity.

"Watch out for the trees at the end of the runway," Durand cautioned. After you lift off, raise the nose until you approach stall--the maximum angle of attack. We won't see obstacles until we are right on top of them, so we need to gain altitude rapidly."

Pushing his doubts aside, Weber nodded, grasped the throttle, and retracted it fully. The engine roared, and the Nieuport catapulted into the darkness. Within moments, they were airborne. Weber pulled on the stick until the nose was well above the pink clouds atop the eastern horizon and then eased off on the throttle. That distant glow was a reminder that dawn was in the offing. Weber took comfort in that fact.

Minutes passed before Weber took in a lungful of air. He'd been holding his breath, waiting for branches to appear out of nowhere, crash against the wings, and foul the prop. But that hadn't happened. That meant that the Nieuport had cleared the tree line at the end of the runway, and they had overcome their mission's first major hurdle. The next challenge was to stay airborne until there was enough illumination to find their bearings and set a course for the luftschiffhafen. To do that, Weber knew he had to find an altitude that would keep them well above the undulating landscape of western France and eastern Germany. Rising to the task, he pulled out the throttle, eased back on the stick, and held his breath again as the plane gained airspeed and altitude.

Just as Weber's confidence rebounded, there was a heavy thud on the plane's right side. A split second later, a series of rapid-fire thumps accosted the front of the Nieuport. The engine sputtered, and the aircraft stalled and began to roll. Weber knew he needed to act quickly before the plane went into a spin, but he could no longer see the controls. A dark, thick, slimy substance made his goggles opaque. He jerked his goggles up and off his flight cap and inspected them. A heavy layer of blood and feathers covered both lenses.

Durand shouted, trying to make himself heard over the engine noise. "Watch your attitude! Ease up on the throttle! Stick forward! Left rudder! I think we hit a gaggle of geese."

Weber did as Durand directed, and the Nieuport gradually recovered and began to gain altitude. Both men breathed sighs of relief.

Weber scanned the horizon and saw that the Nieuport had drifted off course in the confusion of the bird strike. They were flying north instead of east. He pushed the stick to the right, added some rudder, and brought the nose around so that the Nieuport again faced the brightest location on the skyline. The clouds that hovered there had shed their pinkish glow and now wore bright shades of red and orange.

The increment in ambient illumination prompted Weber to lean over the fuselage and peer at the terrain passing under the plane. The phantom shapes he'd seen dancing in the moonlight had retreated, and in their place were hills, trees, and other fixed features of the German landscape. The sight buoyed his mood. Plunging through the darkness without trustworthy visual referents had unnerved him. He had begun the mission confident that he could rely on his internal compass--his sense of equilibrium--to maintain the plane's rotational orientation. Soon after takeoff, however, that self-assurance had morphed into pure, unadulterated terror. Every time clouds obscured the moon, he'd had the sensation that the Nieuport was upside down and rushing headlong into the ground.

Now, with a stable frame of reference, Weber recovered his bearings. He flew several broad arcs, searching for familiar landmarks. After spying a familiar hilltop village, he put the Nieuport on a course that would intercept the German aerodrome.

Ten minutes later, the tents of the German's temporary airbase appeared. Parked alongside the tents were numerous airplanes. Weber eased up on the throttle, got Durand's attention, and pointed at the planes.

"The base is just ahead; we're approaching from the southeast. I will come in low, parallel to that road they're using as a runway. Get your camera ready."

"Get me close enough to those planes so I can photograph them. The place looks deserted--those scumbags must still be asleep. Let's give them a rude wake-up call."

Weber nodded his assent. He banked the plane until it was parallel to the farm road. Then he leveled off, cut power, and edged the stick forward. The Nieuport's nose dropped slightly and settled into a quiet, downward glideslope. Weber maintained that angle until they hovered just above the road. Then he retracted the stick and added power.

The Gnome engine roared to life, shattering the predawn stillness. The thrust pushed Weber and Durand against their seats and stabilized the plane on a low, horizontal trajectory. As they thundered down the road, only a few meters off the ground, Durand began snapping pictures of the approaching hangars and planes. Then, something unexpected happened. A partially clad German stepped out of a latrine, drew a pistol, and started shooting at the Nieuport. Durand dropped his camera, grabbed his sidearm, and returned fire. He and the German exchanged fire until the Nieuport was well out of range.

"Bring us around again, Weber! I want to drill that bastard!"

"Be sensible, Durand, we just poked a hornet's nest. If we buzz them again, we're going to get stung. And if we don't leave immediately, every fighter on that base will be up here trying to blow us out of the sky."

Durand opened his mouth, about to object, but then thought again. He turned, took a final look at the enemy base, and settled back in his seat. "Alright, Weber, do what you must."

Spring 1915: Temporary Luftschiffhafen, Southeastern Germany

Göring bolted upright in his cot, awakened by the intensifying wail of an aircraft engine. It was a familiar sound but not one he expected to hear at this hour of the morning. Planes produced that howl when pilots pegged the throttle and the prop spooled to maximum RPM. However, no pilot in his right mind would risk a takeoff at this hour. There wasn't enough daylight. Another thing that didn't make sense was the plane's apparent trajectory. Its yowl was growing stronger, implying the aircraft was approaching rather than leaving the aerodrome. Perhaps this wasn't a takeoff but an aborted landing. Maybe the pilot had come in too fast and was now standing on the throttle, trying to climb out so he could circle the base and try again. Still, if that's all it was, why was his gut telling him something sinister was about to happen?

Gunfire erupted, ending Göring's conjectures. He shouted at the men who were still sleeping in their cots. "Raus, raus! We are under attack!"

Göring found his pants, hurriedly pulled them on, and ran outside. What he witnessed in the predawn light shook him to his core. An enemy aircraft was bearing down on him, hugging the ground, and closing fast. Göring knew instantly that unless he took evasive action, the plane would cut him to pieces. Instinctively, he dropped to his knees and put his hands over his head.

The ground vibrated as the plane roared overhead. Göring tensed, fearing that the aircraft's propeller or landing gear would decapitate him. Instead, all he felt was the blast from the plane's prop wash. The gust was so strong that it knocked him flat on his back.

Göring got back on his feet and appraised the enemy aircraft as it circled away. The craft appeared to be Nieuport--a single-engine biplane with two cockpits. Seated behind the pilot was an observer, and that man was trading fire with someone on the ground. Göring stood transfixed, watching the duel unfold, until he heard a bullet ricochet off a nearby rock. He dove behind a fuel tank and cursed his stupidity after taking stock of what he had done. If the tank took a round, he'd be toast. He fled the tank and found cover behind a nearby plane.

When the Nieuport was a distant speck in the predawn sky, Göring returned to the tent where he had spent the night. He expected to find it empty and was surprised to see Rolf lying on his cot with a blanket over his head.

"Rolf, wake up! Surely, you didn't sleep through that. You must have had one too many schnapps last night. Can you believe the enemy stooped this low? Strafing our base and before sunrise, no less. And they think we are barbarians?"

When Rolf failed to respond, Göring felt a twinge of anxiety. He marched over to Rolf's cot and slowly peeled back the blanket. A flinty odor accosted his nostrils. Blood and pulp were draining from a ragged hole just above Rolf's ear. The dark ooze trickled down through Rolf's hair, across his cheek, down his neck, and onto his pillow. Göring knew, from the quantity of blood that had soaked into Rolf's pillow, that his friend had bled out. This was his first encounter with death, and the sight and smell of it made him wretch.

◆◆◆

The following morning, Göring accompanied Rolf's body to a nearby rail station. He watched as the casket was loaded into a freight car, then found a seat in a second-class coach and settled in for the five-hour ride to Munich. He made this trip to spare Rolf's wife and children some needless suffering. Protocol called for burying Rolf in a temporary grave behind the aerodrome. The military, while at war, considered it impractical to retrieve and preserve bodies or ship them long distances from battlefields. Instead, Hauptman Schmidt would promise Rolf's wife that the military would exhume and return her husband's body after the war.

Göring had been friends with Rolf since childhood and was acquainted with Rolf's wife. He knew he'd never be able to face Rolf's wife if he allowed the military to dump her husband's corpse in a pasture. He had argued with Hauptman Schmidt and eventually been granted a leave to transport Rolf's body to Munich. Before departing, he had called Rolf's wife, told her the bad news, and suggested that she make funeral arrangements. She had fallen apart like most wives who had suddenly become war widows. Later, after she had composed herself, she had agreed to meet Göring at the Munich Hauptbahnhof, or central rail station.

Göring was angry and disillusioned when he returned to the aerodrome from Munich. He accused Loezer of betraying him when he discovered that Loezer had invited Karl, Rolf's former observer, to accompany him on missions. Loezer resented Göring's accusation but apologized nonetheless, and the two men put aside their differences and began flying missions again. Loezer soon discovered that Göring was not the same man he had known previously. The new Göring was outspoken and stubborn. He frequently questioned Loezer's judgment and refused to obey orders during missions.

At first, Loezer was merely annoyed with Göring's obstinate and erratic behavior, but as time wore on, he began to lose patience and question his comrade's fitness for flight duty. Göring, Loezer believed, had become untrustworthy and dangerous. He had sought counsel from other pilots, and they had urged him to end his relationship with Göring. Something had to be done, he realized, and soon. But what? He feared how Göring would react if he refused to fly with him.

One night, things came to a head when the men were drinking schnapps after the evening meal.

"So Göring," Karl asked, "did you comfort Rolf's widow while you were in Munich?"

"Unlike you, Karl, I am not a reptile," Göring replied. "Rolf was my friend. I wouldn't take advantage of his grieving widow."

"Me, a reptile? From what I hear," Karl countered, "you have become cold-blooded."

"Why? Because I told Hauptman Schmidt that we should cross the border, find the enemy's aerodromes, and kill the French and British aviators while they're sleeping?"

"But it's more than that," added Gerhard, another of the squadron's pilots. "You don't follow orders. After you and Loezer leave the base, you try to take control of the mission and the plane. You tell Loezer to ignore the Commandant's instructions. You're only an observer, but you're ordering the pilot to do things that will get you both killed."

Friedrich, one of the more senior pilots, turned to face Göring. "Is this true, Göring?"

"It's not what you think. Two days ago, we were scouting enemy artillery positions when a Nieuport strayed into our airspace. I demanded that Bruno pursue the Nieuport and shoot it down. It was a righteous kill. The bastards in that plane could have been the ones who strafed our base and killed Rolf."

Friedrich frowned and shook his head. He scanned the faces of other pilots, trying to gauge their reactions. "Let me see if I understand, Göring. You abandoned your mission to avenge a grudge--and risked Loezer's life and his plane in the process?"

"Look, we have to change our tactics if we want to win this war. The German pilot's code of honor has outlived its usefulness. It's archaic and makes us look weak. We must be just as cunning and savage as the enemy, if not more so."

"Define cunning and savage, Göring. How exactly would German pilots project strength rather than weakness?"

"If you were a strong pilot, you would see the enemy for what they are-

-vermin to be eradicated. A true warrior would shoot the enemy pilots and observers on sight. It's not enough to blow Allied planes out of the sky. We must crush invaders in a way that makes them and their leaders fear us. It is the only way to destroy an enemy's will to fight and prevent future attacks."

Karl had heard enough. "Göring's never flown a plane, let alone served as a combat pilot, yet he knows what's best for Germany's aviators."

"But Karl," Göring retorted, "you are the one who said that the Allies think of us as animals--an inferior race that should be eliminated from the face of the earth. To survive as a people, we must demonstrate our superiority, even if it means stooping to the Allies' level and mimicking their brutal tactics."

"Big talk for an observer, Göring. I think you should put up or shut up," Karl sneered.

"What do you mean by that?"

"Go to flight school and learn how to fly. When you can keep a plane in the air, come back and prove to us that you're worthy of this rhetoric you're spewing."

Göring nodded. "No need to bait me, Karl. I've already enrolled in a flight school. We'll soon see who's the superior pilot--you or me."

Chapter 2

Winter 1920: Stockholm, Sweden

"Throw him out of the plane when you're high over the Baltic."

"Carl, be serious," Weber replied. "You know I can't do that."

"Ok, then make it look like an accident. Don't buckle his safety harness during the preflight check. Wait until you're offshore, and then tell him you will do some aerobatics. Bank into a barrel roll and, when you're upside down, let the bastard eject and drop like a rock. Be sure the plane's at maximum altitude so he'll have plenty of time to shit his pants before he splashes down and is eaten by sharks."

"Carl, what did I tell you about that kind of language?"

"Well, 'bastard' is the only English word that truly fits Sigge. Would you prefer that I call him 'Skit för Hjärnor'? That's what my Swedish friends call him."

"Look, you're missing the point. You can't harm people just because you dislike them, even if you try to make it look like an accident. And, I am offended that you'd implicate me in a murder. I am not an assassin."

Carl shrugged. "You killed people in the war."

"Don't change the subject, Carl," Weber countered.

"Yes, but Sigge hurt me first. He is a bully, and turnabout is fair play."

"Look, we talked about this. If you retaliate, Sigge will do something worse to you. The feud won't stop; it will escalate. If you want things to improve, you must change the nature of your relationship with Sigge."

"I don't have a relationship with that turd. Sigge and I are enemies."

"You do have a relationship with Sigge, just not a positive one."

"Yeah, I positively hate him."

Weber had picked up his son, Carl, at the end of the school day and was driving toward a western suburb of Stockholm where he and his wife, Anna, had purchased a home. Carl was six years old and attended Vasa Elementary School. Several evenings ago, at the dinner table, Carl had announced that a classmate named Sigge was bullying him.

"Look, Carl, I'll repeat what I told you, but I want you to stop plotting revenge and get on board with our plan. Agreed?"

"Yeah, I guess so."

"Tell me again what Sigge does to you."

"Plenty. He pushes me around. He tells other kids that I'm weak. He takes my lunch money. Should I go on?"

"All right, *why* do you think Sigge does those things? What is he getting out of it? What's in it for him?"

"I don't know. Who knows what goes on in a gorilla's mind?"

"Come on, Carl. I am waiting for an answer."

"Uh, maybe he needs money. Or, maybe he does it for fun."

"Could it be that your suffering makes him feel powerful? Maybe he tries to make you appear weak so that other kids will think he's strong and fear him. If there's one thing I learned in the war, it's that bullies try to make themselves feel powerful by dominating others."

"Most kids are scared of Sigge. I am afraid of him, too."

Weber smiled at Carl and gave him an affirming pat on the back. "I know, son. But our plan is going to fix that. Just stick to our plan."

"I don't see how airplane rides will fix this."

"Trust me. At the core of every relationship, there's an exchange system. Sigge's given you a raw deal, so we will change how he does business and shake up the exchange system in your relationship with Sigge.

"But how?"

"We're going to remake your image and change what Sigge wants from you. If all goes according to plan, Sigge will soon find it difficult, if not impossible, to bully you."

When Weber arrived at his house, he parked in the driveway and ushered Carl through the front door. His stomach growled as he stepped inside--the entire house smelled of freshly baked bread. A smile creased Weber's face. Anna was home. She must have punched out early and spent the day baking. He glanced toward the kitchen and shouted a greeting.

"Somebody's been baking! When do we eat?"

"Wash up, both of you, and make yourselves presentable," Anna replied. "Only well-groomed men are welcome at the table. Scruffy men will go hungry!"

Weber glanced at Carl and feigned a grimace.

"Son, we just received our marching orders. Do your duty and meet me at the dinner table in 10 minutes."

Anna's tone of voice reminded Weber of the day he met her. Near the war's end, he moved to Stockholm and took a job as a pilot for the fledgling Svensk-Luft Trafik Airlines. One of his regular routes was a round-trip flight from Stockholm to Copenhagen. One morning, he arrived at the Stockholm airport and found it socked in with fog. To wait out the delay, he had driven to a nearby café, ordered breakfast, and waited for conditions to improve. When the fog finally lifted, he returned to the airport, completed his preflight check, and boarded the plane. Upon entering the cockpit, he was surprised to find a woman sitting in the copilot's seat.

Weber would never forget what happened next. Politely, he ordered the woman out of the cockpit and told her to find a seat in the aircraft's cabin. The woman bristled, looked him straight in the eye, and refused. After a long, uncomfortable silence, the woman spoke. "You need to read your flight schedules more carefully, Mr. Weber. I just joined Svensk-Luft Trafik Airlines as a copilot and will accompany you to Copenhagen. Now, take your seat and prepare for takeoff."

Weber couldn't admit it then, but he had been smitten instantly. Anna was a Nordic beauty. She was blonde, blue-eyed, and svelte, and never failed to turn heads when she walked into a room. He had apologized to Anna before the flight reached Copenhagen and invited her to dinner that evening. In the following weeks, he worked hard to win Anna's heart. They dated for a while and then married. Nine months later, Carl arrived.

When the meal finished and Carl went to bed, Weber joined Anna in front of the fireplace. Anna put her arm around Weber, cocked her head, and looked inquisitively into his eyes.

"When will you tell me about this plan that you and Carl have hatched?"

"Now is as good a time as any. We modeled our plan on a classic military maneuver. The first step is to separate Sigge from his troops. Then, once Sigge's defenseless and vulnerable, we'll lure him in and disarm him."

"You understand that these are 6-year-old boys, don't you? And Sigge is a childhood bully, not Attila the Hun."

"Look, the plan's principles are sound. We have to adjust the tactics to suit 6-year-old boys."

"So, how do airplane rides figure into your plan?"

"Carl will ask each of Sigge's toadies if they'd like an airplane ride. Boys his age find airplanes irresistible. He'll start with Sigge's best friend, then invite another friend, and so on. Once Sigge's friends have flown above the clouds, they won't stop talking about it. Sigge, of course, will be envious. He'll soon realize that Carl is his ticket to an airplane ride and that bullying Carl isn't going to win him an invitation. If he's smart, he'll change tactics and try to befriend Carl, even if his intentions are insincere. When that happens, we'll have disarmed the little tyrant. Sigge will stop bullying Carl because he'll see that it's a losing proposition. He won't risk bullying Carl if it means forfeiting the plane ride."

Anna nodded tentatively, not entirely convinced. "What happens after Sigge gets an airplane ride? Will he bully Carl again?"

Weber wasn't in the mood to discuss the plan's limitations, so he changed the subject.

"Hey, we'll cross that bridge when we come to it. By the way, did you see that Svensk-Luft is adding a nonstop flight to Tromsø? Some wealthy fur traders do business there. It will be the company's first destination north of the Arctic Circle. The weather is unpredictable, particularly in the winter, so we will face significant flight challenges. I imagine you and I will be asked to fly that route occasionally."

"That might be the case, Robert, but promise me something. Don't be the first pilot to volunteer for that route."

Winter 1920: Svensk-Luft Trafik Airlines, Morning Staff Meeting

A detour during Robert's and Anna's morning commute made them late for the Svensk-Luft staff meeting. When they arrived, Oscar Johansson, the airline's owner, stood at the front of the room, addressing a small group of company employees, including pilots, ground crew, and sales personnel. Johansson acknowledged the Webers and directed them toward two empty chairs.

"Glad you could join us, Robert and Anna. Now, what was I saying? Oh, yes. Demand is up, and new routes are forthcoming, so the airline must add personnel and planes. I'm going to review company policy because there are new employees in our group today. First, this is a business; if Svensk-Luft Trafik Airlines doesn't turn a profit, it will cease to exist, and you will lose your jobs. Second, passengers are our lifeblood; if you don't meet their expectations, they will take their business elsewhere, and you will lose your job. Any questions?"

No one said a word, so Johansson continued.

"Pilots, I know many of you flew during the war, but the war is over, and you must eschew radical flight tactics. This is a commercial airline. Passengers want smooth, comfortable flights. They don't want to be jostled, bounced off bulkheads, and forced to puke in their laps. Also, you must conserve company resources—when possible, cruise at higher altitudes to reduce wind resistance and save fuel. The same goes for engine speed;

throttle back during descents and cut to idle once you've established a glide path. Copilots, when you're airborne and on a stable flight path, check on passengers and attend to their needs. Passenger safety is your responsibility. Ground crew, work on speeding up the turnarounds. There have been too many delayed departures and late arrivals lately. Sales staff, don't offer passengers discounts without my approval. *Now,* are there any questions?"

The room was silent.

"Hearing none, I want to introduce new personnel. Hermann and Gunter, will you please stand?"

Two men stood briefly near the front of the room, nodded toward the group, and then sat down again.

"Hermann Göring and Gunter Meissner are German citizens, but they come to us from Denmark, where Hermann's made a living testing Fokker aircraft and selling airplane rides to the public. Gunter is a former pilot who works as a flight engineer for Fokker Aircraft in the Netherlands. He will evaluate our aircraft maintenance, find ways to make our flights safer and more economical, and help us test some new Fokker aircraft that will handle more passengers and fly longer distances."

Spring 1920: Svensk-Luft Trafik Airlines Maintenance Hangar

Even though it was Weber's day off, he got up early and drove to his office at the Stockholm airport to complete some unfinished paperwork. He parked outside the Svensk-Luft hangar, went inside, and strode through the maintenance area toward his office at the rear of the building. Halfway there, he noticed "his" plane--the Junker F.13 that he regularly flew--parked in the left rear corner of the building, with its nose angled against the wall. The sight struck him as odd because his plane wasn't due for maintenance until after his next round-trip to Copenhagen. He glanced around the hangar, searching in vain for a maintenance crew member. Then something caught his eye: a guy in dirty overalls stood under his plane's nose.

Weber surveyed the plane as he approached it. Someone had removed the cowl, leaving the engine bay exposed. Various mechanical bits and pieces, many of them engine parts, lay scattered about on the hangar floor. Baffled, he tried to make sense of what he was seeing. No form of routine maintenance called for this level of engine disassembly. So what was going on?

Concerned now, Weber rushed toward the front of the plane. As he rounded the right wing, a man holding a wrench turned to face him. It was Gunter.

"Gunter, what is the meaning of this? My Junkers is not due for service;

even if it was, there is no call for tearing down the engine. This Mercedes 6-cylinder doesn't have enough flight time to justify an inspection of its pistons."

Gunter dropped the wrench and reached for an object hanging from a chain he wore around his neck. He fingered the object as Weber approached.

"Relax Weber. This isn't your plane; it belongs to Johansson. He hired me to make his aircraft more efficient. This Junkers will burn less fuel when I'm finished with it."

"Why wasn't I notified?"

"You're just a pilot. Flight jockeys only care about whether a plane takes off, stays in the air, and lands. I am an aeronautical engineer, and I don't answer to you. Talk to Johansson if you don't like it."

Weber looked for Johansson but discovered that he was away on business. He finished his paperwork, drove home, and told himself to forget about Gunter. But that was easier said than done. Something about Gunter's behavior bothered him. The German seemed surprised to see him and, when confronted, reacted like a kid caught with his hand in a cookie jar. Why had Gunter been so defensive? Was he hiding something? Weber decided to find out.

Later that evening, Weber returned to the airport and found his plane parked outside the Svensk-Luft hangar. The Junkers appeared intact, but Weber knew that appearances could be deceiving. He walked around the plane and scrutinized it. Nothing seemed amiss. When he reached the plane's nose, he lifted the cowl flap and inspected the engine. The sleek Mercedes 6-cylinder appeared to be unharmed. Weber ran his eye over the fittings, checking to ensure that Gunter had reinstalled each one correctly. After all, Gunter wasn't the only aeronautical engineer who worked for this airline. Weber had decided to keep mum about his technical abilities--no sense triggering a pissing match with Gunter. And, if Gunter was up to something, it made sense to conceal his skills and use them to his advantage--just as he was doing now.

Finding nothing amiss, Weber conducted a preflight check, crawled into the cockpit, and fired the engine. The true test of the plane's fitness, he knew, would be a test flight. He edged the Junkers onto the runway, pulled the throttle back full, and let it accelerate until the cool evening air enveloped the wings and lifted the plane off the ground. He kept the plane low--skimming a few feet above the airport's empty runways. He wanted to be near the ground if the plane suffered engine failure or experienced some other unforeseen problem. But the test flight went off without a hitch. Weber landed the plane and returned it to its position outside the hanger. Perhaps, he concluded, Gunter was on the level. Maybe he should cut the man some slack.

Spring 1920: Business Office, Svensk-Luft Trafik Airlines

Weber knocked on the door to Johansson's office and waited for a response. He knew the boss wanted to see him, but he wasn't sure why. Whatever it was, he hoped Johansson would keep it brief. He only had an hour before his regularly scheduled flight to Copenhagen and needed to finish his preflight check. Just as Weber reached the end of his patience, Johansson replied.

"Come in."

"Boss, you wanted to see me?"

"Yes, sit down, Weber. I summoned you because I want you to help me grow this airline. Our Junkers aircraft accommodate only four passengers. Demand for air travel is increasing, and Svensk-Luft would become more profitable if we could transport more people. Gunter tells me that Fokker is developing a new aircraft--called the F7--that will seat 12 passengers. I want you to test-fly a prototype of that aircraft on some of our routes and see if it suits our needs. Are you willing to do that?"

"Sure, boss. When will the plane be ready?"

"Gunter will ferry the plane to Stockholm this weekend, and you can start testing next week. Schedule some flight time with him and learn how to fly the plane. The F7 is a complex and demanding aircraft--it has three engines and is considerably larger and less maneuverable than the Junkers. Not all of our pilots will be able to master the F7, but I know you can, and I want you to be honest with me about the plane's airworthiness and suitability for our flight routes. We're fortunate to have Gunter on our staff, but the man is a Fokker factory representative with a vested interest in selling us the aircraft."

"OK, boss. I'll work with Gunter and let you know what I think."

After completing the return leg of his Copenhagen run, Weber returned to his desk in the Svensk-Luft hangar and updated his flight log. While he wrote his last entry, a distant buzzing or droning interrupted his concentration. The sound had an odd harmonic quality that defied comprehension. The only association that came to mind was a swarm of angry bees.

As minutes passed, the sound grew louder, and its resonance increased to the point that it triggered vibrations in the hangar's ceiling girders. Weber got out of his chair, ran outside, and peered at the sky. He was just in time to see a huge aircraft--a plane of unimaginable proportions--roar overhead. As Weber watched in awe, the pilot banked and aligned the aircraft with the nearest runway and initiated a long, slow descent. The plane eventually touched down and taxied toward the hangar.

Weber scrutinized the aircraft as it approached. So this is the F7, he thought to himself. The plane had a single wing mounted on top of the fuselage, a wide body, and three large radial engines--one under each wing and another on the aircraft's nose.

When the pilot reached the hangar, he parked the F7 alongside Weber's plane and powered down the engines. The massive F7 made the Junkers look like a toy.

The cockpit door opened, and Gunter stepped out on the wing. He glanced around, saw Weber, and waved. Weber reluctantly returned the gesture. Although the F7 intrigued him, he had a feeling that flying it with Gunter would be insufferable.

◆◆◆

From the pilot's seat of the F7, Weber kept an eye on the cold front that had appeared north of their current position. The day's forecast contained no mention of severe weather, but dark clouds nonetheless had materialized and drifted into their flight path.

He and Gunter were on the return leg to Stockholm after having flown the F7 to Copenhagen. Gunter, who sat in the copilot's seat, had actively coached Weber during the first leg of the trip. Now, for the journey home, Gunter sat back and let Weber fly the plane. He kept a careful eye on Weber's actions but gave him sufficient leeway to explore the plane's capabilities and learn from his mistakes. He only barked directives or took over the controls when Weber was about to commit an egregious error.

After finding an altitude relatively free of turbulence, Weber trimmed the plane, set a course for Stockholm, and settled in for the remainder of the flight. Now that the aircraft had a stable cruising altitude, it practically flew itself. It wasn't long before the constant drone of the engines, and the absence of discourse between the pilots threatened to put both Gunter and Weber to sleep. Gunter, recognizing what was happening, broke the silence.

"You catch on quickly, Weber. Where did you learn to fly?"

"In the United States, near Boston."

"I figured as much from your accent."

"Your instructors must be proud, Gunter. You're an accomplished pilot."

Gunter smiled and nodded. “I was an ace fighter pilot during the war, and so was Hermann.”

“Tell me about Göring. Sounds like you’ve known him a long time.”

“Yes, we roamed the streets of Munich together as kids. I learned to fly in Munich, and Hermann attended flight school in Freiburg during the war and qualified as a Jagdflieger--a fighter pilot. We served together in Jagdstaffel 5 and flew the first twin-engine fighters. It was an exciting time that I sorely miss. Unlike me, Hermann became a true hero. His actions and speeches raised the morale of fighter pilots everywhere. By the war’s end, he commanded Baron von Richthofen’s former squadron and had shot down more than 20 Allied planes. He won many awards, including the Verdienstorden or Blue Max in March of 1918. You probably know it by the French name--the Pour le Mérite.”

“Impressive.”

“So, Weber, did you fly during the war?”

“I did.”

“With whom?”

“The French Air Service.”

Gunter’s nose wrinkled as if accosted by a putrid odor. “Really? You flew with those arrogant, unethical FAS pukes?”

“Look, Gunter, the war is over. Let bygones be bygones.”

“Easy for you to say, Weber. Your people didn’t have the Treaty of Versailles shoved down their throats.”

“Look, Gunter, everyone who served during the war suffered. No one emerged unscathed. But it’s over now, and the wounds won’t heal if you keep picking at the scabs.”

“Don’t be naïve, Weber. How can wounds heal if they’re ignored and left to bleed?”

Suddenly, the F7 hit turbulence and heaved Weber hard against his seatbelt. Taken by surprise, he shifted his gaze away from Gunter, looked through the windscreen, and surveyed the sky in front of the plane. Everywhere he looked, there were dark, angry clouds. The cold front had accelerated its southern sweep, slammed into the prevailing warm air, and set off a massive thunderstorm. Weber chided himself for attending to Gunter’s whining. While he’d been distracted, the plane had flown headlong into the storm.

Now in the thick of it, the F7 pitched, yawed right, and threatened to stall. Gunter gestured wildly and began spewing obscenities. Weber ignored Gunter’s rant and concentrated on bringing the big bird back under his control. He throttled up all three engines, gently retracted the yoke, and peddled the rudder leftward. The plane leveled and began to recover, but then lightning struck the nose, and the forward engine burst into flames. Thick, black smoke funneled back onto the windscreen, obstructing Weber's view. The acrid stench of burning wires filled the cockpit.

As Weber fought for control, Gunter fell silent and blankly stared through the windscreen. He opened his shirt collar, withdrew the chain that hung around his neck, and began fingering some kind of pendant. Curious, Weber briefly took his eyes off the instrument panel and glanced at Gunter's fingers. He was manipulating a dark copper object that resembled a shell casing.

As they flew deeper into the storm, Gunter became more agitated. He stopped fingering the pendant, shoved it in his mouth, and held it under his tongue. He fidgeted in his seat for several minutes, then unbuckled his seatbelt, grabbed the upper rim of the instrument panel, and levered himself up against the windscreen. After scanning the airspace in front of the plane, he spat out the pendant and started shouting.

"Two o'clock high, Loezer! Enemy fighter on approach. Take evasive action now! And look there: ninety degrees and closing--two FAS grunts in a Nieuport."

Hurriedly, Gunter reached into his pockets and withdrew a handful of metal objects that bore the same coppery color as his pendant. He inserted the metal objects into his mouth one by one until his cheeks resembled those of an overfed chipmunk. Then he reached into his flight bag, withdrew a pistol, and released the weapon's ammo clip. One by one, he spat bullets into his hand and inserted them into the clip. When the clip was full, he shoved it into the gun, retracted the slide, and chambered a round.

Weber realized that he couldn't sit there and do nothing. Gunter had a loaded gun in his hand, and he was waving it around and shouting gibberish about enemy fighters. His flight instructor had become a lunatic.

"Gunter, what is the matter with you? What are you doing?"

"Obey orders, Loezer, or I will have you court marshaled!"

"Who the hell is Loezer? Give me the gun, Gunter, and sit down and shut up! You're out of your mind and endangering this flight. Get a grip! You're going to get us killed."

Gunter showed no sign of yielding, so Weber stood, grabbed the gun, and wrenched it out of Gunter's hand. Gunter cocked a fist and lunged, his face contorted in wild-eyed fury. Without thinking, Weber slapped Gunter across the face with the back of his hand, shoved him into his seat, and wrapped the seatbelt around his torso. He winched the belt around the armrest and held it tightly until Gunter stopped struggling. When he was satisfied that Gunter was no longer a threat, he released the belt and returned to his seat.

The plane, fortunately, had retained its trim and remained on course. It had passed through the worst of the storm, and heavy rain had extinguished the engine fire. Weber offered a prayer of thanks and raised his estimation of the F7's flight capabilities. The plane had successfully navigated weather that surely would have brought down his Junkers.

Weber's estimation of Gunter, on the other hand, plummeted. The man was a loose cannon, and it would be a cold day in hell before he'd fly with him again. After he subdued Gunter, the German had pulled a flask from his flight bag, quaffed a large volume of schnapps, and fallen into a drunken stupor. Weber had to finish the flight and land the plane in Stockholm without Gunter's assistance.

◆◆◆

After returning to Stockholm safely, Weber tried to avoid Gunter. He debated reporting the incident to Johansson but held his tongue. Days passed without incident and then he ran into Gunter on the hangar floor late one afternoon.

"What do you have to say for yourself, Weber?"

"Nothing you'd want to hear, Gunter."

"You know, Weber, our flight taught me something about you. Something I suspect you'd like to keep hidden."

"Oh, and what's that?"

"Stress brings out the worst in you. You're erratic under pressure and have a strong propensity toward violence."

"Me? That's a projection, Gunter. You're attributing your personality flaws to me instead of recognizing them in yourself. I did what was necessary to keep us airborne and alive. When the engine caught fire, you lost touch with reality and started yelling about imaginary bogies. Then you loaded a pistol and waved it in my face. Come on, Gunter, what choice did I have? You were a danger to me and yourself."

"Ach, so now I see another hidden aspect of your character. You not only hit coworkers but spin lies to cover up your aggression. You are an aggressor and a liar."

Weber shook his head in disgust and walked away. An hour later, he was in Johansson's office describing how Gunter had reacted to the engine fire. Johansson listened but didn't appear sympathetic.

"Listen, Weber. Gunter was just here telling me that you flew directly into a storm and lost control of the plane. He said you panicked under pressure, and when he tried to help you regain control of the plane, you punched him and tied him to his seat."

"That is a bald-faced lie."

"These are serious charges, Weber. Gunter was in command of that flight, and you were an apprentice copilot. If what he says is true, you struck a superior officer, restrained him against his will, and seized control of the plane. In maritime circles, you'd be guilty of mutiny. Consider yourself lucky that I don't fire you."

"Fire me? Are you joking? Think about how long I have worked for you, Johansson. You just hired Gunter--how much do you actually know about him? He isn't the man you think he is; if you keep him around, you will regret it. The man is imbalanced and shouldn't be flying airplanes. Hell, he shouldn't be allowed to drive an automobile. Don't say I didn't warn you."

Chapter 3

Spring 1920: Stockholm, Sweden

The Hökens Näbb reeked of cigarettes and stale beer. Weber could almost feel the cloying stench seeping into his skin. He hadn't intended to stop at a pub on the way home from work, but Göring had insisted, and he'd felt obligated to accept the invitation.

He and the other employees of Svensk-Luft Trafik Airlines had driven to the pub after sitting through another of Johansson's mind-numbing staff meetings. Johansson, as always, had talked about the company's financial woes and asked the staff to help him devise ways to improve the airline's revenues. One ground crew member had suggested expanding the timetable to include evening or night flights, and Johansson had asked the pilots whether such an undertaking was feasible. Avionics had improved since the war, but instrument-dependent flight remained risky during daylight hours, let alone at night when obstacles such as buildings, towers, and mountains were shrouded in darkness. A few aviators scoffed at the idea, but others seemed receptive and asked for more time to consider the proposition.

Once inside the Hökens Näbb, Weber spotted Göring, Meissner, and several other aviators at a corner table. A few members of the ground crew sat amongst them. The men were swilling vodka, telling vulgar jokes, and laughing raucously. Weber was glad he'd encouraged Anna to forgo this social event. He knew the men's alcohol-fueled repartee would only become more vulgar as the evening wore on.

Weber walked to where the men were sitting and greeted them with a brief nod. He found a vacant chair across from Meissner and Göring, seated himself at the table, and signaled the waiter for a beer. Gunter glanced at Weber and then muttered something indecipherable in Göring's ear. Göring smiled, nodded, and then looked intently at Weber.

"Glad you could join us, Weber. Where's your lovely wife?"

"She had a previous engagement but sent her regards."

"Too bad. I wanted to ask her opinion about night flights."

Göring swiveled in his chair and systematically scanned the faces of the other men at the table. The men fell silent as Göring's intimidating glare fell upon them. When Göring had everyone's attention, he looked back at Weber. "So, Weber, let's hear your thoughts about night flights."

"Can't say that I favor the idea. Pilots who depend entirely on instruments or fly without visual referents increase their flight risks."

A quizzical look appeared on Göring's face. "Are you speaking hypothetically or from experience?"

"I am giving you my opinion, but it's based on a night flight I did during the war."

"I see. Tell us about that, will you?"

Weber didn't want to talk about the war, especially in the company of men who had fought for Germany, so he tried to deflect Göring's question. "There isn't much to tell. Let's hear what others at the table have to say."

"You can't be coy, Weber, and expect the men at this table to respect your opinions. Speak your mind, and damn the consequences. Others can speak in a moment."

"Alright, if you insist. On this particular occasion, I took off just before dawn on a night with a full moon. I could see the plane's body in the moonlight, but once I gained altitude, I couldn't see anything on the ground. The plane's instruments were meager by today's standards and often malfunctioned. I relied on them as best as I could, but I frequently lost my bearings and had the sense that the plane was slipping into a roll, losing altitude, or angling toward the ground."

"Chilling, Weber. Tell us more."

"That's about it."

"Oh, come on. Surely, there's more to this story. Were you alone in the plane?"

"No, I was accompanied by an observer."

"What was your mission?"

"We were tasked with finding German aerodromes."

"I see. And what were you supposed to do if you found one?"

"Take pictures. It was a reconnaissance mission."

"So, did you find any aerodromes?"

"Just one. We had to abort the mission and return to base."

Göring hunched his shoulders and arched his eyebrows, feigning surprise. "Now you've got us on the edge of our seats, Weber. What went wrong?"

"I came in low, skimming along a farm road that the German pilots used as a runway. When I got alongside a large canvas hangar, some soldier stepped out of a latrine, drew a pistol, and started shooting. I was practically eye-to-eye with the guy and directly in his line of fire, so I maxed the throttle and did a steep climb out."

Göring paused and glanced at Gunter. Gunter replied with a slight, almost imperceptible nod. Göring stroked his mustache and then looked back at Weber.

"So tell me, Weber, did this disruption keep you from taking photos?"

"My observer got a few pictures before he had to abandon his camera and return fire."

"So your reconnaissance assignment became a combat mission."

"Let's just say that we found it necessary to defend ourselves."

"Did your observer neutralize the man who was shooting at you?"

"Not that I remember. He fired on the guy repeatedly, but the plane was pitching around, and most of his shots went wild."

There was silence at the table when Weber stopped talking. Weber glanced around, trying to gauge the men's reactions. As he did, Gunter slid out of his chair, stood, and walked toward the rear of the pub. Göring followed.

◆◆◆

Gunter entered the men's room, went to a mirror, and combed his hair. When Göring walked in, he turned and put his finger to his lips. Then he tiptoed to the rear of the room, where the toilets were located, and checked inside each stall. Satisfied that they were alone, he signaled Göring to bolt the door to the men's room.

The two men eyed each other silently for several seconds, and then Gunter spoke.

"Hermann, I think we found Rolf's killer. Would you agree? Weber as much as admitted it."

"I wouldn't call his story a confession, but I suspect you're right."

"What do you want to do about it?"

Göring drew a deep breath and stared at Gunter without really seeing him. His eyes darted back and forth as suppressed memories flooded into his consciousness. He recalled Rolf lying dead on his cot, blood cascading down his face and pooling on his pillow. That image triggered memories of Rolf in his casket, the long rail journey to Munich, and the widow's grief over her husband's death.

Sadness welled up inside Göring, nearly bringing him to tears. Then, that surge of emotion mutated into a deep, burning rage in the blink of an eye.

"Gunter, I'm so angry I can hardly speak. I've seethed over Rolf's pointless death ever since the war, but I've never had anyone I could direct my anger against—someone I could blame for killing Rolf. Now, I have a specific object for my rage; I will see Weber's face whenever I think of Rolf. His countenance will forever be etched in my mind as Rolf's killer."

As a gesture of support, Gunter put his hand on Göring's shoulder. "I share your grief and your anger, Hermann."

Göring shifted his gaze and looked Gunter directly in the eye. "So, tell me, my friend, how am I supposed to work with this murderer? Each day when I go to work, I'll see Weber and be reminded of the fact that he killed my dear friend Rolf. It will be unbearable."

"It doesn't have to be that way."

"Be realistic, Gunter, nothing can be done. I have no choice but to live with it."

"Not necessarily."

"What do you mean?"

"Say no more. I'll fix this."

"But how? What can you possibly do?"

"Don't ask. It's better if you don't know. Be patient. Let it be a surprise."

"All right, Gunter, do as you wish. I trust you."

Winter 1920: Stockholm, Sweden

Weber put Carl to bed and joined Anna in the kitchen, where she was washing dishes. He picked up a wet plate, began drying it with a towel, and thought about how he should break the news.

Johansson had summoned him at the end of the workday and abruptly announced that he'd scheduled the two of them--Anna and Weber--for a weekend flight to Tromsø. Several wealthy fur traders had pressing business in the Great White North. Travel to that part of Scandinavia was treacherous at this time of year, but the traders were flush with cash, and Johansson had an insatiable appetite for Kroners.

Weber knew that Anna considered it unwise to fly across the Arctic Circle after October and would balk at Johansson's request. Over the years, she had repeatedly begged Weber not to volunteer for the Tromsø flight during the winter months. Thus far, he had respected her wishes, even though he thought she was overestimating the risks.

Today, however, Johansson hadn't given Weber a choice. He hadn't asked whether Weber and Anna would fly the route; he had ordered them to do so. Rather than argue, Weber had simply nodded his assent. He knew that

Johansson had pocketed the traders' Kroners and wouldn't let a big payday slip through his fingers. Weber screwed up his courage and blurted out the news.

"Anna, Johansson called me into his office today and insisted we fly some wealthy fur traders to Tromsø this weekend. I know how you feel about that flight, especially this time of year, but Johansson isn't giving us a choice."

"Robert, who will care for Carl if something happens to us?"

"Nothing's going to happen to us, Anna. I checked the forecast, and there's no sign of severe weather along the route. Plus, Göring made it in and out of there last month without difficulty."

"Göring did it four weeks ago and didn't get killed. Am I supposed to find that reassuring?"

◆◆◆

Weber parked in front of a stately house in the heart of Stockholm. Anna exited the car, retrieved a suitcase from the trunk, and escorted Carl up the walkway toward the front door. As they approached the house, Linnea, Anna's younger sister, emerged and invited Anna and Carl inside her home. Weber glanced at his watch and wondered how long it would take Anna to schmoose with Linnea, bid Carl farewell, and return to the car. He was grateful to Linnea for agreeing to watch Carl, but they were overdue at the airport. In less than two hours, they needed to be in the air and on their way to Tromsø.

When Anna returned, there were tears on her cheeks. Weber patted her arm, murmured a few reassuring phrases, and then pulled away from the curb. During the remainder of their commute, they talked about Carl.

"Robert, do you remember that student-teacher conference I attended while you were in Copenhagen? I don't think I told you what Carl's teacher said."

"No, you didn't. Is Carl doing OK? What did Mr. Bjornson say?"

He said that Carl is very bright and shows a special aptitude for mathematics. Though he is still very young, he is already performing beyond other children in arithmetic. Where do you think this ability came from?

"Really? That's great! Well, you know, neither of us did poorly in math, and my great-grandfather was a math professor. He won an award for solving some supposedly insoluble math problem."

"I didn't know that."

"Did Mr. Bjornson have any recommendations?"

"He wants Carl to participate in a math enrichment program. Later, perhaps in a few years, he thinks Carl should attend a special school that would challenge his abilities. With the right preparation, he said, kids like Carl often earn admission to top-flight universities and become scientists and engineers."

"A special school--like one of those boarding academies? That would require Carl to live away from home. Could he handle that? Could *you* handle being separated from Carl?"

"Just drive, Robert. I don't want to think about that right now."

◆◆◆

Weber looked over the vast expanse of ice-covered tundra stretching below the plane. The F7 was at cruising altitude, a little over an hour from Tromsø, flying on a northwesterly heading. All three engines were spooled above the company's recommended cruise RPMs. Johansson would disapprove, but boosting the plane's airspeed was the only way Weber could compensate for lost time. They were behind schedule because one of the passengers, a Mr. Ollie Svensson, had arrived late at the Stockholm airport. Weber had argued for leaving without him, but Johansson had vetoed the idea.

Thus far, the flight had annoyed Weber, but it had been particularly unpleasant for Anna. It wasn't as if the plane was overloaded. There were only four passengers aboard--all men. But one of the men--Svensson--had been drunk and disorderly from the start.

After takeoff, Anna introduced herself to each passenger. She learned that three men were fur traders, and the fourth--Svensson--owned a company that marketed pickled herring. She had laughed to herself when Svensson described his occupation because the rotund and balding Swede was as pickled as the product he was peddling. Every few minutes, he would withdraw a flask from his suit pocket and pour alcohol down his throat. He had been obnoxious when he boarded the plane and had become increasingly belligerent as the flight progressed. Before takeoff, he had ignored Anna's safety instructions. As the aircraft encountered turbulence, he refused to take his seat and buckle his seatbelt. Anna, who had positioned herself in the cabin to assist passengers, threw up her hands in disgust and marched into the cockpit.

"I've had it, Robert. Let me take the controls, and you can go into the cabin and deal with Svensson. I'm so pissed off I could scream. That drunk annoys the other passengers and is a danger to himself. He ignores everything I say."

"We should be on the ground in 45 minutes."

"Robert, did you hear me?"

"Yes, okay, you take the plane, and I'll go back there."

Weber left the cockpit and entered the cabin. Svensson was out of his seat, bellowing at one of the fur merchants--a man named Lars Sodergaard. Weber walked to where Svensson was standing, grabbed him by the arm, and hauled him back to his seat. Svensson started to protest, but Weber forcibly pushed him into his seat and fastened the seatbelt.

"Remain seated with your belt buckled. If I find you out of your seat again, I will crack that hatch and toss you out of this plane. If you survive the fall, you'll have to slog across two hundred miles of frozen tundra to reach Tromsø. You hear me, Svensson?"

The color drained from Svensson's face. He raised his arm, gave Weber a pathetic salute, and then whimpered. "Yes, captain. Whatever you say, captain."

When Weber returned to the cockpit, Anna greeted him with a scowl and pointed toward the windscreen.

"Robert, take a look at the horizon. That's more than a squall. It's a massive storm, and it's headed right for us."

Weber looked past the nose of the plane. Anna was right. Dead ahead, heavy black clouds churned along the entire length of the horizon. Weber inhaled sharply and felt the adrenaline kick in. Not to worry, he told himself. I've been in tighter spots during the war. Besides, this tough old bird can handle a bit of rough weather. It's not like someone's shooting at us.

After propping up his confidence, Weber shifted into problem-solving mode. His first thought was to find an escape route, but after scanning the horizon more thoroughly, he lost his resolve. There didn't seem to be a ceiling at the base of the storm, nor was there room to maneuver above the clouds. The storm front was one continuous wall that stretched from the tundra to the highest reaches of the stratosphere.

Weber's indecisiveness unnerved Anna, so she attempted to take control of the situation. "Robert, there's no going back because we're past the point of no return. Normally, I'd search for an alternate heading to take us around the storm. But this is a big storm, and we're low on fuel. Also, I don't know any place to put down besides Tromsø. Do you want to try to set down on the tundra before visibility drops to zero?"

Before Weber could consider that option, the left engine coughed and began to decelerate. It whined for several minutes as it lost RPMs. Then it sputtered and quit.

"What the hell!" Weber yelled. He scanned the fuel gauges. The tanks were low, but none were out of fuel. Anna feathered the prop and attempted to restart the engine, but it failed to catch. The left wing dipped, tilting the flight deck, so Anna boosted the right engine's throttle and leveled the plane.

Now, Anna's self-assurance began to falter. "Talk to me, Robert. What should we do?"

"With one engine out, we'll burn less fuel and gain some additional flight time. The storm is moving west, so I propose that we fly east and hope we can find its terminus. Maybe we'll get lucky and find a place where the winds have died down enough to cross the storm front."

"But this is an immense storm, Robert. We have no idea how long it might take to find its eastern boundary."

"I know that, Anna, but an eastern flight path will keep us over land. Plus, it's better than putting down on a surface as uneven as the tundra. The landscape looks smooth from the air, but jagged ice and rock outcroppings are everywhere."

"Okay, I'm bringing us around to a 90-degree heading. We'll fly east, perpendicular to the storm, and try to preserve enough fuel to travel an alternate route if we find one. Stay alert, and watch for a path through the storm or a safe place to put down."

"What should I tell the passengers?"

"Pass Svensson's flask around and tell them to quaff some liquid courage. Everyone but Svensson is going to need it."

Anna maintained the plane's altitude and easterly heading while Weber kept an eye on the northern horizon. After forty minutes of flight time, Weber still had not seen a break in the storm. He tried to remain optimistic, but their predicament's seriousness was chipping away at his confidence and eroding his composure. Not only had the plane lost an engine, but it was low on fuel. Worse still, they had abandoned their flight plan and were hundreds of miles off course.

As a professional pilot, Weber had never felt so uncertain about his aircraft's location and the availability of alternative flight routes. It wasn't as though he'd lost track of the F7's location. He knew they were on an easterly heading. The problem was that, besides Tromsø, he knew of no other airports in the vicinity. Further, he couldn't rely on visual referents to establish his bearings because they were flying over uninhabited and featureless landscapes. Worse still, daylight was fading, making it impossible to tell whether they were passing over land or water. He figured that the plane had crossed the Arctic Circle some time ago and that their heading would eventually take them over the northernmost reaches of Norway, Sweden, Finland, and Russia. That region, he knew, contained some of the most treacherous and unforgiving terrain on the planet.

"Anna, get some rest and let me take the plane. We can't remain on this heading any longer. Flying further east is reckless and probably suicidal. We should backtrack or take our chances and fly through the storm."

"Reversing course seems foolish," Robert. Tromsø isn't directly west; it has to be northwest of our current position. Given our fuel levels and accounting for magnetic declination, I suggest we bring the plane to 285 degrees and take our chances with the storm."

"Agreed. Now trade seats with me."

Anna got up, walked into the cabin, and told the passengers to remain seated and fasten their seatbelts. Then she returned to the cockpit and buckled up.

Weber throttled up the right engine, spooled down the nose engine, and elevated the left flap. The plane banked and circled. Weber found the new heading and restored power to the nose engine. Instead of generating more thrust, the nose engine wheezed, sputtered, and then decelerated. Several seconds later, its prop stopped spinning. Weber cursed. Why, he wondered, would the nose engine die in nearly the same way as the right engine? It didn't make sense. The probability that two engines would fail the same way had to be near zero.

The F7 immediately rolled left, forcing Weber to push his disbelief aside and focus on regaining control of the aircraft. Before he could react, the nose dropped sharply, and the plane plummeted. Weber raised the nose too quickly, and the airplane stalled. Thrust from the right engine swung the plane sideways, and the F7 tilted into a dangerous downward spin.

Catastrophic images flashed through Weber's mind as he fought to extricate the plane from its downward spiral. Unless he stabilized the F7 immediately, the aircraft would twist into the ground like a corkscrew.

At first, Weber's control inputs did nothing. The plane dropped like a runaway elevator, falling into a deep, dark mineshaft. Anna moaned as gravity relinquished its grip on her body and weightlessness clawed at the pit of her stomach. Weber tried every trick he knew to raise the nose and restore lift to the wings. After what seemed like forever, the sound of air blasting against the windscreen diminished, and the plane's controls became more responsive. Weber gradually leveled the plane and added throttle, but seconds later, the right engine lost power, recovered briefly, and then quit.

"Anna, prepare for landing!"

Anna, still dizzy from the freefall, gave Weber a vacant look. "But Robert, what about all those ice formations and rock outcroppings?"

"Come on, Anna, get a grip. We have no choice but to put down."

"But how, Robert? You can't see anything in this blackness."

"I am going to raise the snout so we don't come in nose first, glide as long as possible, and hold my breath until the landing gear touches down."

"Ah, that's a great strategy for Stockholm's concrete runways. What makes you think our gear will withstand the tundra's harsh, rugged surface?"

"Got a better idea, smartass? Would you feel better if I said that the tundra is going to rip the belly out of the plane, ignite the fuel tanks, and burn us all alive?"

"Robert, I'm trying to help you solve this problem."

"Yeah, I know. Sorry, I snapped. Now brace for landing."

Weber sat bolt upright with his head cocked to the side, listening for a strut to strike the tundra's surface. The waiting was killing him. He was already tense and sitting stock-still in the cockpit, anticipating disaster. The waiting was testing the limits of his sanity. His imagination was not helping matters. He kept picturing some of the worst crashes he had witnessed during the war.

Minutes passed as the plane slipped quietly through the darkness. With the F7's engines silenced, all Weber could hear were whispers from the air rushing past the windscreen and muted howls from the storm's retreating winds. Why, he wondered, hadn't the plane touched down? Weber retracted the yoke slightly to maintain the plane's angle of approach.

"Anna, did you tighten your seatbelt?"

"Of course, Robert, I've checked it a hundred times."

"Stay relaxed; impacts cause more injuries when you're tense."

"Oh, for God's sake, Robert! You're not telling me anything I don't know."

"Anna, I couldn't bear it if anything happened to you. I don't think I'd survive."

"Focus, Robert. Get us through this."

Then it happened: a deafening boom from under the plane's left side followed by the screech of twisting metal. The aircraft shuddered and lurched rightward. Weber pulled hard on the yoke, and the plane vaulted upward like a bullet ricocheting off a boulder.

Anna blew out a long breath and tried to regain her composure. "That was frightening, Robert. What do you think happened?"

"I'm not sure. I suspect that whatever we hit sheared off the port strut. If that's true, we'll be lopsided for our next touchdown. The starboard wing will hit the deck and dig in. Not the safest scenario for our final landing."

"What do you mean by 'final,' Robert?' Are you speaking metaphorically?"

"We don't have enough airspeed to lift off again," Weber stated matter-of-factly. "After this hop, we're down for the count."

Weber fought to keep the plane aloft, but it was a losing battle. He watched the altimeter's needle unwind and braced for the inevitable.

The right strut slammed against the tundra with a heavy thud. The F7 shuddered violently, took a bad hop, and came down leaning left. Weber struggled to level the plane, but it didn't have enough airspeed for him to lift the left wing. The aircraft dropped like a rock, buried its wingtip in the tundra, and pivoted on that fulcrum until it spun sideways. Centrifugal force further rotated the plane until the accumulating torsional stress snapped the right strut. The F7 crashed onto its belly and hurtled across the tundra's coarse surface, bucking like an out-of-control bronco.

The violent bouncing eased suddenly when the plane coasted onto a flatter, slicker surface. Weber relaxed a bit, thinking that the worst was over. Then the F7 careened over a ledge, dropped several meters, twisted sideways, and slammed against a hidden, stationary object. The right or starboard wing instantly disintegrated, and then the right-facing fuselage imploded, crumpling bulkheads and shattering windows. Had Weber and Anna not worn their seatbelts, the abrupt impact would have ejected them through the cockpit's starboard windscreen. As it was, the force of the collision nearly snapped Weber's neck. It hit Anna harder because she sat on the cockpit's starboard side.

The cockpit, which had been loud and chaotic a few seconds ago, was dark and deadly silent. Still reeling from the impact, Weber released his seatbelt, retrieved a flashlight from an overhead bin, and stumbled over to Anna. She was breathing but not conscious. Blood oozed from her shoulder where her seatbelt had sliced through her blouse and into her skin. Weber shook her gently but got no response. He unbuckled her seatbelt, lowered her onto the floor, and stanched her bleeding shoulder with his handkerchief. Then he draped his flight jacket over her prone body.

Muffled moaning from inside the cabin prompted Weber to check on the passengers. As he entered the cabin, his foot caught on something, and he nearly fell headlong on the floor. After regaining his equilibrium, he focused the beam of his flashlight on the flight deck and saw Svensson sprawled against the forward bulkhead. The inebriated Swede had a fractured cranium, and blood and bits of brain matter were splattered on the flight deck and across the bulkhead.

Weber's insides roiled, but he quickly steeled himself; he'd seen worse during the war. "Had to get out of your seat again, didn't you, Svensson," he scolded. He pushed his forefinger against Svensson's neck but didn't find a pulse.

Weber stood, shone his flashlight around the cabin, and tried to understand what he saw. Ice shards littered the floor alongside a sharp-edged hunk of frozen rock that had ripped through the plane's belly. The gash belched frigid air.

A large section of the starboard fuselage jutted into the cabin, so much so that it had crushed one of the passenger's seats. Even from where he stood, Weber could tell that the man buckled into that seat hadn't survived. Who, he wondered, was that unfortunate soul--Lars Sodergaard? He'd have to ask Anna when she regained consciousness. Then, it occurred to him that Anna might not wake up. Tears spilled down his cheeks. He drew a deep breath and reminded himself that, as the flight's captain, he was responsible for all the passengers on this flight.

One of the passengers groaned, so Weber went to see if he could assist. This passenger, he discovered, was short, overweight, and probably close to fifty. Other than a scalp wound, the man seemed relatively unscathed.

"How are you, sir? I'm Weber, the captain of this aircraft."

"Damned poor pilot, aren't you? Roughest landing imaginable. Call me a cab and tell the driver to take me to the Hotel Tromsø."

The peculiar retort took Weber off guard, but he soon realized the man was confused and in shock. "Would you mind telling me your name, sir?"

"None of your business who I am. Shut up and do what I say. Now!"

Weber retrieved the plane's first aid kit and bandaged the man's scalp. He flashed the man a smile, nodded politely, and then walked away.

The remaining passenger fit Weber's image of a fur trapper. He was tall, sturdily built in a Bunyanesque way, and sported a bushy beard.

"Sir, I'm Robert Weber, the captain. How are you?"

"Shaken, captain, but alive. My name's Johan Osterlind. Where are we? What the hell happened?"

"I can't answer your first question. I can tell you that a massive storm ran us off course, and the aircraft suffered multiple engine failures."

"A grim situation, to be sure. So what do we do?"

"Good question." Weber nodded toward the man he had just bandaged.

"Do you know that man?"

"Yeah, that's Anatoly Pushkin. He runs a Russian fur business. Difficult fellow."

"I noticed. The thing is, Pushkin's in shock. He's out of his mind."

"I'll help you keep an eye on him."

Pushkin stood and began punching the air with his fists and yelling commands. "You incompetent dolt! Where's my taxi? Let me off this plane!"

Weber approached Pushkin, smiled, and addressed him in a soft voice.

"Mr. Pushkin, we are lost somewhere north of the Arctic Circle, and the plane is inoperable. It's probably below zero outside, so you must remain on this aircraft or what's left of it.."

"Damned lies! Open that door! I'm going into the terminal, and then I'm calling the police."

"Pushkin, there's no airport out there. No police either. Just hundreds of miles of tundra."

Pushkin balled up his fist and took a swing at Weber. Weber dodged the blow and summoned Osterland. Osterlind came running, and together, the two of them restrained Pushkin. Pushkin, however, continued to shout curses and demand that Weber allow him to disembark.

His patience spent, Weber shrugged, strode over to the hatch, cracked it ajar, and let it swing out over the plane's remaining wing. Ice crystals and frigid air gusted into the cabin. Pushkin watched Weber like a hawk but didn't move a muscle.

"What are you waiting for, Pushkin? Look out there and tell me if you see an airport."

Pushkin walked to the door, past Weber, and onto the wing. He stood silently for several seconds, staring into the darkness as if rooted in place. Then he gestured at something and gave Weber a smug look.

"There it is. Right there! Bring my bags. I'm going to my hotel to get some rest."

Peshkin slid off the wing and bounded toward the rear of the plane. Weber and Osterlind slid through the hatch, sprinted after Peshkin, and hauled him, kicking and screaming, back inside the cabin.

◆◆◆

Weber checked on Anna before settling in for the night. He was dismayed to see that she hadn't regained consciousness. Crestfallen, he returned to the cabin, and he and Osterlind took turns guarding Pushkin. Eventually, however, both men fell asleep. When Weber awoke the next morning, sunlight was streaming through the cockpit windows, and Anna was awake. Elated, he kissed Anna on the forehead and helped her to her feet. She took a few wobbly steps and dropped into the pilot's seat.

"Are you OK, Anna?"

"I think so. My shoulder aches, and I've got a monstrous headache."

Weber handed her his canteen. "Here, drink this. You're probably dehydrated."

Relieved that Anna had regained consciousness, Weber observed her closely for several minutes and then re-tied his handkerchief around her shoulder. The wound still bled but not as profusely. When he felt confident she was stable, he went to the cabin to check on his other patient--Pushkin. Pushkin, however, had disappeared. He woke Osterlind and inquired about Pushkin's whereabouts.

"Johan, where's Pushkin? Is he outside taking a piss?"

"I don't know Robert. He was here before I fell asleep."

Weber walked to the hatch and found it ajar. He pushed it open, stepped onto the wing, and surveyed the landscape that surrounded the plane. Rays from the morning sun danced on the surface of a large body of water about fifty meters in front of the plane. Remnants of what appeared to be an iceberg stood between the plane and the water. The plane's right side was jammed tight against the iceberg. As far as the eye could see, stretching around the other sides of the plane were flat expanses of white, frozen tundra. The tracks the F7 had cut into the tundra on its journey to its icy grave stretched out behind the plane.

Osterlind joined Weber on the wing and surveyed the landscape. "It's fortunate that we hit that pile of ice, Robert, or we'd have ended up in the water."

"I agree, although I wouldn't have said that last night."

"Any sign of Pushkin?"

"Not so far, but I haven't searched yet."

"I'll give you a hand. I've done plenty of tracking in this part of the world."

"Sure, let's see what we can find."

Weber and Osterlind headed off in different directions. After forty minutes of searching, Weber returned to the plane and found Osterlind sitting on the wing. "Any sign of him?" Weber asked.

"Footprints, I assume Pushkin's, extend south of the plane into the heart of the tundra. That idiot is off his rocker. The way he's dressed, he's dead already. In these temps, and without food or water, even an experienced tracker would be lucky to survive."

"So, does that mean you plan to stay with us? You know, remain with the plane?"

"Depends. I can't promise. Well, to be honest, I doubt it."

"Gees, Osterlind, don't do us any favors. What chance do we have without you?"

"You're better off without me. I'll consume your provisions."

"What provisions?"

"Look, you can melt ice for drinking water. I'll teach you how to catch fish from that ice ledge by the shoreline. After that, you're on your own."

"What are you going to do?"

"Like I said. I'm an experienced tracker. I'll follow the shoreline and use the same tactics to survive. It's risky, sure. Hopefully, I'll get lucky and run into a settlement or something."

Weber stood, opened the hatch, and climbed into the plane. "Bastard," he muttered under his breath. The warmth he expected to feel inside the aircraft was absent, and in its place was bone-chilling cold. Residual engine heat had kept the cabin temperature above zero after the crash. Not any longer. Now, the engines were as cold as the iceberg that had gutted the F7, leaving it to die on the tundra. He knew immediately that he had to reorder his priorities. If he didn't take immediate action, his passengers would freeze to death. The temperatures in the Arctic were survivable during the day but plunged dangerously at night.

Chapter 4

Winter 1920: North of the Arctic Circle

Weber walked through the plane and made a mental inventory of the available resources. He and Anna had flight jackets, and there were a couple of blankets, a tarpaulin, a first aid kit, and some tools and spare aircraft parts in one of the overhead bins. Clearly, he didn't have much to work with; a couple of blankets and a tarp wouldn't protect them from the Arctic cold.

Then it came to him: some avgas were still in the F7's tanks. Avgas was a kerosene derivative and, if properly wicked, would burn rather than explode. He decided to siphon some from the tanks, pour it into his canteen, and stuff a cloth into the canteen's spout. If he was lucky, the cloth would function as a wick--much as it did in a Molotov cocktail--and sustain combustion as long as the container wasn't damaged or broken.

He opened the bin, retrieved the tools, and went through the cabin and outside the plane. After reaching the F7's nose, he opened the engine cowling, located the forward fuel tank, and separated the end of the fuel line from the tank. As he retracted the tubing, he noticed an odd kink in the line about ten centimeters away from the tank. A metal clamp held the kink in place, so Weber removed it and let the fuel line flex back into its original shape. As the fuel line relaxed, Weber heard a metallic ping. Something had fallen out of the tube and landed on the floor of the engine compartment. He looked for the object and was shocked to discover that it was a casing--a brass-colored bullet casing.

Consumed with curiosity, Weber crawled up on the left wing, lifted a flap, and inspected the fuel line for the port engine. He found it immediately: the same kind of kink, held in place by an identical metal clip. He pulled the line from the tank, removed the clip, and shook the line. Out dropped another casing. Now he knew: this was no accident. Someone had deliberately crimped the fuel lines--not enough to stop fuel from reaching the engines, but just enough so that a small cylindrical object, like a bullet casing, could jam the line and cut off the fuel flow. The casing must have lain in the bottom of the tank until fuel spikes--caused by hard acceleration--had sucked it into the fuel line and driven it against the kink. As Weber contemplated that scenario, he remembered that each engine failure had occurred just after he'd maxed the throttle and spooled the engine toward full power.

Weber's anger flared. He had a damn good idea who had sabotaged his plane. If he survived this debacle, he would visit Gunter and exact some payback. He pictured himself choking the bastard until he begged for mercy. Hell, maybe he'd throttle the guy until he croaked.

One thing bothered him, however. Why would Gunter do this? Gunter was one of his colleagues. What motive could he possibly have?

Ever the pragmatist, Weber soon realized that his anger wasn't doing him or Anna any good. Right now, survival was all that mattered. He tried to quell his anger and focus on the task at hand. He siphoned avgas from the port engine's tank and poured it into his canteen. Now he had to find a way to make the canteen generate enough heat to help them survive the night.

Osterlind roused Weber early the next morning. Somehow, Weber's jury-rigged canteen heater had gotten them through the night.

"Get up, Weber. Time to catch breakfast."

"Breakfast, Johann? You can eat shark shit for all I care."

"Your choice, Weber. Come with me or starve. Either way, I'm leaving after breakfast."

Weber begrudgingly followed Osterlind to the shoreline and watched as the trapper dropped a thin strand of wire into the frigid water. Osterlind had fashioned a hook from some heavy-gauge wire he'd filched from one of the plane's engine bays and tied it to a flimsy strand of control wire. The two men crouched on the ice ledge along the shoreline and prayed that some edible sea creature would snatch the bait.

"What are you using for bait, Osterlind?"

"Half of Svensson's big toe. The bloody half."

"You desecrated Svensson's corpse?"

"Relax, Weber, he won't use his toes anymore."

"Nice rationalization, Osterlind. I guess only sensitive men become trappers."

"Look, would you rather eat or starve?"

"Hey, why settle for fish when we could be eating marinated liver? Svensson's not using his, and it's already pickled."

The line jerked and Osterlind reeled in a sizeable mackerel. The men dragged their catch back to the plane, where Osterlind gutted the fish. Weber made a fire from detritus he'd scavenged from inside the cabin. Osterlind seared the mackerel over the fire, and then the three starving survivors--Weber, Anna, and Osterlind--greedily wolfed down most of the fish. When they finished, Osterlind packed the leftovers and prepared to depart.

Weber cornered the trapper before he could leave. "Osterlind, do me one last favor. Help me carry Svensson's and Sodergaard's corpses out of the cabin and onto the wing. The cold will preserve their bodies."

Osterlind grudgingly agreed but complained incessantly while he and Weber moved the bodies. When the task was finished, the trapper spat on Sodergaard's corpse and, without saying a word, turned and walked away from the crash site. Weber tried to conceal his disgust. Anna wasn't fooled.

"What's bothering you, Robert?"

"I'm glad we're rid of that ass, but now we're alone in this God-forsaken wasteland."

A wave of anxiety flickered across Anna's face. Then her expression hardened. "Alright, Robert, let's make a survival plan. We must find a way out of here before one or both of us ends up alongside Svensson and Sodergaard."

"That's not funny, Anna."

"I didn't mean it as a joke."

"All right, let's hear your plan."

"I haven't got one."

"I think we should stay with the plane, at least initially. When you're shot down in enemy territory, you take cover near your plane and wait to be rescued."

"This isn't enemy territory, Robert, and we're probably too far off course for search teams to find us."

"I know, but what's the alternative? Do you want to imitate that Neanderthal, Osterlind, and try to hike our way out of this frozen hell?"

"I think we should prepare for that contingency. Stay with the plane for now, but be ready to trek across the tundra if help doesn't materialize."

"Prepare how?"

"I'm no survivalist, but why not search the plane and pack anything that might help us survive a week or two on the tundra."

Weber glanced around the plane, trying to envision Anna's plan. "Ok, let's get started. Go strip Svensson's and Sodergaard's corpses. We'll need their clothing."

"Are you serious, Robert? Those men have soiled themselves, and I'd have to look at their man parts. I won't do that!"

"Ok, sorry, I'll do it. Why don't you take the fishing tackle and see if you can catch our dinner?"

Anna located the makeshift fishing tackle, exited the plane, and proceeded toward the ice ledge. Weber retrieved a knife from the toolset and began harvesting Svensson's and Sodergaard's clothing. He worked quickly because the stench was overpowering, even in the sub-zero weather. He salvaged two coats, one shirt, a rucksack, and some cigars. The remainder of the dead men's possessions were soiled or useless.

Later that night, Weber exited the plane to relieve himself and was surprised to find the corpses missing. He searched around the plane and then went inside and woke Anna.

"Anna, you won't believe this, but Svensson and Sodergaard have vanished."

"What do you mean, vanished? They couldn't have walked away. Has Osterlind returned? Why didn't he wake us?"

"It's inconceivable, Anna. I'll search again tomorrow, but I found nothing in the moonlight. There's no one out there, not even the corpses."

"Robert, you're scaring me."

"Sorry, but I thought you should know. I'm baffled."

◆◆◆

A week passed before Weber began to feel pangs of despair. He had convinced himself that rescue was imminent, but when days passed and nothing happened, he began to suspect that Svensk-Luft Airlines had abandoned their search for the F7.

With hope fading, Weber's optimism dwindled, and his mood turned gloomy. Neither he nor Anna had anything to look forward to; they were simply marking time. Each day was like the last, except the daylight hours became progressively shorter, and the nights grew colder.

Lacking other options, the two pilots occupied themselves with the business of survival. Anna fished for food, and Weber broiled their meals with avgas. He tried not to think about what would happen when the avgas ran out. He'd already drained the nose tank, and now the wing tank was almost empty. Soon, he concluded, they'd be consuming raw fish. The thought made his gut roil.

Having dismissed the prospect of imminent rescue, Weber started thinking about Osterlind. Had that jerk found his way back to civilization? He still despised Osterlind but had to admit that the trapper's survival strategy no longer seemed foolish. Leaving the crash site contradicted his military training, but so did mindless devotion to a doomed tactic.

Weber rededicated himself to Anna's contingency plan: he scoured the plane for things that might enable them to survive a long trek across the tundra. His search wasn't productive initially, so he paused to envision them hiking across miles of frozen terrain and sleeping out in the open in sub-zero temperatures. The bleak realities he imagined helped to focus his search. Among the items he salvaged was a pair of steel rods. He figured those could be propped under the tarpaulin, like tent poles. He also stripped strands of control wire from the F7's bulkheads. Anna could use those for fishing line.

The latter discovery reminded Weber that Anna was standing on an ice ledge trying to catch their dinner. Three days ago, she had hooked a monstrous fish, and it had nearly pulled her into the icy water. She'd released the line, and the fish had dragged the gear--hook, line, and sinker--into the sea. Now, she used tackle that Weber had reconstructed from spare plane parts. He decided to check on Anna and see how the new gear worked.

Weber exited through the hatch, climbed off the wing, and walked toward the water. He scanned the shoreline and spotted Anna on a ledge near the iceberg that had become the F7's final resting place. As Weber approached, he noticed a shadow appear from the rear of the iceberg. Something was behind the iceberg, blocking the sun's rays and casting a shadow on the surface of the shoreline. When the shadow's perimeter suddenly expanded and moved in Anna's direction, Weber knew his wife was in trouble.

A massive polar bear bounded from behind the iceberg sped along the ice ledge and launched himself at Anna. The beast caught her between his front paws, wrapped his powerful arms around her, and careened off the ice ledge into the freezing water. There was a thunderous splash as the bear, clutching Anna tightly against his chest, hit the water and disappeared under the surface.

Aghast, Weber yanked out his knife, sprinted to the ice ledge, and dove into the bear's wake. The freezing water nearly incapacitated him, but the arc of his dive brought him to within a few feet of the bear. He stabbed at the bear with his knife, but the icy water slowed his movements and stole the power that he put behind each blow. He redoubled his efforts, and the blade cut a furrow in the bear's rump. Blood and fat gushed from the wound, clouding the water. Weber lost sight of the bear and broke off his attack. Sensing his advantage, the bear spun around and batted Weber with one paw, ripping a deep gash between the pilot's shoulder blades. The blow's force pushed Weber deep below the sea's surface.

◆◆◆

When Weber finally pulled his bleeding body onto the ice ledge, he wasn't sure what hurt worse--the gaping wound between his shoulder blades or the shock of Anna's death. One thing he felt certain about was that life, as he knew it, was over. If the wound didn't kill him, trying to survive without Anna probably would. Then, there was the non-trivial matter of extricating himself from this frozen hell and finding his way back to civilization. Amid his grief, he wasn't sure he wanted to survive.

That night, Weber slept alone in the F7. He had dragged himself back to the plane, cleaned his wounds as best he could, and then passed out on the cabin floor. During the middle of the night, the pressure of a full bladder awakened him. Groggy and in pain, he pulled himself to his feet and stumbled toward the hatch. As he reached for the handle, some unidentifiable sound caught his attention. He paused to listen. There it was again—a faint scratching sound. Weber tried to localize the source. It sounded like it was coming from somewhere under the fuselage.

The scratching stopped. Weber stood immobilized, disgusted that he'd allowed himself to be spooked by some innocuous sound. Still, this was the first time since the crash that he had heard any noise from under the plane.

Cautiously, Weber reached for the handle on the hatch. As he wrapped his fingers around it, the plane quaked violently, knocking him to the floor. A series of thuds followed, each one triggering a seismic aftershock that rocked the entire plane.

Weber crawled to the starboard window, lifted the canvas flap, and peered outside. An enormous polar bear stood on the wing, just outside the hatch. Weber couldn't believe his eyes. Was this Anna's killer? That question triggered another. Did this bear steal Svensson's and Sodergaard's corpses? A sick feeling formed in the pit of Weber's stomach. The bear was feeding on the crash survivors, and Weber was his next meal.

The bear changed tactics. He padded over to the hatch, reared up, and slammed his body against the fuselage. The hatch and surrounding fuselage sections quaked, groaned, and threatened to give way. Between body slams, the bear raked the side of the plane with his claws. Weber cowered like a caged animal, awaiting slaughter. He figured he had minutes, if not seconds, to live.

As Weber contemplated his imminent demise, he had an epiphany. He wanted to survive, even if it meant living without Anna. Anna's death had made him question whether he wanted to live or die, but the bear had usurped those options by threatening him with certain death.

That twist of fate energized Weber. He wasn't going to let the monster that had taken Anna's life take him, too. Besides, if the bear devoured him, what would happen to Carl? In his pain and grief, he'd selfishly focused on himself and forgotten about Carl. Anna would never have done that. She would have put Carl's needs above hers. His too, probably. Weber decided to do whatever was necessary to return to Stockholm and raise Carl.

Winter 1920: North of the Arctic Circle

Weber's resolve had given him a purpose but not a plan. Just a few days ago, he had thought it imprudent to abandon the downed plane. Now, he was more than willing to flee the crash site and risk everything to cross the tundra. As he saw it, Tromsø was the first step in the journey back to Stockholm, and he was determined to go there even if he had to eat raw fish and slog through blizzards on his hands and knees.

Impatient to get started, Weber focused on practical considerations, such as packing supplies and finding a route to Tromsø. While weighing potential routes, he was forced to admit that he couldn't take the journey's first step. Unless he got past the bear, he wasn't going anywhere, and outsmarting this bear would be no easy task. This ursine predator knew where to find his next meal. He'd tried to peel the fuselage like a sardine can, and when that failed, he'd hidden under the wing to ambush Weber. The bear, Weber conceded, had him cornered.

Weber tried to face facts; he was trapped without food or water and couldn't even leave the cabin to relieve himself. To fend off panic, he busied himself with chores. "First things first," he muttered. He walked to the rear of the cabin and peed against the wall. Relief washed over him; his bladder had been about to burst. Next, he found Svensson's rucksack and stuffed it with the gear he'd earmarked for the trek. Before packing the steel rods, he used a file from the tool kit to sharpen the ends. Besides his knife, the rods were the closest thing he had to a weapon.

"Too bad Gunter didn't make the trip," he muttered under his breath. "I'd relieve him of his gun, put a bullet in his brain, and then shoot the damned bear."

After Weber had finished packing, he went to the window and looked for the bear. At first, he saw nothing but vacant tundra. Then, the beast's head popped out from under the wing. Weber's anxiety ratcheted up a notch. The ursine predator was still crouched under the wing, lying in wait.

Weber racked his brain, trying to think of a way to slip past this ogre and evade his brethren once he was out on the tundra. Finally, an idea came to him. He went to the spare plane parts cabinet and pulled out a rubber inner tube. Fixing a flat tire was the least of his worries now. He sliced the tube in half with his knife and knotted one end. After retrieving his canteen, he poured all the remaining avgas into the open end of the tube and then knotted that end, too. To test his creation, he squeezed the tube. The bladder-like section between the two knots swelled until it looked like a half-deflated balloon. Pleased, he grabbed an awl from the tool kit and punctured a small hole in the middle of the bladder. Then he retrieved a cigar from the rucksack, lit it, and placed it in his mouth. Now, he was ready.

Weber slung the rucksack on his back, picked up the bladder, and opened the hatch. As he stepped outside, the bear growled, dashed out from under the wing, and reared up directly in front of him. Weber stood firm and tried to conceal his fear. He raised the bladder, squeezed it, and directed a narrow stream of avgas at the bear. The bear snorted, dropped on all fours, and retreated a foot or two, apparently repulsed by the scent of petroleum.

Weber cautiously advanced and sprayed another stream of avgas at the bear. This time, the bear stood his ground. Not to be deterred, Weber squeezed the bladder again, and as the avgas arced toward the bear, he stuck his cigar into the stream. The avgas ignited with a low whump and instantly morphed into a river of fire that jetted aloft and descended onto the bear. The beast yelped, recoiled, and sought cover under the wing. Weber waited a beat, wondering whether the bear would circle under the wing and attack from the rear. When that didn't happen, he jumped off the wing and ran like hell into the dark, frozen tundra.

Weber didn't look over his shoulder until he arrived at the ice ledge next to the open water. There was no sign of the bear; apparently, the flames had discouraged the beast from pursuing him. He said a prayer of thanks and made his way west along the shoreline, hoping, as Osterlind had, that he'd eventually stumble into something that resembled civilization.

◆◆◆

Several hours later, Weber paused and sat on a rock alongside the shoreline. He'd come a long way since he left the F7. The sun had disappeared hours ago, but the illumination from a partial moon had allowed him to find his way along the coast. His feet ached from all the miles he'd hiked on the tundra's icy, uneven surface. After retying his boots, he glanced rearward and saw no other footprints in the snow but his. He hadn't seen any sign of Osterlind since he'd left the plane. Had the bear made a meal of that dirtbag as well? The thought made him cringe. The crash and the bear had killed everyone on the Tromsø flight but him. Now he was alone with the bear in this frozen hell. Had he ever been more alone? Certainly, he knew, he had never been lonelier.

Still, he was determined to find Tromsø, and the sooner the better. Buoyed by the brief respite, Weber stood, hoisted the rucksack onto his back, and set off along the shoreline in a westerly direction.

Ten minutes later, however, Weber's determination crumbled. He tried to push on, but his body protested. His feet ached, his legs cramped, and his back spasmed. On top of that, he was ravenously hungry and deathly tired. Grudgingly, he surrendered to his body's wishes and set up camp. "Guess what's for dinner," he muttered dejectedly. He pulled the fishing tackle from the rucksack, found an ice ledge along the shoreline, and threw the line in the water. Then he lowered himself onto the ledge, dangled his feet over the water, and waited for a fish to bite. None did. After an hour, he returned empty-handed to his hastily improvised camp.

When Weber awoke the next morning, a foot of snow had fallen on top of his makeshift tent. Before going to sleep, he had hammered the sharpened metal rods into the ice and draped the tarpaulin atop them.

He pushed the canvas aside, cleared a path to the shoreline, and dropped the fishing line into the inky black water. Sunrise was two hours away, and until then, it would be necessary to prepare for the day's journey in the fading light of a receding moon.

Weber stood patiently on the ice ledge, staring at the water. The idea of eating fish for breakfast sickened him. He'd dined on nothing else since leaving the plane, and the thought of the scaly, slimy creatures made him want to wretch.

When large bubbles broke the surface a few feet from the shoreline, Weber gripped the line tightly and braced himself, assuming he was about to hook a large fish. Instead, a gigantic, snarling polar bear exploded out of the water and lunged for him. Instinctively, Weber recoiled, turned, and ran for the campsite, his feet fighting for traction on the ice. The bear pulled himself onto the ice ledge with his powerful limbs and gave chase.

When Weber arrived at his campsite, he ripped the tarpaulin off the makeshift tent, yanked both metal rods out of the ice, and swiveled to confront the oncoming bear. As the bear raced toward him, Weber puffed himself up and struck a defiant pose. He was surprised when his posture spooked the bear. The wary predator pulled up short, swiveled his head sideways, and eyed Weber malevolently.

Now that he was eye to eye with the bear, Weber was frightened senseless. Inwardly, he bargained with God to save his life. Outwardly, he donned his war face and parried the rods about himself like swords. Jousting with a hungry polar bear wasn't on his bucket list, but it might as well be because that was exactly what he was about to do.

The bear lowered his head, growled, and crept forward. As he drew closer, Weber noticed a gash on the bear's butt and some blotchy discolorations on its otherwise ivory-colored fur. "Wait a minute," he muttered. "I know you. You're the SOB that killed Anna and trapped me inside the plane. Those dark patches are scorch marks--places where I burned you with avgas!"

A fiery rage supplanted Weber's fear. He cocked his right arm and waited for the bear to come closer. When the beast opened his jaws and lunged, Weber jammed the rod down his throat. The bear's eyes went wide. He wheezed, coughed, and shook his head violently, trying to dislodge the rod.

At first, the bear's predatory instincts sustained his attack. Even while struggling to cough up the rod, the beast took a swipe at Weber and knocked him to the ground. The rod, however, didn't budge, and eventually, the beast fell to his knees, rolled onto his back, and writhed on the ice. Weber slid backward until he was safely away from the bear. Then he got to his feet and bolted like a scared jackrabbit into the tundra.

Weber ran until his legs gave out. There was a large rock formation to his left, so he dashed into the boulders, hid, and waited for nightfall. He passed the remaining daylight hours, shivering and agonizing over his plight. One thing was clear: he couldn't survive without his gear. That meant returning to the campsite.

He waited for the moon to rise, found his footprints in the snow, and cautiously retraced his steps toward the campsite. The last thing he wanted was another confrontation with the bear.

When the campsite came into view, Weber paused. An image of the bear crouching under the plane popped into his head. Was the beast hiding somewhere, waiting for him to return? He circled the perimeter and scanned every centimeter of the campsite. The bear, it seemed, had departed.

He inched his way toward the campsite. The tarpaulin was dead ahead, half-covered with snow. Off to the right, he saw a circular area resembling a miniature ice rink- probably where the bear had polished the surface with his backside. A bloody metal rod lay nearby. He picked up the rod and then searched for the rucksack. When he found it near the tarpaulin, he packed it with gear strewn about the campsite. Satisfied that he had salvaged most of his gear, he returned to the shoreline and resumed his westerly journey. While plodding along in the moonlight, he suddenly experienced a sense of elation. He was alive, damn it, and there was still a chance that he'd see Carl again. He pushed his hand into his pocket and fingered the bullet casings. Yeah, and maybe he'd see Gunter again, too.

Chapter 5

Winter 1920: Tromsø, Norway

Weber's eyelids fluttered, then opened fully as he regained consciousness. That's odd, he thought, where's the grey Arctic sky? Sensing that he was lying flat on his back, he pushed his hands beneath him, expecting to feel the rugged, icy tundra. Instead, his fingertips sank into something soft and warm. What the hell? Unnerved, he swiveled his head left and right, running his eyes over everything around him, demanding that his brain make sense of his surroundings. At first, nothing made sense. Then comprehension dawned. He hadn't awoken on the tundra, lying on the bone-chilling ice, as had been his custom for the past several weeks. No, he was alone in a windowless room, reclining on a narrow bed, staring at a wood plank ceiling.

Weber lay there silently for several minutes until his curiosity got the best of him. He rolled to one side, intending to pull himself out of bed. He slid his right leg over the side, toward the floor, but when he tried to move his left leg, something clutched his ankle and held it firmly. Stunned, he yanked off the covers and peered at his foot. Encircling his ankle was a shiny steel shackle--the kind hunters used to trap game. Connected to the shackle was a stout chain securely tethered to the bed's iron footboard.

Weber kicked his left leg up and down, hoping to break the shackle or dislodge the chain. The tactic proved futile. The shackle tore a deep, bloody gash in his shin, and the chain rattled against the bedpost and refused to release its grip.

Seconds later, a bearded man burst into Weber's room through the door. "What's going on in here?"

Rather than acknowledge the man, Weber busied himself with his wounds. He tore off a piece of bedsheet and painstakingly wrapped it around his bloody shin. When finished, he raised his eyes and scowled at his captor. The man was tall, lean, and blonde. His beard was bushy and unkempt, and his hair was matted against his head. The stench of body odor was overpowering. Weber wondered if the man had ever taken a bath.

"How dare you imprison me!" Weber snarled. "Do you know who I am?"

"Shut up, Ivan! You're not the first Russian we've caught sneaking across the border. Why can't you Russkies stay where you belong? You're not welcome in Norway."

"My name isn't Ivan, and I'm not Russian."

"Prove it. All you had in your pockets when Oskar pulled your frozen ass out of a snowbank were a few shell casings. That's what border jumpers do—they don't carry anything that could be used to identify them. And don't tell me you're Swedish because your accent says otherwise."

"Look, whoever you are, my name is Robert Weber, and I'm an American, not a Russian. That's why I speak Swedish with an accent."

"Robert Weber, eh?" Well, I'm Per Nilsson, the constable of Tromsø. I'm holding you on suspicion of entering Norway illegally. You say that you're an American. What would an American be doing in this part of the world?"

"I'm a pilot for Svensk-Luft Airlines, and during a flight to Tromsø, my plane went down in a storm. The wreckage is somewhere northeast of here, above the Arctic Circle."

"Wow, that's some yarn. You're a better liar than most Russkies."

"I am not lying. Wire my boss in Stockholm, and he will vouch for me."

Nilsson scoffed and left the room.

Nilsson returned several hours later, grasping a narrow slip of paper. "Alright, Weber, I did some investigating. A Svensk-Luft Airlines flight failed to arrive in Tromsø several weeks ago. The wire I received from the airline's owner confirmed that Robert Weber piloted that plane. However, he further indicated that your wife—Anna Weber—and four passengers were aboard that flight. That's five additional people. Where are they?"

"Two passengers died on impact, another went crazy and fled the crash site, and the fourth—a trapper named Osterlind—trekked across the tundra in search of a settlement. Anna, my wife, was eaten by a polar bear."

"A polar bear ate your wife? Are you serious? Polar bears rarely prey on humans."

"Well, this one did."

"And you say Osterlind abandoned the crash site to search for a settlement? Let me tell you something. People here know Osterlind. Some local trappers told me he hadn't been in Tromsø for months. Are you going to tell me that he was eaten by a bear, too?"

"I don't know for certain, but I think it's likely."

"So you were the only lucky one, eh Weber? You didn't die in the crash, go crazy, or get eaten by this phantom bear. Is that what you're telling me?"

"Why don't you believe me?"

"No need to convince me. I've decided to hold you until our itinerant magistrate arrives. You can spin that yarn and see if the judge believes you. Personally, I think that fairytale is going to earn you a long jail term."

◆◆◆

Weber ran. He escaped after midnight when one of Nilsson's assistants escorted him to an outdoor privy. While inside the outhouse, supposedly relieving himself, he forcibly removed some loose planks from the rear wall and slipped unnoticed into the night.

Tromsø, he soon discovered, was located on an island and consisted of a labyrinth of dimly lit streets surrounded by low wooden buildings. was situated on an island and consisted of a maze of dark streets surrounded by low wooden buildings. He stumbled up one street and down another, searching in vain for a harbor, his only hope of escape. After hours of fruitless wandering, he spied an unusual building with three towering pillars rising from its roofline. He assumed the shafts were flag poles, but as he came closer, he realized they were masts. There was a ship moored behind that building! He had found a harbor!

Weber scanned the building for signs of life and, seeing none, walked to the rear, where he found a clipper ship moored alongside an immense wooden dock. Rows of barrels sat atop the pier and across the clipper's lower decks, awaiting placement in the ship's cargo holds. Weber crept up the ship's gangplank and worked his way along a lower deck until he reached the first cargo hold. Next to the open hold was a row of barrels and a toolbox. Weber searched the toolbox, extracted a hammer, and used it to pry the lid off one of the barrels. Darkness prevented him from seeing what was inside the barrel, but he had no trouble identifying the stench that accosted his nostrils--it was the unmistakable smell of dried fish.

Weber knew what had to be done but cursed his luck nonetheless. He rolled the barrel to the edge of the deck, lowered it onto its side, and dumped the fish into the ocean. Then he righted the barrel, rolled it back into place, and used the hammer to knock a small hole in one of the staves. After saying a short prayer, he drew a deep breath, climbed inside the barrel, and secured the lid.

Winter 1920: Stockholm Sweden

The better part of a month passed before Weber reached Stockholm. The clipper he'd secretly boarded had sailed southwest from Tromsø along the coast of Norway. Before climbing out of the barrel, he'd waited until the ship was well out to sea. It wasn't long before a crew member caught him pilfering scraps from the mess hall, accused him of being a stowaway, and summoned the captain. A tense confrontation followed, during which Weber offered to pay for his passage by working as a deckhand. Begrudgingly, the captain had agreed.

Weber's sea voyage ended when the clipper docked in Bergen. Still destitute, he searched for a job during the day and slept on the streets at night. Eventually, the owner of a dogsled team hired him to help ferry supplies to isolated farms in the southern, snow-covered regions of Norway and Sweden. When one trip brought him near Stockholm, he abruptly quit and made his way home.

Weber went directly to his house on the outskirts of the city. To his chagrin, he found no comfort there. His homecoming fantasies had kept him alive on the tundra, helped him endure incarceration in Tromsø, and buoyed his spirits during the arduous sea journey. Now, as he walked through the house, that dream tormented him. Everything he saw reminded him of Anna and their life together--a life he could no longer live. A life that Gunter had stolen.

Ambushed by his anguish, Weber's lucidity crumbled; his mind took a nosedive and spun out of control. He saw the bewildered expression on Anna's face when the polar bear pounced. He heard Anna's screams as the beast tackled her and propelled her limp body into the icy water. Then, after the waves swallowed Anna's cries, he saw something else: Gunter. He watched Gunter open the F7's engine cowlings and stuff shell casings into the fuel lines. There was a wicked grin on Gunter's face. That image sent Weber into a murderous rage. He went upstairs to the bedroom where he and Anna had slept and pulled a locked box from under the bed. Rather than search for the key, he used his hunting knife to force open the lock, withdrew his service revolver, and shoved it into his coat pocket. As he made his way downstairs, he pictured himself aiming the gun, pulling the trigger, and watching Gunter's head explode. The image stopped him in his tracks. No. No way. A bullet in the head wouldn't be as painful as being eaten alive by a bear. Weber retraced his steps, retrieved his hunting knife, and then made tracks for the airport.

◆◆◆

It was midday when Weber reached the Svensk-Luft hanger. He stomped inside and headed for the service bay where Gunter and Göring routinely parked their aircraft. As he approached the bay, he shoved his right hand into his coat pocket and wrapped his fingers around the hunting knife. The handle felt cool against his hot, sweaty palm. Now, he told himself, I will dispense some long-overdue justice. Gunter is going to feel my wrath.

Before Weber could take another step, someone shouted his name. It was Johansson.

"Weber--is that you? I thought you were dead!"

Weber let go of the knife, withdrew his hand from his coat pocket, and turned to face Johansson. "Death stalked me many times since I last saw you, Johansson. By some twist of fate, I'm still alive."

"Do you know what you've put me through, Weber? Do you realize what you've done to this airline? Svensk-Luft may never recover. I'm nearly bankrupt!"

"What did I put *you* through? Listen, you ungrateful miser, what you've suffered is nothing compared to what I've been through. We crash-landed north of the Arctic Circle in a desolate, icy hell. Passengers died, and I had to dispose of their corpses. The survivors, faced with starvation, wanted to eat the dead. A polar bear massacred my wife, and I couldn't do anything but watch. The same bear, after ingesting Anna, relentlessly hunted me. The crash site was hundreds of miles from Tromsø. It took me three weeks to walk, crawl, and claw my way across the tundra to get there. Need I say more?"

"A bear ate Anna? Um, well, I had no idea."

"Now you do. And that's just half of it. Be thankful I don't regale you with the gory details. Now, where's Gunter? He and I have a score to settle."

"Gunter? He and Göring are flying the Copenhagen route today. I don't expect them until late this afternoon."

Weber grimaced, did an about-face, and walked away.

"Where are you going, Weber? Now that you're back, we have much to discuss."

Weber ignored Johansson. He left the hangar, got back in his car, and slammed the heels of his palms against the steering wheel. "You dunce!" he screamed. "Where are your priorities?" He sped away from the airport, parked in front of Linnea's house, and knocked on the front door. There was no response, so he pounded harder. Seconds later, the door opened, and Linnea appeared. He watched the color drain from her face.

"Robert, I thought you were dead. Anna too. Where is Anna?"

"Sadly, Anna *is* dead. She died after our plane went down in the Arctic. I'm lucky to be alive. Where's Carl?"

"Carl? Oh my God! Carl thinks you're dead, too."

"Is he here?"

"No, he's at school."

◆◆◆

Weber didn't sleep that night. He lay awake in his bed, trying to discern a way forward. What, he asked himself, do I do now? How do I raise Carl alone? What will we do for money? To console himself, he thought about how Carl had reacted when he'd stormed into the school and embraced his son. Carl, at least, had confidence in him. He'd been overjoyed to see his father and couldn't wait to pick up the pieces of their lives. Rather than returning to Linnea's house, Carl accompanied Weber home and insisted they celebrate his father's resurrection. Weber was happy to oblige but couldn't find it in himself to celebrate a homecoming that didn't include Anna. He'd put on a good front for Carl, but his heart wasn't in it. On the other hand, Carl did not mention his mother and seemed genuinely happy. Weber suspected that Carl hadn't fully absorbed the loss of his mother.

Helping his son grieve, Weber realized, would be another of the daunting challenges that lay ahead. Now, perhaps for the first time, he began to understand what it meant to be a single parent. As the weight of that responsibility settled on his shoulders, he realized he'd misconstrued his priorities. It had been foolish to stalk Gunter. Letting his rage dictate his actions would only land him in prison, and there wasn't much he could do for Carl from a jail cell. Rather than avenge Anna, he'd have to be a responsible adult and concentrate on making a living and caring for Carl. As far as he could see, that left him only one option. He'd have to return to being a commercial pilot. How else could he earn a decent wage? That prospect, however, was fraught with unknowns. After what had happened in the Arctic, would Johannson take him back? Perhaps more to the point, could he bring himself to fly an airplane after what happened in the Arctic? There was only one way to know. He would get up early the next morning, return to the Svensk-Luft hanger, and find out.

◆◆◆

Weber entered the Svensk-Luft hanger just after dawn and went directly to a vacant F7 aircraft. He cracked the entry hatch, crawled inside, and crawled into the pilot's seat. The cockpit felt a bit claustrophobic, so he unlocked the starboard window and slid it open. As he sat there, inspecting the controls and trying to tamp down bad memories, voices drifted up from the hangar floor.

"Johansson says the American has returned. How is that possible? When he departed for Tromsø, you told me it would be his last flight. You said he'd never return—that you'd fixed this problem."

"I am as surprised as you are, Hermann. That flight was doomed--no one should have survived."

"Well, now, who's doomed? Will he suspect you, or worse still, me? You must contain this situation before it gets out of control."

"Of course. I'll fix this."

"That's what you said last time."

Weber waited until the two Germans had departed, climbed out of the F7, and looked for Johansson. He found him sitting at his desk, drinking coffee and inspecting the day's flight schedule.

"I need to talk to you, Johansson."

"Alright, Weber, but first things first. I want to know what happened on your flight to Tromsø. Why did you crash on the tundra, and why were you so far off course?"

"Still looking for someone to blame, eh? Let me be brutally honest. The plane was off course because Anna and I were trying to circumnavigate a massive storm. The crash, however, was Gunter's fault."

"Gunter? You can't be serious. He didn't have anything to do with that flight."

"He as much as admitted it. I just overheard him talking to Göring. I'm not sure why, but the two of them want me dead."

"So you're not just blaming Gunter, but Göring too? How do you expect me to believe that? Did the crash scramble your brains?"

Weber reached into his pocket, withdrew a shell casing, and placed it on Johansson's desk.

"Guess where I found this. I inspected the F7 after the crash and found this jammed inside the fuel line for the main engine. There was one of these inside the fuel lines for each wing-mounted engine, too. They're just small enough to get sucked into the fuel lines under hard acceleration. Have you ever noticed what's hanging on that chain that Gunter wears around his neck? One of these--a shell casing exactly like this one."

"That could be a coincidence--it doesn't prove anything."

"Come on, Johansson, wake up. Pilot error didn't cause this crash. Gunter sabotaged the plane."

"I can't say I believe you, Weber, especially in light of your previous altercations with Gunter. Besides, there isn't enough proof. Nothing you've said would stand up in court. But here's what I will do. I'm short-staffed, and if your skills as a pilot check out, I'd consider rehiring you. I'd probably put you on short runs at first. Are you interested?"

"Only if you promise I'll never have to fly with Gunter or Hermann."

"Done."

◆◆◆

Weber did a check-ride with another of Svensk-Luft's pilots, received Johansson's approval, and then eased himself into the flight schedule as a copilot. Three weeks later, Svensk-Luft took delivery of four new aircraft, and Johansson elevated Weber's status to first officer. Ready or not, Weber was back in his role as captain, flying short hops from Stockholm and occasional overnighters to Copenhagen, Olso, and Helsinki.

Spring 1921: Stockholm, Sweden

Returning to the cockpit had been a struggle, but so far, Weber had managed to overpower the demons that assaulted him every time he boarded an aircraft. Invariably, flashbacks of the Arctic crash and Anna's death replayed in his head. He deadened the images by focusing on Carl and telling himself he had to earn a living. Even so, images of Gunter intruded on his thoughts during the day and invaded his dreams at night. Against his better judgment, he decided to investigate the sinister Germans, if only to find out why they wanted him dead.

As a first step, he slipped into Johansson's office after hours and read Gunter's and Göring's files. He found nothing interesting, but the gambit assuaged his demons and strengthened his resolve. Having crossed that boundary, there was no turning back. Soon, he was using his days off--every available minute while Carl was in school or sleeping--to follow Gunter and Göring and track their movements.

During his first week of surveillance, Weber discovered that the two Germans were nearly inseparable during the daylight hours. Gunter and Göring shared an apartment, traveled about the city in the same car, and routinely dined together in various restaurants. After dark, however, the two men's lives diverged. Göring, Weber observed, tended to spend his evenings in clubs and bars, drinking and flirting with an assortment of women. Gunter often stayed home, but when he did accompany Göring in the evenings, he kept to himself and watched his friend's romantic escapades from the sidelines.

After three weeks of surveillance, Weber felt confident he could predict Gunter's and Göring's movements. The Germans, however, abruptly proved him wrong. Suddenly, Gunter's and Göring's seemingly parallel lives were no longer in sync. Weber rarely saw Göring enter or leave his apartment, and Gunter routinely ate breakfast and lunch alone. One evening, he found the two men in a bar, and it was immediately apparent that Göring's behavior had changed. Gone was his characteristic carousing. Instead, Göring fawned over one particular woman, a slim, well-dressed, brown-eyed brunette. When the evening drew to a close, Göring left with her on his arm.

Weber followed Göring out of the bar, secreted himself behind a lamppost, and watched his quarry escort the unidentified woman toward a large, black limousine. When the pair reached the vehicle, a chauffeur stepped from the shadows and opened the rear door. Göring helped the woman into the car, crawled in beside her, and pulled the door closed behind him.

As the vehicle sped away, Weber stood in the shadows, wondering about the identity of Göring's companion. The woman looked familiar, but he couldn't place her. She was attractive, well-dressed, and radiated a snobbish self-assurance. Most likely, he figured, the woman was some aristocrat, and if that was the case, she shouldn't be difficult to identify.

While Weber investigated Göring's companion's identity, he continued to track Gunter's movements. It was immediately apparent that, when deprived of Göring's company, Gunter led a far more solitary existence. Except for work and meals, he rarely left the apartment. Two outings, however, piqued Weber's curiosity. Both were trips to the Polis Högkvarter, or police headquarters in central Stockholm.

◆◆◆

Weber climbed out of the F7, did his post-flight inspection, and carried his paperwork toward Johannson's office across the hangar. He had just completed a flight to Oslo, his third this week, and he was dead tired and looking forward to dinner with Carl. When he reached Johansson's office, his boss waved him inside and told him to shut the door.

"Look, Weber, I'm not sure if I should be telling you this, but Gunter is having you investigated."

"What do you mean, investigated?"

"You heard me. He's talking to the police--says he's convinced the cops that you committed crimes in the Arctic."

"Crimes, what crimes?"

"He met with some Norwegian constable named Per Nilsson in Tromsø during one of his recent flights. Evidently, Nilsson told Gunter that you're wanted for murder in Norway and that you fled custody to escape prosecution."

"Murder, that's absurd! I explained to Nilsson how Anna and the others on that flight died. Their deaths were caused by the crash and the harsh conditions we endured on the tundra. They all died of natural causes. No one was murdered."

"Look, I believe you, or I wouldn't be telling you this."

"Thanks, I guess. I can't believe this is happening. I told you that Gunter is out to get me. I just don't know why."

"So you know Nilsson, eh?"

"Well, yeah. One of his flunkies found me unconscious on the tundra. They thought I was an illegal Russian immigrant and locked me up. I explained who I was and told Nilsson to contact Svensk-Luft Airlines. I assumed he did because he stopped accusing me of being a Russian and started asking questions about the crash."

"And you did a runner rather than try to clear your name?"

"I had to. Nilsson as much as said that he didn't believe me. He swore he'd make sure that I served a long sentence. I felt certain that I wouldn't get a fair shake."

"Well, Weber, the police haven't contacted me yet, but Gunter told me to expect them. He said that the cops want you for questioning. If I were you, I'd do something to protect myself. Tell the police your side of the story before they arrest you, and this mess spins out of control."

◆◆◆

Weber returned to the nightclub where he had spotted Göring and the mysterious brunette and quizzed the bartender about the woman's identity. The bartender laughed at Weber's naiveté. "Have you been living in a cave? I thought everyone around here knew the Baroness. Baroness Carin von Kantzow is practically a celebrity in Sweden, and so is her husband, Count Eric von Rosen."

Weber inhaled sharply. "Her husband?"

"Hey, wait a minute, smart guy. What do you have in mind? Forget it, buddy; she's out of your league. You don't have a chance with her."

Armed with this information, Weber reordered his priorities. He stopped following Gunter and spent every available minute shadowing Göring. He soon discovered that Göring began and ended each day at the Grand Hôtel near Gamla Stan, Stockholm's old town. This, Weber realized, explained why Gunter lived alone in the apartment the two Germans had occupied. But why had Göring taken up residence in a hotel? There was only one way to find out.

Late one evening, Weber hid in the hotel bar until Göring arrived and then discretely followed him through the lobby, up several flights of stairs, and down a hallway. When Göring paused in front of room 321, Weber stooped to tie his shoe and slyly watched as the German slotted his key into the lock, opened the door, and disappeared into the room. Weber noted the room's number, returned to the lobby and booked the room next to Göring's. Across the next few days, he spent several hours with his ear pressed against the wall that adjoined Göring's room. What he heard surprised him. Göring, it seemed, had a new roommate--the Baroness. Weber could listen to them talking at all hours of the day and night, and sometimes, they were doing a lot more than talking. It was obvious that Göring and the Baroness had embarked on a romantic relationship and were living together in the Grand Hôtel. Weber wondered how Count von Rosen felt about that or whether he even knew that he'd been cuckolded.

Chapter 6

Spring 2021: Stockholm, Sweden

"Dad, I heard a noise--it woke me up." Carl stood at the foot of his father's bed, trying to rouse him from a deep slumber.

Weber gradually opened his eyes and peered at Carl, wondering why he had left his bedroom to summon him in the middle of the night. "Go back to your room and get some sleep, Carl. You probably had a bad dream."

"No, Dad, I heard the stairs squeak--you know, the creaky ones at the bottom of the downstairs staircase."

"Well, I don't hear anything, so go back to sleep."

Then something caught Weber's eye near the bedroom door--a faint, momentary reflection cast by a shiny object. Sensing danger, Weber bolted upright, grabbed Carl, and yanked the boy onto his bed. He hugged Carl tightly and rolled sideways until they tumbled off the bed onto the floor.

As Weber pulled Carl under the bed, there was a muzzle flash and a deafening explosion. A bullet thudded into the mattress just above Weber's head. Instinctively, he ran his hand along the underside of the bed to see if the round had pierced the mattress. It hadn't. That meant the shooter was using a small-caliber pistol, like Gunter's. Weber pivoted toward the security box that contained his sidearm, withdrew the weapon, and fired a round parallel to the bedframe, hoping to hit the shooter in a foot or an ankle. The shot must have missed its mark because the shooter dashed down the stairs and out of the house.

Weber pulled Carl out from under the bed and cradled him in his arms. He held the boy tight, let him sob, and waited for his panic to drain away. While comforting Carl, his mind replayed the near-death experience they had just endured. Clearly, he had underestimated the threat that Gunter posed and couldn't delude himself any longer. It wasn't just his life that was at risk, but Carl's as well. They were both in mortal danger. It was time to take evasive action--he needed to put aside his feud with Gunter and Göring and get Carl out of harm's way.

Early the next morning, Weber retrieved a worn military duffle bag from his closet and handed it to Carl. "Carl, go pack some clothes and a few of your favorite things--you know, pictures of your mother and a couple of toys." He then packed some of his essential gear in a single suitcase. After a quick bite to eat, the pair loaded the car and departed for central Stockholm. Weber watched for a tail as he wove his way through traffic. Seeing none, he made his way to Linnea's. Her stately home sat well back from the road in a copse of trees ringed by an ivy-covered stone wall. Weber turned into the driveway, sped through the front gate, and parked the car out of sight in the rear of the house.

Linnea was startled to find Weber and Carl on her doorstep. Father and son looked haggard and unkempt, like a couple of street beggars from a Dicken's novel. "Robert and Carl--this is a surprise. What are you doing here?"

"Hello, Linnea," Weber replied sheepishly. "Listen, we need a place to hide. Will you help us?"

Linnea graciously ushered Weber and Carl into her home. After settling the boy in a spare bedroom, she made Weber a cup of coffee and invited him to sit at her kitchen table. She sat down beside him and gently placed her hand on his arm. "Robert, you look like death warmed over. What's happening?" Weber's eyes filled with tears. After a long pause, he bowed his head, took a deep breath, and tried to explain why he had come to her for help. Words, however, failed him--his muddled thoughts produced a jumble of words that sounded like some farfetched plot from a second-rate murder mystery. He tried to make Linnea understand, but he was too distraught to provide a coherent account of the multitude of events that had culminated in Gunter's murderous attack.

Hoping that he had given Linnea sufficient background to justify his appearance on her doorstep, Weber addressed the problem at hand. "So you see, Linnea, Gunter is a homicidal maniac. He is tracking our movements and won't hesitate to harm Carl. Moreover, he's told the police that I'm a murderer, and now they're hunting me too. I'm scared, Linnea," Weber confessed. "I don't have a plan, but I think Carl and I must get out of Sweden."

Shock and dismay registered on Linnea's face as she listened to Weber's tale. "It's a lot to take in, Robert. First, Anna dies, and now all this. I can't pretend to understand what you've been through, but fleeing Sweden seems extreme. I don't see why you think leaving the country is necessary."

Chagrined, Weber paused. Even though he had kept the details to a minimum, or perhaps because he had, Linnea was struggling to understand. It *was* a lot to grasp--a complex plot filled with seemingly disconnected events and undecipherable motives. Hell, even he didn't fully understand why Gunter and Göring were trying to kill him. And the implications were dire. Perhaps Linnea feared that he had put her life at risk. "Look, I don't want to endanger you. Perhaps Carl and I should leave."

Linnea dismissed that suggestion. "No, Robert, I care about you and Carl and want you to stay. Carl is all I have left of Anna. Let's talk about this further, and perhaps my grasp of the situation will improve, and we can figure out what you should do."

◆◆◆

Weber spent several days talking with Linnea about everything that preceded the circumstances that now endangered his and Carl's lives. He began with the day that Gunter and Göring had joined Svensk-Luft Airlines and then recounted the events associated with the Arctic crash, Anna's death, his trek across the tundra, Per Nilsson's accusations, his escape from Tromsø, the journey back to Stockholm, and the ongoing plot by Gunter and Göring to discredit and kill him.

Weber experienced a range of emotions as he talked with Linnea, often cycling from intense anger to extreme sadness in a matter of moments. Linnea was a good listener, and Weber soon discovered that sharing his pain was cathartic and perhaps even healing. On some occasions, such as when Weber described Anna's death, he and Linnea broke down, cried, and fell into each other's arms. The intimacy of these moments was overpowering, and Weber soon began to recognize that he was developing feelings for Linnea. He wondered how much of what he felt was attributable to Linnea's appearance. She resembled Anna physically and possessed many of her mannerisms. Even Linnea's scent reminded him of Anna because she wore the same perfume. Although he found it difficult to admit, he felt aroused when Linnea's shapely and supple body was pressed against his.

◆◆◆

There was a solemn look on Linnea's face at breakfast the next morning. "Robert, I understand why you want to leave Sweden. I wouldn't say I like the idea, but I agree that protecting Carl is necessary. I'll lend you some money, and I have some thoughts about how you could distract Göring and Gunter so you can sneak out of the country."

Weber stared at Linnea, dumbfounded. It was suddenly clear to him that his fantasies about her had overcome his desire to leave Sweden. Foolishly, he had allowed his feelings to cloud his judgment. Linnea, in contrast, didn't seem burdened by such illusions and was instead focused on the realities of their situation. It was time he did likewise. He struggled to quell his emotions, put aside his fantasies, and listen to what Linnea was saying.

"Robert, I have a friend who works at *Stockholms-Tidningen*, one of the most influential newspapers in the city, and I think you should tell her what you know about Göring and Baroness Carin von Kantzow. Making their affair public would scandalize Göring, distract Gunter, and perhaps force them to leave the country. While they cope with the fallout, you and Carl could slip into Denmark and then book passage to a safer destination such as England or America."

◆◆◆

The morning the story about Göring and the Baroness broke, Weber called Johansson at Svensk-Luft Airlines and asked to pilot a flight to Copenhagen. He purposely didn't mention Carl because he didn't want his son's name to appear on the flight roster. Several anxious moments passed as his boss contemplated the request. Weber figured that Johansson had misgivings about letting him fly one of his airplanes out of the country because his boss knew he was at odds with the police and likely suspected he was seeking safe passage out of Sweden. After what seemed like an eternity, Johansson consented and scheduled Weber for a flight later that day.

Having arranged passage to Denmark, Weber contemplated his next move. The first step of his plan had come off without a hitch. He'd soon have Carl out of harm's way. The cowering, waiting, and hiding were nearly over. All he had to do now was pack, drive to the airport, and sneak Carl on the plane. So why was he feeling such a strong sense of foreboding? It irked him that he couldn't isolate the source of his discomfort. Did he resent fleeing and leaving everything behind--Sweden, his job, and all he owned? Or was he afraid that Gunter was crouching in the shadows, waiting to pounce? Perhaps it had something to do with Linnea? Whatever it was, there was no turning back now. He needed to steel himself and forge ahead. "Get moving," Weber muttered to himself. "Pack, load the car, and drive to the airport. All else be damned!"

Weber went to the bedroom he'd occupied in Linnea's home and started packing. Linnea appeared in the doorway as he stuffed some shirts into his suitcase. She didn't say anything; she just stood there with her head resting on her shoulder and a faraway look in her eyes. Weber had the feeling that she wanted to say something but couldn't. He walked to where she was standing and looked into her eyes. "What is it?" he asked. Without replying, she reached out, pulled him against her, and pressed her lips against his. Weber didn't resist; he wrapped her in his arms and held her in a long and passionate embrace.

When Linnea let go, Weber stared at her in disbelief. What had just happened? What did it mean? What should he do? He looked into Linnea's eyes, hoping for answers, but found only tears and sadness. He considered asking Linnea why she had kissed him but couldn't muster the courage. Sadly, he realized, the moment's meaning might be lost forever. He was late for his flight. He had a deadline to keep.

◆◆◆

Weber bundled Carl and their belongings into the car and sped toward the airport. He kept watch for pursuers but saw none. When they arrived, he parked near a side entrance to the main hangar and snuck Carl inside. Glancing around, he spotted the plane for the Copenhagen flight--an F7--sitting in front of the main doors, ready to be rolled out onto the runway. But where was the crew? There didn't seem to be anyone in the building. Then he heard voices from the rear of the hangar and realized that the crew was taking a coffee break. There was no time to lose. He quickly ushered Carl to the F7 and secreted the boy inside a cockpit storage compartment.

An hour later, Weber retracted the F7's throttle and taxied onto the runway. His co-pilot, Per Jameson, completed the preflight checklist, and Inga Ryerson, the sole flight attendant, prepared the six passengers for takeoff. Weber radioed to obtain clearance but received a terse response. "Flight aborted. Return to the hangar." The instructions took Weber by surprise, and he was immediately suspicious. "Confirm and explain," he replied. "Police on premises; permission to leave Sweden revoked," he was told.

It was now or never, Weber told himself. He wasn't going to chance a confrontation with the Swedish police. Furthermore, he wouldn't run the risk that the Danish police had been alerted and would be waiting for him in Copenhagen.

Weber revved the three engines, released the brakes, and let the big bird rocket down the runway. Jameson, the copilot, started shouting. "What the hell are you doing? Return to the hanger!" Weber ignored the outburst and retracted the yoke. The F7 lifted off, angled its nose skyward, and quickly gained altitude. When the craft reached ten thousand feet, Weber leveled off and set a course for Oslo. Jameson, his face now contorted with rage, resumed his tirade. "Where are you going? You're off course! Copenhagen's the destination, not Oslo. No, forget that--land immediately! The flight's been canceled. Are you nuts?"

Upon arrival in Oslo, Weber released Carl from the storage compartment. Then he dismissed the passengers, took on a full complement of fuel, and took off for London. Once on British soil, he relinquished the F7 to Jameson and booked passage for himself and Carl on a ship bound for the United States.

Spring 2021: Stockholm, Sweden

Gunter arrived at the Grand Hôtel precisely at 7 AM, dashed up three flights of stairs, and pounded on the door to room 321. Inside the room, Göring and the Baroness slept on a plush, oversized bed, dead to the world after partying until the wee hours in Gamla Stan's bars. The prolonged pounding eventually penetrated Göring's drunken stupor and roused him to something resembling consciousness. The Baroness, lying prone beside him, moaned like a sick cow and pulled a pillow over her head. As the pounding grew louder, Göring cursed, swung his feet over the edge of the bed, and stumbled toward the door.

"Who the hell is making this thunderous din?" Göring roared as he flung the door open and let it crash against the wall. "Gunter! You're lucky I don't shoot you where you stand."

Gunter pulled a folded copy of the *Stockholms-Tidningen* from his coat pocket, leafed through the paper until he found the front page, and then shoved it in Göring's face. "Hermann, you've disgraced yourself again. Thanks to his article, everyone in Sweden knows about your affair with the Baroness."

Göring's shoulders slumped, and his angry expression faded. He stepped aside, allowing Gunter to enter the room, then walked to where the Baroness was sleeping and pulled the sheets over her prone, partially-clad body. Motioning toward the room's far end, Göring led Gunter to a table by the window. He pulled back the curtains and winced as the morning sun streamed into the room. Grunting loudly, he slumped into a chair and read the *Stockholms-Tidningen's* account of his affair with Baroness Carin von Kantzow. Gunter pulled up a chair and quietly steeled himself while waiting for his friend's reaction.

As Göring read the story, he shook his head, groaned, and muttered curses. "Scheisse! Where did the reporter get these details? Someone's been spying on us! I want you to find out who is responsible for this, Gunter!"

"That's a fool's errand, Hermann. The bull's already out of the barnyard."

"Once a farmer, always a farmer, eh Gunter? Spare me your bullshit proverbs."

"I'm not to blame, Hermann, and insulting me won't make this disappear."

"Alright, my mistake. But how can I protect the Baroness unless I silence the spy?"

"The damage is already done, Hermann. But if you insist, I can tell you something that could be a clue. One of the bartenders at a pub you frequent told me he saw a man fitting Weber's description hanging around outside the building."

Göring's eyes narrowed, and his cheeks reddened. "Weber! That murderous swine! Why is he still breathing, Gunter? You promised me you'd 'fix' that problem. Isn't it enough that he killed Rolf? Now he's spying on us."

"Calm down, Hermann, you're jumping to conclusions. We can't be sure that Weber is spying on us or talking to reporters. Many people in Stockholm have witnessed your escapades with the Baroness."

"I suppose you're right. But you didn't answer my question. Why is Weber still harassing us?"

"I'm working on it. That fool should have perished in the Arctic with his wife. He's still telling people that I sabotaged his plane, but, fortunately, no one believes him. A few weeks ago, I tried to shoot him in his bed in the middle of the night. But I became distracted when I saw a young boy in Weber's bedroom. My shot went wild, and I had to retreat when Weber returned fire. I didn't know Weber had a kid, and I don't kill children."

"So another of your maneuvers has failed? There's no excuse for poor planning and execution, Gunter. What in heaven's name will you do now?"

"I told the Swedish authorities that Weber committed crimes in Norway. The police investigated and are now trying to apprehend him for questioning. If all goes well, Weber will be extradited to Norway and sentenced to a long jail term."

"I liked it better when I thought he was dead. Someday, he'll be released and make trouble for us again."

"Perhaps that can be arranged once Weber's incarcerated with other violent inmates."

"I see. I suppose it wouldn't seem suspicious if Weber succumbed to some form of deadly mayhem while he was in prison."

"That's my thinking, exactly."

"Alright. Keep me informed. Now, how do you think I should handle this vile newspaper article? Few intelligent people read this gossip rag, and those who do will dismiss the story as rumor and innuendo. There's no sense in worrying about it. The whole thing will blow over in a day or two."

"I wish that were true, Hermann, but let's not forget what happened in Denmark. In that case, your married paramour was discreet and quietly asked you to leave the country. This time, your amorous adventure has attracted national attention. Not only is the Baroness married, but she has an 8-year-old son. People will see you as a homewrecker. There will be a public outcry and, to save face, Nils von Kantzow--the Baroness's husband--will be forced to act. He's a high-ranking military officer who has political connections. He and his powerful friends will probably have you deported."

"Maybe you're right, Gunter. But this isn't some minor dalliance. I love Carin deeply and will do whatever's necessary to protect her. I'll even leave Sweden if that will prevent her from being disgraced."

"You'd give up your pilot's job?"

"Gunter, it's time I looked for opportunities elsewhere. Investigate some locations for me, will you? Germany would be my first choice, but only if the economic and political climate has improved. Maybe explore Denmark and Austria."

"OK, but let's be realistic. You're not going back to Denmark. Denmark is out of the question."

◆◆◆

Gunter traveled abroad searching for job opportunities and returned several weeks later to report his findings. He found Göring in the same room at the Grand Hôtel, living an isolated existence.

As Gunter entered Göring's hotel room, he couldn't help but stare at his friend. Göring's demeanor and appearance had deteriorated; the man looked stressed, pale, and older than his years. The room was littered with detritus and reeked of body odor, spoiled food, and stale beer. There was no trace of the Baroness.

"Hermann, what's happened to you? Are you alright?"

"My friend, I hope you have good news because I want to leave Sweden. I seem to have worn out my welcome here. My finances are dwindling, and I have no means of support. Johannson fired me! Can you believe that? Sometimes it feels like all of Stockholm is against me."

"I'm sorry to hear that, Hermann. Unfortunately, the news is not good. Germany is racked by chaos and verging on disintegration. Austria's not much better. The entire economy is in shambles, and jobs are scarce. The aviation companies I visited told me that no one is hiring pilots. The so-called Weimar Republic is despised for honoring the Versailles treaty. Politicians are spending so much money on war debt that it is bankrupting the German economy. Runaway inflation has devalued the German mark to the point that it's practically worthless. As a result, people are starving; they seek food, not airplane rides. There is widespread disillusionment with the government, undermining the traditional political parties and fomenting unrest. Extreme left- and right-wing factions have emerged, and there is talk of strikes, assassinations, and rebellion."

"What, then, is to become of us, Gunter?"

"We are German citizens, Hermann. Let's return to Germany and accept our fate."

Summer 1921: Washington DC

Weber and Carl's Atlantic voyage ended in New York. It had taken one week to cross the Atlantic and three additional weeks to clear US customs and secure Carl's residency. When all the paperwork was finished, they spent some time sightseeing and then took a train to Washington, DC.

Upon arrival in Washington, DC, Weber contacted some former friends and asked them to help him find a job and a place to live. One friend, a former MIT classmate named Curtis Taylor, used his connections to get Weber a job with Martin Aircraft in Middle River, Maryland. Another friend, Will Prescott, leased him an apartment in a house he owned that overlooked the Potomac.

Weber was grateful for his new job, but it required him to reinvent himself and prove his worth as an aeronautical engineer. It had been a long time since he had worked in that capacity. Flying planes for an airline was one thing, but designing innovative, airworthy, and profitable aircraft was another.

Martin Aircraft was a fledgling company whose primary objective was to design and build commercial aircraft. Weber was assigned to a team of engineers in a department tasked with developing a new breed of engines that would power bigger and faster aircraft. The man who ran the department, Arthur Dunlevy, was a demanding boss with ambitious production goals. Dunlevy had been poached from another aircraft company and had made it his mission to surpass not only his former employer but all other aircraft manufacturers. Dunlevy rode his engineers hard to achieve his ends and expected the impossible. His daily motto was, "What have you done for me lately?" He told his engineers that he didn't want them to develop an "improved" aircraft engine; he expected them to create a revolutionary device--something astounding--a true technological breakthrough.

Weber soon distinguished himself by devising engine components that his fellow engineers thought were innovative yet feasible. One such invention, a revised air intake that increased engine power and efficiency, was exceptionally meritorious and even won Dunlevy's praise.

As much as Weber liked the work, the constant pressure and long hours began to take a toll. Carl complained that he never saw his father, and his schoolwork suffered. Weber had no life outside of work and ached for some personal connection or intimacy. Occasionally, he met with Curtis or Will for a drink or a meal, but those engagements were few and far between and did nothing to dispel his loneliness or satisfy his amorous longings.

His unresolved feelings about Sweden exacerbated these threats to his emotional well-being. Fleeing the country under duress had been difficult, and Weber was still dealing with the emotional fallout. Every aspect of his being--his job, his relationships, his routines--had been abruptly severed and transformed into raw, painful wounds that refused to heal. Among the worst were the heartaches caused by Anna's demise and his unresolved feelings about Linnea. Those unrelenting injuries plagued him day and night and interfered with his efforts to care for Carl and do his job.

Summer 1921: Munich, Germany

Gunter stepped off the train onto the third platform inside the Munich Hauptbahnhof or central train station. He glanced up and down the crowded platform, searching for the baggage car. There was no time to lose. He had to claim his solitary suitcase and Göring's many trunks, crates, and boxes before somebody stole them.

Gunter hadn't been able to rouse Göring when they arrived in Munich, so he'd abandoned his friend, figuring that the conductor would eventually find Göring and throw him off the train. Leaving Göring on the train, asleep in his seat, didn't sit well with Gunter, but he had no choice. His friend drank heavily after leaving Stockholm and then slept like a corpse during the remainder of the journey. The alcohol-induced coma was Göring's way of coping with the reverses he'd experienced after his affair with the Baroness had been exposed. Stockholm's upper class fired him from his job and scorned him. Worst of all, Carin von Kantzow had retreated from their relationship, saying that her husband's rage and public censure made it impossible for her to continue the affair. Divorce, she had insisted, was not an option, even though she and Nils von Kantzow had been estranged for some time. Göring, depressed and disillusioned, had crawled out of Stockholm like a dog with his tail between his legs.

Gunter found the baggage car at the rear of the train and paid a porter his few remaining Swedish Kroners to load his suitcase and Göring's belongings onto a pushcart. He tried not to think about the future as he wheeled the overladen trolley toward the coach where he had abandoned Göring. He was about to enter the city of his birth--not as a war hero or a renowned aviator--but as a forlorn and destitute beggar. There was nothing for him in Munich: his parents were dead, he had no siblings, and the bank had repossessed his family's farm. Worse still, he had no money, job, or place to live.

Göring's prospects, by comparison, were far rosier. Although his father was retired and living on a state pension, his mother had prospered from a prolonged affair that she pursued with a wealthy physician named Dr. Hermann Epenstein. Epenstein had gifted Frau Göring and her five children a small castle called Veldenstein. It was also to Göring's benefit that he was known throughout the country as a war hero and winner of the prestigious

Pour le Mérit. These circumstances made it likely that he, unlike Gunter, would survive and perhaps even prosper during the lean years of the Weimar Republic.

Chapter 7

Fall 1921: Washington DC

At the end of a particularly difficult week, Weber got a call from Curtis Taylor. Taylor suggested they meet for Sunday brunch to discuss a recently announced government initiative. Weber hated to leave Carl alone on the weekend but agreed because he valued Taylor's friendship and was curious about the initiative.

Sunday morning, Weber drove to the Wilson-McKinley Hotel, took the elevator to the top floor, and searched for Taylor in The Odyssey--one of the establishment's restaurants situated outdoors on a west-facing portico. The Wilson-McKinley was located in the heart of Washington, and its top-floor outdoor portico provided a bird's eye view of Washington DC, including the White House and its surrounding grounds. Weber found Taylor sitting at a table next to the railing that skirted the outer edge of the portico.

Weber greeted Taylor, seated himself at the table, and gazed at the cityscape below. The view was breathtaking. He felt like a bird perched high above the city, looking down on the marble and granite metropolis--the epicenter of one of the world's most powerful countries. Mesmerized by the sights, he sat back in his chair and felt himself relax. It was a warm, sunny day, and the open-air portico was the perfect place to share a meal and socialize with a friend. This was precisely what he needed. Slowly but surely, his job pressures receded into the background.

Taylor put down his coffee cup and smiled. "Greetings, my friend. Glad you could make it. How've you been?"

"Thanks to you, Curtis, Carl and I have re-established our lives after a very arduous transition. The job at Martin Air made all the difference. I don't know where we'd be if it hadn't been for you."

"I'm sorry the transition was so difficult. To be honest, I was surprised that you returned to the States. I knew you took a job with Svensk-Luft Airlines after the war. Some years later, I heard that your wife died. Did you leave Sweden so Carl could be closer to your stateside family?"

"No. We didn't leave Sweden by choice. We had to sneak out of the country--like a cople of rats fleeing a sinking ship. If we stayed, we'd have been killed."

Taylor was stunned. "What? Killed? Surely you exaggerate!"

"No. I'm deadly serious. A man named Gunter Meissner broke into our house during the middle of the night, pulled a gun, and took a shot at me. He nearly hit Carl. We hid at Anna's sister's house until I could arrange a flight out of the country. The flight was scheduled for Copenhagen, but I diverted to Olso and then to London once we were airborne. Because of that incident and another predicament, I'm wanted by the authorities in Sweden and Norway."

"This guy--Gunter--was he trying to rob you? Why'd you let some petty thief run you out of the country?"

"Gunter's not some petty criminal. He's a diabolical, cold-blooded killer. This wasn't the first time he'd tried to kill me, and the bastard murdered my wife, Anna."

"What? Robert, this is inconceivable! Are you saying that this maniac hunted you and your family? But why?"

"It's complicated, Curtis. I can tell you what happened, but I don't know exactly what's behind it. A string of troublesome events occurred over many months, and I'm still trying to understand how they're connected. It started shortly after two German pilots joined Svensk-Luft Airlines. One of the pilots was Gunter Meissner, and the other was a friend of his named Hermann Göring. My boss, Johansson, hired them because they were experienced aviators; both were combat pilots during World War I. Johansson was particularly interested in Gunter because he was a flight engineer for Fokker Aircraft and was in a position to help the airline acquire new planes."

Taylor nodded. "So these Germans had known each other for some time?"

"Yes," Weber agreed. "I had the impression that they had been friends for many years and were stationed together during the war."

"Ok, so tell me what happened."

"I'll tell you the sequence of events as best as I can remember. Not long after the Germans were hired, I entered the hangar and found Gunter working on my plane's engines. Gunter hadn't notified me, and the plane wasn't due for service. When I confronted Gunter, he became defensive and said that Johansson had hired him to make the aircraft more efficient and that he'd found a way to make my plane burn less fuel. When he was done, I carefully examined and tested the plane and found nothing wrong.

A few weeks later, Gunter arranged for Svensk-Luft to acquire a new F7, and Johansson asked Gunter to train me on the plane during a round trip to Copenhagen. During the outbound leg, Gunter told me that he and Göring had been German aces during WW1 and inquired about my wartime service. When I told him I'd flown for the French Air Service, he wrinkled up his nose and called the FAS pilots a bunch of arrogant, unethical pukes. On the return flight, Gunter fell asleep just before we flew into heavy weather.

When I shook him awake, he screamed obscenities, called me 'Loezer,' and nervously fingered a shell casing that hung from a chain around his neck. Soon after, he saw imaginary warplanes attacking us and pulled out a pistol. He loaded the gun and was going to shoot through the windscreen to 'down the bogies.' I had to tie him to his seat to keep him from crashing the plane. Later, Gunter informed Johansson that I had panicked under pressure and nearly lost control of the plane. When I told Johansson what really happened, he chided me for criticizing a superior officer."

Curtis leaned toward Weber and half-whispered, "Wow, this guy sounds unstable. He has no business flying a plane."

"You haven't heard the worst of it yet. Several weeks later, the Svensk-Luft crews went to a pub after a staff meeting, and Göring asked my opinion about flying after dark. Johansson had suggested adding night flights to boost revenue and asked the pilots for feedback. I told Göring that I'd flown a sortie by moonlight during the war, and he and Gunter questioned me relentlessly about the mission. I didn't want to discuss the war because I knew it would be divisive, but they kept pushing me. They were obsessive in their quest for details. I couldn't figure out why they were so interested."

"I assume this night mission was carried out against the Germans. Maybe that's why it interested them so much."

"Maybe, but I wondered if their goal was to embarrass me--to make me out to be one of those 'arrogant, unethical FAS pukes.'"

"Hard to say, but I suspect these guys are still bitter about losing the war. Gunter, in particular, doesn't seem to have gotten over it--hell, he's trying to shoot down imaginary bogies. The man doesn't have his head screwed on straight."

Weber looked at his shoes and took a deep breath. "Now comes the part I find difficult to talk about--Anna's death. Bear with me." Weber gasped and covered his face with his hands. "No, that's the wrong choice of words--I didn't mean to say 'bear.' He tried to speak but was so choked up that words failed him. After a few moments, he regained his composure. "Sorry. Let me try again. Anna and I piloted a winter flight to Tromsø, and while we were flying the first leg, we ran into a massive storm. We flew east toward Russia, trying to do an end-run around the storm, but to no avail. One by one, we lost power in all three of the F7's engines. Unlikely, eh?"

Taylor shook his head in disbelief. "Three engine failures? The probability of that is infinitesimally low."

"Yeah, that's what I thought too. But it happened. One by one, the engines quit, and, in each case, the failure occurred under hard acceleration. To make a long story short, we crashed in a desolate location on the tundra only a few yards from the Arctic Ocean--the plane slid right up to the shoreline and lodged against an iceberg. There were six souls on board: four passengers plus Anna and me. One passenger died on impact, and another lost his mind and went walkabout on the tundra. Anna was injured and unconscious but eventually recovered. We nearly froze the first night, so I decided to siphon avgas from the plane's fuel tanks. While I was at it, I examined the engines. The first engine I inspected had a kink in the fuel line secured with a metal clip. When I disconnected the fuel hose, a metal object fell out. It was a shell casing identical to the one Gunter wears around his neck. That bastard had crimped the fuel line so that, under full throttle, the bullet casing was sucked from the tank into the fuel hose and jammed against the metal clip--starving the engine of fuel. I found the same setup on all three engines."

Taylor, who had been listening quietly, was now wild-eyed and red-faced. He lost his composure, slammed his fists on the tabletop, and bellowed. "That bastard! He deliberately tried to kill you." The outburst drew the attention of other diners. Everyone in the restaurant turned and stared at Taylor.

Undaunted, Weber continued. "Well, Gunter chose to kill indiscriminately, didn't he? It wasn't just me that he tried to murder, but everyone on the plane."

"Yes, but I thought you said that Anna recovered?"

"She did regain consciousness and partial use of her injured shoulder, but she was later attacked and eaten by a polar bear. Her death was the direct result of Gunter's sabotage. As far as I am concerned, he murdered her."

"Oh, Robert, how awful! What a horrible way for Anna to die. You must have been devastated."

"That's putting it mildly. But the story doesn't end there. Several months after I returned to Svensk-Luft Airlines, I overheard Gunter and Göring talking in the main hangar. Göring was angry that I'd survived the crash in the Arctic and returned to Stockholm. Gunter told him that he'd find another way to get rid of me. I don't know if Göring knew he was talking about murder, but it was clear that the two of them were conspiring against me."

"So, Gunter is guilty of premeditated murder. But why--what was Gunter's motive?

"As I said before, I'm at a loss. I haven't been able to figure it out. Do the events I just described suggest anything to you? I was hoping that you might be able to infer something from their actions."

"No, not immediately, but I'll think about it. So, what happened next?"

"The final episode occurred when Gunter broke into our house and tried to shoot Carl and me. That's when I decided that we needed to leave Sweden."

"Whew, that's a hell of an ordeal. I'm glad that you and Carl survived."

"Thanks. I'm grateful that chapter of our lives is over. However, I must admit that I contemplate revenge--I fantasize about finding Gunter and settling the score."

"I understand, but the Swedish authorities should handle that. Did you report this to the police? These are serious offenses, and Gunter deserves a long jail sentence."

Weber shrugged and threw up his hands. "Well, no, I couldn't do that. As I said, besides absconding with one of Johansson's planes, I'm wanted by the Swedish and Norwegian police for another incident. After the crash in the Arctic, I trekked across the tundra to Tromsø, Norway. When I arrived, a constable named Per Nilsson accused me of being an illegal Russian immigrant and threw me in jail. He made it clear that I wouldn't get a fair trial, so I broke out of jail and stole passage on a ship bound for Bergen. Somehow, Gunter found out I was wanted in Norway and told the Swedish police that I was a fugitive from justice. So, you see, I couldn't report Gunter because I was trying to avoid a confrontation with the Swedish police and possible extradition to Norway."

"What a tangled web of betrayal, deception, and scheming! No wonder you fled Sweden."

"Well, I did exact a modicum of revenge. I embarrassed Göring in the press by exposing his affair with a married Swedish baroness. A journalist--a friend of Anna's sister, Linnea—planted the story in a Stockholm paper when Carl and I left Sweden. We used the story as a diversion to cover our escape."

"Pardon me for saying this, Robert, but that punishment does not fit the crime. Look, I want to do whatever I can to help you balance the scales. Right now, I'm so angry that I'd volunteer to help you kill this guy. But that's just my anger talking. We're civilized men, not savages. We can't sink to their level. Realistically, I'd like to help you bring this bastard to justice and help you recover your reputation."

"I appreciate your offer, Curtis, and I'll call on you if the opportunity arises. Now, let's talk about something else. No sense spoiling a sunny day with my dreary misfortunes."

Spring 1922: Munich Germany

Several months had passed since Gunter and Göring had arrived in Munich. Göring had bid Gunter goodbye at the rail station and hadn't communicated since. Gunter had struggled to find work and housing and eventually cobbled together a meager existence. Because there had been no word from Göring, Gunter was concerned about what might have happened to his friend. He ultimately heard through a mutual acquaintance that Göring was living in his family's castle, Veldenstein, located in Hochkreuth near Bayrischzell. He sent a note through the post and arranged to meet Göring at the Bratwurstglöckle, a beer garden in the Marienplatz in central Munich.

"Hermann, how goes it? I haven't seen you since we arrived in Munich."

"Times are hard, but I am surviving, Gunter. How about you?"

"The first month was difficult. I lived on the streets and slept in the gutters. Then, I found a job as a porter at the Bayern Hof Hotel. Two weeks later, I started working nights here as a bartender. Neither job pays well, so I supplement my income occasionally by picking the pockets of passersby in the Marienplatz. You haven't told me what you are doing, Hermann. Have you found employment?"

Göring smiled sheepishly, broke eye contact, and gazed out a nearby window. "No, I haven't, Gunter. I am attending the university and reading political science. I love aviation but want to be more than a pilot. I aspire to do something noble."

Gunter felt his pulse rise and his throat tighten. He put down his beer stein, rose from the table, and turned to leave. As he departed, he glanced over his shoulder. "Hermann, sometimes I find it difficult to be your friend."

◆◆◆

After finishing work at Bayern Hof hotel, Gunter walked to the Bratwurstglöckle, tied a dirty, beer-stained apron around his waist, and began waiting on tables. No sooner had he entered the beer garden's main hall when customers, the majority of whom were men, started shouting his name. Gunter cursed under his breath and tried to restrain his temper. It seemed everyone had an empty stein and an unquenchable thirst for beer.

Gunter was acquainted with most of the people who frequented the Bratwurstglöckle and had deliberately cultivated ties with noteworthy members of the Munich community, such as merchants, city officials, and aspiring politicians. A good listener, he often overhead the conversations of his intoxicated customers and, therefore, knew a great deal about community affairs and city politics.

As Gunter moved about the room, greeting customers and taking orders, he noticed a man with a familiar face sitting alone at a table along the wall. It was Göring. He hadn't seen him for over a year and resented their last encounter. Hesitantly, he approached Göring's table and greeted him.

"Hermann, what are you doing here?"

"I came to apologize, Gunter. I've neglected our friendship. I knew you were having trouble resettling in Germany, and I did nothing. I want to make it up to you. I want us to be friends again."

Gunter closed his eyes, drew a deep breath, and sat across from Göring. "How can I say no, Hermann? I've known you since we were children. We fought together in the war, and we flew together in Sweden. I know your secrets, and you know mine."

"I promise that things will be different now, Gunter. We can meet more often because I'm living in Munich. My wife and I just moved here."

"You're married, Hermann?"

"Yes, to Carin--the former Baroness von Kantzow. Not long after we returned to Germany, she came to visit my mother, and after spending time with us at Veldenstein, she decided to divorce her husband, Nils. We were married earlier this year--on the third of February--and settled near Bayrischzell. We moved to Munich two weeks ago and rented a flat near the Marienplatz."

"What will you do in Munich?"

"I became interested in politics during my stint at the university, and I want to work to restore Germany's honor and prosperity. As you well know, the Treaty of Versailles is a national disgrace and has taken a great toll on the German people. Backstabbers and defeatists run the government. Something has to be done."

"Hermann, I know someone you should meet. I met him here at the Bratwurstgölckle when I was refilling patron's beer steins. He and his friends gather here on Monday nights to talk about politics and Germany's future. His words attracted me like a magnet, and now, whenever I have a Monday off, I attend his meetings. He hates the Treaty of Versailles as much as we do and believes that the cowards in Berlin are destroying Germany. I admire him because he's more than a doomsayer--he has a vision for Germany's future and is taking steps to achieve it. Let me introduce you to him. His name is Adolph."

Fall 1922: Munich Germany

Göring followed Gunter's advice and introduced himself to Hitler in the fall of 1922. The two men enjoyed each other's company and established a robust and enduring relationship. Göring was immediately enamored with Hitler's political vision, aspirations, and objectives. Hitler, in turn, saw Göring as an asset for his budding political ambitions. He understood that Göring's stature as a war hero would not only enhance the legitimacy of the NSDAP, or Nazi party, but also endow him with a loyal and respected functionary. During the closing months of 1922, Hitler conspired with Göring to develop the military arm of his party--the SA, or stormtroopers. Göring's performance proved exemplary, and his success was about to pay dividends in the form of a militia that was strong enough to march on Munich and depose its corrupt leadership.

Fall 1923: Munich Germany

Gunter cinched his gun belt around his waist and slid his Walther-4 sidearm into its holster. He donned his greatcoat and checked to ensure the pistol was entirely concealed. Satisfied that no one would know he was armed, he walked out of his flat, descended three floors to street level, and sat on the front steps. He was expecting Göring to arrive momentarily. While he waited for Göring, he watched the sun rise over the eastern horizon and begin its slow ascent into the morning's clear, blue skies.

Gunter greeted Göring upon his arrival and walked with him to the Bürgerbräukeller, Munich's largest beer hall. He could hardly contain his excitement. Finally, after months of dithering, the NSDAP--or Nationalsozialistische Deutsche Arbeiterpartei, or National Socialist German Workers Party--was about to flex its muscles. He and Göring, along with nearly three thousand other men clad in brown shirts, would march to the Marienplatz, storm the Defense Ministry, and seize control of the Bavarian government. Like their compatriots in the NSDAP, Gunter, and Göring despised the Bavarian leaders almost as much as the scum that perpetuated the Weimar Republic in Berlin.

The march had been hastily scheduled after a failed coup attempt the previous evening at the Bürgerbräukeller, where the Prime Minister of Bavaria, Gustav Kahr, spoke to a crowd of prominent city officials and businessmen. Both maneuvers were the result of intense and sustained political scheming by the founder of the NSDAP--a man named Adolph Hitler. Hitler's agenda was to seize control of Bavaria and use it as leverage against the national government in Berlin.

◆◆◆

Gunter was getting impatient. He, Göring, and a phalanx of stormtroopers had been standing on the streets that bordered the Bürgerbräukeller for more than an hour, waiting for the march to begin. What, he wondered, had happened to Adolph? Without a leader, the troop was rudderless and likely to disband. Rumors began to circulate, the most pernicious of which was that Adolph had fled the city to escape the consequences of the prior evening's failed beer hall putsch.

Gunter turned toward Göring and whispered in his ear. "Hermann, you are the leader of the SA. I think you should step up and take charge."

"Word about this march didn't reach me until this morning, Gunter. Adolph hasn't asked me to take charge, and I don't want to usurp his authority. He's sensitive about things like that. We have no choice but to wait for his orders."

Suddenly, the men sitting near Gunter and Göring stood, strode into the street, and began following a column of marchers walking down Rosenheimer Street toward the Ludwig Bridge. Gunter and Göring hurried after the men and worked their way to the front of the column. There, they saw an old man leading the marchers. He was dressed in a tattered WWI uniform and carrying a saber.

"Hermann, that's General Ludendorff--the World War I hero. He was with Adolph last night at the Bürgerbräukeller. The General is sympathetic to our cause."

"Yes, but why is *he* leading this march, and where is he taking us?"

At that moment, Hitler appeared, brandishing a pistol, and fell into step next to Göring. Several other NSDAP leaders, including Rudolph Hess, joined him.

"Göring, my friend," said Hitler. "Today, we will prevail. We will march to the War Ministry in the city's center and oust Klar and those other backstabbers."

Göring, surprised by Hitler's arrival, eyed him suspiciously. "Adolph, why is Ludendorff leading this march?"

"It was his idea--a tactic for recapturing the momentum we lost last night. The old fool believes he's invincible. He thinks that Kahr's goons in the Bavarian police and military won't shoot him."

As Ludendorff led the procession across the Ludwig Bridge, a phalanx of armed police officers confronted him. He raised his arm, and the marchers came to a halt. In a show of support, Hitler and Göring stepped forward, joining Ludendorff at the head of the column. Göring shouted at the officers.

"Stand aside! We've taken several government officials hostage, and we'll shoot them unless you let us pass."

The police officers conferred for several minutes, and then they slowly broke ranks and walked off the bridge. The stormtroopers cheered, and Ludendorff waved them forward. As the march resumed, Ludendoff and Hitler took up positions at the front of the procession, as did Göring, who walked on Hitler's left. Gunter re-holstered his pistol, assuming that the worst was over. He pushed through the crowd and took a position directly behind Göring.

After crossing the bridge, the marchers proceeded down Zweibruckenstrasse, or Two-Bridge Street, toward the Marienplatz, where the War Ministry was located. Emboldened by their victory over the police, the troopers sang Nazi songs as they marched, oblivious to any further obstacles that might impede their progress.

As Ludendorff and the other leaders approached the Marienplatz, they led the marchers down Dienerstrasse, a narrow street that emptied into an even narrower avenue called Residenzstrasse. The route made Gunter uncomfortable, and as the streets grew narrower, he began to feel claustrophobic. He couldn't shake the feeling that the buildings that lined the streets were closing in on him. The tone of the march had changed, too. The stormtroopers were no longer singing; instead, they were pushing and shoving each other, trying to preserve their positions in line as the streets narrowed, letting fewer of them pass.

Pffffft. Bang! Pffffft. Bang! Gunter ducked and ran for cover, reacting without a moment's thought. He knew that sound all too well, having been conditioned by it during the war. It was the nearly imperceptible hiss of a bullet blasting past his head at supersonic speed. Unfortunately, the war had also taught him that the hiss of a bullet told you nothing about the shooter's position. Lying prostrate in the gutter, he glanced forward, backward, and left and right, searching for a muzzle flash. He saw nothing. All he could conclude was that one or more shooters had fired on them.

The gunfire abruptly resumed, this time with greater intensity. The marchers scattered. Gunter shifted his gaze toward the men leading the procession at the front of the column. He saw Hitler roll sideways and land on his left shoulder. Then Göring stumbled, dropped to his knees, and fell on his face.

Several nearby troopers lifted Hitler to his feet, escorted him to the rear of the column, and pushed him inside an automobile. The vehicle's engine roared, and the car sped away. Gunter rose from the gutter and ran to Göring's side. One glance told him that his friend was seriously injured--a rapidly expanding pool of blood encircled Göring's groin. Gunter summoned two nearby troopers, and together, the men carried Göring around a nearby street corner, out of the line of fire. Gunter used his handkerchief to staunch the wound, and then he and the troopers carried Göring several blocks to his flat.

◆◆◆

Carin was standing outdoors, anticipating Göring's return. She saw the men coming and ushered them inside. As the men eased Göring into bed, Carin saw her husband's blood-soaked groin and panicked.

"Mein Gott, Gunter! What happened? Will Hermann be OK? Who did this? You were supposed to protect him!"

◆◆◆

Two days after the march, Hitler was arrested and charged with sedition. Stunned by the news, Gunter immediately made plans to sneak Göring out of the country. However, every means of escape he contemplated was fraught with challenges, some of which seemed insurmountable.

Göring's frailty would make travel difficult. Although his wounds had been dressed during a clandestine trip to a nearby clinic, they continued to drain and fester. His legs were discolored, his entire body was wracked by pain and fever, and his mobility was compromised. He couldn't stand, let alone walk. Even if Göring could travel, Gunter had severe misgivings about transporting an injured fugitive across an international border. Austria was the obvious destination because Salzburg was only 116 kilometers from Munich. However, reaching Salzburg meant traveling by train or car through border checkpoints where guards inspected travelers' passports.

The problem was solved when Carin convinced friends from Salzburg to drive to Munich, transport her and Göring across the border, and shelter them in their home. Gunter hid Göring under a blanket in the car's trunk, and, to his relief, the Austrian border guards admitted them without incident.

Hitler wasn't as fortunate. He was tried, convicted, and sentenced to five years in Landsberg prison. That development convinced Gunter that Göring must remain outside Germany for the foreseeable future. However, with Hitler in jail, Göring feared for the future of the NSDAP and wanted to return to Germany. Gunter eventually prevailed by convincing Carin that her husband risked prison unless he remained outside the reach of the German authorities. Carin agreed and put her foot down. Göring sulked but soon accepted his fate. He was too ill to do otherwise. With that settled, Gunter helped Carin find temporary housing in Austria and offered to help her relocate Göring if it became necessary to seek asylum elsewhere.

Spring 1924: Munich Germany

The phone rang in Gunter's Munich apartment. It was late, and he had just arrived home from a long shift at the Bratwurstglöckle. He thought about ignoring the call, but his imagination got the better of him. What if it was Adolph? He picked up the phone, barked a curt greeting, and was astonished when he heard the voice of Göring's wife, Carin, on the line.

"Gunter, can you come to Innsbruck? Hermann isn't well. His wound won't heal. It's been quite some time since he was shot, and he's suffering terribly. He moans and cries because the pain is unbearable. Even morphine doesn't help him. We're also in dire financial straits--our bank accounts are empty, and the authorities in Munich won't let us sell our house. Can you help us?"

"Of course, Carin. I'll take an overnight train and arrive first thing in the morning."

Spring 1924: Innsbruck, Austria

Carin greeted Gunter when he arrived at Göring's apartment. She immediately escorted him to the bedroom, where Göring lay flat on his back, moaning.

As Gunter entered the bedroom, Göring opened his eyes, propped himself up on one arm, and then extended his hand, attempting to greet his friend. Halfway through the gesture, he winced and fell back into bed, exhausted.

Gunter was shocked and dismayed; he'd expected Göring to be in bad shape, but his condition was far worse than he had imagined. The formerly vigorous war hero was pale, bloated, and corpulent--he looked like his days were at an end. He glanced at Carin, who, in turn, returned his gaze and shook her head in a gesture of futility. Unsure what to do, Gunter walked to Göring's bed, sat on the edge of thc mattress, and waited for his friend to speak.

"Gunter, I'm glad you're here. I need your help. I must return to Munich to sell our house and then go to Landsberg to visit Adolph in jail. Carin and I are desperately short of money. The Nazis here in Austria have been taking up collections for us, but even so, we are deeply in debt and can't pay our bills."

"No, Hermann. Listen to me carefully. If you return to Germany, you will be arrested and jailed. How will languishing in prison improve your financial situation? And imagine what it would do to Carin if you're incarcerated!"

"It's not just the money, Gunter. With Adolph in prison, the Nazi party is leaderless and in danger of dissolution. We've come too far and accomplished too much to have it all fall apart. Carin visited Adolph at Landsberg and said he was writing a book to publicize his political positions and reinvigorate the party. However, someone has to step up, provide some leadership, and hold the party together while he's incarcerated."

"Maybe so, Hermann, but you can't do that--let Adolph find someone else. Carin tells me that you're addicted to morphine and prone to violent mood swings. And look at you! You're unwell, and you've gained a lot of weight. Face it, Hermann, you must stay here and do whatever is necessary to regain your health. I will keep you posted on developments in Germany."

Chapter 8

Winter 1926: Washington DC

The months and years had passed quickly since Weber had arrived in Washington, DC, because he'd worked incessantly and had little time for anything else. The long hours spent at Martin Air were taking a toll on him, and his time with Carl had dwindled to almost nothing. His once close relationship with Carl had become more distant, and Carl had responded to the estrangement and lack of supervision by disengaging from school, spending his days wandering the city, and fishing in the Potomac. Weber felt he needed to improve the situation, but he wasn't sure what to do. One night, feeling particularly concerned, he called Curtis Taylor and arranged to meet him for breakfast the following morning.

Weber arrived at the Wilson-McKinley Hotel, looking forward to another breakfast at the Odyssey restaurant with his friend, Curtis Taylor. It was a chilly Tuesday morning, and a blanket of fresh-fallen snow covered the city. Shivering after trekking across the city, Weber welcomed the warmth that enveloped him as he entered the hotel. He took the elevator to the top floor and entered the restaurant's indoor banquet hall, where the smell of fresh coffee greeted him. The open-air portico was closed during the winter months, and meals were served indoors. Curtis had arrived and was sitting in a west-facing alcove overlooking the White House.

Weber greeted Taylor and took a seat at the table. They chatted for a few minutes, and then Taylor raised his hand, signaling the waiter that they were ready for breakfast. He ordered eggs, toast, and juice, and Weber requested oatmeal and coffee.

"So, Robert, how has Carl been adjusting to life in the States? I suspect he's had to deal with many changes—a new country, new language, new home, new school, and new peer groups. Has he adapted well or been struggling with acculturation shock?"

"The hours I work seem to stress Carl more than the cultural shift. Although he was already fluent in English and never struggled with schoolwork, he hasn't been able to adjust well to the new environment. He doesn't seem to enjoy school and hasn't made any close friends yet, but he's trying to socialize more. Recently I've discovered that he has been skipping school to spend time fishing in the Potomac. His main complaint is that he never gets to see me because I'm always at the office."

"I understand. These days, aeronautical engineering is a high-stress occupation. The aircraft industry is expanding rapidly, and companies are increasingly competitive. Production demands have skyrocketed because the public has recognized the advantages of air travel, and governments are discovering new aircraft applications. I suspect that aviation's glory days are just over the horizon."

Weber sighed. "Yeah, tell me about it. My boss, Dunlevy, is obsessed with beating the competition and pushes us like there's no tomorrow."

"Sounds like you need a change. Why don't you take a day off and attend a meeting with me?"

"Weber scowled. I'm sure Dunlevy would object. What's the meeting's purpose?"

Taylor lowered his voice to ensure he wouldn't be overheard. "Some people in the government think that aircraft will play an increasingly important role in future wars, and they want to investigate military applications for civilian aircraft."

"Military applications? You mean like turning passenger planes into bombers?" Weber asked.

Taylor shrugged his shoulders. "I don't know exactly. A friend on the committee, Troy Furst, said they want to gather ideas from aircraft engineers. We'd learn more about the Committee's goals if we attended the meeting. Do you want to go?"

"I like to, but I doubt I could convince Dunlevy to give me a day off."

"Just play up the competitive angle and appeal to his profit motive. Tell Dunlevy that engineers from other aircraft manufacturers will be there and, if the committee pursues military applications, it could lead to substantial government contracts."

Weber nodded his agreement. "Good thinking. I'll give it a try."

The next day, Weber screwed up his courage and spoke to Dunlevy. "Look, Mr. Dunlevy, I only need one day off, and, as I explained, the meeting might lead to some lucrative new business."

Dunlevy eyed Weber suspiciously. "I might let you go for the morning. You'd have to report for work after lunch."

Weber had anticipated that ploy. "I'd miss the deliberations and recommendations that the committee will make when the meeting concludes."

"Oh, all right," Dunlevy conceded. "Under one condition. I want you to schmooze with the reps from other aircraft companies and find out as much as you can about their production plans and goals."

This directive caught Weber off guard. "What, you want me to spy on them?"

Dunlevy grinned slyly, pleased with himself for having devised such a clever scheme. He looked like a kid eying a candy jar. "Of course! This is the perfect opportunity to snoop on our competition. I expect a full report when you return to work."

Weber was at a loss for words. He drew a breath, exhaled a derisive snort, and then walked away. He would not commit industrial espionage to satisfy his boss's greed.

◆◆◆

Weber met Curtis Taylor at the main entrance to the Department of Labor Building on B Street. He had decided not to let Dunlevy's stipulations interfere with his desire to spend time with Curtis and attend the meeting on aircraft initiatives. Dunlevy's insistence that he spy on colleagues still rankled, but he figured it was possible to satisfy his boss's greed without compromising his principles. He wouldn't stoop to snooping; instead, he'd summarize the meeting's agenda and colleague's proposals without revealing competitors' plans, proprietary information, or trade secrets. If all else failed, he'd feed Dunlevy some crap and let him choke on it.

Weber and Taylor entered the building, followed signs to the meeting room, and searched for empty seats. The room was nearly full; Weber did a quick body count and figured that at least fifty engineers were in attendance. Taylor pointed toward the front of the room and then ushered Weber toward two empty chairs.

At 9 AM, Taylor's friend Troy Furst entered the room with six other men. Furst proceeded to a podium in the front of the room, and the committee members took seats at adjacent tables, facing the audience. Furst began by introducing his colleagues; two were members of Congress, and four held senior positions in the War Department. He then introduced himself, saying he was a liaison between the Executive and Legislative bodies of government. Next, Furst turned to a nearby blackboard and wrote a list of categories: (1) airframe design and static, dynamic stability, (2) navigation and sighting systems, (3) exterior hatches and doors, (4) engine power, fuel capacities, and aircraft speed and range, (5) incorporation of weapons systems, (6) wingspan, sweepback, lift, and payload capacities, (7) deployment mechanisms for parachutes and heavy equipment, and (8) wheelbase and landing gear placement.

Furst explained that the committee was assembling a "talent roster" that Congress and the military would utilize if there were a need to ramp up military aircraft design and production. After pausing briefly to let his audience absorb that mandate, he passed around a sign-up sheet and asked the attending engineers to self-nominate for each category.

What Furst left unsaid hung like a black cloud over the room--the implication was that high-level government officials thought a war was in the offing. Weber glanced around the room and saw nothing but frowns and scowls. His fellow attendees were troubled by the idea that the government might draft engineers to prepare for that eventuality. For the remainder of the meeting, Furst and committee members asked attendees to consider the listed design categories, suggest specific modifications, and indicate whether those alterations could be assimilated into contemporary aircraft or achieved only by developing new aircraft.

Weber left the meeting feeling a mixture of apprehension and anticipation. On the one hand, the prospect of another war was disturbing, but on the other hand, an international armed conflict would revolutionize aircraft design, expand manufacturing, and boost employment. He'd seen it happen before, but on a much smaller scale, during WWI. In the next war, aircraft would be indispensable, and production demands would expand the aviation industry exponentially. As much as he'd welcome those changes, he couldn't help but count the costs--those gains would be accomplished on the backs of thousands, if not millions, of dead people. Accepting that compromise seemed akin to making a deal with the devil.

Taylor and Weber exited on the Ohio Avenue side of the Department of Labor building. As they walked up E street, Taylor inquired about his friend's reaction to the meeting. "You look displeased, Robert. Care to share your thoughts?"

"I love aviation, Curtis. It's my passion. And there was a time in my life when I wanted combat experience. But the last war taught me some hard lessons. Now, it bothers me that aviation's future will be tied so closely with death and destruction."

"Taylor nodded in agreement. "That concerns me too, Robert, but what can we do? Once a technology exists, some people will exploit it for nefarious purposes. Perhaps we need to ensure that our military planes exceed the capabilities of our enemies' aircraft. Air superiority could be an effective deterrent."

Weber slowed his pace, contemplating Taylor's suggestion. "OK, I see your point. But that couldn't be accomplished unless you knew the capabilities of your enemies' planes. Aircraft design is a progressive process, so you'd also have to monitor innovations and improvements. You'd have to watch your enemies constantly and beat them at their own game, so to speak."

"I agree. That would be essential."

"So what are we talking about, Curtis? This doesn't sound much different than what Dunlevy asked me to do--spy on competitors. You know, engage in industrial espionage." Taylor stopped walking, turned, and glared at Weber. "Come on, Robert, there's no comparison! Dunlevy's out to make a buck and enrich his reputation. Surely, you see more at stake here than profits and personal ambition. You said it yourself. This is about shaping the future of aviation and, I might add, other nontrivial goals such as protecting our country."

Spring 1926: Washington DC

It was a tough morning for Weber, and things were about to worsen. During breakfast, he argued with his son Carl about a school project the boy had failed to complete. Carl's teacher had called the previous evening to inform Weber that his son had failed to submit a homework assignment on Napoleon Bonaparte. The teacher said that Carl wasn't taking school seriously and implied that Weber was an inattentive parent who wasn't committed to his son's education. The criticisms stung and added to Weber's guilt about uprooting the boy after losing his mother and prioritizing his Martin Air duties over his parenting responsibilities.

The escalating guilt simmered overnight and ignited at the breakfast table the next morning. Weber lost his temper and unloaded on Carl. The boy responded by slamming his fist on the breakfast table and sweeping his half-finished plate of pancakes onto the floor. A heated shouting match ensued, after which Carl dashed out the door without looking back. Weber wasn't sure if the boy was headed toward school or another destination. He decided not to worry about it because he didn't have time to chase him. Carl would probably play hooky, and he'd get another uplifting call from the boy's teacher. Swell.

As he drove to work, Weber ruminated about the altercation. Perhaps he had been too hard on Carl. However, something had to be done regardless of who was to blame. Carl had been an outstanding student in Sweden, but now he often neglected his homework and was frequently truant. More than once, Weber had caught him fishing from the banks of the Potomac on a school day. That had to stop. But what was the solution? Try as he might, he couldn't come up with one.

When Weber arrived at Martin Air, Dunlevy pounced on him with a list of jobs and insisted that he drop everything and complete his demands by the end of the day. Weber thought about telling Dunlevy to go to hell but restrained himself. Barely. Weber threw himself into work to contain his anger and tried not to think about Carl. The ploy, however, failed to accomplish its intended purpose. He was still fuming when lunchtime rolled around.

At noon, Weber entered the lunchroom, bought a peanut butter sandwich, and approached three engineers from his workgroup sitting at a table near the back of the room. The men were engaged in conversation but fell silent when Weber sat down. "Sorry to interrupt," Weber said, feeling somewhat self-conscious. "What's up?"

"Nothing much," remarked Elroy Harnett, the engineer seated across from Weber. "If you must know, we were discussing a rumor that Dunlevy's eliminating staff at Martin Air to cut costs. We're wondering how many in our group might get the ax."

"This day just gets better and better," Weber snorted sarcastically.

A hush fell over the lunchroom as Weber took a bite of his sandwich. He and the other engineers glanced around, trying to determine what had precipitated the silence. The cause was soon apparent. Dunlevy stood in the doorway to the lunchroom, scowling.

"Weber," Dunlevy barked. "Phone call. Curtis Taylor wants to talk to you. Make it snappy. That daft bloke is tying up my line."

Weber stood, excused himself, and followed Dunlevy out of the lunchroom. Once inside Dunlevy's office, Weber picked up the phone. "Hello," he stammered into the mouthpiece, feeling awkward and uncomfortable. Dunlevy stood there glaring; he wasn't about to give Weber any privacy.

"Robert, it's Curtis. We need to talk immediately."

"Sure, but I can't talk now. I'll call you tonight." Weber put down the phone and turned to leave. Dunlevy cornered him before he could get out the door. "So, Weber, what did Taylor want?"

"None of your business, Dunlevy."

"Is Taylor trying to lure you away from Martin Air? Are you considering another job?"

"Nothing was said about jobs, Dunlevy."

"Look, Weber, I know that Taylor helped you get this job. Taylor thinks he's a big deal in the aircraft industry because he knows Mr. Martin. Well, let me tell you something, Weber. I am a bigger deal than Taylor. Mr. Martin and I play golf together! You remember that."

"Believe me, Dunlevy," Weber growled, "I won't forget."

Instead of returning to the lunchroom, Weber left the building, walked to a nearby payphone, and called Curtis Taylor.

"Sorry, Curtis. Dunlevy was listening to our conversation. I'm at a payphone. What did you want to talk about?"

"Robert, Troy Furst wants to talk to you. Right away--preferably early tomorrow. Can you attend a 9 AM meeting at the War Department in the Munitions Building on Constitution Avenue?"

"Wait a minute," Weber replied. The War Department? I thought Furst was some government liaison."

"All will be revealed tomorrow, Robert. Meet us in room 221."

"Curtis, what am I supposed to tell Dunlevy?"

"Say nothing. Skip work and come to the meeting."

"Easy for you to say, Taylor." The irony wasn't lost on Weber. He thought of Carl and then chided himself. "Now, who's playing hooky?"

◆◆◆

When Weber left home and drove toward the Munitions Building, the horizon was alight with a pinkish-orange glow. He was getting an early start to avoid central city gridlock and ensure he was on time for his 9 AM meeting. One of his favorite restaurants was only a few kilometers from the War Department. Stopping there for coffee would allow him time to gather his thoughts and prepare for whatever lay ahead.

Fortunately, this day was off to a better start than yesterday. Breakfast with Carl had been civil, perhaps even pleasant. The flashpoint that had kindled yesterday's conflagration had not reignited--there had been no additional incendiary phone calls from Carl's teacher. To Weber's amazement, the boy hadn't played hooky after he stormed out of the house; he'd gone to school and attended his classes. Thank God for small miracles.

Whether his fortuity would endure depended on what happened next with Troy Furst. Admittedly, he didn't know what to expect. Curtis Taylor had been less than forthcoming about the meeting's purpose, leaving him feeling uneasy. What could the Department of Defense want with him? No sense speculating because he didn't have a clue.

◆◆◆

An Army lieutenant motioned to Weber as he approached the reception desk at the main entrance to the Munitions Building. The lieutenant stood ramrod straight and wore a crisp, freshly-pressed khaki uniform. The uniform's drab color was offset by a raft of multi-colored ribbons clustered over the lieutenant's left front shirt pocket. The officer checked Weber's ID and then escorted him through a maze of hallways until they reached room 221. The nameplate on the door read "Troy Furst, Colonel, Army Intelligence." Weber gawped at the inscription, momentarily baffled by the realization that Furst was an intelligence officer and a high-ranking one. Alarm bells began to ring in his head, and his heart skipped a beat. What, he wondered, had he gotten himself into? He tried to conceal his unease as the lieutenant stepped forward and knocked on the door.

Furst opened the door, greeted Weber, and then turned toward the lieutenant and snapped off a dismissive salute. As Weber entered Furst's spacious office, he saw that the walls were covered with aerial photographs of military airports, most depicting installations built on remote, challenging landscapes such as mountains, tundra, and deserts. At the rear of the office was a large window that overlooked Constitution Avenue. Centered in the room was a conference table surrounded by eight chairs. Curtis Taylor was sitting at the far end of the table. Furst took a chair opposite Taylor and motioned for Weber to take one of the six remaining seats.

"You're probably wondering why I asked you here today," Furst intoned. Pardon all the mystery, and just so you know, I forbade Curtis from telling you anything about this meeting. What we discuss today must remain confidential. Therefore, before I say more, I must insist you sign a nondisclosure agreement. The agreement is an extension of the Espionage Act of 1917 and is patterned after Britain's Official Secrets Acts of 1911 and 1920. By signing it, you agree not to disclose restricted information and acknowledge the penalties for doing so."

Weber hesitated, trying to decipher Furst's ploy. The meeting hadn't even started, and Furst was asking him to sign a gag order without telling him what he couldn't talk about. "Let me get this straight. You want me to promise that I won't talk about something that you haven't told me yet? Is that what you're asking me to do?"

"Yes, that's right. Curtis has already signed an agreement because he and I have been working together. He knows very little, however, about the purposes of today's meeting. Once you sign, I will elaborate, and we will all be on the same page."

Weber looked at Taylor, who nodded his approval. Weber shrugged. "Well then, I guess I'm in good company. Pass me the form, and I'll sign it."

After Weber signed, Furst countersigned the agreement and placed it in a file cabinet. "I will begin, Mr. Weber, by offering you a job. Would you be interested in working for the government?"

"Perhaps," Weber replied, "but I can't say without knowing more about the job. Does this have to do with developing military applications for civilian aircraft?"

"Not exactly," Furst replied. "People at the highest levels of our government have asked me to assemble a comprehensive picture of military aircraft production in another country. Typically, gathering data on foreign aviation industries is not too difficult. However, in this case, the country in question isn't supposed to have military aircraft, let alone be in the business of building warplanes. My superiors are concerned that this nation might secretly do so using disguised or concealed facilities.

Weber had already guessed that Furst was talking about Germany. The Treaty of Versailles at the end of WWI discredited Germany, restricted the country's economic and military capabilities, and plunged the nation into chaos. For many Germans, the enduring humiliation and financial hardship had been a bitter pill to swallow, and the sour aftertaste had only grown stronger over the years. Gunter's rants had made that abundantly clear. Any mention of Germany's defeat or war reparations had transformed Gunter into a seething mass of anger and resentment.

Furst continued. "To put this in perspective, aircraft manufacturing might be just one component of an extensive, underground rearmament effort that includes the production of many types of military equipment and munitions. Although it is important not to lose sight of the bigger picture, this office has been tasked with a single objective--to gather intelligence on military aircraft production. I think you are the man to help me accomplish that goal."

Perplexed, Weber stared at Furst, momentarily at a loss for words. Both Furst and Taylor eyed him expectantly, waiting for a response. Finally finding his voice, Weber stammered, "Me? Why me?"

Furst nodded. "With Curtis' help, I have assembled a dossier on you, Weber. You're an impressive individual and, we think, uniquely qualified for this mission. You design airplanes for a living, and you're one of the most inventive aeronautical engineers in the business. You innovate aircraft, which means you'd recognize others' attempts to do the same. And, you've been a combat pilot, so you're familiar with warbirds, air skirmishes, and the differential requirements of military aircraft compared to commercial planes. You've also been a commercial airline pilot, so you're familiar with civilian flight rules and regulations and could be employed as a transport pilot. Your family heritage is German, and you speak German. Curtis, have I left anything out?"

Curtis said, somewhat sheepishly, "Robert, I apologize for giving Troy personal information without your knowledge. This mission is essential to the future of our country, and we're convinced that you can succeed where others cannot. You may disagree. To that, I would say: put your misgivings aside and be a patriot--your country needs you."

Weber glared at Taylor. "Are you questioning my courage, my patriotism?"

Sensing that Taylor may have overstepped, Furst took over. There's another reason, Robert. Our plans dictate that we recruit an unattached person; as fate would have it, you're not married. My condolences, by the way, on the death of your wife."

"Gees, you guys don't miss a trick. What's next, you want me to change my sexual orientation?"

Furst chuckled, hoping to break the tension. "No, nothing like that. I assure you."

Weber, however, was not amused. He rose from his chair, walked to the window, and stared outside. After a few uncomfortable moments, he pivoted and marched to where Furst was seated. "Look, Furst, enough about me, and stop talking in generalities. Maybe you better tell me what you have in mind for this widowed spy. What exactly would you have me do?"

"Certainly," Furst replied. "I'll describe how we envision this mission--what we see you doing as an operative, and what we hope to accomplish--but please understand that our plans are not fixed or finalized. It's important that the operative fits the mission and the mission fits the operative. You're well suited for this mission, but we want your help designing the operation so that it fits you."

Weber returned to his chair, sat down, and exhaled. "Alright, I'm listening."

"We'd devise new identities for you and Carl and set you up in Berlin," Furst explained. "Once established, you'd investigate the German aircraft industry and determine whether steps are being taken to design, produce, or test military aircraft. Infiltrating you into that industry as an engineer might seem a reasonable way to access that information, but our sources advise against that strategy. That tactic, they say, would be risky and problematic. Fabricated engineering credentials might not withstand scrutiny. Plus, new engineers are usually assigned to a particular job at a specific facility and don't have the freedom or clearance to explore concealed or secret enterprises, such as warbird production. It seems safer to gain access indirectly, through covert channels or roles that would not invite scrutiny or suspicion.

Taylor chimed in, "Toward that end, we would provide you with multiple identities. As your primary identity, you'd be a visiting American clergyman. You'd also possess two other sets of forged papers--one identifying you as a German citizen with a pilot's license and another portraying you as a Swedish national employed by a commercial airline."

"A charming deception--and one you probably think is foolproof," Weber said sarcastically. "And who would Carl be in this scenario?"

Furst smiled. "The son of a clergyman--a preacher's kid. Think about it. It's genius, don't you think? No one would suspect a preacher and his pious son!"

"Why stop there?" Weber retorted. "Why not give Carl a German

Shepherd that genuflects or a parrot that prays in German? Seriously, are you guys off your rockers? What business does a preacher have with the aircraft industry? You think his dog collar will get him past security at secret installations?"

The room was silent for several seconds. Taylor squirmed in his chair, coughed, and cleared his throat. "Well, Robert, that's where your marital status comes into play. The plan is that you would court and perhaps even marry a woman who's highly placed in the German aircraft industry--one of the country's foremost female aeronautical engineers."

Weber bristled. "Surely you're not serious. You want me to woo a woman and perhaps even marry her so that I can spy on her? I can't think of anything more disingenuous and despicable."

"Let's be honest, Robert," Furst replied. "Men do that all the time--feign interest, spin lies, and even promise commitment so that they can have sex with a woman."

"And you think me that kind of man?"

"No, I am not saying that. I am asking you to play a role. One that might seem contemptible but done for a noble purpose. You'd do this for your country's greater good and future."

"Oh," Weber retorted, "so reprehensible acts are OK as long as they are cloaked in the flag? How's that any different than what you're accusing the Germans of doing?"

Furst appeared irritated and leaned forward in his chair as he addressed Weber in a firm tone. "Come down off your pedestal, Robert. I am not going to argue with you about the ethics of spying. This mission is predicated on a simple premise: fewer people will die if we can prevent another war."

Weber pushed his chair back from the table and stood, preparing to depart. "I am sorry to disappoint you, gentlemen, but I cannot imagine doing this."

Taylor rose and looked Weber in the eye. "Robert, if you can't do it for us or your country, then do it for Carl."

Weber glared at Taylor. "Do it for Carl? Why would I move to Berlin and become a spy for Carl's sake?"

"Robert, it's no secret that you're concerned about Carl. You've said as much, and it's written all over your face every time we meet. Maybe DC isn't the best place for Carl. He's a gifted kid, and his school isn't meeting his needs. Plus, how can you be a good father when Dunlevy's sucking the life out of you?"

"That's a low blow, Curtis--using Carl and my parental guilt as leverage. You know I'd do anything to help Carl. I can't believe you'd take advantage of my vulnerability as a father."

"Come on, Robert. I'm speaking as your friend. You're a good father, and I empathize with your concerns about Carl. I'm not some narcissist who would exploit your vulnerabilities to suit my purposes. I believe it would be in Carl's best interests to accompany you to Berlin."

"You better explain yourself because I fail to see how anything about this mission would benefit Carl."

Furst, having refrained from interfering in the deliberations about Carl, now stepped in on Taylor's behalf. "Berlin has an outstanding tech-focused high school that we think would be perfect for Carl. The school specializes in math and science and accepts only high-aptitude students. Nearly all its graduates attend university and work as scientists and engineers. Isn't it possible that a gifted kid like Carl would be better off in a school that focused on his strengths and challenged his abilities?

Weber felt tears form in the corner of his eyes. Furst had struck a nerve; his concern for Carl's future had knifed through his defenses and stabbed him in the heart. For the first time that morning, he considered Furst's proposal.

"Well, Furst, let me ask you something. You said you'd set us up in Berlin. What exactly does that mean? Would you cover our expenses and also pay for Carl's schooling?"

"Yes, of course, plus you'd receive a salary."

"Would it be comparable to what I make at Martin Air?"

Furst nodded affirmatively. Make that one of your conditions for accepting the job. In fact, ask for a raise."

"Why would I need multiple identities? What's your thinking on that?"

"Your first identity, as a visiting clergyman, would be your primary cover. Some Protestant churches have fellowship exchange programs, and we'd use one to place you in a large Berlin parish. We chose that occupation because it's not likely to invite scrutiny or arouse suspicion. Who would suspect that a clergyman, in actuality, is an aeronautical engineer who's spying on the German aviation industry?"

"Agreed, but I doubt I'd be convincing in that role. I have no background or preparation for a religious vocation."

"Not to worry. We know people who could coach you, and we'd find you a mentor in Germany."

Furst paused, and Taylor took over. "We devised the other two identities to facilitate investigative activities and travel. As a German citizen with a pilot's license, you'd have the flexibility to travel around the country and visit sites you deem worthy of investigation--such as factories or airfields. As a Swedish commercial airline pilot--a job you're already qualified to do--you'd be able to leave Germany expeditiously, should the need arise. It would also serve as an avenue for smuggling documents or other contraband to a neutral country and as a destination for meetings with a controller or other agents."

"Have you forgotten, Curtis, that the Swedish authorities want me?"

"No, Robert, I haven't. We'll have more to say about that if you undertake this mission."

Weber scratched his head, opened his suit jacket, and straightened his tie, all the while looking like he was lost in thought. Several moments later, he squared his shoulders, leaned forward, and made eye contact, first with Taylor and then with Furst. "Gentlemen, I can't give you an answer now. I'll need a few days to contemplate your proposal. It's a big decision, and I want to discuss it with Carl. Plus, if I were to accept this mission, there are certain things I'd need you to do for me."

"Make a list, Robert," said Furst. "Let's meet again and discuss your decision and conditions."

◆◆◆

Over the next few days, Weber tried to imagine himself as a spy disguised as a clergyman, living in Berlin with Carl. At first, he couldn't envisage himself in that role--it was too much of a stretch--one that would necessitate acting in ways totally out of character. Later, however, when he tried to picture some of the more adventurous aspects of the mission, he felt his resistance diminish. There was no denying that he felt an emotional pull underneath all his intellectual objections--the same kind of magnetism that had drawn him to aviation and made aerial combat seem enticing. He chided himself for allowing such primitive feelings to enter into his deliberations. After all, he wasn't a kid anymore; he was an adult and owed it to Carl to act like one. Still, he asked himself, didn't mature and honorable individuals put others' welfare--"the greater good" --above their self-interest? Hadn't Furst justified the mission in precisely that way?

He wondered, however, if Furst's logic was flawed. After all, the United States was not at war with Germany--Furst was basing his argument on a hunch--he believed war was inevitable. Or, did Furst know more than he was letting on? Perhaps Army Intelligence had incriminatory political or military information that Furst hadn't shared with him. Even after signing a nondisclosure agreement, he felt that Furst wasn't telling him everything. Both Furst and Taylor had deliberately sidestepped some of his questions. It was quite possible, therefore, that Furst did have additional information about Germany's military situation but had chosen to keep it secret. Why else would the government risk placing an undercover agent in Germany's capital? Surely, it would embarrass the United States and, perhaps, even cause an international incident if the Germans uncovered it. That thought triggered a darker realization. Suppose the mission *was* exposed--what would the Germans do to him? Worse still, what would they do to Carl? The scenarios that came to mind were particularly unsettling.

Coupled with those disturbing thoughts was the prospect of seducing some female aeronautical engineer. Weber found that aspect of the mission particularly distasteful. He felt sure he didn't have the scruples or the skills to pull that off. That realization made him wonder whether the mission's risks outweighed its benefits. Alternatively, perhaps he was focusing too much on the negatives and losing perspective. Rather than let his misgivings multiply and kill his interest in the mission entirely, he decided to discuss his concerns with Curtis Taylor.

◆◆◆

The two friends reprised their lunch at the Odyssey. Weber arrived early, ordered coffee, and procured a table on the perimeter of the outdoor portico. As he gazed out over the city, a warm breeze ruffled his hair and tugged at the lapels of his suit jacket. Shadows created by easterly-drifting clouds skimmed across the buildings and monuments that lined the avenues below.

Taylor arrived and pulled up a chair, snapping Weber out of his reverie. "Sorry I'm late, Robert; I've had a busy morning."

"Thanks for making time to meet me, Curtis. I need your advice. I'm interested in the 'job' that Furst offered me, but I have some concerns. Would you be willing to step out of your Army Intelligence role so that we could talk as friends?"

Taylor's eyes narrowed. "Admittedly, the line demarcating those roles has blurred, but I'll do my best, Robert."

"I am concerned about the risk this mission poses for Carl. He might pay a heavy price if I'm exposed."

"Realistically, you'd both be at risk, but I understand your concern as a parent. Perhaps Furst could create some safeguards for Carl, like a pre-arranged emergency escape route. That way, if Carl's in danger or the operation unravels, you could send him out of the country to a safe location."

"Good idea, but how foolproof would that evacuation plan be? It would have to be reliable for me to consider it." Weber turned, glanced over his shoulder, and lowered his voice. "Another aspect of the assignment that bothers me is having to seduce some woman."

"Yeah, that's rough duty. Maybe you should ask Furst for hazard pay."

"Enough with the jokes, Curtis. I'm serious."

"Okay, I knew you'd balk at that. I can sympathize because that wouldn't come easily for me either. We're not those kinds of guys. But perhaps you're looking at this objective in the wrong way. Instead of construing it as 'seduction,' which has tawdry overtones, why not think of it as pursuing a romantic relationship? There's nothing improper about courting a woman. You could try to strike up a friendship based on common interests and see where it leads."

"You make it sound easy. I'm still grieving the loss of my wife. Do you know how long it's been since I've dated? Besides, I might already have feelings for a woman I knew in Sweden."

"Do tell, Robert!"

"Curtis, we're not in junior high school. Would you focus, please? My love life--or lack of one--is irrelevant."

"Alright, but try to lighten up, will you? You're wound tighter than a coiled spring."

"Of course, I'm tense! There's a lot at stake. Just hear me out, okay? Maybe I'll be able to relax after you help me work out my concerns."

"Okay, okay. So what else are you concerned about?"

"Curtis, in all the years we've known each other, have I ever seemed like someone who was cut out to be a clergyman?

"Robert, I don't mean to offend you, but I don't think I ever thought of you that way."

"That makes two of us. My family's not religious, and I had no formal religious training as a kid. I've been to church a few times but never attended consistently or felt drawn to religious literature or activities. I wouldn't call myself an atheist, but I'm not what you'd call a 'believer' either. I guess I'm an agnostic."

"Well, I've got you beat there, Robert. I'm Jewish, and my father is a rabbi. I had many years of religious training and spent a lot of time in synagogues. I rebelled against my father and my faith when I reached adolescence because I resented being a 'rabbi's kid.' I felt confined by the role and wanted to avoid its expectations and strictures. Now, as an adult, I can see that I overreacted; like most adolescents, I just needed some autonomy so I could figure out my identity."

"Well, then, perhaps you could advise me. You know, teach me what to say and do so I'd appear religious. Help me learn the rules that clergymen are expected to live by, like the Ten Commandments, so my actions would conform to people's expectations."

"There's a lot more to it than that, Robert. I might be of some help because Judaism and Christianity are related, but I'd recommend that you follow Furst's advice. In Berlin, you'd apprentice with a mentor--a senior German clergyman. You'd be a novice at the outset, so no one would expect you to know everything. Your mentor would coach you until you learn the role."

"I suppose you're right, and I find your perspective helpful, but I still have doubts. My overarching issue is that I'm uncomfortable with all the duplicity and deception this job requires. Not only would I have to sneak around spying on the Germans, but I'd also need to seduce some woman and masquerade as a member of the clergy."

"Here's a thought, Robert: Another agent I work with told me that spies are like actors who play a specific character. They create a role and script suited to a mission's objectives and then invent a character to act out the role. The trick is to 'become' the character so you never step out of the role or compromise your identity. That tactic might also enable you to divorce yourself from the character you're playing so that you could do things you dislike or feel ill-prepared to implement--like wooing a woman you aren't attracted to or pretending you're a man of God."

Weber nodded and shifted forward in his chair. "I'm also concerned about some basic logistics. I'm unsure how long I could 'stay in character' to use your analogy without needing respite. I'd need to step out of the role occasionally, maybe even leave Germany sporadically, to escape the pressures of maintaining a false identity. Living all those lies would wear me down, and I'd need an occasional reprieve."

"Of course. I'd be your contact person and arrange for us to meet regularly in Berlin or outside Germany. Furst will facilitate those meetings because he wants you to smuggle classified information to Army Intelligence. But I'd be willing to rendezvous with you anytime you need a break. Hey, what if we met somewhere near that woman you like in Sweden?"

"Oh, so now you're a matchmaker, eh? Here's another complication, Curtis. Remember what I told you about Gunter and Göring--the two Germans who want to kill me? As I said, I don't know what they have against me, except maybe I flew for the FAS, and they're still nursing grudges about the Versailles treaty. My concern is that if I ran into these guys in Germany, there's a good chance they'd recognize me. That could scuttle the mission and put Carl in danger."

"That is a concern, Robert--one I am unprepared to address. You should raise it with Furst and see what he suggests."

◆◆◆

Still feeling ambivalent, Weber decided to broach the subject with Carl. The boy's appraisal mattered more than his. The mission wasn't worth considering unless Carl was receptive and felt he'd benefit from the move.

The following morning, Weber shouted up the stairwell to wake Carl for breakfast and then returned to the kitchen to finish preparing one of his son's favorite foods--pancakes. Shortly after, Carl bounded down the stairs, entered the kitchen, and sat at the table. He smiled as his father placed a plate of pancakes before him.

"This is odd, Dad. Don't get me wrong, I love pancakes. But you're usually too rushed on workday mornings to make them. What's up?"

"Tell me something, Carl. What would you miss if we didn't live here, in DC?"

"Fishing."

"Really? Is that all?"

"Yes."

"Not friends? Not school?"

"No, I don't have any friends. Definitely not school."

Well, I've been offered a job in Berlin, Germany. Do you think you'd be interested in living there? The city has a world-class high school with a curriculum focused on math and science, much like the school you attended in Sweden. I wondered if a school like that would be better for you. Maybe you'd be more interested in school again and feel happier. You might even make some new friends."

"It couldn't be worse than here."

"Wow, that's a ringing endorsement! Come on, what do you really think?"

"Would we have to speak German?"

"Yes, but you could do that. You'd probably have to learn some new words and practice a bit, but it wouldn't be much different than talking with your grandparents."

Carl nodded but then frowned. "Wait a minute. Who's offering you a job? What would you do there?"

"I'd be exploring a new career and doing part-time consulting work in the aviation sector for the United States government."

"New career? Really? What kind of new career?"

"I know this will sound strange, but I've considered entering the clergy. There is an internship exchange program in Berlin that would allow me to try it on an exploratory basis. The program is for Americans who want to do coursework in theology and work as apprentice pastors in Germany."

"Really, Dad? Is this a joke? You've always been interested in airplanes. You eat, sleep, and breathe aviation. For heaven's sake, you work 24 hours a day at Martin Air. I can't imagine you doing anything else."

"Well, Carl, our lives have been upended, altering my perspective. Given all that's happened, I've had to reassess what's important."

"What's happened that would change you so much, Dad?"

Weber felt his throat tighten, and his mouth went dry. "Well, uh, it's complicated," he stammered, flustered by Carl's rapid-fire interrogation. He'd expected Carl to ask about Berlin, the new school, and other aspects of German culture. Instead, the boy was skeptical about Weber's proposed career plans and questioned his father's motives and state of mind. Carl's reaction made Weber wonder whether he should be forthright about the mission--perhaps tell his son some of the less classified details. Carl was no fool, and attempting to mislead him might backfire and put them both at risk. But how much should he disclose? His better judgment told him to say nothing until he'd consulted with Taylor and Furst. For now, he'd try to answer his son's questions as honestly as possible and steer clear of unnecessary subterfuge.

"As you might guess, Carl, the experiences I had in the Arctic after our plane went down altered my outlook on life. Witnessing your mother's demise and contemplating my own while trying to survive on the tundra made me acutely aware of the fragility of life and the imminence of death. That heightened existential awareness led me to question whether God exists, whether there is an afterlife, and whether we will see our departed loved ones again. I had good reason to ask myself those questions, as I suspect many people do at some point in their lifetimes. I so longed to be with your mother that I wasn't sure I wanted to survive. Ultimately, my love for you kept me alive and brought me home. But the angst and vulnerability provoked by those events and the resulting soul-searching that I did on the tundra changed me--for the better, I hope. Those experiences are partly what makes me interested in exploring the clergy. Are you following what I'm saying?"

"I think so, Dad. Mom's death changed me, too. You know, there was a moment when you and Mom were missing in the Arctic when I could feel Mom's presence. Like she was in the room with me. I was alone in my bedroom at Linnea's house. I didn't know Mom was dead, but I wondered if something bad had happened to her. It seemed like she was saying goodbye. Is that what you're talking about--seeing our departed loved ones again?"

"Oh, Carl, thank you for telling me that! We'd both be better off if we could talk about your mom and how much we miss her. I don't know how to interpret your experience, but I'm glad you feel an intimate connection with your mother. An experience like that is something to remember and cherish. I wish I could feel that close to your mother again. She has been in some of my dreams, but that's not like being with her again."

◆◆◆

Weber removed a crinkled piece of paper from his inside suit pocket, unfolded it, and placed it on the conference table. Furst nodded toward the paper. "So, Weber, you've returned and brought a list. Does this mean you're interested in the mission and ready to negotiate?"

"It does, although I still have some reservations. I'm not ready to make a firm commitment, but I am willing to take the next step and see where that leads," In actuality, Weber felt more certain than he was letting on because he now knew that Carl was committed to the move and would likely benefit from it. The conversation he'd had with Carl about Berlin had taken an unexpected turn when it provoked an intimate and emotional discussion about Anna's death. It was the first time Carl had talked about the loss of his mother, and Weber had immediately understood the significance of that detour. He'd abandoned his original aims and encouraged Carl to express his grief. That catharsis made the two of them feel closer, and Carl eventually announced that he wanted to move to Berlin.

Furst opened a folder, withdrew a sheet of paper, and picked up a pencil. "OK, Weber, what are your terms? What will it take for you to agree to this mission?"

"There are some assurances and provisions that I'd need from you. Let me start with risk management. It's clear to me that this mission is inherently dangerous. I want an around-the-clock, fail-safe evacuation plan for Carl so that he would be transported to Sweden immediately if I decide he is in danger. I'd arrange for his aunt in Stockholm to be his guardian. For the same reason, I want an airplane to be located at a private airport in Berlin so that Carl and I have a means of escape that wouldn't depend on public transportation or expose us to border inspections. I'd also use the plane for mission objectives, such as investigating remote factories or airstrips, using my identity as a German pilot."

"Certainly, Weber. Carl can use our emergency flight service, and access to an airplane was already part of the plan."

"How reliable is your emergency flight service?"

"Don't worry, Weber, it's dependable--you can count on it. Now, what else is on your list?"

"I'd like permission to share information about this mission, as needed, with my son. Carl is highly intelligent and observant. Eventually, my behavior will give me away, or he will see through my excuses and lies. I'd rather him understand that I am working covertly, so he will know to keep mum and perhaps even run interference for me occasionally. I'd only tell him what he needs to know--just the basics. I wouldn't reveal specifics or divulge classified information."

"That request concerns me, Weber. I'm sure you understand that secrecy is essential for your safety and the success of this mission—the fewer people who know about your mission, the better. Plus, informing your son puts him at risk. Have you considered that?"

"Yes, but I'm convinced that deceiving Carl, or attempting to, is even riskier."

"Alright, fine, Weber. I hope you know what you're doing. Your life and your son's hang in the balance. What's next on your list?"

"A secure location outside of Germany where I can receive assistance and deliver my intelligence reports."

"Your friend Curtis Taylor has agreed to be your contact person or handler. He'll be available in Berlin occasionally, and for document transfer or personal reprieve, I can arrange for him to meet you in Sweden or Switzerland."

"When I need to leave Berlin, I'd like to meet Curtis in Stockholm because I have a close friend there--my former wife's sister. The same person who'd be Carl's guardian if that becomes necessary."

"Done. What else?"

"I want to receive double my current salary, with half paid to me in Berlin and half paid to a numbered bank account in Zurich."

"No problem. We'll also provide an expense account and finance any operations you deem necessary to accomplish your mission. Anything else?"

"I want frequent situation reports on the whereabouts of Hermann Göring and his right-hand man, Gunter Meissner. Those two Germans want to harm me and perhaps Carl, too. The last I knew, they lived in Stockholm and worked for Svensk-Luft Airlines. Göring, however, was involved in a public scandal around the time I left Sweden, and he and Gunter may have fled the country. I'd need to monitor their whereabouts to avoid those bastards."

"I understand, but the current sophistication of our intelligence network in Scandinavia and Germany might not permit that kind of surveillance. I'll look into it and get back to you."

"That's it for now."

"So, Weber, have you reached a decision?"

"Pending what you discover about your surveillance capabilities, I'm cautiously optimistic. The assurances you've offered have eliminated most of my concerns."

Chapter 9

Summer 1926: Berlin, Germany

Weber and Carl arrived in Berlin on a warm August afternoon after a long and exhausting journey. Weber had given his notice at Martin Air, and he and Carl quickly packed their belongings, sublet their apartment, and took a train from Washington DC to New York City. In New York, Weber booked a passage on a ship bound for Hamburg, Germany. After a week at sea, they reached Hamburg, and Weber took Carl to a hotel where they spent the night. The next morning, Weber purchased train tickets for Berlin, and they endured a seemingly never-ending rail journey to reach the city.

On the following day, crates filled with their personal belongings, which mostly comprised clothing, personal items, and some small pieces of furniture, arrived via freight train and were kept in storage. Before leaving Washington, Weber had contemplated how much of their personal items they should bring to Berlin. Ultimately, he decided to ship as few of their possessions as possible. Furst had advised him to retain his Washington apartment and depend on his expense account to purchase everything he needed in Berlin.

Weber rented a flat on Victoria Strasse just south of the Tiergarten--the forested, former animal preserve--and two blocks west of the Potsdamer Bahnhof, or rail station. The apartment's location suited him because it had a garage and was near the Stadt Mitte, or city center. To reach downtown Berlin, he only had to walk north through the Tiergarten and then east on Unter den Linden.

Carl accompanied Weber on several shopping trips, and together, they finished furnishing the apartment. Weber's next order of business was to enroll Carl at the BTA or Berlin Technological Academy. On the first Monday morning in September, he woke Carl early and made them breakfast. Then he and Carl walked north on Sieges Allee through the Tiergarten, across King's Square by the Reichstag, and over the Spree River to the BTA, located on Invaliden Strasse near the Lehrter Bahnhof.

Carl was registered and attending his first day of classes in no time. Weber breathed a sigh of relief as he returned to the flat. He'd registered Carl using his German identity papers, and no one had questioned his credentials or Carl's ostensibly German citizenship during enrollment. He'd simply completed an application, presented his passport, and paid the fall term's tuition. Further, the staff welcomed Carl and introduced him to some of his new classmates. Most reassuring of all was Carl's reaction to the school. The boy seemed eager to attend and interested in the BTA's curriculum.

Weber's next priority was to locate his mentor, the Reverend Dr. Dieter Schreiber, and begin his internship. To reach Dr. Schreiber's office near the Kaiser Wilhelm Cathedral, he walked southeast through the Tiergarten, crossed Budapester Strasse, and proceeded east on the Kurfürstendamm. He found Schreiber's office on the second floor of a three-story Romanesque building adjacent to the Cathedral.

Schreiber's office door was open, so Weber knocked and uttered a greeting. Schreiber rose from his desk, returned the salutation, and motioned for Weber to enter. The clergyman was tall and thin and looked to be in his fifties. He had a full head of chestnut-colored hair, a closely cropped beard, and a warm smile. Except for a white clerical collar, he was dressed entirely in black. He offered Weber a chair and asked if he'd like a coffee. Weber gladly accepted.

Schreiber went in search of coffee and returned with two steaming mugs. He handed one to Weber and then sat in a nearby chair.

"Welcome to Berlin, Mr. Weber."

"Thank you. I'm pleased to be here. As you might guess, I'm German by heritage. Please call me Robert. Shall I address you as Reverend or Doctor Schreiber?"

"Ah, yes. Weber is a common German surname that connotes 'weaver.' And, let's dispense with formalities. Call me Dieter."

The conversation continued, and when the men were better acquainted, Weber asked about his internship. Schreiber nodded and struck a thoughtful pose.

"Robert, are you prepared to fully embrace this internship and not enter it halfheartedly?"

"I am," he replied, his words betraying his true thoughts and feelings. It was a shameful lie, but he couldn't tell Schreiber that he'd be using the internship to conceal a plethora of duplicitous acts--this being the first of them.

Schreiber seemed satisfied. "Your intention for the internship, as stated in your application, is to explore the clergy as an occupation. But I hope it will change you as a person. You see, the ministry is more than a vocation; it's a calling. It's about serving God and people. Can you relate to that? More importantly, can you commit to that?"

Probably not, Weber thought. I'll be serving a master named Troy Furst and doing my utmost to deceive you and nearly everyone around me. You seem like a nice guy, and I regret that I can't be honest with you about this charade. But that's not possible, so I'll tell you what you want to hear. "Certainly, Dieter, I'll do my best."

"Excellent. The internship focuses on your head, hands, and heart to impact how you think, act, and feel. As an illustration of the latter, most interns become less self-centered and more compassionate. Here is your first assignment. I want you to compare the meanings of two passages and analyze their implications for individuals and society. The first is found in Thucydides, Book 5 of the History of the Peloponnesian War: *"Right, as the world goes, is only in question between equals in power, while the strong do what they can and the weak suffer what they must."* The second is Micah 6:8 in the NIV Bible: *He has shown you, O mortal, what is good. And what does the LORD require of you? To act justly, love mercy, and walk humbly with your God."* Let's discuss your conclusions over lunch one week from today."

Weber agreed and recorded the appointment, passages, and references in a compact diary he'd purchased for intelligence-gathering purposes. After that, he bid Schreiber farewell and left his office feeling perplexed and wondering whether accepting the internship had been a mistake.

◆◆◆

Having established his cover, Weber initiated preparations for his mission. His knowledge of Berlin was limited, so he began by familiarizing himself with the city. After Carl left for school in the mornings, he journeyed into the city and made mental maps of streets and buildings. He sketched in his diary those landmarks that proved difficult to memorize.

Weber also took steps to maximize his mobility. He could rely on walking and public transit within the city, but trips elsewhere, particularly when it would be necessary to travel incognito or locate and surveil secret facilities, would require a car or a plane. Furst had promised to supply a plane and asked Curtis Taylor to make the arrangements. If all went according to plan, he'd hear from Taylor soon. Locating and purchasing a car, however, was Weber's responsibility.

Finding an automobile proved elusive until chance intervened while Weber walked through a residential neighborhood in the Wedding district of Berlin. As he passed a large, two-story home, a dark blue Mercedes-Benz 630 roared down the street, jumped the curb, and nearly ran over him. The driver--a middle-aged man wearing a German military uniform--stepped out of the car and apologized profusely, explaining that he'd overshot his driveway. The man introduced himself as Captain Horst Wesselman. Weber caught a whiff of alcohol on the soldier's breath but doubted that he was intoxicated. The sincerity of Wesselman's remorse convinced Weber to hold his temper and accept the man's apology.

During their conversation, Wesselman invited Weber into his home for coffee and indicated he was interested in selling his car. The Benz, Wesselman explained, was powered by an in-line six and had a 4-speed manual transmission. The car suited Weber's purposes, so he took it for a drive and found it in good condition. He bought it on the spot, drove it home, and locked it in his garage.

◆◆◆

The following week, Weber received a phone call from Curtis Taylor. Taylor had just arrived in Berlin and suggested they meet in his room at the Hotel Adlon that evening. Weber agreed and asked if he had news about the airplane. Taylor began to reply but then demurred, saying he'd prefer to discuss operational details in the privacy of his room. Weber felt mildly chastised but said nothing because he didn't want to disrespect Taylor's tradecraft.

When evening arrived, Weber walked east on Unter den Linden to the Brandenburg Gate, crossed Wilhelmstrasse, and entered the Aldon Hotel. He found Taylor waiting in the lobby and followed him up several flights of stairs to his third-floor room.

Once inside the room, Taylor greeted Weber warmly and offered him a beer. "Robert, my friend, it's good to see you. Let's talk business first, and we can catch up later. I know you just arrived in Berlin, but Furst is expecting a report. So, please update me on your progress. What have you accomplished, and what do you need?"

"It's early days, Curtis, so there's not much to report. I've secured an apartment on the city's east side and purchased a car. Carl's in school, and I've started my internship. I'm learning my way around the city. Regarding support, I need a plane--have you found one?"

"I'll get to that, but first, tell me your plans. What's next on your agenda?"

Weber's smile disappeared, and his expression soured. "I suppose I should start searching for female aeronautical engineers."

Taylor laughed. "Robert, try to restrain your enthusiasm!"

"You know how I feel about this, Curtis."

"Perhaps I can help. Furst's assistants researched the German aircraft industry and found three names. I've listed them for you." Taylor handed Weber a folded sheet of paper. "Burn that when you're done with it."

Weber glanced at the names. "Frau Obermaier, Frau Lichtmann, and Frau Dortmunder. All very charming, I'm sure. I can't wait to meet them." Weber frowned as he pocketed the paper. "So where do I find these women?"

"Sorry, but I can't help with that. We only know that one works for German's primary air service, Deutsche Luft Hansa or DLH, and another works for the manufacturer Ernst Heinkel Flugzeugwerke or Heinkel Aircraft. We don't know anything about the third woman."

"That's not much to go on. But it's a start. Now tell me about the plane."

"Ok. I've been working in Paris and came across a relatively new Potez 25. It's an open-air tail dragger with tandem seating and 451 horsepower. Should serve you nicely. I flew it to Johannisthal Air Field, which is about 15km southeast of Berlin, and rented a hangar."

"Did Furst send you to Paris?"

"I thought you wanted to know about the plane."

"So, you're working with other agents besides me?"

"Robert, that's privileged information--not something you need to know. Suffice it to say that I do what Furst tells me to do. Remember this: You're one of my closest friends. You can count on me--I'm here for you, no matter what."

"All right, thanks, and pardon my faux pas. But I hope you understand: I'm here alone with a kid, doing things I've never done before and pretending to be someone I'm not. It's disconcerting, to say the least."

"Sure, I understand. How can I help?"

"I can't talk to anyone about what I'm doing in Germany and sometimes I need to weigh options or solve unexpected problems."

"Are you struggling with something now--other than finding the female engineers?"

"Yes, the internship. I know it's my cover, but it's distracting and time-consuming. The first assignment I received from my mentor, Dr. Schreiber, was some kind of philosophical analysis of two literary passages. I haven't the foggiest how to complete it. I'm an engineer, not a philosopher."

"What are the passages?"

Weber took his diary from his pocket and read both passages. "So, what would you say are the implications of those passages for individuals and society?"

"Robert, I'll share some thoughts with you, but I think these writings merit your consideration, especially in the aftermath of World War I. You were there--you saw what happened--the gross inhumanity, the millions killed, and the senseless destruction."

"I remember all too well. The nightmares still haunt me. So, tell me your ideas."

"This is my interpretation, but I see different perspectives in these passages about the forces that organize human relationships and maintain social order. Thucydides believes that brute power or strength is the basis for both, as in the animal kingdom, where predators dominate prey. At a societal level, strong countries subjugate weak ones. For individuals, the tough guy overpowers the weakling, or the bully beats up the victim. In contrast, the Biblical passage I learned during my childhood implies that social order stems from respect for a Higher Power, God, and a society's or person's choice to follow God's principles. So, we're still talking about power, but in this case, Power acts in a prescriptive or advisory capacity rather than a coercive or predatory one.

"What's justice and mercy have to do with it?"

"Justice usually means fairness. Disputes, for example, would be resolved according to what is considered fair or right, not because one party--a country or person--has the power or strength to dominate the other. Mercy refers to compassion and forgiveness. Mercy is shown, for example, when a country or a person commits an offense but is not penalized but rather given a chance to apologize, make amends, or provide restitution."

"What if restitution is forced on one country by other countries, such as when a war's winners force the losers to pay for it?"

"I wouldn't call that mercy."

"Nor would I. It's more like rubbing the loser's nose in it. I think that bankrupting the losers and preventing them from saving face ultimately becomes an impetus for revenge."

"Sounds like you're speaking from experience."

"Remember what I told you about Gunter?"

"Yes, now that you mention it."

"That's a painful subject, so let's not dwell on it. I've been buoyed by your visit and benefited from your ideas. But what if something else comes up?"

Taylor pulled a pen from his pocket, grabbed Weber's hand, and scribbled a number on his palm. "I'm currently on assignment in Paris, and you can reach me at this number."

◆◆◆

Emboldened by Taylor's visit, Weber pondered how best to become acquainted with each female engineer. He knew where two of the three engineers were employed but couldn't think of a plausible reason for contacting them. What woman would be interested in an anonymous man who showed up unannounced in her workplace? He couldn't think of a ploy that wouldn't arouse suspicion. Upon further thought, he realized that romantic liaisons typically didn't begin that way. What he needed was an indirect approach--a way of meeting a woman or becoming acquainted that wasn't contrived--something like a chance encounter. But how exactly did one "stage" a chance encounter?

Fall 1926: Berlin Germany

Creating a romantic liaison was only one of several mission-related tasks that Weber now had to balance against his parental duties. The first week or two in Berlin had been relatively relaxed, and he'd spent considerable time bonding with Carl over common activities such as shopping and sightseeing. That time had been a welcome respite from the pressures he'd endured in his Martin Air job and had helped him re-establish his relationship with his son. But now, the demands on his time were increasing, and his life was quickly becoming more complicated. He didn't want to lose sight of his relationship with Carl, so he prioritized staying abreast of the events in his son's life by talking with him each evening.

One thing Weber learned during these father-son conversations was that Carl was far more engaged with his BTA schoolwork and classmates than he had been in Washington, DC. This change was also evident in Carl's time at school; he frequently stayed late to participate in organized peer activities. It pleased Weber that Carl was more involved in school but he was also curious about the boy's extracurricular activities. Although Carl made mention of the activities, he was rarely forthcoming about what he and his classmates did during their after-school hours. One evening, Weber sat down with his son and broached the subject.

"Carl, tell me more about what you do after school."

"A lot of the guys get together to do stuff."

"By guys, I assume you mean boys. No girls?"

"Yeah, just boys."

"What kinds of 'stuff' do you do?"

"The leaders plan stuff for us, like exercise and calisthenics. Sports activities, too, like soccer, marching, and archery."

"What leaders? Do you mean adults? Are they BTA teachers?"

"No, not teachers. Men from HJ."

"What is HJ?"

"Hitlerjugend. It's just for boys between the ages of 14 and 18."

"Why didn't you tell me about this before?"

"We are the future of the Fatherland. What we do for the Fatherland is nobody's business but ours."

"Who told you that?"

"The men from HJ."

Carl's admission took Weber by surprise. At a loss for words, he stood and paced the room, struggling to face this unexpected development. He didn't know what concerned him most- that his son hadn't been open about his activities or the robotic manner in which Carl had parroted some jaundiced partisan dictum. Apparently, his son had been caught up in some political counterculture without his knowledge. He couldn't let that happen without investigating the HJ and determining how its ideology and activities might affect his son. As a first step, he decided to visit the BTA headmaster.

◆◆◆

"As you know, Mr. Weber," said Headmaster Bauer, "boys' groups have been popular in Germany for some time, and religious or political organizations sponsor most. Some of our students participate in the HJ or Hitler Youth, and others have joined the Young Protestants, the Young Conservatives, and other such organizations."

"Why was I not informed?"

"Please understand that the BTA does not endorse any youth organization. Organizations promoting physical exercise and sports can use our facilities during after-school hours because we believe those activities build character and foster health."

"Still, I did not grant permission for my son to join the HJ."

"Are you sure he's a member? Often, boys' friends invite them to participate informally when they need additional players or perceive someone as an asset to their team. Is your son good at sports?"

"That's beside the point. Tell me about the HJ. What's their ideology--what are their goals for adolescent boys?"

"I can't speak for them, Mr. Weber. I suggest you contact one of the organization's leaders. However, there is another matter that I'd like to discuss with you."

"I'm listening."

"The government is sponsoring internships for boys especially talented in mathematics and science. Carl certainly qualifies--he excels in both domains. The internship encourages boys to pursue science and engineering degrees and ultimately join those sectors of the German workforce. Trainees work with established scientists and engineers on major government projects and acquire practical experience that helps them gain admission to Germany's best universities."

"To what extent are the internships matched to students' interests? Would Carl be allowed to choose a project?"

"Perhaps not a project, but he could choose an engineering specialty. The current offerings are in naval and aviation engineering. Might Carl be interested in ships or airplanes?"

"I couldn't say without talking to Carl. I'll do that and get back to you. Thanks for telling me about this opportunity, Mr. Bauer."

◆◆◆

Weber parked the Benz alongside a strip of hangars that lined the western edge of Johannisthal Air Field. He'd waited for a clear, sunny morning to make the journey so that he could inspect the Potez 25 and conduct a test flight. The airfield was active and larger than he'd anticipated. Two perpendicular runways were oriented to accommodate east-west and north-south takeoffs and landings. Currently, three planes were queued up for takeoff on the north-south runway. Along its eastern edge, along the opposite side of the airport, was a collection of garages, workshops, and oversized industrial hangars with signs denoting different aircraft companies and flight services.

As Weber walked down the row of hangers, the early morning sun projected his shadow against the façades of the closely spaced buildings, making it appear that he had an accomplice. He found hangar 15--the one Taylor had rented--near the end of the row and swung open its massive door. Inside, the Potez crouched like a bird of prey poised for flight. The biplane's short struts hugged the tarmac, and its fuselage hunched forward like an eagle preparing to pounce on its prey.

Weber inspected the plane, climbed into the cockpit, familiarized himself with the controls, fired the engine, and taxied onto the runway. After holding for cross-traffic, he revved the engine, released the brakes, and let the Potez sprint down the runway and ascend into the morning sky. As Taylor promised, the Potez 25 proved fast, responsive, and agile. Pleased with the plane's performance, Weber circled back to the airport, landed, and taxied toward the row of hangars. As he approached his hangar, he noticed that two additional hangars stood open, but both had been closed at the time of his departure.

After parking the Potez, Weber walked to the nearest open hangar. Glancing inside, he saw an Albatros L 77v with its cowling raised and a man in coveralls working on the engine. He introduced himself and asked whether the man owned the plane.

"No, I work for Flug Mechanicals and I'm servicing this plane for Herr Luftig."

"I see. Are you taking new clients? I just moved my Potez 25 into hanger 15."

"Possibly. What kind of work did you have in mind? For major repairs, you'll need to contact one of the aviation companies on the other side of the airport."

"Just basic maintenance, although my plane is airworthy at present. Say, have you ever worked for Frau Dortmunder, or would you know if Frau Obermaier or Frau Lichtmann keep planes at this airport?"

"Well, Frau Dortmunder's husband keeps their plane in hangar 3. I've seen Frau Obermaier park her plane in hangar 8. I don't know Frau Lichtmann."

Weber decided to observe Obermaier's hangar and introduce himself when she made an appearance. He'd eliminated Frau Dortmunder from consideration because of her marital status.

◆◆◆

After eight days and as many nights of sitting in the Benz across from Obermaier's hangar Weber had nothing to show for his efforts. He was exhausted and frustrated that there had been no sign of Frau Obermaier. On the afternoon of the ninth day, however, something unexpected happened. He'd just been lulled to sleep by the boredom of sitting idly in the Benz when the deep, resonant roar of tandem aircraft engines awakened him. Willing himself awake, he turned toward the noise and saw a sleek, two-engine monoplane glide out of one of the larger, industrial-sized hangars on the opposite side of the airport. Unable to identify the plane, Weber exited the Benz and walked toward the runway to look closer. It was immediately apparent that this was a unique aircraft. Single-wing aircraft were becoming more common, but Weber had never seen one with this plane's sweptback design, dual wing-mount engines, and multiple arrays of gun ports in the nose, wingtips, and tail. This was undoubtedly an advanced warbird and a formidable one at that.

Intrigued, Weber returned to the Benz, drove to the other side of the airport, and parked behind the large industrial hangar where he'd seen the monoplane exit. The oversized hangar was sandwiched between two buildings that belonged to different aircraft manufacturers, Fokker and Heinkel. Weber walked through an alley between the hangar and the Heinkel structure until he reached a side door that opened into the hangar. The door was ajar, so he cautiously opened it and peered inside. Several aircraft were parked in service bays, and among them were two more planes like the warbird he had seen leave the hangar. These planes, however, lacked any form of armaments. One wore Luft Hansa insignias and appeared to be a commercial aircraft. The other had no markings whatsoever.

Realizing that he'd stumbled upon an important piece of intelligence, Weber cautiously retreated to the Benz and drove toward the opposite side of the airport. As he tried to make sense of what he'd seen, he was reminded of Furst's objective for the government aviation meeting he had attended with Curtis Taylor: converting commercial aircraft into military aircraft. Based on what he had just witnessed, he wondered whether the Germans were doing the reverse, which was manufacturing military planes and passing them off as commercial aircraft.

As Weber arrived at hangar 15, he saw a woman struggling with the door to hangar 8. He hopped out of the Benz, strode to the hangar, and asked the woman--who he assumed was Frau Obermaier--if she needed assistance.

"This damn hangar door," the woman fumed. She quickly kicked the door and then spun toward Weber and barked imperiously, "I suppose you think you can close this door when I can't. I'd like to see you try."

Weber was mildly offended by the woman's tone but attempted to help her anyway. He braced his shoulder against the door and gave it a mighty push. There was a loud squeal, and the door retracted an inch or two and then ground to a stop. Weber pushed again, but the door remained jammed in place.

"Just as I thought. Another man who thinks he can solve problems with brute force rather than finesse. What's next? Will you try to ram the door shut with your car?"

Weber was tempted to ask Frau Obermaier how that approach would be any different than kicking the door, as she had done. Instead, he shrugged his shoulders and walked away, regretting that he'd offered to lend a hand. At least he now knew she wasn't suitable for a romantic relationship. So, where did that leave him? Two down and one to go. His only remaining option was to find Frau Lichtman.

Chapter 10

Fall 1926: Berlin, Germany

At Weber's second internship meeting, Dr. Schreiber asked if the assigned literary passages had prompted any conclusions. Weber nodded affirmatively and then summarized Taylor's analysis without crediting his source. His report seemed to please Schreiber, but it left him feeling guilty. Guilt, it seemed, would be his constant companion in these meetings.

Schreiber then changed the subject and asked Weber if he had ever weathered the loss of a loved one. Weber shrugged and threw up his hands, thinking he'd misheard the question. Then, reflexively, his teeth clenched, and his mouth went dry as images of Anna's death rose from their resting places and took center stage in his consciousness. "What do you mean?" Weber said, stalling to regain his composure.

Schreiber wasn't to be deterred. "You lost your wife not long ago, didn't you?"

"Yes, but what's that got to do with this?" Weber pleaded. Schreiber pressed on, seemingly oblivious to Weber's discomfort.

"Your last assignment drew upon your intellect and yielded some insight or knowledge. It was more about your head than your heart. For this assignment, I want you to explore what the Bible says about pain and suffering and potential remedies for those maladies. You'll need to examine your heart and apply what you learn to your feelings of loss. Be open to experiencing your emotions. You can tell me what happens next week."

Feelings of dread descended on Weber as he walked back to his flat. He'd buried his feelings about Anna's death deep inside and didn't want to dig them up and release all that pain. Doing so, he feared, would unleash a suffocating agony that would strangle his will to live.

◆◆◆

When Weber returned the following week, Dr. Schreiber inquired about his search of the Bible and whether he had been able to apply any of its revelations. Weber reported that he'd had a difficult week emotionally but that the activity had been informative and given him some comfort and hope. He'd actually avoided dealing with his feelings about Anna and called Curtis Taylor for help with the assignment.

Taylor characterized pain and suffering as inescapable aspects of the human condition, perhaps even intended by God as humbling experiences that motivated people to seek Him for solace and when merited, healing. The Torah or Tanakhic texts, he'd said, characterized God as caring for those who suffered most, such as widows and orphans, the poor and oppressed, and those victimized by abuse and injustice. Weber glanced at portions of the New Testament and discovered that Jesus healed the infirm and that his followers in the early church cared for the sick and suffering. The text clarified that this compassion was atypical because it contradicted longstanding cultural norms. He paraphrased all this in his report to Schreiber, who briefly offered some observations and gave Weber another assignment.

"So, if we combine this with what you learned in your first assignment, we see that it's the church's role to compensate for injustice, have mercy on sinners, and care for those who suffer. Your next assignment is to lead a group in which you commune with people who've suffered lost or broken relationships. You'll use your head and heart to offer them a helping hand."

Surprised, Weber glowered at Schreiber. "Me? Surely you are kidding. How would I do that?"

"Post some notices around the city inviting people to attend a small group meeting here in the church annex. At the meetings, tell people what happened to you and encourage them to tell their stories and talk about their feelings. Adhere to these simple rules: (1) All are encouraged to share; (2) Everyone is respected; no one denigrates anyone else; (3) Give so that you may receive: people who give support tend to receive it; (4) Pray for each other.

Weber bristled. "No, I don't think I can do that."

"Surely you jest, Mr. Weber. You're here to serve others. Why else would you have come to Berlin?"

If only you knew, Weber thought. "Alright, but you never know what people will say or do. What if I lose control?"

"Of your feelings? That's to be expected when you share grief. However, if you're worried about managing the group, follow my rules and call me if things get out of hand. I'll help you. Be alert for people who might want to harm themselves. Notify me if anyone appears suicidal, or better yet, take them immediately across the street to the hospital."

Weber seethed as he left Schreiber's office. Some cover, he thought--surrounding myself with grieving people while I struggle to constrain my misery. My imitation of a clergyman is going to cover me so deep in desperation and despair that I'll lose my undercover moxie and wind up shackled in Spandau Prison.

◆◆◆

One by one, people arrived at the cathedral, entered the annex, and seated themselves in chairs that Weber had arranged in a circle. When the time came for the session to begin, there were thirty-some people in the room, two-thirds of whom were women. Weber was surprised by the turnout because he'd spurned his mentor's advice and posted only a few notices in inconspicuous locations within the city. So much for passive resistance.

Weber began with introductions, first himself and then each participant in turn. He then recited Schreiber's rules for group decorum and asked for a show of hands. "Which of you are here tonight because you're struggling with a lost or broken relationship?" Everyone in the room raised a hand.

Weber nodded, drew a deep breath, and proceeded to describe the events surrounding Anna's death. When he told of the plane crash, he paused to brush away tears. When he spoke of Anna's injuries, his voice cracked. Then, when he described how a polar bear pounced and dragged Anna into the depths of the Arctic, he broke down entirely and sobbed.

The room fell silent except for the sounds of Weber's sobs. Several participants withdrew tissues from their pockets or handbags and dabbed at their eyes. When Weber regained his composure, he looked from one participant to the next, pausing briefly to make eye contact, hoping to find someone ready to share their misery.

Then, a woman to his left cleared her throat, and all eyes turned toward her. "My husband was hit by a train. The police said he committed suicide, but I don't believe them." This woman's tale of woe inspired others who, in turn, shared their heart-wrenching stories of separation, abandonment, divorce, death, and suicide. Weber felt his soul was collapsing under the collective weight of the participants' burdens. Only later did he realize that his pain felt more bearable because the participants' afflictions were like his affliction, and their heartaches were like his heartache.

When the meeting concluded, several participants approached Weber to pay their respects. He greeted them individually and listened to their comments. Most told him that they valued the meeting and planned to return.

One woman remained seated and approached him only after all the other participants had departed. She was tall and slim, about Weber's age, and had dark wavy hair, bright blue eyes, and an infectious smile. Weber remembered thinking she was attractive when he saw her arrive for the meeting.

"I sympathize with your loss, Mr. Weber. Your wife, Anna, was a talented woman, and it's obvious that you loved her very much."

"Thank you. I noticed that you were silent during the meeting. Did the others make you uncomfortable?

"No, I'm suffering, like those who spoke this evening, but I value my privacy. We live in challenging times, Mr. Weber. It's best not to be too open about one's past."

Intrigued, Weber asked her to elaborate, but she demurred. She studied his face briefly as if taking his measure and then added, "Perhaps someday when I know you better."

"Ah, that implies we might become better acquainted," Weber countered. "Is that a possibility?"

"Perhaps." With that parting remark, she turned and walked toward the door.

Weber watched her leave, wondering if he'd see her again. "Wait! I don't know your name."

"It's Anna", she replied. Then she opened the door, turned to give Weber a parting glance, and disappeared into the night.

Winter 1926: Berlin, Germany

When the evening meal was finished, Carl washed dishes, and Weber dried and stacked them carefully inside the kitchen's ancient, narrow, and shallow cabinets. Many of the apartments' accouterments had earned Weber's appreciation during their residence. The kitchen wasn't one of them.

When the chore was completed, Weber asked Carl what he had done in school that day. It was his way of initiating the nightly father-son conversation hour. Carl groaned in mock protest and said he'd skipped school and had nothing to report. Weber laughed. The days when Carl skipped school were long past.

"So, my favorite son, what's new in school?"

"Favorite? You mean 'only,' don't you?

"Ok, so you're my only favorite son. Would you like some competition? I might be able to arrange for you to have a baby brother."

"Oh yeah? How, exactly, would you do that? Or should I say with whom would you do that? And could you explain the mechanics of that undertaking--you know, from an engineering perspective?"

"Shut up, wise guy. Come on, fess up. What's new?"

"I started the government internship today. Some men in military uniforms drove me and a few schoolmates to an office in the Reichswehr downtown. They asked what type of engineering I wanted to learn, and I said aviation. I'm not interested in ships. That pleased one of the officials, and he took me to another building and showed me some prototypes for ultramodern propellers, wings, and landing gears."

Weber, who'd been only half-listening, perked up and gave the boy his full attention. "So, taking after the old man, eh? We'll be able to talk shop; I'd like to hear more about those projects."

"I'm not sure how much I'll be able to tell you. One of the officials asked if I could keep secrets. He said they were working on confidential, proprietary designs, and I'd have to complete a trial period to prove I was trustworthy before they'd grant me a security clearance. Once I have clearance, they'd allow me to work on complex problems and advanced designs. Real cutting-edge stuff."

After Carl went to bed, Weber thought about the implications of his son's internship for his mission. The aviation initiatives that Carl described had all the earmarks of a covert operation. If that supposition proved accurate, he might have stumbled upon an indispensable inroad into the government's illegal aviation projects--an investigative avenue too valuable to be ignored. However, choosing that path would ensnare him in a quandary that pitted his investigative priorities against his parental responsibilities. Try as he might, he couldn't envision a scenario where he could capitalize on Carl's knowledge without endangering him. He wrestled with the dilemma for the remainder of the night without reaching a decision. Finally, when morning came, he decided against doing anything until he was sure Carl had been granted a security clearance and was working on classified military projects.

◆◆◆

Several weeks later during another father-son conversation hour, Carl announced that some men in long, black leather coats had appeared at BTA and interviewed some of his classmates. Weber asked Carl if he knew who the men were and why they had come to his school.

"It was strange, Dad, because most of the kids they interviewed were friends of mine. I talked to them after school, and they said the men pressured them to snitch on me. Some of my friends were asked whether I ever discussed my internship or talked about airplanes. Another friend, Bruno, told them I liked airplanes, so they demanded that he write down everything I had ever said about aircraft. When Bruno finished the list, they grilled him about everything he wrote. Another friend, Horst, said that after the men interviewed him, they warned him to keep his mouth shut or they'd come back and cut his balls off."

"You know what these men were doing, don't you?"

"Checking up on me, I guess."

"I suspect so, but I don't admire their methods. These guys' approach to vetting you for a security clearance was as subtle as a bull in a china shop. I wouldn't want to cross these guys--they seem more than willing to use crude, heavy-handed tactics to get what they want."

"Yeah, my friends felt intimidated and pressured and are now upset. I'm not sure my friends like me anymore."

"It's not your fault. Give them time, and they'll get over it."

◆◆◆

After listening to people share their relationship sorrows, losses, and failures for what seemed an eternity, Weber drew the meeting to a close and watched as the participants mustered the courage to resume their lives. Most departed, but, as before, several participants remained behind to chat and pay their respects. The woman who'd said her name was Anna waited until the room had emptied to make her approach. Weber smiled and greeted her.

"Hello Anna, how have you been?"

"As well as can be expected. I hadn't planned to attend this meeting but discovered I was looking forward to seeing you again."

Anna's admission took Weber by surprise. He'd felt the same way but had tried to quash those emotions. His amorous feelings toward her were verboten because he needed to find and court the elusive Frau Lichtmann. Just seeing Anna again, however, spontaneously rekindled his yearning. He tried to keep his head and play it cool. "I'm pleased to see you again, too."

"That keen, are you? I've had cats greet me with more enthusiasm."

"Sorry, I was looking forward to seeing you but thought saying so would be unprofessional."

"Well, you certainly succeeded by that criterion, but, as a woman, I find your demeanor off-putting. Last time, you said you hoped we'd become better acquainted. I suppose that remark was just another of your professional pleasantries?"

"No, not at all. It's just that…" Weber hesitated, realizing that he couldn't finish that sentence. Speaking the truth would compromise his mission, leaving him nothing to say but lies, and he didn't want to be dishonest with this woman for some reason. "Look, could we start over? I'm ashamed of myself, and I want to apologize."

"I'll accept your apology if you take me to dinner."

Weber swallowed his misgivings and agreed.

◆◆◆

"So, tell me about yourself," Anna said as the waiter seated her at a table for two in a softly illuminated corner of the Rosengarten, a classy restaurant attached to the Berliner Ausblick hotel. Weber smiled as he pulled up a chair across from her, pleased he'd been able to reserve a table in the most romantic section of the restaurant.

"There's not much to tell. I came here from Washington, DC, to do an internship. I'm considering a career change and wanted to explore the clergy."

"You are a remarkable individual, Mr. Weber. Isn't it uncommon for airline pilots to become clergymen?"

"Please call me Robert. May I call you Anna? And, yes, I suppose it is unusual."

"Perhaps it has something to do with the death of your wife."

"Yes, of course. That, and my struggle to survive the crash and carry on in her absence."

"I sympathize."

"Sorry, but I'm at a disadvantage. I appreciate your sympathy, but I don't know what enables you to empathize with my plight. My sorrow must remind you of some misfortune in your life."

Anna blanched, averted her eyes, and took a long sip from her wineglass. She was uncomfortable with the direction of the conversation and immediately changed the subject. Her discomfort threw Weber off balance, but he masked his reaction and tried to shift the conversation toward mundane, trivial topics. After some initial fumbling, he rekindled the ambiance, and Anna regained her composure. She persisted, however, in saying little or nothing about herself. Eventually, the burden of steering the conversation toward trite themes and inanities wore Weber down, and he returned to talking about himself and his family.

"Settling in Berlin has done wonders for my son, Carl. He's a bright boy and wasn't challenged by the school he attended in Washington. He's now attending the BTA and doing very well."

Anna's face darkened again. "You have a son?"

As Weber continued to talk about Carl, Anna's composure deteriorated, and her features took on a wistful appearance. Her eyes moistened. A tear formed, clung briefly to an eyelash, lost its grip, and slid down her cheek.

Again, taken off guard, Weber struggled to interpret Anna's emotions. This time, I've blown it, he thought. I've revealed that I'm not only a single parent but the father of a teenager, no less. He knew that many women avoided that kind of entanglement, preferring to conceive and raise a child of their own. It was a law of nature--a basic tenet of the biological imperative. Why perpetuate another woman's genes when you could ensure the survival of your own?

Weber's discomfort and Anna's melancholy receded when the waiter arrived with their meals. Grateful for the distraction, Weber talked about the food. During the silences, he tried to think of ways to salvage the evening.

When the meal concluded, Weber asked Anna if she'd like coffee and dessert at his apartment. He'd made the gesture simply to demonstrate that he harbored no hard feelings. Only afterward did it occur to him that she might interpret the invitation as a clumsy attempt to get her into bed. He braced himself for a chilly refusal and was astonished when she brightened and accepted his offer.

After the waiter cleared their plates and Weber paid the bill, they left the restaurant and proceeded on foot toward Weber's apartment, which was located approximately ten blocks to the west. It was well after dark on a warm night, and they made their way from block to block using the random patterns of illumination created by intermittent street lights and after-hours store lighting. When they reached the Tiergarten, however, darkness descended upon them. Weber stopped, took Anna's hand, and waited for his eyes to adjust. Anna moved closer, leaned against Weber, and nestled her head against his shoulder. When his night vision improved, Weber squeezed Anna's hand and led her into the Tiergarten. Now, woodlands rather than buildings hugged both sides of the street, and other than their footsteps, they heard no sounds but the wind in the trees and crickets chirping.

Weber and Anna were relieved when they rounded a corner and saw street lights ahead. Weber turned toward Anna and whispered, "My apartment is only a few hundred meters ahead on the right side of the street." Anna sighed and picked up the pace.

Moments later, the couple arrived at their destination, ascended the front steps, and entered the apartment. Carl rose from the couch, greeted Weber, and then cowered beside his father, apparently too shy to speak to Anna.

"Carl, this is Anna, the woman I met for dinner tonight. You've heard me speak of her--she's been attending my group."

Carl managed to squeak out a greeting. "Hello Anna, welcome to our flat."

Carl returned to the couch, and Anna followed him. She sat beside the boy, smiled attentively, and put her hand on his. Carl seemed to enjoy the attention. He grinned at Anna and remarked that his mother's name was the same as hers. They talked for a long time and ignored Weber entirely.

"So much for coffee and dessert and the intimacies that could have developed after a cozy stroll through the Tiergarten," Weber grumbled to himself. He understood why Carl was so interested in this woman's attention--Anna was an attractive woman who doted on him and shared his mother's name. What he didn't understand was why Anna was so interested in Carl.

Spring 1927: Berlin, Germany

Weber's search for Frau Lichtmann faltered. He hadn't unearthed a single clue as to the woman's whereabouts, even though he'd tried to cover all the angles and leave no stone unturned. Perhaps the task exceeded his abilities as an investigator, or the woman had vanished without a trace. Accepting either conclusion undermined his mission, so he told himself that failure wasn't an option and redoubled his efforts. To his chagrin, nothing changed. He eventually tired of chasing down dead ends and focused on other priorities.

Anna was one of those priorities. Although Weber knew his feelings for Anna were misplaced and would eventually interfere with his efforts to find and court Frau Lichtmann, he couldn't bring himself to end the relationship. He struggled to carve out an hour or two from his busy schedule to spend with Anna each week. She, likewise, had little time for liaisons and, to make matters worse, was often secretive about her commitments.

Even though Weber and Anna met infrequently, often only for a brief walk in the Tiergarten or a hasty lunch in a café, they nonetheless grew closer. By necessity, the bond they developed was more emotional than physical. They'd shared few physical intimacies besides a brief kiss in the Tiergarten. It wasn't passion that was lacking but rather opportunities to meet in private places and spend time alone. Anna was averse to meeting at her apartment, although she never explained why. Perhaps she had a roommate. Weber didn't want to leave Carl alone in the evenings and didn't think it appropriate for Anna to stay in his apartment overnight. That kind of behavior didn't set a good example for his son, and it was inimical to his cover as a budding clergyman.

Growing tension over this predicament prompted Weber to raise the issue during a hastily arranged lunch. He made a reservation at the Obstmarkt, a small café in central Berlin, and when he arrived, a waiter seated him at a table in the window. The restaurant was decorated with still-life paintings of fruit and smelled of freshly baked bread. Weber's table offered a voyeur's perspective on the foot traffic in front of the restaurant. As he watched passersby traverse the downtown streets, Anna came into view, entered the restaurant, and seated herself across from him.

"This is a good table for people-watching, Robert, but I feel like I'm sitting in a fishbowl."

Weber caught a waiter's attention and asked to be seated in the rear of the café. The waiter obliged, found them a less conspicuous location, and placed menus on the table.

`"Thank you, Robert, this is much better."

"You're welcome. Anna, we don't have much time, so let me get to the point. Are you happy with the way things are going between us?"

"I like you, Robert, and I'm not unhappy. To be honest, I don't know where our relationship is going. Intimacy doesn't seem to be a priority, and perhaps that's okay. I sense we're just coasting along, snatching moments together when opportunities arise."

"You make it sound like our relationship has no purpose or direction like wind-tossed ships passing in the night."

"Are you saying that you want more than that, Robert?"

Anna's question shifted Weber's perspective. Quite unintentionally, he was pushing Anna to define their relationship. He had slipped into the pursuer's role, chased Anna, and backed her into a corner. Was that wise? Did he want the relationship to progress toward some kind of commitment? What about Frau Lichtmann? Was he letting his heart or, perhaps, another part of his anatomy lead him in a direction that would subvert his mission? Sobered by these realizations, Weber retreated. "I don't know what I want. Do you?"

"Wow, that's some reversal. So, the onus is on me now, is it? Look, I'm taking it slow because I want to be cautious."

"No kidding. As if I hadn't noticed! You're so cautious that I hardly know anything about you. I don't even know your surname."

"Resorting to accusations won't make me more forthcoming, Robert. Besides, I don't remember you asking. My name is Gabel--Anna Gabel."

"So, Anna Gabel, why must you be so cautious?"

"Robert, I'm guarded because I've been burned before. It's put me on the defensive and changed the way I live. I'm careful about what I disclose because I need to control what people know about me and my life."

"So, you're hiding from life and licking your wounds?"

"Don't make it sound so attractive. Would you like me to diagnose your pathologies?

"I didn't know I had any."

"This isn't helping, Robert. Let's not lose sight of why we're here."

"Sure, but answer one thing first. Why are you putting caution aside to take a chance on me?"

Embarrassed, Anna's face flushed. "Well, she stammered, I like many things about you. You're handsome. Plus, I like that you were a pilot, have a son, want to work for the church, and are an American. Foremost, I think you're different."

"What do you mean different?"

She smiled coyly. "You're going to make me be specific? You're different than the men I know. You're not like men from my past, the men I work with, or those who live in my apartment building. You're not like German men in general."

Weber laughed heartily. "I didn't realize I was so atypical of my gender and so different than men in your culture."

"You need to be more observant, Robert. If you paid attention to what's happening in this country, you'd see an angry, vengeful mood sweeping the nation. Losing the Great War humiliated Germans, and to recover their pride, they're turning to aggressive nationalism, embracing militarism, and rekindling predatory Germanic stereotypes. They're looking for something or someone to blame for the sins of the Weimar Republic--economic decline, moral decay, paying reparations to former oppressors--and using racism and ethnocentrism to identify scapegoats. German men, in particular, have fallen prey to these dangerous ideologies and fallacies. A woman in my apartment building says that losing the war emasculated German men, and they've chosen to regain their virility by marching around in jackboots, saluting the flag, and declaring themselves invincible."

They might be doing more than that, Weber thought. They might be building warplanes.

Nonetheless, the picture Anna was painting did illustrate what he'd been seeing in the streets.

"Robert, we've strayed off topic again. Here's an idea. Why don't we commit to spending more time together and see where that leads? Instead of just scheduling a few minutes here and there, why don't you plan something fun that we can do together--like visiting a museum or going to the zoo? Getting to know each other better will build trust and allow us to reveal more of who we are."

Chapter 11

Spring 1927: Berlin, Germany

The Potez 25 stretched its wings, extended its tail, and pointed its nose skyward as it soared like an eagle on the early morning thermals over the fields south of Johannisthal Air Field. Weber let the Potez coast into a patch of mist and then nosed the plane over so that it arced away from the clouds and into the clear, dry air below. Sitting ahead of Weber in the forward cockpit, Anna focused on the horizon to maintain her bearings and fend off vertigo.

Outings such as a museum or zoo trip hadn't interested Weber, so he'd proposed a plane ride, and Anna had readily accepted. When they reached the airport, Weber opened the hangar door, and Anna gasped. She thought that Weber had hired a pilot or rented a plane and was stunned when she realized that the Potez 25 was his. Her first question was, "How does an aspiring clergyman afford a plane like this?" Weber lied and told her that he'd purchased the plane during his tenure as an airline pilot and that a friend had ferried it to Berlin. It was his first lie and he hated himself for being dishonest. But what choice did he have? Anna looked at him skeptically but let the matter drop because she was too excited to let her doubts spoil the outing.

Weber landed, taxied to the hangar, and throttled the engine back to idle. He climbed down from his cockpit and asked Anna if she wanted to trade seats.

"What do you have in mind, Robert? Surely you don't expect me to fly this thing?"

"No, but I thought you might like to sit at the controls and learn how they work."

Anna climbed into Weber's cockpit, seated herself, and played with the stick and the yoke, pretending to 'fly' the plane. Weber laughed, amused by Anna's antics. He crawled into the passenger's seat, reached into Anna's cockpit, and retracted the throttle slightly. The engine droned as its RPMs increased, and the plane edged forward. Weber started shouting instructions.

"Don't make any large or sudden adjustments to the controls. Just push down on both foot pedals to slow the plane. Ease off the pedals to let the plane roll forward. To angle left, push harder on the left pedal. To turn right, give it more right pedal."

Anna did as directed, and the plane eased along the paved strip that fronted the hangars. Weber told her to stop when she reached the end of the strip, where the runway began, so he could take over and return the plane to its hangar. Anna nodded.

When the Potez reached the end of the strip, Anna slowed the plane but didn't come to a complete stop. Instead, she pivoted the aircraft onto the runway and yanked hard on the throttle. The engine screamed, and the Potez rocketed forward, slamming her and Weber against their seats. Weber yelled, "No, don't touch the throttle," at the top of his lungs, but the engine's roar drowned out his words. He waved his arms frantically, trying to signal Anna to stop the plane. He was still yelling and waving when the Potez lifted off and rose into the crisp morning air.

After achieving sufficient altitude, Anna banked in a tight turn and didn't level the plane until she had achieved a northwesterly heading. Then she raised the nose, throttled up to maximum RPM, and held on as the Potez angled sharply skyward and gained altitude rapidly. Weber continued to flail and sputter, but Anna silenced his outbursts with extreme maneuvers. When he waved his arms, she rolled the plane, forcing him to reach for a wing strut and hold on for dear life. She spooled up the engine when he yelled and cursed and let the slipstream muffle his words.

When the novelty of the stunt wore off, Anna flew back to the airport, landed, and parked the plane in its hangar. Red-faced and fuming, Weber jumped down and dashed over to Anna's cockpit, spoiling for a fight.

"Who the hell are you?"

"Calm down, Robert, and move aside so I can climb down."

Grudgingly, Weber stood aside but continued the harangue. "Wipe that smile off your face. Do you think this is funny? What's next? Are you going to tell me that you were married to Baron von Richthofen and became a fighter ace in his squadron?"

Anna climbed out of her cockpit and stood facing Weber. "Be serious, Robert, women didn't fly combat missions in that war, and I'm too young to have served. Besides, isn't this what you wanted? You've been complaining that I'm too guarded and that you know nothing about me. Well, now you know that I can fly a plane. That's why I said I liked that you were a pilot."

"Why didn't you tell me instead of pulling this crazy stunt?"

"Where's the fun in that? This way, you've learned more about me and experienced my skills firsthand."

Weber's anger cooled, and he began to recover his composure. "So, when did you learn to fly?"

"My father taught me when I was a teenager. My family has a large farm in southern Germany, and my dad uses a plane to check on his crops and livestock. Some of his fields are high in the Alps."

◆◆◆

Weber returned intermittently to Johannisthal Air Field to search for the phantom warbird he'd seen exit from the hangar between the Fokker and Heinkel buildings. The sleek, two-engine monoplane's existence was the most important piece of intelligence he'd obtained thus far. Still, his initial search of the industrial-sized hangar hadn't yielded clues about its origins. As far as he could determine, the hangar was a service facility. That meant the Germans were building the plane elsewhere, and his only hope of finding the manufacturer was to find the aircraft and follow it.

He'd spent the day at the airfield, sitting in the Benz with nothing to show for it. Bored and dispirited, he resigned himself to another failure. Like all his previous stakeouts, this one had been a waste of time. He was beginning to think the plane was a figment of his imagination. Preparing to leave, he got out of the Benz, strode to his hangar, and retracted the door. On the way back to the car, he heard a rumbling sound, like thunder in the distance. He turned toward the sound and scanned the horizon but saw no clouds. Then the rumble intensified, and Weber recognized the deep, resonant roar of tandem aircraft engines.

The phantom warbird came into view, touched down briefly on the east-west runway, and then took off again. Weber watched as the plane circled, did a second touchdown maneuver, and then sped off on an easterly heading. "What are you waiting for?" Weber muttered to himself, "That phantom bogie is getting away." He opened the hangar, fired up the Potez 25, and taxied onto the east-west runway. Seconds later, he ascended into an easterly headwind and put the plane on a course to intercept the warbird. Minutes passed before the monoplane appeared on his windscreen. As if aware of his presence, the bogie suddenly banked to the south. Weber imitated the defensive maneuver but couldn't close the distance between the planes. The warbird surged ahead, its engines howling, widening the gap and leaving him behind. A cloud of exhaust enveloped Weber, and when it cleared, there was no sign of the warbird. Crestfallen, Weber broke off his pursuit and returned to the airfield.

After returning to his apartment, Weber called Curtis Taylor in Paris and described his airborne encounter. Taylor was both concerned and curious about the incident and suggested they meet to discuss it at the Hotel Adlon in two days. Weber agreed.

◆◆◆

Weber arrived at the door to Taylor's room, knocked, and was ushered inside. After greeting Taylor and engaging in small talk, Weber got down to business.

"The dual-engine monoplane is my best lead thus far. At a minimum, its existence implies that the Germans are building and testing advanced airframes and weaponry. It's also possible they've moved beyond prototypes and scaled up production. If so, they might soon possess a formidable, secret air force."

"This is valuable intelligence, Robert. I informed Furst, who authorized me to supply you with a newer, faster plane. I obtained an experimental Dewoitine D-500 in Paris, flew it here, and parked it in your hangar. It's a French monoplane with a modified tandem cockpit, a V-12 engine, and 691 horsepower. It's far more capable than the Potez 25 and should enable you to outrun and perhaps even outmaneuver this phantom German aircraft. I'll fly the Potez 25 back to Paris."

"That's great news. Please thank Furst for me."

"You might not feel so thankful when I tell you what else Furst had to say."

Taylor's ominous tone implied that Furst was displeased, so Weber braced for bad news. "Crap, what else did he say?"

"Besides reporting this phantom plane, he's wondering why you failed to report anything about your other mission objectives. Is tracking this phantom plane your only viable means for gathering intelligence?"

"It is so far."

"Where do things stand with Frau Lichtmann?"

"She doesn't exist."

"Be reasonable, Robert, I can't tell Furst that. You'll have to elaborate."

"Alright, I can't find her. And it's not for lack of trying. I've exhausted every avenue."

"Look, Furst's aware of your objections to this part of the plan. He'll roll you up if he thinks you've deliberately scuttled it. You'll be replaced, or the mission will be canceled."

"Curtis, trust me. I've looked for the woman, and she's nowhere to be found."

"All right, Robert, I'll fabricate a story to buy you some time. But what will you do now? Can you fall back on some other source or tactic? Surely, there must be another way for you to gather the intelligence we need."

Weber told Taylor about Carl's internship with the German Air Ministry. He didn't mention Anna.

◆◆◆

Carl spent most of his after-school hours at the Air Ministry and regularly brought assignments home to work on in the evenings. His initial assignments had focused on basic principles of aerodynamics, and having mastered those, he'd been assigned more challenging tasks. Carl had sought

Weber's assistance occasionally, and as the work became more complex, he did so more often.

"Dad, the Air Ministry has moved me to projects requiring security clearance. My mentors asked me to work on a prototype for a plane they plan to build. I probably shouldn't consult with you, but I need your advice."

Weber cringed. Here it is, he thought, my first opportunity to steal secrets from my son. Am I going to stoop so low? "Sure," he replied to Carl. "How can I help?"

"They've specified a payload for a commercial airliner, and I'm supposed to devise a plausible airframe that would have sufficient strength, power, and lift to handle that load. But the stipulated payload is 8000 pounds or 4 tons. That doesn't make sense--it seems excessive. The airliner is supposed to seat 10 passengers, plus the pilot and copilot. Even if I overestimate at 250 pounds per person, that's 3,000 pounds, and fuel adds another thousand. Surely, another two tons of capacity isn't needed for luggage and extras. Do you think the payload specification is an error? What would all that extra capacity be needed for?"

Bombs, Weber thought, big bombs.

◆◆◆

Over time, as Weber and Anna grew closer, they began to do things as a couple and establish routines. Weber found the courage to ask Anna to stay the night, and soon after that, she shared his bed, helped with meals, and saw Carl off in the mornings. Carl was pleased with his newfound family. He knew that this 'Anna' could never replace his mother, but he'd welcomed her affection, fallen under her spell, and begun to think of her as his stepmother.

Weber and Anna let down their guard as their relationship deepened, relaxed their boundaries and inhibitions, and became more open. Weber told Anna about his experiences during the war and his years as an airline pilot. He avoided painful topics such as his wife's demise and Gunter's murderous escapades. Likewise, he didn't mention his contacts in Washington, DC, nor say anything about his mission. Anna, in turn, talked about her childhood in Bavaria and told stories about her parents and siblings. She mentioned her occupation but didn't detail her duties or employer. She told Weber that she worked as a government architect in downtown Berlin. What she didn't talk about was the heartbreak that had motivated her to attend Weber's group at the cathedral.

Summer 1927: East of Munich, Germany

"So, what are your intentions regarding my daughter?" It was the question every suitor dreaded, and Weber was no exception. The inquisitor was a big, burly farmer named Aaron Gabel. Gabel was Anna's father, and he was seated across from Weber at the dinner table in his Bavarian farmhouse. Anna and her brother, Luka--a strapping adolescent about Carl's age--sat beside Weber. Ruth Gabel, Anna's mother, was seated across the table next to her husband.

Weber froze in the chill of Gabel's icy stare. He wanted to express his feelings about Anna, but his mind seized, and his thoughts stopped flowing. An awkward silence ensued while Weber sat dumbfounded, at a loss for words. Gabel eyed him suspiciously, and as the seconds passed, his visage darkened: his jaw muscles twitched, his forehead furrowed, and his eyes protruded like the business end of a double-barrel shotgun. "Well, young man? Have you no idea what you're doing with my daughter? Surely, she must mean something to you."

Anna wrapped her arms around Weber and told her father to back off. "That's enough, father, you're scaring him."

"He should be scared if his intentions aren't honorable. Damn scared. I don't want him toying with your affections like that other jerk did."

"I'll be the judge of that, father. I'm a grown woman. Mind your own business and stay out of my affairs."

With dinner over, Anna and Weber retreated to the rear of the house and sequestered themselves in a bedroom that had been Anna's when she was a child. The room contained a large poster bed, a desk, a dressing table, and an ornate armoire. The walls were pink and covered with pictures of horses and airplanes. A large window overlooked the rear of the property where Weber saw a barn with a fenced corral, an airplane hangar, assorted farm machinery, and several smaller outbuildings. Beyond that was a rolling pasture that stretched for miles up toward the Alpine foothills.

"You won't be able to sleep here," Anna said. "My mother wants us to have separate bedrooms."

"I'll bet your father had something to say about that. I don't think he likes me. I'm embarrassed that I let him intimidate me at dinner."

"That's okay. My father means well, but he's concerned about my welfare, which sometimes makes him overprotective."

"What is he trying to protect you from? Did some previous suitor abuse you?"

Anna shrugged. "It's ancient history. I had a relationship when I was young that ended badly. It's not worth talking about. The problem is that my father still thinks of me as an adolescent. Let's talk about something else. What would you like to do tomorrow?"

The next morning, Weber rose at daybreak, found his way outside, and walked to the airplane hangar behind the farmhouse. The Dewoitine D-500 sat where he had parked it the previous day on the airstrip that fronted the hangar. He had traveled with Anna to Bavaria because she wanted him to meet her family and see where she'd grown up. The flight was the first time Weber had piloted the Dewoitine, and it performed flawlessly. With Anna aboard, he'd refrained from testing the aircraft's capabilities, but its power and maneuverability had exceeded his expectations even during routine maneuvers. Taylor had chosen well; he felt confident that this plane, unlike the Potez 25, would be a better match against the German's phantom warbird.

An unexpected noise caught Weber off guard, and he spun around, searching for its source. His eyes were drawn to the motion of the hangar door as it began to retract. Seconds later, Aaron Gabel walked out of the hangar, holding a hammer in one hand and a wrench in the other. Weber's first thought was that Gabel intended to dispense with an unwanted suitor. He soon discovered, however, that Gabel had other ideas.

"That's some plane you've got there, Weber. Why would a guy like you need such a powerful plane?"

"Tell me something, Gabel, is confrontation your only way of relating to people? Because, I have to tell you, I'm getting tired of it."

Gabel laughed, and the tension between the two men eased. "Touché, Mr. Weber, I'll bury the hatchet for the moment. But, I must tell you, I'm not sure I like you."

"Fair enough, but I'd appreciate a chance to earn your trust."

"We'll see. Tell me something. It's obvious that you can fly planes, but are you good at fixing them?"

Weber decided not to tell Gabel he was an aeronautical engineer because it could blow his cover. "I'm no mechanic, but I did repair aircraft during the war. All pilots did--it was the only way to keep those rickety planes in the air. Why do you ask?"

"My plane's kaput. It's been out of service for months, and I need it to check on my crops and cattle."

Weber glanced inside the hangar and saw a Caspar C32 parked nose forward. The biplane had tandem open cockpits and was fitted for aerial spraying. Its cowling had been removed, and numerous engine parts lay on the floor under the nose of the plane. "What seems to be the problem with your plane, Mr. Gabel?"

"Look, let's dispense with the formalities. Just call me Aaron."

Weber smiled at Gabel's concession. Had the curmudgeon's icy disposition begun to thaw? "Ok, Aaron. My name is Robert. Why don't we have a look at your plane?"

When Gabel turned and walked toward the Caspar, Weber noticed his gait was uneven, seemingly because he favored his left leg. It struck him as odd that he hadn't noticed it before. Perhaps it was because the impediment was nearly undetectable--Gabel had a slight hitch in his step, not a pronounced limp. Weber wondered what might have caused Gabel's limp but decided it would be impolite to inquire.

Weber leaned into the Caspar's engine bay and did a cursory inspection. It was immediately apparent that essential parts were missing from the engine. He found most of them lying on the hangar floor, including a cracked cylinder head and a couple of burned-out magnetos. Weber's hopes for getting the Caspar back in the air dimmed. The plane needed extensive repairs and would take weeks, if not months, to complete them. He picked up the damaged cylinder head and handed it to Gabel. "I suspect you know this already, Aaron, but this part, and most of the others lying here on the hangar floor, will have to be replaced before the Caspar will be airworthy."

"I know, but it's impossible to get replacements. The damn Nazis have restricted the sales of airplane parts."

"Why would they do that?"

"Who knows? Do you think it would be possible to rebuild these parts?"

"Not likely. You'd need a well-equipped machine shop and new electrical and mechanical components specific to this plane."

"Just as I figured. Maybe it's time I sold this farm."

"That seems drastic, Aaron. Let me search for parts when I return to Johannisthal Air Field. I met a mechanic there who services planes for Berlin's elite. I'll bet he can get parts for your Caspar."

"Thanks, Robert. I'd appreciate that."

"My pleasure. Say, Aaron, Here's a thought. The morning's still young, so why don't we take the Dewoitine and check on your crops and cattle?"

Gabel smiled and nodded affirmatively.

The Dewoitine lifted off the dirt runway with both men aboard and ascended several thousand feet over Gabel's farm. Weber established a southwesterly heading toward the Alps and let the plane drift over the vast swaths of rich, green farmland below. Gabel pointed toward fields that varied in color and texture--some darker shades of green and denser than others--and shouted the names of crops in a vain attempt to make himself heard over the ambient wind and engine noise. "That's wheat. Rye over there. Barley up ahead." As far as Weber could tell, the crops looked robust and healthy.

When they reached the foothills, the cropland gave way to rolling pastures. To compensate for the rising terrain, Weber retracted the Dewoitine's yoke, added power, and watched as the altimeter spooled up and the plane gained altitude. After leveling off, he glanced below and saw that this portion of the farm was populated with livestock. Cattle were grazing in meadows, clustered around ponds, and huddled under trees. He flew a circular pattern over the pastures while Gabel examined his livestock. All appeared in order, so Gabel directed Weber to fly higher into the Alps.

Weber again throttled up the Dewoitine and raised the nose to overcome the rapidly rising Alpine slopes. When they reached the first of Gabel's Alpine meadows--a broad slope just below the snow line covered with short grasses, gold clover, and lichens--he descended to an altitude that allowed Gabel to inspect his livestock. Cows, most with bells hanging from their necks, were scattered throughout the meadow.

Gabel tapped Weber on the shoulder and pointed toward a rocky outcropping where several cows lay in the dirt, bloated and lifeless. He leveled his palm and made a slashing motion across this throat. Weber nodded affirmatively. *Dead cows*. Next, Gable cocked his arm, swept his hand downward, and made a bouncing motion with his palm. Weber nodded again. *Descend and... Wait, what? Is he suggesting that I land the plane? Where?* Gabel, anticipating Weber's unspoken question, pointed northward, further up the slope. Weber nodded and resumed an upward trajectory.

Minutes later, Weber saw a long, steep trail leading to an alpine hut that was built against a tall cliff. Gabel motioned toward the trail and repeated the gesture Weber had interpreted as 'land the plane.' He wanted to oblige, but his instincts as an aviator argued against landing the Dewoitine on a surface that looked more like a footpath than a runway. Descending to look closer, he saw that the trail skirted a meadow and appeared free of rocks and debris. Faint outlines of tracks were also visible, which, Weber assumed, marked where Gabel had been landing his plane. Landing now seemed less risky, so Weber throttled back the engine, lowered the flaps, and let the plane gradually descend until it touched down, bumped along the trail, and rolled to a stop.

Weber and Gabel climbed out of the plane and hiked across the meadow until they reached a rocky ledge. Under the ledge, they found four dead cows; all had their throats ripped open and were partially eaten. "Wolves," Gabel said, "probably launched themselves off the ledge onto the cattle. I haven't been able to get up here to cull those marauding bastards."

When they arrived back at the plane, Gabel pointed toward the cliffside cabin and asked Weber if he'd like a cup of coffee. Weber accepted, curious to see the cabin's interior. Gabel pulled some firewood from a rack mounted on the side of the cabin, unlocked the door, and led Weber inside. The cabin's interior consisted of a single room with plank floors, a beamed ceiling, and walls constructed from rough-hewn logs. Along one wall, two rocking chairs stood in front of a large fieldstone fireplace. Next to the fireplace, on an adjoining wall, was a rudimentary kitchen with an ancient woodstove and a single-lever hand pump mounted over a cast iron sink. A screen partially concealed a bed and washstand in a corner at the rear of the cabin.

Gabel started a fire in the woodstove, placed a tarnished coffee pot on a burner, and retrieved two mugs from a cabinet next to the sink. Twenty minutes later, the two men sat in the rocking chairs, drinking coffee and gazing the fire in the fireplace. Curious about his host, Weber steered the conversation toward Gabel's past.

"Have you always been a farmer, Aaron?"

"No, Ruth and I built a successful business in Munich. We owned a nice house near the Marienplatz and raised Anna there. When times turned against us, we sold our home and business and bought this farm."

Weber thought it odd that Gabel had mentioned Anna but not her brother, Luka. He also wondered what kind of adversity had forced Gabel to leave Munich. "What happened in Munich that made you leave? Did it have something to do with the postwar economy--the ravages of the Weimar Republic?"

"Perhaps indirectly. But, let's just say that ill winds were blowing, and we didn't want to stick around for the storm."

Sensing that Gabel was uncomfortable, Weber pivoted to what he thought would be a more agreeable topic.

"I bet moving to the farm pleased Anna."

Now, Gabel looked even more distressed. He swiveled in his chair and eyed Weber suspiciously. "What has she told you about that period of her life?"

Weber realized that he'd stepped on a landmine and backtracked immediately. "Not a thing, Aaron. I'm sorry if I upset you. I was just trying to make conversation."

Gabel stood, demanded Weber's coffee mug, and prepared to leave. "Take me back to the farmhouse. I have chores to do."

Chapter 12

Summer 1927: Berlin, Germany

On the journey back to Gabel's farm, the Dewoitine cruised at ten thousand feet on a northbound heading when Weber noticed a speck on the horizon. The speck quickly grew and took on the shape of an approaching aircraft. This was the first airborne plane Weber had encountered since leaving the Alpine hut. He calculated that the approaching aircraft traveled at a similar speed and altitude on a diametrically opposed heading. He monitored the approaching aircraft's progress for several minutes and began to feel concerned as it drew closer without changing course. He struggled to make sense of the situation until it occurred to him that the oncoming pilot intended to intercept the Dewoitine. To test his assumption, Weber changed his course from 5 degrees north to 45 degrees northwest. As expected, the intruder followed suit and shifted to a bearing that would intercept his flight path.

As the interceptor drew closer, Weber saw it was a monoplane fighter like the one he had seen at Johannisthal Air Field. The distance between the planes closed rapidly, and soon, the warbird bore down on him without deflecting from its collision course. Weber turned toward Gabel and motioned for him to hold tight. He banked hard starboard until the plane's heading reversed, then instituted a sharp climb and leveled off. They were now flying on a parallel heading above and to the side of the German plane. The warbird passed harmlessly below them and then slowed. Weber figured the German pilot had overshot his target, lost sight of the Dewoitine, and paused to regroup. Recognizing his advantage, he banked and descended laterally until the Dewoitine was directly behind the warbird. Then he edged alongside and locked eyes with the pilot. The German pilot, taken by surprise, became unhinged. His face contorted in rage, and he began shouting and shaking his fists at Weber.

Weber felt smug until he glanced rearward and saw four more German fighters approaching. As the interceptors swarmed around him, Weber inspected their wingtips and saw that, unlike the phantom he'd seen at Johannisthal Air Field, the gun ports on these planes were fitted with cannons. It was a disturbing sight and left him with no choice but to assume that these planes were armed. He felt like he'd poked a bee's nest and was about to get stung, perhaps repeatedly.

The newly arrived planes edged closer and took up positions surrounding the Dewoitine--one above, one below, and one on each side of the aircraft. The initial interceptor positioned itself directly in front of the Dewoitine, blocking the way forward. Weber realized too late that he had lost control of the situation; he hadn't reacted quickly enough, and now he was boxed in and had no room to maneuver. The pilot on Weber's right waved to get his attention and motioned toward the ground. Weber vehemently shook his head from side to side, trying to clarify that he had no intention of landing. The Germans responded by banking in unison, forcing Weber to follow their lead.

Maintaining a tight formation, the German planes kept the Dewoitine confined like an eagle in a cage. They pivoted in perfect synchrony, settled on an easterly heading, and then flew into a remote region of Bavaria. Soon after that, an airfield appeared in the distance. Weber felt a tap on his shoulder and turned to see Gabel leaning forward and pointing toward the distant airfield. He started shouting directly in Weber's ear.

"Robert, do something. Don't let them force us to land at that airport."

The prospect of forced landing didn't please Weber either, but he didn't see any way around it. The situation seemed hopeless--he was trapped and out of options. Or was he? He chided himself for feeling helpless and tried to formulate a means of escape. There was no way to get past the lead plane; the path forward was blocked. Banking to port or starboard would slam the Dewoitine against the planes beside him or jam its wingtips into the escorts above or below him. Those maneuvers would be deadly. Was there no way out? Then it occurred to him that his rear was unguarded; no plane was behind him. Most likely, the Germans figured that if he decelerated, they could slow to match his speed, maintain formation, and keep the Dewoitine in its cage. That thought, however, triggered an idea.

Weber depressed the throttle, cutting power to the engine, and then swiftly retracted the yoke. The Dewoitine pitched up sharply, stalled, then dropped its nose precipitously and dove toward the earth. Gabel screamed and writhed in his seat, unaware that Weber had intentionally executed the dive. The maneuver surprised the Germans; in just a few seconds, the Dewoitine had slowed, slipped behind its underside escort, and dropped out of sight.

After allowing the Dewoitine to fall several thousand feet, Weber pulled out of the dive, leveled off, and then repeated the maneuver. Repetition of the maneuver reduced the risk of an extended dive; the longer the dive lasted, the harder it was to recover. When they were only a few thousand feet off the ground, he leveled the plane for the last time, maxed the throttle, and set a course for the mountains. If his luck held, the Alpine topography would help to shield him from German pursuers.

Once within the Alps, Weber hugged the contours of the mountains, often flying inside valleys and basins to escape detection. The route was slow and circuitous, but it enabled them to reach Gabel's farm without incident.

As the Dewoitine coasted up to the hangar, Gabel jumped out and started shouting instructions. "Stop here so you don't block the hangar. We need to get my plane out so we can hide the Dewoitine. We can't leave it on the runway where the Germans can see it." Weber brought the plane to a stop and climbed down. He followed Gabel into the hangar, and together, the two men rolled the Caspar onto the runway and put the Dewoitine in its place.

Gabel closed the hangar door and told Weber to wait while he went to the farmhouse to get them a beer and something to eat. Weber nodded and eased into a chair beside Gabel's workbench, exhausted from the ordeal. When Gabel returned, the two men sat at Gabel's workbench, poured themselves a beer, and feasted on cheese and sausages.

The men laughed and joked as they ate, their humor dispelling accumulated stress. Then, quite abruptly, Gabel's mood turned somber. "We had a close call today, Robert. I don't think you understand how dangerous it would have been if the Germans had forced us to land at that airfield."

"I figured we were in trouble when I saw your reaction to that airfield. However, you're right; I don't understand why putting down there would have been so dangerous."

"There are things I'd like to tell you, Robert, but first, I need to know that I can trust you. German politics are treacherous these days, and I need to be sure that you won't repeat anything I say to the authorities."

"The authorities? Who exactly are you talking about?"

"All of them, but the Nazis in particular."

"Believe me, Aaron, you can trust me. I have no sympathy for the Nazis. I'll keep everything you tell me in the strictest confidence."

"Alright, let me start at the beginning. You asked me why we left Munich and I obfuscated. Well, now I'm going to tell you the truth. The Nazis drove us out. You see, Ruth and I are Jewish, and the Nazis are blaming the Jews for Germany's problems. They made life miserable for us. We had to sell our business because they intimidated our customers. The last straw was when one of them accosted me on the street one night when I took the day's proceeds to the bank. The sniveling little swine stabbed me and stole my money. I'm lucky I survived. The wound was serious; it severed nerves in my back and left me with a limp. We changed our names, fled the city, and used our savings to buy this farm."

"Aaron, that's terrible. You're lucky you weren't killed."

"After we left, the political situation in Munich deteriorated. It became a haven for right-wing extremists who disavowed the Treaty of Versailles, resisted Berlin's authority, and advocated the overthrow of the Weimar government. One particularly heinous group, the Nationalsozialistische Deutsche Arbeiterpartei, or the Nazi party, was led by a former army corporal named Adolph Hitler. He and his henchmen plotted together for years in a Munich beer hall, spreading lies and specious propaganda. Among other things, they argued that Jews, Marxists, and the ruling class conspired to bring about Germany's WWI defeat and that the Weimar politicians were 'backstabbers' because they accepted the Treaty of Versailles, which led to the country's economic, moral, and political decline. They formulated a nationalist platform in which they advocated for deposing the Weimar government, stripping Jews of citizenship, and forming a "Greater Germany" that included former Austro-German regions such as Prussia and Austria.

The party grew in size and political strength, and Hitler formed a private army called the Sturmabteilung--the SA or brown shirts. He did it by recruiting disgruntled ex-soldiers and appointed a former war hero named Göring to organize and train those thugs in the woods outside Munich."

Weber flinched when he heard Gabel mention Göring's name. "Wait a minute, Aaron. Göring? Would that have been *Hermann* Göring?

"Yes, his name was Hermann Göring."

"What do you know about him?"

"Göring grew up near Munich and became a WWI flying ace. He lived in Sweden after the war and returned to Germany in the early 1920s. Hitler used his status as a war hero to legitimize his political ambitions."

Now visibly shaken, Weber stood and began pacing the hangar floor. "Damn, I wondered what happened to him. I have some history with Göring, and none of my memories are pleasant. Where is he now?"

"I don't know, but rumor has it that, after his injury, he and his wife absconded to Austria."

"Injury? What happened?"

"Hitler attempted a putsch at a beer hall where Munich's political leaders were meeting. When it failed, he and Göring mustered the SA and marched into Munich, intending to overthrow the regional government. The Nazi mob was met by an armed detachment of police and troops who opened fire on them. Göring was among the wounded--he took a bullet in the groin. Hitler stood trial for treason and received a five-year sentence. Göring avoided arrest by fleeing the country."

"Do you know whether a man named Gunter was involved?"

"Not to my knowledge."

"Where do things stand now?"

"Hitler served only a few months in prison, and during that time, he wrote a rambling, muddled treatise called *Mein Kampf* in which he asserted his jaundiced view of Germany's problems and his ignominious, prejudicial recommendations for the country's future. That book, unfortunately, placed Nazi ideology on the national stage. Before that, Nazi lies and violence were largely limited to Bavaria. I fear for Germany if the Nazis acquire power at a national level."

"Do you think another war is likely?"

"Certainly, if Hitler has his way. His plan to create a greater Germany suggests that he is willing to bring about reunification and create Lebensraum, or living space, by any means necessary, including military intervention. But it isn't just the Nazis that make another war likely. Conditions throughout Germany are conducive to another war. The Allies' enforcement of the Treaty of Versailles made life difficult for all Germans. Many, if not most, are destitute and disillusioned, and they blame the Allies for their plight. That's why, at this very moment, the German government is secretly rearming, even though the Treaty of Versailles specifically forbids rearmament."

Weber's mission objectives immediately sprung to mind. "Does that include rebuilding military aviation?"

"It does."

Now, Weber was on the edge of his seat. "And is that related to why you vehemently opposed landing at that airfield?"

"It is."

"I'd like to hear more about that, Aaron."

"I'm sure you would, but I shouldn't say anything before consulting with my collaborators."

"If you have collaborators, I think you belong to some resistance movement working against rearmament. Is that the case?"

"Alright, I'll trust you with a few details. But you must keep your promise not to betray us."

Weber nodded his agreement. "I promise. I won't divulge anything you tell me."

Gabel drew a deep breath and glanced around the hangar as if he was searching for spies. Then his expression hardened. He looked Weber in the eye and began speaking resolutely. "I am a member of a small group working to prevent Germany from rearming and waging another war. We not only oppose the Nazis in Bavaria but also fight against the broader national efforts to rearm Germany secretly. Our ranks disagree on whether we should inform the Allies of these illegal activities. For now, we work in secret. We gather information and do what we can to impede the government's rearmament activities."

"Are you talking about sabotage?"

"We conduct those kinds of operations occasionally, but on a small scale. We're not commandos, nor are we well-armed. Principally, we gather information about covert, illegal activities and use it to coerce those engaged in rearmament--primarily government agencies and manufacturers--by threatening to expose their actions.

"Is aviation included in this underground rearmament initiative?"

"Yes, but it's been a challenge to distinguish between legitimate versus banned activities. The Treaty of Versailles bans only the building of military aircraft and the creation of an air force. Germany is free to engage in civil aviation and develop aeronautical technology, which includes aircraft design and instrumentation. What the government and manufacturers cannot do is develop, test, or utilize those aspects of aviation for military purposes."

"From what you've said, I assume your crew knows how the government or industry uses aviation technology for military purposes. Is that correct?"

"I can't go into specifics, but yes, our 'crew' has some evidence that would be of interest to the Inter-Allied Control Commission--the organization that enforces the Treaty of Versailles--and it's damning enough to precipitate additional sanctions against Germany. For one thing, there appears to be a shadow agency within the government that instigates and coordinates rearmament projects. We think they work closely with German aeronautical researchers and manufacturers. But, what we suspect and can prove are two different things. There are a lot of illegal activities that remain to be uncovered.

"What kinds of illegal activities have you exposed?"

"What we've found suggests that rearmament efforts include misappropriating ultramodern aviation technology and using it for military purposes. German scientists and engineers produce some of the best avionics in the world, such as radios, gyroscopes, and altitude indicators, and they market them to the manufacturers of civilian aircraft in Germany and elsewhere. However, governments in other countries purchase this technology not just to improve their civilian aircraft but also to improve their military aircraft. So, Germany is advancing other nations' military capabilities while their armed forces languish. Strategically, that puts them in a vulnerable position. Hence, the rearmament agency seizes a portion of these ultramodern avionics and redirects them to facilities where they are adapted for use in secret warplanes."

"So, the Allies know that Germany is developing some of the world's best aviation technology, but they don't object because they need it to modernize their armed forces, and they believe that Germans only use the technology to improve their civil aviation?"

"That's correct. It's not illegal for Germany to develop and test instruments for civilian aircraft. However, as I have just told you, we have it on good authority that ultramodern avionics are finding their way into military aircraft."

"Ok, what else?"

"Manufacturers are designing and building military aircraft, such as fighters and bombers, and passing them off as civilian planes. They devise innovations, such as swept-back wings, large cargo holds, and metal fuselages, ostensibly to improve civilian aircraft, but the real design purpose is to enhance the capabilities and performance of military aircraft. For example, manufacturers build what appear to be airliners, but, in actuality, the planes have been engineered as bombers. Moreover, they assemble the planes in ways that make it easy to convert them into military aircraft."

"That's a serious allegation."

"And that's not all. The rearmament agency appears to have an operational arm charged with building and running secret "ghost" airbases. We know very little about this aspect of the initiative, but we think they use some bases to assemble warplanes--by converting civilian aircraft, modifying avionics, and installing armaments--and they use other bases to test warplanes, train pilots, and practice combat tactics.

"Okay, Aaron, now I think I know why you didn't want us to land at that airfield."

"I am certain it's a ghost base where fighter aircraft are assembled. A source told me that someone was building a secret airbase near my farm, so my team and I located it and observed its operations. We couldn't get inside the base because its perimeter was heavily guarded, but we spotted some trucks delivering aircraft parts to one of the hangars." Gabel paused, retrieved several photographs from a wall safe, and handed them to Weber. "Take a look at these. This is why the Germans intercepted the Dewoitine and forcibly escorted us to the airfield. We accidentally entered their airspace, and they suspected us of being spies."

They'd have been right, Weber thought. He laughed and feigned disinterest. "Imagine that!"

"I'm serious, Robert. If we'd landed there, our fates would have been sealed. We'd have been detained, or worse yet, silenced permanently."

Weber fell silent, and his expression became solemn. "Aaron, I have a favor to ask. I want to borrow some photographs showing aircraft parts arriving at the base. Would you do me that favor?"

"So, the man with the powerful plane wants pictures of illegal aircraft parts arriving at a secret airbase! That makes me wonder, Robert, if you are being honest with me about your reasons for being in Germany. Would you care to explain?"

"You're a perceptive man, Aaron. I want to be more forthcoming, but I'm not at liberty to do so. For now, let me say that I know some people in Washington, DC, who would be interested in these pictures, and their goals are consistent with yours. Trust me when I say that sharing these photos would further your cause rather than hinder it."

"Will there come a day, Robert, when you can be truthful with me?"

"I think so, yes. For now, let me say that I'm indebted to you, Aaron. You've gathered an amazing amount of intelligence. Some of it seems like top-secret information. However, I have a question for you. You mentioned that a source informed you about the secret base, and you have gathered significant data on Germany's rearmament activities. Who is your source for all of this intelligence?"

"Some of it comes from my team's covert operations. Beyond that, I can only say that I have a highly placed source inside the Wehrmacht's Aviation Coalition."

"And who might that be?"

"I have secrets to protect, just as you do. I can't reveal my source. That channel is sensitive, and the information that flows through it is too valuable for me to risk exposing it."

◆◆◆

That evening, in the farmhouse, Anna and Weber ate dinner with her family and then retired to her bedroom to prepare for the journey back to Berlin. While Anna started packing, Weber went to his separate bedroom, gathered his belongings, and brought them to her room. He had just started folding his clothes when Anna turned and spoke to him in a soft, faltering voice. There were tears in her eyes.

"Robert, I want Luka to live with us in Berlin."

The request took Weber by surprise. He'd been thinking about Gabel's revelations when Anna's request abruptly refocused his thoughts. "What? Why, Anna?"

"Luka will soon be an adult, and his options here are limited. He's smart, and his life would be wasted as a farmhand. I want him to attend BTS with Carl."

Weber's mind spun as he considered the implications of adding a second teenager to the growing assortment of people living in his apartment, potentially complicating his mission. "Anna, your brother's life isn't your responsibility. Luka's future is your father and mother's concern."

"But the farm isolates him from other boys his age. He's alone too much and needs a friend. I think he and Carl would get along famously."

"Oh, now it's Luka's social life that concerns you. Come on, Anna, level with me. What's this really about?"

Anna fell silent, turned away, and stared out the window. As Weber waited for her to respond, an uneasy feeling welled up in the pit of his stomach. Unable to tolerate the suspense any longer, he broke the silence. "Well?"

"Robert, this isn't easy for me to talk about. You see, Luka isn't my brother; he's my son."

"Your son?" Weber's mouth dropped open as he stared at Anna in disbelief. At a loss for words, he stepped backward, bumped against Anna's bed, and sat down hard on the edge of the mattress. He struggled to make sense of Anna's confession, but comprehension eluded him. "How can that be?"

"He just is. Please don't grill me. Can't you just accept this?"

"No. I'm sorry, but I think I deserve an explanation."

"Luka is why my father is so concerned about you toying with my affections. I had him when I was only sixteen. Remember when I told you that I had a relationship that ended badly? Well, I left out the part about why--I got pregnant."

"So, if you're Luka's mother, why did your parents raise him? Why did he grow up here on the farm?"

"I was trying to protect him."

"From what?"

"From myself, partly. I was an adolescent and didn't know anything about being a parent. And because I was afraid that he'd be harmed by people who saw him as a Jewish teenager's bastard child."

"You mean the Nazis?

"Certainly, the Nazis! I wanted to protect him from those malicious racists and all the other faultfinders who are quick to judge a woman who has a child out of wedlock."

Weber nodded, signaling that he understood, and then he dropped his head, stared at the floor, and rubbed his forehead. The full weight of Anna's plea rested on his shoulders, and he wasn't sure how to unburden himself. He knew he needed to choose his words carefully because the future of their relationship likely would hinge on the next few utterances that came out of his mouth. "Be reasonable, Anna. You're raising a complex issue on the cusp of our departure and expecting me to make a split-second decision! How is that fair? I need time to think."

Several moments passed as Anna stood silently, trying to collect her thoughts and regain her composure. Then she sighed, walked to the bedside where Weber was seated, and sat beside him. "Alright, Robert," she said, her voice quavering slightly. Her lips curled into a smile, but the expression seemed forced and didn't hide the disappointment in her eyes. "Let's stay here another day or two. Why don't you spend time with Luka and get to know him? Perhaps that will help you make up your mind."

Chapter 13

Fall 1927: Munich Germany

The news broke while Gunter was helping one of Bayern Hof's wealthy clients, Herr Obermaier, settle into a top-floor hotel suite. Obermaier was a Fokker Aircraft engineer visiting Munich to consult with the Bayerische Motoren Werke about new engine designs for his company's aircraft. After placing Obermaier's bags in the closet, Gunter opened a window and turned down the bed. Then he approached Obermaier, made eye contact, and waited expectantly for a tip.

"Is there anything else I can do for you today, Herr Obermaier?

"Find me a copy of today's Münchener Post. President von Hindenburg made an announcement today about political amnesty, and the details will be printed in the paper."

Gunter obliged. He went to the hotel lobby and purchased a copy of the newspaper. On the way back to Obermaier's suite, he read the article about von Hindenburg's announcement. Shortly after that, he placed a call to Göring.

"Hermann, your days of living in exile are over. President von Hindenburg has just announced a political amnesty. You can return to Germany."

"Gunter, that's the best news I've heard in years. Carin has fallen ill and is unable to make the journey. When she recovers, she plans to visit her family in Sweden. I, however, have regained my strength and will take a train to Munich immediately. Tell our friend Herr Hitler that I'm returning and get me an appointment with him."

"You won't need an appointment, Hermann. Adolph and his closest associates still meet at the Bratwurstglöckle on Monday evenings."

Göring's trip to Germany took longer than expected. He had little money and was forced to beg his Austrian supporters for train fare. The few marks he had scrounged got him as far as Salzburg, where he spent the night on a public bench. The next morning, he used his last coin to call Gunter, who reluctantly agreed to drive to Salzburg and transport his penniless friend to Munich. When they arrived, Gunter graciously allowed Göring to stay in his apartment.

The following Monday evening, Göring accompanied Gunter to the Bratwurstglöckle, where he approached Hitler and his cronies. Hitler wasn't pleased to see him. "What do you expect me to do for you, Göring? You're broke. You'd be a drain on the party. We do not need beggars who are looking for handouts. I'm also concerned about your loyalty. You left the country while I was in prison, and our friends in Austria say you maligned me while you lived there."

"Adolph, you don't understand. I was seriously injured when we marched on the Marienplatz. Gunter knew that if I were hospitalized in Munich, they'd let me bleed to death. So he and my wife took me to Austria, and we stayed there because I was gravely ill and the German authorities were hunting us. I apologize if I said anything untoward about you or the party. I was delirious for months and spouted a lot of nonsense."

"Come and see me when you've got something to offer the party. Get a job and earn your keep. Your penury is a disgrace. Now leave us."

Gunter tried to cheer the dejected Göring as they walked to his apartment. "Adolph's bad-tempered these days because the party is a shamble and nearly insolvent. Don't take his criticisms personally. He needs money to bolster the party's resources, grow its membership, and improve its political prospects. He's desperate to become a legitimate politician, and to accomplish that, he's vowed to fill the Reichstag with Nazis in the next election."

"I should be one of the party's candidates, Gunter. Tell Adolph that when you see him again. Who better than a war hero could win the hearts and minds of the German people?"

"This isn't the time, Hermann. Right now, Adolph wouldn't let you clean his toilets, let alone represent the party as a Reichstag candidate. You need to show him you can be the man you used to be. Better yet, prove to him that you can do something that he and his henchmen can't, like earning the respect of Germany's corporate leaders and political elite. Adolph has no experience with the ruling class and wouldn't know how to relate to the titans of industry. You, my friend, are educated and could do that in your sleep."

"What exactly are you suggesting, Gunter?"

"Do I have to spell it out for you, Hermann? Where's your initiative? Have you forgotten who you are? Did that bullet blow a hole in your confidence?"

"Don't preach at me, Gunter--not until you've taken a bullet in the groin and watched your life disappear while an excruciating, festering infection devours your body and mind."

"Alright, enough. You know I don't respond well to guilt tactics. Here's what I suggest. Go to Berlin and try to get a job in the aviation industry. The people who buy and sell planes will know you by reputation. Impress them with how much you know about airplanes and then ask them for a job."

Winter 1927: Berlin, Germany

Göring slogged through the heavy snow that an early winter storm had dumped on Berlin's streets. He'd had no choice but to walk to his morning appointments because nothing motorized was moving. The U-Bahn was shuttered, and cars and trucks sat like snow sculptures along the roadsides, frozen in place until the plows arrived. He was making good progress until a sudden gust of wind knocked him sideways, nearly pushing him into a snowbank. After regaining his balance, he pulled up his coat collar and picked up his pace. He was a professional now, and determined to be on time for his appointments even if his clients were late.

He hated to admit it, but Gunter's advice had been providential. After arriving in Berlin, he'd met with a former colleague, Erhard Milch, a senior executive at Lufthansa Airlines. Milch had put him in touch with companies that did business with the aviation industry, and in less than a month, he had been offered not one but three jobs. He was now a sales representative for Bayerische Motoren Werke, Heinkel, and a Swedish parachute company. As his income rose, he'd rented a small office on the city's edge and taken on a business partner named Paul Koener. He'd known Koener, another airman, during the Great War. Together, they'd worked hard and grown a successful business.

Göring's success as a businessman hadn't blunted his political aspirations. As spring approached, he began thinking about the elections. He was in a very different position now than when he'd first returned to Germany and begged Hitler to reinstate him in the Nazi party. He'd made something of himself in Berlin; his fortunes had improved financially, and he was on a first-name basis with many of Berlin's elite, including those who spent their days in the lofty corridors of government and finance.

By late February, Göring had made up his mind. The 1928 election was scheduled for May, and unless he declared his candidacy soon, there would not be sufficient time to mount a campaign. He asked Koener to cover his appointments and traveled to Munich to confront Hitler.

Spring 1928: Munich, Germany

It was loud and crowded in the Munich Hauptbahnhof when Göring arrived. He stepped down from his coach into the crowd of passengers on the platform waiting to board the train. Several impatient boarders pushed past him, eager to stow their luggage and claim the best seats in the coach's compartments. Hearing someone shout his name, he scanned the crowd and spied Gunter leaning against an empty luggage cart. He waved, walked to where his friend stood, and greeted him with a handshake.

Gunter invited Göring to stay in his apartment and, the next morning, showed him the way to Hitler's flat. Göring was intimated by the prospect of confronting Hitler and asked Gunter to attend the meeting. Gunter demurred and said that Hitler would interpret his presence as a sign of weakness--a perception that might prevent him from endorsing Göring's candidacy. He suggested instead that Göring join him in a nearby café when the meeting was over.

Göring proceeded to Hitler's flat at 41 Thierschstrasse, just south of the Marienplatz and east of the Isar River. He climbed the stairs to the second floor, knocked on the door, and was greeted by one of Hitler's aides who ushered him into the two-room flat. The larger of the two rooms contained a sofa, a bed, and a small kitchen. The aide led Göring into a smaller room that Hitler used as an office. As Göring entered, Hitler, seated behind a desk, looked up and gestured toward an empty chair.

Hitler began the meeting by asking a series of questions that, from Göring's perspective, felt like an interrogation. "Why are you here, Göring? Are you still looking for a handout? What's changed since the last time I saw you? Why should I trust you to represent our interests in the Reichstag? What can you do for the party that others can't?"

Göring tried to maintain his composure while he answered Hitler's questions, but he eventually tired of the browbeating and lost his temper. "Shut up, Adolph, and try to reign in your arrogance. You think you're clever, but I have some tricks up my sleeve that you haven't considered. You need me but can't see why because your vanity blinds you."

Hitler exploded. His jaw tensed, his face flushed, and his eyes grew as large as saucers. He bounded to his feet, paced the office floor, and screamed curses until his voice grew hoarse and spittle ran down his jowls.

Göring squirmed uncomfortably in his chair, waiting for Hitler's tantrum to subside. When Hitler regained a modicum of composure, Göring mustered his courage and made a case for his candidacy. "Adolph, if you want the Nazi party to succeed outside of Bavaria, you will have to do more than woo working-class Germans. You'll need to make inroads into the business and professional classes; there's no future for you in national politics without their support and money. Who within the Nazi party can help you achieve that? I can. My business dealings in Berlin bring me into contact with many types of professionals daily: the captains of industry, uppermost government officials, scientists, political pundits, and media moguls, to mention a few."

Göring paused to gauge Hitler's reaction. He sensed immediately that the dynamics of the meeting had shifted. Hitler had stopped raving and started listening. Göring's confidence surged, so he decided to make one more pitch he thought would seal the deal. "There's one more thing, Adolph. What if I knew something that could enhance your political clout--a secret that would embarrass Germany's top politicians if it were to be publicized?"

Hitler leaned forward, anticipating Göring's next words. "Well, spit it out. What is this secret?" Göring smiled inwardly. He'd pulled it off. The Nazi's top dog was eating out of the palm of his hand. "I'll tell you, Adolph, but first, you must promise me I will be one of the party's candidates for Reichstag."

"Alright, consider it done. Now, what's the secret?"

"The government is secretly rearming Germany. Their actions violate the Versailles Treaty and, if made public, would destabilize the current government and the country's economy. Think of the leverage that would give you. I can't think of a better cudgel for you to wield against the Weimar backstabbers in the next election."

"Why should I believe you, Göring? How did you come by this information?"

"I sell equipment to aviation manufacturers. Behind closed doors, they are asking me to source items such as machine guns and bomb sights. When I ask why such equipment is needed, they refer me to some obscure government official who never returns my calls. When I deliver the equipment, they tell me to dispose of receipts and eliminate any paper trail. I'm not a fool. There's a reason for the secrecy--they aren't installing that gear in civilian aircraft."

"That's useful to know, Göring. I can see now that I've decided wisely about your future. But then, as you said, I'm a clever man. The party will benefit from your return."

Chapter 14

Fall 1927: Berlin, Germany

Upon returning to Berlin after the trip to visit Anna's parents in Bavaria, Weber resumed his duties as an intern and labored to pick up the threads of his mission. His life had become complicated; consequently, he'd made his mission less of a priority. The mission was the principal reason he and Carl moved to Berlin. If he was honest with himself, he knew that his decision to pursue a relationship with Anna was primarily responsible for the shift in his lifestyle and priorities. Rather than lament that choice, however, he'd considered his new life a mixed blessing.

The portion of his life devoted to parenting had expanded dramatically, and the amount of time he spent on childrearing responsibilities had nearly doubled because there were now two teenage boys living under his roof. After acquiescing to Anna's request, he'd welcomed Luka into his household and introduced him to Carl. It had taken Carl a while to adjust, but as Anna had surmised, he eventually took to Luka, and the two boys had become close friends. Weber was pleased that Carl now had a close friend but wasn't thrilled about the prospect of fathering two teenage boys.

His relationship with Anna consumed another sizeable portion of his life and the ties he had formed with her parents while in Bavaria added a further layer of complications. Still, Weber had to admit that the trip to Bavaria had exponentially expanded his knowledge about Germany's underground aircraft programs. In a matter of days, Aaron had taught him more about Germany's aviation rearmament than he had learned from weeks of investigation on his own in Berlin. That information brought him several steps closer to accomplishing his mission objectives and provided numerous leads that would increase the effectiveness of his investigation. In retrospect, he decided, the value of Aaron's contribution was inestimable. Perhaps meeting Anna and spending time with her family was not a mixed blessing but a blessing in disguise.

◆◆◆

As Weber struggled to find his bearings and reestablish his priorities, he couldn't help but notice that Anna was happier than he had ever seen her. Returning to Berlin with her son, reunited at long last, had done wonders for her emotional well-being and outlook. Her newfound happiness had spilled over into her interactions with Weber and improved their romance as well, a development that Weber hadn't anticipated but gladly embraced. She seemed to enjoy being a parent and had taken an authoritative hand in Luka's upbringing and everyday activities.

One of the first things Anna did after returning from Bavaria was to seek admission for Luka at the Berlin Technical School, where Carl was a student. She and Luka visited the school and met with an admissions officer who arranged for Luka to take an entrance exam. The test revealed that Luka had a superior intellect and above-average aptitudes in math and science. The admissions officer congratulated Luka and informed Anna that BTS would accept her son and allow him to begin school immediately. Anna thanked the officer and said she needed to discuss the opportunity with Luka before deciding.

Carl and Weber threw a party for Luka at dinner that evening to celebrate his admission. Anna joined the merriment but warned the revelers that she would not allow Luka to attend BTS unless he agreed to some ground rules. No one inquired about the rules for fear of spoiling the party, but when bedtime came, Luka broached the issue with his mother. Anna told Luka that she had three non-negotiable stipulations and would not allow him to attend BTS unless he promised to honor them. Luka frowned but then threw up his hands in submission and asked his mother to disclose her conditions.

Anna stood, put her hands on Luka's shoulders, and looked him square in the eye. She paused briefly for effect, then, with a stern visage and a firm tone of voice, she listed her conditions. First, she demanded that Luka conceal his religion and his Bavarian upbringing from everyone at BTS, including his teachers and classmates. Second, she insisted that he list only their Berlin address and his German citizenship on his application. Third, she asked Luka to promise he would not participate in the Hitlerjugend or the Air Ministry's internship program. Of the three demands, the latter elicited the most pushback from Luka. He objected strenuously, and when that failed, he floated several counterarguments, chief among them the allegation that Weber had allowed Carl to participate in both programs. Ultimately, Anna overruled Luka's objections and threatened to return him to Bavaria unless he agreed to her conditions. Luka capitulated, although begrudgingly, after which Anna agreed to let him begin school at BTS.

Spring 1928: Berlin, Germany

Weber arrived at Johannisthal Air Field shortly after sunrise, parked the Benz next to his hangar, and walked south along the access road until he reached the manager's office. Upon entering the office, he greeted the manager and handed him a check.

"Hello, Hans. Here's the rent payment for my hangar."

"Good morning, Robert. I'll credit these funds to your account. By the way, a guy came in a few days ago asking whether a Dewoitine was parked in any of our hangars. He seemed a little shifty, so I asked him why he wanted to know, and he mumbled something about registration rules for non-German aircraft. That struck me as odd, so I asked the guy for his credentials, and he bristled and demanded to see my supervisor. I snubbed the guy, and he lost his temper, called me foul names, and said he'd come back with a warrant. I haven't seen him since, but I thought you should know."

"Hans, when I registered my plane, nothing was said about non-German aircraft. What was this guy talking about?"

"Damned if I know. It's suspicious, isn't it?

"Yes. Would you call me if you see this guy again?"

"Sure, Robert, you can count on it."

Weber felt uneasy as he drove back into the city. Something wasn't right. Hans had sensed it, too. Someone was searching for his plane. He couldn't shake the feeling that the shifty guy was connected to the incident near the Bavarian ghost base. Perhaps the fighter pilots had identified the Dewoitine when they tried to force it down, and now their superiors were hunting for his plane. That spelled trouble because if they found the Dewoitine, it would lead them directly to him.

Before Weber arrived at his apartment, he stopped at a public phone booth and called Curtis Taylor. Until now, he hadn't endeavored to conceal his actions, but it seemed prudent to step up his tradecraft in light of the morning's developments.

When Taylor answered his phone, Weber requested a meeting and said it was urgent. "Curtis, I have new information and need to swap planes."

"I'll meet you at the Johannisthal hangar at noon tomorrow. What are your requirements for the aircraft?"

"German built with performance similar or better than the Dewoitine."

◆◆◆

Weber watched as Taylor's plane came into view, flew parallel to the south side of the airfield, and then banked sharply and descended onto the east-west runway. Even at a distance, he could tell that the aircraft was newer and more advanced than the Dewoitine. It was a single-prop, tandem monoplane with a sleek fuselage and enclosed cabin. He waited patiently as Taylor taxied to the south side of the airfield, pivoted onto the access road, and parked next to his hangar. Seconds later, the cockpit door opened, and Taylor crawled onto the wing, slid to the ground, and stood facing his friend.

"Right on time as always, Curtis! Thanks for making the trip on such short notice."

"Well, as they say, 'a friend in need' and all that. What's the emergency?"

Weber turned and pointed toward the hangar. "Come inside, and I'll fill you in." He led the way into the hangar, pulled two stools to his workbench, and sat facing Taylor. "Here's the problem, Curtis. I began a relationship with a woman named Anna, and we visited her parents recently in Bavaria. I took her father up in the Dewoitine, and we were intercepted by a squadron of fighters--planes like the one I have been chasing but armed with wing-mounted guns. To make a long story short, we escaped before they forced us down, but now some shifty character is snooping around this airfield trying to find Dewoitines. How many other Dewoitines do you think exist in Germany--especially ones configured like mine? My guess would be zero. Later, I learned that the interception occurred near a secret air base. I suspect the Germans thought we were aerial spies."

"Wow, Robert, that's a lot to digest. Let me get this straight. You've met a woman, and from what you've said, it sounds like you're in a serious relationship. You flew to Bavaria, met her parents, and found a secret air base. A bevy of fighters from that airbase intercepted your plane and nearly forced you down. Have I left anything out? Oh, yes, now you're being hunted by some suspicious person you can't identify."

"That's about the size of it."

"Alright, it makes sense to swap your plane. Finding a late-model German aircraft was difficult, but I managed to locate an experimental Junkers JU 49. Don't ask me how. It's a single prop plane with a Junkers L88a V-12 engine with 800 horsepower. It should be faster and more maneuverable than the Dewoitine."

"I'm impressed. You've outdone yourself, Curtis."

"Don't mention it. Now, what else did you want to tell me? It sounds like you stumbled onto a secret airbase. I'm curious about that, and Furst will be too."

Weber told Taylor about Gabel and his crew and showed him some photos the resistance group had taken of trucks delivering aircraft parts to the ghost base. He went on to explain what the crew had discovered about the German rearmament strategies. When he finished, Taylor pursed his lips and whistled softly. "Robert, you've struck gold. If all this checks out, your mission will have been a resounding success. But that doesn't mean you're finished. No, nothing of the sort. It means you've proven yourself to be a successful, productive agent. So, don't stop, keep digging."

"What exactly are you suggesting, Curtis? If I dig much deeper, I might lose my footing and fall into a hole."

"Isn't it obvious? Team up with Gabel and his crew, sneak into the factory at that airbase, and photograph the entire operation, including the armaments they're installing on those fighters."

"I'll tell you what's obvious, Curtis. My mission's becoming more dangerous because an agent from that base is hunting me, and you're raising the risk level even further by sending me back there for a photo shoot."

"I think you're overestimating the risk, Robert. Gabel and his crew sound like experienced operatives who are familiar with the base. If you collaborate with them and plan the job carefully, your chances for success should outweigh the risks."

"It's more complicated than that, Curtis. You're proposing that I involve Anna's father in a covert operation that could get him captured or killed. If I put Gabel in harm's way and something bad happens to him, can you imagine how that would impact Anna? Think of what that would do to our relationship!"

"Look, Robert, protecting this German woman is not your priority. Your mission comes first. We didn't send you to Germany to find a spouse or a stepmother for Carl."

"Curtis, for a friend, your perspective seems rather callous."

"At the moment, I'm not speaking as your friend but as Furst's intermediary and your field manager. Do I need to remind you of the importance of this mission to your country? Have you forgotten its implications for global stability? There's much more at stake here than your personal needs and romantic aspirations."

Weber bristled. He'd had enough of Taylor's condescending tone, skewed perspective, and ill-considered advice. He stood, pushed his stool under the workbench, and turned to face his friend. "Look, Curtis, let's adjourn because I can't chance being seen with you. Help me move the Dewoitine." He pointed toward the plane, signaling his desire to hasten Taylor's departure.

Weber's abruptness and demeanor took Taylor by surprise. A mixture of dismay and chagrin flickered across his countenance as he stood and followed Weber toward the plane. Nothing more was said as the two men rolled the Dewoitine out of the hangar and replaced it with the Junkers.

Spring 1928: Berlin, Germany

After the school day ended, Luka sat on a park bench watching Carl and his team compete in a soccer game against another group of Hitlerjugend boys. It wasn't the first time he'd warmed this bench, waiting for Carl and his classmates to finish their game. It pained him to watch others play and not be able to participate, and it was becoming increasingly difficult to manage his emotions while he waited. He felt a strong sense of yearning at the outset of each game, and as the matches progressed, that longing turned into anger and then escalated into a seething rage against his mother. How dare she ban him? What did she have against the Hitlerjugend? It wasn't fair. He was as talented as Carl, if not more so, and soccer was one of his favorite pastimes.

When the game ended, Carl joined Luka, and the two boys picked up their belongings and began walking across the Tiergarten toward home. Carl could sense that Luka was in a foul mood, so he tried to distract him, hoping it might soothe his friend.

"Just think, Luka, this place--the Tiergarten--used to be some old guy's game preserve. You know, some bigwig like Fredrick Wilhelm or one of his lot. We read about it last year in my BTS history class."

"Carl, I'm German. Remember? Translated, Tiergarten means 'animal garden.' And more than one Fredrick Wilhelm resided here as one of Berlin's rulers."

"Sure, I knew that. The Tiergarten was here a long time before it became a park. When the wildlife disappeared, people decided to build statues of animals and famous people."

"An oversimplification if I ever heard one. You haven't retained much knowledge about the Tiergarten from your history class."

Carl sighed. Distraction wasn't helping, and Luka's attitude was making him angry. It was time to take the bull by the horns.

"Alright, Luka, what the hell is the matter with you? Are you angry at your mother again?"

"Who else? Why did she bring me here? She moved me to Berlin, encouraged me to be your friend, and then told me I couldn't be like you. How does that make sense? Her restrictions are ruining my life."

"Maybe you should talk to her about it again. See if you can change her mind."

"I've got a better idea. What if I joined the Hitlerjugend and didn't tell her? Would you keep your mouth shut?"

"Yes, because once you're a member of the Hitlerjugend, you can apply to join the Air Ministry's internship program. That would be fantastic because we could work on aviation projects together."

"My mother doesn't want me to do that either."

"If you're going to hide one thing from her, why not two? The punishment probably wouldn't be much worse if you get caught."

Luka smiled. It was a twisted logic, but he found it reassuring because it supported the course of action he'd already decided to pursue.

◆◆◆

With the addition of Anna and Luka as residents in Weber's apartment, quiet evenings were no longer the norm. The foursome regularly ate dinner together and engaged in animated conversations throughout the meal about things they'd experienced earlier in the day. It was a ritual that Anna had insisted on because she had been raised to believe that such gatherings were the cornerstone of family life. During her time on the farm, her family had dined together religiously, and she had many fond memories of the conversations they'd shared while discussing the events of their lives.

The only remaining remnants of this evening's meal were the dirty dishes that Carl was washing, and Luka was drying. The boys were in a jocular mood, telling jokes and laughing about their school-day antics and escapades. When the chore was finished, Carl told Luka he had 'homework' to do. He retrieved his briefcase, withdrew a sheaf of papers containing drawings and calculations, and spread them across the kitchen table. Luka sat down beside him and began inspecting the drawings.

"Carl, this plane is one of my favorites, but I think the wings have a problem. I know it's supposed to be a sweptback design, but the angle seems off. The slant seems too sharp, and the draft too shallow to provide sufficient lift for a plane this size. Have you done the calculations to evaluate the aerodynamics yet?"

"No, not completely. I was hoping that we could do that together this evening." Carl pointed to a sheet of paper near where Luka was sitting. "See those calculations? I started working on the problem but didn't get far. The math is complex, and I can't get the equations to work out. See what you can do, would you? Why don't you work on it? Maybe you can figure out where I'm going wrong."

Luka nodded, picked up the paper, and began inspecting the equations. "I see what you mean, Carl. This is a challenging problem."

While the boys were busy working, Anna entered the kitchen, walked to the table, and peered over Luka's shoulder. "What's this, Luka--it can't be schoolwork--these are aircraft drawings and calculations. This looks like work that Carl has brought home from his Aviation Coalition internship. Why would you be working on this?"

"Mom, I'm good at math, and Carl asked for my help. That's all."

Anna eyed Luka suspiciously, trying to decide whether his explanation was believable. "Oh really? Do you ever go to the Aviation Coalition with him when he's working on his internship?"

"Of course not, Mom."

Anna decided to give her son the benefit of the doubt. "Ok, just checking. That place is off-limits.

"If it's off limits, why can Carl go there?"

"That's between Carl and his father. I'm your mother, and you will do what I tell you. Understand?"

Luka nodded and then muttered something.

"Speak up, young man. Was that backtalk? Are you disrespecting me?"

"No, of course not, Mom."

Anna started to walk away, but something on the table caught her eye. She turned, picked up the sheet of paper Luka had been working on, and carefully inspected it. "There's an error here in your calculations, boys." She picked up a pencil, scribbled something on the page, and placed it in front of Luka. "Here, try this. I think you'll find it works."

Weber was standing in the doorway watching Anna interact with the boys. He had been in the living room, reading the paper, when he overheard the conversation in the kitchen and decided to investigate. It struck him as odd that an architect knew enough about aerodynamics to spot errors in complex calculations. He didn't know much about architecture, but he understood aerodynamics well enough to know that only an experienced engineer could successfully debug the kind of equations that Carl and Luka were working on. Something was amiss. His first impulse was to confront Anna, but caution prevailed. Why make a scene in front of the boys? Perhaps there was a reasonable explanation--something he hadn't considered or didn't know about Anna's past. He let the matter slide and returned to the living room to read the paper.

Chapter 15

Summer 1928: Berlin, Germany

It had been two weeks since Weber met with Curtis Taylor, and he still had no plan. It wasn't for lack of trying. He'd devised numerous schemes but ultimately rejected them all. Every plan he formulated seemed fraught with flaws---nothing seemed feasible. Perhaps he wasn't trying hard enough or needed to accept that no plan was foolproof. No matter. Plan or no plan, it was time to act.

He could understand why Taylor wanted him to return to Munich and photograph the secret airbase. Pictures of an illegal arms factory and banned warplanes would prove that Germany was rearming and convince the world that the Versailles Treaty had been violated. The Allied Commission would be forced to act, and retribution would be swift and merciless. It was precisely the leverage Furst sought and the principal reason for sending Weber to Berlin.

Having reminded himself of his mission's purpose, Weber asked himself why he was so uneasy about this particular assignment. He had already asked himself this question multiple times but couldn't figure out why he was uncomfortable. He had clearly stated to Taylor that any operation involving Aaron Gabel would put Gabel's life at risk and endanger his relationship with Anna. Those risks alone were enough to justify his discomfort. However, Weber felt something else was bothering him, which he couldn't quite identify. Whenever he thought about the assignment, he felt an ominous feeling that was hard to shake--a gut-wrenching sense of foreboding.

◆◆◆

Weber slept fitfully and awoke with a start. Rays from the early morning sun were darting through slits in the window blinds and perching on his eyelids. He rolled onto his side and reached for Anna but remembered that she had risen early, bid him farewell, and departed for work. It was his turn to wake the boys and prepare them for school. He dragged himself out from under the covers, stumbled down the hall to the boys' bedroom, and announced that breakfast would be served in half an hour. Then he went to the kitchen, mixed up some batter, and started making pancakes.

After breakfast, Weber packed the boys a lunch and ushered them out the front door. Then he returned to the kitchen and stared at the telephone. Unbeknownst to Anna, he was about to telephone her father and beg him to participate in a dangerous, covert operation. He'd mentally rehearsed the call many times but still felt uncertain about how to approach the subject with Gabel and solicit his participation. What did you tell your prospective father-in-law to convince him to risk his life and livelihood? He picked up the phone, dialed, and waited for what seemed like an eternity. Finally, Gabel answered.

"Gabel here."

Hello Aaron, it's Robert. Do you have time to talk? I have a favor to ask--a rather large favor."

"Robert, it's good to hear from you! How are Anna and the boys?"

"Very well, thanks. They send their regards."

"Excellent. Now, what can I do for you?"

"I can't discuss details over the phone, but I wonder if you and your associates would help me take some photographs. I'm doing a feature on the German agricultural industry and want to take pictures of the new farm equipment manufactured in Bavaria. I want to go inside tractor factories and get some shots of the manufacturing process. Factories like that one we almost visited on the way back from your Alpine meadows."

There was a long pause before Gabel responded. "Tractors, you say?"

"Yes. You know how much I love tractors. Remember that time I tried to fix your tractor? I found a crack in a cylinder head if I remember correctly."

"And you want to tour a tractor factory?"

"Yes, like that one where they build innovative tractors that few farmers have ever seen. Tractors with the newest designs that have little known or previously undisclosed features and equipment."

Gabel snorted. "Oh, that factory. Uh, well, that might take some doing. They don't let just anybody tour those factories. I'd have to confer with my associates and find out if it might be possible to arrange a plant tour. I suspect that we can work something out."

"Great. Anna and the boys will likely want to make the trip with me. They aren't interested in farm machinery, so can you help me think of some other pretext for the trip?"

"Well, how about this? Luka will have a birthday soon. Tell Anna and the boys we've invited them here for a party."

"Good idea. I'll do that. Until then, let's keep this between us. No one else needs to know."

"As you wish, Robert. It will be our secret."

That evening, Weber told Anna about her father's invitation and asked if she'd like to travel to Munich a day or two before Luka's birthday. The proposal surprised Anna; initially, she seemed intrigued by the idea, but after a few moments of contemplation, her forehead wrinkled, and she began to shake her head. "No, Robert, I'm sorry, but my firm has scheduled an important meeting on those days, and I have to attend. However, why don't you and the boys make the trip? I will join you after my meeting."

Summer 1928: Munich, Germany

Two weeks later, Weber and the boys arrived at Gabel's farm around midday. Gabel and his wife, Ruth, greeted the threesome warmly and invited them inside for a hearty lunch. During the meal, while Luka and Carl told stories about their recent after-school exploits, Gabel caught Weber's eye and nodded discreetly.

After the meal, Gabel told Ruth and the boys that he had some chores to finish in the hangar and invited Weber to accompany him. The men left the house, walked through the yard to the rear pasture, and entered the hangar. Gabel motioned toward some stools next to his workbench and, after Weber was seated, cleared his throat and began speaking in hushed tones.

"I've made arrangements. We'll go tonight unless you think that's too soon. Are you ready, Robert? Did you bring a high-resolution, low-light camera?"

"Yes. I'm ready, and the sooner we go, the better. The anticipatory tension has been gnawing at me, and I'd like to put this behind us before it eats me alive. I do have a suitable camera."

"Try to relax, Robert. Five of the best men in my cell have agreed to accompany us. They've done some initial reconnaissance and advised me that the factory should be quiet after midnight. The aircraft assembly work typically scales down in the late afternoon, and the maintenance shift finishes just before midnight. After that, the plant is on standby and nearly empty. We shouldn't have to contend with more than a skeleton crew and a few guards who monitor the plant's perimeter. Plus, we have one man on the inside--a recently hired friend who works the night shift."

"That's reassuring, Aaron. I appreciate the prep work that you and your team have done."

"You're welcome. However, I think it is time you leveled with me, Robert. You're asking my team and me to take a significant risk, and we don't know why."

"Aaron, as I said before, I know people in Washington who are interested in these pictures, and their goals are consistent with yours."

"Come on, Robert, that's just not good enough. I've been open and honest with you about my resistance activities, which, for all I know, has put my team and me in jeopardy. At least you could do me the courtesy of returning the favor."

"Well, Aaron, I haven't been more open because I've signed a nondisclosure agreement patterned after Britain's Official Secrets Acts."

"That tells me something, Robert. I suspect you're a spy working for a foreign government, and given your Washington contacts, I'd guess you're working for an American intelligence agency."

"You are a perceptive man, Aaron. Alright, I'll come clean with you. I'm a US Army Intelligence agent whose mission is to infiltrate the German aviation industry. Specifically, I am here to determine whether Germany is building warplanes or engaged in other types of aviation activities that would violate the Versailles treaty."

"Just as I suspected. We can proceed now that I know why you're asking my team to enter that ghost base. Our goals are consistent, so we will support you and keep your identity a secret."

◆◆◆

Having laid awake until just after midnight, Weber slipped out of bed cautiously so as not to wake Ruth or the boys and went to the kitchen where Gabel was waiting. Gabel put a finger against his lips and then turned and led Weber out the farmhouse's front door and down the driveway, using only hand gestures to point the way. Weber, attempting to emulate Gabel's stealth, struggled to silence his boots' crunching sound on the gravel.

As Weber walked through the inky darkness, he understood why Gabel had scheduled the mission for this particular night. The sky was clear and moonless, providing a nearly impermeable canopy of darkness that would help to conceal their movements.

When the two men arrived at the end of the driveway, Gabel stopped and looked east, toward Munich. Weber followed his gaze but couldn't see or hear anything except the sound of crickets. They waited a few minutes, and Weber eventually leaned against a fencepost, almost dozing off. Suddenly, two bright lights appeared on the horizon and moved in their direction along the road.

Gabel grunted and muttered something under his breath. Then he turned toward Weber and motioned for him to join him at the road's edge. Weber approached him just as they heard the pitched growl of an engine struggling under a heavy load. The lights that Weber had spotted earlier had transformed into headlights and were much closer.

A few moments later, a large truck emerged from the darkness and rumbled to a halt next to Weber and Gabel. The truck had a spacious crew cab in front and a long flatbed at the back, stacked high with enormous wooden crates. The driver's door opened, and a man wearing a black hat and dark clothing stepped out of the cab and walked over to Gabel. Gabel started grousing before the man had a chance to speak.

"You're twenty minutes behind schedule, Clutch."

"We're here, aren't we? Stealing this truck took longer than expected. But, at least we got away clean--no one followed us. What do you think, Boss--will this truck suit our purposes?"

"It depends. What's in the crates?"

"Hopefully, aircraft parts. The truck was parked in the railyards beside the platforms where they unload shipments from aircraft manufacturers. We just snatched the truck--opening the crates would have attracted attention and looked suspicious."

Gabel frowned and shook his head. "Alright, I've heard enough excuses, let's get moving." He pointed to Weber. "Clutch, meet 'Weaver,' the man who initiated this mission." Once we get him inside the ghost base, he must photograph the entire operation. Now find him a seat in the truck and introduce him to the rest of the crew."

As Clutch reached the truck, he opened the door on the passenger's side of the cab and motioned Weber inside. As Weber slid in amongst the occupants--four burly men and two Alsatian dogs--a rank stench of cigarette smoke, sweat, and damp dog hair accosted his nostrils. He resisted the urge to cough and pushed his way to the rear of the cab, where he seated himself between two men. To his left was a large, heavy-set man who didn't react when Weber sat down. His eyes were closed, and his head was propped against the seatback. However, the man to his right was awake and alert and greeted him warmly. He smiled, extended a hand, and introduced himself as 'Blade.' Blade had an angular face, a wiry build, and was dressed entirely in black. Cocked sideways on his head was a ragged stocking cap that was matted with dog hair.

The dogs, both of whom had been dozing at Blade's feet, woke, rose from their repose, and sniffed Weber's clothes. After taking Weber's measure, the Alsatians eyed Blade whimpered and waited for a response. Blade, clearly the dogs' master, made a fist and gestured toward the floor; immediately, the dogs lowered their heads, crept back to Blade's side, and curled up by his feet.

Clutch got in the truck and slid into the driver's seat. Gabel entered from the opposite side and sat in the passenger's seat. Clutch gunned the engine, shifted into first, and swung the truck around to head back toward Munich. They rumbled along for twenty minutes, and then Clutch took a sharp right and drove south on a narrow, rutted road that led into a mountainous pine forest. For the next hour, the truck took a terrible beating; it pitched, swayed, and shuddered as its wheels slammed into one pothole after another.

Weber was used to turbulence, but even he began to feel twinges of motion sickness. Blade, the man sitting to his right, rolled down a window and heaved the contents of his stomach along the side of the road. Mercifully, Clutch drove only a few more miles and then stopped the truck. Woozy and weary, the men and dogs stumbled out of the cab, crouched by the side of the road, and tried to recover their composure.

Weber glanced around, surveying their surroundings. It was pitch dark, but from what he saw in the glare of the trucks' headlights, it appeared that Clutch had parked on the crest of a hill surrounded by dense pine forest. Massive craggy boulders lay amongst the pines, and a footpath wove amongst them, providing what appeared to be a southern descent.

After the men regained their bearings, they returned to the truck, pulled several overstuffed duffle bags from under the seats, and stacked them by the side of the road. When all the equipment had been offloaded, Gabel assembled the men at the truck's rear and began speaking. "Now that you're on your feet and, hopefully, awake and fit for duty, I'll introduce our sponsor and initiate tonight's assignments." Gabel paused and placed a hand on Weber's shoulder. "Gentlemen, this is Weaver. He is funding this mission, and it is to our advantage that he succeeds. I want you to understand his objectives so you can help him accomplish every facet of his mission. He's here to photograph the entire ghost base, including all phases of aircraft production and examples of the finished products--fully assembled and armed warplanes. Let me be clear. We do not leave that base until all aspects of this mission have been accomplished. Got that?"

Heads bobbed, and there was a murmur of agreement among the men.

Gabel continued, "Weaver, meet your fellow operatives. As you may have guessed, security necessitates that we use nom de guerres. To your left are Clutch and Blade, whom you already know. Standing next to Blade is Armor, and to his left is Scorch. The dogs' names are Tracker and Trooper, and you can tell them apart by the markings on their faces. Only Trooper has a white patch of fur under his left eye."

Weber reached out and shook hands with each of the men. Then, after asking Blade for permission to approach the dogs, he stooped and extended a closed fist toward the animals. The dogs stood, advanced toward Weber, and took turns sniffing his hand. They again eyed Blade, who nodded his approval. Satisfied, albeit somewhat unenthusiastically, the dogs retreated to their master's side and sat at his feet.

Gabel began issuing orders. "Scorch, pack the heavy munitions so we can transport them safely. Armor, distribute the weapons and ammunition. I'll need my sidearm and find a suitable pistol for Weaver. Apportion the ammunition among the men and inspect everyone's armaments--equipment malfunctions cause casualties.

Armor left the group and began opening duffle bags and extracting weapons and boxes of ammunition. Shortly after that, he returned and handed sidearms to Gabel and Weber.

Gable strapped on his sidearm and then looked at Clutch. “At 14:00, drive the truck to the base and attempt access. Timing is critical, Clutch, so keep one eye on the clock.”

Clutch nodded, got in the truck, and started the engine. As the truck pulled away, he raised his hand and snapped off a salute. Gabel returned the gesture.

Next, Gabel turned and pointed toward the nearby footpath. “Blade, Armor, Scorch, and Weaver: at 14:30, you and the dogs will accompany me on that footpath. We’ll have a 45-minute window to descend the mountain and approach the ghost base from the south. Put the dogs on point and maintain strict operational silence. Comprehend?” The men nodded in unison.

“Alright, any questions?” Gabel growled. Weber raised his hand.

“Yes, Weaver, what is it?”

“I don’t mean to second guess you, Boss, but secrecy is paramount. If we go in armed to the teeth and shoot up the place, the Germans will know that we’re aware of their rearmament program. Worse still, if they realize that we’ve documented the production of illegal warplanes, they’ll take immediate steps to hide or dismantle this base and every other facet of the aviation industry that’s covertly supporting their efforts to rearm. We must get in and out of that base without being detected.”

A momentary look of annoyance flashed across Gabel’s countenance. He drew a deep breath and exhaled loudly. “Yes, of course, Weaver, that’s understood, and the men have been briefed accordingly. It’s a central element in our plan. But surely you don’t expect us to go in there unarmed? We have to be prepared for every contingency. If God forbid, we’re discovered and confronted, we’ll need to defend ourselves.”

At first, Weber stiffened and locked eyes with Gabel. He was angry and struggling to contain the foreboding he’d experienced early on while contemplating this mission. He waited a few seconds until his anger subsided and then relented and nodded his agreement. “Alright, Boss, we’ll follow your plan and hope for the best.”

Gabel didn’t look convinced but dropped the matter and spoke instead to his crew. “Men, we’ll depart in twenty minutes. Use this time to camouflage your faces, check your equipment, and mentally prepare yourselves for covert operations and, if need be, combat.”

◆◆◆

Preceded by the dogs, the four men walked single file down the trail, silently weaving through the trees and boulders. Blade was on point, just behind the dogs, followed by Boss, Armor, and Scorch. Weber walked a few paces behind Scorch, bringing up the rear. Each man carried a shielded penlight, a weapon, and a backpack loaded with gear.

After the first several hundred yards, the trail turned and wound its way edgewise along the mountain's rim. As the troop entered this semi-level stretch, Blade let the dogs run ahead to search for threats. The men picked up their pace, following in each other's footsteps while maintaining light and noise discipline.

The trail sloped to the right and over the rim before descending on the mountain's southern side. As the men crested the rim, they found the dogs lying on the trail, waiting for them to arrive. Blade waved a greeting to the dogs and then patted his right thigh. Trooper and Tracker rose and dashed forward on the trail, resuming their role but remaining within earshot. The men followed suit, but as the trail became steeper and more uneven, they slowed their pace to prevent falls and conserve energy. Weber felt pressure on his knees as he adjusted his gait to compensate for the angle of descent. Within minutes, he, like the other men, was respiring faster and harder and found it necessary to take countermeasures to suppress the sounds of his breathing.

The dogs and men cleaved to the trail, following its every twist and turn as it snaked its way down the side of the mountain. The footing was sometimes uneven, and other times, it was downright treacherous. At one point, Gabel tripped on a rock outcropping, lost his balance, and tumbled over a ledge and down an embankment. His backpack, fortunately, lodged between some trees and kept him from sliding further toward what appeared to be a precipice. Blade halted the group and told Scorch to toss Boss a rope. Weber held his breath, watching the scene unfold, wondering whether this was why he'd experienced such a strong sense of foreboding about this mission. A shiver ran down his spine as he imagined himself telling Anna that her father had fallen off a mountain while assisting him with an operation that he'd deliberately hidden from her and the boys.

Scorch uncoiled a rope and lowered one end until it dangled next to Gabel. Gabel fumbled around but eventually grabbed the rope and tied it around his chest and under his arms. Scorch then dragged Boss up the slope, lifted him onto the trail, and helped him regain his footing.

Gabel untied the rope, brushed himself off, and then sat on a large rock while muttering a string of curses. The men watched and waited; no one spoke for fear of incurring Boss' wrath. Gabel took several deep breaths and, after regaining his composure, he stood, cinched his backpack, and signaled for the men to resume their journey.

The troop moved on, continuing their downward trek without further incident until they reached the mountain's base. There, the trail intersected with several others that, collectively, branched off into myriad directions. Gabel pulled out his compass, rotated it until he found magnetic north, and then pointed toward a leg of the trail that led northward across what appeared to be rolling but still heavily treed terrain.

Blade and the dogs marched forward, and the remainder of the men followed close on their heels. The troop had progressed no more than fifty yards when the dogs suddenly froze and dropped to the ground, refusing to move. Blade spun around and motioned for everyone to take cover. The men and dogs scattered. Weber dashed into a copse of trees, found a large stump, and stooped behind it.

Weber crouched there, motionless and trembling, listening for errant noises and watching for signs of intrusion. As the minutes passed and nothing happened, he glanced around, taking stock of the situation. He couldn't see where Boss and the others had gone but assumed they'd found similar ways to blend into the landscape. To his surprise, he saw Trooper lying on the ground a few feet to his left, but there was no sign of Tracker. The trail he'd abandoned lay twenty yards to his right, and if memory served, that meant that the intersection they'd just passed through lay only a short distance from where he was hiding.

Five more minutes passed uneventfully, and Weber began to lose patience. Why hadn't Gabel reassembled the group? They were on a tight timeline; unless they got moving, the operation would fail. They couldn't afford to be cowering in the darkness when it was clear that the dogs had made a mistake. His indictment of the dogs prompted him to glance at Trooper, who, he saw, was still lying motionless on the forest floor nearby. Was that damn dog sleeping? Maybe he and Tracker had conspired to take a nap and pulled one over on Blade. As Weber stared at the dog, Trooper slowly--nearly imperceptibly--tilted his head eastward.

Then Weber heard it--faint voices, men speaking German. The voices grew louder and seemed to be approaching his position from the east. Trooper tensed but didn't move or make a sound. Soon, Weber was able to overhear snippets of conversation between what sounded like two men "…a shitty beer garden…they charge too much…the singers can't carry a tune…the musicians can't play…" The sounds of the men's footsteps grew louder and then faded as they trudged past one of the trails that passed through the intersection.

After several minutes of silence, Trooper stood, tilted his head to one side, whimpered, and then ambled toward the trail. Weber drew his pistol and followed the dog. As he approached the trail, he saw the faint glow of a penlight. It was Blade. The dog's handler stood on the trail facing him and summoned Trooper with a silent dog whistle. Next to him stood Tracker.

Blade nearly jumped out of his skin when Trooper emerged from the darkness with Weber in tow. "Gees, Weaver, I wasn't expecting you," he whispered. "Walk up the trail about fifty yards and look for a clearing on your right. The men are gathered there."

Weber nodded his assent and then walked until he saw the glow of several penlights dancing in the forest several hundred feet off the right side of the trail. He left the trail and, guided by the illumination, picked his way through the trees until he found Boss and the others standing in a clearing.

Scorch was pulling packages out of backpacks and stacking them in piles on the forest floor. He greeted Weber and handed him a package wrapped in brown paper.

"Glad you are back, Weaver. Hang on to this package--it stays here."

Weber shone his penlight on the package and saw the word 'Süden' written across the top. He shifted the penlight's beam to the other packages stacked on the ground nearby and saw that they were labeled 'Ost,' Norden," and 'Westen.' Confused and questioning what the packages had to do with the mission, he glanced to where Boss was standing, hoping to find answers.

Boss, however, was busy giving orders. "Scorch, go deliver your parcels. Keep an eye on the time. Clutch and Armor, you do the same. Blade, you and the dogs stay here." Boss then looked in Weber's direction. "Weaver, bring that parcel over here and give it to Blade. Blade, see those two trees over there--those with adjoining trunks? Shove that parcel between the trunks. Make sure it's jammed in there tight."

Weber handed his package to Blade and then eyed Boss suspiciously. "Boss, I don't remember anything about packages or parcel deliveries in our plan. What's going on?"

"Just a little extra insurance. I'll explain later--we're behind schedule thanks to that ski trip I took coming down the mountain. Blade, take Weaver and the dogs, and push north on this trail toward the ghost base. Prime the dogs so they'll warn you about any guards roving around the base's perimeter."

Gabel's last order struck Weber as pointless. Trooper and Tracker had just demonstrated that they could detect intruders long before they were threats and were equally capable of evading detection or capture. In his opinion, the dogs deserved more credit. He was about to point this out but then saw the grumpy expression on Gabel's face and decided otherwise. He commented instead on his brush with the guards. "Speaking of roving guards, two walked past my position a few minutes ago near the place where the trails intersect, and they were headed west."

Gabel nodded but changed the subject. "Okay, but the base is north, and we're wasting time. Take the dogs and move out! I'll catch up with you momentarily."

The dogs were quivering in anticipation, awaiting Blade's command. Trooper and Tracker pawed the ground and swiveled their heads back and forth, first eyeing Blade and then glancing up the trail. Blade put them out of their misery by tapping his right thigh. The dogs spun around and bounded northward up the trail.

Weber and Blade slung their backpacks over their shoulders and followed the dogs toward the base. After hiking for several minutes, Weber asked Blade if he knew what was in the packages and why Gabel was so secretive. A pained expression appeared on Blade's face. "It's not my place to say, Weaver. Boss only tells people what they need to know." Blade had no sooner uttered those words when the ground shuddered, and Weber heard a massive explosion behind him. He whirled around and looked back along the trail in the direction they had just traveled. An orange glow hung over the forest, and underneath it, a curtain of flames rose from the forest floor and danced in the treetops.

Weber glanced at Blade, who shrugged his shoulders. "Well, Weaver, I guess that answers your question."

In the illumination created by the conflagration, Weber saw the faint outline of a man running in their direction. Several seconds later, Gabel staggered up and stood beside him. He nodded a greeting, caught his breath, and then spoke. "OK, Weaver, about those packages. I figured we should give the guards something to investigate besides us. That diversion should keep them busy for the next several hours."

"I suspect so, Boss," Weber replied. "But our mission is no longer shrouded in secrecy, is it? You've just announced our presence."

"Not necessarily. Unless we get caught, the most the guards can infer is that an unexplained forest fire occurred south of the base."

No sooner had the threesome begun walking toward the base when Trooper and Tracker bolted out of the darkness and dropped at Blade's feet. Rather than sitting quietly, the dogs squirmed, fidgeted, and whined. Concerned, Blade bent down to comfort the dogs.

Weber figured something was up. The dogs were upset about something--he'd not seen Tracker or Trooper this agitated before. Just watching the pair made him feel uncomfortable.

Blade stood abruptly and gestured to his left into the forest. He quickly led the dogs off the trail and into the trees, silently motioning for Gabel and Weber to follow. Once inside the forest, Blade ran to a knoll, ducked behind it, and dropped to a prone position. The dogs shadowed Blade and curled up beside him. Weber and Gabel hunkered down next to the dogs.

Seconds later, Weber heard footfalls on the forest floor, a succession of thuds that emanated from the north and grew louder by the second. "Guards," Blade whispered, "probably on their way to investigate the fire."

Gabel nodded. The dogs huddled up to Blade, laid their heads flat on the ground, and didn't make a sound. Weber lifted his head slightly and peered over the knoll, hoping to glimpse the intruders.

Four men, all dressed in military uniforms and carrying shovels, sprinted southward along the trail past the troop's position. From what Weber could discern, the soldiers' movements were focused and determined--they ran with eyes forward, seemingly uninterested in their surroundings, occasionally glancing skyward at the orange glow that hung over the forest.

As the sounds of the footfalls faded, Gabel stood and congratulated himself. "How's that for a successful diversion? We can proceed without further interference now that we've eliminated one of our primary threats."

Blade looked skeptical, and as he stood, he tapped his thigh, signaling the dogs to take point and remain on alert. Trooper and Tracker willingly obliged, and after their departure, the men gathered their gear and trudged northward up the trail.

◆◆◆

Gabel's pronouncement proved to be prophetic. After a twenty-minute hike without further intrusions, the men stood on a low hill overlooking the ghost base. Weber surveyed their objective, mentally assessing the feasibility of various avenues of approach and infiltration. The base was surrounded by a high barbed-wire fence supporting rows of industrial lights illuminating the grounds. The factory lay due north of their position, and a runway ran from east to west between them and the factory. To enter the factory, they'd either have to skirt the runway--which would entail a substantial end-run detour to the east or west--or scale the fence and try to sneak across the partially illuminated runway undetected. The latter plan, Weber figured, would make more sense if it were possible to kill the lights. But was that an option?

Neither Gabel nor Blade had uttered a word since their arrival, which led Weber to believe that his companions were also plotting an approach to the base and were likely mentally reviewing the same scenarios he'd just considered. He nudged Gabel to get his attention.

"What's our first move, Boss?"

Gabel nodded absentmindedly, then exhaled and rubbed his forehead. "I say we go left, circle the runway, and approach the plant from the west. It's tempting to breach the fence and cross the runway, but the risk of exposure and capture is too high. Better to remain concealed and not lose our edge."

Weber nodded his agreement and looked to Blade for confirmation. Blade reciprocated the gesture. "Ok," Weber whispered, "It's settled. Let's get started."

They hiked around the runway, staying well back from the fence, remaining in the shadows. The dogs led the way, but Blade kept them close, making sure they didn't stray more than a few yards in front of him. Eventually, they stood at a dimly illuminated portion of the wire fence that fronted the western end of the factory. Gabel pulled a pair of wire cutters from his backpack and snipped a segment along the ground large enough for the men and dogs to crawl through. Once under the fence, Blade got down on all fours and crawled toward the building with the dogs creeping close behind him. Weber and Gabel watched and waited, half expecting to hear an alarm bellow or a sentry shout.

When Blade reached the building, he stood, rounded up the dogs, and hid behind a low partition that sheltered an assortment of runway equipment. Weber and Gabel then crawled to the partition, slipped inside, and seated themselves on the ground with their backs against the building next to Blade and the dogs.

Weber tilted his head toward Gabel and whispered, "So far, so good, Boss. What's our next move?"

Gabel lifted his right arm and spun his hand clockwise, circularly. "Exit out of this storage area to the right and then cut back to your left. Proceed along the side of the building until you come to a single pedestrian door adjacent to a couple of large overhead hangar doors. If we're lucky, that door will be unlocked in preparation for our arrival. Wait outside--don't enter the factory. I repeat, wait outside the door for Blade, the dogs, and me to join you."

Irritated, Weber cursed under his breath. "What's with you, Boss? Are you hiding things from me again? Why would you think that door would be unlocked?"

"Compartmentalization, Weaver. You can't tell the enemy what you don't know."

"But this is my operation," Weber retorted.

"Yes, but you asked me to plan it, remember? My experience with these thugs has taught me to take that responsibility seriously."

Weber frowned but stifled his annoyance and pulled on his backpack. He slid around Gabel and then crawled past Blade and the dogs. As he passed the dogs, Tracker and Trooper edged away from the wall and sniffed his torso and legs. Blade whispered a gentle reprimand, and the dogs desisted.

After passing through the partition, Weber pressed his back against the building and moved slowly along the factory's west wall until he arrived at a single pedestrian door. He looked past the door and saw two large overhead doors, both big enough for a fighter plane to pass through. Curious, he took hold of the handle on the pedestrian door and pulled it. He heard a click, and then the door opened slightly, slipping its latch. Weber knew the door might be unlocked, but he was still taken aback when it opened with ease. Unsure of what to do next, he stood with the door ajar, allowing air inside the factory to waft through the opening and cascade against his face. The air carried an odor that he recognized immediately--a pungent mix of oil, metal, rubber, kerosene, and glass--elements that routinely existed inside aircraft hangars and factories.

Weber reached to close the door but then resisted the impulse for fear of making unnecessary noise. Instead, he pulled off his backpack, wedged it against that doorjamb, and waited patiently for his co-conspirators to arrive. He didn't have long to wait; within minutes, Gabel, Blade, and the dogs crept out of the shadows and crouched by the door.

Gabel glanced around and then grimaced. "I see you opened the door," he growled. "Did you enter the building too?"

"Calm down, Boss. I just tried the handle to see if the door was unlocked, and when it yielded, I used my pack to prop it open. No harm done."

Gabel pulled the door further ajar and glanced inside the factory. Nothing seemed amiss. He exhaled, blowing out his cheeks, and then made eye contact with Weber. Some of the tension etched on his face dissipated. "Ok, no harm done," he whispered. "But from now on, damn it, don't improvise. Clear everything with me first. Got it?"

Irritated by the reprimand, Weber nearly lost his temper and spewed a string of expletives. The urge, fortunately, passed quickly, squelched by his fear of endangering the mission. He chastised himself for a momentary lapse in judgment, bit his tongue, and nodded.

Mollified, Gabel whispered further instructions. "Now listen up because I will pinpoint our position, designate assignments, and establish avenues of infiltration. He stooped to the ground and scratched the shape of a 'T' in the dirt using his index finger. "This is a map of the factory's floorplan." He pointed at the top of the T. "The main door and delivery area are here, in the center of the area represented by the T's crossbar. To the left and right of that area, as you move toward the ends of the crossbar, are the factory's offices and storage areas. The assembly line runs down the shaft of the T and ends here, at these hangar doors, right next to where we're standing."

Weber and Blade nodded, signaling that they understood. Boss continued speaking in a low whisper. "Blade, you, Trooper, and Weber will work your way up the assembly line. Let the dog scout ahead for threats, and after you secure each leg of the route, you can photograph at will. I will take Tracker and proceed up the assembly line until we reach the delivery area. If all goes according to plan, Clutch and our inside man will be there, unloading the truck."

Blade opened the door wide enough for Trooper to enter and followed the dog inside the factory. Weber waited a few seconds and then slipped through the door.

Once inside, Weber found himself at the foot of a long, wide corridor. Overhead was a latticework of metal trusses--row upon row stretching as far as he could see. Mounted to the trusses was a corrugated steel roof. Strings of industrial-sized fluorescent lights, only a small portion of which were illuminated, hung from the trusses and cast a dull greyish light on the factory's walls and floor. Stalls filled with aircraft parts lined both sides of the corridor, and carts filled with tools were parked alongside the stalls.

After allowing his eyes to adjust to the ambient light, Weber spotted Blade crouched behind a workbench. Taking care to silence his footsteps, he went to the workbench and squatted next to Blade. He scanned the area around the workbench, expecting to find Trooper, but the dog was nowhere to be seen.

"Trooper's on the prowl," Blade whispered. Sit tight until we know whether the coast is clear." Weber nodded an acknowledgment, withdrew his camera from his backpack, and began taking pictures of aircraft parts stacked in nearby stalls. No sense in wasting time. One of the stalls contained upholstery and seat frames, and another was filled with paint cans and spray gear.

Moments later, Trooper appeared and nuzzled up to Blade. Blade smiled, stroked the dog, and signaled Weber that it was safe to advance. Reassured, Weber stood and proceeded down the corridor, stopping at each stall he passed to photograph the contents.

Blade slipped back outside, retrieved Gabel and Tracker, and escorted them down the corridor to where Weber was snapping photos. The three men conferred briefly, and then Gabel and Tracker continued their journey toward the delivery area at the far end of the corridor.

Blade and Trooper marched ahead to scout the next section of the corridor, and Weber turned to his left and began inspecting stalls on the east side of the building. He didn't find much worth photographing in the first few stalls, but then he came to one that contained landing gear and another that was filled with Perspex windscreens and port-hole-shaped windows. He photographed the contents of both stalls, figuring that even if the parts didn't prove that the Germans were assembling warbirds, they nonetheless provided essential clues about the aircraft's design.

Moving on, Weber came to a door that led into a room filled with electronics. There were workbenches along the walls and, above them, cabinets and shelves containing gauges, switches, levers, wiring harnesses, and other types of avionic equipment. One particular cabinet captured his attention because it contained a critical piece of contraband: bombsights.

Weber felt his pulse quicken. Of all the types of equipment he'd hoped to find, bombsights were at the top of his list. What better proof was there that Germany was producing military aircraft? Munitions would support the same conclusion, and he hoped to find items such as bombs and wing-mounted machine guns and photograph them as well. Bombsights, however, were especially incriminating because they provided irrefutable proof that the manufacturer intended to use the aircraft to attack and destroy adversaries for offensive purposes. Weber pulled one of the devices down from the cabinet, placed it on a nearby workbench, and photographed it from every angle. When finished, he returned the bombsight to the cabinet and took pictures of the other avionic equipment stockpiled in the room.

Weber heard noises from behind while working at the back of the room. He spun around and looked toward the door where he'd entered the room. In the doorframe stood Trooper, silhouetted against the flinty haze of the corridor's fluorescent lights. The dog stood riveted in place, eyeing Weber intently. Weber acknowledged Trooper by nodding, and the dog responded by lowering his head and whimpering faintly as if beckoning him. Weber didn't hesitate. He stuffed his camera in his pocket, strode to the doorway where the Trooper was standing, and glanced up and down the corridor. To his surprise, nothing seemed amiss; he didn't see or hear anything. So, where was Blade? Then, Trooper began pushing against his legs.

Weber exited the room and walked northward, intending to proceed up the corridor toward stalls he hadn't photographed. Trooper, however, slipped past him, blocked his path, and began pushing him in the opposite direction. Figuring that the dog knew something he didn't, Weber reversed course and let Trooper lead the way. The dog bounded southward, hugging the corridor wall as he led Weber toward the door where the troop had entered the factory. Along the way, Weber questioned the dog as if Trooper somehow could explain what was happening.

"What is it, Trooper? Where are you taking me? Where's Blade? Damn it, what's happening?" Each time Weber spoke, the dog glanced rearward but didn't break stride. Trooper's only concern, it seemed, was to make sure Weber was following him.

The dog stopped at the end of the corridor and stood by the pedestrian door that led outside toward the runway. Weber saw Trooper come to a halt, so he broke off the chase and cautiously walked to the door where the dog was standing. Trooper seemed agitated, so Weber crouched and patted the animal's head while he caught his breath and contemplated the dog's actions. Why had Trooper been so determined to bring him here? Had something happened, or was something about to happen? There had to be a reason. Weber stood and did a slow pirouette, scanning the entire area. He didn't see anyone and couldn't hear anything but the faint hum of machinery.

Having found nothing, Weber decided to go outside to check the grounds. As he approached the pedestrian door, Trooper stood, whimpered faintly, and scratched at the door. As if by magic, the door swung open, and Blade entered the corridor. "Blade," Weber exclaimed, "where have you been? Trooper's been looking for you, and so have I."

"Trooper alerted me to noises outside the building, so I went outdoors to investigate. I sent Trooper to fetch you in case there was trouble."

"Are we in trouble? What's happening out there?"

"Nothing seems amiss within our immediate vicinity. But I did hear some indistinct, rhythmic noise off in the distance. Humming or buzzing or something--nothing I could identify."

Weber frowned and rubbed his chin while he pondered Blade's report. Something about it didn't sit well with him. The base was isolated, and it was late at night--he couldn't think of anything that could account for the distant humming or buzzing. "Maybe I should go outside and see if I can identify that noise. It was quiet when we arrived, so it's odd that you'd hear those sounds now."

Weber opened the door, walked outside, and surveyed the grounds surrounding the factory. He heard a faint buzz and considered the possibility that it was caused by distant aircraft but dismissed the idea because the noise didn't seem distinct from the factory's maintenance equipment. Reassured, he returned to the door, intending to reenter the building. As his fingers touched the door handle, a dark figure sprang from the shadows, grabbed him from behind, and wrapped an arm around his throat. Weber instinctively thrust his elbows rearward, jamming them hard into his attacker's gut. A guttural hiss followed a muffled grunt as air erupted from the aggressor's windpipe. Sensing his advantage, Weber broke free, pulled his sidearm, and shoved the barrel against his attacker's chest. "Move, and you're dead. And be forewarned: I've got a twitchy trigger finger."

"Ease up, Weaver. I didn't recognize you. I thought you were a guard."

"Scorch, is that you? I thought *you* were a guard. You're lucky I didn't blow a hole in your chest."

"Point taken, but shut up and listen, will you? Do you hear that droning in the distance? Aircraft are approaching, and we must take cover in case they're headed for this base."

Weber listened again and realized that the buzzing had grown louder and now resembled the resonance produced by aircraft engines. He looked Scorch in the eye and gave him an affirmative nod.

Scorch turned toward the west and whistled softly. Armor emerged from the shadows and strode to where Weber was standing. "You gave us a scare, Weaver."

"Likewise, Amor," Weber remarked as he shifted his gaze back to Scorch. "Alright, Scorch, what do you propose? Boss and Tracker are at the other end of the factory looking for Clutch. Blade and Trooper are just inside the door."

"If those planes descend here, we'll probably be illuminated by their landing lights. Unless it's unsafe, I suggest we go inside the factory and observe developments from there."

"Agreed," Weber said as he turned and walked toward the factory.

Once inside the building, Weber and his companions were greeted not only by Blade and Trooper but also by Gabel and Tracker. "Boss," said Weber, with a hint of surprise in his voice, "what are you doing here?"

"Change of plan," Gabel replied. "We've got visitors. Two limousines arrived at the front gate, underwent a brief inspection, and then motored toward the building's main entrance. We didn't wait around to greet the occupants. Clutch drove the truck out of the factory while the guards were still inspecting the limousines. Tracker and I escaped down the corridor so we could warn you guys.

Scorch interrupted before Gabel could continue. "Same here, Boss. We've got incoming aircraft. Most likely landing within the next five minutes."

Gabel shook his head, blew out his cheeks, and threw up his hands. "We'll have to improvise. We anticipated a skeleton crew, but obviously, something unexpected has happened, and we'll soon be confronted by a larger number of adversaries. Weaver, have you accomplished your mission, or do you need more photos?"

Weber grimaced. "I've gathered some formidable evidence but don't have photos of armed fighters. I need some shots of completed warbirds."

Now it was Gabel's turn to grimace. "That could be a tall order, given our current situation."

Gabel's thoughts were interrupted by the sound of an aircraft touching down on the base's runway. Weber opened the door a crack and peered outside. "One plane heading this way--on approach to the hangar--arriving momentarily." As he spoke, bright shafts of light streamed through the windows of the hangar doors and played across the factory walls.

Gabel reacted immediately. "Scorch, you and Armor retreat. Exit under the fence, find a thicket in the forest and wait for us to join you. Take Tracker with you and stay out of sight. Weaver, we need a place inside the factory where you, Blade, Trooper, and I can hide."

Gabel's orders produced a flurry of activity. Scorch, accompanied by Armor and Tracker, dashed to a window on the building's west side. He unlocked the window, slid back one of the panes, and crawled outside. Armor picked up Tracker, passed him through the window to Scorch, and exited.

Weber grabbed Gabel's arm and pointed up the corridor. "Follow me. There's an avionics room ahead on the left where we can hide." Before Weber finished speaking, Trooper bounded up the corridor.

Weber ran after Trooper with Gable and Blade close on his heels. As he neared the avionics room, he heard noises from behind--first a series of mechanical clicks and then the shrill whine of an electric motor straining to lift the hangar door. He glanced over his shoulder and saw the hangar door inch upward, gradually allowing light and sound from the approaching aircraft to penetrate the factory's interior.

The hangar door continued to rise, and once it cleared the aircraft's nose, bright beams of light streamed up the corridor. Weber forgot where he was and started yelling at his companions. "There's the door to the avionics room! Get inside before you're lit up like a Christmas tree!"

Moments later, Weber stood pressed against a wall in the avionics room with Gabel and Blade beside him. Trooper sat dutifully at Blade's feet. There was a deafening roar as the aircraft entered the hangar, rolled up the corridor, and stopped outside the avionics room. Bewildered, Weber looked at Gabel and swore. "What the hell? What kind of a pilot operates a plane inside a factory?" Gabel shook his head in disgust but didn't reply. Now that the mission had spun out of control, he was at a loss for words.

Fumes laden with the scent of burnt kerosene wafted through the doorway and fouled the atmosphere inside the room. Weber resisted the urge to cough but succumbed, as did Gabel and Blade. Only Trooper remained silent. The fumes worried Weber--they were caustic and toxic--but he was even more concerned that their coughing would be overheard. He ran to a row of windows that lined the room's outside wall, opened several glass panels, and sucked fresh air into his lungs. His coughing soon subsided. Gabel and Blade followed suit. The three of them remained there, with their heads hanging out of the windows, until the plane's engines stopped and the fumes dissipated.

Noise from the corridor piqued Weber's curiosity, so he crossed the room and listened beside the half-open door. He heard men speaking in German, but their voices were muffled, and he couldn't discern what they were saying. He also heard mechanical noises that he assumed were coming from the plane. To improve his vantage, he slipped into the open space between the door and the wall and eased his head forward until his right eye cleared the doorframe and rendered an unobstructed view of the corridor.

Weber could hardly believe his eyes. The aircraft parked in the corridor wasn't a fighter, as he'd expected, but a transport plane. The aircraft was surrounded by five men, each busy performing different tasks. One man shoved chocks under the plane's wheels while another slung ropes over the props to secure them. A third man wheeled a generator toward the front of the aircraft. The remaining two men pushed portable stairs to the plane's right side and positioned them under the main hatch.

While Weber waited for the hatch to open, Gabel wedged in beside him and stuck his head into the corridor. Weber put his hand on Gabel's shoulder, wrenched him back into the room, and whispered a rebuke. "Come on, Boss, you know better than that. If you stick your big noggin into the corridor, you'll give us away."

"Sorry, my tradecraft slipped a notch when our plan went to hell. I'll do better. So what's happening out there?"

"The plane's a transport; it's attended by five men. The passengers are still aboard, waiting for the hatch to open. Got your binoculars? Keep them trained on that hatch and see if you can identify any passengers as they disembark."

Gabel dropped to the floor, positioned himself so that only the tips of his binoculars protruded beyond the doorframe, and fiddled with the viewfinder until he had a clear view of the hatch.

The situation remained static until one of the ground crew climbed the portable stairs and pounded on the hatch. After several seconds, the hatch opened a crack, retracted slightly, and then pivoted toward the inside of the plane.

The first person to step through the hatch was a man in uniform. Weber stared at the man--something about him seemed familiar. Gabel gasped--he apparently recognized the man as well. Weber poked Gabel and pointed at the binoculars. Gabel reluctantly relinquished them.

Now, through the binoculars, Weber saw the uniformed man's face. A chill ran up his spine--it was Gunter! Reflexively, he drew his sidearm and aimed it at Gunter's head. As he was about to pull the trigger, Gabel glanced up and saw what was about to happen. He grabbed Weber's right leg and pushed him off balance. "What are you doing, Robert--I mean Weaver?"

"I'm killing a cockroach," Weber replied.

"Don't be foolish. You'll jeopardize the entire mission. Those Nazis will shoot us on sight."

Then, a second person climbed through the hatch--a woman. Weber didn't need the binoculars to recognize her--it was Anna. What the hell was she doing here? Stunned, he lowered his gun, slumped back against the wall, and tried to make sense of what he'd just seen. First, Gunter steps off the plane, and then Anna? Had he taken leave of his senses? Even his worst nightmare paled by comparison.

Chapter 16

Spring 1928: Berlin, Germany

With Hitler's support, Göring, along with other Nazi Party members including Joseph Goebbels, declared his candidacy for the Reichstag and campaigned throughout Germany before the May 1928 election. It was a difficult and lonely time for Göring because he lived alone, separated from his wife, Baroness Carin von Kantzow. Carin had worked tirelessly to help Göring recover from his injuries and addictions while the couple was exiled from Germany, and the strain had taken a toll on her health. After suffering exhaustion, she fell ill and returned to her ancestral home in Sweden for medical care.

By late spring, shortly before the elections, Carin's health improved, and she returned to Berlin to live with her husband. Her return energized Göring, who spent nearly all his waking hours debating politics with party members, campaigning against adversaries, and courting wealthy industrialists.

◆◆◆

At the end of Election Day, May 20th, 1928, Göring arrived at his flat at 16 Berchtesgadenerstrasse, entered the kitchen, and dropped into a chair at the dinner table. "Carin, say hello to a Reichsminister! I have just been elected to represent Bavaria in seat 54 of the Reichstag. Goebbels was elected as well."

"Congratulations, Hermann, it is indeed a fortunate day for Germany and the Nazi Party!"

"Thank you, Carin, but the party's prospects aren't as bright as Adolph hoped. I just came from a meeting at Hitler's flat, and the mood there was less than celebratory. The Nazi Party trailed the Social Democrats by more than eight million votes and won only 12 of the 491 seats in the Reichstag. Adolph expected better and vowed that he'd vanquish the party's detractors and win a majority of seats in the next election."

Summer 1928: Berlin, Germany

Sitting in his new office near the Reichstag, Göring picked up his phone and called Munich. After several rings, a familiar voice came on the line.

"Hello, this is Gunter Meissner speaking. How can I help you?"

"Gunter, this is Hermann. Where are you and what are you doing?"

"I'm in the lobby of the Bayern Hof Hotel. I just started my shift. I can't talk long because I have rooms to clean."

"My friend, why don't you quit that job, move to Berlin, and work for me?"

"Believe me, Hermann, I'm tired of cleaning toilets and washing people's dirty linen. And serving beer to drunks and wiping up their vomit is getting tiresome, too. But what are you offering me? I couldn't quit without stable employment and sufficient income to live in Berlin. It's expensive there."

"You must know by now, Gunter, that I am a Reichsminister. My position in the Reichstag includes funds for an assistant, so I could employ you full-time throughout my term and, hopefully, beyond if I am reelected. If need be, I can find you a job in my company. The business is doing well, and my partner, Paul Koener, will manage it during my absence."

"When would I start?"

"Pack your bags and get on a train, Gunter. You can start work tomorrow."

◆◆◆

Carin opened the door and greeted Gunter when he arrived at 16 Berchtesgadenerstrasse. A look of surprise registered on Gunter's face because, the last he knew, Carin had been living in Stockholm with her family after falling ill and moving there from Austria. He hadn't realized she had recovered and returned to Berlin to live with Göring.

"Carin, how wonderful to see you again. Welcome back to Germany! Thank goodness you are well and no longer forced to live in exile."

Carin smiled and led Gunter into the kitchen where Göring was eating breakfast. He stood and offered Gunter a seat at the table.

"Gunter, come, sit, and eat with us!"

"Hermann, you didn't tell me that Carin had recovered and was living with you in Berlin."

"Yes, after a long separation, we are together again. Here, my friend, have some coffee and strudel, and then we'll talk."

After the two men finished breakfast, they bid Carin goodbye and walked to Göring's office. Along the way, Göring talked about the election, his goals as a Reichsminister, and what Gunter could do to help him achieve those goals.

"I assume you saw Adolph after the election, Gunter. If so, you know how dissatisfied he is with the results. He expected that the Nazis would gain a hundred or more of the 491 seats in the Reichstag, but they won only twelve. It was a dismal showing, especially after all of Adolph's speeches and the popularity of his book. Goebbels and I were elected, which, perhaps, wasn't a surprise given all the campaigning he and I did in Berlin."

"Yes, I saw Adolph when he came to Munich to meet with his cronies at the Bratwurstglöckle after the election. He was in a foul mood but buoyed somewhat by the fact that you and Goebbels won. So, what will you do now that you're a member of the Reichstag?"

"Broadly, my area will be communications as it applies to transportation, but my chief responsibility will be aviation. To begin, I will push for creating a separate division of the Reichswehr called the Air Ministry and appointing a full-time Air Minister. And I'll repay Erhard Milch by ensuring Lufthansa receives more funding."

"I don't see how I can help you with that."

"No need, Gunter, those are just preliminaries. My foremost objective is to strengthen and improve military aviation. Once established, I will argue that Germany must invest more in aviation because it has fallen behind in aircraft design and production and is no longer competitive in the airline industry. That's what I'll say publicly. Privately, I'll contend that it's also making us vulnerable militarily."

"Hermann, your plan is ambitious, but will you take action beyond political advocacy?"

"Yes, of course, and that's why I need your help, Gunter. I want to attack this problem from several angles. Nothing can be accomplished without money, so one of our tasks will be to court investors. Substantial funding will be needed to build, equip, and staff a large and formidable Luftwaffe. To secure that financing, we'll have to convince the leaders of industry and government--the people who control the purse strings in the German economy--to fund aviation's bank account, so to speak, to the tune of millions of Reichsmarks. Our efforts to solicit funds must be conducted secretly, and the funds themselves must be hidden and administered without public knowledge. For this to succeed, it will be necessary to create a clandestine consortium of wealthy industrialists, aircraft manufacturers, and government officials."

"Ok, so we'll bilk rich Germans of their Reichsmarks and deposit them in a secret bank account. Then what?"

"Once we've obtained sufficient funds, we'll use them to further efforts to build a shadow or "ghost" Luftwaffe. Bringing a truly advanced yet secret air force to fruition will take creativity and be a prolonged and complex undertaking. However, as I will explain in a moment, some of the fundamentals are already in place, and we can accomplish a great deal by building on that foundation."

"But Hermann, how do you propose to build an entire military branch and conceal it from the public and the Allied Commission?"

"Well, Gunter, that's why I'm using the term 'ghost Luftwaffe.' Work is already underway to create a Luftwaffe that the Allied Commission will not see as an air force or an arm of the military. I want to support and extend that work. Some of what I hope to accomplish would be done in the open, and other operations would be hidden or conducted in secret. If necessary, we'd engage in covert operations, subterfuge, distraction--whatever means necessary to conceal the enterprise's true purpose."

"So, how would you go about this? What would you do first?"

"To acquire a modern, competitive Luftwaffe, we'd have to accomplish three things. First, we'd have to design and build ultramodern military aircraft, including fighters and bombers. Second, we'd have to constantly improve those planes to maintain an edge over our adversaries, and for that to happen, we'd need to find gifted young men and women--Germany's wunderkind--and train them to be aeronautical engineers. Third, we'd have to recruit and train a corps of flight personnel--pilots, navigators, bombardiers, and flight engineers--to fly those planes and do so effectively under combat conditions."

"You're right, Hermann, that's a huge undertaking. I wouldn't know where to start."

"I have some strategies in mind, but before we discuss them, let me give you some background. Please remember that what I am about to tell you must remain secret. I've learned through my business contacts that the government and the aviation industry are collaborating on a secret rearmament program. I'm told that it began as a small operation in 1925 and has expanded substantially since. Because of my position, I can't engage with these people directly or have it appear that I'm supporting an illegal undertaking. I want you to be my proxy, that is, function as my covert representative. You'd consult with these people, travel to their sites, inspect their work, and monitor their progress. Above all, you'd keep me informed. I'd expect regular reports. Does that sound like something you could handle?"

"Of course, Hermann. I'd consider it my patriotic duty."

"Your first assignment is to investigate the ongoing rearmament activities in the aviation sector, particularly in aircraft production. The objective of your investigation is to determine the extent to which the creation of a modern Luftwaffe has been achieved, including the design and construction of ultramodern military aircraft. Your task is to find out where the manufacturing facilities are located, who is managing the operations, what has been accomplished so far, and what is in the pipeline. I want to know if they've produced any fighters or bombers and developed technologies to give us an edge over our adversaries. Figure out what these operations need to stay productive and make note of obstacles and problems.

Oh, and this is important: evaluate security at each facility. It is imperative that these operations remain confidential. Begin immediately and document everything in confidential status reports, and report to me regularly so we can discuss your findings and plan accordingly."

Gunter was stunned by Göring's forcefulness and self-assurance. Who was this man? He didn't know whether to salute or laugh at his friend. This was a different Göring than the moaning, corpulent, delirious scrounger that he'd visited in Innsbruck. "Certainly, Hermann, I'll get on this immediately. I do have one question, however. Where do I start? Can you direct me to someone familiar with this program--a confidential source?"

"I will do my best to assist you, but I must admit that my knowledge of the Reichswehr, or the German military establishment, is incomplete. It is a vast and complex organization, and we must navigate through it to find the appropriate sources and identify individuals who can collaborate with us. As my investigator, I hope you can help me with this task."

"Hermann, I'll do my best. I asked where to start because the Reichswehr has no Air Ministry."

"Correct. When the Reichswehr was formed after the Treaty of Versailles, there was no provision for an aviation branch separate from the army or navy. However, the postwar chief of the Reichswehr, Colonel General Von Seeckt, made sure that aviators and aviation specialists were represented in the Reichswehr by integrating them into the various divisions, such as the Truppenamt, or Troops Office, or the Waffenamt, or Weapons Office. Von Seeckt's successors, including General Georg Wetzel and General Werner von Blomberg, sustained this policy. Over time. people began to refer to the organization of aviation interests and personnel within the Reichswehr as the 'Aviation Coalition.'

"Do you know anyone in the Aviation Coalition who could be a good initial point of contact?"

"I know from my business dealings that the Waffenamt has a testing department. Captain Kurt Student is the director, and I suggest you begin by talking to him. Rumor has it that he manages some aspects of the rearmament program, including aviation-related sections."

"Okay, Hermann, I'll contact Captain Student and proceed from there."

One month later, Gunter knocked on the door to Göring's office. A draft of the confidential status report he had assembled on Germany's aviation rearmament operations was safely concealed inside his briefcase. Göring opened the door, invited Gunter inside, and poured him a cup of coffee. Then, the two men sat at a small conference table opposite each other.

"Welcome back to Berlin, Gunter. How were your travels?"

"Productive, I think." Gunter opened his briefcase, extracted a file folder, and handed it to Göring. "German air power is not entirely outdated, Hermann. There is more to be done, of course, but there are reasons to be optimistic. Rearmament activities are more extensive than I imagined."

Göring opened the thick file folder and stared at its contents. Stapled to one side of the folder was a lengthy, typewritten report. Clipped to the other side was a sheaf of maps and photographs.

"My Gunter, you have been thorough. It will take me hours to read and digest all this information, and I don't know when I'll have time to do that. Politicians, it seems, spend all their time in meetings. Do me a favor. I have time now, so would you brief me on your findings?"

"Of course, Hermann. There is one base inside Germany located near Munich where military planes are assembled and tested. This base is disguised to look like a factory operated by a commercial aircraft manufacturer."

"What about aircraft? Have they produced any fighters or bombers?

"Yes, there are prototypes of both, but only the fighter is airworthy. It's a single-wing aircraft with a sweptback design, dual wing-mount engines, and multiple gun ports. I'm no engineer, but I suspect this plane is more advanced than other nations' fighters. However, I wasn't briefed on the fighter's test-flight performance or avionic equipment, so I can't speak to its actual capabilities or suitability for combat. Further, the people I spoke to were unwilling to discuss the plane's provenance or production history. Consequently, I know nothing about who designed the aircraft or how it was manufactured. I think we need to look closer at who is engineering these aircraft and how they are building them."

"Why were the people you spoke to so closed-mouthed? What was the reason for their recalcitrance?"

"I don't know. I told them I was your investigator, and they said they had heard of Reichsminister Hermann Göring, but they were extremely cagey nonetheless."

Göring slammed his fist down on his desk. "Do these people think they can defy me? That is going to change, and soon. Now, tell me about security at these bases."

"It appears tight, but the personnel at the Munich base reported one breach. In addition, two suspicious flights have been reported."

"What do they mean by a breach?"

"There was a break-in at the Munich base. Windows were broken, and tools were stolen. One of the guards thought he saw someone taking pictures of delivery trucks loaded with airplane parts. There's no hard evidence of spying; the break-in might have been part of a robbery."

"Possibly, but the guard's report bothers me. What if the 'robbers' were there to photograph the new fighter? A leak like that could be dangerous.

Now, tell me about the suspicious flights. Is there evidence of aerial spying?"

"On two occasions, our test pilots had close encounters with suspicious aircraft. One incident occurred near here at Johannisthal Air Field. The test pilot was practicing touch-and-go maneuvers when someone in a Potez 25 took off from that airfield and chased him. The Potez was no match for the new fighter, and it soon fell behind and disappeared. The other incursion was near the Munich airbase. In that case, a test pilot intercepted a much more powerful plane--a Dewoitine 500--as it approached the air base. Four other fighters were dispatched, and they formed up around the Dewoitine and tried to force it down at the airbase. The intruder, however, pulled some fancy maneuvers and escaped."

"The first incident could be attributed to curiosity--perhaps some plane buff wanted to scope out an unfamiliar aircraft. But the latter incident is suspicious. Judging by his escape, that pilot was an expert at evasive maneuvers. That's exactly the skill you'd expect a spy to have. Who but fighter pilots and spies possess that kind of skill?"

"My thoughts exactly, Hermann. What do you want me to do?"

"Find this Dewoitine. It's a French plane and shouldn't be that common in Germany. Track down the owner when you find it. I want to interrogate that spy for information. If he's not forthcoming, we'll persuade him to cooperate."

"Certainly, Hermann, I'll start work immediately. However, have you considered how long it will take to find this Dewoitine and its owner? There must be thousands of aircraft in Germany, and to inspect them all, I'd have to visit airports in every major city and those in rural areas. It could take months."

"You're right, and this isn't the most important task on our agenda. What would you suggest we do?"

"What if we could simultaneously speed up the search process and raise money for our ghost Luftwaffe? As a Reichminister, you could create a National Aircraft Registry and require owners to register their planes and pay a fee to utilize German airspace. Airport administrators would be required to register planes and collect appropriate fees officially. A portion of those funds could be utilized to employ agents who enforce compliance through regular inspections at airports and private facilities. These agents would be instructed to notify us immediately if they encounter any Dewoitine aircraft."

"Gunter, that's a brilliant idea. I'll draw up a plan, get it approved, and we can administer the Registry through my office until a full-time Air Minister is appointed."

"I'm pleased that you like my idea, Hermann. To expedite matters, I'll travel to some airports near where the Dewoitine was intercepted and make inquiries. Perhaps I'll get lucky and find the spy within the next few days."

Gunter drove to Tempelhof Airport, where Göring kept a Fokker D.XII fighter plane. The plane was the only one of its kind in Germany. The Versailles Treaty made it illegal for Germans to own fighters, but Göring had purchased this plane while working as an aircraft sales representative and had the manufacturer modify it so he could fly it legally in Germany.

After retrieving the Fokker, Gunter flew south to Munich and landed at Atzenhof Airport. He parked the plane near the control tower, entered the administration building, and strode into the airport supervisor's office. No one was there to assist him, so he muttered a few expletives, sat in a shabby chair, and surveyed his surroundings. The place looked like it hadn't had a fresh coat of paint since the Great War. The carpet was threadbare and reeked of cat urine. The walls were adorned with faded pictures of ancient biplanes, and an archaic desk sat in the center of the room, surrounded by dilapidated file cabinets.

Gunter drummed his fingers on the chair's armrest as his patience waned. He finally stood up to leave when an older man with a beard walked in and looked at him. "Can I assist you, sir?" he asked.

"I doubt it. The service here seems poor, but I'll give you one chance to prove me wrong. I'm a government agent, and I'm trying to locate a specific plane - a Dewoitine 500, to be exact. Do you have a Dewoitine hangered here, or have you seen one recently?"

"I can't say that I have, Mr. uh…what did you say your name was?"

"I didn't. But here's my business card. Call me immediately if you see or hear of a Dewoitine 500 in this area."

"What's this all about? Is there some issue I should be aware of?"

"The government plans to institute a National Aircraft Registry, and in preparation, I'm conducting a census of non-German aircraft."

"Don't politicians have anything better to do than harass the long-suffering citizens of this country with another needless tax?"

"I'm going to pretend I didn't hear that."

"So why are you looking for a particular Dewoitine 500? There are a lot of planes in Germany that were manufactured in other countries, like that Fokker you are flying."

"None of your business. Just do as you're told or suffer the consequences."

On returning to Berlin, Gunter stopped at several other airports but failed to unearth anything about the Dewoitine. He was frustrated by his lack of progress and concerned that Göring would be disappointed when he found out he had little or nothing to report. The only thing he had learned thus far was that airport personnel were a disagreeable lot--at best, they were uncooperative, and at worst, they were rude and surly.

As Gunter neared Berlin, he decided to extend his investigation to one more airport-- Johannisthal Air Field. He landed the Fokker, taxied to the terminal, and parked alongside the Heinkel Flugzeugwerke building. After entering the terminal, he roamed the halls until he found the Superintendent's office at the top of the stairs on the second floor. There was a sign on the door with the name HANS WOLKEL engraved in large letters.

Gunter didn't knock; he pushed the door open and marched into the office. A man bent over a desk looked up and frowned but greeted Gunter nonetheless.

"Hello, and welcome to Johannisthal Air Field. How may I assist you?"

Gunter stood with his hands on his hips and asked, "Are you Hans?"

"Yes, sir."

"Well, Hans, I'm a government investigator here to obtain some information. It would be in your best interest to cooperate with me."

"No need to get testy--what do you want to know?"

"I am looking for non-German aircraft, specifically a Dewoitine 500. Have you seen one at this airport? Has anyone parked one in your hangars?"

"Could I see your credentials, sir? I couldn't release that information without checking with the owner."

"Are you trying to obstruct my investigation? I want to speak to your supervisor, Hans. Now!"

"Look, whoever you are. We're done talking, so leave my office and don't come back."

"You Schwein! Dummkopf! Arschloch! You will regret this because I'll have a warrant for your arrest when I return!"

◆◆◆

The next time Gunter met with Göring, he was gloomy and defensive. He arrived late and said little when Göring invited him into his office. Eschewing eye contact, he trudged to the conference table at the center of Göring's office and slumped into a chair.

"No time for pleasantries today, Gunter? What's the problem?"

"I've failed, Hermann. My search for the Dewoitine led nowhere; I know nothing more now than when I started."

"Tell me what happened."

"Well, those verdammt airport administrators are to blame. All of them were uncooperative; not one was willing to help me. I suspect one or more of them knew about the spy plane, but they kept schtum. And their reactions to the idea of a National Aircraft Registry were anything but supportive."

"That is disappointing, Gunter, but perhaps not surprising. That plane could be anywhere, and you're working alone and haven't had a chance to visit many airports. Please keep looking, as you have time, but I have other priorities that need your attention. When the Registry is approved, I'll hire an army of agents, and they will scour the country until the Dewoitine's owner is found."

"So, which of your priorities shall I work on next?"

"As I mentioned in our last meeting, we can't build a progressive Luftwaffe that consistently outperforms our adversaries unless we find gifted young men and women and train them to be aeronautical engineers. I want to know if the managers of the current rearmament program are working on this objective and, if so, what they're doing to address it. Report to me as soon as you know something."

"I'll start immediately, Hermann, but where do I begin? Can you direct me to an appropriate source in the Reichswehr?"

"This time, you'll want to speak to someone in military education, preferably the person whose job is to recruit and train students for aircraft design and engineering. Again, my contacts in the Reichswehr are limited, but I suggest you speak to Captain Horst Wesselman.

Gunter took the S-Bahn to the center of Berlin, transferred to the U-Bahn, and got off when he reached Reichswehr headquarters. After finding the Truppenamt's main office, he asked to see Captain Horst Wesselman and a receptionist directed him to an obscure office on the top floor. Gunter ascended five flights of stairs, walked through a labyrinth of hallways, and eventually found Wesselman's office in a dark corner of the building. The door was open, so he entered and found Wesselman writing mathematical formulas on a large chalkboard.

"Are you, by chance, Wesselman?"

"Who wants to know?"

"Look, let's not play cat and mouse. My name is Gunter, and I am Hermann Göring's assistant. He sent me to ask you some questions."

"Ah, Germany's famous World War One ace. I understand that Hermann was elected to the Reichstag. What does he want to know?"

"He wants to know if the Reichswehr is recruiting talented young men and women and training them to be aeronautical engineers."

"And why would he want to know that?"

"Because he doesn't think Germany can have a world-beating Luftwaffe unless we find our nation's wunderkind and train them to build it."

"But surely you know it's illegal for the Reichswehr to build an air force."

"Officially, yes. But what about a ghost Luftwaffe?"

"Ah, I see that you are well-informed. Are you cleared to discuss military secrets?"

"I'm granted that privilege as Göring's assistant, and I'm fully aware that the Reichswehr has been collaborating with the government and airplane manufacturers to build a ghost Luftwaffe. Hermann supports that program, but he believes its success depends on finding the talent necessary to design and build the next generation of warplanes--specifically, warplanes that supersede the capabilities of our adversaries."

"I can't fault Hermann's foresight. Moreover, his support would benefit our development efforts. Alright, let me tell you what we are doing--both officially and unofficially."

◆◆◆

Shortly after talking to Wesselman, Gunter met with Göring to report what he had learned. Göring listened attentively.

"My meeting with Wesselman was very informative, Hermann, and I think you'll be pleased with what I've discovered. Horst and a few of his colleagues in the Reichswehr operate official programs that benefit aviation, such as pilot training, airborne competitions and war games, aerial warfare instruction, and foreign air power analysis. Perhaps more importantly, they also sponsor ostensibly legitimate activities that are a cover for schemes that benefit the ghost Luftwaffe. Among those are government-sponsored internships in aeronautical engineering and aircraft design for high-aptitude high school students."

"So, it's Horst now. You must have hit it off with Wesselman. So, tell me, Gunter, how do Wesselman and his crew find students for those internships? And, what purpose does the internship serve?"

"Horst and his colleagues work with the Hitler Youth and the technical high schools to find students who exhibit superior abilities in math and science. The students they identify are interviewed and vetted, and candidates embark on a trial period during which Horst and his colleagues assess their work and loyalty. If students prove their worth during the internship, they are granted a security clearance, assigned to actual engineering teams, and allowed to work on projects contributing to the ghost Luftwaffe. Horst also arranges for his protégés to attend Germany's best universities and has the Reichswehr pay for their coursework in engineering."

"I like what I'm hearing so far, Gunter. I want you to work more closely with Wesselman. See if there are ways to extend and improve this program."

The following week, Gunter asked Wesselman if he could observe and perhaps even participate in their student recruitment and internship programs. He explained that the endeavor fit Göring's plans for German aviation and that he, as a Reichminister, wanted to study it to expand and improve the program.

Wesselman searched Gunter's face for signs of treachery or deceit but, seeing none, nodded his agreement. "Alright, but how do you propose to study the program?"

"Horst, I'm interested in every aspect of your program--the entire operation. Unless you have a better idea, I'd like to work with you directly. Take me to the schools and the Hitler Youth meetings so I can meet your contacts and see how you recruit the best students. Show me how you vet the students, evaluate the quality of their work, and assess their loyalty. Let me meet some of the interns and watch them as they work with the design and engineering teams. And, at every step of the way, point out the problems you've encountered and tell me how you think the program could be improved. Hermann will do everything he can to help you overcome those obstacles."

◆◆◆

Gunter spent a month shadowing Wesselman and his staff. It had been one of the busiest four weeks of his life; he'd spent countless hours interviewing staff, traveling to youth meetings and schools, reading student records and internship reports, and writing progress reports. Overall, he was pleased with the way the investigation was progressing. Horst had been true to his word and allowed him to observe every aspect of the internship program. He knew Göring would be interested in the results of his investigation, so he called his boss and arranged a meeting.

When Gunter met with Göring, he tried to restrain his enthusiasm so he wouldn't risk overstating the value of Wesselman's internship program. He'd grown fond of Horst and developed a favorable perception of Wesselman's leadership and accomplishments. Even so, he recognized that the internship program had problems and could benefit from improvements. He owed it to Göring to provide a balanced perspective.

"Hermann, I haven't completed my investigation, but what I've seen thus far makes me think you'd be wise to invest in Wesselman's internship program. Like any enterprise, it has strengths and weaknesses, but, overall, I think the program's benefits outweigh its limitations."

"What do you see as the program's strengths?"

"Wesselman, for one; Horst believes--as you do--that the Luftwaffe will only be as good as the people who build it, and he's convinced that there are youth within Germany who can build an invincible Luftwaffe. Toward that end, he's recruiting intelligent youth, turning them into top-flight engineers, and then utilizing them to build a shadow Luftwaffe--the precursor for an ultramodern air force."

"I like Wesselman's perspective, and his leadership is an obvious asset. Are there other strengths?"

"I think the program will improve German aviation eventually. What's unclear is whether the pace and scale of operations are sufficient to produce a ghost Luftwaffe within the next decade."

"Timing is important, Gunter, so that's a serious limitation. Ideally, we need to design and build prototypes of all essential military aircraft within the next five years. Why can't the program progress more quickly?"

"Horst has recruited a small number of talented youth from Berlin and surrounding communities. Only about 20% of this group completed the internship successfully; the remainder were eliminated, typically because they were unreliable, incompetent, or disloyal. So, in its current state, the program will expand the ranks of outstanding aeronautical engineers, but perhaps not in sufficient numbers to establish the foundation for a modern, military air force."

"It seems we've pivoted to considering the program's limitations, so what other weaknesses did you detect? And, if you have recommendations for how the programs' limitations could be addressed, I'd like to hear them."

"Alright, Hermann, I'll begin where I left off. The program's size limits its effectiveness, and we could address that by making it a national rather than a local enterprise. With your resources, we could recruit talented youth nationwide instead of just in Berlin."

"I'll consider that. What else?"

"Horst's methods for finding talented youth are subjective and piecemeal, and, as a result, he's probably overlooked some high-quality candidates. He asks teachers and youth group leaders to identify applicants and seems unaware that those informants aren't always reliable judges of students' mathematical aptitude. He should augment those recommendations with objective indicators of students' aptitude for math and science. For example, he could obtain students' scores on math tests or evaluate samples of their work."

"I concur, Gunter. Are there other limitations?"

"There's one more, Hermann. Internship applicants aren't properly vetted. Horst and his staff build a student profile by interviewing applicants and examining their school records. They evaluate loyalty and security by interviewing the applicants' friends and checking to see whether the applicant has disclosed classified information. That's a reasonable approach as far as it goes, but it's not what I'd call a thorough background check. At a minimum, they should be tracing the applicant's family history or lineage, examining the applicant's political views, and checking police reports to see if the applicant has engaged in delinquent or criminal behavior."

"That's especially concerning, Gunter. We can't have spies infiltrating this program, nor can we tolerate security leaks. The risks are just too great.

What if the Allied Commission caught wind of this program? Wesselman would be jailed, we'd be disgraced, and the ghost Luftwaffe would be kaput."

"So, Hermann, how should we proceed? What should I do next?"

"Alright, Gunter, hear me out. Suppose you told Wesselman that I'm concerned about these limitations and want to address them by expanding the program beyond Berlin, incorporating objective selection techniques, and tightening background checks. How do you think he'd respond?"

"I can only guess, Hermann, but I don't think Horst would object to upgrading his selection tools and expanding the program, especially if you're willing to fund those improvements. However, I know he'd scream bloody murder if we asked him to conduct enhanced background checks on his current interns and future applicants."

"Why would Wesselman object to expanded background checks? Surely, he understands that everyone who works on this project needs to be thoroughly vetted."

"I'm sure he does, but there's a fly in ointment, so to speak. Horst has an exceptional intern named Luka, whose contributions to aircraft design could prove extraordinary. The problem is that the kid won't talk about himself; he says his parents won't allow him to disclose personal information. Horst pressured the kid until Luka threatened to quit the program. That spooked Horst; he couldn't bear losing the kid. Ultimately, he told Luka that he'd passed his preliminary exams and was promoted to one of the design teams."

"That's unacceptable--it's a clear breach of protocol! What makes this kid so special?"

"Several things, from what I understand. To start, the kid's a bit of a nonconformist, perhaps even an eccentric in the way geniuses often are. When he began working with a design team, the experienced engineers didn't know what to make of him. His ideas are unorthodox, and his approach to aircraft design is unconventional—for example, the kid's obsessed with drag--that is, aerodynamic drag. Reducing drag, he says, will make planes fly faster and maneuver better. To prove his point, he does crazy things such as taping strands of ribbon on the wings and fuselage of airplanes and then watching how the ribbons flutter and flap when the planes take off, cruise, and land. Now he's telling Wesselman to build a wind tunnel modeled on Eiffel's work in Paris--but one that's large enough to encompass an entire airplane."

"Clearly, the kid's imaginative, but is his work of any consequence? Does it produce meaningful discoveries--ones that have practical applications?"

"It's too early to tell, Hermann, but Wesselman's expecting big things. He says the kid is using his observations to refine the formulas for aerodynamic drag. If substantiated, his formulations could help us design and build unique, unrivaled military aircraft. The bottom line is that the kid could potentially transform aircraft design. He's earned the respect of his teammates; even the seasoned engineers are intrigued with the kid's approach and findings."

"I am beginning to understand why Wesselman has bent the rules to keep this kid. However, we can't afford this kind of precedent. We know nothing about this kid. Make sure this kid's background check is completed. Do it yourself if you have to."

"Ok, don't worry, Hermann. I'll fix this."

Chapter 17

Fall 1928: Bavaria, Germany

Weber was in shock as he tried to process what he had just witnessed. Perhaps his eyes were playing tricks on him. He eased his way back into the doorframe and glanced up the corridor at the woman who had just exited from the transport plane's rear hatch. There was no denying it; Anna was standing on the platform next to Gunter.

Weber felt an overwhelming urge to dash into the corridor and scream, "What are you doing here?" but his better judgment kept him rooted in place: that and Gabel's vice-like grip on his ankles.

Gabel was still lying on the floor next to Weber, positioned so he could observe the transport plane through his binoculars. The moment he'd spotted Anna and heard Weber gasp, he'd dropped the binoculars and wrapped his arms tightly around Weber's ankles.

Weber looked down at Gabel and sighed. "Alright, Boss, you can let go now. I'm not going to do anything foolish." As Gabel uncoiled his arms, Weber studied the look on Gabel's face. He couldn't be sure, but he saw nothing in the contours of Gabel's expression to suggest that he'd just experienced a shock. Hell, the man didn't even appear to be perplexed. The fact was that Gabel had been composed enough to anticipate Weber's response and react accordingly. Anna's appearance hadn't surprised Gabel as much as it had focused him on the possibility that Weber's reaction might give away their position.

Suspicions aroused, Weber backed away from the doorframe, spun around, and walked toward the center of the avionics room. Gabel observed Weber's movements and then stood up and followed him. When the two men stood face to face, Weber balled up his fists and glared at Gabel. "Do you know what's going on here? What is your daughter doing with those Nazis?"

Gabel stared at his feet, unable to look Weber in the eye. "Well, it's a complicated matter," he sputtered, "and we were trying to protect you. I told Anna you'd be better off if you didn't know."

"Know what? Dammit, the cat's out of the bag, so you better come clean."

"Uh, remember I told you I had a highly-placed source in the Reichswehr's Aviation Coalition? Well…

Ruth Gabel called her husband, the two boys, and Weber to the dinner table as she put the finishing touches on the evening meal. She had spent the day preparing a feast of sauerbraten, gravy, and spätzle in honor of Luka's birthday. And, for the party that would begin after dinner, she baked a three-layer birthday cake with 17 candles.

Aaron Gabel said a quick blessing, and then he and Ruth picked up the platters of meat and spätzle and passed them around the table. When the food reached the corner of the table where Luka and Carl were seated, the boys scooped food onto their plates until the platters were nearly empty. Aaron chuckled and reminded the boys that others at the table were also hungry. "Luka and Carl, I know you're growing boys, but would you mind leaving a few scraps for the rest of us?" After partially refilling the platters, the boys smiled guiltily and passed the food to Weber.

Weber put some meat and a few dollops of spätzle on his plate and began eating. He'd no sooner taken his first bite when the front door slammed. Seconds later, Anna strode into the dining room, dressed in an overcoat and clutching a briefcase. Weber dropped his fork, pushed his chair away from the table, and stood facing Anna. "So, tell us, Anna, how was your business meeting?"

Before Anna could reply, Aaron Gabel leaped from his chair, dashed across the room, and positioned himself between Weber and Anna. "Before you say anything else, Robert, I have something to discuss with my daughter. Sit down, eat your dinner, and be quiet."

Weber stood his ground, glaring at Gabel, but held his tongue. Gabel took Weber's silence as a sign that the confrontation had ended, so he turned toward Anna, put his hand on her arm, and led her out of the room. Weber muttered something quietly to himself as he watched Gabel and Anna depart, and then he sat back down at the table.

Ten minutes later, Gabel returned to the dining room and sat at the dinner table. Anna was nowhere to be seen. Weber looked across the table, expecting an explanation, but Gabel said nothing. Instead, he forked a piece of meat, put it in his mouth, and began chewing. After he swallowed, he laughed and asked Luka if he was enjoying his twelfth birthday party.

"Oh, Opa," Luka replied. "You think you're so funny. You know I'm seventeen, not twelve."

Gabel laughed again. "Oh, surely you're not that old, are you? Mein Gott, you'll be interested in girls soon."

"For your information, Opa, that happened long ago." Gabel feigned surprise and then laughed again.

Weber wasn't amused. Gabel's contrived insouciance had ripped a hole in the thin veil of patience he'd managed to muster. He slammed his fist on the table and shouted, "Where is she, Aaron?"

Gabel's jocular expression disappeared, and an angry frown took its place. "Robert, don't ruin Luka's birthday party. Can't you put aside your petty grievances for an hour or two?"

"Petty grievances? Are you serious?"

"You're blowing this out of proportion."

"Don't downplay this, Aaron. I'm angry, and I think I'm owed an explanation."

"All right, if you must--Anna's in her bedroom, changing her clothes for the party."

Weber stormed out of the dining room and marched toward Anna's bedroom. Meanwhile, Gabel continued to admonish him from the dining room. "Robert, it's not what you think. You owe it to Anna to listen to her side of the story. She's not to blame here--this whole business is far more convoluted than you know."

Upon reaching Anna's bedroom, Weber found Anna standing in the doorway, hands on her hips, jaw clenched, and a scowl on her face. He was speechless when he saw her confident and unwavering gaze. This wasn't the person he'd envisioned himself confronting--he'd expected to find Anna prostrate on the bed, crying and begging for forgiveness.

"You've been spying on me," she intoned. "Where's your integrity? You're not the man I thought you were."

"Me? How dare you malign *my* character! I can scarcely fathom the depths of deceit to which you've sunken. You've lied to me, you've lied to Carl, and you've even lied to Luka. What kind of mother lies to her son about basic things like her occupation? You're an architect, all right--an architect of lies. You've built a mammoth web of lies."

"Yes, I have concealed things about my identity, but only out of necessity. I've never acted maliciously, nor have I ever wanted to deceive you, Robert. All my actions have been motivated by self-preservation and a desire to protect Luka."

"So, tell me what you do for a living."

"What did my father tell you?"

"Come on, be straight with me. Your father says a lot of things. I want to hear it from you."

"I'm an aircraft engineer."

Weber took a step back and covered his face to conceal his reaction. The parallel between Anna's occupation and his covert identity had surprised him. "You're what?"

"You heard me. I design airplanes for a living. I grew up flying my father's planes and was good at math and science. I studied aeronautical engineering in college, and after earning a degree, I went to work in the aircraft industry."

"But why would you help the Nazis?"

"It wasn't by choice. I took an engineering job in the Reichswehr during the Weimar years and eventually became a member of the Aviation Coalition. That was long before the Nazis gained influence and tried to control Germany's covert rearmament programs. After Göring and his cronies showed up, everyone in the Aviation Coalition had to bow to their wishes. Those who objected to their policies were forced to resign."

"Still, I don't understand how you could work with a man like Gunter Meissner. How well do you know him?"

"I've known Gunter a long time and Hermann Göring too. I grew up with them, and we went to the same schools in Munich. Gunter's an insecure farm boy who's never had any scruples. He's always been Göring's toady, shamelessly promoting Hermann's nefarious schemes by any means necessary, impervious to the harm he inflicts upon others."

"So, you knew Göring too?" Weber said, trying not to look surprised.

"Yes, we were classmates and traveled in the same social circles when I was in high school. We even dated until I realized he was chasing other girls behind my back."

"What a prince."

Anna smirked. "What a pair--Gunter always covered for Göring, helping him hide his indiscretions."

Weber thought about all the times he'd seen Gunter clean up after Göring's messes, and his anger began to cool. "Yeah, what a twosome. It seems like neither Gunter nor Göring has changed much. How do they handle the fact that you're Jewish? Doesn't that cause problems?"

"In the past, they tolerated me because of our shared history and the importance of my contributions to the rearmament program. Now that Nazi ideology has gained a foothold in Germany, they've started to look at me as an outsider. I fear it won't be long before they think of me as an undesirable or one of the 'Untermensch.' When that happens, they'll fire me or perhaps do something worse. They're already restricting the projects I work on and monitoring my activities more closely."

"Is that what motivated all this duplicity--you thought you could protect yourself by pretending to be someone you're not?"

Anna wrung her hands, looked away, and drew a deep breath. The anger etched on her face dissolved into a wistful expression. "Oh, Robert, it's much more complicated than that. Yes, I did it to protect myself but also to safeguard my family. My parents left Munich and changed their names to escape people like the Nazis--brutal, small-minded bigots. That's when I became Anna Gabel and began to use that identity to shield my family. The people I work with, like Gunter and Göring, still know me as the girl they grew up with--Anna Lichtmann. So, essentially, I'm leading a double life.

To you and everyone I know outside of work, I'm Anna Gabel. Inside the Reichswehr, I'm Anna Lichtmann. My apartment in Berlin is registered to Anna Lichtmann because the Reichswehr employment application required a home address. Even though I live with you, I keep that apartment in case someone from work tries to find me. Moving in with you allowed me to live in Berlin as Anna Gabel and be reunited with my son. Keeping the two strands of my life separate has been challenging, but so far, I've managed to keep them from intersecting. That is, until now. You are the first person to unmask Anna Gabel."

Weber stood silently, trying to absorb what he'd just been told. It was a lot to take in, and he suspected that there was more to come. Quite unexpectedly, Anna had mentioned a name that brought to mind a person he'd searched for during the early days of his mission. He'd scoured the aviation industry looking for a woman named Lichtmann but never found her. Now he knew why. "I think I'm beginning to understand. But how's your father figure into this--he told me that you are his highly-placed source within the Reichswehr."

"It's our hedge against the Nazis. It's obvious what they have in mind for Germany. They're plotting revenge against the countries that imposed the Versailles Treaty. They see the Allies as predators that bled Germany like a stuck pig and won't rest until they've extracted their pound of flesh. They also despise the Jews and blame them for Germany's misfortunes. If the Nazis gain power politically, they will marginalize the Jews, strip them of their citizenship, and heap abuse on them. We can't stand by and watch that happen. We're doing everything we can to ensure they fail."

"Are you telling me that you're a spy and passing information about the Aviation Committee's secret rearmament program to your father?"

"That's exactly what I am saying."

Anna's confession confirmed what Weber had suspected, but it nonetheless left him stunned. He paused for several moments, trying to gather his wits. Then his investigative instincts triggered a thought: perhaps he should ask Anna how her secrets were being used so that he could compare her rendition with the explanation he'd obtained from her father. "So, what does your father do with that information?"

"We've agreed that he will use it to obstruct and embarrass the Nazis. Exactly how he does that is his secret. We compartmentalize or conceal certain things from each other. It's safer for both of us. But I'm curious, Robert, why do you want to know?" Why would you be interested in what my father does with that information?"

Weber chided himself. Acting on his investigative instincts had been a mistake. Doing so had turned the tables on him, and now he was on the defensive. "Uh, well, no reason, I guess. I was just curious."

"Now, who's being disingenuous? I just bared my soul, and you have the gall to lie to me? It's time you leveled with me."

"About what?"

"I'm not stupid, Robert. Did you think I wouldn't decipher the subtext of your accusations and questions? By accusing me, you've revealed yourself. For starters, explain what you were doing in that aircraft factory. When you finish that, you can tell me how you know Gunter Meissner."

"Your father and I have been working together. He probably thought you didn't need to know."

"I don't care what my father thought. I want to know what *you* were doing and why you concealed it from me."

"Okay, fine. I was inside that factory gathering information about German rearmament, specifically the production of military aircraft. I didn't tell you because I'm not at liberty to discuss what I'm doing."

"Are you telling me that you're a spy pretending to be an apprentice clergyman?"

"That's exactly what I am saying."

"Gee, Robert, where have I heard this before? What's good for the goose is good for the gander, eh?

Weber thought that Anna's attempt to equate their indiscretions meant she didn't plan to interrogate him further. He thought he'd found a way to escape his predicament and tried to make light of the situation. "Wow, this is an amazing coincidence, Anna. Here we are, two spies living under the same roof, engaged in similar missions, but neither knows what the other is doing."

"Not so fast, Robert. Who do you work for, and why are they interested in German rearmament?"

Weber pulled Anna into the bedroom, closed the door, and motioned for her to sit with him on the edge of the bed. "Look, I'm breaking an oath by telling you this, but given what you've just revealed, I guess it's only fair that I reciprocate. I, too, am an aeronautical engineer, and I was recruited by US Army Intelligence to spy on the German aircraft industry. The purpose of my mission is to determine whether Germany is violating the Versailles Treaty by building military aircraft. I didn't accomplish much until I met your father. His information was so valuable that my handlers now consider my mission a success. Now, however, I realize that you, more than your father, are the source for most of the intelligence that I've acquired."

Weber paused, turned toward Anna, and looked into her eyes. Anna nodded but said nothing, her expression inscrutable. Fearing that his disclosures had alienated her, Weber screwed up his courage and floated a proposition. "Perhaps we should work together. How would you feel about that?"

Anna closed her eyes, put her hand to her face, and pinched the bridge of her nose. "I don't know, Robert. Let me think about it. Maybe I can give you an answer after I hear what you have to say about Gunter."

There was a pregnant pause as Weber thought about what to say. As he gathered his thoughts, his anger grew; his lips tightened, and his face flushed. "I'm not sure I can talk about Gunter without it sounding like a diatribe."

"It's alright, Robert, you can speak freely."

"Well, where should I begin? To put it succinctly, the man has no redeeming qualities whatsoever. He has endeavored to ruin my life and has come close to succeeding." Weber went on to describe how Gunter had sabotaged his Svensk-Luft aircraft, ultimately killing his wife and most of his passengers and leaving him to die on the tundra. Then he recounted how Gunter had broken into his house during the middle of the night and tried to kill Carl and himself while they were sleeping. He concluded by explaining how Gunter had conspired to have him arrested by the Swedish authorities, forcing him to flee the country. "I could tell you more, but I won't belabor the point. The man's a treacherous swine."

"My God, that's unbelievable! But why, Robert? Why would Gunter pursue you so persistently and try to harm your family?"

"I wish I knew--I've repeatedly asked myself the same question but never found an answer. I overheard Gunter promise Göring that he'd get rid of me one way or another, but nothing he said offered insight into his motives. The one thing I do understand is that he won't rest until I'm dead."

Tears formed in Anna's eyes. She reached out, wrapped her arms around Weber, and kissed him. "Oh Robert, no man should endure what you've been through. I knew your wife died in a crash, but I had no idea that Gunter was complicit in her death. Then he tried to kill Carl? That reprobate has put you through hell."

"I'm sorry I didn't tell you sooner, but I didn't want to burden you with the dismal details of my life story. I couldn't see how anything would be gained by subjecting you to the pain and sorrow that I've been forced to endure."

"I understand, but I wish you had told me. You shouldn't carry this pain alone--that's what I'm here for--I love you. Carl, too."

Now, it was Weber's turn to get misty-eyed. He held Anna in a tight embrace and kissed her softly. "Let's not let things like this come between us again. Okay?"

Anna hesitated. She searched Weber's face as if the answer to his question was hiding somewhere in his features. Then she looked away and nodded.

Chapter 18

Fall 1928: Berlin, Germany

"I'm sorry, Mr. Meissner, but I can't give you that information. The contents of a student's record are confidential, and neither I--the Director of the Berlin Technical Academy--nor any other member of the BTA staff will release student data without the parent's consent."

Gunter scowled; his patience was wearing thin. He'd asked politely, and that had gotten him nowhere. He leaned over the Director's desk, placed both hands on the desktop, and looked the headmaster directly in the eye. "Look, Mr. Barren, I won't ask you again. Just tell me where the kid lives. What is Luka's home address?"

"Who do you think you are, Mr. Meissner? Men like you don't intimidate me. Please leave--you have no legitimate reason for being here."

"No legitimate reason? Are you deaf? I told you that Reichsminister Göring asked me to do enhanced background checks on all BTA students who accept internships with the Reichswehr Aviation Coalition. What could be more legitimate than that?"

"BTA and the Reichswehr are separate institutions and have their own rules and regulations. I suspect the Reichswehr collects demographic information on their personnel, so perhaps you and Reichsminister Göring should visit them. Ask to see Horst Wesselman; he's our contact for the internship program. If anyone is qualified to do background checks, it's Wesselman. Conversely, you have no such authority and have done nothing that would earn my trust. As far as I know, you're some charlatan masquerading as a government official."

Gunter was seething with anger and finding it hard to control his urge to strike Barren. "Reichsminister Göring will hear about this, Mr. Barren. I promise you."

"Do I look worried? Get out of my school."

Gunter stomped out of the school. As he descended the front steps, he heard a commotion coming from somewhere behind the building. Curious, he decided to investigate. When he reached the rear of the property, he saw a group of boys filing out of the school onto a grassy playing field. They were shouting and laughing, releasing stress that had accumulated during the school day. Several men dressed in Hitler Youth garb stood in the field, awaiting the boys' arrival. One of the men tossed a soccer ball on the ground and motioned for the boys to join him.

Figuring he'd just stumbled upon a golden opportunity, Gunter strode to where one of the men stood and asked him if he knew a boy named Luka. The man nodded but refused to say more until Gunter identified himself.

"Who are you, and why are you interested in Luka?"

"My name is Gunter Meissner. To whom am I speaking?"

"Lothar Speilman."

Gunter flipped open his wallet and showed Lothar his Nazi Party identification card. "Lothar, like yourself, I'm a member of the Nazi Party. I work for Hermann Göring, a newly elected Reichsminister. Göring asked me to do background checks on students working as interns at the Reichswehr. Luka's one of those students."

"I see. Well, there's not much I can tell you. Luka's a quiet, cautious kid. He doesn't say much about himself."

"Surely you know more than that. What else can you tell me?"

"Well, he and Carl Weber are friends. Those two are inseparable."

Gunter snorted an acknowledgment. "That doesn't help me much, Lothar."

"Sorry, Mr. Meissner, that's all I know."

"Well, point him out for me, will you? And while you're at it, identify the Weber kid."

Lothar obliged.

Frustrated by his lack of progress, Gunter paced the sidelines, eyeing Luka and Carl while he waited for the boys to finish playing soccer. His only remaining option, it seemed, was to confront Luka and force him to talk.

◆◆◆

Carl and Luka stood next to each other on the soccer pitch while the HJ coaches disputed a penalty called against one of their teammates. Carl leaned toward Luka and whispered. "Hey, a guy on the sidelines has been staring at you. Do you know him?"

Luka glanced at Gunter and then replied. "He looks familiar, like someone I've seen at the Reichswehr. But why would someone from the Reichswehr be here?"

"I don't know, but the guy is watching you, and he looks angry."

"What do you suppose he wants?"

"Who knows, but I think you should steer clear of him."

When the match ended, Luka and Carl rushed off the field, picked up their belongings, and set off for home. They'd only walked a short distance when the man they'd seen on the sidelines stepped from behind some bushes and blocked their path.

"Hold it right there, boys. You're not under arrest, but you will be if you don't answer my questions."

Carl was the first to speak. "Under arrest? For what? We haven't done anything wrong."

The stranger took a step toward Carl and made a menacing gesture. "Shut up, Carl. I'm here to question Luka."

Now, it was Luka's turn to protest. "Who are you, and how do you know our names?"

"Luka, you've omitted important details in your application for an internship at the Reichswehr. You haven't been forthcoming about yourself, your family, and your political affiliations. I don't think it's because you're slipshod or negligent--I think you did it intentionally, and I want to know why."

Carl nudged Luka, and the boys took off running. The man chased them, yelling their names and cursing, but he soon tired and fell behind. The boys ran together until they reached the Tiergarten, and then they split up and hid among the trees.

◆◆◆

The next day at soccer practice, Carl spotted the same man standing on the sidelines, watching Luka closely. He pulled Luka aside, pointed out the stranger, and suggested a plan.

Just before practice ended, the boys grabbed their gear, ran inside the school, and exited from a door on the opposite side of the building. Seeing no one, they walked down a side street toward Invaliden Strasse. As they approached the intersection, Carl turned and saw the stranger about a hundred yards to the rear, keeping his distance but following them nonetheless.

"Luka, the snoop is tailing us. He's about a hundred yards back. Turn left when you reach Invaliden Strasse and head for Lehrter Bahnhof." Luka nodded.

When the boys reached the train station, they bought tickets, dashed through turnstiles, descended to the platforms, and jumped aboard an eastbound train. As the train pulled out of the station, they saw the stranger standing on the platform, peering into the windows of the coaches as they sped past him.

Carl nudged Luka and pointed out the window toward the stranger. "We've given him the slip again, but this is getting tiresome. We need to get this guy off our backs. Maybe we should report him to Mr. Barren."

"No, Carl. That's just as bad as letting this troublemaker follow us home. Barren will contact my mother, and then she'll know I've joined the HJ. She might even discover I'm interning with you at the Reichswehr. We can't let this snoop find out where we live. There's got to be another way."

"All right. Maybe if we put our heads together, we can come up with a solution."

◆◆◆

Göring appeared disappointed and asked Gunter if he had learned anything about Luka, the young prodigy who could potentially influence the future of German military aviation. "Are you telling me you've learned nothing about our wayward wunderkind?" He glared at Gunter, waiting for a response. He had summoned Gunter to his Reichsminister's office and was anxious to find out whether Gunter's background check had been productive.

Gunter stared at his shoes, afraid to look Göring in the eye. "Well, I found out that Luka has a friend at BTA who's interning with the Aviation Coalition."

"Is this the kind of information I'm to expect from your 'enhanced' background checks? If so, the endeavor is worthless--nothing but a waste of time and money."

"Calm down, Hermann. It's early days--I'm just getting started. I'll know more in a week or two."

"You don't have a week or two because I am changing your assignment. My investment in Germany's aviation sector has begun to pay dividends. As a result, my priorities have changed, and I need you to gather some intelligence for me."

"What kind of intelligence?"

"I want you to investigate the capabilities of our adversaries' military aircraft. If we hope to beat the Allies in the next war, we'll need to build warbirds that are more capable than theirs. Our fighters must be faster and more maneuverable. Our bombers must fly further and carry heavier payloads. The only way to ensure that our planes are superior--to guarantee that our aircraft dominate the skies--is to benchmark them against the Allies' best warbirds and then build ours to a higher standard."

"How exactly would I obtain that information? The Allies don't publicize the capabilities of their military aircraft--they keep that information under lock and key. Warbird specs are top secret."

"Here's my plan. Our best pilots will fly to Allied countries for a 'vacation,' and once there, they will locate the Allies' elite warbirds and test their capabilities by attempting to outmaneuver them in the air. Our pilots will then file a report that details everything they observed in those encounters."

Gunter scratched his head while he contemplated Göring's scheme. "Outmaneuver them how?

"Do I have to paint you a picture? Surely, an experienced pilot like yourself knows how to create an aerial provocation or force a confrontation. Many tactics come to mind: You could intercept the Allied planes, block their flight paths, compel them to engage in evasive maneuvers, or try to force them down. Don't worry about the consequences. If things go badly and our pilots are caught or prosecuted, they can claim they were intercepted, rudely provoked, and forced to defend themselves."

"It's a perilous plan, Hermann. Shouldn't we work out the specifics and eliminate some risks before implementing it?"

"No. You will go to England and France and gather intelligence on their best warplanes. Check weather conditions, service your plane, and pack your bags. I want you to leave immediately."

Gunter drew a deep breath and exhaled, blowing out his cheeks. Grudgingly, he acquiesced. "All right, Hermann, I'll do as you say."

"Good. After you return and the other pilots have filed their reports, I want you to schedule a meeting with our best engineers and get to work on improving our existing aircraft and designing new warbirds. Have the meeting in a secure place. Use the secret base in Bavaria again."

◆◆◆

Anna left work early, rode the S-Bahn to Lehrter Bahnhof, and walked to the apartment she shared with Weber. She wanted to discuss something with Weber before the boys arrived home from school. Upon entering the apartment, she found Weber reading the newspaper in the living room.

Weber was surprised to see Anna; he dropped the paper and stood to greet her. "Anna, what brings you home at this hour?"

"I heard something at work today that I think you should know about--a spy operation that Göring and Gunter are undertaking."

Inwardly, Weber smiled. This was a first. He'd suggested to Anna that the two of them collaborate, but thus far, she'd been evasive and hadn't done anything to support his mission. This disclosure implied that she had made a decision, or perhaps had conquered her fears and doubts, and was now ready to work with him. If so, he welcomed the opportunity.

"What kind of spy operation are those thugs planning?"

"Göring's devised a scheme for gathering intelligence on Allied military aircraft. He's sending German pilots to Allied countries to assess the capabilities of the Allies' most advanced aircraft. Gunter, for example, will fly his plane to Britain and France to spy on their latest fighters. After the pilots complete their missions, Göring will use their reports to engineer and build aircraft superior to their Allied counterparts."

"Anna, if I might be so bold, let me just say this is a daft plan. How are the German pilots going to access this intelligence? Are they going to steal the specs from aircraft manufacturers, break into military bases, kidnap some aeronautical engineers, or hijack Allied aircraft?"

"I don't know, Robert. Nothing was said about that in the conversations that I overheard."

◆◆◆

Weber and Anna sat across from Taylor at a table inside the Weissbrot Café. Weber had reserved the table even though he'd considered it an odd meeting place. Taylor had insisted that they break their pattern of meeting at the Hotel Adlon and gather at a nondescript, public location where there'd be little risk of surveillance.

As Weber looked across the table at Curtis Taylor, he noticed some subtle changes in his friend's appearance. Taylor's posture was hunched, his forehead creased with deeper stress lines and his eyes darted about when he spoke. His speech was clipped, and he had a stern, brusque disposition that had replaced his usual friendly demeanor.

"It's good to see you again, Curtis. How was your trip?"

"It wasn't easy. The Germans are restricting flights into the country and tightening security at airports. They thoroughly searched me and my plane when I landed in Berlin."

"That's a bad omen. It's going to make it more difficult for us to meet."

"Yes. We'll need to change the way we exchange information. But let's focus on the matter at hand and discuss that later."

Weber placed his hand on top of Anna's. "Curtis, I'd like you to meet Anna. She's the reason for this meeting. As I explained, Anna is an aeronautical engineer inside the Reichswehr and is privy to Germany's secret rearmament plans and activities."

"I'm pleased to make your acquaintance, Anna. I realize that you're taking an enormous risk by working with us. I am indebted to you, as is my boss, Troy Furst. If you need anything, or there's something I can do for you, please don't hesitate to ask."

"Thank you, Mr. Taylor; I will keep that in mind. Robert arranged this meeting because I've become aware of a spy operation needing immediate attention. A newly-elected Reichsminister, Hermann Göring, spearheads the movement to rearm Germany's air force. He and one of his henchmen, Gunter Meissner, have developed a plan to spy on Allied warplanes and utilize the data to build aircraft that surpass their rivals. They aim to ensure that Germany achieves air superiority in the next war."

Taylor frowned and squirmed in his chair. "That's very concerning, Anna. When will this operation commence, and how will Meissner gain access to classified aviation specs?"

"Meissner will fly to England sometime this week, and from there, he'll travel to France. Unfortunately, I don't know the mechanics of the spy operation."

Taylor shifted his gaze toward Weber. "Robert, if this plan succeeds, the Allies could be seriously disadvantaged in the next war. I'll advise our international counterparts and suggest they tighten security at aviation facilities. But stopgap measures might not be enough to neutralize this threat, so I want you to shadow Meissner and find out how and where he gathers intelligence. Stay in contact with me in case Furst wants you to intervene or stop this operation. If things get out of hand, he might want you to terminate this operative."

"If it comes to that, Curtis, you won't have to ask me twice."

Taylor nodded and then turned toward Anna. "Anna, I have a favor to ask, and it's a rather large one. We'd like to know more about the rearmament program and, specifically, the work you and your colleagues are doing to advance military aviation. Your position inside the Reichswehr and your access to aircraft development and production make you an incomparable source. Would you be willing to provide us with that information?"

Anna inhaled sharply, and the color drained from her face. She pushed back her chair, stood, and walked toward the women's WC, mumbling about freshening her makeup.

Aghast, Taylor looked toward Weber for reassurance. "Did I overstep, Robert? I didn't mean to frighten her. What should we do?"

Weber considered pursuing Anna but decided against it, figuring she needed time alone to regain her composure. His supposition proved accurate when, a few minutes later, Anna returned to the table, appearing calm and collected. She seated herself and stared at Taylor as if looking right through him. "I'll think about your proposition, Mr. Taylor, but I can't make any promises. What you're asking me to do is dangerous--not only for me but also for my family, and I won't do anything that might endanger my family."

"I understand, Anna. Please give it some thought and let me know what you decide."

Rather than reply, Anna stood, buttoned her coat, and slung her handbag over her shoulder. "Sorry, gentlemen, but I must depart. I have appointments to keep. Robert, I will see you at home this evening." She briefly made eye contact with Weber, then turned and walked out of the café.

There was an awkward silence at the table as Weber and Taylor struggled to come to grips with Anna's abrupt departure. Taylor chastised himself for backing Anna into a corner and struggled to think of ways to restore his credibility and earn her trust. Weber worried that Taylor's botched recruitment attempt would erode the newfound trust he and Anna had developed and dissuade her from participating in his mission.

Eventually, Taylor grew tired of wrestling with his guilt and spoke. "This is my fault, Robert. I should have been more sensitive. I didn't consider what Anna might be ready to handle; I just assumed that she'd sell out her colleagues and betray her country. I pushed her too hard and too fast."

"I agree, Curtis. We may have fractured her trust, so we must be patient and see where the pieces fall. Treason isn't what she's concerned about; it's protecting her family. She's no friend of the Nazis and has already committed espionage to thwart their military ambitions. Her hesitancy stems from her relationship with Hermann Göring and Gunter Meissner. She grew up with those men, and something about her history with them makes her worry about her family's safety. She says it's their animosity toward the Jews, but I think it's more than that."

"I sympathize with her situation. Please inform me of her decision. I need to depart soon so I'd like to discuss changes in our mode of communication. During my recent trip, I realized that it might not be feasible to fly across the border to meet with you in Germany. If I can't be your courier, we must find an alternative way to transfer documents and share confidential information. Unless you have a better idea, you or someone you trust will have to bring classified information out of Germany and deliver it to a predetermined neutral location. Sweden and Switzerland seem like good options, as France is crawling with German agents. Of course, if you choose to go to Sweden, you will have to travel by air or sea, whereas Switzerland can be accessed by car, train, or even on foot. You will need to explore these options and assess the risks involved, especially if Anna decides to provide you with classified information. Please let me know if there is anything I can do to help."

Taylor's instructions and admonishments had a sobering effect on Weber's mood. He already felt isolated, working as an enemy agent in hostile territory, and now his connection to his former life had been cut or severely curtailed. As Taylor finished his lunch and prepared to leave, Weber felt alone and vulnerable. He wondered whether he'd ever see his friend again.

◆◆◆

After topping up his wing tanks with Avgas, Weber crawled into the cockpit of his Junkers JU 49 and taxied onto Johannisthal Air Field's north-south runway. Gunter's plane, the Fokker D.XII that belonged to Hermann Göring, had just taken off from the same runway. Weber maxed the throttle, waited until the Junkers gained sufficient speed, and retracted the yolk. The Junkers rose smoothly from the runway and ascended rapidly into a partly cloudy sky. Weber searched the horizon until he spotted Gunter's plane and then brought the Junker's nose around until it was on the same heading as the Fokker but positioned at a higher altitude.

Weber settled in for what he thought would be a long flight. He was convinced that Gunter was going to England to spy on Allied aircraft. He'd followed Gunter twice before and been disappointed. This time, he'd bribed the airport manager and learned that Amsterdam was Gunter's destination. It was a short hop from Amsterdam across the North Sea to London.

◆◆◆

After a brief layover in Amsterdam, Weber tailed Gunter across the North Sea and kept the Fokker in his sights until it landed at Croydon airport, south of London. He circled the airport multiple times to ensure that Gunter had time to park his plane and leave. Then he landed the Junkers and parked it behind a hangar, well out of sight of Gunter's plane. It was a short walk to the terminal, and once there, Weber hailed a cab and asked the driver to find him a hotel nearby. The driver obliged, and after renting a room, Weber turned in for the night.

Weber arose before dawn, took a cab to the airport, and searched for Gunter's plane. When he found it, he looked for a place to observe the Fokker surreptitiously and await Gunter's arrival. It proved challenging to find a suitable location, so he positioned himself under a large truck parked about halfway between Gunter's plane and his own.

Sleep overcame Weber's vigilance, and he awoke to the roar of an engine. He struggled to localize the sound and realized, to his dismay, that the source was just overhead. The thunder was coming from the truck's engine bay. Soon, there were additional sounds--the hiss of a hydraulic clutch and the clank of a gearshift--and then the truck lurched forward. Weber instinctively rolled sideways to avoid being crushed by the behemoth's massive tires. Once clear, he got to his feet, ran for cover, and resumed his vigil from the alcove of a nearby building.

Gunter arrived shortly after dawn and inspected the Fokker. When his flight check was completed, he fired up the engine, taxied onto the runway, and took off to the east. Weber waited until Gunter had departed, then dashed to the Junkers and gave chase.

Once in the air, Weber again positioned the Junkers well above and behind Gunter's Fokker. Over an hour passed as the planes cruised across the English countryside in an easterly direction toward Norwich, a coastal city in England's Norfolk County. As the aircraft neared the coast, the Fokker began to descend. Weber hung back and circled overhead, angling the Junkers to observe Gunter's destination.

While the Junkers sustained a holding pattern, Weber withdrew a hand-drawn map from his flight jacket and tried to pinpoint his location. Before leaving Berlin, he'd visited the library and sketched the locations of aerodromes and airports in the southern portion of England. From the Fokker's position, he guessed that Gunter was approaching Mousehold Heath, a former WWI aerodrome still serving as an English air base.

Movement on the horizon caught Weber's attention, so he shifted his focus and scrutinized the approaching object. It was an RAF fighter traveling inland from the coast, flying on a westbound heading toward Mousehold Heath. It was apparent that Gunter had also spotted the plane because he banked the Fokker and put it on a heading that would intercept the fighter.

Weber watched in horror as Gunter flew the Fokker on a head-on collision course with the approaching fighter. As the gap closed, the fighter broke off, arced skyward until it was inverted, then rolled upright, reversing its heading. Undeterred, Gunter adjusted course and pursued the fighter, pushing the Fokker until the planes were abreast of each other. He banked aggressively, tipping the Fokker's nose and propellers toward the fighter's wings.

The pilot of the fighter plane took immediate evasive action, this time by descending precipitously, allowing the Fokker to pass overhead harmlessly. This adept maneuver, however, failed to shake off the seemingly crazed attacker. Gunter circled and set the Fokker on another collision course, this time with the midsection of the fighter's fuselage.

Weber felt helpless because there was nothing he could do to stop the attack. He'd have blown the Fokker out of the sky if his plane had been armed. But it wasn't, so he could only shout and curse, even though he knew Gunter couldn't hear him. "Du verrückter Nazi! Scheiße fürs Gehirn! Du gehörst in eine Anstalt!"

The aerial brawl continued for what seemed like hours, and then suddenly Gunter withdrew and put the Fokker on a westerly heading toward London. Weber breathed a sigh of relief, wiped the sweat from his brow, and watched the Fokker retreat. When the Fokker became a distant speck on the horizon, he banked the Junkers to the west and set a course for Croydon airport.

The next day was a repeat of the former, only this time Gunter pounced on a squadron of RAF fighters on maneuvers off the coast of Cornwall, on England's southwestern coast. The pseudo-dogfight ended quickly because the RAF fighters outnumbered Gunter, and they dominated every aspect of the encounter. Even so, Gunter forced the pilots to perform defensive maneuvers that revealed the fighters' capabilities during quasi-combat conditions.

Gunter's sorties continued unabated, and the audacity of his attacks grated on Weber's nerves. It angered him to stand by and watch Gunter bully English pilots with impunity. Something had to be done. But what? He began to channel his anger into fantasies in which he sabotaged Gunter's plane or murdered him in his sleep. But then it occurred to him that those were the same tactics that Gunter had used to harm his family. Suitably chastened, he steadied his nerves and soldiered on.

Early the next morning, British MPs wheeled into Croydon and began inspecting aircraft. Weber had just topped up the Junker's tanks when a sergeant approached and asked what he was doing in England and why he was flying a German plane. Weber showed the constable his US diplomatic passport and explained that he was an agent of the US government stationed in Berlin. The constable seemed satisfied, and as he turned to leave, Weber asked what had precipitated the inspection. The sergeant explained that they were searching for a rogue German plane--one that had violated British air regulations. Weber turned to point out Gunter's plane but then noticed that it was missing. "Sergeant, I think you're looking for a Fokker, typically parked next to that grey hangar. It's gone now, but you'll probably find it there this evening." The constable nodded and then walked away.

Weber gunned the Junkers onto the runway, took off, and eventually found Gunter's plane south of the airport. He fell in behind the Fokker and told himself to relax; he was seething because Gunter had eluded the MPs' dragnet and was free to continue his campaign of aerial confrontations. However, Weber was spared further torment when Gunter deviated from his usual pattern and flew south to the white cliffs of Dover, out across the English Channel, and on toward the port of Le Havre. Weber surmised that Gunter had completed his work in England and was moving to France. From their flying route, he guessed that Paris was Gunter's destination.

◆◆◆

After landing at Paris-Le Bourget airport, Weber purposely situated the Junkers near a service facility opposite the airport from where he'd seen Gunter park. The facility was located alongside a runway in an oversized warehouse that doubled as a repair shop and hangar. Weber entered through a tall corrugated steel door, found the manager, and rented hangar space for the Junkers. While the ground crew towed the Junkers into the hangar, he asked to use the telephone and called Curtis Taylor. Taylor greeted him warmly and suggested that Weber take a cab to his apartment at 25 Place du Panthéon in Paris' fifth arrondissement.

Taylor's apartment was far more opulent than Weber had imagined. It took up two floors in a neo-classical building directly across from the Panthéon. A marble staircase connected the first and second floors with a gilded gold leaf railing. Inlaid tile, arranged in artistic patterns, covered the floors, and original artwork adorned the walls. Each of the ten rooms was filled with sculptures and expensive furniture.

"What a charmed life you lead, Curtis. I didn't realize you had such aristocratic tastes. How can you afford this place?"

"It belongs to Furst's wealthy French friend Claude Leman. I'm looking after the place while he's tending his vineyards in Provence."

Taylor took Weber to lunch at a nearby café, and as they dined, Weber recounted his experiences in England. "Gunter Meissner's a menace, Curtis, and not just because his spying is furthering Göring's rearmament ambitions. He endangered many pilots in England, and now he's going to perpetrate the same madness here in France. Please ask Furst to let me end this fiasco."

"What do you have in mind?"

"Just ask if I can put an end to Gunter's operation. If Furst agrees, we can discuss tactics."

For the next few days, Weber obtained some much-needed rest and entertained himself by wandering the streets of Paris, admiring the architecture and sampling the cuisine in local cafes. It was the first opportunity he'd had in months to let down his guard, shed his role as a spy, and be himself. It was a welcome respite, easing his worries and shifting his priorities. He was no longer obsessed with Gunter and the threat he posed to Allied pilots. Those thoughts receded into the back of his mind and were supplanted by musings about his life with Anna, Carl, and Luka.

His reverie ended early one morning when Taylor pounded on the door to his bedroom. "Robert, I heard from Furst, and he wants you to resume your surveillance immediately. He's specified some conditions for the remainder of your mission. Get up, and I'll fill you in at breakfast."

The two men walked to the Café du Cinq Cours and sat at an empty table next to a pedestrian walkway crowded with passersby. Service was slow, but a bearded man wearing a stained apron eventually arrived at their table, poured coffee, and took their orders.

"Furst didn't endorse your request, Robert. He doesn't see how you can end Gunter's mission without causing an international incident. An unauthorized skirmish with a German agent could worsen the tense diplomatic relations between the United States and Germany. That's his official position. Off the record, however, he stopped short of prohibiting the undertaking entirely. He said he found it difficult to imagine how you'd pull off that kind of operation without triggering an incident and blowing your cover."

"So Furst won't authorize the operation officially, but he wouldn't object if it were accomplished surreptitiously?"

"It depends on what you mean by surreptitious. Furst said the operation couldn't appear premeditated, nor could any aspect of it be traced back to you or the United States government. That means no witnesses, and it rules out assassinations. Basically, you couldn't leave bullet holes in Meissner or his plane. You don't have any realistic options."

"So it would seem, Curtis. But let me think it over and get back to you."

At dinner the following evening, Weber presented Taylor with a list of demands. "I need two things from you, Curtis. First, loan me some French francs so I can do some repairs on my plane. Second, help me find an old friend named Françoise Durand. I flew with Durand during the First World War, and if my luck holds, he's still living in France, perhaps even in Paris.

Taylor said he'd use his connections to search for Durand. Then he extracted a wad of bills from his wallet, but before handing them to Weber, he looked his friend in the eye. "Please tell me you're not going to do anything foolish." Weber smiled, and then Taylor sighed and handed him the money.

Weber returned to Paris-Le Bourget airport and scheduled some time to work on his Junkers in one of the service facility's repair bays. The manager kindly loaned him some tools and sold him an assortment of supplies, including a sheet of scrap aluminum, some small-gauge control wire, and a parachute. Using the aluminum, Weber fabricated a two-foot square box and riveted it under the Junker's tail ahead of the elevators and trim tabs. He left open the side of the box facing the plane's front and covered the opposite, rear-facing side with a hinged flap. Then, he mounted one end of the control wire to a latch located on the bottom of the flap and ran the remainder of the wire alongside the fuselage and into the cockpit.

That evening, Taylor told Weber that he'd located Françoise Durand and arranged for them to meet at Durand's office the following day. He said Durand was now a major in the French military Armée de l'Air and kept an office at the Vélizy-Villacoublay Air Field, thirteen kilometers southwest of Paris. He wished Weber success at rekindling his friendship with Durand but urged him not to reveal classified information until he was sure Durand could be trusted.

Weber rose shortly after dawn, borrowed Taylor's car, and drove to Vélizy-Villacoublay Air Field. The guards at the security gate asked to see his papers, made a call, and then waved him through. He parked in front of an office complex next to a three-story military hangar, then went inside and found Durand's office. An adjutant sitting in an outer alcove told Weber that

Durand was teaching a ground school class for recruits but would return shortly. Weber found an empty chair and took a seat.

When Durand appeared, Weber rose to greet him. “Françoise! How long has it been? You don’t look like the FAS grunt I knew all those years ago. You’ve put on a few pounds, and you’re an officer now--a major, no less.”

“And you, Robert, no longer smell like Avgas and look like the wet-behind-the-ears American kid who begged me to help him become a combat pilot.”

“Alright, let’s dispense with the compliments, Françoise. My ego isn’t tough enough to handle all that Gallic praise.”

Durand chuckled. “Listen, Robert, why don’t we have dinner this week and discuss old times? Unfortunately, I have another meeting in twenty minutes, so we should get down to business.” Durand led Weber into his office and closed the door. “Sit, Robert, and tell me what brings you here.”

“Françoise, am I right in thinking you’re one of the more senior officers in the Armée de l'Air?”

“That’s correct.”

“And would you, or perhaps your superiors, be concerned if a foreign agent was spying on your most advanced military aircraft?”

“Yes, of course, we would. What is this about, Robert--what do you know? And, perhaps more importantly, how would you possess that kind of information?”

“Let’s just say that I work for the United States government.”

“Why so evasive, Robert?”

“I don’t have clearance to say more. Perhaps later, depending on what we’re able to negotiate.”

“What is it that you want?”

“I want to mount an operation to bring down this spy, and I was hoping you’d help me. If you’re interested and your superiors approve, I will brief you on everything I know.”

“I can’t run this up the chain of command without some kind of proof. The brass will want to know if this is a credible threat.”

Weber handed Durand some photographs that he’d taken of Gunter’s aerial confrontations in England. “Show them these photos. Then tell them to ask their counterparts in England whether they’re searching for a rouge pilot who's been attacking British fighters.”

“I’m intrigued, to say the least, Robert. Give me a few days, and I will reply.”

Two days later, Weber received a call from Durand’s adjutant instructing him to return to Vélizy-Villacoublay Air Field for a late afternoon meeting. When Weber arrived, Durand told him that his superiors had approved the mission on the condition that they receive a full report of the operation and its outcome.

"The brass want to purge this spy, Robert, and they also want to know who he's working for. So do I. Now that we have an arrangement, what can you tell me?"

Weber told Durand about Göring's plan and Gunter's strategy for gathering intelligence on Allied aircraft. He explained that he monitored Gunter's exploits in England and followed Meissner to Paris. Durand was incensed.

"It is just as I expected. The Germans are spying on us. It's further proof that another war is in the offing. Remember the last war, Robert? We're lucky we survived. How can we possibly endure another one?"

"The people I work for want to prevent that from happening. Are you free for dinner? We can catch up, and I'll tell you what I have in mind."

Weber drove Durand to Café Le Chat Rouge and ordered champagne. "Françoise, let's toast to surviving the Great War." They tapped their flutes and drank deeply.

Then Durand proposed a toast. "To surviving the night we strafed a German aerodrome." He held up his glass and searched Weber's face for signs of recognition. "Do you remember that night, Robert?"

"How could I forget? It's rarely far from my consciousness, Françoise. In fact, I knew these same two Germans--Hermann Göring and Gunter Meissner--when I worked for Svensk-Luft Trafik Airlines in Sweden. We were at a bar one night, and they wanted to know if I had any experience with night flights. I told them about our trip to the aerodrome, and they reacted very strangely."

"For some, war breeds an enduring contempt for one's adversaries."

"I suppose so. They made it clear that anyone who flew for the French Air Service was beneath contempt. After they found out that I flew for the FAS, they treated me like dirt and tried to harm my family. Meissner tried to get me arrested by the Swedish authorities, killed my wife by sabotaging our plane, and attempted to murder my son and me in our sleep."

"Mon Dieu, quel diable! Now I understand why you are so determined to stop this scoundrel. Your motives are personal as well as professional. Meissner isn't just a spy; he's an assassin."

"Meissner plans to gather intelligence on France's newest fighters by observing their capabilities during defensive maneuvers. He'll intercept new or experimental military aircraft while airborne and try to knock them out of the sky. I've seen him try to bump, ram, and crash into aircraft."

"What's your plan, Robert? How can we rid France of this menace?"

"François, could you book some flight time in an advanced or experimental military fighter? If so, here's my plan: I'd like you to be a decoy. You'd take off in that plane, cruise the skies, and let Meissner find you. When he does, you'd lure him into a chase across France until his plane approaches the German border. I'll take over from there."

Durand ate the last bite of his meal and downed the last few drops of champagne. Then he stood and motioned toward the door. "Robert, take me back to the airfield. There's a plane I want to show you."

When they arrived at the base, Durand led Weber inside the three-story hangar and pointed to a parked plane in a service bay. The aircraft's cowling had been removed, and a crate containing an aircraft engine was on the floor underneath the front of the plane. Weber whistled. "That looks like a modified Dewoitine 500."

"That's right. You were always good at identifying aircraft, Robert. Notice how the cockpit's been enclosed and the wings have been reshaped? See how the tail section's been streamlined? Now, take a look at the engine that's in that crate under the nose. That's a modified V-12 that will produce over a thousand horsepower. The former mill was plenty capable; it produced 691 horsepower. But with this boost in power and the craft's enhanced maneuverability, few fighters will stand a chance against it."

"I'm impressed, Françoise! Is this the plane you'll use to entrap Meissner?"

"One look at this bird, and he won't be able to resist. He'll follow me anywhere."

"I suspect you're correct. I happen to know that Göring's agents are searching for a Dewoitine, so this plane will certainly get his attention."

"The mechanics should have the engine installed in a day or two. Two mules or test planes were used to develop and evaluate the modifications, so I know this plane will be airworthy."

"Great. Check your schedule, give me a day and a time, and we'll embark on this operation."

◆◆◆

Weber was seated at a Louis XIV-style Giltwood table in Taylor's sumptuous dining room, preparing to consume the first course of the evening's meal. Usually, he and Taylor went to a café for their meals, but

Taylor had decided that tonight's dinner conversation was too sensitive for that venue.

Weber helped himself to a large portion of Chateaubriand while Taylor filled their champagne flutes. When the flutes were full, Taylor raised his and proposed a toast. "To the success of your mission, Robert."

Weber lifted his flute and tapped it against Taylor's. "Here, here."

Taylor sipped some champagne and then asked Weber to give an account of the classified information he had shared with Françoise Durand. He also wanted to know how Durand had responded to the news that a German was spying on France's military aircraft.

Weber summarized his meetings with Durand, but the phone rang before he could explain that Durand and his military superiors had approved his plan to end Gunter's mission. Taylor answered and handed the phone to Weber, saying the call was from Durand.

"Hello Robert, there's been a development. A French pilot was harassed by Meissner today and was killed when his fighter spiraled into the ground. My commander is furious and he wants the German found and prosecuted immediately. He's not going to wait for us to execute our mission. A squadron of gendarmes has been dispatched to Paris-Le Bourget airport to arrest Meissner and impound his plane."

"Françoise, I understand your commander's anger, but sending a squadron of gendarmes to search an entire airport seems misguided. That tactic is not only predictable, but it lacks finesse. The gendarmes don't have a description of Gunter or know his plane's location, so their search will be indiscriminate and conspicuous. The English police used the same tactic when I was in London. Gunter saw them coming and absconded long before they could find and detain him."

"I suspect you are right, Robert, but I don't have a say in the matter. The commander's issued orders, and the search is underway."

"Well, I wish him luck. Let me know what happens."

◆◆◆

Weber met Durand for breakfast the following day. "Any news, Françoise?"

"Some, but none of it good. The gendarmes searched every square inch of the airport and found neither Gunter nor his plane. That sewer rat seems to have vanished into thin air. My commander is still livid."

"Yeah, it's just as I suspected. Gunter's a bit of a magician when it comes to vanishing acts. Now that he's in the wind, our chances of finding him are slim."

"Robert, we can't let this setback defeat us. Couldn't we modify your original plan so that it's still viable?"

◆◆◆

Weber stood on an elevated platform at Paris-Le Bourget airport, watching sightseers file past the Armee de I 'Air's newest fighter. The aircraft--a modified Dewoitine 500--was parked inside a fenced-off quadrant of a secondary runway. It was the same plane Durand had shown him at Vélizy-Villacoublay Air Field earlier that week.

Durand had convinced his superiors to use the Dewoitine as bait and then placed an article in Paris-soir inviting the public to view the aircraft the day before its maiden flight. He and Weber had concocted the ruse to lure Gunter out of hiding. They figured that Gunter would surveil the Dewoitine while it was on display and then ready his Fokker so he could intercept the fighter during its maiden flight. If the ruse worked as planned, it would give them two chances to capture Gunter: one if he visited the showing and another if he stalked the Dewoitine during its maiden flight.

The airport show was well attended; a crowd materialized, and people roamed around, gawping and pointing at the Dewoitine. Weber scanned the throng, hoping to catch a glimpse of Gunter. He thought it unlikely that Gunter would attend the show but couldn't dismiss the possibility that Meissner could blend into the crowd and remain unnoticed in a turnout this large. He watched the onlookers closely for several hours, but eventually, fatigue set in, and he was forced to concede defeat. The first stage of their plan had failed. Now, he and Durand would have to pin their hopes on the operation's second stage.

Shortly after dawn the next day, Durand fired up the experimental Dewoitine's powerful new engine, taxied onto Paris-Le Bourget's east-west runway, and took off toward the east. The plane rose effortlessly into the brisk morning air; its nose pointed directly into the rising sun. Durand shielded his eyes from the glare, maintaining his bearings by glancing out the port and starboard cockpit windows. When the Dewoitine achieved cruising altitude, he trimmed the plane, checked the compass to ensure he was headed toward the German border, and began searching the surrounding airspace for aircraft. He spotted Weber's Junkers high and behind the Dewoitine's position. Weber had taken off shortly after he did and was following at a discreet distance.

Durand further checked the skies, hoping to identify Gunter's Fokker, but no other aircraft was in sight. He felt a twinge of anxiety as it occurred to him that the German might not show up. "Where are you, Meissner, you damned Boche spy?" he muttered. Then, embarrassed by his breach of military etiquette, he told himself to calm down, get a grip, and give the German time to reveal himself. "Where's your composure, Major Durand?" he reminded himself, "You've only been airborne for ten minutes." The rebuke helped him refocus but did nothing to ease the pressure he was under to find Meissner and bring him to justice.

Weber, on the other hand, wasn't thinking about justice. He was mentally rehearsing each step of his plan for terminating Gunter's mission--and Gunter too if need be. If he implemented it successfully, the plan would end Meissner's mission abruptly, perhaps even disastrously. And if Gunter perished in the process, so be it. After all, he rationalized, there was only so much he could control. He would do the job to the best of his ability and damn the consequences.

Realizing he was lost in thought, Weber refocused on the skies surrounding the Junkers. Ahead, in the distance, he could see Durand's plane cruising on the same heading at a lower altitude. A visual sweep of the airspace surrounding the Dewoitine revealed nothing but an empty sky. It seemed that Gunter hadn't tracked their departure or given up the chase. Perhaps after downing a French pilot, Gunter realized that he was a wanted criminal and had fled to Berlin.

Durand, meanwhile, decided to take matters into his own hands. He banked sharply, swung the Dewoitine around a hundred and eighty degrees, and set a course for Paris-Le Bourget airport. His best guess was that Gunter hadn't observed their departure and was searching for the Dewoitine somewhere near Paris. If that was the case, it made sense to turn around; continuing on an easterly course would only take him further from his quarry.

Weber was surprised to see the Dewoitine reverse course but followed Durand's lead, figuring that his friend had decided to backtrack and search for Gunter near their point of departure. He found it easier to survey the westward airspace because the sun was now at his back, and forward objects reflected the sun's rays. His eyes moved rhythmically, sweeping the skyline every few seconds. Several minutes passed, and then a glint on the horizon caught his eye. He stared at the reflection until the familiar shape of a Fokker fighter came into view.

Durand also had spotted the Fokker, and he changed course to intercept it. Now that Meissner was in his sights, he was determined to force a confrontation. He put Dewoitine on a collision course and spooled up the V-12. As he drew closer, the Fokker banked away from the Dewoitine, descended several thousand feet, and flew underneath Durand's flight path.

Durand gave chase. He initiated a steep dive, pivoted, and then closed in on the Fokker. The German slowed, allowing Durand to approach, and then banked the Fokker directly into the Dewoitine's flight path. Durand shifted course, evading a collision, then signaled Weber by waggling his wings. He was sure now that Gunter had taken the bait, so he put the Dewoitine on course for the German border. For the next hour, he and Gunter engaged in a series of skirmishes, all of which Durand sidestepped by out-accelerating the Fokker. Throughout the confrontations, Durand maintained an easterly course, and as time wore on, the planes passed over Reims, then Metz, and eventually arrived at the German border near Saarbrücken.

Weber remained above the fray by concealing the Junker's position while he tailed the clashing fighters. He assiduously kept his distance to escape detection, flew at a higher altitude, and varied his flight path. Now, as Durand and Gunter approached the German border, it was time for him to break cover and put an end to Gunter's mission.

The bottom fell out of Weber's stomach as he pushed the Junker's yoke forward and maxed the throttle. The ensuing descent thrust him against his seatback, jiggled the flesh in his cheeks, and popped his ears. The plane shook and yawed as it plunged through thermals, descending on a trajectory that brought it a few thousand feet above Gunter's Fokker.

Durand saw the Junkers drop from the sky, level off, and slip into position above Gunter's Fokker. That maneuver, he knew, signaled the end of his role in the operation. It was time for him to withdraw and let Weber take over. He banked the Dewoitine and put it on an easterly course toward Paris.

◆◆◆

Weber noticed Gunter attempting to follow Durand by banking his Fokker, so he initiated the next step of his plan. Before Gunter could bring the Fokker's nose around, Weber descended and positioned his Junkers directly in front of the Fokker. The tactic forced Gunter to level off, slow down, and fall behind the Junkers. Weber waited until the Fokker was several meters behind and then pulled the control wire connected to the aluminum box riveted under the Junkers' tail. He heard a dull thump as the flap opened and the parachute inside the box blew out. Then there was a muffled whomp as the parachute hit the slipstream behind the Junkers, burst open, and enveloped the Fokker's spinning propeller. The Fokker's prop whined but kept spinning as its blades slashed through the parachute's thin silk. But then the chute's suspension lines and harness cords caught in the prop's blades and wound around its shaft, seizing the propeller and stalling the Fokker.

Weber watched the Fokker plummet toward the earth. The plane's nose and canopy were covered in parachute fragments, which flapped violently against it as it picked up speed. Weber guided the Junkers into a holding pattern, allowing him to monitor the Fokker's descent and witness Gunter's demise. The terrain below made it unlikely that Gunter would survive; it was rugged, hilly, and largely forested--an unforgiving topography for an emergency landing.

As the Fokker approached the ground, it began to move in an unsteady and unpredictable manner, indicating that Gunter had lost control of the aircraft. The plane pitched and yawed over the treetops until it struck a tall pine, spun end to end, and crashed into the woods. Weber flew over the forest to assess the damage, but all he could see was a dark plume of smoke emanating from the crash site and a few shreds of parachute silk caught in some tree branches. Weber was convinced the ordeal had ended, so he turned his plane towards the east, gained altitude, and set course for Paris.

◆◆◆

Taylor lifted his eyes from the eggs he'd been pushing around on his plate and scowled at Weber. "I've been trying to assess the fallout from your operation with Durand. Furst is demanding a full report."

Webber shrugged. He sat across from Taylor at one of their usual breakfast haunts, the Café le Croissant Doré. "Ah, so that's what you're upset about. I thought you were displeased with your breakfast."

"You knew Furst's position, and I warned you about the risks. Now, you'll have to live with the consequences."

"What consequences? What have you learned so far?"

"Not much. The French border authorities found Meissner's plane, or what was left of it after it crashed and burned, but they didn't find a body. The cockpit was crumpled and charred, but there was a blood trail leading into the forest, suggesting that Gunter survived the crash, at least temporarily. The fact that they haven't found him, even after a thorough search of the surrounding area, implies that he's still alive, although probably injured."

"OK, so you have a situation report. What about the fallout?" I assume Furst is concerned about adverse publicity, particularly the German government's reaction to the crash. Any news about that?"

"An article appeared in a small French daily--the local newspaper in a border town near the crash site. It's reported in the article that the pilot of a German plane hit a parachutist on the French side of the border and that the parachutist is missing and presumed dead. The local gendarmes are searching for the parachutist and issued an arrest warrant for the pilot."

"That construal suits our purposes, doesn't it? It's a benign interpretation of events that minimizes the likelihood of blowback. It doesn't implicate you, me, or the US government. Furst can swallow that story without getting indigestion."

"Ever the optimist, eh Robert?"

"So, enlighten me, Curtis. What's the pessimist's perspective?"

"Suppose the gendarmes find Meissner and arrest him. Worse still, suppose he talks, and it becomes known that he's a German spy stealing French military secrets. That, my friend, is a spark that could ignite a global conflagration."

"It won't come to that because Gunter will never admit he's a German spy. He'll spin some falsehood such as claiming that he works for Fokker, a Dutch aircraft manufacturer, and came to France to sell aircraft to rich Frenchmen."

"You see my point, though, don't you, Robert? The fallout, or blowback as you call it, is still brewing and could still blow the cover off our operation."

"Alright, point taken. But you and Furst should be pleased with how Durand and I engineered the operation. We brought down a spy without leaving a trace--no bullets, no witnesses, and no one to blame but the spy himself. As far as anyone can tell, some careless German pilot crashed after hitting and allegedly killing a French parachutist. The blame for that egregious act falls squarely on Gunter's shoulders. If there are political recriminations, they'll be leveled against Germany rather than France."

Chapter 19

Fall 1928: Skies East of Paris

Gunter was elated. He had not only discovered the experimental Dewoitine aircraft, but the French pilot had also chased after him and was now demonstrating the plane's capabilities without any prompting. The pilot seemed unaware he was revealing France's military secrets to an enemy. The irony of the situation amused Gunter so much that he laughed out loud.

As he laughed, Gunter felt some of the tension accumulated over the past few days dissipate. It was a welcome relief because the mishaps and hardships that he had endured had been no laughing matter. The debacle began when, somewhat unexpectedly, his aerial provocations downed a French fighter, killed the pilot, and instigated a nationwide search for his plane. After that, he'd been unable to return to Paris-Le Bourget or any other French airport, so he'd taken refuge in a rural area south of the city. He'd risked landing and refueling at a small-town airport and then flown over vast swaths of farmland searching for an isolated, barren meadow. Upon finding a suitable pasture, he'd landed the Fokker and hid it under some trees that bordered the field.

The pasture's turf made for rough landings, but it was firm enough to support the Fokker. For nearly a week, he'd slept under the plane at night and resumed his mission the following morning, taking off shortly after daybreak. However, on the morning that the experimental Dewoitine was scheduled for its maiden flight, nothing had gone according to plan. He had intended to arrive at Paris-Le Bourget airport just after dawn and circle the airport, waiting for the Dewoitine to depart. But circumstances at the pasture conspired to keep him from reaching the airport in time. First, he'd overslept because a mouse had awoken him repeatedly during the night by nibbling on his earlobe. Then, a rainstorm drenched the pasture, and the Fokker's wheels had become mired in the mud. It had taken several hours for the sun to evaporate enough moisture for him to free the aircraft and take off. When he finally reached Paris-Le Bourget airport, the Dewoitine was long gone. He'd searched the area, and then, as he was about to give up and return to the pasture, the Dewoitine had appeared on the horizon and provoked a confrontation.

Gunter glanced rearward and saw the Dewoitine coming up fast on his tail. He eased off the throttle, and when his pursuer came alongside, he banked sharply toward the Dewoitine. The skirmish ended quickly when the French pilot dodged the impending collision, accelerated, and blew past the Fokker. Baffled, Gunter watched as the Dewoitine's profile receded into the distance and became a blip on the horizon. Had he ever seen an aircraft move and maneuver that swiftly? He thought not. He put the Fokker on a heading to intercept the Dewoitine and maxed the throttle. Then he got out his camera and reached for his flight log. He knew Hermann would be interested in this plane, so he needed to document its capabilities.

Catching the Dewoitine proved difficult, and outmaneuvering it was next to impossible. Each time Gunter approached to provoke a confrontation, the French pilot anticipated his actions and slipped away unscathed. No matter how hard Gunter pushed the Fokker, it couldn't out-accelerate or out-maneuver the Dewoitine. Regardless, he continued to pursue the experimental aircraft while photographing the plane and making notes in his flight log. However, while observing and documenting the Dewoitine's capabilities, he failed to notice that, each time his quarry emerged from a skirmish, it returned to an easterly heading.

When Gunter finally paused to check his bearings, he was surprised to discover that he was flying over France's easternmost départements, or counties, and quickly approaching the German border. He berated himself for losing his position and letting the Fokker drift into unfamiliar territory. He glanced at his fuel gauge and calculated that he could reach nearby French or German airports but didn't have enough avgas to return to Paris. While he was pondering his predicament, a German plane—a Junkers—appeared out of nowhere. It cruised overhead, quickly overtaking the Fokker, and descended directly into Gunter's flight path. It was an aggressive maneuver—much like the tactics that Gunter had used to intimidate Allied pilots.

Gunter exploded. "What the hell are you doing? You've deliberately blocked my flight path!" He began to bank starboard as a countermeasure, but before the Fokker could lift a wing, a balloon-like object inflated in front of the plane and blew against the prop. The Fokker's propeller thrashed the object, ripping holes in what appeared to be a lightweight, silky fabric. Gunter assumed that the Fokker would slice through the object and emerge unscathed, but, to his dismay, cable remnants tightened around the propeller's shaft and fabric enveloped the windscreen. The engine whined as it lost RPMs; then it stalled, the prop halted, and the Fokker nosedived.

Gunter's seatbelt cinched against his torso as the cockpit angled downward, and the Fokker spiraled toward Earth. As the plane spun, his throat filled with bile, and his acuity diminished. He fought to maintain his bearings and composure; panic, he knew, would only disorient him further. He needed to pinpoint the horizon and locate visual referents to avert a crash, but he couldn't figure out how to do that when the cockpit windows were covered with fabric. He scratched and pounded on the cockpit windscreens as if that might lift the veil that prevented him from seeing the outside world.

As the Fokker picked up speed, fabric thumped against the fuselage. The rhythmic pounding unnerved Gunter—was this his death knell? The Fokker was in free fall, and he was flying blind with no way to clear the windscreen. The drum beat against the fuselage became more rapid and intense as if building to a crescendo that would proclaim his imminent demise.

Then, the fabric shifted in the wind, positioning some small holes near the center of the forward windscreen. Gunter pressed his face against the windscreen and peered through the holes. He couldn't see much, but it was enough to establish his bearings. He reached for the yoke and flap levers and fought for control of the plane. Eventually, he leveled the Fokker's wings and established a shaky but relatively stable glide path.

Squinting through the fabric holes, Gunter saw that the Fokker was descending into a hilly, forested area. As the Fokker approached treetop level, he retracted the yoke, but the plane continued to descend unabated. Moments later, there was a loud boom when the starboard wing slammed into a tree. The impact caused the wing to break off, and the Fokker spun sideways, flipped over, and crashed into the forest.

When Gunter awoke, he was hanging upside down, suspended by his seatbelt. A searing pain emanated from the back of his scalp. Blood ran down his neck, across his face, and onto the cockpit's ceiling, which was now underneath him. His last thought before losing consciousness was that he needed help, and soon.

Dense smoke, intense heat, and flames greeted Gunter when he regained consciousness. The Fokker was ablaze, and the cockpit would soon be an inferno. Even in his groggy state, Gunter knew that, unless he acted quickly, he would be roasted alive. He mustered his remaining strength, twisted sideways, slipped out of his seatbelt, and dropped onto the cockpit ceiling. The hot metal surface burned his legs and hands through his clothing. Ignoring the pain from the burns and his injuries, he stood, pushed open the inverted cockpit door, and stumbled outside.

The forest was dark, but the conflagration illuminated the area around the crash site. Gunter crawled into the forest, trying to escape the heat and smoke and shield himself from an explosion. He only now realized that he'd lost all sense of time. The crash had occurred during daylight. How long had he been trapped inside the Fokker? He lapsed into unconsciousness before he could arrive at an answer.

◆◆◆

Hounds barking and people shouting roused Gunter from a deep sleep. He glanced around, trying to make sense of his surroundings. He was lying on a bed of pine needles underneath a cluster of trees, the tops illuminated by the early morning sun. As his head cleared, he grabbed a low-hanging branch, pulled himself up, and propped his torso against a tree trunk. That was when he saw it: the Fokker's smoldering wreckage. Now he remembered—the crash, the fire, and his retreat into the forest. He quickly inspected his wounds and then stood and tested his limbs. The gash on his forehead had stopped bleeding, and although it hurt to move his arms and legs, no bones appeared to be broken.

As the barking and voices grew closer, Gunter realized that people—probably the authorities—were searching for him. It stood to reason that the crash and fire had been reported, and emergency crews were searching for survivors or casualties. He had survived, thankfully, but he was a fugitive and didn't want to be apprehended. He gazed skyward to check the sun's position and began a westerly retreat toward the German border.

It was the dogs that worried him most. Once they had his scent, it would be challenging to stay ahead of them, and, in his condition, he could neither jog nor run. He had to distract the hounds or find a hiding place to mask his scent.

He limped and stumbled through the forest, using a tree branch as a crutch, somehow staying ahead of the dogs. It had been twenty minutes or more since he'd heard any barking; perhaps the dogs were still at the crash site, nosing through the wreckage.

Eventually, he came to a fence that fronted a pasture populated with cattle. He climbed over the barbed wire and approached a small barn in the middle of the field. Once there, he slipped inside and reclined on some hay that was strewn on the floor in a corner of the barn. Curling into a fetal position, he tried to rest. The hike had taken every ounce of his strength, and the barn was as good a refuge as he was likely to find. If the dogs came, they'd have trouble distinguishing his scent from those of the cows. Having been raised on a farm, he'd seen that firsthand. Comforted by that knowledge, he fell asleep.

A sharp kick in the ribs awakened him. He expected to see a gendarme with a gun standing over him, but instead, he saw cattle. He was surrounded by cows vying for the hay he was lying on. The impatient bovines had devoured all the straw around him and were nudging him aside to reach the few strands under his body. Rather than risk further blows to his ribs, he rolled off the hay, slid to a wall, and flattened himself against the side of the barn.

Sleep beckoned again, but he resisted the urge and remained alert. The barn had served its purpose, and it was time to formulate a plan and move on. He considered his circumstances and arrived at several conclusions. The cows were inside the barn, so it must be dark outside; farmers sheltered their livestock at night. Further, the animals were hungry, so dawn must be approaching; cows were fed and milked in the morning. If those suppositions were correct, someone would arrive soon to tend to the cows. That left him with only one option—to leave immediately and get as far away from the barn as possible.

Gunter stood and walked between the cows toward the door where he'd entered. When he was halfway to his destination, a flap on the side of the barn opened, and bales of hay slipped through the opening and dropped to the floor. The sound of the hay hitting the floor triggered a minor stampede; the herd turned and scampered toward the bales. In their zeal, the cows knocked Gunter to the floor. He wriggled from side to side, trying to dodge oncoming cows, but the animals trampled him nonetheless. When the dust settled, Gunter lay in a lifeless heap on the barn floor, bruised and bloodied.

This time, when Gunter awoke, a man dressed in overalls stood over him. "Qui êtes-vous, monsieur, et que faites-vous dans ma grange? Gunter didn't understand the farmer, so he shrugged, smiled, and replied using one of the few French phrases he knew. "Je ne parle pas français." Undeterred, the farmer prattled on in French, his voice growing louder and more insistent. Gunter stayed silent, afraid that if he responded in German, the farmer would call the police and have him arrested.

The farmer eventually threw his hands in the air, shook his head, and walked out of the barn. A few minutes later, he returned with a sponge and bandages and dressed Gunter's wounds. When finished, he helped Gunter to his feet, escorted him to the barn door, and pointed toward a path that led out of the pasture. "Allez maintenant et ne revenez pas, les vagabonds les bienvenus ici." Assuming the farmer had wished him well, Gunter said "au revoir" and departed.

Grateful that he hadn't been recognized or arrested, Gunter continued his westward trek toward the German border. Hobbled by his injuries, he walked like a decrepit old man. Perhaps it was for the best, he reasoned. Better to be seen as an elderly invalid than a fugitive German aviator.

Emboldened by his encounter with the farmer, Gunter journeyed along country roads during the day and slept in parks or roadside huts at night. Three days later, he arrived at Carling, a small village on the French side of the German border. As he entered the town, he saw a sign for "Allemagne" with an arrow pointing east. A wave of relief swept over him; once he returned to his homeland, he'd no longer be a fugitive.

He walked westward along the Rue des Prés, and when he came to the center of town, he entered a café and ordered a croissant and a cup of coffee. He knew it wasn't wise to be seen in public, but he discounted the risk because he was hungry and Carling was a tiny village. It was unlikely, he thought, that the crash would have been publicized in such a remote locale. But as he finished his coffee, he saw a man open a newspaper at a nearby table. He could hardly believe his eyes: a picture of himself was on the front page! It was an old picture—one taken during the days when he'd flown with Svensk-Luft Trafik Airlines--but it captured his features well enough for people to identify him.

Gunter stood, walked to the rear of the café, and entered the WC. Once inside, he crawled through a window and walked down an alley until he came to the Rue de la Frontiére. From there, he traveled east until he found a park across from the border control station.

He sat on a bench and watched the guards inspect traffic as it passed from France into Germany. Security was lax, just as he'd suspected. Small towns had less cross-border traffic and more lenient border guards than larger cities. Not that it mattered, Gunter grumbled, because he had no papers; the fire in the Fokker had burned them and all his other personal belongings. To get into Germany, he'd have to wait until dark, find an isolated stretch of fence line, and sneak across the border.

When darkness fell, Gunter walked along the border, searching for an isolated place to scale the fence. He moved south along the Rue de Bois Richard until he reached the Rue d'Uberherrn Courte and turned east. After that, he followed dirt roads and cow paths until he came to a remote, unguarded section of the fence. He threw his coat over the top of the barbed wire and then hoisted himself up and over the fence, landing on his feet unscathed. As he walked away from the fence, he congratulated himself. Finally, he exulted, I'm on German soil!

Gunter spent the remainder of the night in an abandoned roadside hut and, in the morning, hitched a ride with a farmer to Saarbrücken. After some searching, he found the Nazi Party headquarters and asked an adjunct to let him speak to a senior official. The adjunct, who wore a corporal's Sturmabteilung uniform, looked at him suspiciously and asked to see his identification papers and membership card. When Gunter explained that he'd lost all his papers in a fire, the adjunct asked him why he wanted to speak to a senior official.

"Look, Herr—uh, what was your name?"

"Meissner. Gunter Meissner."

"What do you want, Mr. Meissner? Why do you want to see a senior official?"

"I need a transit visa and enough money to buy a train ticket to Berlin."

The adjunct chuckled. "Is that all? Are you sure you don't want a bottle of schnapps for the trip?" Look, Mr. Meissner, we can do nothing for you, so please leave. Beggars and ne'er-do-wells are not welcome here."

"I'm not a vagrant. I work for Reichminister Hermann Göring in Berlin."

"Liars are not welcome either. Next, you'll be telling me that Adolph Hitler is your uncle."

"Don't use that tone with me, trooper. I've known Adolph for years. He's a friend of mine."

"The Hitler who wrote *Mein Kampf*?"

"Yes. I visited him in Landesburg prison while he was writing that book."

Doubt crept into the adjunct's eyes, and his demeanor softened. He raised his arm, scratched his scalp, and then got up from his desk and walked away. Moments later, he returned with another man wearing a Sturmabteilung uniform adorned with sergeant's stripes.

"Mr. Meissner? My name is Truppführer Jāger. Scharführer Kraus tells me that you work for Reichminister Göring and are acquainted with Adolph Hitler. Is that correct?"

"Yes, it is."

"Well then, perhaps you can tell me why someone with those connections would appear on my doorstep without papers, begging for a transit visa and some Reichsmarks?"

"Reichminister Göring sent me to England and France on an assignment, and while I was in France, my plane crashed, and I lost all my belongings. I exfiltrated through Carling and made my way to Saarbrücken. I need to travel to Berlin and report to Reichminister Göring."

"What, exactly, were you doing in England and France?"

"I'm sorry, but that's classified. I've told you as much as I can."

"Perhaps you can't tell us anything more because you haven't had time to fabricate a story?"

Gunter's temper flared, but he resisted an angry outburst. "Look, Truppführer Jāger, let me save you some embarrassment. Call Reichminister Göring's office and confirm my story. He will authorize a travel visa and reimburse you for a train ticket."

Jāger pointed toward the phone on Scharführer Kraus' desk. "You make the call, Mr. Meissner. Let's see if you know Reichminister Göring."

Gunter picked up the phone and dialed confidently. Göring's secretary answered.

"Reichminister Göring's office. To whom am I speaking?"

"This is Gunter Meissner. Please put Hermann on the line." There was a pause, and then Göring's voice could be heard.

"Hello, Gunter? Where are you?"

"Hermann, I've had an accident and lost my papers. I'm at the Nazi Party office in Saarbrücken, and I need you to convince the commander, Truppführer Jāger, to issue me a travel visa and buy me a train ticket to Berlin. I'll explain everything when I get there."

"Be forewarned, Gunter. You've got a lot of explaining to do. But, all right, let me talk to Truppführer Jāger."

Gunter handed the phone to Jāger, who introduced himself by repeating his name and rank. When Göring began speaking, Jāger cringed and held the receiver away from his ear. Göring spoke so loudly that Gunter could hear every word he said.

After hanging up the phone, Jāger was visibly shaken. He apologized profusely and instructed Kraus to prepare a transit visa. Then he withdrew his wallet from the inside pocket of his military tunic, extracted a wad of Reichsmarks, and handed them to Gunter.

"Please accept these Marks with my compliments, Herr Meissner. There's enough here for a ticket to Berlin and some meals along the way. You don't need to reimburse me; just give Reichminister Göring my apologies."

Gunter chose to act kindly. He saluted Jāger and then took the Reichsmarks and put them in his pocket. When Kraus completed the travel visa, he pocketed it and left the office to look for the train station.

◆◆◆

Gunter could tell by the stern look on Hermann Göring's face that he was in deep trouble. Shortly after he'd arrived in Berlin, Göring had called and demanded a meeting. He'd begrudgingly acquiesced, and now he was sitting in Göring's office, mentally rehearsing the excuses he'd created during his rail journey across Germany.

Göring began the inquisition by asking what had happened to his beloved Fokker fighter plane. "Where's my Fokker, Gunter? I hope you haven't damaged it. You know I love that plane."

Gunter squirmed in his chair, searching for words to ease the blow. Try as he might, he couldn't think of a euphemism that would shield him from Göring's wrath. Göring was expecting to hear about 'damage,' but terms like 'destroyed,' 'obliterated,' and 'burned beyond recognition' better described the Fokker's fate.

"I guess there's no easy way to say this, Hermann. The Fokker crashed and burned. It's a smoldering wreck."

Göring's lip quivered briefly, and then his face hardened. "How could you let this happen? I trusted you."

"It wasn't my fault, Hermann," Gunter explained what transpired, but when he described how a parachute had mysteriously appeared and engulfed the Fokker, Göring scoffed. "Are you trying to tell me that someone deliberately parachuted into the Fokker's prop?"

"Well, yes. Except there was no parachutist—not that I could see. Only the parachute."

Göring slammed his fists on the tabletop and bellowed. "Do you expect me to believe that? How gullible do you think I am?"

"Implausible as it sounds, that's what happened, Hermann. But hear me out. I'll fix this. I'll go to the Netherlands and ask my friends at Fokker to build you another, better fighter. Then I'll fly it to our base in Munich and have cannons installed in the wingtips. You'll like the new plane because it will be an actual fighter with functioning armaments—real firepower."

Göring unclenched his fists and sat back in his chair. Like the calm after a storm, the dark clouds in his eyes dispersed, and the thunder in his voice diminished. Gunter's proposition had captured his interest. Still, there were pragmatics to be considered. "Owning a real fighter appeals to me, but what about the cost? How would you pay for it?"

"We could use some of the proceeds from our newly implemented National Aircraft Registry to purchase the plane. The purchase would be justified because we need a plane to travel to airports throughout Germany for compliance inspections."

Somewhat mollified, Göring spoke in a conciliatory tone. "All right, make the arrangements, and I'll obtain the funds from the Registry's account. Now, tell me about your mission. What evidence did you obtain that will help us build aircraft superior to the Allies' fighters?"

Gunter's mouth went dry, and when he spoke, his voice cracked. "Uh, well, you see…" he stammered, pointing to his head, "it's all up here. I need some time to write it all down."

"What are you telling me?" Göring said, his anger flaring again. "Didn't you document your observations in a flight log or take photographs?"

"Yes," Gunter replied sheepishly. "Of course I did."

"Well then, where are they?"

"They were burned, incinerated. When the Fokker crashed, the fire consumed everything—my flight log, camera, and personal belongings."

Göring turned toward his desk, withdrew a Lugar from a drawer, and placed the pistol on the table. The color drained from Gunter's face; he didn't know whether to sit tight or run. Göring stared at the gun for several minutes, then picked it up and pointed it at Gunter's chest. Beads of sweat formed on Gunter's forehead, and his hands started shaking.

"Please, Hermann, I know I've disappointed you, but I don't deserve this. We've been friends since childhood, and I've always done everything you asked me."

Göring diverted the Lugar's barrel from Gunter's chest and pulled the trigger. There was a loud click as the firing pin struck an empty chamber. Then he smiled. "My Lugar needs servicing; the trigger sticks. Take it to a gun shop and have it repaired. If you disappoint me like this again, I might need to use it."

One week later, Göring called Gunter to his office for another meeting. Ever the dutiful assistant, Gunter arrived on time and asked Göring how he could assist.

"Now that you've returned from England and France, I want you to focus on two tasks. First, resume the expanded background checks you began on the interns at the Aviation Coalition. Start by finishing your investigation of the wunderkind, Luka, or whatever that kid's name is. Wesselman's been hounding me—he's called the office repeatedly, saying that he can't utilize the kid on sensitive projects until his security clearance is finalized. Second, compile the surveillance data that our pilots gathered on Allied planes and work with our best engineers to design new warplanes. Ensure the engineers understand that our next generation of warplanes must be more than competitive. For every class of aircraft—fighters, bombers, seaplanes, and so on, German planes must exceed the capabilities of Allied aircraft on every dimension germane to warfare--speed, maneuverability, weaponry, and payload."

"I'll investigate the wunderkind immediately. That should soothe Wesselman's ruffled feathers."

"Good. Let me know what you find out."

Gunter nodded, opened his briefcase, withdrew Göring's Lugar, and placed it on the table. "Here's your pistol, Hermann. It's been repaired: the trigger no longer sticks. To ensure I don't disappoint you again, I need to understand your expectations for the aircraft redesign project."

"What don't you understand?"

"I have a couple of questions."

"Ok, shoot," Göring said, picking up his Lugar and fingering the trigger. When he saw the fear etched on Gunter's face, he chuckled. "Sorry, I didn't mean that literally."

"What should we do with the experimental planes developed previously in the secret rearmament program? Like the fighters we are building at our secret base in Munich?"

"Modify them to meet our new standards or scrap them and start over if that's not feasible. I don't want any compromises."

"All right. How do you want the design process to proceed? At what stages do you want to see results, and what should we aim for as the final product?"

"Begin by designing fighters and then proceed to bombers. I want to see the blueprints for every aircraft that the engineers propose. I'll inspect the designs and make changes; every aircraft design will undergo multiple iterations before settling on a prototype. Your ultimate goal is to build an aircraft portfolio—a collection of plans for the next generation of German military aircraft. When that's finished, we can discuss production—building and testing the prototypes."

◆◆◆

Gunter went directly to Horst Wesselman's office and requested to see the files of the interns working for the Aviation Coalition. Before handing over the files, Wesselman's secretary, Frau Schmidt, examined Gunter's identification papers and balked at his request.

"Herr Meissner, I must deny your request because your security clearance isn't current."

Gunter fought back the urge to eviscerate Schmidt and hissed through gritted teeth: "Get Wesselman out here. Now!"

Schmidt snorted derisively and then went in search of Wesselman. She returned with him several minutes later. The sour look on Wesselman's face betrayed his attempt to conceal his irritation.

"Ah, it's you, Meissner. I should have known. Only you would have the audacity to bully my staff and interrupt my morning meeting. What's the emergency?"

"My audacity? It's your insolence that has precipitated this crisis, Wesselman. You've aggravated Göring by repeatedly calling his office and complaining about unfinished background checks on Luka and other interns.

I need to inspect your files to determine what's missing on the intern's application forms and complete the extended background checks."

Wesselman demurred and instructed his secretary to hand over the files. Reluctantly, Schmidt complied. Gunter packed the files in his briefcase and left the office.

Gunter went to a coffee shop in downtown Berlin, seated himself in an empty booth, and spread the files across the tabletop. He began inspecting the files and making lists of the information he needed to gather for each intern. When he came to Luka's file, he scanned the contents and uttered a curse. "Scheisse, there's nothing in this file!" Luka's application form was practically blank. All the kid had written on the form was his last name—Gabel, his age—17, and the name of his school—The Berlin Technical Academy. He'd left everything else blank, including his home address, birth date, place of birth, political affiliations, and parents' names.

Gunter shook his head in disbelief—he was appalled by the kids' brazen disrespect for authority. His disgust soon gave way to anger when he considered how much work he'd have to do to complete the kid's background check. But it wasn't just the workload or the drain on his time that bothered him. No, there was more to it than that. Something about 'Luka the Wunderkind' didn't sit right. Why, he wondered, would an intelligent, ambitious young man deliberately omit essential personal information on a government application? It was suspicious, to say the least. Most likely, the kid was hiding something.

He waved over a waiter, asked for more coffee, and then debated the best way to complete Luka's background check. He hadn't admitted to Göring that the BTA Director had refused to let him see Luka's school records or that Luka and his friend Carl had given him the slip every time he'd tried to follow them home. Not only had those strategies failed, but they had made him look like a fool. He wasn't about to endure that kind of humiliation again. This time, his plan would be foolproof, even if it meant taking some risks.

He left the coffee shop after sunset and walked at a leisurely pace across the city so he would arrive at the Berlin Technical Academy well after dark. Once there, he circled the building, keeping to the sidewalks along the school's perimeter, occasionally shouting, "Here Brutus, come Hündchen," as if searching for a lost pet.

The building seemed deserted. He'd circled it twice and hadn't seen a soul. Some hallways were illuminated, but all of the classrooms and offices were dark. Convinced that it was safe to proceed, he terminated the 'lost dog' charade and began to look for ways to break into the school.

He strode to the nearest door and tried the handle. It failed to yield, so he traveled around the building and tried each door in succession, only to find all the outside doors locked. Next, he pulled out his flashlight and shone it on windows, hoping to find one open or ajar. No such luck. He swore under his breath and racked his brain, trying to think of other ways to gain access. Then he noticed a row of windows underneath the building's first floor, just above ground level. It hadn't occurred to him that the school had a basement or that he could access the building through a cellar.

Gunter walked to a window cloaked in the shadow of a large tree, took aim with his boot, and gave the pane a swift kick. The glass shattered, and shards flew inside the building and crashed against the basement floor. Caught unawares by the din, he ran to the nearby tree, pressed himself against the trunk, and waited to see if the clamor would go unnoticed. After several minutes of silence, he returned to the window and used his flashlight to knock out the few remaining shards embedded in the frame. Then he lay on the ground and crawled backward, feet-first through the empty window. When his hands reached the window frame, he grasped it tightly and lowered himself against the interior wall of the basement. Once his entire body hung against the wall, he let go of the frame and landed on the basement floor with a thud.

It was pitch dark in the basement but not silent. Gunter stood frozen in place, trying to make sense of the noises he heard coming from indistinct locations. He resisted the urge to switch on his flashlight, preferring to wait until he was sure the sounds weren't caused by a custodian, a guard, or someone who had overheard his intrusion. Several minutes later, he stopped holding his breath when he realized that the sounds were mechanical and likely caused by plumbing, heating, and ventilation systems. He switched on his flashlight but covered the lens with his fingers so that only a trickle of illumination escaped into the room.

He inched into the dark, cavernous basement until he came to a narrow corridor in front of four large furnaces, each crowned with a duct system that snaked into the ceiling. Behind the furnaces was a massive tank with large, insulated pipes extending from the top and bottom. At the end of the corridor, he came to a heavy steel door that opened into a stairwell. He opened the door and climbed the stairs cautiously, silencing his footsteps, until he reached a lobby on the building's first floor. He did a slow pirouette, scanning the adjoining hallways and nearby offices and classrooms. Nothing seemed amiss; the place was as quiet as a morgue. Turning to the left, he saw a sign pointing to the Main Office. He walked in that direction.

The door to the main office was open, so Gunter entered and searched for a room where student's records might be stored. He proceeded through the reception area to an internal hallway lined with offices and began reading the names posted on each door. At the end of the hallway, he found a room labeled "Records Repository." He opened the door and flipped on a light. Rows of dark wooden file cabinets filled the center of the room, and bookcases lined three of the four walls. Gunter searched among the cabinets until he found one marked "current students." The second drawer was tagged "G — I," so he pulled it open and flipped through folders until he found one marked, Gabel, Luka. The folder was thinner than most and contained only one form: Luka's application for admission. To Gunter's dismay, the application was incomplete and contained hardly any details about Luka or his family. There were, however, a few entries that he hadn't seen in Luka's internship application. He discovered Luka was born in Munich, Germany on December 10th, 1912. His mother's name was listed as A. Gabel, but the spaces for his father's name and current home address were blank.

Gunter left the building feeling embittered by how little he'd learned about Luka; it was a tiny reward relative to the effort he'd expended, but at least he'd found the kid's birthplace. He'd be traveling to Munich soon to meet with the Aviation Coalition's engineers, and while he was there, he'd make time to visit Munich's Standesamt, or civil registration office.

Chapter 20

Fall 1928: Berlin Germany

When Anna arrived home from work, Weber knew something was troubling her. She stomped into the living room, barely said hello to Carl and Luka, and flung her briefcase on the floor.

"Tough day at the Reichswehr, Anna?"

Anna grunted a reply but didn't elaborate. Weber was concerned but decided against asking what was wrong; the expression on Anna's face told him that she wanted to be left alone.

Besides some banter between Carl and Luka, the evening meal was a quiet affair. Weber tried to steer the conversation toward topics that would elicit Anna's participation, but she said little and rarely smiled. After dinner, Anna picked up the empty plates and carried them into the kitchen. Weber followed; he'd given Anna some space, but now he'd run out of patience and needed to know what was bothering her.

When he entered the kitchen, Anna was rinsing plates in the sink. He approached and stood beside her, but she didn't acknowledge his presence. "What's the matter, Anna? Care to talk about it?"

Anna tensed and lost her grip on the plate she was washing; it slipped from her hands, fell into the sink, and shattered. She stared at the broken pieces of pottery for several seconds and then turned and looked into Weber's eyes. Her head bobbed slightly before she spoke. "Okay, Robert, but not here. The boys might overhear."

"All right," Weber replied, trying to imagine the troubles that Anna might want to hide from the boys. Whatever had happened, he realized, must be serious. "Let's go someplace where we can have some privacy. How about a walk in the Tiergarten?"

"And leave the boys here alone?"

"I'll tell them to do their homework. We won't be gone long. They're old enough to take care of themselves."

Weber put his arm around Anna's shoulder as they strolled through the Tiergarten. She paused, turned to face him, and pulled him close in a tender embrace. Weber felt tears falling on his shoulder, so he tightened his embrace until he felt the tension in Anna's body ease. Then he pulled a handkerchief from his pocket and dabbed at the moisture on her cheeks.

Those few moments of intimacy restored Anna's equanimity and loosened her tongue. "Robert, I'm worried about our future and what will happen to our boys."

"Those are weighty concerns; worries like that can crush your spirit. What's making you feel that way?"

"I see troubles coming, Robert, on so many levels: for Germany, for my parents, for you and me, and our sons. The cumulative effect of all those worries overwhelms me; it's paralyzing."

"Where are these worries coming from, Anna? What makes you think that the future is so dire?"

"The signs are everywhere, Robert, but I see them most clearly in my workplace. The assignments are changing for the Aviation Coalition and the Reichswehr as a whole. Based on what we're being asked to do, it's not hard to infer what lies ahead. Secretly, the Nazis are preparing for another war, and, toward that end, they are accelerating the pace of rearmament."

"That's worrisome, I agree. I've suspected as much from the inquiries that I've conducted, but you're in a better position to observe armament trends than I am."

"If that weren't enough to worry about, I have to cope with the fact that I'm helping the government create the very future that I abhor."

"It must be difficult to reconcile your love of airplanes with the military's aviation objectives, but you've been doing this job for a while. Plus, you and your father have been conspiring against the Nazis. Why have you suddenly developed a full-blown crisis of conscience?"

"Well, until recently, I've told myself that it's not immoral to design and produce new planes; it's only wrong when people use those aircraft for nefarious purposes--like to wage war. And, I've been able to embrace the rearmament program because it seems only fair for Germany to maintain parity with other nations--to preserve the balance of power militarily. However, when Nazism gained a political foothold, people who were in a position to influence the course of military aviation--like Hermann Göring--insisted that the Reichswehr develop aircraft for offensive rather than defensive purposes. Consequently, Aviation Coalition engineers have been told to scrap previous designs and concentrate on attack aircraft. Now, the only way I can do my job is to disassociate my work from its ultimate purpose."

"Perhaps you shouldn't worry so much about the future. As ominous as these trends may seem, it will take time for them to play out, and intervening events may alter the outcomes. Try to take comfort in the fact that these vicissitudes won't immediately affect our lives."

"Oh, but they will, Robert. I haven't told you what happened at work today. A revised duty roster was distributed for the Aviation Coalition, and most of the engineers, including me, have been given new work assignments and locations. That intensified my 'crisis of conscience' and made me worry about what will happen to us and our boys."

"Who's behind this, and what prompted the restructuring?"

"Gunter Meissner came into the office around noon and made the announcement. He said he was acting on Göring's orders. He didn't take questions or solicit feedback, so it's pretty clear that there's no room for negotiation."

"So, Gunter's still alive and back in Berlin. When his Fokker crashed in eastern France, I didn't think he'd survive. I'm amazed that he did."

"Yes, from what you told me about your mission, I wasn't expecting to see him again. He must have been injured in the crash because his arm was bandaged."

"How will your job be affected by the changes that Gunter announced? What are they asking you to do?"

"I, along with most of the Coalition's senior engineers, will be part of a design initiative that Göring and Gunter oversee. Our orders are to design the next generation of German military aircraft and create a portfolio of assault planes, including fighters and bombers. We'll be given intelligence data to ensure that every plane we design exceeds the capabilities of its Allied counterparts. After Göring has approved the designs, we'll move to the secret air base near Munich and begin developing and fine-tuning prototypes.

"Wow, that's a massive undertaking--the Nazis are laying the groundwork for an entirely new air force--one intended to decimate Germany's adversaries. I'd like to get my hands on that portfolio. Can you imagine how Curtis Taylor would respond if I told him that we've filched the plans for the entire German Air Force?"

"Is that all you can think about, Robert? What about us? What about the boys? You've been away in England and France for weeks, and now I'm leaving for Munich for God knows how long. Surely, there are more important issues at stake than your mission."

Weber apologized immediately. "Of course, Anna, you're right. I got caught up in thinking about the design initiative and its strategic implications. The sheer boldness of the initiative says something about the Nazi's plans for Germany's future--the political implications are enormous. It clarifies how Göring and his cronies aim to restore Germany's position as a world power: they plan to use the secret rearmament program to build a strong military to defeat their adversaries and thereby overturn the Versailles treaty."

"I'm still waiting for you to ask me when I'm leaving and how that will affect our relationship and parenting responsibilities."

"Of course--forgive me for not asking sooner. When are you leaving?"

"Gunter is giving the Aviation Coalition engineers two months to create a portfolio of fighter and bomber designs. All designs must be reviewed, tweaked, and approved by Göring before we travel to the secret base in Munich. Once there, we'll live and work at the base until we've fabricated and tested all the components for each design, evaluated aerodynamics, and assembled working prototypes."

"That soon, eh?"

"Yes. What are we going to do?"

"When you leave for the base, I'll take the boys to Munich to stay with your parents until you finish this assignment. That way, when you're not working, we can see each other and do things as a family."

"It's too dangerous, Robert, especially in light of Gunter's other announcement. He said he's conducting extended background checks on Aviation Coalition employees. Göring not only wants to tighten security but also ensure that people who work for the Coalition have attitudes and backgrounds consistent with Nazi ideology."

"Why is that risky? Gunter and Göring already know your background. They've known you and your family since childhood--they went to school with you."

"They weren't Nazis then. The rise of fascism has cast aspersions on my family background, and even if they wanted to overlook my Jewish origins, it would be politically risky for them to do so. Gunter will investigate everyone's ethnicity and political affiliations, so he'll search for my family and try to interview my parents."

"But your folks left Munich and changed their names, so he's not likely to find them."

"I'm sure he will question me about their whereabouts. I'll probably tell him that they died a few years ago, but I'm not sure he will believe me. That's why I don't want you and the boys to stay with my parents. I couldn't visit you while I'm working in Munich because if Gunter or one of his operatives were to follow me, it could lead them directly to my parents."

"Yes, I see your point. It's too bad you can't opt out of this design initiative. If Göring's planning a purge based on people's ethnicities and political affiliations, it seems like you'd be one of the first to be discharged."

"I agree. I suspect I've been protected thus far by my history with Hermann and Gunter and my engineering skills. However, once Gunter finishes the extended background checks, my days with the Aviation Coalition may be numbered."

"Okay, Anna, the boys and I will stay in Berlin while you're away. I'll miss you, but it's probably best for Luka and Carl to stay in school and be with their friends."

Winter 1928: Secret Air Base Near Munich

Anna removed socks and underwear from her suitcase and arranged them in small piles in the top drawer of a dilapidated wooden dresser. She put the rest of her clothing, including military-style blouses and trousers, in the other drawers. After unpacking, she sat on a nearby cot and surveyed her surroundings. The room was small, no bigger than 3 by 4 meters, and looked like a jail cell. The entire enclosure was concrete; nothing adorned the dull grey walls. There was no carpet on the floor; the only light source was a single light bulb hanging from the ceiling. The room had a small window above a desk at one end, an exposed sink and toilet on the wall across from her, and a windowless door that opened into a corridor lined with rooms like hers.

She'd arrived with fourteen other Aviation Coalition engineers at the secret airbase early in the evening. The only other passengers on the plane were Gunter and the pilot. After she and the other engineers disembarked, Gunter led the group to a large workroom where he'd announced room assignments and given a brief orientation. He'd told the engineers to report to the workroom promptly for breakfast at 5 AM and be ready for work at 6 AM.

Thoughts of Weber and the boys kept Anna from falling asleep. She missed them terribly and wished she'd taken Robert's advice and quit the Aviation Coalition. Now, she had no choice but to subsist in this squalid cell and comply with Gunter's demands. She tossed and turned, wondering how many more nights she'd have to lie awake, staring at the concrete walls and ceiling like a prisoner in a jail cell.

The next morning, Anna arrived at the workroom before the other engineers and found Gunter rearranging tables and chairs. He'd created five workstations, each comprised of a large table surrounded by five chairs. Each chair had a name tag, and on each table was a copy of the design portfolio and an assortment of pencils, graph paper, and slide rules. Near the entrance to the room was a food cart that contained coffee, milk, muesli, doughnuts, and a selection of cold meats and cheeses.

Anna poured herself a cup of coffee and speared a slice of cheese with a toothpick. When she looked up, Gunter was standing next to her. He moved closer, invading her space until his shoulder touched hers, and then he whispered into her ear.

"I have some things to discuss with you."

Anna winced and took a step back, alarmed by Gunter's effrontery. "Look, I'm still half asleep. I need some coffee; we can talk later when the other engineers eat breakfast." She quickly walked away, mumbling about 'the call of nature' and needing to find the WC. She glanced behind her, concerned that Gunter might be following, and was relieved when she saw him turn to greet another engineer who had entered the workroom. At least she wasn't alone with Gunter now.

Upon Anna's return, the workroom was bustling with activity. All of her coworkers had arrived and were scattered around the room in small groups, enjoying coffee, eating doughnuts, and chatting. Gunter was at the front of the room, behind a podium, organizing his notes. Determined to keep her distance from Gunter, Anna walked to the back of the room and joined a group of colleagues who were engaged in conversation.

Several minutes later, Gunter asked the engineers to assemble themselves into workgroups by finding their designated seats. Anna, the only woman in the room, seated herself at a table with four male colleagues--Heinz Albrecht, Wilhelm Graf, Helmut Wolff, and Hans Dietrich--engineers she worked with regularly and whose specialty was airframe design. She felt comfortable with these men; it hadn't mattered to them that she was a woman and the only female engineer in the Aviation Coalition--they'd accepted her from the start and, over the years, had come to appreciate her unique talents.

Albrecht was the oldest of the crew--a tall, balding, fatherly figure that Anna respected and often relied on for advice. Aircraft engines were his specialty, and he was known for having created some of the most advanced powerplants used in German aircraft. He was also an experienced pilot; he'd flown for the Luftwaffe during the Great War, piloted commercial planes, and competed in civilian aircraft races. Albrecht knew more about airplanes and how to fly them than anyone Anna had ever met.

Graf was the group's math wizard. He could calculate complex equations in his head and loved math puzzles. Bearded and bespectacled, he looked and acted like an absent-minded professor. He'd spend hours working on complex problems, often so lost in thought that he forgot to eat or sleep.

Wolff had a background in metallurgy and was an expert on using lightweight metals in the design and fabrication of fuselage components, including frames, trusses, and skins. He had a tall, slender build and stooped posture, often making him appear tense or edgy. An introvert by nature, he rarely talked unless spoken to, had a limited social life, and was more of a follower than a leader. Work was his life's focus; he was more comfortable with planes than people and tended to avoid conflict with coworkers and eschew social gatherings.

Dietrich was a year or so older than Anna and, like a rowdy brother, teased her occasionally in a friendly, good-natured way. Physically, he was an attractive man--tall, blue-eyed, and blond--the Aryan ideal--but he didn't flaunt his looks. Like Anna, his specialty was wing and fuselage design, and when the two of them worked on a joint project, he would often challenge Anna to see who could create a better design. Anna typically won those competitions, and, for the most part, Dietrich smiled and acknowledged her victories.

After glancing at his notes, Gunter cleared his throat and began the meeting. "The five workgroups in this room have distinct areas of expertise, including aerodynamics, propulsion, structure and payload, controls and instrumentation, and weaponry. The members of each workgroup are to collaborate as needed to achieve an optimal prototype for each design in our portfolio. Be sure to review the research findings and surveillance reports on Allied aircraft so that every prototype we create and test will exceed the capabilities of its Allied counterpart."

Anna raised her hand. "Our portfolio contains no aircraft that are optimized for defensive applications. As I've said, we can't create a well-rounded air force with only attack planes."

"And as I've told you before, Frau Lichtmanm, the best defense is a good offense. You're to work from the perspective that a superior offensive aircraft can be utilized, or adapted if necessary, for defensive purposes."

There was murmuring throughout the room following Gunter's ultimatum. Others in the room agreed with Anna and grumbled about Gunter's assertion.

Gunter ignored the discontent and resumed his directives. "To fabricate and test design applications, I have hired a team of craftsmen who will live on-site and be available twenty-four hours a day. They can be used as needed to generate and evaluate design iterations; they have the tools to construct mockups, scale models, wing prototypes, engine parts, and so on. The resources you will need to build and test design modifications are also on-site, including woods and metals for fabrications, work stands for model wings and empennages, and an assortment of contemporary instruments and engine parts. The aircraft manufacturers collaborating with our rearmament program will, upon request, supply us with other types of machines, tools, and parts that they are using to build commercial aircraft. I also plan to create novel devices to improve the design process and ultimately help us create radically sophisticated aircraft that will outstrip anything the Allies possess."

Hans Dietrich, the engineer sitting to Anna's left, looked at her in askance. He whispered, "Novel devices? What's he talking about?" Anna shook her head, so Dietrich repeated the question aloud for everyone to hear.

Gunter did not attempt to conceal his irritation. "Hold your questions until I am done speaking," he barked. "But since you asked, Dietrich, I'll ignore your impertinence and give you an example. I will have a large fan installed in one of the corridors to propel air across aircraft surfaces such as wings, control surfaces, and fuselages. One of our interns suggested the idea as a way of studying aerodynamic lift and drag. This isn't the time to go into details, but you can ask me about the specifics later."

Undeterred, Dietrich fired off another question: "So, where is this intern?" Why isn't he or she here to contribute to the design and fabrication process?"

"I would have thought that obvious, Dietrich. The intern is a kid--he's still in school. Furthermore, he has no security clearance because his background check hasn't been completed. Now, shut up, and let me continue."

As Anna left the workroom at the end of the day, Gunter cornered her in the corridor. "Meet me in my room after dinner this evening. No excuses!" She pushed past him without responding and defiantly marched toward her room. Once inside her room, she locked the door, sat on the edge of her cot, and ruminated about Gunter's invitation. She hated to admit it, but she was frightened and repulsed by the idea of meeting Gunter in his room. What, she wondered, does that reprobate want?

After the evening meal, Anna approached Gunter's room and stood trembling in front of the door. She felt defenseless and alone; her only protection was a table knife she'd stolen from the breakfast cart and placed in her purse. However, she was under no illusions about the knife's worth as a defensive weapon; that morning, it had proven too dull to cut through a piece of cheese.

She knocked on the door and heard a voice say, 'Enter.' She swung the door open and saw Gunter sitting on his cot. He smiled and greeted her. "Anna, come sit here, next to me." He patted the space beside him on the cot.

Anna glanced around the room, desperate to find somewhere else to sit. She spied a chair beside Gunter's desk and walked to it. "Thanks, but I prefer to sit here."

"My, my, Anna. You were a lot friendlier when we were kids in Munich."

"I'm not a kid anymore, Gunter. I don't normally visit men alone in their rooms at night. It gives them the wrong impression if you know what I mean."

"But I intend you no harm, Anna."

Anna swiveled the desk chair so that she faced Gunter. "So, what do you want to discuss?"

Gunter reached under his cot and pulled out a tray containing a bottle of schnapps and two glasses. "First, let's toast to old times." He filled both glasses, passed one to Anna, and then raised his glass. “To our misspent youth!”

Anna grudgingly accepted the glass but placed it on the floor next to her feet. “No offense, Gunter, but I don’t mix business with pleasure.”

Gunter poured himself a second glass of schnapps and downed it. “Tell me something, Anna. Why have you never married? It seems odd that an attractive woman like yourself lacks male companionship.”

Internally, Anna felt a sudden discomfort. She wasn't expecting the conversation to take this turn, making her uneasy. She tried to come up with a response to steer the conversation away from Gunter's advances. “My job is the most important thing in my life. It gives me a sense of purpose and fulfills my needs. Men and their desires are just distractions.”

“But I thought you liked men. You certainly acted like you did when we were teenagers in Munich.”

“I’m not attracted to women if that’s what you’re asking.”

“You’ve never wanted a child? You must have had the urge—it’s instinctive for women. Plus, the party is encouraging women to have children. You belong to the Nazi party, don’t you?”

Rather than lie through her teeth, Anna nodded and tried to change the subject. “Surely, my personal life is of no importance. The design initiative is what matters. So, let’s get down to business.”

Gunter, however, wasn’t to be dissuaded. “Having a child is a patriotic duty, Anna, and no man’s more virile than I am. Surely you can see that. And few men can offer you my kind of genes—good Aryan genes. My child would have blue eyes and blond hair and grow into a warrior.”

‘God, spare me,’ Anna thought to herself. Gunter downed another glass of schnapps and droned on. The more he talked, the more Anna wondered where his harangue was leading and what he would do when she rejected his overtures. Rather than find out, she cleared her throat, stood, and walked toward the door.

Gunter ceased talking, rose from the cot, and stood in front of the door, blocking Anna’s retreat. “Not so fast. I assure you that my intentions are honorable.”

“That implies that you have a code of honor. What I’ve heard about your exploits would suggest otherwise.”

“A lesser man would take offense at that remark, Anna, but I will let it pass—this time. However, I must caution you against insulting your superiors. Now, sit down, and let me tell you why I invited you here.”

Anna suspected this was another ploy, but with Gunter blocking the door, she had no choice but to swallow her fear and return to her chair. Once seated, she slid her hand into her purse and wrapped her fingers around the table knife. It was a worthless piece of metal, but somehow, it made her feel stronger. She screwed up her courage and bellowed: "So, knock off the bullshit, farm boy, and tell me why you invited me here."

Gunter inhaled sharply; his eyes narrowed, and his face flushed. He stood, shook his fists at Anna, and yelled, "How dare you call me that!"

"Why not? Hermann gave you that name when we were kids. It was your nickname, wasn't it?"

"What did I tell you about insulting your superiors?"

"It wasn't an insult. A nickname is a term of endearment. Don't be so thin-skinned. Now get to the point, Gunter. Is there something you want to discuss with me or not?"

Gunter paced the floor, glowering and muttering curses under his breath. After several minutes, he regained his composure and returned to his cot. "All right, there's something I want you to do for me—an errand that needs to be done in the city—in Munich—not during the work day, but in your spare time."

"What spare time? An errand? Does Göring know about this? I'm sure he'd think my time was better spent working on the design initiative."

"I'm in charge here, and Göring expects you to obey my orders. He's asked me to do extended background checks on the staff, starting with the interns who work for the Aviation Coalition. You're familiar with Munich and acquainted with people who live there, so I want you to go to the Standesamt, the civil registry office, and search for a birth certificate."

"Birth certificate? But why?"

"I'm investigating one intern in particular--the kid I mentioned in today's meeting. He failed to report his parents' names on his application, and I think he's trying to conceal his ancestry. I have it on good authority that he was born in Munich, so you should find his birth certificate at the Standesamt, and his parents' names will be listed on the document. Bring me a copy of that certificate."

Anna opened her purse and withdrew a notepad and pen. "What is this intern's name?"

"Luka Gabel."

Anna was so stunned that she couldn't speak. She tried to conceal her reaction, but Gunter realized something was amiss.

"Do you know this boy? Wesselman recruited him from the BTA but hasn't allowed him to work in your sector because he's not cleared for classified projects."

Anna stalled for time, hoping to muster her thoughts and regain her composure. She fumbled with her notepad and, in the process, dropped her pen on the floor. She stood, walked to where the pen had rolled, and 'inadvertently' stepped on it. A sharp crack occurred as the barrel snapped, and ink leaked on the floor. "Oh, how clumsy of me. Do you have something I can use to wipe up this ink?"

Gunter sighed, went to his dresser, and extracted a hand towel from the bottom drawer. He tossed it on the floor near Anna and then searched for another pen. When he found one on his desk, he handed it to Anna and repeated his question. "So, are you acquainted with this boy?"

"Uh, no. No, I'm not. Tell me how to spell his name so I can find the correct record at the Standesamt."

"You're going to need more than a name," Gunter replied. "Fortunately, I have the boy's date of birth."

Anna quickly jotted down the necessary information in her notepad and then left Gunter's room with a sense of relief. She walked down the corridor towards her own room, all the while muttering to herself, "You foolish boy, what have you gotten yourself into?"

◆◆◆

Anna borrowed a car from the base's motor pool and drove to Munich, where she parked on a side street near Marienplatz. She walked to the Neues Rathaus, crossed under the arch below the ornate clock tower, and entered the building through its ancient front doors. Inside, she found herself in a dimly lit, wood-paneled lobby adorned with oil paintings of former city officials. There were hallways on either side and a central staircase ahead of her. A sign pointed Anna toward the Standesamt, or civil registration department, on the building's second floor. Anna climbed the central staircase, found the office, and greeted a clerk who was busy making notations in a ledger while bent over a desk.

The clerk stood and asked Anna how he could assist. Anna introduced herself and asked to see all of the Standesamt's birth records for the month that Luka was born. She spoke authoritatively to fend off potential objections.

The clerk, Herr Otto Schmidt, eyed Anna with suspicion. "Do you realize how many documents you're asking for, Frau Lichtmann? Might I ask why you need to see so many birth records?"

"No, you may not, Herr Schmidt. Please just do as I ask."

The suspicious look on Schmidt's face shifted to one of contempt. He retrieved a document from his desk and handed it to Anna. "Complete this application. I don't care who you are or why you're here. You can't look at that many public records until you've completed this application and paid a fee of 25 Reichsmarks."

Anna took a pen from her purse, sat in a nearby chair, and completed the application. Most of what she wrote was accurate, although she did fudge replies to some items and left others blank. When she finished, she handed the application and 25 Reichsmarks to Schmidt.

Schmidt scanned the application without reading most of Anna's entries. "I cannot approve your application, Frau Lichtmann, but I will accept your fee." He smirked and pocketed the cash.

Anna thought about berating Schmidt or asking to see his supervisor. The man was a corrupt, officious bureaucrat and deserved to be disciplined. In the end, she settled on a more expedient approach. She opened her purse, withdrew 100 Reichsmarks, and waived them under Schmidt's nose. "Suppose I contribute to the Standesamt's emergency beer fund? Might that persuade you to approve my application?"

"Why, yes, Frau Lichtmann. I'm sure our overworked employees will gladly assist you in return for such a generous contribution."

Schmidt disappeared through a doorway at the rear of the records office and returned several minutes later carrying a bundle of files. "Frau Lichtmann, there were seventy-five births during that month." He gestured toward an adjoining room. "You may use this room to inspect the files; it will afford you some privacy. You may take notes, but do not write on any documents." Schmidt led Anna into the room and dumped the files on a large, rectangular table.

Anna sat at the table and began looking through the files. Four hours had passed since she'd left the air base, and thus far, she'd accomplished nothing. Perhaps now she'd find what she was looking for—a birth certificate for another child named Luka, who had been born in the same month as her child. Luka was a common forename, and she figured that if she found another 'Luka' who was born near her son's birthdate, she could use that child as a decoy. She'd steer Gunter toward the decoy and thus prevent him from looking for her child.

After examining fifty birth certificates, Anna found only one infant named Luka, and that was her child, Luka Lichtmann. Listed on that certificate were Luka's forename and surname, ethnicity and eye color, and parents' names and addresses—information she desperately wanted to conceal from Gunter.

With only twenty-five files left to search, Anna began to lose hope. What were the chances of finding a birth certificate for another child named Luka? The odds, in her estimation, were slim to none. But she kept searching anyway, and in the sixty-seventh file, she found what she was looking for—a birth certificate for a child named Luka Bergmann. The Bergmann child's birthdate was ten days after her son's, but it was close enough to suit her purposes. She copied the Bergmann child's birth certificate information into her notepad. Then she packed her things, returned the files to Herr Schmidt, and went to her car. She needed to do one more thing before she returned to the base.

Anna drove to the address that was listed on the Bergmann child's birth certificate and parked in front of a decrepit apartment building. The number on the building corresponded to the one listed on the birth certificate, so she went to the front door, found a directory, and read the names listed for the current occupants. She was pleased to see that Bergmann was not among them. It was precisely what she'd hoped to find. Anyone who used this address to trace the Bergmann child—including Gunter Meissner—would find nothing. The address was a dead end.

As Anna drove back to the base, the pessimism she had been feeling about her son's future diminished and was replaced with a growing sense of optimism. She'd found a way to mislead Gunter, and if all went as planned, his extended background check on Luka would founder and reveal nothing about her son's parentage and ancestry. Now, as the final step in her plan, she needed to extricate Luka from the Aviation Coalition's internship program and hide him in a place where Gunter and his Nazi thugs wouldn't find him.

When she reached the outskirts of Munich, Anna stopped at a hotel and called Weber. The telephones at the base were monitored, so this was her only opportunity to tell Weber what had happened and enlist his help with Luka. When Weber answered the phone, Anna breathed a sigh of relief and got to the point without explaining the reason for her call.

"Robert, I don't have much time, so listen carefully. I need you to prevent Luka from participating in the Aviation Coalition's internship program and find him a safe hiding place."

"What? But Luka didn't join the internship program. You forbid it, remember?"

"He's deceived me—joined the program behind my back. Now Gunter is investigating Luka—searching for his parents—and that puts everyone in my family in danger. Even you and Carl may be at risk."

"All right. Try not to worry—I'll start immediately. The boys are in school, but I'll go there now and get Luka. Where do you want me to hide him?"

"Take him to my parent's farm and ensure no one follows you. Tell my dad not to let Luka out of his sight. If things go according to plan, Gunter won't find him there."

"Okay, I'll fly him down there tonight after dark."

"Thanks, Robert. I'd like to tell you more, but I don't have time. I don't know when I'll be able to contact you again. Kiss the boys for me and keep them safe."

◆◆◆

Gunter cornered Anna at breakfast the next morning. "What did you find out in Munich?"

Anna held her tongue, her mind racing, as she tried to think of a way to deflect Gunter's inquiry. Her plan to mislead him about her son's identity was nearly complete, but she needed time to finalize the details. She glanced around the workroom and nodded toward the other engineers eating breakfast nearby. "Is this the proper venue for that kind of conversation? I can tell you what I discovered, but there's a good chance someone will overhear. Isn't there a need for discretion in this situation?"

"Yes, of course, Anna. What was I thinking? Come to my room at seven this evening. We'll talk then."

Anna stepped away from Gunter, silently chastising herself as she walked toward her workstation. Her attempt to stall Gunter had backfired. The last thing she wanted was to be alone again with that serpent in his lair.

That evening, when Anna returned to Gunter's room, she was carrying a stiletto in her purse. She'd seen it in a shop window near where she'd parked her car in the Marienplatz. After her last visit to Gunter's room, she'd prioritized protecting herself with something better than a dull butter knife. This time she'd be ready if that Nazi lowlife tried it on with her.

Gunter greeted her with a smarmy smile as he opened the door. Anna didn't hesitate; she jammed her fist into his shoulder and stiff-armed him aside without saying a word. While Gunter struggled to maintain his balance, she slipped past him, bolted across the room, and perched on the same chair she'd occupied during their previous meeting. Once Gunter regained his bearings, he whirled toward Anna and assumed a threatening stance.

"Pushy broad, aren't you? Maybe someone needs to teach you some manners."

"You don't do well with assertive women, do you, Gunter? Do you need a few minutes to puff up your ego?"

Gunter cursed her under his breath. But rather than take the bait and escalate the confrontation, Meissner stepped back and changed tactics.

"You look tense, Anna. Is something the matter?"

"I have a lot on my mind. Shut the door and sit down so I can tell you what I discovered in Munich."

"Yes, I can see you're tense. Perhaps this time you'll have a drink with me. I have an expensive bottle of peppermint schnapps—vintage quality. I assure you that it will take the edge off your frayed nerves. Just a few sips, and you'll forget your cares."

"I can take care of myself, and I didn't come here to drink with you. Now listen carefully because I'm not going to repeat this. I checked the name and birth date you gave me against the Standesamt's records and didn't find a child named Luka. I thought perhaps the birth date was wrong, so I looked at all the children who were born that month. That search turned up a child named Luka Bergmann, born ten days after the date you gave me. How reliable is your information? Could Bergmann be the kid you're looking for?"

Gunter scratched his chin and stared at the ceiling. Several moments passed before he shifted his gaze back to Anna. "I think you're on to something. I've been suspicious of this Gabel kid from the start. He deliberately omitted information on his application and was evasive when I questioned him. I feel certain that he's trying to conceal his identity and prevent us from learning about his family. It wouldn't surprise me if the kid lied about his name and birth date--in fact, I think that's likely. So, this Bergmann probably is the kid I'm trying to find. He's using a false name and calling himself Luka Gabel. Good work, Lichtmann."

Early the next morning, Gunter called Wesselman at the Reichswehr in Berlin. "Listen, Horst, I have reason to believe that Luka Gabel is using a false name. I want you to interrogate him and see if you can get a confession. The kid's real name is Bergmann, Luka Bergmann."

"I'd like to help you, Gunter, but the kid's disappeared. He hasn't reported for work, and none of the staff have seen him. He's always punctual--never been late for work, let alone miss a day."

"Find him, Wesselman! Search for the kid yourself or get some of your staff to help you. Don't make me come back there to look for him. I'm already on a short fuse because the engineers are behind schedule with the design initiative. Building and testing parts for each prototype takes more time than anticipated. If I have to return to Berlin, it will put us even further behind, and then, I assure you, there will be hell to pay. Am I making myself clear?"

Wesselman's throat went dry, and he was suddenly tongue-tied. "I…I…I…understand and will start searching for Gabel, Bergmann, or whatever the kid's name is immediately."

After a fitful night, Anna woke late and arrived at the workroom after breakfast. She'd been awake most of the night worrying about Luka and what would happen if Gunter found him. She figured that the ruse she'd hatched--sending Meissner after a decoy--would buy her some time but couldn't shake the feeling that it wouldn't prevent Gunter from finding her son. The man was a predator--like a shark circling its prey, anticipating a feeding frenzy--he wouldn't stop until he found Luka.

Wearily, she trudged to her workstation and greeted Albrecht, Graf, Wolff, and Dietrich, who were busy discussing modifications to a fighter prototype. The men paused, glanced toward Anna, and nodded. Albrecht remarked on Anna's drowsy demeanor. "You look terrible, Anna. Are you all right?"

"Thanks for the compliment, Heinz."

"I didn't mean to offend you. I'm just concerned."

"I understand; no offense taken. I slept poorly, and I'm irritable--I probably look like a wreck."

Anna sat down next to Helmut Wolff. "So, where's Gunter? Have you seen him this morning?"

"I saw him in the corridor early this morning," Wolff replied. "He was leaving for business in Munich and asked me to keep an eye on things while he's away."

Everyone at the table turned and looked at Wolff. Anna was the first to speak. "What—Gunter left you in charge—is that what you're saying? You're going to report on us when he gets back?"

"Well, not exactly."

"Well, which is it, Helmut?" said Graf. "Are you snooping on us or not?"

"Look, it's not like that," Wolff replied.

Heinz Albrecht stood and pounded his fist on the table. "Well, how is it then, Helmut? Does Göring's henchman have you on a short leash? Explain yourself."

Wolff drew a deep breath and hung his head. "I'm sorry. This isn't what I wanted—Meissner backed me into a corner and threatened me. It started with a few drinks after work. His room is next to mine, and one evening, he came to my door with a bottle of schnapps and asked if I'd like a taste. It seemed harmless enough, so I agreed, and before long, he was at my door repeatedly, bottle in hand, expecting to sit in my room and drink until the middle of the night. One night, after I'd had a few too many, he interrogated me--asked a lot of personal questions—said he was conducting background checks and wanted to know my political views and whether I was a member of the Nazi party. When I said I wasn't a party member, he asked if I wanted to keep my job. I said that party membership wasn't a requirement for Reichswehr employment. A few days later, he said he'd found something irregular in my background—evidence of sedition—and unless I submitted to his demands, he'd terminate my employment and have me jailed."

Albrecht groaned and shook his head in disgust. "That treacherous swine." Anna and the others at the table quickly agreed and offered support. "That certainly rings true, Helmut," said Anna. "Gunter's made similar overtures toward me."

"Will you help me?" Wolff pleaded. "I don't know what to do."

"Let's turn the tables on Meissner," Anna suggested. "We could work as a group--the five of us. We'll obstruct Meissner and prevent him from coercing and extorting other members of the Coalition."

"That sounds dangerous," Albrecht said. "If Meissner caught on, he wouldn't need to fabricate evidence of sedition."

"That's true," Anna said, "but what's the alternative? Will we sit idly by while he and Göring coerce us into doing their bidding? Will we let them oust engineers who disagree with their political and military agendas? There will be no turning back once they gain the upper hand."

"She's right," said Dietrich. "The only option in this situation is to anticipate Meissner's moves and outmaneuver him. How else can we protect ourselves and our colleagues?"

Anna nodded and made eye contact with each man at the table. No one disagreed with Dietrich's assertion. "It's settled then," she said. "Helmut, find out as much as possible about Gunter's plans and activities and keep us informed. The five of us will analyze your reports and devise sabotage strategies. At the very least, we'll invent false but plausible narratives for you to embed in your conversations with Gunter--webs of lies that will protect our staff and subvert his plans.

Wolff appeared relieved and nodded in agreement. "I thought all of you would hate me! It's a relief to confess my blunder and admit I'm ashamed of myself. I'll do as you say. Perhaps the first thing I should tell you is that Gunter's going to Munich to investigate an intern named Luka. He is the same kid who suggested using fans to study aerodynamic drag. Instead of appreciating the kid's intellect, he's convinced that something in the boy's background disqualifies him from participating in the intern program. Maybe he thinks the kid won't make a good Nazi."

Wolff's disclosure put Anna in a quandary. What, if anything, should she say about Luka? Divulging her secrets could put Luka in danger, but keeping them posed risks as well. Rather than stay silent, she decided to confess to her involvement in Gunter's search but conceal Luka's identity as her son. "I knew Gunter was investigating that intern because he sent me to the Munich Standesamt to search for the kid's birth record. He wouldn't divulge his reasons except to say that the search was part of an extended background check--which we know is a euphemism for the despicable charade that he and Göring have concocted to segregate the Aviation Coalition staff based on their ancestry and political views."

That news took Wolff by surprise. "So, I'm not the only one Gunter's sucked into his nefarious schemes. How did he coerce you?"

"He threatened to father a child with me--sire an offspring that would possess his outstanding Ayran genes."

There was a collective gasp from the other engineers. "Surely you jest," Albrecht declared. Dietrich was indignant: "How could any man sink so low?" Graf cursed: "Lecherous bastard!" Anna laughed disingenuously to defuse the tension, but her false levity failed to lighten the mood.

"Look," Anna said, "I propose dividing the leadership responsibilities for our resistance activities. I'll be the point person for this case, so notify me immediately when you learn anything about Gunter's search for this particular intern—Luka." Glances were exchanged around the table, but no objections were voiced. Anna took that as consent and then addressed Wolff directly. "Helmut, I expect to hear from you as soon as Gunter returns from Munich."

◆◆◆

At the end of the day, exhausted from work and lacking sleep, Anna dragged herself back to her room. She could barely keep her eyes open. Eating didn't appeal to her, but she forced herself to consume some stale bread and cheese that she'd saved from breakfast and then prepared for bed. As she was reclining on her cot, there was a knock on the door followed by a hoarse whisper. "Anna, are you in there? Open the door!"

She got up, opened the door, and saw Wolff standing in the corridor. "Can this wait? I was going to bed." Wolff put his index finger against his lips and slid past her into the room. Anna closed the door and faced Wolff, making no effort to hide the sour expression on her face. "What do you want?"

"I'm doing what you asked--updating you about Gunter's activities."

Anna's sour expression vanished as energy surged through her body. She pulled her shoulders back and stood erect. Her eyes opened fully, and the muscles around her jaw tightened. Wolff had her full attention. "Yes, of course, Helmut. Come sit on my cot and tell me what's happened."

"Gunter's not returning to the base tonight. He's staying at a hotel in Munich. When I asked why, he said something cryptic like, 'The trail's gone cold; I need to get an early start in the morning.'

Anna thanked Wolff and ushered him out the door. As she returned to her cot, she contemplated Wolff's news. His report was encouraging, and it made her feel slightly smug. 'So, Gunter,' she mused, 'after all you're sniffing around, the trail's gone cold? Marvelous. Nose around all you like tomorrow--see if you can pick up a scent. Then run yourself ragged until you realize you're traveling down blind alleys toward another dead end.'

Chapter 21

Winter 1928: Munich Germany

The alarm next to Gunter's cot rang an hour before dawn, jolting him awake. Sleepy-eyed, he rose and stumbled to the exposed sink across from his cot, where he washed his face, combed his hair, and shaved. Then he slipped into his skivvies, stepped into his trousers, leg by leg, and pushed his arms through the sleeves of a white dress shirt. While he dressed, his thoughts--few as they were at that early hour--were focused on only one thing--a steaming mug of coffee. He chided himself for thinking about creature comforts when there was an important job to be done. Had he gone soft? Where was the discipline he had learned in the Luftwaffe and practiced for so many years?

Dismissing the self-recriminations, he reached under his cot, grabbed the shoulder holster containing his Walther PPK, and slung the cross straps over his head and around his back so the weapon hung just under his right armpit. It had been a long time since he'd worn a sidearm, and its weight and bulk felt unfamiliar, even mildly uncomfortable. He thought briefly about leaving the pistol behind but decided against it. Who knew what the day would bring? His journey would bring him into contact with many unfamiliar people, and even though he wasn't expecting trouble, there was always the chance that someone would require a little extra incentive to cooperate.

He fumbled through the drawers of his dresser until he found an anorak large enough to conceal the PPK and slipped it on. Then he went to his desk, pocketed his notes about the Bergmann boy, and exited the corridor. As he locked his door, Helmut Wolff--his gullible and spineless neighbor to the left--greeted him.

"You're up early, Gunter. On your way to a meeting?"

"What makes you say that?"

"You're not in your usual attire--you're wearing dress clothes."

"How observant of you, Helmut. If you must know, I will be in Munich today. I will return by this evening at the latest. While I'm away, I want you to keep an eye on things. Remember our arrangement? I'll keep you out of trouble as long as you do as I say. Verstehst du?"

"Ja wohl, Herr Meissner! I haven't forgotten."

"Good--see that you don't. Watch the engineers carefully. Make sure they do their jobs and don't slack off. I'll expect a full report when I return."

Upon arriving in Munich, Gunter stopped at a café for breakfast and asked the waiter for directions to the address Anna had given him for the Bergmann boy's parents. The waiter scratched his head and said he thought the address was on the city's west side. He drew Gunter a crude map and wished him luck.

It was overcast and raining as Gunter left the café; the streets were wet, and light streaming from the headlights of passing vehicles danced along the pavement and reflected off the windows of nearby buildings. He zipped his anorak as he walked toward his car to shield himself and his PPK from the dampness.

Once in the car, he started the engine, pulled away from the curb, and threaded his way west through the morning traffic. It was slow going because the streets were slick and choked with vehicles and pedestrians. Gunter soon lost patience and began cursing everyone and everything in his way.

His mood improved when he reached the city's west side, where traffic eased, and he could speed past slower vehicles. However, he soon began fuming again because the map the waiter had given him brought him to an empty parking lot. He cursed the waiter, parked in the lot, exited the car, and searched for assistance. Down the block, he found a policeman directing traffic at a cross street. The officer told Gunter that his destination was nearby and gave him explicit directions.

Following the policeman's directions, Gunter arrived at a rundown apartment building in a seedy area. The place appeared to be in worse condition than Gunter had anticipated, but upon checking the address against his notes, he confirmed that he had arrived at the correct location. He parked across the street and surveyed the building; shutters and flowerboxes hung at disparate angles, trash was strewn everywhere, and a large, vicious-looking dog prowled around in the detritus. Gunter didn't like the looks of the place and wasn't in the mood to brawl with the dog. But he reminded himself, as he had earlier in the day, that comfort wasn't his priority. He pushed aside his reluctance and focused on his objective. He wasn't going home empty-handed. Before opening the car door, he unzipped his raincoat and fingered off the safety on the PPK. Then he climbed out of the car and crossed the street.

As Gunter neared the building's entrance, the dog stopped snuffling through the trash, eyed him suspiciously, and growled. Without making any sudden movements, Gunter paused, eased his right arm inside his anorak, and gripped the PPK. He rarely backed down from a fight, but this time, he decided that he had nothing to gain by shooting a stray but everything to lose if he killed a dog that, unbeknownst to him, happened to be the Bergmann's pet. So, to avoid provoking the dog, he kept still and didn't make eye contact with the animal. The dog soon lost interest and began pawing through the trash again.

Gunter proceeded to the building's entry foyer, where he found a directory listing residents' names and apartment numbers. To his dismay, Bergmann was not among the names in the directory. He cursed his luck and tried to think of another way to locate Luka's parents. Maybe, he thought, the Bergmann's had lived here recently but had found an apartment elsewhere in the city, perhaps in a better neighborhood. It certainly seemed possible--anyone in their right mind would be motivated to flee this dump. If that was the case, then perhaps the Bergmann's left a forwarding address with one of their neighbors.

Gunter knocked on doors, searching for someone who would talk to him. His first few queries were fruitless, leading him to suspect that people were either absent or unwilling to open their doors to strangers. Then, as chance would have it, he ran into an elderly couple in the hallway returning from a shopping trip.

"Excuse me, I was told that the Bergmann family lives in this building, but I can't find them. Would you know where they reside?"

The elderly man extended an arm in front of his companion as if shielding her from a threat. "Who's asking?"

"My name is Gunter, and I'm a friend of the Bergmann's."

The old man snorted. "If you're a friend--which I doubt you are--you'd know how to find them."

"Well, I'm an old friend from childhood, and I lost touch with the Bergmanns years ago."

"So, you've not been a reliable friend then, have you? Serves you right."

Gunter shook his head in disgust. Anger burned inside his chest and made him want to shoot the old man. But what would that accomplish? Maybe he could get what he wanted by intimidating the geezer. He unzipped his jacket, leaned forward, and let the PPK slide out of his raincoat. "Look, old man, just tell me what I want to know before someone gets hurt."

The old man looked at the gun, glanced at his companion, and then shifted his gaze back to Gunter. To convince the old guy that he was serious, Gunter pulled the PPK out of its holster and held it at his side. The old man went white and backed up a step. It looked to Gunter as if the old fart had lost his resolve--there didn't seem to be any fight left in him.

"All right, the Bergmanns used to live here- in apartment 4C--but they're gone now."

Gunter made a menacing gesture with the PPK. "What do you mean 'gone?' Where are they?"

"Well, the father--Klaus--died. He worked for the railroad and was killed in a train accident."

"What about the mother? Where is she?"

"I don't know. Helga left after Klaus died. Rumor was that she remarried, but we never saw her again."

"They had a kid named Luka. What happened to him?"

"Luka? Ah, well… I don't know anything about him either."

The old man's hesitation made Gunter suspicious. "I don't believe you. You know something about the Bergmann kid. Tell me before I do something you'll regret."

"Look, stranger, we're not political. We keep our opinions to ourselves. Too many people take offense these days."

"What's this got to do with politics?"

"Well, Luka joined the Hitler Youth, and you know what the Nazis are like."

Gunter bristled again. "What have you got against the Nazi party? Are you saying that there's something wrong with Nazis?"

"Uh, well, no. Of course not, and I can prove it. I own a copy of *Mein Kampf*, and I've read it twice." The old man wanted to say he hadn't understood it either time, but he kept that thought to himself.

"All right, but what does politics have to do with the Bergmann kid?"

"He went climbing in the Alps with the Hitler Youth, fell off a cliff, and died of his injuries."

"Are you sure that's what happened? The press would have reported a tragedy like that, and I don't remember reading about it."

"That's because the Nazis hushed it up. They kept the story out of the papers."

"Oh yeah? How do I know that you're not lying to me?"

"I'm just telling you what I heard. But it stands to reason that if Luka's dead, then he must be buried somewhere. Right? So, if you want proof, look for his gravesite. Hell, dig him up for all I care and see if his bones are in the casket."

"Careful, old man. Don't get smart with me."

"I've told you everything I know."

"So where is Luka buried?"

"I remember someone saying that Luka was buried north of the city somewhere. I don't know which cemetery. Now leave us alone."

"One more thing, and then I'll go. Whose dog is that out front, nosing around in the trash?"

The old man grimaced. "Is that dog loose again? He belongs to a neighbor."

"Well, tell your neighbor that he almost lost his dog today. The only thing that dog is good for is sausage. The mutt will be bratwurst soon unless he takes better care of him."

"You brute!" shrieked the old man's companion. She flung her handbag at Gunter before the old man could restrain her. Gunter sidestepped the projectile, moved toward the woman, and shoved the PPK against her forehead. "Bang, bang," he snarled menacingly. The old lady fainted.

Driving north, Gunter debated whether to trust the old man's information about the Bergmann family. The old guy's statements had, after all, been obtained under duress--at gunpoint, no less. The old fart might have spun an elaborate yarn just to keep from getting beat up or shot. He imagined himself traipsing through cemeteries and tripping over tombstones only to discover that the old man had sent him on a snipe hunt. Enraged by that thought, he gritted his teeth and swore an oath: "If you've sent me on a fool's errand, old man, I'll put a bullet in your brain."

A large cemetery appeared on the right side of the road, and Gunter stopped to investigate. He had driven this far--to the north side of Munich--why give up without looking? He drove through the outer gates and immediately came to a large, domed building with a sign that read: Nordfriedhof Cemetery. He pulled into a parking lot and entered the building through the centermost of five archways that faced the cemetery's entrance.

A burly middle-aged man in a dark suit and tortoise-shell glasses greeted him at the reception desk. The man had a full head of bushy red hair and a fleshy face peppered with amber freckles. "Good day, sir. My name is Horst Doppelsbühl. How may I assist you?"

Gunter nodded an acknowledgment as he glanced around the lobby, leisurely surveying his surroundings. The receptionist drummed his fingers on the top of his desk, waiting for Gunter to reply, and when no response was forthcoming, he cleared his throat and voiced his annoyance. "I am a busy man, sir. Would you be so kind as to tell me why you're visiting Nordfriedhof?"

Gunter shifted his gaze to the receptionist and noticed the name tag on his lapel. "Good day to you, Herr Doppelsbühl. My name is Meissner. Gunter Meissner. I'm looking for the gravesite of a teenager named Luka Bergmann. Can you tell me if he was buried here?"

"Your request is not a trivial one, sir. Do you see those volumes?" The receptionist pointed to a string of floor-to-ceiling bookcases covering one entire reception hall wall. The shelves were filled with leather-bound books. "Those volumes contain personal data for the more than 30,000 souls buried in this cemetery. Finding the name of one person who's been interred here could take weeks."

Gunter made his irritation known by sighing loud enough for Doppelsbühl to overhear. "The challenges of your job don't interest me, Doppelsbühl. Complain to your boss if you think it will help. In the meantime, do what I ask--find out if the Bergmann kid is buried here. It's a simple question--unless you're a dunce, it shouldn't take weeks to find an answer."

Doppelsbühl's lips tightened, his eyes bulged, and his face flushed crimson. "How dare you speak to me that way! Do you think you're the only person who needs my assistance? The best I can do is put you on my waitlist--there are about thirty people in front of you. Come back in two weeks, and I'll tell you how far you've progressed in the queue."

"That won't do, Herr Doppelsbühl. I'm here on government business and insist you expedite my request."

"Oh, I see. In that case, come back in *three* weeks, and I'll tell you how far you've progressed in the queue."

Gunter seethed. He unzipped his jacket and leaned forward, letting the PPK slip into view. "I think it would be in your best interests to reconsider."

The color drained from Doppelsbühl's face. He gasped and raised his hands in a gesture of surrender. "What was that name again--the young man you are searching for?"

"Luka Bergmann."

Doppelsbühl opened his desk drawer, took out a pencil and paper, and wrote down the name. "And when did this Bergmann youth pass away?"

"I can't be certain--anywhere between 5 and 15 years ago."

Doppelsbühl frowned, snorted in disgust, and tossed his pencil on the desktop. "This is unbelievable. You can't be any more specific than that?"

"Don't get testy, my friend, or I'll do your job for you." Gunter stomped from Doppelsbühl's desk to the wall of bookcases, pulled a volume off a shelf, and tossed it on the floor. He drew back his right foot and kicked the book with the full force of his heavy jackboot. The book sailed through the air, split along its spine, and discharged pages as it flew across the room and crashed against the opposite wall. Gunter picked up some pages that had fallen from the book and pretended to read them. "I don't see anyone named Bergmann on this page. And there's no Bergmann on this page, either. Let me try another volume." He walked to the bookcases and reached for another book.

"Stop that, you ill-bred son-of-a… Ah, sorry, I meant to say, please stop, mein Herr. I beg of you."

Gunter smirked and returned to the reception desk. "Look, Doppelsbühl, I'm a reasonable man. I'll give you some time to work on my request. When I return tomorrow, I expect you to tell me whether Luka Bergmann is buried in this cemetery. Will you do that for me?"

"Yes…tomorrow…I'll search for Bergmann and have something for you then."

Gunter was irritated that his search for Bergmann had been delayed, and the thought of driving back to the base only to make the trip again the next day further irritated him. What appealed to him instead was staying the night in Munich and eating his evening meal at his favorite beer garden, the Bratwurstglöckle. Nothing wiped away the day's troubles like a cold beer and a bratwurst, except maybe several cold beers and bratwurst.

He pulled out of Nordfriedhof Cemetery's parking lot and drove toward the Stadtzentrum or the center of the city. His mood improved as he considered staying at the Bayern Hof Hotel and dining at the Bratwurstglöckle. If he were lucky, Adolph would be holding court at the Bratwurstglöckle, and he and his cronies would be talking politics and making plans to improve Germany's future. What could be more uplifting than that? That would certainly take his mind off his troubles.

Shortly after arriving at the Bayern Hof, Gunter called Helmut Wolff at the base. "What happened at the base today? Are there any problems I should know about?"

"Everything's fine, Gunter. Nothing to be concerned about."

"Good. I need you to oversee base operations for another day or two. I'm staying in Munich tonight and won't return until tomorrow or possibly the next day. Make sure the engineers stay focused on the design initiative. I will expect you to inform me of their progress."

"Of course, but why have you been delayed, Gunter?"

"I've run into some difficulties with the background check for the Bergmann boy. I haven't found his family or been able to trace his ancestry. Let's just say that the trail's gone cold; I must start early in the morning."

"I understand, and I'll manage things in your absence. Best of luck with your investigation."

◆◆◆

As Gunter motored toward Nordfriedhof Cemetery the next day, he thought about the night he'd spent in Munich. To say that it was a disappointment was putting it mildly. Nothing had turned out the way he'd expected. The Bratwurstglöckle had been closed for repairs, so he'd eaten his evening meal in a second-rate beer garden; the beer was watered down, the bratwurst tasted like dog meat, and neither Adolph nor any of his crew were in attendance. Instead, the place was full of social democrats who were spouting lies about the Nazi Party. Listening to those malcontents had driven him to the edge of insanity, and, in retrospect, he was thankful he'd left the PPK in his hotel room. Had he possessed the firearm, he probably would have permanently silenced those communists and pseudo-liberals and ended up in prison.

The debacle continued when he returned to his room at the Bayern Hof Hotel. Some idiot in the room next to his had thrown a party, and the raucous music and voices had kept him awake all night. He'd complained, but the night manager told him nothing could be done because the revelers were wealthy patrons who regularly spent large sums of money in the hotel.

Was it any wonder that now, as he drove north through morning traffic, he was in a foul mood? The combination of bad food, offensive people, and a sleepless night would make anyone irritable, and, on top of that, he was about to have a return engagement with that dunce, Doppelsbühl. He shuddered to think of what would happen if Doppelsbühl tried his patience again. Even the slightest provocation would prompt him to thrash the bureaucrat.

Moments later, the cemetery came into view, so Gunter eased out of the bumper-to-bumper traffic, made a right turn, and parked in front of the Nordfriedhof reception center. He strode through the arched entryway, entered the domed building, and spotted Doppelsbühl removing volumes from the floor-to-ceiling bookcases and stacking them on a cart. Other patrons were standing in a line at the reception desk, but Gunter was in no mood to wait, so he called across the room to get Doppelsbühl's attention.

"I'm back, Doppelsbühl. What did you discover about the Bergmann youth?"

Doppelsbühl stopped what he was doing, wheeled his cart to the reception desk, and told the people waiting in line that he would return shortly. Then he snatched a paper from the top of his desk and walked to where Gunter was standing.

"I can answer your question now, Herr Meissner. Luka Bergmann *is* buried in this cemetery. He lies in rest in plot L-162. Now, will there be anything else? I hope that your next request won't be made at gunpoint."

Gunter guffawed. "You have an overactive imagination, Doppelsbühl. My gun never leaves its holster unless I'm threatened or in danger, and you don't scare me in the least. However, I have another question: How do I find plot L-162?"

Doppelsbühl grunted derisively and then, in a sarcastic tone, said, "So you're having trouble figuring out the plot, are you, Herr Meissner? Why am I not surprised? Some people are slow to catch on." He then walked to a window at the rear of the reception area and pointed toward the back of the cemetery. "See that copse of trees toward the rear of the park, standing on the top of a knoll? As you ascend that knoll, you'll find L-162 about halfway up. If you reach the trees, you've gone too far."

Gunter exited at the rear of the building, and proceeded northward on a gravel path that wound its way through the tombstones toward the rear of the cemetery. As he journeyed along the path, he glanced at the headstones and was amazed to see that some of Nordfriedhof's denizens had been interred as far back as the late 1800s.

Further along, he came to a section filled with WWI dead. The sight made him think of Göring's friend, Rolf, and he wondered whether this was the place where Rolf's wife had laid the dead pilot to rest. That thought triggered a stream of distressing memories, like the morning when Göring had discovered Rolf lying dead on his cot with a bullet in his head. He could still picture that Allied plane strafing the aerodrome just before dawn. Rolf's death had transformed Göring--he'd lost all sense of reason and became maniacal about finding and killing those Allied pilots. That passion had gone unrequited until, years later, they'd discovered that one of their colleagues at Svensk-Luft Trafik Airlines, Robert Weber, had conducted the raid. Having stumbled across Rolf's killer years later in Sweden was the shock of a lifetime. That recollection reminded him that he'd failed his friend, Hermann. He'd promised Göring that he'd deal with Weber, and although he'd tried to make good on that pledge, he'd failed. That wasn't like him--he wasn't accustomed to being outwitted by an adversary--and on three occasions, no less. At least he'd managed to kill the thug's wife.

Gunter considered searching for Rolf's gravestone but then dismissed the idea. Solving one mystery was hard enough, and the Bergmann kid took priority. He promised himself he'd search for Rolf's final resting place some other time.

When he reached the knoll, he trekked up the southern slope, pausing occasionally to read the names carved on gravestones. Rather than searching systematically, he wandered from marker to marker, expecting to find the gravestone in a central position on the face of the knoll. That expectation proved wrong; after nearly an hour of searching, he'd encountered an assortment of German surnames, but Bergmann wasn't one of them.

Gunter again entertained the idea of thrashing Doppelsbühl as he descended the knoll. The man was incompetent—he'd sent him to search for Bergmann in the wrong sector of the cemetery. Perhaps nothing Doppelsbühl said could be trusted; hell, the Bergmann kid might not even be buried in this cemetery.

At the bottom of the knoll, Gunter walked laterally along a row of tombstones until he came to the gravel path that led to the reception center. As he stepped onto the path, he saw a small inlaid marker with the numbers L56 to L96 on it. He paused to ponder the meaning of the numbers and then realized that they referred to the plots within the row that he had just traversed. Why hadn't that dunce Doppelsbühl told him a plot index was situated at the beginning of each row?

Gunter ascended the knoll once more, but this time he walked along its outer edge, inspecting the plot indices as he passed the rows. About halfway up the slope, he reached a marker that read L148 to L188. He turned and walked down that row, counting plots until he came to L162. Initially, the plot seemed empty of a gravestone, but upon closer inspection, he spotted a small marker that was flush with the ground and concealed by tall grass. He knelt down, moved aside the greenery, and examined the gravestone.

What Gunter saw took his breath away. Inscribed on the marker was the name Luka Bergmann. He could hardly believe his eyes. He sat back and reflected on the implications of his discovery. "The old fart was right," he thought. "The Bergmann kid is dead and buried. That means Luka Gabel and Luka Bergmann are not the same person. So then, who is Luka Gabel?"

Gunter dashed to his vehicle, drove out of the cemetery, and returned to the Bayern Hof Hotel, where he called Wesselman. "Horst, there's something I need you to do immediately. Bring the Gabel kid into your office and make him tell you his real name and birthplace. Force him to comply, if you have to, using any means necessary. His real name isn't Bergmann because the Bergmann kid is dead. I'm still convinced that Gabel's an impostor, but I don't have a single scrap of evidence that I can use to trace his identity."

"Sorry, Gunter, I can't help you. Luka Gabel is still missing."

Gunter flew into a rage. "You still haven't found him? What have you been doing—sitting on your hands?"

"I resent that, Meissner. Casting aspersions on your coworkers is no way to earn their cooperation. Despite what you think, my crew and I have searched for Gabel daily since you ordered us to find him. We've looked everywhere, spoken to everyone who knows him, and come up with nothing. He's abandoned his internship at the Reichswehr, and the BTS headmaster told me that Gabel hasn't attended school for nearly a week. I spoke to some of Gabel's classmates, and none of them knew his whereabouts. The kid's vanished; there's just no trace of him."

Gunter didn't want to hear any more excuses, so he hung up on Wesselman and returned to his car. Along the way, he cursed Wesselman for his misfortune. "You fool! You have singlehandedly ruined my investigation!" But as he continued to blame Wesselman, thoughts about his culpability crept into his consciousness.

Upon reaching the car, Gunter slid behind the wheel, but instead of starting the engine, he leaned his head against the seatback, stared at the fabric liner that stretched across the vehicle's ceiling, and thought about his plight. What was he to do now? He'd reached a dead end and exhausted all his options. He decided to go over everything he had done so far while investigating the Gable kid. As he mentally reconstructed his steps, he asked himself whether he had overlooked something, taken a wrong turn, or made an error in judgment. Maybe this predicament wasn't entirely Wesselman's fault.

Slowly, the white-hot rage he'd felt toward Wesselman cooled; even the wrath he felt toward the Gabel kid diminished. As the armor that his anger provided fell away, an onslaught of self-doubt descended upon him. A voice in his subconscious accused him of ineptitude. "After all," the subliminal homunculus opined, "what have you learned about Luka Gabel? You know nothing more about him now than you did before you started your investigation. Your efforts to unmask the Gabel kid haven't produced a single piece of new information."

The accusations sent Gunter into a downward spiral. Instead of feeling tough and efficacious—his usual state of mind—he felt vulnerable and powerless. He'd always been a stranger to those feelings, and for good reason. For him, they were anathema.

He did what he always did when those feelings crept into the periphery of his awareness. To bolster his flagging bravado, he'd analyze the dilemma and use his insights to invent a new solution to 'fix' it. He'd learned that coping strategy while growing up on the farm, and it had enabled him to reinvent himself and surmount dire circumstances like the interval during his school days when Hermann had saddled him with the nickname 'farm boy' and his classmates had teased him mercilessly. This situation was no different, he told himself. Just reassess the dilemma and change course.

The problem, as he saw it, was that Gabel was remarkably cagy. The kid had given Wesselman the slip. Had Gabel outfoxed him as well? He knew the kid was intelligent, but perhaps he'd underestimated his cunning. After all, hadn't Gabel and his friend eluded him more than once when he'd tried to follow them home after school?

Even so, the whole of Gabel's ploy--the collective ruse that the kid seemed to have perpetrated--struck him as too intricate and calculated for someone of his age. The deceptive maneuvers that had preceded Gabel's disappearance--such as the deliberate omission of personal and family details from his school and internship applications--suggested that someone older and wiser than the kid was orchestrating his moves. The more he thought about it, the more the whole situation smacked of collusion.

It was time to face facts, Gunter told himself. He began by asking himself some hard questions. How much of what I know about this kid is true? For example, is 'Luka' his real name? The kid's surname appears to be a sham, so why not his forename? And what about his date and place of birth? Maybe he's older than he looks. What if he wasn't born in Munich? As he pondered those possibilities, he realized that he hadn't known anything about the kid's birth until he'd broken into the BTS records office. Gabel hadn't reported those facts on his internship application. Chances were, then, that the kid's parent or guardian had provided the BTS birth information. In Germany, petitions for school admission were submitted by parents; no school would accept a student without an application that had been completed and signed by the child's legal guardian.

He wondered how likely it was that a parent would falsify their child's birth date and place of birth. It was possible--especially if the parent had something to hide--but it seemed unlikely when one considered the ease with which such data could be verified. Then again, that was precisely what happened when Anna attempted to verify Gabel's birth data at the Munich Standesamt. Not only had she been unable to confirm Luka Gabel's birth date and location, but she'd also failed to authenticate his name.

As Gunter pondered over Anna's findings, he realized that he couldn't trust anything he knew about the Gabel kid. This created a seemingly insurmountable problem: he had nothing to work with, no evidence to continue his search. He had to determine whether anything he knew about the kid was accurate or believable. But what could that be? He tried to imagine how a parent would try to hide their child's identity in a school admissions application. He thought that it would be more likely for a parent to change the child's surname rather than their given name. By the time children start school, and especially by adolescence, their first names are deeply ingrained in their minds. It would take weeks or months for a child to internalize and respond to a new name. Surnames, on the other hand, are shared with other family members and aren't typically used to distinguish a child from their siblings. First names are more personal and related to the child's developing sense of identity.

That line of reasoning led Gunter to a tentative conclusion: the name 'Luka' was his best clue. He knew the clue's credibility was shaky--it was based on a supposition rather than evidence--but it gave him a place to start.

Then he had an epiphany. Perhaps he hadn't overlooked something, taken a wrong turn, or made an error in judgment--maybe Anna had. Especially if the Gabel kid's parents had lied about his birth date. He'd assumed when he sent Anna to the Munich Standesamt to search for Gabel's birth record that the birth date he'd given her--the one he found in the BTS application--was accurate. She might not have found anything because she'd focused on that date and only looked at records for infants born a few weeks before and after. The obvious next step, Gunter now realized, was to go to the Munich Standesamt and search the birth records more thoroughly for infants whose parents had named them Luka.

Energized by his insight, Gunter started the engine, drove downtown to the Marienplatz, and parked near the Neues Rathaus. Once inside the neo-Gothic structure, he ascended the stairs to the second floor and entered the civil registration department. A clerk seated behind a desk rose to greet him. "Good day, sir; how may I help you?"

Gunter walked to where the man stood and read the name tag above his left shirt pocket. "I'm pleased to make your acquaintance, Herr Otto Schmidt. My name is Gunter Meissner, and I'm here on government business. I need to inspect birth registrations for all families who named their infant Luka over the past twenty years. I need to see these records as soon as possible, and I'm willing to pay you or one of your assistants to scour your files and compile the relevant records."

Schmidt ran his eyes over Gunter, sizing up his quarry. "Greetings, Herr Meissner. You say you're willing to pay? How much compensation are you offering? Considerable time and effort would be required to sort through twenty years' birth records."

"I'm willing to negotiate. As a government employee, my funds are limited, but I'm sure we can agree on a figure."

Schmidt pictured his pockets full of Reichsmarks and smiled. "Yes, of course. I'll call my assistant, and he can begin working on this tomorrow."

Gunter nodded. "Excellent!"

"You know, Herr Meissner, it's odd because another person made a similar request just a few days ago. A woman wanted to see birth records for infants who'd been named Luka."

Gunter feigned surprise even though he knew Schmidt was talking about Anna. "Ach, what a strange coincidence. Did this woman find any relevant records?"

"She initially requested records for a specific date but then expanded her search to include several weeks before and after that date--about an entire month. And, yes, she found birth records for two children named Luka."

Now Gunter was genuinely astonished. Anna had told him she'd found only one such record--the one for the Bergmann boy. "What? Are you sure she found two cases?"

"Yes, Mein Herr. I am certain because I scrutinized the certificates before refiling them in our archives. In both cases, the parents had named their child Luka."

Gunter was unsure what to make of Schmidt's revelation, but his suspicions were aroused. "Herr Schmidt, I'd very much like to see those records--can you find them for me?"

Schmidt gave an affirmative nod and pointed toward a door marked 'Archives' at the rear of the records office. "Follow me, please." Gunter trailed Schmidt through the door and into a large room that contained row upon row of file cabinets. He waited as Schmidt wandered up one aisle and down the next, scrutinizing the index labels affixed to each cabinet. When Schmidt found the cabinet he was looking for, he paused, opened a file drawer, and motioned for Gunter to join him.

Gunter watched as Schmidt thumbed through file folders, working his way toward the back of the drawer. Schmidt eventually selected a folder and handed it to him. "Here's one of the records. Look at this one while I search for the other one." As Schmidt walked away, Gunter opened the folder and inspected its contents.

There were just two pages in the file. One was a copy of a birth announcement that had appeared in the local paper, and the other was an official birth certificate. Gunter ignored the announcement and examined the birth certificate. He quickly determined that the document was for the Bergmann boy; the date of birth was ten days after the one he'd found for Gabel in the BTS application, and the parents were listed as Klaus and Helga. "Just what Anna told me," Gunter muttered, "now let's see what she didn't tell me." He scanned the room for Schmidt and spotted him several rows away, bending over a file drawer. "Say Schmidt, I'm keen to see the other birth certificate. Have you found it yet?"

Schmidt lifted a folder over his head and waved it in the air. "I found it; come take a look." Gunter hustled over, snatched the file from Schmidt's hand, and flipped it open. A birth certificate was inside, and what was written on it shook Gunter to his core. "Mein Gott! No, this can't be! There must be some mistake."

Schmidt glared at Gunter; his pride was injured. "Sir, my predecessors and I have been scrupulous in our record keeping. I assure you that these records are accurate."

Schmidt's protests were ignored. Gunter was too stunned to listen; his mind was reeling, trying to understand what he'd seen. He stuffed the certificate into his pocket and dashed out of the archives room. His abrupt, unexpected departure took Schmidt by surprise. "Wait, Herr Meissner, that's an official document. You can't take it out of this room. And what about the Reichsmarks you promised me?"

Gunter sped back to the Bayern Hof Hotel and called Wolff at the air base. "Helmut, something unexpected has come up, and I need you to manage things for another day or two. I'm taking the first available train to Berlin and, if all goes well, I'll return tomorrow. While I'm away, I want you to watch Anna Lichtmann closely."

Wolff interrupted before Gunter could continue. "Anna? What exactly did you have in mind? Do you want me to spy on her?"

Gunter sighed. "No, Helmut, nothing like that. Just make sure she doesn't leave the base."

"But I don't understand. She's more dedicated to the design initiative than most of our engineers. Why would she want to leave the base?"

"She's interfered with the background check I've conducted on the

Gabel boy. I sent her to the Munich Standesamt last week to research birth records, and today, when I visited that office, I discovered that she tricked me into searching for the wrong family. I will initiate disciplinary action against her while I'm in Berlin. Now stop asking questions, Helmut. I'll explain later."

"That doesn't sound like Anna. Are you sure you haven't made a mistake?

"There's no mistake. She concealed the boy's parentage information so I couldn't complete the background check."

"Still, Gunter, there's something fishy about all this, and I'm not comfortable doing what you're asking me to do."

"You're trying my patience, Helmut. Remember our pact? Just do as I say."

"All right, Gunter, you have me at a disadvantage. I don't believe Anna will desert her colleagues, but what do you want me to do if she tries to leave?"

"Hopefully, it won't come to that, but if she talks about leaving or tries to flee the base, confine her to quarters. Lock her in her room and post a guard outside."

"Lock her up? You've got to be kidding."

"This is serious, Helmut! I'm not joking around. If you don't obey my orders, I'll lock you up too."

◆◆◆

Wolff searched for Anna and found her conversing with the other team members in the workroom. He approached the team's workstation, caught Anna's eye, and motioned toward the door. Then he left the workroom and waited in the corridor.

The other engineers at the workstation--Albrecht, Graf, and Dietrich--stopped talking and watched Anna to see how she would respond. When she stood and walked toward the corridor, they followed her.

Wolff intercepted the foursome as they exited the workroom. "Let's meet in my room. There's been a development that we need to discuss in private."

After they were settled in Wolf's room, he told them about his conversation with Gunter.

Anna panicked. "What?" she shrieked. "Meissner was at the Standesamt looking at birth records? Oh my God, no!"

"Yes, and Gunter's planning to take disciplinary action against you for derailing his background check on the Gabel boy. He said you concealed information and deliberately tricked him into searching for the wrong family."

The other engineers stared at Anna, concerned but uncomprehending. None of them understood the reason for her distress, nor could they appreciate the significance of Gunter's discovery.

Anna's panic attack worsened. Her chest tightened, and bile rose in her throat. She choked back tears, attempting to maintain her composure, but then crumbled when waves of nausea rolled through her insides. She wrapped her arms around herself, doubled over, and vomited onto the floor.

Aghast, the engineers did what they could to comfort Anna. Wolff handed Anna a handkerchief, Albrecht held her head, and Graf grabbed a towel and began wiping up the mess. Dietrich murmured a few comforting phrases. However, neither the handkerchief nor the sympathy allayed Anna's fears.

What Anna feared most had come to pass: Gunter knew about Luka--he'd discovered what she'd spent decades trying to hide. She knew he'd act on that knowledge, and nothing would ever be the same; her world would tilt off its axis and spin out of control.

That knowledge killed her longstanding hope for her son's future. Luka's destiny was sealed; she felt powerless to prevent what she knew would happen. Now that Gunter had acquired Luka's scent, he would chase him down, like a bloodhound, and corner him. Even though she'd taken great pains to hide Luka, Anna knew it would only be a matter of time before Meissner found him. There was too much at stake for Gunter to do otherwise.

Chapter 22

Winter 1928: Munich, Germany

"Heinz, I need a handgun, preferably one that I can conceal in my purse," Anna confided to Albrecht. She had come to Albrecht's quarters shortly after the members of her engineering team had met in Wolff's room. Albrecht's eyebrows arched as he stared at Anna in disbelief. "Have you taken leave of your senses? Why do you need a pistol? Is someone threatening you?"

"Well, in a manner of speaking, yes. Meissner's traveling to Berlin to take disciplinary action against me, and I plan to alter his journey by adding an early terminus."

"But Anna," Albrecht pleaded, "Gunter's dangerous; this plan of yours might get you killed. Besides, I doubt that the bureaucrats in Berlin will take Gunter's complaint seriously. You're too good of an engineer and too important to the rearmament program for them to fire you."

"I'm not afraid of losing my job. The threat is more serious than that, Heinz. Gunter discovered something that endangers my family, and I must prevent him from reaching Berlin. Now, do you have a gun I can borrow? I've got a train to catch."

Albrecht sighed. "If you weren't in such a hurry, I'd ask you to tell me what Gunter's done. But, I'll help you, even though it's against my better judgment." He went to his dresser, reached inside the top drawer, and withdrew a Beholla semi-automatic pistol stuffed inside a sock. "I've had this pistol a long time; it was issued to me by the German Imperial Army during the Great War. Don't make me regret that I've loaned it to you."

Anna nodded as she placed the pistol inside her purse. She bid Albrecht farewell and then returned to the workroom, where she slipped a copy of the design portfolio into her briefcase. Then she exited the building, misappropriated a staff car from the parking lot, and sped toward the Munich Hauptbahnhof.

There were no parking spaces near the Hauptbahnhof, so Anna ditched the car behind a beer garden and set out for the train station on foot. When she arrived at the sprawling complex, she strode to the archway marked AUSGANG and pushed through the turnstiles. Once inside the station, she went directly to the departures board and scanned the schedule for Berlin-bound trains. Her eyes settled on an intercity express scheduled to leave for Berlin in forty minutes. She felt confident that Gunter would choose that train because all the other options were slower commuter lines that stopped frequently and required passengers to change trains in larger cities.

She went to the ticket counter, purchased a one-way voucher, and then found a table in a café across from the platform where the express train would arrive. She ordered coffee and then used a newspaper that she found on the table to shield her face while she watched people arrive at the platform and queue up for the train. If all went according to plan, she'd spot Gunter when he arrived, sneak onto the train after he boarded, and then shadow him until she could arrange his untimely demise.

A waiter appeared at Anna's table to refill her coffee cup and asked whether she wanted to order from the menu. She glanced at her watch before refusing; the intercity express was due in five minutes, and Gunter was nowhere to be seen. Had she made a mistake and chosen the wrong train? As she paid the waiter and stood to leave, a man with a familiar gait carrying only a briefcase passed the café and strode onto the platform where travelers awaited the intercity express. Anna knew it was Gunter even though she hadn't seen the man's face.

Anna waited until Gunter reached the far end of the platform, and then she crept into the crowd of travelers and hid behind a signpost. Moments later, a train displaying the yellow and black Deutsche Reichsbahn insignia arrived, and passengers streamed out of its coaches and onto the platform. Anna waited patiently until she saw Gunter board a first-class car near the front of the train, and then she stole her way onto a second-class coach that was several cars to the rear.

The train departed from the station, and as it gained momentum, Anna worked her way forward to the coach just behind Gunter's and took a seat that allowed her to observe him without being noticed. Because his seat faced the front of the train, she had a clear view of the back of his head.

She hunkered down into her seat, fingered the pistol in her coat pocket, and contemplated a plan of attack. The only time she'd used a gun was to kill vermin at her parent's farm, and the prospect of shooting another human being unnerved her. Was she capable of committing murder? It was a question she'd prefer not to answer, and she'd certainly never thought of herself as an assassin. For her to commit such a heinous act, even for a righteous reason, she'd have to act quickly or lose her nerve. Her impulse was to walk up behind Gunter, shove the pistol against his seatback, and pull the trigger. It was an audacious, brutish plan, but what it lacked in finesse, it made up for in expediency and effectiveness. It would all be over in seconds, and Gunter wouldn't even see it coming.

However, that plan's appeal soon faded as Anna thought about what would happen after pulling the trigger. It wasn't hard to imagine: she'd be standing next to a blood-spattered corpse, smoking gun in hand, surrounded by a host of passengers who'd witnessed her every move. Plus, she'd be stuck on a speeding train without hope of escape. The authorities would descend upon her like a pack of wolves craving fresh meat, and she'd wind up dead or in jail. Where would that leave Luka?

Anna restrained her impulses, took stock of her surroundings, and tried to think of a plan that would not only silence Gunter but also preserve her life and liberty. She was soon frustrated, however, because every plan she devised suffered from one glaring flaw: there was no way to conceal her crime. Firing a handgun on a public conveyance without attracting attention was impossible. Too many potential witnesses would connect the sound of a shot with the shooter.

While Anna was lost in thought, a woman sitting in a nearby row stood, walked up the aisle, and entered a WC at the rear of Gunter's coach. That event gave Anna an idea: Gunter would eventually use the same WC, and when he did, she could sneak up from behind, shove him inside, lock the door behind her, and shoot him where he stood. There'd be no witnesses, and hopefully, the closed quarters would muffle the gunshot. She'd position the body on the toilet and place an 'out of order' sign on the door as she exited the WC.

She called the porter and asked to have a large stein of beer anonymously delivered to Gunter. The sooner he had to urinate, the better.

Half an hour later, Anna sensed movement in the forward coach, so she raised her head and peered over the seatback. Gunter was in the aisle, walking rearward toward the WC. Anna slid across her seat, crouched at the edge of the aisle, and withdrew the pistol from her coat pocket. When Gunter turned to enter the WC, she hastily crept up from behind and threw her weight against the door as it swung closed. Just as her body impacted the door, there was a loud thump as the door's internal locking mechanism engaged. Anna pushed harder, but the door failed to yield; it was firmly bolted and too stout to give way.

Surprised and frustrated, Anna banged her fist on the door and cursed. She heard a voice from inside the WC shout, "Occupied! Wait your turn!" When she turned to leave, several passengers stared at her. A young boy sitting with his mother pointed at her and laughed. "Mom," he said, "That woman really has to pee. Is she going to wet her pants?"

Embarrassed and defeated, Anna returned to her seat. Her plan had failed, but the upside was that Gunter was none the wiser—he hadn't seen her face. And, none of the passengers had seen the gun she'd concealed in the palm of her hand. Exhausted, she rested her head against the seatback, and as the adrenaline wore off, she inadvertently fell asleep. When she awoke, the train was only 30 minutes from Berlin.

Anna chastised herself for falling asleep. "How did you let this happen?" she muttered to herself. "You're running out of time, and Gunter is still breathing. Luka is done for if Gunter gets off this train in Berlin."

Energized by a sense of urgency and resolve, Anna extracted the Beholla semi-automatic from her coat pocket and ejected the clip. She counted seven rounds in the magazine and then pushed the clip back into the gun's handle. Even though the gun was fully loaded, she hadn't imagined needing more than one or two bullets. Now, with everything spinning out of control, she was glad to have the additional firepower. She chambered a round and then promised herself that Gunter wouldn't live to see Berlin come hell or high water.

Anna palmed the Beholla and anxiously awaited an opportunity to use it. She kept a close eye on Gunter, hoping he'd make a last-minute trip to the WC, but those hopes were dashed when the train slowed, and the conductor announced that the train was arriving in Berlin. Passengers nearby began collecting their belongings and pulling their suitcases from overhead racks. Gunter, however, remained seated.

Anna's heart pounded, and her respirations became rapid and shallow; she'd exhausted her options and run out of time. Rattled and desperate, she tried to calm herself and clear her head. At the moment, it seemed she had no choice but to mirror the actions of the people around her, preparing to get off the train. She slipped the gun into her purse, retrieved her briefcase, and stepped into a line of passengers forming in the aisle.

When the train came to a stop, the door between Anna's and Gunter's coach retracted, and people ahead of Anna streamed forward and began descending the stairs that led to the platform alongside the train. As Anna approached the doorway, she saw Gunter stand and reach for his briefcase in the bin above his seat. As he swung the briefcase down from the rack, he turned toward the door, and his eyes met Anna's. A look of recognition and surprise appeared on his face.

Anna instinctively knew it was now or never. She withdrew the Beholla from her purse, pointed it directly at Gunter's chest, and pulled the trigger twice. Two deafening blasts rang out, amplified by the close quarters inside the coach. The passengers behind Anna screamed and pushed forward, nearly knocking her down as they stampeded toward the exit, desperate to get off the train.

Anna regained her footing and let the thundering herd of frightened passengers push her down the stairs and onto the platform. There, she blended into the crowd of people fleeing toward the central part of the station. She stripped off her coat and threw it on a nearby bench to reduce the chances of being recognized.

The mob surged along until it reached the end of the platform and then pivoted onto the walkway that led to the station's center. Anna kept pace until the throng arrived at another platform where people were boarding a train bound for Dresden. She could see that the platform was situated such that it would offer an unobstructed view of the train that she had just fled. She worked her way toward the crowd's edge, veered onto the platform, and boarded a first-class coach.

Anna found a seat on the side of the train that faced the intercity express and gazed at the coach she had traveled in, desperate to discover Gunter's fate. In the scuffle sparked by the gunshots, she'd lost sight of him and didn't know whether he had survived the attack.

An ambulance was parked on the platform, and first responders, including police and emergency personnel, rushed in and out of the coach. As Anna watched, two men climbed down from the coach carrying a man on a stretcher covered with a blanket. She assumed Gunter was alive because the blanket wasn't draped over the man's head. The men placed the stretcher on a gurney and wheeled it into the ambulance.

Anna got off the train and returned to where the platform joined the walkway leading to the station's center. She stood there momentarily, watching people pass, wondering what to do. She was dismayed that Gunter was alive and toyed with the idea of finishing the job but couldn't think of a foolproof way to get inside the ambulance and silence him permanently. It pained her to admit it, but there was nothing else she could do. She resigned herself to what would now become a waiting game, waiting to see whether Gunter died of his injuries or survived and came after Luka.

She exited the station, hailed a cab, and told the driver to take her to the apartment she shared with Weber on Victoria Strasse, near the Tiergarten. Her only solace was knowing that Weber would be there to comfort her. It would be awkward initially because she had a lot of explaining to do. She'd need to level with him about her past and all that had transpired in Munich and on the train to Berlin. That wouldn't be easy, but once they got past those complications, she felt confident that Weber would help her find a way to protect Luka.

◆◆◆

Gunter awoke with a start, his eyes instinctively darting from side to side, scanning his surroundings for threats. Before he understood what was happening, pain flooded his consciousnesses—a pain so sharp that it took his breath away. The torment raged within his right shoulder and exploded down his arm and into his fingertips. Tears ran down his face, and he moaned involuntarily as he slipped back into unconsciousness.

Three days later, when Gunter opened his eyes again, he realized he was lying on a bed in a small, windowless room. A woman in a white uniform was standing next to him with a syringe in her hand. "You were moaning in your sleep, so I increased your morphine dosage." Gunter twisted his lips into what he thought was a smile; he was grateful that his pain had lessened, even if it meant that his awareness had been reduced to a drug-induced stupor. "Where am I?" he croaked.

The woman glanced around the room as if appraising it for the first time. "Don't you recognize these surroundings? You're in a Berlin krankenhaus--the Charité hospital. How much do you remember of what happened to you?"

Gunter closed his eyes and tried to summon images from his recent past. He saw himself getting on the train in Munich and traveling in a first-class coach toward Berlin. Then he saw Anna Lichtmann's face and a muzzle flash. He winced, and his body convulsed. The woman in the white uniform gasped and moved to restrain him; out of habit, she reached for his shoulders, but upon seeing the bandages, she instead clutched his torso and held his abdomen tight against the mattress.

Three weeks later, Gunter awoke to find Göring sitting beside his bed. Groggy from sleep, he croaked a greeting. "Hermann, I'm so glad you found me."

Göring smiled and put his hand on Gunter's arm. "A nurse from the hospital called me and said you'd been shot. My phone number was in your wallet. You've been in a coma and you're lucky to be alive. How the hell did this happen?"

"I took the intercity express to Berlin to bring you an important message—something I couldn't say on the phone. But I almost didn't make it because Anna Lichtmann shot me as I was preparing to exit the train in the Berlin Hauptbahnhof."

Göring stared at Gunter disbelievingly and shook his head. "Gunter, your mind is playing tricks on you. Surely, that's the morphine talking. Anna's in Munich working on the design initiative. Besides, we've known her since childhood; she doesn't have a treacherous bone in her body."

"I'm as surprised as you are, Hermann, but believe me, she did this—she hid aboard the train and followed me to Berlin because she was trying to stop me from talking to you. She's been hiding something from us."

Now, Göring's suspicions were aroused. His skeptical expression shifted to one of concern. "What has she been hiding?"

"No, I can't tell you here—it's too sensitive—it's best if I tell you privately."

"All right, we can meet where we usually do—in my office—as soon as they release you from the hospital."

Gunter sighed. "When will that be? Have you talked to my doctor? I need to get out of here; I'm sick of lying on my ass, contemplating my navel."

"Soon, Gunter, probably at the end of this week. Be patient. You've got a hole in your shoulder the size of a Reichsmark, and you'll need time to wean yourself off morphine."

◆◆◆

Two more weeks passed before Gunter left the hospital. His release was delayed by another setback—this time, a severe case of sepsis. His wound became infected, and he'd spiked a high fever, become delirious, and wandered the hospital hallways searching for a man named Bruno Loezer. Fearing that he might harm himself, the nursing staff strapped Gunter to his bed until the hallucinations subsided.

When Gunter finally left the hospital, he took a taxi to his apartment, changed his clothes, and walked directly to Göring's office. A secretary greeted him and asked if he had an appointment. "No," he growled. "Just tell him it's Meissner. He'll see me."

When Göring opened the door, he stepped back, ran his eyes over Gunter, and tried to conceal his astonishment. He hardly recognized his friend. Gunter was thin and pale as a sheet, his posture was stooped, and his right arm hung in a sling. At a loss for words, Göring attempted to say something upbeat. "Gunter! I'm glad you're upright and mobile, even though you look a little worse for wear."

Gunter grunted, pushed past Göring, and seated himself at the conference table in the center of the room. "Get me a beer, Hermann. You're going to need one too. After you hear what I have to say, you might need several more."

Göring sent his secretary to a nearby beer garden and then seated himself at the table across from Gunter. "So, what do you know that would make Anna Lichtmann want to kill you? It must be important if she's willing to commit murder to silence you."

"I learned something when I was investigating the Gabel kid's ancestry. Anna Lichtmann is his birth mother. Luka Gabel is her son."

"What? This wunderkind in the Aviation Coalition's internship program is her son? Do you mean she allowed her son to participate in the internship program without telling us? I don't understand. Why would she hide this from us?"

"I discovered the kid's parentage when I searched the birth records at the Munich Standesamt. I first sent Anna to find the Gabel kid's birth certificate, but she told me that no child named 'Luka' had been born on the date I had given her. The only Luka she'd found, she claimed, was born ten days later and christened Luka Bergmann. I searched for the Bergmann boy only to discover that he was deceased. Realizing that I'd been duped, I went to the Standesamt, and, with the director's help, I found a birth certificate for Luka Lichtmann."

"Ah, I see. The kid we know as Luka Gabel was born Luka Lichtmann, and someone—probably Anna—changed his name. But why would she change his name to Gabel?"

"To keep you from finding him."

"Me? What are you implying?"

"On the birth certificate, the name listed for the father is H. Göring."

Dumbstruck, Göring stared at Gunter in disbelief. The color drained from his face, his eyes glassed over, and his jaw muscles drew taut. His lips moved but didn't produce any sounds.

Gunter shook his head and cleared his throat before continuing. "Could this be true, Hermann? Does she have any basis for this claim?"

Göring's temper flared. "Are you asking me if I screwed her? She was my girlfriend in high school, and we dated for several months. So, yes, I had sex with her, but infrequently, and she never said anything about being pregnant. We were teenagers, for God's sake. It happened so long ago that I barely remember my sexual encounters with her."

"Well, apparently, Anna remembers them and decided you fathered her child. I take it from your reaction that she documented paternity on the birth certificate without consulting you."

"Yes, of course. She never said a word to me. I had no idea she'd been pregnant, let alone had a child. How do we know she isn't lying?"

"We don't, but what reason would she have for falsifying the child's paternity, especially when she's kept the kid a secret and never asked you for child support?"

"I still think she's lying. But, all right, suppose that I am Luka's father. Now that Anna realizes you've uncovered her secret, what will she want from me?"

"I don't think she'll want anything from you. She's spent nearly two decades trying to hide the kid. She doesn't want you to know he exists."

"Why do you think that is?"

"Well, for a start, her family's Jewish. How would you have reacted if she'd told you that you had a Jewish son?"

"I don't know, but that certainly poses a bigger problem now than it would have in the past. Imagine what Adolph would say. My credibility with the Nazis will be shot to hell."

"Yes, Anna's lit the fuse on this time bomb, and it could blow up at any time. That's why I rushed to Berlin to warn you. If this gets out, your reputation will be indelibly tarnished—you'll never be able to expunge the stain. You'd become a pariah and be drummed out of the party."

"Must you torture me with the detestable details, Gunter? You're not helping me by painting a bleak picture of my future. I'm already upset, and you're making things worse."

"Well, Hermann, you need to face facts. This situation is explosive; you must act quickly and decisively to contain it. We must deactivate this bomb before it explodes and engulfs you in a firestorm of criticism and disgrace."

"Yes, of course, I understand that. But how can we keep this bomb from detonating? For all we know, Anna may have shared this information with other people, like her parents. If Anna's not the only person who knows about my paternity, then others would need to be silenced as well. The scale of that kind of containment operation seems unmanageable if not infeasible."

"What I've discovered suggests that this is a well-kept secret. I very much doubt that Anna discussed Luka's parentage with anyone outside her family. Even though we can't know for certain, I think we should assume that Anna has told only her parents and Luka that you are the boy's father. Thus, there's a good chance this bomb can be defused if we silence Anna and her family."

"Silence the entire family? I don't see how that's possible unless.... Surely, you're not suggesting mass murder?"

"Not as such; certainly not as a deliberate act. But a lot can happen when you attempt to arrest someone. As a rule, people don't surrender willingly; most refuse to be taken into custody and, if they're armed, they often get shot while resisting arrest."

"I can see how that might happen, especially if you provoke people or take them by surprise."

Gunter smiled. "Exactly!"

"I wouldn't lose any sleep if that fate befell Anna and her parents, but I'm not comfortable with orchestrating my son's death. After all, Luka is my flesh and blood."

"Well, you're Luka's biological father, but that's exactly the problem, right? If you claim him as your son, the Nazis will roast you like a pig on a spit over an open fire. You can't have it both ways."

"Isn't there some other, peaceable way to compel Luka's silence?"

"Don't be naïve, Hermann. If you can't smooth out this little bump in the road, you have no business being a Reichsminister for the Nazi party."

"Tell me something, Gunter. If Luka were your son, would you be this callous and ruthless? I suspect not."

Gunter fell silent, sat back in his chair, and pondered Göring's accusation. "All right, Hermann, perhaps there is another option. What if we captured the kid and sequestered him at the secret air base in Munich? There are plenty of spare rooms that could serve as cells. We'd essentially incarcerate Luka in a secret prison. No one would know he was there, and he couldn't communicate with the outside world."

"I can't say I like the idea of imprisoning my son, but it's certainly the lesser of the two evils. You have my permission to proceed with that plan."

"Good; then it's settled. There's no need for you to give this matter another thought. I'll fix this."

◆◆◆

The cab pulled to the curb when it reached its destination on Victoria Strasse, and Anna gathered her things, paid the driver, and entered the apartment. "Robert," she called out, "I'm home!" When there was no reply, she wandered the apartment searching for Weber. As she moved from room to room, finding no one, her disappointment intensified, and she fought back tears. "Where are you, Robert?" She'd been anticipating her reunion with Weber since she left the train station, and his absence threatened to unleash her barely controlled panic. "Damn it, Robert, why aren't you here when I need you?"

Upset, frustrated, and tired, Anna went to the bedroom, threw herself on the bed, and cried herself to sleep. She awoke two hours later to find Weber sitting next to her. "Oh, Robert, you're home. Where have you been?"

"I flew the return leg from Munich this morning after taking Luka to your parent's farm, and then I did some routine maintenance on the plane after I landed in Berlin. It was a good trip overall. Luka initially struggled with the move, but your parents are helping him adjust. They also convinced me to stay a few days, and I helped your Dad with some chores. Now, tell me, why are you here? I'm surprised you're back so soon. Are you on leave from the base?"

"Yes," Anna sheepishly replied, "but it's not official leave—you might say I'm AWOL from my job."

Weber flinched involuntarily but then tried to mask his surprise. Something was wrong—seriously wrong. Anna was a committed member of the Aviation Coalition and would never have left the base without permission. "What happened?"

"Oh, Robert, I don't even know where to start. My life is a mess. I've done things you won't like—embarrassing things that are out of character for me. There's a lot I haven't been able to tell you because I'm afraid you'll hate me."

"I'm not going to hate you. I have skeletons in my closet, too—I've done plenty of things I'm not proud of. Just tell me what's happened."

Anna began to sob. "Over the past few days, my past has returned to haunt me, and now it's threatening not just Luka but me as well. Everything's spiraled out of control."

Weber wrapped his arms around Anna and embraced her. "Please calm down and stop talking in generalities. I can't help you if you don't level with me. Start at the beginning and take me through it step by step."

Anna nodded and tried to compose herself. "It all started when I was in high school in Munich. I was just a kid—a teenager—and a naive one at that. I dated a boy in my high school, and he convinced me to have sex a few times, and then I discovered I was pregnant. My father wanted to confront the boy, but he couldn't because he'd been stabbed and robbed in an alley a few weeks earlier and was too weak to pursue the matter. I was relieved because I was having trouble fitting in at school and didn't need that kind of embarrassment. My mother suggested an abortion, but I decided to have the child and not tell the baby's father or anyone else about the pregnancy. A few months before Luka was born, my family left Munich, changed their names from Lichtmann to Gabel, and settled in a rural community where no one knew my past. My parents raised Luka as their son, and I became Luka's older sister, and no one was the wiser until I told you my secret."

"I figured something like that must have happened but decided to respect your privacy and not pry. That happened a long time ago, and teenage pregnancies aren't that uncommon, so why is this causing problems for you now?"

"Because Gunter discovered that the boy he knows as Luka Gabel is my son. Luka foolishly joined the Aviation Coalition internship program without my knowledge, and someone asked Gunter to do a background check so that Luka would be eligible for a security clearance. While stationed at the base, Gunter unwittingly sent me to the Munich Standesamt to find Luka's birth certificate and identify his parents. I found my son's birth certificate but misled Gunter by telling him that no record existed for Luka Gabel. I suggested he search instead for the family of another boy named Luka Bergmann, born around the same time."

"How diabolical! So, Gunter didn't realize that the woman he sent to the Standesamt was the mother of the boy he was trying to find?"

"No, he didn't. But he became suspicious when he discovered that Luka Bergmann was deceased and couldn't be the same person as Luka Gabel. He asked the Director of the Munich Standesamt to do a thorough search of the birth records that were recorded around the time of Luka's birth and discovered that Anna Lichtmann—the name I go by at the Reichswehr—gave birth to a child named Luka Lichtmann."

Weber scratched his head, looking quizzically at Anna. "So, based on that, Gunter inferred that Luka Lichtmann and Luka Gabel were the same person?" he asked.

"Of course. It didn't take much of an intuitive leap for him to arrive at that conclusion. In all the years Gunter's known me, he's never suspected I had a child. Once he saw the birth certificate, he knew that I'd not only hidden Luka for decades but also lied about the existence of his birth certificate."

"I see. So now Gunter knows that you had a child, and he realizes that the person he's been investigating—Luka Gabel—is your son. I can see why he'd be miffed because you didn't trust him with that secret, but I don't understand why that's such a big problem. Why would Gunter's discovery of your son's existence make you this upset and so fanatical about protecting Luka?"

"I've kept Luka's existence a secret to protect him from the man I believed to be his father—Hermann Göring. I neither trusted Hermann nor thought he would be a good influence on my son. So, I decided not to tell him about Luka, and now, looking back, I can see that it was the right choice. Can you imagine what would happen if the public learned that a former war hero and recently-elected Nazi Reichsminister fathered a son with a Jewish woman out of wedlock?"

Weber put his arms around Anna and embraced her. "My God, Anna, I had no idea. No wonder you're upset. But why did you say you *believed* that Göring was Luka's father? Did you have reason to doubt that he was the father?"

"I dated Hermann in high school, and I fell pregnant around the time our relationship ended. I knew that if I told him I was pregnant, he would assume he was the father. As I said, I didn't tell him about Luka because he wasn't the kind of man I wanted as a father for Luka. But there was another reason, too. One night, my girlfriends and I drank at a beer garden with Hermann and some boys from our high school. After all of us got drunk and lost our inhibitions, one of the boys suggested we leave the beer garden and go on a hay ride. Sometime during the hay ride, I had sex with a boy named Rolf. Rolf and I had developed romantic feelings for each other, but he was already engaged to a girl named Maria, who was also a friend of mine. After our tryst, Rolf felt guilty and requested that I keep it a secret. Despite being in a relationship with Hermann at the time, I also didn't want to hurt Maria, so I had my own reasons for keeping the affair under wraps. However, when Luka was born, I had to list the father's name on his birth certificate. Given my history with Hermann and because Rolf and I were intimate only once, I put Hermann's name on the certificate. I believed that Hermann was Luka's father until he became an adolescent and resembled and acted more like Rolf. I am now convinced that Luka's father was Rolf, not Hermann."

"Weber looked at Anna with a confused expression as he tried to understand the complicated story she had just told him. "If I understand correctly, Gunter is under the impression that Hermann Göring is Luka's father, but that's not true. Is that what's upsetting you?"

"Yes, that's one of the reasons. Gunter believes that Göring is Luka's biological father, and he will go to any lengths to keep this information hidden from the public. That's why I am so fixated on ensuring Luka's safety. My son's life is in danger, and I must do everything possible to protect him."

"That's just one of the reasons? What else is causing you distress?"

"I'm afraid my distress is not solely caused by Gunter's propensity to use extreme measures to safeguard Göring. During my trip from Munich to Berlin, I did something that has worsened the situation and made it more complicated."

"Are you saying there's more to this story? How could things possibly get any worse?"

"Oh, Robert, I'm afraid it gets much worse. Gunter and I were traveling on the same train today—the intercity express from Munich to Berlin—and I shot him as he was preparing to get off the train in Berlin."

Shock registered on Weber's face. His mouth fell open, and he was speechless for several seconds. "Shot? Do you mean with a gun? You tried to kill him?"

"I just did what was necessary—pulled the trigger twice. I knew that Gunter was traveling to Berlin to tell Göring that he'd fathered my son."

"Those two rounds you fired—did either hit Gunter?"

"I think so, but chaos erupted when the shots rang out, and stampeding passengers swept me off the train before I could determine Gunter's fate. I escaped by blending into the crowd of people running from the train. Later, I saw an emergency crew remove Gunter on a stretcher. I need to find out where they've taken him and whether he's survived."

"Oh, Anna, no wonder you're upset. The police will be looking for you."

"I know, and we need to be ready in case they find this apartment. I'll take my belongings to my former apartment, so nothing here indicates that I've been living with you. Also, we need to remove all of Luka's things—completely clean out his room. We need to dispose of anything that might tie him to this apartment. Can you do that for me?"

"Yes, of course. Then what?"

"I need to find out where Gunter was taken—if he's still alive, he'll be a patient in one of the Berlin hospitals. If he is hospitalized, then I'll monitor his condition and see if he survives. If I have to, I'll finish the job before he can tell Göring what he knows."

"Look, Anna, before you start plotting another ambush, you should rest and give us time to think. This situation is dangerous, and we need to handle it smartly. Acting rashly will only make things worse."

Chapter 23

Winter 1928: Berlin, Germany

Weber ruminated about Anna's predicament and its ramifications for their family. Obviously, Anna's actions would have repercussions—she'd stirred up a hornet's nest, and everyone would get stung unless they all ran for cover. Weber knew that Anna and Luka were most at risk, but he feared that Göring's reprisals would also endanger Carl and jeopardize the success of his mission. After further thought, he concluded that the cost of doing nothing was more than he was willing to pay and that the onus was on him to protect his loved ones. He felt sure that, when threatened, Göring would be a cunning and dangerous foe. The Reichsminister had the resources of the Nazi party at his disposal, and, with Gunter out of commission, he could call on other thugs to do his dirty work, including a bevy of stormtroopers.

Anna and the boys were no match for that threat, especially given Anna's fragile state of mind. Her maternal instincts had overridden her common sense and spycraft; like a mother bear whose cub was in danger, she was determined to protect Luka by any means necessary, risks be damned. Carl and Luka were too young and inexperienced to defend themselves against the Nazi horde, let alone safeguard their parents. That meant that the responsibility for protecting his family fell to him. He had no choice but to step up and take charge.

As a first step, Weber decided he couldn't allow Anna to search for Gunter in the Berlin hospitals. If passengers on the train had witnessed the shooting, then it was likely that the police had Anna's description and perhaps even a composite sketch. He concluded it would be much safer if he searched the hospitals and Anna stayed out of sight.

But as Weber pictured himself prowling hospital corridors, he questioned the merits of Anna's plans. What would he gain by finding Gunter, and would the benefits outweigh the risks? Even for him, searching for Gunter posed specific hazards. For all he knew, Göring's cronies had staked out Gunter's hospital room and were waiting, ready to pounce.

Still, it could be important to know whether Anna's ambush had prevented Gunter from telling Göring about Luka. If he discovered that Gunter was dead or in a coma, then he would know that Anna and Luka weren't in immediate danger, and the entire family, including Anna's parents, would be safe, at least temporarily. It would also afford him peace of mind and time to evaluate their predicament, confer with Curtis Taylor, and devise a foolproof escape plan. Those advantages, Weber realized, made it imperative that he find Gunter and determine whether he had survived and was in good enough condition to inform Göring about Luka.

That evening, after making Anna promise not to leave the apartment, Weber walked into the city to begin his search of Berlin hospitals. His first stop was the Charité, Berlin's oldest and largest hospital and the closest medical facility to the train station where Gunter had been shot. Odds were good, he figured, that the emergency squad had brought Gunter to the Charité.

His hunch proved correct. The clerk at the reception desk confirmed that Gunter had been admitted to the hospital but was hesitant to share information about his condition. To persuade the clerk, Weber said his name was Ulrich Meissner and that he'd traveled from Heidelberg to visit his brother. The clerk nodded and told Weber to go to the nurses' station on the second floor and ask whether Gunter was well enough to receive visitors.

Weber did as directed, and when he arrived at the nurses' station, the night supervisor told him that his brother was in critical condition. "I'm sorry, Mr. Meissner, but your brother is in a coma and cannot be disturbed. You can check with us tomorrow to see if Gunter's condition has improved."

"Thank you, I'll do that. Has my brother been conscious at any time since his arrival? Has he had any other visitors?"

The night supervisor opened a file and flipped through some pages. "I'm checking your brother's case notes to see if I can answer your questions. Ah, yes, I see here that he was unconscious upon arrival and hasn't awakened since. As far as I can tell, you're his first visitor and the only person who's inquired about his condition."

As Weber returned to his apartment, he contemplated the implications of Gunter's survival. Experience had taught him not to underestimate Meissner; the man was a wily adversary who, like a cat, seemed to have nine lives. Prudence dictated that he plan for every eventuality. He imagined various assault scenarios and formulated defensive schemes that he thought might help him safeguard Anna and the boys. One scheme in particular--suffocating Gunter in his hospital bed before he regained consciousness--appealed to him because it would prevent Göring from learning Anna's secret and would immediately eliminate the threat to his family. He also considered eliminating Göring. That scheme was also attractive: Why not just cut off the head of the snake? Eventually, he realized those schemes' appealed to him for their expediency more than their feasibility or sensibleness.

In the end, discretion prevailed, and Weber dismissed both schemes; he abhorred that kind of violence and didn't want it on his conscience. The only eventuality that merited consideration, he decided, was one in which Göring found out about Luka from Gunter and then marshaled his considerable resources to silence everyone who was aware of his paternity. As frightening as that prospect was, he knew he needed to plan for it because it could become a reality if Gunter regained consciousness.

When he arrived at the apartment, Anna was pacing the floor, anxiously awaiting his return. He barely got in the door before she confronted him. "Did you find him, Robert?" Weber nodded affirmatively.

"Oh my God, that means he's still alive!" Anna shrieked. She slumped onto the couch, put her head in her hands, and burst into tears. Weber sat beside her and tried to comfort her. "Listen, Anna, it's not as bad as you think. Yes, your actions have led you down an unfamiliar path, and storm clouds are gathering, but we must look for the silver lining. Even though Gunter's still alive, you haven't committed murder, and it looks like you've prevented him from speaking to Göring."

Now more curious than upset, Anna turned toward Weber and searched his face. "What are you talking about? How is that possible?"

"Gunter's been unconscious since he arrived at the hospital and hasn't had any visitors. That means we have some time to think through how we want to handle this situation and respond in a way that will protect not only Luka but all of us, including your parents."

"Why are you concerned about my parents? Do you think they're in danger too?"

Playing into Anna's fears didn't seem wise, so Weber tried soft-pedaling the risk. "Most likely not—only a slim probability at best. But to be safe, I think we should assume that Göring will be guided by his suspicions and will cast a wide net. If he suspects that your parents are aware of his paternity—which is a reasonable assumption—then he might attempt to silence them."

Silence them? Just how serious is this, Robert? What do you think he's going to do?"

Realizing that he'd not only ignited Anna's fears but doused them in gasoline, Weber tried to extinguish the blaze. "Well, Anna, remember that Göring may never find out. Gunter's been in a coma for quite some time, and he may never wake up. He may die before he regains consciousness. I'm just suggesting that we think ahead and develop a contingency plan."

The look on Anna's face—a mixture of fear and uncertainty—implied that she wasn't entirely convinced, but she gave Weber the benefit of the doubt. "All right, Robert, how should we prepare ourselves if Göring decides to go on a rampage and 'silence' us? How do we defend ourselves against a Nazi onslaught?"

"Let's not get carried away, Anna. It won't help to focus on the negatives or exaggerate the risks. Let's keep our cool and think about this rationally and intelligently. Between the two of us, we have more collective brain power than Göring and all of his Nazi minions combined."

Anna went to a writing desk beside the apartment's front windows and picked up a notepad and pencil. "You're probably right, Robert. My emotions are coloring my judgment and making it hard for me to concentrate on what you're saying. So, tell me how you think we should prepare, and I'll take notes."

Curiously, now that Weber had the floor, he hesitated and told Anna he needed a moment to organize his thoughts. It wasn't that he lacked ideas; he had plenty to say. Since leaving the Charité, he'd spent every waking hour strategizing—much like playing a mental chess game—imagining tactics Göring might use to find and silence Anna and her family, and then devising countermeasures for their escape and evasion. These machinations helped him formulate a complex, multi-layered plan with alternatives for anticipated contingencies and unforeseen events.

He hesitated because he wasn't sure how to present the plan without upsetting Anna. He knew she would resist any plan that would upend her entire life, and the scheme he was about to propose would do just that. To soften the blow, he decided against a didactic approach, as lecturing Anna had proven to be a recipe for disaster. Instead, he chose to use a Socratic strategy. He hoped that, as she wrestled with the realities of a Nazi manhunt, she would independently arrive at many of the same conclusions that he had.

"Okay, Anna, why don't we think about this from Göring's point of view? Suppose that he and his cronies, or the authorities for that matter, try to find you. How do you think they'd do that?"

Anna spoke without giving the matter much thought. "I suppose they'd organize some kind of search, " she said.

"Can you be more specific? Where do you think they'd look first?"

"Well, if we assume that Göring's spoken to Gunter, then he'll know I'm not at the base in Munich. He'd most likely send someone to my Berlin apartment—to the address listed in my employment records at the Reichswehr."

"I agree. But you haven't been living there for a while, and they'll discover that if they speak to your neighbors."

"That's good, isn't it? Göring will stumble into a dead end and get nowhere."

Weber shrugged his shoulders. "That depends. Do any of your neighbors know you're staying here with me?"

"No. I've been careful not to share any details about our lives."

"Good. Now, do you suppose there's a way we could use that apartment to our advantage?"

Anna wrinkled her nose and cocked her head sideways. She thought for several minutes before responding. "We could concoct some kind of cover story to tell my neighbors—a tale that would misdirect Göring's minions so they'd look for me in ambiguous locations that would take weeks or months to search."

"That's an excellent idea. But your neighbors might not be trustworthy. If the Nazis rough them up, they might admit that you told them to lie. So, here's another thought. Is there someone you trust who might like to rent your apartment--someone reliable enough to collaborate with us? A trustworthy house sitter could spread the bogus cover story and alert us when someone comes looking for you at your apartment. It would be like an early warning system for us."

Anna pondered the idea and then said, "Hanna Keller might be interested. She's one of my friends at the Reichswehr who's astute and trustworthy. I'll ask her."

"Good. Now, how would we respond if Hanna warns us that someone suspicious is searching for you?"

A quizzical look appeared on Anna's face, and then she abruptly stood, tossed the pencil and notepad on the couch, and pointed her finger at Weber. "All right, Robert, I know what you're doing. Stop this nonsense, and tell me your plan. It's obvious that you've thought long and hard about this, and we're wasting time because you're mollycoddling me."

Weber laughed. "There's no fooling you, is there, Anna? I was afraid that you wouldn't consider some plan elements because they could disrupt your life or change the nature of our relationship."

"Just tell me the plan—lay it out from beginning to end. Once I know what you're proposing, we can discuss how it might affect our life together."

Weber stood and paced the floor, gathering his thoughts."Okay, here's what I think. If Gunter recovers, you should leave Berlin and live with Luka on your parent's farm. It might be wise to do that now, regardless. You can't return to your job, and the Berlin police are probably looking for you."

"But Robert, I want to stay here with you."

"If you stay, you'll be living like a caged animal. You won't be able to go anywhere. It probably isn't safe for you to leave our apartment. You'll risk being seen."

Anna frowned, closed her eyes, and put her fist against her forehead.

"You were right. I don't like this plan."

"Come on, Anna. You wanted me to lay out the entire plan, so just hear me out. Brace yourself because I will dispense with hypotheticals and discuss the plan as though we will do it. If the plan seems more realistic, we'll be better able to spot flaws and make it foolproof."

Anna drew a deep breath and nodded affirmatively. "I'm listening."

"To get to Munich, I want you to steal one of the Aviation Coalition's planes, fly it to your parent's farm, and conceal it in your father's hangar. Two aircraft will provide us with more avenues of escape than one. If and when I join you, I'll use my plane so we'll have a third aircraft."

"What do you mean 'if' you join me?"

"Let me finish, please. After arriving at the farm, ask your father and Luka to help stockpile provisions. Purchase enough food for a month and get enough climbing gear to outfit everyone. Fly it to your father's Alpine shack and store it there. Then, find someone in Munich who can forge false papers for you, Luka, and your parents. If possible, have two sets made: one with Swedish names and the other with Swiss names. Make sure the papers look authentic; they must be good enough to pass a border inspection."

"Don't talk so fast, Robert. I'm having trouble writing all this down." Anna scribbled furiously in her notepad, filling an entire page.

"Next, see if you can find a short-wave radio to use at the farm. You might have to shop for one in Munich, or perhaps your father can get one from someone he knows. The guys in his crew are savvy and have connections; one might have a short-wave or know how to get one. I'll find one that I can use here. If I can't purchase a short-wave radio in Berlin, I'll arrange to meet Curtis Taylor at the border and get one from him. I'll ask him for two radios in case you have trouble finding one in Munich."

"The radios, I assume, are for us to communicate."

"Yes, it will be safer than using the telephone. It might also allow us to monitor Göring's communications if he uses radio transmissions to manage his search teams."

"All right. Then what?"

"I'll stay here in Berlin, monitor the situation as best I can, and use the short wave to stay in touch with you. I'll visit the Charité daily to check on Gunter's condition. If he makes enough of a recovery to speak to Göring, or I discover that Göring's begun to search for you and Luka, I'll contact you immediately. We should interpret either of those events as tripwires that tell us to activate this plan. If Göring closes in on me, I'll send Carl to Sweden, using Curtis's exfiltration network, and fly to the farm alone. But if his thugs fail to find our apartment, I might join you but have Carl remain in Berlin so he can stay in school."

"So, you will definitely join us at the farm?"

"That's my intention, but we'll have to see how things develop."

"What would keep you from joining us, Robert? Is it your commitment to your mission and your loyalty to Curtis Taylor?"

"Well, yes, I want to honor that commitment, so it is a consideration."

"I know how you can do both, Robert—help me and my family and honor your commitment."

"Are you serious? How would I do that?"

"I'll make you a deal. If you help me and my family leave Germany, I will give you a design portfolio that Göring has commissioned. It contains the blueprints for the next German Air Force—fighters, bombers, seaplanes, reconnaissance planes—all of the aircraft being developed for the next war. It's what I was working on at the secret base in Munich with the engineers from the Aviation Coalition—the aviation arm of the secret rearmament program."

◆◆◆

The intercity express was halfway between Stuttgart and Strasbourg as Weber lay in the upper berth of a double occupancy sleeper compartment, wishing he could go back to sleep. Since the train had left Stuttgart, he'd slept in fits and spurts, intermittently awakened by the man in the bunk below him who snored louder than a foghorn.

Earlier in the day, he'd driven Anna to Johannisthal Air Field and bid her farewell as she reluctantly began her sojourn to Munich to reside at her parent's farm. Anna had requisitioned one of the Aviation Coalition's planes, loaded her gear in the cargo compartment, and filed a flight plan for the secret air base near Munich. Strictly speaking, she didn't have clearance for the flight, but Gunter was in no position to object, and her senior status within the Reichswehr rearmament program gave her the authority to utilize government aircraft for official duties and testing purposes. Once she was in the air, no one could stop her from changing course and diverting to her parent's farm.

The separation had been emotionally painful for Weber and Anna; neither knew when they'd see each other again. Anna had been in tears when she'd climbed into the cockpit, and Weber had hung around at the airport, grieving as he waited for her plane to depart. When the aircraft had left the runway, he'd waved his arms like a madman even though he knew Anna couldn't see him. He wondered who was the idiot who'd said that parting was such sweet sorrow. Sorrow was all he had felt; nothing was sweet about it.

Upon leaving the airport, Weber had taken a cab to the Berlin Hauptbahnhof and boarded an intercity express that would take him westward across the country. The train would soon arrive in Strasbourg, where he'd arranged to meet Curtis Taylor and take delivery of two short-wave radios and a pistol. They'd agreed on Strasbourg as a meeting place because the city's location on the French-German border was ideal for a covert exchange. The ancient town was situated on the left bank of the Rhine along a trade route that had thrived for centuries. The constant influx of travelers would make it easy for operatives like themselves to masquerade as tourists and blend into the crowds without attracting attention. Furthermore, Strasbourg was an interesting destination; its proximity to two disparate cultures endowed the city with a diverse population, a cosmopolitan atmosphere, and a wide selection of markets, cafes, and restaurants. Its blended Franco-German heritage was a direct result of shifting nationalities—throughout its history, Strasbourg had sometimes belonged to Germany and other times to France. Currently, it was a French city, having been annexed by France after WWI under the Treaty of Versailles.

Rail wasn't Weber's favorite mode of transportation; he'd much preferred to have flown his plane to Strasbourg, but with security tightening at airports, he'd decided not to take that risk. Curtis had insisted that he knew how to pack the contraband so the railroad cops and border guards wouldn't find it. Not entirely convinced, Weber had reminded his friend that he'd be the one to pay the price if anything went wrong. However, Curtis refused to take his concern seriously, even after Weber had restated his misgivings. To his chagrin, nothing he'd said had put the slightest dent in Curtis' confidence. Ultimately, he'd had no choice but to trust his friend.

Winter 1928: Strasbourg, France

Weber arrived in Strasbourg on a clear, sunny and unseasonably warm day. He took a cab from the train station and instructed the driver to take him to the Bonne Chance café, the place Curtis had chosen for their meeting. The driver sped through a maze of busy, narrow streets, grumbling about pedestrians and other drivers who got in his way. When the cab finally slowed, Weber glanced out his window and saw the Bonne Chance come into view. The café was situated on an escarpment overlooking the Rhine.

Weber paid the driver, exited the cab, and strolled into the café, where he was greeted by the host, an attractive French-speaking woman who asked him whether he'd prefer a table in the dining area or on the deck behind the café. Before responding, he glanced around to see if he could spot Curtis. The café's interior consisted of a modest-sized dining area painted in earth tones with pictures of Parisian cafes hanging on the walls. Tables and chairs were scattered throughout the room, most of which were occupied, and servers were taking orders and delivering food. A large sliding glass door at the rear of the café opened onto an open-air deck where patrons were dining on white wicker tables and chairs under bright red folding umbrellas.

Curtis was nowhere to be seen, so Weber asked the host to seat him on the deck. He followed her through the dining area, and as they passed through the sliding glass door, he spied Curtis sitting at a table that was off by itself next to a protective railing that ran along the deck's perimeter. He thanked the host and walked toward Curtis' table. As he approached the table, he noticed that the deck was suspended high over the escarpment and overlooked a bend in the Rhine. The dark green river with bluish undertones carved a wide path between parallel, tree-covered hills. Several small boats drifted downstream, and one larger vessel fought the current as it rounded the bend and made its way upstream. Other maritime traffic was visible in the distance.

As Weber approached Curtis' table, Curtis looked up and waved him over. "Robert, my friend, how was your journey?"

"It was uneventful, except for the lout in my compartment, who snored constantly and kept me awake. But, all things considered, it went smoothly. I hope my return trip will be just as dull."

Curtis nodded to a nearby waiter, who returned the gesture and came directly to the table. "Oui, monsieur, comment puis-je vous aider?" Curtis ordered coffee and a croissant and then passed his menu to Weber.

Weber didn't bother to look at the menu. "I'll have the same, except make mine a chocolate croissant."

"Excellent choix, monsieur. Les croissants au chocolat are fresh from the oven."

After the waiter departed, Curtis' expression became more somber. "I have the equipment you requested."

Weber glanced at the floor near Curtis' feet and saw a thin, leather briefcase propped against a table leg. "You could have fooled me. Unless you're a magician, I don't see how you could have crammed two radios into that little briefcase."

"Always the comedian, eh Robert? The crate containing those items was delivered to the Strasbourg Hauptbahnhof today and will travel as freight on the train you take back to Berlin. The crate is labeled 'emergency medical supplies' and will be unloaded onto the platform next to your train when you arrive. Pick it up immediately; no one leaves emergency medical supplies lying around unattended. Tell the porters that the crate contains perishable medical supplies and to load it into a cab quickly so you can deliver it to the Charité hospital."

"Emergency medical supplies?"

Curtis removed two papers from his wallet and slid them across the table. “Yes, you’re going to be Dr. Robert Cramer, an American physician traveling to Berlin to deliver needed medical supplies to the Charité hospital. You’re on paid leave from Bellevue Hospital in New York to learn new medical techniques at the Charité. Your supervisor at the Charité sent you to Strasbourg to procure emergency medical supplies and personally escort them to Berlin.”

Weber inspected the pages and saw that one identified him as an American citizen, and the other showed him as an employee of the Charité hospital. He folded the pages carefully and slipped them into his wallet. “Interesting cover story, but I’m not sure I know enough about medicine to pass as a physician if questioned.”

“You’ll manage. Let your identity papers do the talking; they’re top-notch forgeries. However, the hospital ID isn’t as trustworthy as the citizenship document, so use it sparingly. Our forgers have less experience cloning employment papers. If you are stopped and questioned, keep it simple: say only what’s needed to get by, and don’t let them trick you into giving lengthy explanations.

“What about the firearm?”

Curtis lifted the lapel of his suit jacket, exposing a shoulder holster. “Later, we’ll make a trip to the WC, and I’ll pass this to you. You’ll need to figure out how to conceal it while traveling on the train.”

Weber paused to take a bite of his croissant. While doing so, he surveyed the patrons at nearby tables to make sure no one was listening. Then, in tones close to a whisper, he briefed Curtis on his situation in Berlin. "Chances are that I'll need to escort Anna and her son, Luka, out of Germany. I suspect that the police want her, and her situation with the Nazis has deteriorated to the point that she, Luka, and possibly her parents are in mortal danger. She possesses a treasure trove of intelligence about the secret rearmament program—a comprehensive design portfolio for a wide range of military aircraft and detailed information about current development and production activities. The portfolio is Göring’s vision for the future of the German Air Force. She’s instructed me to offer you a deal: if you help her family escape from Germany, she’ll give you the portfolio and tell you everything she knows. Are you interested, or do you need to call Washington and confer with Furst before making a decision?"

Curtis took a moment to digest Weber’s proposal. “Your request for radios and a pistol suggests that you have a plan. Tell me about that. How exactly would you get Anna and her family out of Germany?”

“I do have a plan--a layered set of plans based on foreseeable contingencies. At the moment, our main concern is Gunter Meissner. He’s in a coma, and it’s unclear if he’ll recover. Anna shot Gunter to prevent him from revealing a family secret that could seriously damage Göring’s future with the Nazi party. If Meissner recovers and tells Göring what he knows, he and his Nazi cronies will do everything in their power to silence Anna and eradicate her entire family."

"Wait a minute. Did you say that Anna shot Meissner? That seems extreme, even for her." "What do you mean, 'even for her'? Wouldn't you go to extremes to protect your child?" "Okay, point taken. So, you're saying that the deal depends on what happens to Meissner. There's no immediate need for Anna to leave Germany."

"That's correct. I am monitoring Gunter's condition, and Anna and Luka are sequestered on her family's farm west of Munich. We'll use the short waves to keep each other apprised of developments. The moment I discover that the Nazis have initiated a search, I'll put my plan in motion."

"So, if the Nazis do come after Anna, then what?

"Time's running short--my train departs in an hour, so I'll spare you the details. The gist is that we'll assemble at her family's farm and use three planes to fly everyone to Sweden or Switzerland. If Carl's in danger, I'll use Furst's emergency evacuation route to send him to Sweden to live with his aunt."

"All right, I'll clear this with Furst and see what resources he will provide for Anna's family. Keep me updated by short wave and stay off the telephone. I've got a high-powered short-wave radio in my Paris apartment that I use to communicate with Furst."

"Understood."

"I wish we had time to schmooze, but you've got a train to catch. Wait two minutes, and then meet me in the WC."

◆◆◆

The intercity express to Berlin left Strasbourg in the late afternoon and was halfway to Stuttgart before Weber dared to inspect the firearm that hung in a shoulder holster inside his jacket. He'd kept his arm pressed against his side the entire time for fear that the rig created an unsightly bulge that someone would notice. Rather than wait for that to happen, he'd buttonholed the conductor and booked a sleeping compartment--a single occupancy berth. This time, there'd be no snoring in this compartment unless he did it.

After moving his suitcase into the sleeper, he took off his jacket, removed the shoulder holster, and unsnapped the strap that secured the gun. Pulling the pistol from the holster, he saw a miniature stiletto protruding from an inside pouch. He extracted the knife, palmed it, and then flung it toward his bunk. The stiletto flew end over end, struck the mattress, and buried its three-inch blade up to the hilt; it was as sharp as a razor. Impressed, Weber raised his arm, put his hand against his forehead, and snapped off a salute to his friend. "Das ist fantastisch, Curtis." Something was reassuring about a weapon that could kill without making a sound.

Next, he examined the pistol—a Revolveur Modele 1892—the type used by the French army in World War I. He flicked a lever on the right side of the gun, and the cylinder swung out from the frame, revealing six 8mm rounds. It was an old gun, but it would serve his purposes if push came to shove.

He put the gun back in its holster and searched for a place to hide it but soon discovered that there wasn't a nook, cranny, or recess anywhere in the compartment that would withstand even a cursory search. Then his gaze fell upon the stiletto stuck in the mattress, giving him an idea. He pulled out the bed, lifted the bedsheets, and used the stiletto to cut a ten-inch slit in the side of the mattress that faced the wall. Then he shoved the holster and gun deep inside the mattress, replaced the bedsheets, and pushed the bed back into place.

The evening was approaching, so Weber went to the dining car, ordered bratwurst and a beer, and watched the forested countryside of southern Germany silently slip past his window. When the waiter delivered his food, he took a long pull from the ice-encrusted beer stein and used his napkin to wipe surplus suds from his upper lip. As he placed the stein on the table, he noticed a man dressed in a Bahnpolizei uniform staring at him from across the room. Weber shifted his gaze toward his food and took a bite of his bratwurst, hoping that man would lose interest. When he looked up again, the man was gone.

Weber's beer stein was soon empty, so he ordered another and quickly downed it. After that, he felt drowsy, so he returned to his compartment, crawled into the bunk, and covered himself with a sheet. He slept peacefully until a knock on the door awakened him.

"Bahnpolizei! Open this door!"

Weber groaned and tried to dismiss the pests. "Geh weg, ich schlafe!" To his dismay, the din at his door only intensified.

"Raus, raus! Öffne diese Tür! Hörst du? Open this door, or we will break it down!"

Weber rolled out of the bunk and muttered a string of curses as he stumbled toward the door. When he released the latch, the railroad cop he'd seen in the dining car burst through the door, knocking him to the floor. While Weber endeavored to get to his feet, a second man in uniform entered the compartment.

The two cops hoisted Weber from the floor and slammed him against the wall. The cop from the dining car braced Weber and started shouting. "Papers! Show me your papers!"

Weber started to protest, but the cop shoved his fist against his throat. "You will address me as Sergeant Offenhauser." Offenhauser then pointed at the other man in the room. "And you will call him Corporal Weissman."

"Ja wohl, Sergeant Offenhauser," Weber said sarcastically.

Offenhauser's face turned crimson, and he reached for his sidearm. Weber immediately understood that he'd underestimated the seriousness of the situation, so he wiped the smirk off his face and raised both arms as a sign of surrender. "I apologize, Sergeant Offenhauser. I meant no disrespect. It's just that you've rousted me from my bed in the middle of the night for no apparent reason."

Offenhauser responded by pushing Weber from his compartment into the corridor and then toward the rear of the train. "I will question you further in my office while Corporal Weissman searches your compartment."

Weber, followed closely by Offenhauser, marched through three coaches until they reached Offenhauser's office, located in the forward compartment of a converted freight car. Offenhauser unlocked the door and ordered Weber to sit in a chair bolted to the floor across from his desk.

Weber sat in the chair and then vented his anger at Offenhauser's heavy-handedness. "This is absurd. I haven't done anything wrong," he exclaimed. However, Offenhauser was too busy inspecting Weber's papers to reply. Silence ensued until Offenhauser finally dropped the papers on his desk and looked Weber in the eye.

"So, your name is Weber, and you're an American. Why are you in Germany, Mr. Weber?"

"It's Dr. Weber. I am a physician on leave from Bellevue Hospital in New York, and I came to Germany to learn new surgical techniques at the Charité hospital in Berlin."

"Ah, is that what you'd have me believe, Mr. Weber? Are you aware, Mr. Weber, that we don't particularly like Americans and like them even less when they reside in our country? As Herr Hitler says, 'Germany is for Germans.' Your politicians have proven themselves untrustworthy."

"I am no politician, I assure you."

"Be that as it may, your recalcitrance in responding to my summons to enter your compartment speaks volumes. Why did you ignore my directive? What have you got to hide?"

"I told you why I was slow to respond. I am not hiding anything."

"Perhaps then you will stop challenging my authority and tell me what I want to know. Where did you board this train?"

Remembering what Curtis had told him, Weber kept his replies as brief as possible.

"Strasbourg."

"And what is your destination?"

"Berlin."

"What is the reason for your trip?

"I'm escorting medical supplies from Strasbourg to the Charité hospital in Berlin.

"If you work at a Berlin hospital, why would you go to Strasbourg for medical supplies?"

"The specifics are confidential, but an emergency at the hospital made this trip necessary. All I can say is that Strasbourg was the only place that had the supplies I needed to treat a man with a rare disease."

"You tell a good story, Mr. Weber. It's polished, and your delivery is convincing. I suspect that you've spent considerable time rehearsing it. Yes, it's almost believable."

"Look, Offenhauser, why are you so determined to make trouble for me? I'm just doing my job."

"And so am I, Mr. Weber. Now sit there and keep your mouth shut until Corporal Weissman returns with his search results."

Weber stared at his shoes for what seemed like an hour before Weissman returned. Offenhauser stood as Weissman entered his office."

"Yes, Corporal, what did you find?"

Weissman shrugged his shoulders. "Nothing, sir, no contraband of any kind."

"Are you certain? How thorough was your search?"

"Exhaustive, sir. I found nothing."

Perplexed, Offenhauser rubbed his chin with the back of his hand and sat at his desk. He eyed Weber suspiciously, seemingly at a loss for words. Then, as if he'd experienced a revelation, he jumped to his feet and jabbed his finger accusingly at Weber. "You said that you're transporting medical supplies. Well, where are they?"

"They're in a crate loaded aboard the train in Strasbourg."

Offenhauser shifted his gaze toward Weissman. "Corporal, go look for this crate and report back to me. Let's see if Mr. Weber is telling us the truth."

Weissman left the office and returned twenty minutes later. "Sergeant, there is a crate marked medical supplies in a freight car at the rear of the train. It's wedged among some other freight loaded in Strasbourg--mostly boxes and barrels."

"Good work, Corporal. Get a crowbar out of the tool cabinet and show me this crate. I want to see what's inside. Weber, get on your feet; you're going with me."

Offenhauser marched Weber toward the rear of the train. They passed through two freight cars, and as they entered a third, Weber saw Weissman standing next to a crate with a crowbar. The crate was rectangular--about three feet tall and four feet wide--and clearly labeled 'medical supplies.'

"Pry the lid off that crate, Corporal!"

"Ja Wohl!" Weissman jammed the tip of the crowbar between the crate's upper slats and leaned on the shaft. There was a loud screech as the crowbar's leverage overpowered the crate's wooden slats.

Offenhauser pushed Weber toward the crate and stood beside him, waiting impatiently as Weissman struggled to pry off the lid. "Why is this taking so long, Corporal? Get that crate open." Weber held his breath as he watched Weissman work, praying that Curtis had disguised the radios well enough to keep him out of jail.

Weber saw something like steam escaping from the crate's interior as the lid came off. As the vapor cleared, he peered inside the box and saw a large black cylinder wrapped in blue plastic. Taped to the top of the cylinder were two small unmarked cardboard boxes. As he stared unknowingly at the boxes, questions formed in his mind. Now what, Curtis? What am I supposed to do with these boxes?

Offenhauser glanced inside the crate, pointed at the contents, and then glared at Weber, expecting an explanation. Weber did the only thing he could think of: he improvised. He grabbed the cardboard boxes and tore them open. He found surgical masks inside one, and the other contained rubber gloves. Without missing a beat, he donned both items and then passed each man a pair of gloves and a mask. "Here," he said sternly, "put these on so you don't contaminate my medical supplies."

The two Germans grudgingly obeyed, but the ruse didn't stall Offenhauser for long. He reached into the crate, grabbed the blue plastic liner, and tried to tear it open. The liner stretched but didn't tear, so Offenhauser ordered Weissman to cut it open.

Weissman pulled a small knife from his pocket, slit the liner, and was immediately engulfed in a thick cloud of vapor. He backed away from the crate, snorting, coughing, and waving his arms in a vain attempt to clear the air. Weber smiled and tried not to laugh. "It's a good thing you're wearing gloves and a mask. There's no telling what that stuff might do to your lungs."

Aghast at Weissman's predicament, Offenhauser retreated to the entrance of the freight car, leaving Weber alone by the crate. "Stay where you are, Mr. Weber," he shouted. "I want to see if you survive. If you do, we can continue our friendly chat, and you can show me what's inside that crate." When the air cleared, and Weber still stood, Offenhauser cautiously approached the crate. "Now, Mr. Weber, you will take the risks. Open that black tank so I can see what's inside."

When Weber pulled on the tank's lid, it didn't budge, so he twisted it instead. To his surprise, it rotated--slowly at first and then more quickly--until a lever popped up and freed the lid. He grasped the lever and lifted the lid, releasing another vapor cloud. After setting the lid aside, he peered into the tank. The cylinder was filled with a dark liquid, with a thick layer of burgundy-colored dry ice floating on top.

Offenhauser stood motionless beside the crate, mesmerized by its contents. "Weber, what is that crusty, reddish, gas-producing material floating in the tank?"

"Haven't you seen dry ice before? A French scientist invented it during the last century."

"Yes, but dry ice is white, not red. But I digress. I want to see what's underneath the dry ice. Put your hand in the tank and feel around for whatever you're transporting in there. Lift out the contents so I can see them."

Weber pulled the cuffs of his gloves up above his wrists, then pushed the dry ice aside and plunged his hand into the dark liquid. His fingers brushed against something like a water-filled balloon, so he grasped the object, lifted it out of the tank, and placed it on the floor next to Offenhauser's feet. It was a plastic bag filled with dark red fluid.

Offenhauser stepped on the bag with his boot, and it burst, spraying a syrupy burgundy solution onto his pants and everything else in the immediate vicinity. "Scheisse! Weber, you fool, look what you've done! My uniform has been stained."

Weissman, who'd been watching closely, stated the obvious. "It's blood, sir. You stomped on a bag of blood!"

Deliberately ignoring Offenhauser, Weber reached into the tank again and extracted a white shaft with knurled, knob-like ends that resembled joints. Dark chunks of flesh and knotty blood vessels dangled from the shaft. Weber shook the shaft to slough off the fleshy fragments but only succeeded in casting bits of bloody tissue onto Offenhauser's face and uniform.

Weisman, now clearly unnerved, shrieked, "Mein Gott, that's flesh and bone from somebody's body!"

Offenhauser yelped and sprang back in horror, then dropped to his knees and repeatedly retched onto the floor. When the spasms ceased, he pulled a handkerchief from his pocket, wiped his face, and stood. "Weber, put that bone back and seal the tank immediately! You've deliberately exposed me to something dangerous, haven't you?"

Weber nodded to indicate that he'd understood Offenhauser's orders, but he hoped that the panicking Sergeant had interpreted the gesture as confirmation of his fears. "Well, Sergeant, whenever tissues are exposed, there's a disease risk."

Offenhauser turned an even whiter shade of pale and began shouting at Weissman. "Corporal, get over here and wipe up this mess. There's blood and vomit everywhere, and the stink is unbearable. Do you realize how unsanitary this is? Think of the germs--it's a breeding ground for disease. I'll catch my death in here."

A sense of relief washed over Weber as he tightened the lid on the tank. His seemingly inescapable journey into captivity had taken an unexpected turn toward liberation. Offenhauser had lost interest in him because he was more concerned about survival.

Now that the possibility of going to jail seemed remote, Weber started thinking about his escape plan. He realized that if he came out of this debacle unscathed--which now seemed likely--he had only one person to thank: Curtis Taylor. Weber wanted to salute his friend again as a gesture of respect and appreciation but refrained so as not to blow his cover. Looking back, he realized that he had been foolish to doubt Curtis. The man had an exceptional talent for undercover work.

The freight car lurched suddenly, causing Weber to lose his balance. The train was slowing down, meaning they'd arrive in Stuttgart soon. Weber knew it was time to end this charade and escape Offenhauser's grasp.

"Get a grip, Offenhauser. What were you expecting? I told you I'm a physician, and this crate contained medical supplies. It's not my fault that you have a weak, queasy stomach. Now stop all this nonsense and let me return to my compartment. I must sleep before we reach Berlin, so I'm rested enough to work a full shift at the Charité."

Offenhauser's antagonistic disposition had vanished, and in its place was a more docile version of the tyrant. He waved his hand dismissively, half-ignoring Weber because he was preoccupied with removing the blood and vomit from his face and uniform.

Weber didn't tarry. Before Offenhauser could change his mind, he bolted from the freight car and ran down the corridors that connected the rail cars. When he reached his compartment, he locked himself safely inside.

Chapter 24

Winter 1928: Berlin, Germany

Weber awoke as his train pulled into the Berlin Hauptbahnhof. He packed his things, descended from his coach onto the station platform, and walked toward the train's rear. He'd only taken a few steps when it occurred to him that he'd forgotten to remove his gun from the mattress. Annoyed, he climbed back aboard the train to retrieve the weapon, but to his dismay, a young woman and a child had already occupied the compartment. He introduced himself as the compartment's former occupant and explained that he'd left one of his possessions under the bed.

The woman took the child by the hand and stepped into the corridor, preferring, it seemed, not to be alone with Weber inside the compartment. Weber dashed inside, shoved his hand through the slit in the mattress, and extracted the gun. He kept his back to the woman so she couldn't see what he'd removed from inside the mattress.

More than twenty minutes had passed when Weber resumed his trek toward the rear of the train. He scolded himself for his tardiness; by now, the crate would have been offloaded and left unattended on the platform. When he reached the freight cars, he searched through an assortment of cargo stacked on the platform but couldn't find his crate. He cornered a rail worker inside one of the open freight cars and asked where he might find his medical supplies.

The laborer pointed toward an empty place on the platform. "We put it right there, out front, where it could be seen because we figured it might contain perishable goods. It only sat there a few minutes before two men arrived and loaded it onto a cart. I didn't see which way they went."

"Those guys were thieves—they stole my crate!"

The rail worker's eyes grew as large as saucers. "Hold on while I summon the Bahnpolizei!" He took a whistle from his pocket and blew a shrill alarm; seconds later, a uniformed police officer appeared on the platform. The officer introduced himself as Detective Bruner and nodded when Weber explained that two men had stolen his medical supplies.

"Ach! The damned platform parasites are getting bolder. Your crate must have been sizeable if it took two of them to load it on a cart. For something that large, there are only two ways to exit—left down the platform and out through the station's main entrance or right up the platform and out through the loading docks. The latter option provides more cover, so let's check there first."

Bruner led Weber to the loading docks, and the two men scoured the area outside the terminal. As Weber was about to give up hope, he spotted an empty cart near a large truck pulling away from the curb. "Officer, stop that truck!"

The detective ran out in front of the truck, and when the driver refused to yield, he pulled his sidearm and fired a shot into the air. The blast from the gun ruptured the tranquil evening atmosphere and drew a crowd of onlookers, including three additional Bahnpolizei officers.

Bruner opened the driver's door, pulled the driver out of the cab, and shoved him against the truck's front fender. The driver's companion jumped out of the passenger's door and ran from the station, but the other cops quickly apprehended him and returned him to the truck where Bruner was standing. Bruner took control of the situation and started shouting orders.

"Take both of these crooks to the station and lock them in a closet. Then, contact headquarters to have someone pick them up and charge them accordingly. There is a crate in the back of their truck containing medical supplies that belong to Doctor Weber. Instead of unloading the crate and searching for another vehicle, I am going to commandeer this truck to help him deliver the supplies to the Charité hospital. Does anyone have any questions?" The police officers nodded and escorted the thieves towards the station. Bruner gestured for Weber to get in the truck.

Weber's mind raced as Bruner drove out of the station and merged into evening traffic. He was in a bind: he'd planned to transport the crate to his apartment by cab, but fate had gifted him with a police escort to the hospital, where he'd be forced to surrender the crate. The truck was halfway to the Charité before he hit upon a solution.

"Detective Bruner, would you mind taking a detour to my apartment before we go to the hospital? I want to pick up my car so I can get home after we deliver the medical supplies."

Bruner nodded, requested the address, and rerouted the truck toward Weber's apartment. When he arrived, he parked on the street in front of the apartment and waited while Weber went to get his car.

Weber searched the apartment until he found his car keys. Then he went to the garage, pulled a hatchet off a shelf, and packed it in the trunk of his Mercedes. After backing the car onto the street, he got out and told

Bruner to follow him to the hospital and park beside his Mercedes.

As Weber neared the Charité, he drove along the river until he reached Ost-West Strasse and entered the hospital grounds on Nordstrasse. His next objective was to find an isolated place to park where Bruner could unload the crate and leave him to retrieve the radios without being disturbed. But where? He navigated the maze of streets and buildings until he came to an annex well outside the traffic pattern. He skirted the building and parked in the rear, next to a door in an alcove, relatively hidden from the street.

Bruner parked behind the Mercedes, got out, and started asking questions. "Why are we stopping here? Shouldn't these perishable medical supplies be delivered to the central part of the hospital? Don't you realize we just drove past the main hospital buildings?"

"We are in the right place, Detective Bruner, I assure you. I keep the supplies for my practice and my surgery in this annex. I'll help you get the crate off the truck, and we can place it here by my door." Bruner looked unconvinced but did as Weber asked and then departed.

Weber crawled behind the crate, sat against the door inside the alcove, and waited for nightfall. Once it was dark, he returned to his car and surveilled the area around the annex. Seeing no one, he got the hatchet out of the trunk, returned to the alcove, and chopped off the wooden slats that formed the top and sides of the crate. He discovered that the radios were packed in plastic at the bottom of the crate underneath the black cylinder containing the blood and body parts. He pushed the tank to one side, extracted the radios, and stowed them in the trunk of the Mercedes. "Finally," he muttered, relieved to have taken possession of the radios. Exhausted, he started the car and drove to his apartment.

◆◆◆

Still weary after his trip to Strasbourg, Weber took a day to reconnect with Carl and catch up on his sleep. He'd been concerned about Carl while he was away from Berlin, but, as it turned out, he needn't have been. Carl had managed quite well; he'd made his meals, gotten to school on time, and kept up with his homework. Weber didn't know whether to feel proud or outmoded. Whether he liked it or not, Carl was maturing rapidly and would soon be an independent and capable young adult. Until then, however, it was his duty to safeguard Carl from threats, especially the one posed by Göring and his cronies, even if it required a prolonged separation, which was likely if Carl had to leave Germany and live with his aunt in Sweden. He prayed that it wouldn't come to that.

Toward the end of the day, Weber and Carl went to the kitchen and began making a meal together. Weber was pounding a piece of meat with a tenderizing mallet when Carl motioned for him to stop. "Dad, stop that and listen for a moment. I think someone's knocking on our front door, but I can't tell while you're hammering."

Weber went to the front door, opened it, and found a woman standing on his front porch. She looked upset. He figured it was one of his neighbors who'd come to complain about the noise he was making. "Hello. I'm sorry. Have I disturbed you with all the pounding? I've been trying to tenderize some meat."

The woman looked puzzled and shook her head. "I'm not here about the pounding. My name is Hanna Keller. I'm Anna's friend--the person renting her apartment."

"Oh, yes, of course. Do come inside."

Weber ushered Hanna into the living room and invited her to sit on the couch. "Would you like a cup of tea or something stronger?"

"Thanks. I wouldn't refuse a brandy or some schnapps--I need something to steady my nerves."

Weber went to the kitchen and told Carl about the visitor. A bad feeling swept over him as he poured brandy into a snifter. Hanna was upset, and that meant something was amiss. He wondered whether someone had set off an alarm in their early warning system.

Hanna graciously accepted the brandy and quickly drained the snifter. Weber smiled and tried to maintain a calm demeanor, even though his heart was racing. "So, Hanna, may I ask why you're visiting us today?"

Hanna squirmed on the couch and eyed Weber anxiously. "Some Nazis came to my apartment looking for Anna. They forced their way inside and threatened me. I told them I didn't know Anna, but…" Hanna stopped midsentence, too choked up to continue. Tears rolled down her face, and she struggled to regain her composure. "When I refused to say anything more, the group leader brandished a truncheon and said I should reconsider or I'd be sorry. He told me that he'd return tomorrow for an answer. I'm frightened of what he will do to me if I don't tell him about Anna."

"I'm so sorry, Hanna. Did you know any of these Nazis, or did any of them identify themselves?"

"I think the leader's name was Gunter. That's what the other men called him."

Weber cringed even as he tried to keep a smile on his face. If Gunter had found Anna's residence, how long would it be before he arrived at his apartment? He had to prevent that from happening because it would endanger Carl. But how? Only one solution came to mind: he had to stop Gunter from interrogating Hanna.

"Hanna, is there somewhere you can go or someone you can stay with temporarily?"

"My sister lives in Hannover. I suppose that I could go there."

Weber opened his wallet and handed Hanna some Reichsmarks. "Here's money for a train ticket—go to the station, buy a ticket for Hannover, and leave immediately. Don't go back to the apartment. Leave your sister's number with me, and I'll call you when it's safe to return."

◆◆◆

The following day, Weber rose early, walked to a café, and ordered coffee and kuchen. He bought a copy of the Berliner Tageblatt, sat at an empty table, and began reading the newspaper while waiting for his food. What he saw on the front page took his breath away. Just under the fold were pictures of Anna and Luka with the caption: '*Spies Steal German Military Secrets.*' In the article accompanying the photos, Anna was described as a Reichswehr engineer who had stolen secret military files from a Reichswehr office and disappeared without a trace. Luka was portrayed as an internship student from the Berlin Technical Academy who had helped Lichtmann steal the files by smuggling them past security guards at the Reichswehr facility. The article concluded with a summons: readers were encouraged to contact the police if they had information that might lead to the arrest of either fugitive.

Weber's hands trembled as he set down the newspaper. He leaned back in his chair, trying to process the implications of what he had just read. Could the signals be any clearer? First, Hanna's visit, and now a published allegation of spying and the issuance of an arrest warrant. There was no denying it--Göring was searching for Luka, and Gunter was alive and well and leading the chase. It was time to put his plan into action and get Anna and her family out of Germany.

He left the café, returned to his apartment, and dragged the shortwave radios from under his bed. Each of the two radios was packed in a separate black leather travel case that resembled an oversized attaché. He carried one of the cases to the kitchen table, unsnapped its metal clasps, and removed its contents, consisting of the short-wave radio, a hand-written instruction booklet, and a coil of thin-gauge wire. The writing on the cover of the booklet looked familiar, and as Weber examined it more closely, he understood why: it was Curtis' handwriting. Had Curtis sent him a message? There was only one way to find out. He pulled a chair to the table, sat, and read the makeshift manual.

All but the booklet's last page contained instructions about setting up and operating the short-wave radio. Weber followed the instructions exactly. He opened the back of the radio, identified two thick cables—one black and the other white—and attached them to the corresponding color-coded terminals of the unit's internal battery. Then, he uncoiled a length of the thin-gauge wire, strung it across the kitchen, and pushed one end into an aperture on the top of the radio marked 'antenna.'

Having set up the radio, Weber turned his attention to the manual's last page, which he was surprised to discover contained only gibberish. The page was full of words and numbers strung together in random order. He scanned the page several times, and as he was about to toss the booklet aside, it occurred to him that the message on the last page might be in code. But what code would Curtis have used? Might it be the same encryption method Furst's agents had taught him after he'd accepted the mission to Berlin? He got a pencil and marked off every seventh word on the page. Then, he numbered each seven-word set in order, from beginning to end. He identified the first word for the first set and wrote it on his pad. Then he noted the second word in the second set, which happened to be a number, and transcribed it next to the first word on his pad. He repeated this method of extracting words or numbers for all of the remaining sets, returning to the first word in a set each time he'd deciphered seven complete sets.

When Weber finished, the message was terse but intelligible. It read: *Tune 30.2 MHz, broadcast & receive, M & F, on the hour every other hour, 8 PM to midnight.* He interpreted this to mean that when he wanted to communicate with Curtis, he was to tune the radio to 30.2 MHz and use that frequency to both broadcast and receive messages and that he was to transmit or listen for messages at 8 PM, 10 PM, or midnight on Mondays and Fridays. He felt reasonably confident that his interpretation was correct, but the only way to be sure was to test it. Fortunately, it was a Friday, so he decided to undertake a trial run later that evening.

At 8 PM, Weber turned on the short wave and set the dial for 30.2 MHz. There was nothing but static initially, but then his friend's familiar voice sliced through the ambient crackling and hissing. "Berliner Pilot, this is Parisian Control. Are you receiving?"

Weber replied. "Loud and clear."

"What's your situation?"

"Mission accomplished, although not without duress. The Bahnpolizei intercepted the package, but its contents repulsed the snoops and protected the contraband. The fact that you hear my voice on the airwaves proves that the contraband arrived in good condition."

"So I hear! Congratulations!"

"Thanks. Hey, tell me something. Where did you get the blood, flesh, and bones?"

"An abattoir south of Paris. The owner had an abundance of porcine and bovine carcasses, and I had him pack the tank with bones, flesh, and fluids that resembled those found in humans. You're lucky I didn't have him fill the tank with entrails."

"I'll count myself lucky indeed. There's a Bahnpolizei Sergeant somewhere in southern Germany who isn't feeling quite so lucky."

"Serves him right for interfering with a physician during the performance of his duty."

"Yeah, promise me you'll never ask me to play that role again."

Curtis laughed and then changed the subject. "I have news. The boss has approved your plan. He's playing it low-key, but it's clear that he's desperate to get his hands on that portfolio. The bottom line is that your worth as an agent has risen, and you're in an enviable bargaining position. You can call the shots on this one, so let me know if you want to revise your mission parameters and requirements, and I'll act as your intermediary with the boss."

"That's great news, and I appreciate your support. As you know, it's a fluid situation, and I can't entirely foresee what will happen, let alone anticipate the resources I'll need to surmount unexpected obstacles. But your timing is superb; I know that Göring initiated a search for Luka, so I'll start work immediately on the extraction. I'll fly south tomorrow to deliver contraband to my travelers."

"I'll let Furst know that things are in motion. Mind how you go."

"Will do. I will rethink the entire operation again, but I have a couple of requests offhand. First, see if you can improve my financing—I could use a larger cash infusion. Second, see if the boss can rent my former Washington, DC apartment. If I succeed, the travelers will need a place to stay, recover, and rebuild their lives. Third, alert the boss' local network so they'll be prepared to exfiltrate one traveler to Sweden immediately."

"I'll get on it. Anything else?"

"Let's talk again a week after I've had time to consult with the travelers."

"Sure. I'll contact you next week--same day, same time."

◆◆◆

The experimental Dewoitine D-500 glided over the hills and valleys of southern Bavaria, gently rising and falling as it crossed the thermals created by the sun's differential warming of the undulating landscape below. Weber loosened his grip on the controls, rested his head against his seatback, and cracked open his side window, allowing the crisp morning air to drift through the cabin. Pilots dreamed about days like this one. The sun was perched above the eastern horizon, beaming in all its glory, tinting the wispy, scattered clouds above him a jumble of red and orange hues. The view in front of the aircraft seemed to stretch forever, thanks to an unusually high ceiling and near-perfect air quality. Below, the fields and forests were infused with autumn colors and looked like puzzle pieces, fitted tightly together in myriad shapes and patterns.

When the Gabel's farm came into view, Weber adjusted course and throttled back the engine so that the Dewoitine began a gradual descent. As his destination grew closer, he adjusted the flaps and lowered the nose, letting the plane descend further. Once over the farm, he flew at right angles to the runway, checking wind speed and landing conditions. The wind was from the east, and the runway was dry and clear, so Weber aligned the Dewoitine with the runway and initiated his final descent.

The Dewoitine bounced and shuddered when it touched down on the grass-covered airstrip behind the Gabel's farmhouse. Weber retracted the throttle and let the plane bump along for a few seconds before applying the brakes. When the aircraft approached the end of the runway, he circled to the left, taxied back to Aaron Gabel's hangar, and parked on the concrete apron.

The hangar door opened as Weber climbed down from the cockpit, and Luka stepped onto the apron. Turning to face the boy, Weber shouted a greeting. "Hello, stranger!"

Luka ran to meet Weber, hugged him briefly, and then launched into a series of questions. How's Carl? Do you know how much I've missed you and Carl? When can I move back to Berlin?"

"Whoa, Luka, I just got my feet on the ground. Give me a minute to get my bearings." "Sorry, I'm excited that you're here, and I was hoping you could convince my mother to let me return to Berlin. I don't want to be a farmer; I want to become an aeronautical engineer like you, Carl, and my mother. Why did my mother leave Berlin and make me come back to the farm?"

Weber was taken aback by the number and intensity of Luka's queries and uncertain how to respond. From what the boy was asking, it seemed apparent that Anna had not leveled with Luka about Gunter's discoveries and the dangers he and his family faced. He didn't know why Anna had hidden the truth from Luka but knew it wasn't his place to tell the boy. He decided to hold his tongue until he consulted with Anna. "Look, Luka, I don't have answers to those questions. Perhaps we can discuss these matters later with your mother."

Luka looked disappointed but didn't protest or question Weber's response. "All right, let's go up to the house. Mom's looking forward to seeing you, and Grandma's making lunch."

"Okay, but help me haul some gear to the house." Weber retrieved two carrycases from the plane and handed Luka the one containing the short-wave radio. "That case contains a valuable radio, so don't drop it."

They walked to the farmhouse together, and Weber followed Luka into the kitchen, where Aaron and Ruth Gabel greeted him. Their voices drew Anna from somewhere in the back of the house. When she spotted Weber in the kitchen, she threw her arms around him and kissed him passionately.

The kiss endured until Ruth Gabel lost patience and began putting food on the table. "Come on, break it up, you two; it's time to eat." Aaron and Luka applauded. "Yeah, the rest of us are hungry," Luka quipped.

When lunch and the dishes were finished, Anna invited Weber to her bedroom for some rest and relaxation. Aaron Gabel winked at Anna and chuckled. "Is that what it's called these days?"

"Oh, Dad, must you say everything that crosses your mind? There are some things that you should keep yourself." Anna got up from the table, grabbed one of Weber's suitcases, and stormed out of the kitchen.

Weber politely asked to be excused from the table, thanked Ruth for the meal, and then departed to join Anna in her bedroom. As he walked through the house, his thoughts were focused on rekindling the intimacy that Anna had initiated in the kitchen, but when he entered the bedroom, he found himself quizzing Anna about Luka.

"Luka cornered me when I arrived and asked if he could return to Berlin, so I assume you haven't explained why you moved him to your parents' farm. Why haven't you told him that he's in danger--that his life is at risk?"

"What did you expect me to tell him, Robert? Do you know how difficult it is for me to explain my past? I'm responsible--I've put my son in danger. How do I tell Luka that I made a mistake--that I got pregnant because I was drunk? How do I explain that a Nazi who thinks he's Luka's father and hates my family's heritage wants to dispose of Luka to save himself some embarrassment? You tell me, Robert, what words would I use to say that to my son?"

"Well, who does Luka think is his father? What have you told him?"

"I thought Hermann was Luka's father for most of his life, so I made up a father Luka could respect and kept my story as close to the truth as possible. I told him that his father was a decorated German fighter pilot who died during the war. But as it turned out, what I thought was a lie was closer to the truth than I realized."

"Luka's been told a lot of lies, hasn't he? You've never been very honest with Luka, and now you're deceiving him by concealing the threat that Göring poses."

"That's right, Robert. I've lied to Luka since the day he was born. Why should I stop now?" I gave him a fictitious surname, pretended that I was his sister and not his mother, lied to him about his father, and made up reasons why he had to stay on the farm. His life is based on a lie, and he's been lied to his whole life."

"You say that sarcastically, but maybe it's time that you stopped lying. Luka's old enough to know the truth and strong enough to handle it. Besides, how will you conceal his past when Göring and his stormtroopers come looking for him? They'll hunt him like an animal, and he won't know why. He's more likely to survive if he knows what's happening and can take steps to protect himself."

Anna's eyes flashed with anger, and Weber braced himself for a salvo of harsh words. However, instead of launching a barrage of angry avowals, Anna collapsed onto the bed and wept bitterly.

Having reduced Anna to tears, Weber was overcome with remorse. He sat on the bed beside her and spoke in a conciliatory tone. "You're right, Anna. I've been preachy and critical, and I haven't appreciated how hard this must be for you. I apologize."

"Thank you, Robert, but the truth is that I haven't wanted to hear what you've been telling me. I've nothing to gain and much to lose by denying the truth, so it's time I faced facts and behaved like a responsible parent. Luka deserves to know what's happened and how it will affect his future, and he needs to hear it from me, regardless of how hard it is for me to tell him. I'll speak to him tonight."

◆◆◆

Weber rose early the following day and walked to the hangar behind the farmhouse, intending to inspect Aaron Gabel's plane and the aircraft Anna had pirated from the Aviation Coalition. Preparedness was the linchpin in his plan to protect the Gabel family from the Nazis, and during his time at the farm, he wanted to make sure that Anna and her parents had followed his instructions and were ready to act at a moment's notice. His first order of business was to determine whether all three planes—Aaron's, Anna's, and his—were airworthy and outfitted for lengthy, high-altitude flights. After that, he would check whether Anna and her parents had obtained the specified provisions and equipment and placed them in strategic locations.

Weber turned on the lights as he entered the hangar and was surprised to see Luka curled up on a blanket underneath his grandfather's plane. Awakened by the lights, Luka sat up, rubbed his eyes, and turned to face Weber.

"Robert! What are you doing up so early?"

"Never mind that! Why are you out here sleeping under your grandfather's plane?"

"My mother and I fought last night, just before bedtime. I'm angry with her, and I came out here because I didn't want to see her at breakfast this morning."

"What was the fight about, or would you prefer not to discuss it?"

"She told me that I'm a bastard--that I was born out of wedlock. As it turns out, my real father was a fighter pilot and died in the war. But a Nazi that she works with, a man named Hermann Göring, thinks he's my father, and he'd rather bury me than admit that he has a Jewish son. Talk about a cruel twist of fate! I'll never be able to go back to Berlin. What am I going to do now?"

"Well, before we discuss what you'll do, let's talk about your mother. She loves you very much, you know."

"Don't take her side in this, Robert! She's done nothing but lie to me. You call that love?"

Listen, Luka, you must put this behind you because your family needs you. Your mother and your grandparents are in danger--mortal danger. You and I have to do everything we can to help them."

"Why should I help my mother? She doesn't deserve it. Maybe my grandparents do, but she doesn't."

"Look, Luka. I understand why your mother's confessions have made you angry. It's a lot to take in; she should have told you long ago. I feel for you, and if you let me, I'll do everything I can to help you overcome your past."

"You can help me by telling my mother I will never forgive her."

"That's a bit hard-hearted. Please try to keep your mother's struggles in mind. Her life has been difficult and uncertain since she was your age. However, you were always her reason for living. She chose to give birth to you and raise you, and even though you might not agree with some of her decisions, she did what she believed was necessary to keep you safe from harm. Lying about your father was her way of protecting you from Hermann Göring, a dangerous man who she believed was your father until recently."

"Yeah, whatever."

It was apparent to Weber that Luka was too agitated to listen to reason. Until he mellowed a bit, no amount of cajoling would shift his perspective or overcome his intransigence. Still, he needed to enlist Luka's help; the stakes were too high to do otherwise. But what would motivate the boy? Then he had an idea.

"Luka, I urge you to examine your heart and see if you can find enough compassion to assist me in saving your family. If you do, they will be eternally grateful, and you will be satisfied knowing that you did the right thing--something that truly matters. It is the act of an honorable man, and I believe you are one. Not that it matters, but there's always the possibility that you might profit from saving your family."

Luka, who'd been looking at his shoes, raised his head and made eye contact when he heard Weber mention the word 'profit.' "What do you mean? How might I profit from saving my family?"

"They need to leave Germany; if you help them, you can go with them. I plan to resettle your family in America near Washington, DC. If you lived there instead of here on the farm, you and Carl could attend a school like the

BTA and continue to prepare for an aviation career. Moreover, there are some excellent flight schools near Washington where you could learn to fly and, if desired, become a professional pilot."

Weber could see by the look in Luka's eyes that he was hooked. Part of him felt guilty. Had he just bribed the kid? Yes, he had. But another part of him felt relieved. With Luka's assistance, his plan was much more likely to succeed.

"What would you want me to do, Robert?"

"Help me arrange things here at the farm so that when I give the signal, you and your family can embark immediately on the first leg of your journey to America. Göring's investigator, Gunter Meissner, is searching for them as we speak, and he's very good at his job. Once he has the scent, he'll pounce without warning. If your family isn't prepared to act, they may not escape in time. I brought the short wave to warn you as soon as I know something. I'll teach you how to use it."

"I'd like that, but aren't you going to stay and help us?"

"No, I must return to Berlin to assist Carl and keep tabs on your father and Meissner."

"Okay, you can contact me by radio anytime. What else can I do?"

"I gave your mother a list of provisions and equipment. Do you know if she or your grandparents have stockpiled rations and moved the climbing gear to the alpine cabin?"

"Not that I know of; I haven't seen them purchase any extra food or move equipment."

Weber uttered a curse. "Damn, then I'll need you to do that. I'll give you a copy of my list, and then I want you to take over and get the job done; I'll leave it up to you to figure out how. I bet your grandfather will help you."

"I'll ask him this morning."

"While you're at it, offer to help your grandfather service the aircraft to prepare them for high-altitude, extended flights. Depending on our route, there's a chance the planes could hit their absolute ceilings and prevent us from getting over the mountains. He will need to install high-altitude propellers and auxiliary fuel tanks. It will be a good experience, and you'll learn much about planes."

"Done!"

◆◆◆

Shortly after returning to Berlin, Weber told Carl to pack his bags because he was sending him to Sweden to live with his Aunt. Carl wasn't pleased; he knew that Luka and his family needed to leave Germany but hadn't realized that their troubles would spill over onto him.

"I don't get it, Dad. I'm happy at BTA and can't graduate unless I finish my coursework. I only have a class or two, and I'll be done. Why do I have to leave?"

"Remember the intruder who broke into our house in Stockholm and tried to shoot us while we were sleeping? His name is Gunter Meissner, and he has the same fate in mind for Luka and his family. He's scouring Berlin right now, trying to find them. Hanna told me he'd found Anna's apartment so he could show up soon. If he thinks you know something, he won't hesitate to harm you to get you to talk. I don't want you to be here when he finds us."

Carl blanched. "Dad, I should have told you this before, but a man hung around at my school, watching Luka and me. He tried to follow Luka and me home from school twice, but we gave him the slip."

"What did this man look like?"

Carl's description left no doubt that the man in question was Gunter. "Oh, Carl, why didn't you say something sooner?"

"It gets worse, Dad."

"Worse? How can it get worse?"

"I saw him yesterday. He stood across the street behind some bushes, watching our apartment."

Carl's admission put Weber on edge. He intermittently peered out the front window for the remainder of the day, checking whether anyone was watching the apartment. That evening, after seeing no one, he began to relax. Still, even after dark, he occasionally walked to the window to check for signs of surveillance. All appeared normal until just after Carl went to bed when he spotted something in the trees across the street that made chills run down his spine. It was a pinpoint of light—the orange-red glow of a cigarette.

Alarmed by the sighting, Weber went to his bedroom and retrieved the Revolveur Modele 1892 from his nightstand. He flipped open the cylinder, loaded six 8mm rounds into the chambers, and then shoved the pistol into his hip pocket.

He exited the apartment through the back door and walked eastward through the yards of adjoining residences until he was two blocks downwind of the intruder. Then he crossed the street and backtracked through the densely forested area alongside the street on the opposite side of his apartment. He paused when he neared the place where he'd seen the intruder and scanned the surroundings, hoping to catch a glimpse of the cigarette or overhear a sound that might help him pinpoint the prowler.

He stood motionless for several minutes but didn't see or hear anything that might give away the prowler's position. Redoubling his efforts, he held his breath and listened intently, but to no avail. All he heard were the sounds of leaves ruffling in the treetops. He then dropped to his knees and swiveled his head from side to side, scanning the underbrush centimeter by centimeter, praying that his altered vantage would reveal something he hadn't seen while standing. That prayer, however, went unanswered.

Having run out of options, he crept forward several meters, taking care to sidestep twigs and branches, and hid behind another tree. From this new position, he could look across the street and see the front of his apartment. That meant the prowler was within spitting distance if he hadn't fled. He glanced ahead, and after seeing nothing, he gradually shifted his gaze to the left. That's when he noticed the faint glow of an ember dancing in the air about a meter above the forest floor—got you!

Weber pulled the revolver out of his pocket and crept forward, skirting the place where he'd seen the ember. As he moved in from behind, he spied the outline of a man and pounced. The prowler was crouched next to a stump, and he flinched and grunted when Weber jammed the pistol's barrel against the nape of his neck. "Move, and I'll put a bullet in your head. Who are you, and why are you watching my apartment?"

The prowler said nothing, so Weber shoved the pistol's barrel into his left ear. "You don't think I'm serious?" The man remained mute, so Weber cocked the pistol. The click of the hammer loosened the prowler's tongue.

"Don't shoot! I'm unarmed, and I mean you no harm. A guy hired me to watch this place. He's looking for a boy named Luka."

Before Weber could reply, he felt a steel shaft press against the small of his back. "Drop the gun and get on your knees."

Weber defiantly turned toward the voice. Then something crashed down on his skull, and everything went black.

When Weber regained consciousness, he was still in the forest, and the two men stood over him. He groaned and ran his fingers over his scalp. His head pounded, but it didn't seem to be bleeding.

"Look, Otto," one of the prowlers said. "He's awake."

Weber lay there, unmoving, until Otto kicked him in the stomach and told him to stand. Begrudgingly, he rolled onto his side and slowly got to his feet. As he stood, the man accompanying Otto grabbed him by the collar and spat in his face. Weber raised his hand as if to strike the man but then reconsidered and used his palm to wipe the reeking spittle off his cheek. The brute, whoever he was, must have eaten onions for lunch.

The two men frog-marched Weber across the street, used his keys to open the door to his apartment, and pushed him inside. Otto ordered his partner to restrain Weber. "Put him on the floor and hold him there while I look around." Onion-breath nodded and then told Weber to lie face-down on the floor. When Weber complied, onion-breath placed a foot squarely on Weber's back and pointed a pistol at his head.

Otto was fuming when he returned. "They're not here--neither Luka nor his mother--and I didn't find any belongings suggesting they were here recently."

Onion-breath frowned and shook his head. "Gunter's not going to like that. He told us not to come back until we found them."

"I know that! Do you think I didn't hear what he said? Do you think I'm deaf?"

"Well, what are we going to do?"

Otto kicked Weber again. "I know you've got a kid because I was just in his bedroom. Where is he? We know he's friends with Luka, and we want to talk to him."

Quite truthfully, Weber replied that he didn't know. Inwardly, he puzzled over Carl's whereabouts. Where could he have gone?

Otto told onion-breath to search behind the apartment. "Go outside and check the backyard. Maybe the kid is hiding out there."

The brute returned several minutes later empty-handed. Enraged, Otto shouted at Weber. "One last chance—tell us where to find Luka now, or I'll hunt down your kid and hurt him."

Weber tried not to imagine what Otto might do to Carl, and even though he feared for his son, he chose not to speak. Otto drew back his fist, preparing to punch Weber, but relented when someone began pounding on the front door.

"Open up, Polizei!

Startled, Otto motioned toward the rear of the apartment. He and his accomplice ran through the kitchen and departed through the back door.

Weber got off the floor, opened the front door, and ushered three police officers into his apartment. Before the cops could say a word, he told them what had happened and rattled off a description of the prowlers. "Two men—one named Otto—broke in here and held me at gunpoint. Otto's tall and skinny and has black hair and blue eyes. The other guy is built like a gorilla and stinks of onions. They threatened to harm my son. When you arrived, they ran out the back door. If you hurry, you might catch them."

Two cops departed, and one stayed to take Weber's statement. Weber recounted everything he remembered but didn't mention Luka or Anna. He didn't want to reveal their whereabouts if Gunter or Göring had friends on the police force. When the cop left, Weber got a flashlight and looked for Carl.

He searched the neighborhood without success and then walked along a path that led into the Tiergarten. Once inside the park, he meandered up and down several trails while shining his flashlight into the trees. He saw no signs of life besides one cranky raccoon, so he began to call Carl's name. Several minutes later, Carl strode out of the trees.

"Dad, are you okay? I fled because I didn't want those thugs to capture both of us. I saw them drag you across the street, so I called the police and fled into the Tiergarten."

"That was smart thinking, Carl, but you scared me. Now, do you understand why you have to go to Sweden?"

"Uh, yeah, I guess so."

The next day, Weber called the number Furst had given him for the emergency extraction network. A man with a British accent answered, and after Weber successfully responded to a series of security questions, he was told to hold for an operator. Seconds later, a German woman came on the line and told Weber to state his request.

"My son is in danger and needs safe transport to Stockholm immediately. Can you oblige?"

"Not today, Berliner pilot, but tomorrow. Tell him to stand on the main platform inside the Berlin Hauptbahnhof precisely at 9 AM. He's to wear a red shirt, black pants, and a black Tirolerhut with a red feather in the brim. An agent will make contact and accompany him on his journey."

With Carl's situation sorted, Weber began preparing to leave Berlin and fly to Anna's parents' farm. He mailed a money order to his landlord to cover the next several months' rent so he could keep his apartment and car in case he could return to Berlin. He knew that was wishful thinking, but he liked living in Berlin, and sometimes, his wishes came true. Next, he filled a suitcase with travel gear and then boxed up possessions that would fit in the plane without exceeding its weight limit. After that, he went to Carl's room and helped him pack his things and pick out suitable attire for his rendezvous at the Hauptbahnhof.

Later that Friday evening, Weber made a meal for Carl and stayed awake until midnight when he knew Luka would monitor short-wave transmissions. He kept his message short and obscure to foil eavesdroppers. "Flyboy, do you read me? Anticipate pre-dark arrival tomorrow. Any holdups or glitches at your end?"

The next voice he heard was Luka's. "Message received. Proceed, no snags."

"Understood. Message complete."

Chapter 25

Winter 1928: Berlin and Munich, Germany

Gunter mumbled his reply to Göring's question. "Nothing to report as of yet, Hermann." This was the third meeting in a row where he had given the same response.

Göring lost his temper and began openly berating Gunter, questioning whether he was genuinely searching for the missing boy. "Are you looking for this boy or drowning your sorrows in some beer garden? How hard can it be to find this kid?"

After leaving Göring's office, Gunter was in a foul mood. Göring's insinuations about his work ethic only made things worse. He had done everything he could to protect his friend. He'd rushed across Germany to warn Hermann as soon as he discovered the truth about Luka and even got shot for his troubles. Then, he'd helped Hermann evaluate the risks posed by an illegitimate Jewish son and devise a plan to contain the damage. Now, he was working day and night, trying to find Luka. Was it his fault that the kid had vanished without a trace?

He walked to the nearest beer garden and ordered a tall stein of Doppelbock. "Here's to you, Hermann," he declared sarcastically before taking his first swig of the coppery-brown brew. "Drown my sorrows indeed!" After finishing the first stein, he drank a second, and when the alcohol began to cool his anger, he reflected on his failure to find Luka.

The search had gotten off to a rocky start. He'd obtained Anna's address from the Reichswehr employment records and tracked down her apartment in Berlin, only to find that someone other than Anna lived there--a woman named Hanna Keller. The Keller woman seemed disingenuous--she was tightlipped and claimed to know nothing about Anna or her whereabouts. He knew that was a lie, so he'd threatened the woman. By the time he left the apartment, she seemed suitably frightened.

The threats had the intended effect; Keller fled the apartment posthaste and dashed across town to another residence near the Tiergarten. He'd tailed her there and then staked out the new location. After several hours of surveillance, he spotted Luka's friend from school. It was the same kid who had helped Luka evade him when he'd tried to follow the two boys home from school.

Finding Luka's friend convinced Gunter that Luka was nearby, perhaps even living in the apartment he was surveilling. He'd thought about breaking in and snatching the boy but dismissed the idea because he couldn't be sure that Luka was inside and didn't want to tip off his friend so he could forewarn Luka. Instead, he hired two party members, Otto and Wolfgang, to keep an eye on the apartment and notify him as soon as they spotted Luka. That, he now realized, had been a mistake. Those two dunces had botched the surveillance, spooked his quarry, and attracted unwanted attention from the police.

Now, he was back at square one, drinking beer, twiddling his thumbs, and lamenting the fact that he didn't have a single clue as to Luka's whereabouts. Otto and Wolfgang deserved a good thrashing, but what would that accomplish? It might make him feel better, but it wouldn't help him find Luka. What he needed was a new plan.

Upon reflection, he realized that even though his investigation had failed, he'd discovered that Luka wasn't living in his mother's apartment or with his school friend. There was no evidence of his presence in either location, such as possessions or clothing. Did that mean that Luka wasn't living in Berlin? He hadn't considered that possibility, but now it seemed plausible.

Gunter scratched his chin and pondered ways to broaden the scope of his investigation. He wondered where the boy could have gone if he had fled Berlin. It occurred to him that when he'd grown up with Anna, her family had a business in downtown Munich. Luka might be living with his grandparents in Munich if Anna's parents were still alive and residing there. Gunter knew it was a long shot but thought it was worth investigating. Now that he had a clue as to where he might find Luka, he paid his bar tab and headed for the train station. Although he wasn't thrilled about another rail journey, he knew it would give him time to think and sober up. By the time he reached Munich, he would be ready to work.

◆◆◆

Gunter spent the afternoon walking through the busy streets of central Munich, looking at the names of shops and peering through their windows, searching for Lichtmann's store. He'd already been to the location where he remembered seeing it as a child, but was disappointed to discover an empty storefront. Rather than accept defeat, he presumed that the Lichtmanns had relocated their store and expanded his search to include nearby streets. However, after several hours of searching, he had to admit defeat. None of the establishments he had seen looked even remotely familiar.

Tired and discouraged, he entered a tiny café searching for coffee and pastries. The place was a little hole in the wall with a single window on the street. A couple of tables were inside the front door, and a small counter was at the rear. An older man, whom Gunter assumed was the proprietor, waved to him from behind the counter.

"Willkommen! Wie kann ich dir helfen?"

"Coffee and Kuchen, bitte," Gunter replied.

"Wünschen Sie Kaffee mit Milch oder schwarzer Kaffee?

"No milk, black coffee, please," Gunter replied.

The older man smiled and nodded as he poured the black steaming liquid into a china mug and handed it to Gunter. He then stood back and apprized the man who stood before him.

"You're not one of my regulars, but your accent tells me you're a local. Do you live nearby?"

"I live in Berlin, but I grew up here. I'm trying to find a family I knew as a kid. They used to own a store in this neighborhood, but I can't seem to find it."

"What was the name of this family?"

"Lichtmann. I went to school with their daughter Anna."

"Ah, that was a long time ago. You must be thinking of Aaron and Ruth Lichtmann. I knew them well. Poor Aaron! Some thug stabbed him, stole his money, and left him to die on a street corner. The scum!"

Gunter cringed as the memory of that night came flooding back. He'd always thought of the man he stabbed and robbed as a random stranger. He was stunned to discover that he'd knifed Anna's father.

The older man shook his head and scowled before continuing. "Not long after that, Aaron and Ruth sold their business and moved away. I don't know where they went and haven't seen them since."

Unable to meet the old man's gaze, Gunter nodded and abruptly ended the conversation. He took a final sip of his coffee, tossed a Reichsmark on the counter, and strode out of the shop. The geezer was getting on his nerves—the old man was a meddlesome gossip and would soon have asked why he was trying to find the Lichtmanns. By leaving abruptly, he's saved himself the effort of having to conjure a bunch of lies. Besides, he'd learned what he needed to know. The store didn't exist, so he'd have to find the Lichtmann's another way. But how?

Gunter went to the Marienplatz, sat on an empty bench in front of the Neues Rathaus, and tried to think of a way to locate the Lichtmann family. He was soon frustrated and was about to give up when the sound of a window opening on the second floor of the Rathaus captured his attention. Gazing upward, he saw Herr Otto Schmidt lean out of the window, shake some ash off the end of a cigarette, and blow a plume of smoke into the crisp morning air. He remembered Schmidt from when he'd visited the Standesamt to search for Luka's birth certificate, and that memory triggered an idea.

Gunter entered the Rathaus and climbed the stairs to the second floor. Once inside the Standesamt, Schmidt welcomed him and asked how he could assist. Gunter introduced himself, reminded Schmidt of his prior visit, and stated his request.

"You helped me before, and I hope you can do so again. I came to Munich to find a family I knew as a child. The family's surname is Lichtmann—Aaron and Ruth Lichtmann. I went to school with their daughter, Anna. I haven't found them and wondered if you have any records to help me locate them."

A look of recognition appeared on Schmidt's face. "Ah, yes, I remember you now. I helped you find Luka's birth certificate, and you were surprised that his mother's name was Anna Lichtmann. However, it was the father's name that floored you! Seeing that name took your breath away."

Gunter winced and deliberately ignored Schmidt's comments. He didn't want to reinforce the man's recollection of Göring's paternity. He had to do everything possible to prevent Schmidt or anyone else from publicizing that fact. "Look, Schmidt, can you help me find the Lichtmann family or not?"

"Calm down, Herr Meissner. There's no need to get tetchy. If Aaron Lichtmann lives in Bavaria, his name should be on our tax rolls or property registrations. Do take a seat, and I'll be with you momentarily."

Schmidt went into a room at the back of the records office and returned a few minutes later with a scowl. "I'm sorry, Herr Meissner, but I found no current listings for Aaron Lichtmann."

Gunter cursed under his breath and left the Standesamt. He was getting nowhere and needed time to think, so he checked into the Bayern Hof Hotel. Staying the night would give him some respite and, perhaps, a chance to dine with Adolph and his fellow coconspirators at the Bratwurstglöckle. The prospect of communing with fellow party members helped lift his spirits.

◆◆◆

After a late night of heavy drinking, Gunter felt tired and hungover. Nevertheless, the next morning, he returned to the Neues Rathaus, climbed the stairs to the second floor, and entered the Standesamt. He greeted Schmidt and told him that he needed to ask another favor.

"Herr Schmidt, instead of Aaron Lichtmann, would you search your records for Aaron Gabel?" While drinking with his friends at the Bratwurstglöckle, it had occurred to Gunter that Luka had listed his surname as 'Gabel' on the Aviation Coalition internship application—not Lichtmann.

Schmidt nodded and withdrew into the records depository room. He returned several minutes later carrying a sheet of paper with some scribbled notes. "I found an Aaron Gabel. Our records show that he owns a farm west of the city. I don't have an exact location, just a plot number."

"That's all you can tell me—Gabel has a farm west of here? That's not much to go on."

"No, it isn't. The deed shows a post office box, not an actual address. The farms out that way are expansive, and private roads predominate. Public roads are rare and poorly maintained. I don't envy you for the journey. Driving on private property is risky without a landowner's permission. Rural folks don't take kindly to trespassing."

Gunter thought about Schmidt's warning as he left the Standesamt. It was wise advice. He'd grown up on a farm on the opposite side of the city and clearly remembered the shotgun his father had kept in the kitchen for exterminating pests—not just rodents but trespassers. That memory tempered his desire to find the Lichtmann family. He wondered whether there was someone else he could convince to undertake the search.

After thinking more about it, Gunter decided to call the secret air base and arrange for a staff member to bring a car to his location in Marienplatz. He then tried to think of people who could assist him with his search and concluded that he needed someone to visit the farms before he did to serve as cannon fodder in case things went sideways. He settled on Otto and Wolfgang. They weren't the sharpest arrows in the quiver, but they'd be cheap to employ and expendable if some farmer decided to pepper their hides with buckshot.

Winter 1928: West of Munich, Germany

There was a knock on the door, and Aaron Gabel got up to see who was interrupting his breakfast. He and the entire Gabel clan were gathered around the kitchen table, enjoying an early morning meal of farm-raised eggs, ham, strudel, and coffee. Exhausted from his flight the prior evening, Weber was still asleep in Anna's bedroom.

Irritated by the intrusion, Ruth Gabel called to her husband as he walked toward the door. "Who is it, Aaron?"

"Give me a minute. I won't know until I open the door, will I?"

Aaron cracked the door open, peered outside, and saw his neighbor, Magnus Ekkehard, standing on the porch. Ekkehard owned the homestead directly east of Gabel's farm.

"Magnus, it's good to see you. Come inside and join us for breakfast."

"Thank you, Aaron, but I've already eaten and have cows to milk. Perhaps another time."

"Well, come inside, and I'll pour you a cup of coffee while you tell me why you're here."

Aaron led Magnus into the kitchen and pointed toward his empty chair at the breakfast table. As Magnus sat down, Ruth, Anna, and Luka greeted him.

Having heard the commotion, Weber stumbled into the kitchen, still rubbing sleep from his eyes. He sat down next to Ruth, and she introduced him to Magnus.

Weber bid Magnus good morning and then turned toward Aaron, who was pouring coffee at the sink. "Hey, Aaron, will you pour me a cup, too?

Aaron nodded and returned to the table with two steaming mugs. He handed one to Magnus and the other to Weber. "All right, Magnus," Gabel said, "What brings you here so early in the morning?"

"I thought you should know that two Nazi goons showed up at my farm yesterday. I was spreading hay in my horse stalls and didn't see them coming. Lucky for them because I'd have greeted them with my shotgun."

Weber slammed his mug on the table and bellowed at Magnus. "Nazis? How do you know they were Nazis? What the hell did they want?"

Aaron extended his palm toward Weber as a gesture of restraint. "Calm down, Robert. Let Magnus tell us what he came here to say; this isn't an interrogation."

Weber fell silent, and Magnus continued. "There were two of them—both wore brown shirts with SA insignias—one was tall and skinny, and the other was built like an ape. The skinny one asked me for directions to your farm. He wouldn't say why--just that he was trying to find Aaron Gabel's family. I figured they were up to no good, so I drew them a bogus map and sent them south toward Salzburg. They didn't come back, so I assume they got lost."

Aaron walked to where Magnus was sitting and shook his hand. "Thank you, Magnus, for alerting us. We don't abide Nazis, and we'd appreciate hearing from you if you see them again. I'm going to keep my shotgun loaded and handy. We won't keep you longer because I suspect your cows are getting impatient."

"Right you are," Magnus said as he stood. Aaron accompanied him to the door and bid him farewell.

There was a somber expression on Weber's face when Aaron returned to the breakfast table. "I don't like it, Aaron. Meissner's behind this—those two Nazis match the description of Otto and his pal 'onion breath'—the thugs that jumped me, searched my apartment, and threatened to harm Carl. Gunter is closing in much faster than I would have anticipated. How do you suppose he figured out where to look for your farm?"

Aaron drew a deep breath and blew out his cheeks. "I don't know, but what matters is that he's figured it out and is sniffing around in our backyard. He'll be on our doorstep before long."

Weber angled his head toward Luka. "Remember what I said about being prepared and ready to embark at a moment's notice? Well, this is that moment."

A surprised expression flickered across Luka's face, quickly replaced by an earnest look. "What should we do first?"

Before replying, Weber glanced around the table, making eye contact with Anna, Aaron, and Ruth. "Make your departure preparations quickly. Let's be ready to leave here in three days—by the end of the week at the latest."

◆◆◆

After three days had passed, only Weber and Luka were ready to depart. Aaron was busy making plans with his crew members, Clutch, Armor, Blade, and Scorch, to care for the farm during his absence. Blade and his Alsatians were already patrolling the perimeter, but the other crew members were haggling with Aaron about how to apportion the chores, market the farm goods, and split the monthly proceeds.

Ruth and Anna tirelessly packed the family's belongings. They filled several large suitcases with clothes and personal items and packed keepsakes and heirlooms in boxes. The front door area was already piled high with luggage and boxes, and as time passed, they added more.

Weber and Luka packed their backpacks with a change of clothes, personal items, and survival gear. Together, they prepared the planes for their journey. They fueled all three planes, completed the final inspections, and loaded leftover provisions into the cargo holds. After that, they took brief high-altitude sorties to test the props that Luka and Aaron had installed. Everything was going according to plan, except that half of the travelers were not ready to depart. They couldn't let go of their past lives and embrace an uncertain future.

Weber could see what was happening and knew that disaster was inevitable unless something changed. Someone needed to inject a strong dose of reality into the malignant delusion that was masking Anna's and her parents' fears while it silently bled away their chances for survival. That someone, he decided, had to be him. After screwing up his courage, he asked everyone to meet him at the table after dinner that evening. "We need to meet as a family," he told them, "to identify and eliminate the obstacles preventing us from leaving the farm."

That evening, when Anna, Ruth, Aaron, and Luka were seated around the table, Weber stood and, without smiling, shifted his gaze from person to person until he'd made eye contact with everyone. His stern elicitation had a sobering effect; the collective uneasiness in the room was palpable. Anna found it unbearable. "Robert, you're scaring us."

Rather than reassure Anna, Weber maintained his stony expression and delivered an ultimatum. "I know this will sound brutal, but I must insist that you disengage from this farm, sever ties with your friends, and leave behind your prized possessions. Aaron, it's time you faced facts; the odds are that you will never return to this farm. It would be best to let it go—tell your crew to sell the farm and send you the proceeds. Ruth and Anna, you're being unrealistic; there's no way we can transport that mountain of possessions you've piled by the door. Any cargo we transport must fit in the planes' holds, and survival gear has priority. Am I understood? I expect you to resolve these matters and refocus your efforts immediately, even if you must move heaven and earth to do it. Ready or not, we are leaving in the morning."

Weber's ultimatum elicited a variety of reactions. Aaron frowned and looked away. Anna bit her lip and stared at her hands. Ruth bowed her head and began to sob. Only Luka seemed unaffected; nothing in his expression suggested that he was displeased or distraught.

◆◆◆

The night passed quickly, even though no one slept more than an hour or two between repeated bouts of packing, pacing the floors, sorting through belongings, and then repacking. Much of the unrest stemmed from Weber's insistence that everyone carry no more than a small bag. At one point, Weber saw that Anna was struggling to fit her belongings into a single backpack and asked whether she'd like him to transport the secret aircraft design portfolio. She'd refused. "That's my trump card, Robert, and I'll be the one to play it."

When morning arrived, Weber, Aaron, and Luka hauled everyone's gear out to the hangar, and the three men rolled the aircraft onto the runway. Weber made sure the planes were lined up, one behind the other, per his plan. He positioned Aaron and Ruth's aircraft ahead of the others so they could depart first. Next in line was the airplane Anna would use to transport Luka—the aircraft she'd stolen from the Aviation Coalition. Behind that was Weber's plane, which he alone would occupy. After positioning the three aircraft, Weber opened the cargo holds, and Aaron and Luka stuffed them full of gear. Weber instructed Luka to put one of the shortwave radios in his grandparents' plane and the other in his Dewoitine.

After completing the aircraft preparations, the three men headed back towards the farmhouse. Luka noticed a dust cloud rising on the eastern horizon as they approached the front door. "There's a vehicle approaching rapidly on our access road. Somebody's in a hurry to get here." Although no one spoke it aloud, the word 'Nazi' was on each man's mind.

Weber put his hand on Aaron's shoulder. "Get your shotgun, load both barrels, and hide in the barn. Pick a spot where you can watch the front door to the farmhouse. I'll be the decoy. Count the number of intruders, and don't make your move until you've got the drop on all of them. Luka, find a coil of rope and then meet me inside the farmhouse."

A black Mercedes pulled up in front of the farmhouse, and a brown-shirted man stepped out, strode onto the porch, and pounded on the front door. A holster containing a sidearm hung from his belt. There was no response, so the man pounded on the door again, this time with greater force. When that failed, he started yelling. "Don't be a fool, Gabel. Magnus Ekkehard told me that you own this farm. Ekkehard stopped lying through his teeth after I knocked a few of them out of his head. If I have to break down this door, it will make me irritable, and I might be rude to your wife. You wouldn't want that, would you?"

On the other side of the door, inside the farmhouse, Weber held his tongue and waited for Aaron to get into position and take stock of the intruders. Luka stood beside him, holding a length of rope. "There shouldn't be more than three men," Weber whispered. "Maybe only one if we're lucky." Luka released the breath he'd been holding in his lungs and nodded.

Weber ordered Luka to stand out of sight and then cracked open the front door and squinted through the narrow slit. He recognized the intruder instantly. It was Gunter. In one fluid motion, he flung open the door, lunged forward with his arm extended, and stiff-armed the Nazi.

Gunter spiraled rearward off the porch, landed flat on his back in the driveway, and slid across the rough gravel surface. When his body came to a stop, he lay there, spread-eagled and dazed, gaping at the bloody gashes on his arms and hands.

Aaron rushed out of the barn and shoved his shotgun against Gunter's temple. "What were you saying about being rude to my wife?"

Weber bent down, confiscated Gunter's sidearm, summoned Luka from the house, and took the rope from the boy. He cut off a length, handed back the remainder, and told Luka to tie Gunter's ankles as tightly as possible. While Luka did that, he tied Gunter's hands behind his back.

While Weber was bent over lashing Gunter's hands, the Nazi stared at him like he'd seen a ghost. "You—you're Robert Weber! What are you doing here, you swine? Why are you in Germany?"

Weber ignored Gunter, stood, and shifted his gaze toward Aaron. "What should we do with this scum?"

Aaron lowered his shotgun, relaxed his stance, and angled his head toward the barn. "How about we strap him against the rear wall of a horse stall?"

Weber nodded his assent. "Good idea."

Aaron smirked. "Do you want me to put a horse in there with him? I have a stallion that's very protective of his territory. This Nazi might be in pieces by the time someone finds him."

"Don't tempt me. Gunter is a killer, and it's what he deserves. But why stoop to his level? I'm not sure I want that on my conscience. What's important right now is that we prevent him from following us or alerting anyone who might stop us."

Aaron shrugged his shoulders, and then he and Luka helped Weber carry Gunter inside the barn.

◆◆◆

Strapped in a standing position, Gunter twisted his arms and wriggled his hands, struggling to free himself from the trusses that bound him to the horse stall. He fought for what seemed like hours until blood gushed from the rope burns on his wrists and forced him to stop. How much longer would this torture endure? It would be dark soon, and he was tired, hungry, and in pain. Where were Otto and Wolfgang? He'd told them to follow him to Gabel's farm after they'd buried Ekkehard in a shallow grave. How was he supposed to know that the old farmer had a weak heart?

When night fell, Gunter was still languishing in the horse stall, waiting for Otto and Wolfgang. The barn was so dark that he couldn't see the nose on his face. What he could feel, however, were dozens of rats scurrying around his feet. He kept shaking his trousers to keep the hungry rodents from climbing his legs and chewing on his testicles.

When morning came after a sleepless night, Gunter was still alone. He'd had nothing to drink and was dehydrated and fighting delirium. By midday, his head throbbed, his outlook darkened, and his brain began playing tricks on him. He saw Otto and Wolfgang arrive on a magic carpet and float above him inside the barn, giggling like schoolboys, seemingly oblivious to his plight. "Help me," Gunter screamed, "Cut me loose before I die." To his chagrin, Otto and Wolfgang ignored him.

Then, somewhere inside a dream, Gunter felt waves of icy water crash against his face, and he awoke to see Otto standing over him with a bucket in his hand. "Otto? Am I dreaming, or is that you?"

"Who did this to you, Gunter? We thought you were dead."

Gunter lifted his head and saw Wolfgang standing just outside the horse stall. Wolfgang? Why did it take you so long to find me?"

Wolfgang looked at his shoes and said nothing, so Otto sheepishly explained. "The ground at Ekkehard's place was hard, and it took until nightfall for us to dig a hole big enough to bury that fat old farmer. We figured you'd go home after dark, so we did, too. Had we known you were trapped in a horse stall, we'd have come for you."

"Save your sympathy," Gunter croaked. Untie me so I can get out of these wet clothes. We have to find the Gabels before they get away."

◆◆◆

Weber banked the Dewoitine until the starboard wing dipped enough below his sightline to give him an unobstructed view of the runway stretched in front of the hut below. In contrast to the farm, the alpine climate was colder, and the landscape below was encrusted with the remnants of an early snowfall. He spied two sets of tire tracks etched into the runway's surface, running from south to north and ending near the hut, where two planes were parked.

The scene was as he'd expected; Aaron and Anna had arrived before him and parked their planes at the end of the runway, leaving him sufficient room to land. He aligned the Dewoitine with the runway, extended the flaps, and dropped the nose, and moments later, the plane touched down smoothly.

After the plane rolled to a stop, he reversed course, taxied back to the southernmost end of the runway, and killed the engine. It was a crude but effective strategy; the Dewoitine was now a barrier preventing other pilots from using the runway. No one could access the hut by air.

Weber made his way towards the hut. He kicked the snow off his boots before entering the steeply peaked cliffside structure through its solitary exterior door. As he walked into the lodge's large multipurpose room, a smoky odor accosted his nostrils. He glanced upward as he strode across the rough-cut plank floor and noticed wisps of smoke floating above the massive overhead beams.

While he removed his coat and gloves, Weber surveyed the interior, checking whether everyone had arrived unscathed. The entire Gabel clan was present, and all were engaged in tasks that would make the cabin habitable. Aaron was stoking the hearth, trying to fortify a few flickering flames. Ruth and Anna were rummaging through some cartons, searching for meal rations. Several potatoes lay next to one of the cartons, attesting to their success. Luka stood in the hut's makeshift bedroom, unpacking Aaron's shortwave radio and assembling it on the top of an old wooden dresser.

Anna greeted Weber as he took off his boots. "How was your flight, Robert?"

"Short and sweet," he replied, his breath billowing forth and forming a small cloud around his face. "Wow, it feels colder in here than it does outside! Aaron, how long before you get that fire going?"

Aaron laughed. "Quit complaining, tough guy. A little frostbite never hurt anybody."

Weber smirked. "So that's how it's going to be, eh? Then tell me where to find the schnapps so I can defrost the ice forming in my veins."

Once the hearth was ablaze, Weber helped Anna warm a pot of potato soup over the fire. When the thick liquid began to bubble, Aaron brought five bowls to the hearth, and Anna spooned a generous helping into each one.

The table in the hut was large enough to accommodate everyone, and after seating themselves, the family ate in silence. It was too quiet for Anna; a lively conversation was essential to every meal. Her family had never had a meal devoid of dinner conversation. She held her tongue until she couldn't stand it any longer. "Robert, now that we're all here, what do we do next?"

"Let's take a moment to catch our breath," Robert replied. "We're not as vulnerable here as we were at the farm. You might say we've 'stalled' Gunter, and his lackeys have no idea where we've gone."

Aaron stopped eating and put down his spoon. His lips tightened, and deep lines formed on his brow. "I appreciate your attempt at levity, Robert. God knows we need a bit of stress relief. However, the threat we're facing is no joke. I'm deeply distrustful of the Nazis, and Gunter's proven himself to be a cunning and tenacious predator. I'm not confident that 'stalling' Gunter, as you put it, will stop him from hunting us. I regret that I didn't settle his hash with my shotgun."

"I understand why you feel that way, Aaron, particularly considering your past experiences with the Nazis. However, we managed to escape by plane without filing a flight plan that would have revealed our route. Moreover, we were careful not to leave any clues behind at the farm that could have given away our plans or current location."

"I'd like to trust your appraisal, Robert, but I fear you underestimate our adversary. I thought we were untraceable after we left Munich, moved to the farm, and changed our name to Gabel. But you saw how quickly Gunter sniffed us out. That man's a bloodhound."

Weber tilted his head toward the ceiling and took a deep breath. "Well, perhaps you're right," he conceded. "Better to err on the side of caution. How would you suggest we proceed?"

"Why push our luck? Let's dispense with delays and implement the next step of the plan. Expediency is our most important asset."

Weber rose from the table, retrieved a large envelope from his backpack, and returned to his chair. "All right, let's talk about phase two. But before we proceed, we need to make some decisions. We've made it to the Alps, so our next objective is to leave Germany and enter another country. To do that successfully, we have to cross the German border without getting arrested and seek refuge in a country where the authorities won't detain or prosecute us. In my opinion, the best destinations are Sweden and Switzerland because both are politically neutral. That's why I asked Anna to purchase counterfeit passports for those two countries."

Before continuing, Weber opened the envelope, withdrew two packages of passports, and passed them around the table. "Now, how should we choose between Sweden or Switzerland? Because we are traveling by air, we can fly into either country and avoid the risk of having German border guards inspect our false passports. However, the Swedish border is much further from our current position than the Swiss border. Whereas it would take less than an hour of flight time to reach the Swiss border, it would require several hours to reach the Swedish border and necessitate at least one fuel stop inside Germany. Another consideration is that we'd have to make a high-altitude flight over the Alps to reach the Swiss border, whereas we'd have to fly over the Baltic Sea to get to Sweden. The Baltic prevents the Germans from watching the Swedish border, but the Swiss border is landlocked and closely monitored. Consequently, we're more likely to be seen crossing the Swiss border, and if the Germans spot us, they could muster aircraft and try to intercept us."

Aaron pounded his fist on the table and then stood and began pacing the floor. Weber could tell that the elder Gabel was troubled and waited for him to voice his concerns. After several moments of tortured contemplation, Aaron spoke. "Look, Robert, this is too damn complicated! Our lives are at stake here. How are we supposed to decide?"

Weber got up, walked to where Aaron was standing, and put his hand on his friend's shoulder. "I hate to say this, Aaron, but this gets worse before it gets better."

"There's more?"

"I'm afraid so. We need to choose a friendly country for refugees. We're better off entering a country that won't extradite Anna and Luka to Germany but instead provide temporary housing, transit visas, and permission to book passage on a ship bound for the United States."

Aaron sighed. "And which country would that be?"

"There are risks, but I'd wager that Switzerland is a better bet than Sweden. We'd get there faster, we'd avoid refueling inside Germany, and we could avoid detection by crossing the border at a remote, unpopulated location. The Swiss-German border stretches 400 km along the Rhine River between Lake Constance and Lörrach, Germany, just above the Swiss city of Basel. We could cross the border east of Basel, along a remote section of the Rhine near Schwörstadt, and fly into an uninhabited, heavily forested area just above Aarau, Switzerland. It's too rugged to land there, so we'd have to circle west and eventually put down in Basel."

Anna, who'd be listening attentively, supported Weber's proposition. "I agree. Switzerland makes more sense than Sweden."

Aaron, however, still wasn't convinced. "So, what happens after we land? Will the Swiss authorities give us the things we'll need? You said we'd need housing, transit visas, and passage to the United States."

"I suspect so, but we won't know until we arrive. One problem I foresee with Basel is that the Swiss authorities might detain us if they question the validity of our passports or know that the German police are searching for Anna and Luka. The Germans have closer ties with the Swiss than the Swedes because of the commerce they conduct in Switzerland and their reliance on Swiss banks. If the Swiss knew that Anna and Luka were fugitives, they might hesitate to grant us asylum or even deport them to Germany. We could ask authorities in Basel to take us to the American Embassy, but they might refuse because it's in Bern, the Swiss capital."

Aaron didn't look pleased, but he begrudgingly acquiesced. "I don't like the risks, but I suppose Switzerland is better than Sweden."

"Then it's settled," Weber announced. "Aaron, could you and Ruth be ready to leave in the morning? We should stagger our departure times because multiple planes traveling simultaneously along the same route might elicit surveillance. If you're the first to make the journey, you can report about the route, the border crossing, and the Swiss authorities' reactions to your arrival. Having that information would assist us in determining whether Anna and Luka can safely travel that route without getting arrested or deported when they reach Basel. I will depart soon after Anna to provide emergency support and intervene if she gets intercepted."

The next morning, the family met at the table for breakfast before sunrise. Weber seated himself between Aaron and Ruth, and Anna brought him a cup of coffee and a bowl of muesli. It was obvious that Anna was upset; her eyes were puffy, and her cheeks were moist with tears. He grasped Anna's hand and squeezed it gently.

Weber acknowledged the obvious. "'Aaron and Ruth, your departure makes us sad. We will feel better once you have arrived safely in Basel. Please use the shortwave radio to contact us as soon as it is safe to tell us about your journey and how the Swiss authorities treated you. Now, shall we discuss your route?'"

Aaron left the table and returned with a flight map, which he spread out in front of Weber. He put his finger on one of several lines drawn on the map. "I stayed up late last night plotting flight paths and like this one best."

Weber ran his eyes along the line. "Yes, I see what you mean. This path would take you southwest to Lake Constance while maintaining a safe distance from the Austrian border. You'd fly over the two upper fingers of the lake and then adopt a westerly heading, which would take you along the Rhine until you reach Schwörstadt. You'd pivot south, cross the Swiss border above Aarau, and resume a westerly heading until you reach Basel. It's a good plan, and I think Anna should fly the same route."

Aaron picked up the map, folded it, and stowed it in his flight bag.

"What about fuel? Our planes have different engine configurations, and headwinds might vary. Will we make it to Basel without needing a fuel stop?"

While Weber scratched his head, Anna replied, "I've done some rough calculations, which suggest that all of us will make it unless one or more of us encounters adverse air currents or has to circumvent a large storm or squall."

"That's reassuring," Weber replied. "And thank you, Aaron and Luka, for installing the supplemental fuel tanks. They have extended our range considerably."

Weber waited until the sun had risen in the east, donned his coat, and proceeded to the runway outside the hut. Snow accumulated on the planes overnight, so he brushed off the aircraft and readied Aaron's Caspar C32 for takeoff. He double-checked Caspar's cargo hold to be sure the shortwave was loaded and redistributed some baggage to balance the plane's load.

Moments later, Aaron and Ruth emerged from the hut, climbed into the Caspar, and started the engine. At first, the Caspar's prop squealed and spun sluggishly, protesting against the cold. Then, puffs of smoke blew from the exhaust ports, and the engine roared to life.

Anna, Luka, and Weber waved as the Caspar accelerated down the runway, lifted off, and ascended into the frigid dawn sky. As they watched, the plane gained altitude, and when it was high enough to clear the nearby peaks, it banked sharply toward the west and disappeared over the mountains.

◆◆◆

Gunter drove Otto and Wolfgang to the Munich train station, handed them a wad of Reichsmarks, and bid them farewell. He was glad to be rid of them; after all, those two halfwits had left him languishing in a horse stall overnight. He'd considered defaulting on their wages but dispensed with that idea when he remembered they'd witnessed what he'd done to Magnus Ekkehard.

With that distraction behind him, Gunter rededicated himself to finding Luka and the Gabel family. While tied up in the barn, he'd heard two or possibly three planes take off from the runway behind the farmhouse. The next morning, after Otto and Wolfgang had untied him, he'd searched the farmhouse, the hangar, and all the surrounding outbuildings and found no one. He felt confident that the entire family had escaped by plane so they could hide elsewhere in Germany or leave the country. Finding them would be hell because they could travel great distances by air, and it was harder to trace aircraft than autos or trains. Unless he acted quickly, they'd be beyond his reach in no time.

Shaken by that realization, Gunter slammed his car into gear, left the train station, and sped toward the secret airbase. When he arrived, he buttonholed Helmut Wolff and demanded a status report. Wolff told him that the base had run smoothly during his absence, so he gave Wolff a duty roster and told him to assemble the engineers and resident test pilots in the workroom for a meeting.

Gunter strode to the front of the workroom, turned to face his audience, and demanded to know how many of those present were pilots. "Who in this room can fly one of our experimental warbirds?" Nearly every hand went up. "Good. You will help me find and apprehend Anna Lichtmann, who, along with her son Luka Lichtmann, has stolen our design portfolio. They've absconded in one of the Aviation Coalition's planes and were last seen at a farm west of here. We know they departed this morning and are traveling with other aircraft. Although their destination is unknown, our search will concentrate on predictable routes. Some of you will scout Germany's international borders, including those with Austria and Switzerland. Others will visit nearby airports to see whether Lichtmann stopped to refuel or mentioned her flight plans to airport personnel."

One of the test pilots spoke without raising his hand. "What should we do if we uncover a clue or see one of these spies?"

Perturbed, Gunter scanned the room, trying to identify the speaker. "Who dared interrupt me while I was talking? Identify yourself!" When no one spoke, Gunter continued. "Now, as I was about to say, radio your findings immediately. Wolff will remain at the base to monitor incoming shortwave communications and report your findings. Do I make myself clear?"

Gunter looked around the room and saw other people raise their hands. "There's no time for questions. I gave Wolff a duty roster; see him for your aircraft and duty assignments. Ensure your plane is flightworthy, and then meet me on our east-west runway two hours from now. Look sharp! We must catch these spies before they leave the country!"

While Wolff assigned planes and duty assignments, he discreetly told Heinz Albrecht, Wilhelm Graf, and Hans Dietrich to wait for him in his room. He finished his work quickly, went to his room, and locked the door behind him. The other three men anxiously awaited, wondering why they'd been summoned. Wolff explained. "I've asked you here because I can't, in good conscience, carry out these orders. Do any of you feel likewise?"

Dietrich, Albrecht, and Graf nodded in unison. Albrecht said, "Let me tell you why I won't obey those orders. "Then he shared what Anna had told him: "Gunter's not leveling with us. Anna's no spy. She told me that Gunter discovered something about her family, and he's using it to discredit her."

Dietrich lost his temper. “That sneaky, sniveling weasel!”

Graf was more curious than angry and asked Albrecht to clarify. “What did Gunter discover, and who is Luka Lichtmann?”

“I don’t know, Wilhelm,” said Albrecht, shrugging his shoulders. “Anna didn’t say, but his name is Lichtmann, which suggests he’s a family member.”

“Wait,” said Dietrich, “wasn’t there an intern named Luka?” “Maybe that’s her secret.”

“I doubt it, Hans” Albrecht countered. “That kid’s name is Gable, not Lichtmann.”

Wolff lost patience and ended the discussion. “Let’s not get off track here, gentlemen. It seems clear that we won’t obey Gunter’s orders, so what will we do?”

Everyone was silent for several moments, and then Albrecht spoke. “It seems to me that Hans, Wilhelm, and I have no choice but to fly the assigned missions, but we don’t have to report anything we discover about Anna.”

“Good idea,” said Dietrich. “Don’t prevaricate, just withhold information that might help Gunter find her.”

Graf frowned. “Fine, but I doubt that will keep Gunter from finding Anna. We can be tightlipped, but what about all the other people searching for Anna?”

Wolff spent a moment gathering his thoughts and then proposed a solution. “As the base’s shortwave operator, I’ll receive everyone’s messages before Gunter does. My hearing isn’t what it used to be, so I might miss some messages and hear only snippets of others.”

“Bravo,” quipped Albrecht. “I think we have a plan.”

Chapter 26

Winter 1928: Near Munich, Germany

Gunter's angry voice echoed down the corridor as he criticized the mechanic making final preparations for his aircraft. “Why haven't you finished? This fighter was supposed to be ready an hour ago... What? Speak up! Don't lie to me--I can see that you haven't repaired the tail strut or loaded live rounds into the wing-mounted machine guns.”

It was nearly midday when Gunter's fighter rolled out of the hangar and onto the runway. He watched all of the conscripts in his makeshift squadron take off, and then he powered his fighter down the runway and initiated a steep climb. When he was several thousand feet above the base, he circled and put his plane on a southwesterly heading.

Gunter flew directly to Gabel’s farm and searched for clues to Anna’s and Luka’s whereabouts. Finding nothing, he left the farm and flew towards the Austrian border, approaching the Alps on a southwesterly course. He had a hunch that Anna and her son would try to escape Germany by crossing into Austria, the quickest way out of the country. Despite his determination to stop them, Gunter was frustrated by the harsh reality of the situation. Anna had already escaped from him once at the farm and could have easily made it into Austria by now. She and her son might already be in Salzburg or Vienna, enjoying a coffee in one of the local cafes. That scenario made Gunter so angry that he couldn’t think straight, so he took a deep breath and tried to calm himself. He understood the situation's gravity and realized he needed to reconsider his plans. If he failed to locate Anna and her son before they fled to Austria or another country, they could reveal the truth about Göring’s past and Germany’s covert rearmament program. Moreover, he had a score to settle; the woman had shot him to prevent him from revealing Göring’s paternity. He couldn't afford to let her slip away from him. If he did, he wouldn't be able to get even, and the woman's actions could put his friend, country, and career in danger. Furthermore, if Göring was exposed and expelled from the Nazi Party, it could lead to his expulsion as well.

With the Alps looming ahead, Gunter maxed the throttle and lifted the fighter's nose until its attitude was just below the stall point. It was a risky flight maneuver, but he believed a rapid, steep climb would help him quickly surpass the mountains and reach the border. The plane caught an updraft and ascended swiftly, giving Gunter a panoramic view of the mountain range and its north-facing slopes. However, halfway up, he noticed something strange—a glimmer of light reflecting off an object and movement on one of the slopes. Intrigued, he reduced the throttle, banked to starboard, and brought the fighter down a few thousand meters to get a closer look.

As he circled the slopes, he searched for the mysterious object that had caught his eye. However, the snow cover made it difficult to see anything other than the broader contours of the mountains and sharp ridge lines of the slopes. It was like flying into a cloud. Determined not to give up, he lowered his altitude and made several more passes, but his luck did not improve. Finally, he decided to bank away from the mountain and continue his ascent.

As the fighter ascended to a higher altitude, Gunter was astonished to see the phantom reappear. He maintained his focus on the shimmering object and dove the plane towards it, putting it on a collision course. When the fighter was within a thousand meters of the object, he leveled off and took a closer look. To his surprise, he spotted three aircraft parked on a runway next to a hut, with someone standing on a ladder brushing snow off the wings. One of the planes looked exactly like the aircraft Anna had stolen from the Aviation Coalition.

Gunter circled, came in low, peered through the gunsight, and pulled the trigger.

◆◆◆

Albrecht and the other members of Gunter's squadron, consisting of around twenty engineers and test pilots, waited impatiently in their planes on the runway. They were unsure whether they should depart before their hard-nosed leader arrived. Albrecht, whose plane was at the front of the formation, made the decision to hold the other pilots in their positions. From his perspective, the delay was a windfall because it would give Anna more time to escape.

Gunter's plane emerged from the hangar, and the waiting pilots took off individually toward their assigned destinations. However, Albrecht flew a wide arc around the base, and once Gunter was airborne, he circled around from behind and kept a safe distance to observe Gunter's movements surreptitiously. Although his orders were to patrol the border between Germany and Austria, he had disregarded them to keep an eye on Gunter's whereabouts and monitor his activities. Albrecht knew that Anna's life would be in grave danger if Gunter found her before he did.

Albrecht kept a close eye on Gunter's flight as he flew southwest toward the Austrian border. He expected Gunter's plane to climb and fly over the Alps and was taken aback when Gunter suddenly descended towards a farm in the foothills and landed on a grassy runway. Albrecht decreased the throttle and circled around to observe and try to comprehend why Gunter had made an unexpected stop at the farm.

As Albrecht was trying to understand what was happening, he saw Gunter return to his plane, take off from the runway at the farm, and resume his journey toward the Alps. Albrecht followed him, assuming that Gunter was heading towards the border between Germany and Austria, which was a likely escape route that Anna would take if she intended to flee Germany.

As the two pilots approached the Alps, the air grew colder, and the landscape changed from earth tones to a stark, icy white. Albrecht adjusted the throttle and raised the nose of his plane to match Gunter's angle and pace. However, he was caught off guard when Gunter suddenly changed course and descended towards a nearby slope. Albrecht abruptly banked away and settled into a holding pattern, unsure of what was happening.

Albrecht closely observed Gunter’s movements, trying to decipher his intentions. Gunter had already made one irrational move, but his current actions made even less sense. Suddenly, smoke and flames began to emerge from the gun ports of Gunter's plane. Albrecht shifted his position to get a better view and noticed a hut on the side of a rocky slope with an adjacent runway. Two planes were parked on the runway. Gunter continued to fire, and Albrecht saw the tracers hit one of the planes, causing it to catch fire. A few moments later, there was a massive explosion, and both planes burst into flames, sending debris flying up and down the slope.

Albrecht watched in horror as Gunter's plane veered away from the slope, descended towards the base of the Alps, and flew northeast in the direction of the airbase. Uncertain how to proceed, he maintained his holding pattern and tried to understand what he had just witnessed. He couldn't comprehend what had caused such a brutal and apparently unprovoked attack, but he suspected that it had something to do with Anna. If Anna and Luka had sought refuge in that hut, then Gunter had effectively eliminated their means of escape.

Albrecht raised Wolff on his shortwave. “Helmut, are you alone? I don’t want anyone to overhear this message.”

“Go ahead, Heinz. You can speak freely.”

“Gunter has just fired at two planes parked on a slope near a cabin in the Alps, located approximately 100 km southwest of the base. Although I cannot confirm it, I suspect that Anna and her family took refuge in the cabin and planned to use the planes to escape. If my suspicion is correct, Gunter's actions have disrupted their plans and left them stranded on the mountainside.”

"Sadly, Heinz, I can confirm your suspicions. Gunter just radioed to say that he's returning to base to reload. One of the planes matched the description of the aircraft that Anna stole from the Aviation Coalition depot in Berlin, so Gunter fired on the plane to prevent her from escaping. He's returning to the base to reload, and then he plans to machinegun the cabin and search for bodies."

Albrecht replied by screaming into his microphone. "The hell he will! Find me an armed fighter, load it with ammunition, and have it ready when I return to the base. I'm on my way. Stall Gunter, so he doesn't leave before I get there."

Heinz empathized with Albrecht, saying, "Surely Anna doesn't deserve this. But are you certain you know what you're doing? Going up against Gunter is dangerous. He's an experienced pilot and a war hero. He won't hesitate to blow you out of the sky."

"Just do as I say, Helmut. I can take care of myself."

◆◆◆

Weber turned his head towards the left windscreen and scanned the horizon, trying to locate the source of the gunfire. He caught a glimpse of Durand sitting in the cockpit behind him, looking relaxed as if nothing was happening. Weber was shocked and asked, "Are you just going to sit there, Francöise, while that German pilot tries to shoot us down?" But to his surprise, Durand just laughed. Then, as Weber came to his senses, he realized that he had imagined the entire scenario while having one of his recurring nightmares about the Great War.

Now, as he came fully awake, it became unnervingly clear that the gunfire wasn't imaginary. Along with the drone of an airplane, he heard the unmistakable sound of machinegun fire. Before he could pull himself out of bed, several rounds pierced the roof of the hut and tore into the walls around him.

Instinctively, Weber rolled over and covered Anna's body with his. When the sound of the gunfire receded, he got out of bed and looked for Luka. The boy wasn't anywhere to be found, so he decided to look outside.

Weber braced himself for a blast of frigid air as he opened the door but was greeted instead by a hot breeze carrying burning embers and an acrid odor. He put his hands over his face, stepped outside, and saw both aircraft lying in pieces on the runway, engulfed in flames, burning out of control. The wings of the aircraft, where the fuel tanks were located, were scattered piecemeal across a wide swath of the slope, charred and smoking.

Weber stood there, dumbfounded, berating himself for parking the Dewoitine with Anna's plane next to the hut. He'd inadvertently made the aircraft an easy target for the enemy pilot, who had reduced their primary means of escape to a pile of debris and ashes.

As he approached the damaged planes to assess the fire's aftermath, he heard the sound of revving aircraft engines. He turned around and looked up at the sky, trying to locate the source of the noise. The sound of the engines grew louder, and suddenly, an experimental fighter burst through the cloud cover and raced towards him. One quick look at the plane was enough to tell him that the pilot's intentions weren't benign. Bullets erupted from the gun barrels that protruded from the fighter's wing ports and rained down upon him.

Flames continued to belch from the gun barrels as the enemy pilot fired burst after burst of machinegun rounds. Jagged bits of ice, snow, and rock flew in all directions as bullets struck the ground near Weber's feet. He braced for the sensation of hot metal tearing into his flesh but somehow made it to the side of the hut unscathed and out of the line of fire. Now low and thunderously loud, the enemy fighter buzzed Weber's position and then rapidly arced away from the mountainside. Weber listened to the sound of the fighter's engines, and when they became faint, he assumed that the attack was over.

Shaken but glad to be alive, Weber resumed his search for Luka. He found him crouched and shivering inside a shed Aaron had built next to a trail leading up the mountain to the alpine pastures. The boy's coat was charred, and his hair was singed. Luka explained that he'd been standing on a ladder, cleaning snow off the planes, when he heard gunfire. Then, the fuel tanks ruptured, and he was blown clear of the wreckage. Weber comforted the boy and escorted him to the hut where he dressed his wounds.

◆◆◆

Later that evening, Anna and Weber prepared a meal from their meager remaining provisions and joined Luka at the table. Weber tried not to look as gloomy as he felt, but his contrived expression only succeeded in raising Anna's and Luka's anxiety. "Come on, Robert," Anna said, "get it off your chest. Tell us what you're thinking."

Weber exhaled loudly. "I feel certain that Gunter knows where we are. Hell, he was probably flying that fighter that strafed us today."

Anna made a face of disgust and said, "Let's not talk about that bastard, Robert. We must put ourselves first and determine what we will do."

Weber agreed with Anna and said, "You're right. Staying here is too risky. We don't have much choice now. I'd suggest we leave immediately, but I haven't had time to formulate a new plan. I put too much faith in the aircraft and didn't think enough about how to climb out of here on foot. An extended hike over the mountains seems like our only option now."

Anna was thankful that Luka had purchased climbing gear and brought it to the hut. She said, "Thank God you had Luka bring that gear. I don't know where we'd be without it."

Luka was pleased that he had contributed something that might save their lives. "I stored that gear in my grandfather's shed. It's the one you found me in this morning, Robert. And just so you know, the path by that shed goes up into the Alps and connects with other trails that cross over the mountains. I know because I've hiked those trails."

Weber was impressed. "Luka, you're a godsend. Do you know those trails well enough to draw us a map?"

Luka left the table, grabbed a pencil and paper from his grandfather's desk, and returned to his seat. "Just watch," he said and began drawing a map.

Around midnight, just before bed, Weber turned on the shortwave and listened for transmissions. They couldn't take the radio with them; it was too bulky and heavy to pack out on foot. This was his last opportunity to communicate with Aaron and Ruth.

There was nothing but static on the prearranged frequency. This night, Weber surmised, would be no better than the others that had come before it. Then, to his surprise, he heard Aaron's voice crackling through the speaker. "Alpine Hideaways, come in. Do you read me?"

Weber picked up the microphone and replied. "Loud and clear, Caspar Pilot. What say you?"

"Must be cryptic; current quarters may not be secure. Arrived anticipated destination five days ago; ensnared in red tape thereafter; unable to transmit. The good news: route is safe, and extradition unlikely. Proceed the designated route."

"Copy that, Caspar pilot, but our plan has changed. Transportation is inoperable, so proceeding on foot. Will contact you if and when radio access becomes possible."

"Dirty shame, but understood. Don't stub your toes, beware of rabid Ibex, and mind the crevasses. Out."

◆◆◆

Weber arose before dawn the next day and tried not to wake Anna and Luka. He lit a candle and searched the hut for food, stumbling upon Luka's map on the table. The map was detailed, but Weber noticed no routes on the southern side of the Alps, near the Austrian border. This made him wonder how they would navigate that part of the journey. He started to think about other logistical details, such as the fact that they could no longer travel to Switzerland after losing the aircraft. It was too far away to reach on foot, so they had no choice but to hike south over the Alps and cross the border into

Austria. That route, however, was not ideal because they did not have Austrian passports, and the Austrians were more closely aligned with the Germans than the Swiss.

Rather than dwell on their misfortunes, Weber exited the hut, walked to the shack, and began sorting gear so they'd be ready to leave shortly after daybreak. He laid out the necessities—gloves, goggles, boots, packs, crampons, grappling hooks, ropes, carabiners, ice axes, jumars, tents, and other climbing paraphernalia—and then divided the lot into three piles and tested their respective weights. It could be deadly to overload a climber on a long and strenuous trek.

Satisfied with how he'd distributed the gear, he returned to the hut, where he found Anna and Luka conversing over breakfast, which consisted of an apple and some stale bread. Seeing the paltry rations made Weber aware of another logistical problem; their delayed departure had depleted their stockpile of provisions. How would they survive a trek over the mountains with so little to eat?

◆◆◆

The three novice mountaineers made good progress for the first kilometer as the trail's slope was moderate and even. Since leaving the hut, the path had ascended along gentle slopes, passed over small ridges, and ran along low-lying embankments. No one was out of breath, nor had anyone experienced cramps, vertigo, or other discomforts that often affect amateur climbers.

Eventually, they arrived at the high alpine meadows, where Aaron and Ruth's cows grazed during the summer. Rather than being covered in lush flora and fauna, as Weber had seen the previous summer, the vast, sloping fields were barren, reminding Weber that their supplies were running low and they would soon face starvation. He pushed the thought out of his mind, sat on a nearby rock outcropping, and signaled his companions to join him. "Anna, Luka, come sit with me. We've hiked for over two hours and deserve a short rest."

Refreshed by the break, the group returned to the trail and continued climbing until the alpine meadows were no longer visible. The landscape around them began to change: the snow cover was deeper, the cliffs were higher, the trail was narrower, and the air was thinner. Weber, who was leading, deliberately slowed his pace so that he and his fellow climbers could cope with the increasing challenges.

The trail crossed a knoll and descended into a ravine. It then wound through a field of boulders and continued up the mountainside until it reached a narrow gap between two crags. Weber kneeled and crawled through the gap until he reached a ledge that overhung a crevasse between the crags and the mountainside. The ledge extended along the crevasse until it ended at a cave-like opening in the rock face. Fear gripped Weber as he walked along the narrow ledge, so he distracted himself by imagining what he might find inside the cave. "You'll see," he muttered, "it'll be a cool, dry place where you can make a fire and shelter for the night." But then, a darker image crept into his thoughts. "Or maybe it's a bear's lair, and he'll tear you to pieces and have you for dinner tonight."

When Weber reached the end of the ledge, he shone his flashlight into the cave. The cavern's interior surpassed his expectations; it exceeded the size of Aaron's hut. It had a high ceiling and extended rearward to a fissure large enough to crawl through. Although there was a dank odor inside the cave, the floor was dry, and to his relief, he saw no sign of bears or other predators. He turned off his flashlight, retraced his steps back to the gap where Anna and Luka were waiting, and motioned for them to join him inside the cave.

The climbers brought their gear inside and stored it against the sturdy rock wall at the back of the cave. As Weber put down his pack, he heard a faint droning outside the cave. He caught Luka's eye and motioned toward the mouth of the cave, and the two of them retraced their steps along the ledge, crawled through the gap, and stood on the mountainside, scanning the slopes below them. The droning was louder now, and even though Weber couldn't see the source, he knew the pulsating reverberations came from aircraft—most likely multiple aircraft engines. He put his hand on Luka's shoulder to get his attention and then pointed down the mountain toward the source of the sound. "Good thing we left when we did. I suspect that whoever shot up our planes has returned to finish the job."

As if to confirm Weber's suspicions, a chorus of machine gun fire echoed up and down the mountainside. The bursts continued intermittently for several minutes until a dark plume of smoke rose from somewhere below, coiled up into the late afternoon sky, and dissipated into the stratosphere. Weber traced the trail of smoke with his eyes and then shook his head. "Perhaps our nemesis has crashed and burned."

The two men returned to the cave, where they found Anna preparing a place to sleep. She took a compact blanket from her pack, threw it on the dank floor, and lay on top. "I'm exhausted, Robert; just wake me if you need me."

Weber moved his pack next to Anna, kneeled beside her, and gently kissed her cheek. "Sleep well. I'm going to have a look around before I turn in for the night." He got up and joined Luka by the cleft in the rock that served as the cave's entrance. "Are you alert enough to take the first watch?" Luka nodded. "Good, crawl out to the gap occasionally and listen for intruders, human or otherwise. The cave will shelter us from the elements but limit our situational awareness and mobility. Predators could pounce on us while our soft underbelly is exposed. When inside the cave, position yourself to see both openings." Convinced that Luka understood, Weber pulled out his flashlight and scouted the cave's interior, looking for evidence of prior inhabitants and unwanted pests, such as bats. Besides some mouse feces scattered here and there, he found nothing of concern, so he lay beside Anna and fell asleep.

Bam! A gunshot blast jolted Weber awake. He sat up, saw sunlight shining through the entrance to the cave, and was overcome with guilt because he'd slept through his watch and failed to relieve Luka. He got to his feet and struggled to shake off the aches, pains, and stiffness he'd acquired from sleeping on the hard, uneven, rocky floor.

Anna awoke, yawned, and glanced around the cave. "Robert, what was that noise? Where is Luka?"

"He's gone, and so is the rifle and some of his gear. Stay put, and I'll go find him."

"No, Robert, we can't afford the delay. Pack up, and we'll continue our trek up the mountain. We'll find Luka along the way. I'll leave him a note just in case."

Anna placed a scribbled note on the cave floor, and then she and Weber split Luka's gear between them, exited the cave, and eased their way across the ledge, through the gap, and onto the trail they had climbed the previous day.

The weather had taken a turn for the worse. Dark clouds scudded across the sky, and the air was filled with flurries. Weber stopped short, surprised to see bootprints and animal tracks in the newly fallen snow.

"I don't like this, Anna. These bootprints go up and down the trail. Why would Luka go both ways? Could someone else be prowling around?"

"Were the prints made by different boots?" Anna asked as she studied the trail, hoping for some sign of her son.

"Too much snow has fallen on them for me to tell."

Her patience exhausted, Anna turned and began walking uphill. "Come on, Robert, it's risky to dawdle, so let's follow the uphill prints. Luka wouldn't backtrack."

"Oh, he wouldn't backtrack, but he'd leave in the middle of the night without telling us?"

Anna exhaled loudly and continued hiking up the trail. "I'm already on edge, Robert. Don't make things worse."

The slope became steeper and the snow heavier as the two climbers slogged up the trail. Weber led the way, keeping a close eye on the rapidly disappearing bootprints. The once-deep impressions had become shallow indentations and now were barely discernible outlines. Once the trail vanished entirely, Weber looked up the slopes, hoping to catch a glimpse of Luka, but the snowfall was too dense to see anything more than a few meters ahead.

Weber studied the slope's contours, trying to discern the trail's trajectory, then trudged upward until he came across a ridge. He established a foothold on a low-lying ledge, boosted himself onto the face of the ridge, and then extended his hand toward Anna. As Anna took hold of his hand, a gunshot blast reverberated overhead that knocked Weber off balance. He lost his footing, fell, and crashed into Anna, knocking her headlong into a snowbank. Rather than help Anna to her feet, he pulled her against the base of the ridge, out of the line of fire.

Weber lay there, shielding Anna with his body, until the snowfall eased and visibility increased. Then he got to his knees and peered up the mountainside, searching for signs of the shooter. While he was scanning the slopes, another gunshot rang out, this time from below. "My God, Anna, there are two of them, and it sounds like they're targeting each other."

Anna sat up, crouched next to Weber, and stared at the terrain above the ridge. "I assume that Luka's somewhere above us, but who is the other shooter?"

"I have no idea," Weber replied, "but it's obvious that his intentions are hostile. And, if you're right about Luka's position, we're exposed and need to seek cover on the other side of this ridge."

Anna felt her heart pounding as she and Weber climbed the ridge and continued up the trail. She was expecting to hear a gunshot and wondered whether she'd have time to duck before the bullet tore into her body. But the debacle she'd imagined didn't come to pass; all she heard was the alternating crunch of snow compressing under the soles of her boots.

They pushed onward, fighting for breath while slogging uphill through ankle-deep snow, climbing over fallen trees, and occasionally seeking cover behind boulders. Weber let down his guard after an hour had passed; there had been no further gunfire, and he'd not seen any sign of animals or other climbers. He glanced at Anna and saw from her expression that she was distressed because they hadn't found Luka. He tried to reassure her even though he had doubts of his own. "We'll find him, or he'll find us. He's probably ahead, waiting for us at a higher elevation."

"I know you mean well, Robert, but you have no idea where Luka's gone. Why would he be so far ahead of us?"

Weber was about to protest when he noticed fresh bootprints ahead at a fork in the trail. He drew his pistol and raised his hand to signal Anna, and the two of them took cover behind a nearby boulder. "There are boot prints ahead—one set, and fresh—whoever it is has the high ground and might have seen us coming."

"Put your gun away, Robert; it might be Luka."

"What if it's not?"

"All right, but don't shoot unless fired upon."

Weber nodded without really hearing Anna because he was deep in thought, trying to devise a way to outfox their potential adversary. When he arrived at a solution, he shared it with Anna and then crept up the slope until he reached the fresh bootprints and trod on top of them to conceal his footsteps. After proceeding a hundred meters, he hurdled an embankment and lay in a trough where he couldn't be seen.

Weber had barely lain down in the trough when he heard Anna shout from below, "Help! Please help me!" He lay deathly still, listening intently for a response, but heard nothing. Anna shouted again, and this time, Weber heard the alternating cadence of boots crunching through the snow, growing ever closer, descending along the slope that he had just climbed. Slowly and silently, he rolled into a crouch while keeping his head below the embankment, withdrew his pistol, and prepared to pounce. He waited until the sounds of the footfalls receded down the slope and then vaulted the barrier, dashed toward a lumbering, rifle-toting figure, and shoved his pistol against the person's head. "Toss the rifle, or I'll drop you where you stand."

"Robert, is that you? I thought I heard my mother crying for help. Is she okay?"

"Luka, what the hell are you doing? Your mother's been scared out of her wits. And what's with the gunfire; who's shooting at who?"

Luka started to explain, but Weber motioned for him to stop, grabbed his arm, and led him down the slope. "On second thought, wait until we find your mother, or you'll have to repeat everything."

Anna yelped when she saw Weber guiding Luka toward her. "Luka, thank God you're alive. I'd almost given up hope." She turned away and wiped tears from her face, embarrassed by the strength and spontaneity of her emotions. When she regained control, she faced Luka and spoke calmly but firmly. "Alright, let's hear it. You better have a damn good explanation for what you've put us through."

Luka stood there tongue-tied and looked like he was going to wilt. Weber felt for the kid, so he intervened. "Just start at the beginning."

Luka drew a deep breath. "I was standing watch inside the cave when I heard an animal sniffing around the entrance. I grabbed the rifle and went after it, figuring that I might be able to shoot us a meal. But the beast slipped away from me once it got through the gap, leaving me alone and snow-blind in the middle of a blizzard. I fumbled about in the dark, trying to find my way back to the cave, and got lost, so I holed up under a ledge until morning. When the sun came up, I dug myself out and resumed my search for the cave, but that's when someone took a shot at me. The shooter was positioned below me, so I kept climbing, figuring I'd eventually draw him out into the open to get a clear shot. But the sniper stayed out of sight and kept shooting at me, so I had to keep climbing to get away from him. That's how I got here. It's been quiet for some time—long before I heard mom yell—so perhaps the sniper's gone.

No sooner had Luka finished speaking when a projectile ricocheted off the ledge beside him and sent a sliver of granite spiraling into Weber's forehead. Blood gushed from the wound and ran in rivulets down his face. Echoing in the distance was the delayed report of a high-caliber rifle. Anna pushed Weber and Luka into the snow and kneeled beside them. She retrieved a first aid kit from her pack and stanched the blood oozing from Weber's forehead and then cleaned and bandaged the wound.

When Anna had finished dressing the wound, Weber sat up and looked around, relieved that he only had a headache. Anna and Luka lay next to him, and he instructed them to roll around in the snow until their clothing was covered. He did the same. Once they were as white as polar bears, Weber led the group up the slope, advising them to stay close to snow-covered boulders and embankments to blend in. Though their progress was slow, they eventually reached the top of their first mountain without any incidents. After a short break to admire the view, they descended into a narrow alpine valley and climbed an even steeper slope towards a higher peak.

Winter 1928: Southwest of Munich, Germany

Luther, the mechanic, lay under the fighter's raised wing flap, cursing the overheated machine guns while he struggled to install a bulky ammunition belt. "I told you, Meissner, it's impossible to reload these guns until they cool down."

"Stop making excuses and do your job," Gunter demanded. "Under combat conditions, no superior officer will tolerate your whining. You'd be shot for dereliction of duty. Learn that now, or you will regret it later."

Luther snorted derisively and then climbed down from the wing and walked toward the outer wall of the corridor, where his workbench was located.

"Where do you think you're going?" Gunter screamed. I ordered you to reload immediately! You're delaying my mission! The spies I'm hunting could be escaping as we speak."

"Don't blow a gasket, Meissner; I have to find my gloves."

Gunter withdrew his sidearm and pointed it at the mechanic. "You will address me as Captain Meissner! Do you understand? I won't tolerate insubordination. Reload those wing guns and make this fighter airworthy before I'm forced to do something drastic."

Luther realized he'd delayed Gunter as long as he could, so he reloaded the machine guns and set about preparing the plane for flight. He'd acted on Wolff's orders and had done everything he could to keep Meissner on the ground until Albrecht returned to the base and traded his plane for an armed fighter. Now that he was staring down the muzzle of Meissner's pistol, there was nothing more he could do.

Back in the air, Gunter proceeded west to Gabel's farm and then flew southwest until he arrived at the alpine hut. At one point, he thought he saw an airborne object in the distance and wondered if someone was tailing him, but the speck had disappeared, and he'd seen nothing suspicious since.

Meanwhile, Albrecht was just over the horizon, piloting a fully armed experimental fighter that Wolff had prepared for him when he'd returned to the base. Wolff's friend, a mechanic named Luther, had stalled Gunter long enough for Albrecht to swap planes and return to the air shortly after Gunter's departure. He knew where Meissner was headed, so it wasn't difficult to track his plane and follow it at a discrete distance.

After ascending into the Alps, Albrecht watched in horror as Gunter positioned his fighter for a strafing run and then opened fire on the hut. Tracers streamed from the wingtips and tore into the hut, shattering windows and ripping holes in the roof. The bullets continued to rain down on the hut as the attacking aircraft approached and skimmed over the damaged structure, slicing through a cloud of smoke rising from the roof. The fighter then veered away from the mountainside, circled, and swooped in low for a second pass.

Albrecht imagined bullets raining down on Anna and her family inside the hut. He knew they were in great danger, and unless he acted quickly, they were doomed. He broke cover, put his plane on a collision course with Gunter's fighter, and trained his gunsights on the cockpit. "Take this, you barbarian—here's a taste of your own medicine."

Albrecht's fighter shuddered as his wingtip guns fired simultaneously, spitting flame and smoke and launching a raft of hot lead directly at Gunter's plane. The first round of shots missed their target, but the second burst ripped through the starboard wing and damaged its flaps. The third burst hit just behind the cowl, and shortly after, the propeller stopped spinning. Albrecht had to hold himself back; he wanted to keep firing, but he knew he had disabled Gunter's fighter. He moved away to a safer distance and observed as his adversary struggled to maintain control of his plane.

◆◆◆

Gunter heard gunfire coming from behind him, but before he could identify the attacker, bullets ripped into the starboard wing of his fighter plane, causing him to lose control. He struggled to stabilize the aircraft, but it rolled sideways and descended rapidly. Soon after, bullets hit the engine bay, causing the fighter to lose power. This was a nightmare scenario for any pilot, but Gunter's combat experience during the Great War kicked in as he frantically searched for a safe place to land. He realized that his only option was to land on the same runway he had attacked earlier that day. Unfortunately, the runway was cluttered with aircraft wreckage, making the landing even more dangerous.

Gunter came to the harsh realization that his fighter plane was not agile enough, and the runway was not clear enough to land safely. He only had enough altitude for a single approach; without power, he wouldn't have a second chance. Years ago, his flight instructor had termed it a 'one and done' situation, meaning he had to land successfully on his first attempt.

The fighter plane lurched towards the runway with a nose-heavy and starboard-leaning bearing. Alarmed by how fast the aircraft was descending, Gunter tightened his seatbelt and braced for impact. Suddenly, the plane's right wing scraped the runway's surface, broke off at the fuselage, and disappeared. The aircraft tilted on its side and skidded until debris sheared off the port strut, causing it to drop on its belly. It then rotated off the runway and crashed against the side of the hut.

Gunter struggled with his seatbelt as he attempted to overcome the confusion clouding his judgment. His head had hit the windscreen when the fighter plane crashed into the hut, causing him to lose consciousness briefly. Upon regaining consciousness, he discovered he was unharmed and alive but trapped within the burning wreckage.

As smoke gathered in the cockpit, Gunter worked feverishly to extricate himself before his lungs filled with fumes and choked the life out of him. Nothing he did seemed to matter—he pulled, pushed, yanked, and thrust his body forward and backward, but the seatbelt remained jammed and wouldn't release. Then, as adrenaline pumped into his system and his mind began to clear, he remembered his knife, withdrew it from his pocket, and slashed through the seatbelt.

He crawled to the misshapen opening where the cockpit door had been, pulled his rifle out of its harness, and hobbled onto the runway. Only a few steps from the plane, he slipped on an oil slick and fell headlong onto the tarmac, slid against the burning fuselage, and watched in horror as flames ignited his flight jacket. He struggled to his feet and wriggled out of his jacket, but not before fire had burned through the left sleeve and scorched his arm.

The hut was now an inferno, so Gunter took shelter in a shack next to a trail leading up into the Alps. Once inside, he placed his rifle against a wall, lay his exhausted body on the floor, and slept through the night.

The next morning, Gunter examined the remains of the burnt hut, but he could find no evidence of Anna and her family. While he didn't expect to find survivors, he didn't anticipate the hut being empty. The discovery made him angry; all that effort and firepower had been wasted. He returned to the shack and pawed through trash strewn around the floor. He discovered a worn backpack, climbing gear, and a half-full canteen among the garbage. These items made him suspicious. He was sure Anna and her family had been hiding in the hut. After all, he had seen a boy, likely Luka, brushing snow off the planes he had destroyed. What if Anna and her family had fled on foot while he was reloading at the base? Given the gear he'd just found, that possibility seemed feasible and likely.

Gunter shouldered his rifle and stuffed the gear he had found into the discarded backpack. He then set out on the trail, scanning for footprints or other signs of his prey. Unfortunately, a fresh layer of snow made it impossible to confirm his suspicions. Any footprints that might have existed were long gone. It was discouraging to think that the trail might have gone cold, but he decided to press on and not second-guess his decision.

After walking for several kilometers, Gunter arrived at a broad slope littered with farming equipment and set up camp for the night. The following day, he resumed his search and eventually found three pairs of bootprints covered in light snow shortly after sunrise. He followed the footprints until he reached a gap between two crags, where he noticed a preponderance of bootprints and some animal tracks. All the animal tracks and one set of bootprints continued up the trail and disappeared, but other bootprints went through the gap between the rocks. This made him confident that his target was nearby. He started scanning the slopes above, searching for any signs of movement.

After scanning the mountainside several times, he gave up because the early morning sun's angle created deep shadows that could easily conceal animals or people. He decided to follow the boot prints up the trail, but as he turned to leave, a gunshot echoed, and a bullet ricocheted off a nearby rock. Gunter quickly took cover among the scree that lay at the base of a crag and waited for more gunfire, but none came. As he lay there, he felt increasingly uncomfortable. He knew he couldn't stay where he was; he was too exposed and vulnerable, an easy target for whoever was shooting at him. Summoning his courage, he retreated down the slope to find a more defensible position.

Gunter dashed down the trail at full speed, zig-zagging as often as possible to avoid being hit. He continued until he was several hundred meters below his starting point. Once there, he took cover behind a rock outcropping. After catching his breath, he aimed his rifle at the slopes above him and surveyed the area using the telescopic sight.

The scope's narrow field of view made scanning the mountainside an arduous task. Gunter kept at it until his vision became blurry, and his arms began to ache, but the phantom shooter was nowhere to be seen. He put the rifle down, sat on a ledge, and took a swig from the half-filled canteen. While he was pondering his next move, he heard the sound of voices in the distance. He stood, aimed his rifle toward the voices, and eventually spotted two people with packs and climbing gear standing near the gap where he'd seen all the bootprints.

He stood there waiting for the climbers to turn toward him, and as soon as they did, he recognized them. Weber, the tall one, was standing next to Anna. Now that he had Weber in sight, Gunter thought seriously about pulling the trigger and figured Anna deserved the same fate. He'd long been after Weber, and Anna was as much or more of a threat. However, after careful consideration, he concluded they were unlikely to flee across the Alps without Luka. He realized the most probable scenario was that Luka had fired on him and was hiding somewhere else on the mountain, concealed in the shadows. If this was true, harming Anna and Weber would be counterproductive because he needed them to lead him to Luka. If he didn't find Luka, his entire mission would fail.

When Weber and Anna continued up the trail, Gunter followed at a safe distance while observing them with his rifle's telescopic sight. He walked in the shadows and between boulders to remain hidden from the climbers and the shooter. Several hours passed without incident and then he spotted Weber and Anna attempting to climb a ridge. As he watched the two climbers, he suddenly heard a gunshot, and a bullet flew past his head. He quickly took cover and then carefully aimed his rifle scope uphill to locate the sniper. His attention was drawn to a puff of smoke floating near a ledge that jutted out along a clifftop. He watched the ledge closely, and when he detected movement, he aimed at some nearby rocks and returned fire. The probability was high that Luka was the sniper, and given his promise to Goring, he didn't want to harm the boy but rather deter him from shooting.

When Gunter was confident that the gunfire had ceased, he aimed his scope where he'd seen Weber and Anna and observed them scramble over the ledge and run for cover. Their actions indicated that they were more afraid of the gunman situated downhill, which was consistent with his assumption that it was Luka who was firing at him from above. This insight convinced him that Weber and Anna would lead him to the boy if he were patient. The prospect of finding Luka brought a smile to Gunter's face. Once he had the boy, he could take care of Weber, and he looked forward to that. When he finished with Weber, he'd decide what to do with Anna.

He waited for Weber and Anna to resume their journey, and when they did, he followed them until they reached a fork in the trail. Through his scope, he noticed that Weber had found something, possibly footprints. Soon after, Anna concealed herself behind some rocks, and Weber proceeded alone up the trail until he came across an embankment. He then jumped over it and hid himself in a ditch. Gunter was puzzled by this unusual behavior and didn't know what to make of it.

After several minutes of training his scope on Weber, Gunter spotted Luka approaching Weber's location. As Luka walked past, Weber jumped him from behind and began shouting. Despite Luka's attempt to communicate, Weber didn't listen and grabbed Luka by the arm and led him down the trail to where Anna was waiting for them. A lively conversation between Luka and two others followed, but Gunter couldn't hear what was said. He wondered what they were discussing, but it hardly mattered now that he'd found Luka.

Gunter decided it was time to deal with Weber. He knew hitting such a small target from this range was risky. Though it was a long shot, it wasn't impossible. He brought his scope to bear on the target, lined up the reticles, and squeezed off a shot. The rifle kicked, and there was a loud report. The sound echoed repeatedly as the reverberations bounced off the solid rock walls surrounding him. Looking through the scope, he saw Weber grab his forehead and fall to the ground.

After congratulating himself for his marksmanship, Gunter hurried up the trail to capture Luka. Now that Weber was out of the way, he had nothing to worry about. If Luka resisted, he'd threaten to harm Anna. The kid would have no choice but to follow him back to the base. He'd already prepared a cell and would deal with Anna once the kid was locked up.

Chapter 27

Winter 1928: Southwest of Munich, Germany, Near the Austrian Border

Weber slowed his pace, even though he knew doing so would allow the sniper to draw nearer and endanger his fellow climbers. It wasn't a choice he made willingly; it was something he felt he had to do. The ascent to the second, higher Alp was even more challenging than the first due to the steep terrain, heavy snow, jagged rocks, and loose scree. Despite wearing crampons, all three climbers had fallen multiple times, and each step they took increased their chances of exhaustion or injury.

When Anna fell for the fourth time, Weber helped her to her feet and proposed they take a break to rest and regroup. He pointed to a shepherd's shelter made of rough-hewn logs about a hundred meters ahead and recommended they stop there.

Weber walked towards the ancient shelter, wondering when it was last used. He hoped its previous occupants had been human. Although the sides of the shelter looked intact, the roof was sagging, and half of the structure was buried in snow. After reaching the shelter, he cleared away the snow that had drifted against a ramshackle wooden door. Then he carefully pried open the door, drew his pistol, and stepped inside the dimly lit space. The shack had two windows that faced in opposite directions, both of which were covered with animal hides. Weber removed the hides to let in some light, revealing a sparsely furnished room. He glanced around and saw a small table attached to one wall, a dirty mattress on the floor, and a rough stone fireplace built diagonally into one corner.

After determining the shelter was safe, Weber returned to the doorway and invited Anna and Luka inside. "Well, this place isn't luxurious, but it will serve our needs. Since we're tired and hungry, I suggest we stay here for the night. Does anyone have objections?" Hearing none, Weber looked at Luka and said, "Take the rifle and hunt some game for dinner. Be quick about it, and don't disappear on us like last time. I'll gather some wood and start a fire. Anna, please fill the canteen with snow. I'll warm it over the fire to get fresh water to protect us from dehydration. Then, carve a sturdy branch into a spit so we can roast whatever Luka brings us."

Two hours later, after the fire had warmed the shelter, Luka returned, carrying the carcasses of a fox and two rabbits. Weber congratulated him on his successful hunt and cleaned and roasted the game. When mealtime arrived, the three individuals eagerly devoured the meat as if they had not eaten in days. In fact, it had been two days since their last meal. While the trio savored the food, they drank water from their canteen to replenish their fluids. After finishing their meal, Anna and Luka slept on the mattress while Weber stood guard.

Later that night, Luka kept watch while Weber slept. In the morning, the three climbers ate some leftover food from the previous night and prepared to continue their ascent up the mountain. While packing his gear, Weber stopped and shared a concern he had been mulling. "Listen, Anna and Luka, I think we should talk before we leave. Our original plan to trek across the Alps was made in haste, and now we're mainly driven by the need to escape the sniper. We must clarify our objectives and establish a clear direction for our journey."

Anna looked puzzled. "Our goal is to cross into Austria, isn't it?"

"Yes, but our progress has been slow. We are running short on provisions, we're unfamiliar with the terrain ahead of us, and, to top it off, we are exhausting ourselves trying to stay ahead of a deranged sniper. We never anticipated any of these issues. Additionally, we had to choose Austria by default because we couldn't reach Switzerland without our aircraft. It's not the ideal destination for us; it's rather risky. The closer we get to Austria, the more worried I feel."

"Well, what can we do about that now?" Anna replied.

Luka looked thoughtful and then spoke. "There's a railroad line further up the mountain. I didn't include it on the map because I only considered hiking trails. The route runs towards the east and west. What if we board a westbound train? The train could take us closer to Switzerland, and the sniper won't be able to follow us."

Weber hesitated at Luka's proposal. "It's an intriguing idea, but boarding a moving train is risky," he said.

"I agree," Luka countered, "but trains slow down when they encounter steep, uphill grades in the mountains."

Weber took the map from his pocket, unfolded it, and passed it to Luka. "All right, considering the trail we're on now, show me the quickest way to reach this rail line."

Luka took the map and pointed to their current location. He then traced his finger over a trail further up the mountain that crossed paths with the one they were hiking. "This trail is the quickest way to reach the rail line but also the most perilous one."

"Is it more dangerous than our current trail?" Anna inquired.

Before Luka could respond, Weber interrupted and asked for specifics. "Exactly what makes it more perilous?"

A pained expression flickered across Luka's face. "The trail we need to take goes over a deep crevasse and then runs below a cliff where snow accumulates. Unfortunately, the crevasse is too long to avoid, stretching over a kilometer of impassable terrain. This means we have to cross it at its narrowest point—a place that is about ten meters wide."

Weber looked at Luka skeptically. "Luka, have you ever crossed this crevasse?"

"I've done it several times," Luka replied sheepishly.

Anna inhaled sharply. "You'd have been in serious trouble if I'd known that."

Luka smiled. "I was careful not to mention it."

Weber redirected the conversation towards practicalities. "Luka, do we have sufficient gear to cross this crevasse?"

Luka replied affirmatively. "Yes, we do."

At midmorning, the three climbers set off from the shelter and began hiking up the mountainside towards the route that led to the rail line. Due to the overnight snowfall, the trail was just as treacherous as the day before, if not more so. Weber slipped repeatedly and fell occasionally, as did the other climbers, but fortunately, no one suffered any severe injuries.

After climbing for two hours, Weber reached a point where two trails intersected. He stopped to check his compass and ensure he was headed in the right direction. Their first trail led southward to the summit, but the new trail turned southwest, running parallel to the mountain's face and passing under its peak. Though he thought he was on the right track, Weber wanted to double-check with Luka to confirm their direction.

"Luka, is this the trail we're looking for—the one that leads to the rail line?"

"Yes, Robert, bear to the right here; the crevasse is about two kilometers ahead."

The new trail was not as steep as the former one, but the snow cover was deeper, and neither Weber nor the others had snowshoes. Exhaustion replaced falling as the climbers' principal risk. They pushed on, slogging through knee-deep snow until they were ready to drop, ever mindful that a sniper was hunting them.

After trekking for a kilometer, Weber's resolve flagged, and he questioned the wisdom of taking the new trail. The heavy snow made it difficult to move forward, draining their energy and leaving a conspicuous trail for the sniper to follow. He wondered whether he and the others could make it to the crevasse, let alone the rail line. Images of the three of them lying dead in the snow flashed through his mind.

Anna noticed Weber's diminishing determination and decided to halt the climbers. She pushed through the snow until she reached a ledge and sat on it. "Robert and Luka, come and sit down. It's time we took a break."

Weber responded irritably, "We don't have time to waste. A sniper is after us."

"Don't argue, Robert. I can see what's happening to you. Luka and I are just as weary. Now get over here."

Weber obeyed.

Weber's energy returned as he sat on the ledge, and he began thinking about the next step in their journey. "Luka, we'll be reaching the crevasse soon. Can you explain how we're going to cross it?"

Luka returned to the trail where the trio had dumped their gear, stooped, and began opening packs and rifling through climbing equipment. He selected two coils of rope and a grappling hook, then returned to the ledge and laid it in front of Weber and Anna. "This is the only equipment we'll need. I'll explain how to use it when we arrive at the crevasse; I don't want to give the sniper more time to find us. For now, there are only a few things we need to focus on."

Luka picked up a coil of rope and untangled a part of it. He then held it above Anna's head and asked her to extend her arms and hold onto it like an overhead bar, as if she were about to do a pull-up. Weber was then invited to do the same. After comparing the locations where Anna and Weber had grasped the rope, Luka knotted it in two places, about a meter apart. "I am placing these knots to correspond with the places where Mom's hands grasped the rope. Since Mom's reach is smaller than yours, Robert, we will use that distance to place knots on our suspension cable. Robert, please help me with this. Let's stretch out the rope and tie a knot about every meter along its length. The knots will give us something to grip as we cross the crevasse."

After tying knots in the rope, Weber led the group back to the trail. The three individuals gathered their gear and continued towards the rail line.

The next kilometer was challenging due to the heavy snow, but Weber's vigor increased when he saw the crevasse. He cautiously approached the yawning gap in the mountainside, anchored his boots next to the rim, and peered over the edge. He was stunned by the view in front of him. The crevasse looked like two opposing cliffs that plunged into darkness. He couldn't resist throwing a rock into the abyss. After several seconds, he heard a faint splash from below.

Anna and Luka had lagged behind on the trail but eventually caught up, approached the crevasse, and stood next to Weber. Both were exhausted and stood on the rim, catching their breath while they gazed into the void. Luka was the first to speak. "Crossing will be strenuous, so we should rest before we attempt it."

Still spellbound by the yawning gorge, Anna objected to Luka's terminology, saying that attempting to cross is not the same as making it across.

"I'm confident we'll all make it," Luka reassured Anna. "It's not as dangerous as it looks."

Anna gave a slow nod of agreement, but her expression still betrayed some lingering doubt. Weber understood her trepidation.

The climbers removed their packs, stacked their climbing gear by the edge of the crevasse, and lay down on the snow. As Weber and Anna slept, Luka attached the grappling hook to one end of the knotted rope. He then walked to the crevasse's edge, firmly held one end of the rope, and threw the end with the hook across the void. The hook made a loud clanging sound as it cut through the snow and slammed against the rocks on the other side. Luka then pulled the rope towards himself, allowing the hook to scrape along the stones until it dropped into a fissure between two boulders. Once the hook was securely wedged in the space between the boulders, he tied his end of the rope to some nearby rocks.

When Weber and Anna awoke, Luka stood on the crevasse's other side. Weber got up, examined the suspension rope, and then glanced across the crevasse to where Luka was standing. "What's the procedure, Luka?"

"Sit on the rim, grasp the line firmly, and then push off the edge. Once you're fully suspended, grasp the knot in front of you and pull yourself forward. Then, grab the next knot and repeat the procedure. Reaching hand-over-hand for successive knots will get you across faster, but sliding your hands from knot to knot has the advantage of keeping both hands on the rope at all times. When you get to this side, stick the toe of your boot on this ledge and lever yourself up onto the rim."

Weber beckoned Anna, who was standing close by. "Anna, did you hear that? Are you ready?" Anna put on her backpack, walked towards the crevasse, and sat on its edge. She looked determined and focused as she grabbed the rope and lowered herself into the void.

Anna followed Luka's instructions and moved smoothly across the crevasse until the suspension rope suddenly loosened and dropped a few centimeters. After that, there was a grating sound from Luka's side of the crevasse, and the rope fell a full meter before becoming taut again. The sudden movement caused Anna to bounce up and down like a yoyo. Each time she descended, her body weight pulled against her hands, loosening her grip.

Luka was quick to respond after realizing that the grappling hook had lost its grip on the rocks. He immediately pulled on the rope until the hook was securely lodged between the boulders again. Then, he launched himself onto the suspension line and swung hand-over-hand to where his mother was suspended. He wrapped his arm around her waist and waited for the rope to stop swaying before pulling her across the void and helping her onto the rim. Once Anna was safe, he instructed Weber to tighten the suspension line by retying it on his side of the crevasse.

Watching Luka rescue Anna didn't boost Weber's confidence. He asked Luka to confirm that the hook was secure before he crossed. Luka complied with Weber's request, and then Weber crossed without incident. Once all three climbers were safely across, Luka untied the grappling hook and let go of the suspension line, which fell into the crevasse and dangled down the cliff on the other side.

Weber watched as the rope fell against the cliff on the other side of the crevasse and then turned and gazed at Luka with a perplexed look. "Do you think it was wise to cancel our return journey across the crevasse? What if we need to retrace our steps?" he inquired.

Luka responded, "I understand your concern, but leaving the suspension line intact would benefit the sniper more than us. Don't you think so?"

Weber gave a nod, and the group reloaded their equipment before resuming their journey. Luka, who was familiar with the trail, took the lead. Weber was relieved to have him guide the way, as they had lost sight of the actual trail some time ago due to the heavy snowfall.

The trail climbed steadily from the crevasse and ran underneath a towering cliff extending to the mountain's peak. The snow layer below the cliff was thicker than anything the trio had encountered. Initially, the climbers sank into the snow up to their thighs. As they continued, the snow became even deeper, and they had no choice but to lie on their stomachs and use their arms and legs to crawl across the crusty surface. If it had not been so awkward, Weber would have laughed. They looked like turtles flailing their limbs as they tried to cross an ice rink.

Suddenly, a projectile hit the side of the cliff, followed by a gunshot blast that reverberated off the rock face and echoed down the mountain. As the noise died down, Weber heard a sound like that of breaking eggshells. He looked around and saw that the snow beneath him and his fellow climbers had developed cracks that were spreading. Weber turned his gaze towards the crevasse and noticed that the sniper had somehow crossed it and was now closer than ever. He was aiming the rifle in Weber's direction.

Weber and his companions crawled cautiously toward the cliff, searching for a place to take cover when the sniper fired another shot. The percussive blast echoed off the cliff again, but this time, Weber felt the snow beneath him shift, giving him a sensation of having the ground pulled from under him. Before he could comprehend what was happening, Luka screamed, "Avalanche!"

The climbers watched as the snowpack below them broke apart, sending sheets of ice and snow down the mountainside, creating white tsunamis that crashed into boulders and uprooted trees. As larger sheets broke off and slid away, the entire slope shook. Weber desperately clawed at neighboring rocks, trying to anchor himself to the cliffside. Anna and Luka survived by crawling onto a narrow ledge and securing their gear to rocks before the surrounding snow shifted.

Weber tensed his muscles as the snow began to give way beneath him. He tightened his backpack and held onto a small, rotund granite pillar to avoid being swept away by the avalanche. His effort proved timely; the snowpack beneath him collapsed, and he found himself hanging in mid-air, clinging to the pillar for dear life.

After the avalanche and the accompanying thunder subsided, Luka looped a rope over a rock that protruded from the ledge where he and Anna had taken refuge and rappelled down the cliffside. He descended past the level where the snowpack had been and landed on the almost barren slope beneath it. Anna followed him by climbing down the rope. Once she reached the bottom, Luka shook the rope loose, coiled it, and positioned himself underneath Weber. Weber was holding on to a pillar almost fifteen meters above Luka. "Robert," Luka yelled, "try to catch this rope and tie it to the pillar." He threw the rope forcefully, but it fell short and landed at his feet. He tried again, but the result was the same. Finally, on the third attempt, Weber caught the rope, tied it off, and safely descended onto the slope.

The three climbers stood silently on the slope, gazing at the massive snowfield that had descended the mountain and accumulated on the slopes below them. Anna finally broke the silence. "Thank God we made it through that. Luka and I were fortunate to find a ledge. Are you all right, Robert?"

"I'm shaken, but I'm fine," Weber replied as he turned and looked toward the crevasse, trying to identify the spot where he had seen the sniper. "Wow," he said, pointing to the crevasse with his finger. "I saw the sniper standing next to the crevasse, but he's gone now. Look at how the snow has piled up around the edges of the crevasse."

Luka glanced in the direction Weber was pointing and let out a low whistle. "Unbelievable! The snow around the rim must have risen ten meters since we crossed. That crevasse must have swallowed an enormous amount of snow. What do you think happened to the sniper?"

"No one could have survived that onslaught," Weber replied curtly. "I would bet he's buried under tons of snow at the bottom of the crevasse."

"Good riddance," Anna added with a note of finality in her voice.

Luka heaved his backpack onto his shoulders and began hiking up the trail. Weber and Anna followed closely behind him. The going was easier now because the avalanche had reduced the snowpack, and the trail outlines were more visible. After an hour of hiking, Luka pointed up the trail and yelled, "Look, there's the rail line."

Weber looked ahead and saw railroad tracks running up an elevated embankment toward a trestle bridge that spanned a deep gorge. He came to a halt, placed his hands on his hips, and took a deep breath. He could scarcely believe his eyes—they had made it to the railway line. Now, if only they could sneak aboard a westbound freight.

As the threesome approached the rail line near the mountain's peak, they stood in awe and gazed at the stunning terrain below. Weber sensed the change in elevation because the air was thinner, and the sun's rays felt warmer on his skin. From where he stood with Anna and Luka, the view was astounding. Mountains and valleys stretched as far as the eye could see, creating an incredible vista.

Weber left Anna and Luka and climbed up the elevated embankment to explore the rail line. Upon reaching the top, he stepped onto the tracks, glanced in both directions and marveled at the extensive view. His eyes traveled along the railway line as it snaked through the mountains, negotiating steep ridges, winding around cliffs and hillsides, and even crossing over rivers and through tunnels. Weber was deeply impressed by this engineering marvel. Next, he looked down at the tracks and examined the parallel steel rails and the spikes that kept them in place on the embankment's creosote-infused wooden ties. Based on what he saw, Weber was able to draw a few conclusions about the railroad they were planning to use as an escape route.

As Weber descended the embankment, he caught sight of a roofline to the east that he had missed while surveying the rail line's path across the mountains. The structure was larger than the shack they had stayed in during the second Alp climb. He wondered if the building would be a good place to shelter for the night.

Weber met up with Anna and Luka at the foot of the embankment. He proposed that they hike towards the east to explore the building he had spotted close to the railway line. Anna asked him if he believed the building was inhabited, but Weber said he didn't know because he'd only seen the roofline. Luka was enthusiastic about the idea and immediately set off along the embankment to locate the building and discover what was inside.

Luka spotted the building as he walked along the tracks. It was a two-story structure embedded in the mountainside. The lower level was concrete and had a small door on one side and a larger roll-up door at the front, facing the tracks. The upper level was constructed with logs and had several narrow windows. The steeply angled, slate roof was covered with snow and had long, thick icicles hanging from its corners.

Excited about his discovery, Luka shouted to Weber and Anna, who were several hundred meters behind him. He then hurried to the side of the building and tried to open the small door. That door was locked, so he walked to the front of the building and tried the larger door, which, to his surprise, rolled up and coiled inside its frame.

Upon hearing Luka's shout, Weber and Anna quickly approached and entered the open door. They found themselves in a spacious room with a high ceiling, tall shelves lining the walls, and piles of equipment scattered on the floor. Weber quickly surveyed the room and immediately understood the building's purpose. The floor was cluttered with railroad ties, track sections, welding equipment, and drums of tar and creosote. The shelves along the walls were filled with various supplies, including gloves, sledgehammers, wrenches, switchgear, and steel spikes.

Weber touched Luka's shoulder and gestured towards a door at the back of the room. "Luka, you've found a railroad maintenance building; judging by its size, more rooms exist to explore. Let's check out what's behind that door and see if there's anyone here to welcome us."

Weber pulled out his pistol, opened the door, and eased into the dark interior of another room. Luka followed him inside. They both searched the room blindly until Weber accidentally bumped into a table, causing a chair to fall over. He pocketed his pistol, kicked the chair aside, and felt around the table until his fingers bumped into some objects. "Hold on, Luka. I found some things. I'm going to examine them outside. I'll be back in a second." He picked up as many objects as he could carry, brought them back to the equipment room, and inspected them in the light. One of the items was a small box containing candles and matches. Weber lit a candle and returned to the dark room with Anna.

In the dim light of the candle, Weber discovered another door that led to the outside. Next to the door, there was a fixture with a glass globe on top. When he turned a lever underneath the aperture of the fixture, he heard a hissing sound. He then brought the candle's flame close to the opening and heard a popping sound as the gas stream ignited, filling the room with a blue light.

Weber quickly scanned the room and noticed a fireplace to his left, on the same wall as the door. At the rear of the room, he saw a countertop and sink with cabinets mounted above and below. In the center of the room was a large table and several chairs, while stairs leading to the second floor were positioned opposite the wall where he was standing.

After appraising the room, Weber shifted his gaze toward Luka, who was climbing the stairs toward the second floor. "Hey, hold on. Take this candle with you, and proceed cautiously. Given that this room is designed to feed an entire crew, I suspect you'll find a dormitory upstairs."

Anna stepped outside through the door next to the gas light, found a wood bin on the side of the building, and returned carrying a stack of firewood and kindling. She arranged the wood in the fireplace and began to light a fire.

Meanwhile, Weber searched the cabinets for food and utensils that they could use to make a meal. He found some dried fish and several cans of beans and placed them on the counter. "Anna, we can make a meal out of this if we don't mind roughing it. Should I prepare it?" he asked.

Anna inspected the food and wrinkled her nose. "I might have to hold my nose while I eat, but go ahead. Beggars can't be choosers," she responded.

Weber found a pot, filled it with beans, and heated it in the fireplace. Then he sliced the dried fish, put pieces on plates he had discovered in the cabinets, and arranged the plates on the table. As he poured hot beans onto the plates, Luka returned from searching the building's upstairs.

"It was just as you expected, Robert," Luka announced. "There are five bunk beds upstairs, a couple of closets filled with clothes and blankets, a few pairs of muddy work boots, and some chamber pots and spittoons. It's not what you'd call glamorous accommodations, but it's serviceable."

Weber nodded. "Okay, since this place is unoccupied, I suggest we stay the night."

Anna and Luka agreed, so the threesome sat at the table and ate fish and beans. While they ate, Weber shared his plans for the next steps of their journey. "From what I've seen, we've found an active rail line. The tracks are well-maintained and rust-free, suggesting they're used daily, if not more frequently. However, we don't know what types of trains travel this route or how fast they go past this building. It would be easier and safer to hop on a freight train because they are slower than passenger trains, have fewer people aboard who might notice us, and have more hiding places. So, before we can leave here, we'll need to do some trainspotting. I'll monitor the rail traffic tonight while you two sleep. Perhaps tomorrow, we can plan our departure."

Anna and Luka consented to Weber's plans and bid him good night.

Then they climbed the stairs, crawled into one of the bunkbeds, and fell asleep.

After saying good night to Anna and Luka, Weber searched the lower floor of the maintenance building for a flashlight. He found one in the larger room, on a storage shelf next to the roll-up door. It was a lantern-shaped model with a bracket that enabled it to stand independently. He pocketed the flashlight and then returned to the kitchen, where he donned his coat and exited through the side door.

It was a cold, clear, but moonless night. Weber inhaled deeply and felt the frigid night air nip at his nostrils and throat. He walked to where the railroad tracks passed in front of the building and glanced up and down the tracks. Seeing nothing, he withdrew the flashlight, shone its beam on the tracks and surrounding embankment, and began walking west, uphill toward the trestle bridge.

As Weber walked along the tracks beyond the point he had explored earlier, he noticed footprints in the snow and paused to inspect them. Upon shining his flashlight on the prints, he realized there were two sets of footprints--one made by a person and the other by an animal, probably a large dog. He found it strange that the tracks began abruptly next to the tracks and continued west toward the bridge. Curious, he followed the prints until he reached the bridge, where he discovered some stairs running down the embankment next to the mountain. He climbed down the steps and picked up the trail of footprints at the bottom. He followed them toward the maintenance building, where they disappeared under windswept snow. He wondered why he hadn't seen the tracks earlier. Perhaps it was because they weren't on the side of the embankment he had previously traversed. Plus, it looked like the footprints had been there a while; many had been covered by drifting snow.

Weber continued walking alongside the tracks toward the building, intending to go inside and warm himself by the fireplace, when he heard the sound of a train's whistle in the distance. He stood still beside the tracks and looked toward the sound, hoping to glimpse an approaching train. He saw a gleam on the horizon, and soon after, bright lights illuminated the mountainsides. Weber then spotted two bright beams approaching, making the polished steel tracks look like parallel lightning bolts.

Weber quickly dashed off the tracks and headed towards the maintenance building. He flattened his body against the west wall to avoid being seen and waited for the train to pass. However, to his surprise, the engine's rumbling gradually died, and the train stopped in front of the building. Fearing he might be discovered, Weber quietly walked around the back of the building and entered through the side door. He then climbed the stairs and peeked through a narrow window on the second floor to observe the train. As he looked down the tracks, he saw a line of boxcars and realized it was a freight train.

A door opened on a boxcar, and a man and a dog jumped out and walked towards the front of the train. The man was wearing work clothes and had his dog on a leash. When he reached the locomotive, he waved at the engineer and headed towards the maintenance building. The train slowly started moving, gathered speed, and eventually disappeared towards the trestle bridge.

Weber panicked when he saw the railroad worker and his dog approaching the building. He realized he had no time to wake Anna and Luka and find a hiding place. If the man didn't locate them, the dog certainly would. Weber felt doubtful that the rail worker or his dog would welcome the presence of freeloaders in the building. He realized that his only choice was to anticipate what would occur next. He crawled to the top of the stairwell, drew his pistol, and listened attentively.

The rail worker opened the side door of the building, which creaked on its frozen hinges. His voice echoed up the stairwell: "Panzer, you must stay outside because you have a habit of chewing people's things. Anders is still upset with you for ruining his boots. I'll bring you something to eat later."

Weber let out a sigh of relief. He was glad that the dog wouldn't be able to find them. The door slammed shut, and Weber could hear the sound of boots stomping on the kitchen floor. This was followed by the noise of cabinets opening and closing. The workman then started yelling and cursing about the messy state of the kitchen. "Look at this mess! There are dirty plates on the table, and crap has been spilled on the floor. Temporary work crews are never a good idea. They are nothing but slobs. Scheiss for brains! They have no idea what they're doing! I'm going to report all of you!"

The workman banged around in the kitchen while cleaning and preparing a meal. He kept complaining, "Who the hell ate the beans? Where is the damned dried fish? There is nothing left to eat here!"

Weber waited anxiously, hoping the disgruntled workman wouldn't come upstairs. Fortunately, the man left after twenty minutes, taking his dog with him and hiking up the tracks.

Weber crept down the stairs to the kitchen and stepped outside to see where the workman and his dog had gone. He cautiously moved around the side of the building, scanned the area, and spotted them walking toward the stairs near the trestle bridge. He kept himself hidden and observed as they climbed the stairs and stood on the embankment by the bridge. It appeared that they were waiting for something.

A little while later, a second freight train arrived and stopped on the trestle bridge. The rail worker walked the entire train length, stopping at each boxcar to let his dog sniff the door. After completing the circuit, the worker and his dog returned to the front of the train, opened one of the boxcar doors, and climbed inside. The locomotive sounded a loud whistle, and the train began to move, gradually increasing its speed.

◆◆◆

Weber sat at the kitchen table the next morning, waiting for Anna and Luka. He greeted them and informed them of everything that had happened the previous night.

After hearing all the details, Anna looked surprised and upset. She realized they were in danger and asked Weber if he thought the workman and his dog would return that night. Weber was uncertain but suggested that if they returned, he could use his knowledge of the worker's movements to keep them safe.

Anna then asked if they could outsmart the workman and his dog and sneak aboard the freight train. Weber grinned and said that's precisely what he had in mind.

Weber, Anna, and Luka stayed awake that night, waiting to see if the previous night's events would repeat themselves. They were not disappointed. Shortly after midnight, a freight train stopped outside the maintenance building. A rail worker and his dog climbed out of a boxcar, walked to the front of the train, and waved to the engineer as the train departed.

The threesome quickly exited from the side door and made their way to the rear of the building. They found a hiding spot behind the outhouse. Weber occasionally peeked around the corner of the outhouse to observe the worker's actions.

As before, the worker walked to the side door and tied his dog to the woodbin before entering the maintenance building. The dog expressed displeasure by whining, but the worker ignored it and went inside.

In the darkness, Weber stood motionless behind the outhouse, gesturing for Anna and Luka to do the same. They had rehearsed this tactic earlier, knowing any noise or movement could alert the dog.

After giving the worker a few minutes to settle in, Luka threw a piece of dried fish towards the woodbin to distract the dog. While the dog was investigating the fish, the trio quickly ran to the other side of the maintenance building, crossed the tracks, and went down the far side of the embankment. They were now out of sight from the maintenance building.

The threesome walked west, making their way toward the bridge. On one side of them was a raised rail embankment, while on the other was a steep mountain slope. Weber had decided to walk on the right side of the embankment because he knew that the workman and his dog would be approaching the bridge from the left side of the embankment, between it and the adjacent mountain.

Upon reaching the bridge, they discovered the embankment led to a cliff that plunged into the deep gorge below. Regrettably, there were no stairs on this side of the embankment to ascend to the bridge. The stairs that Weber had discovered earlier were located on the other side of the embankment.

Weber readied his climbing rope by uncoiling it, attaching the grappling hook to one end, and tying knots to make it similar to the suspension line they had used to cross the crevasse earlier. Then, he climbed up the embankment, secured one prong of the grappling hook to the bridge, and rappelled back down to where Anna and Luka were waiting. He looked at each of them and said, “Now we wait.” Then, he crossed his fingers and hoped the worker's actions would not deviate from what he had observed the previous night.

A short time later, a freight train rolled onto the bridge and stopped. Weber waited fifteen minutes, then grasped the rope and pulled himself up the embankment, knot by knot, until he reached the top. He kept his head down, raising it just enough so his eyes could see underneath the train to the other side of the embankment. He scanned the gaps between the boxcar’s undercarriages and the railroad tracks, hoping to catch sight of the workman and his dog as they conducted their inspection tour. But all he saw in those spaces were the huge steel wheels, axles, and coupling hooks suspended under each boxcar's ends.

He waited anxiously, keeping a vigilant eye out for any sign of the workman and his dog. Despite his attempt to remain calm, he couldn't shake the feeling that too much time had passed. “Where are you? You should have been here by now,” he muttered. His mind began to play tricks on him, imagining scenarios where the workman caught him spying and ordered his dog to attack. The thought of the dog only made things worse, as it had sharper senses than the workman and could easily spot him through the gaps under the boxcars.

Weber suddenly heard the sound of boots crunching on the snow. He looked around frantically, trying to locate the source of the sound, but he couldn't see anyone. As he continued to search, the crunching sound grew louder and louder. He wondered whether it was the workman and, if so, whether his dog was looking through the gaps under the boxcars. Suddenly,

Weber saw a boot and a leg appear from behind one set of wheels, striding into the snow. Following that leg was another one that moved in the same way.

Weber suspected the man who had appeared on the other side of the boxcar was the rail worker he'd seen the previous night. His suspicion was confirmed when a dog emerged from behind the boxcar wheels, close on the heels of the workman. The dog dragged his rear feet in the snow and pulled on his chain, resisting the workman's efforts to move forward. The workman said something to the dog that Weber couldn't hear, and the dog whimpered and then stopped resisting and walked dutifully alongside him. When the duo reached the middle of the boxcar, the workman paused, and the dog jumped up to sniff the side before returning to his former position. Then, suddenly, the dog glanced in Weber's direction, pulled against his leash, and began to whine.

Weber swiftly detached the rope and slid down the embankment, gesturing frantically towards Anna and Luka. As soon as he reached the ground, he handed the rope to Luka and guided them over the embankment's edge, down the slope, and behind some large boulders.

As Weber stood behind the boulders, he clenched his fists and listened to the commotion coming from the top of the embankment. The dog was barking and snarling while the rail worker was trying to get it to stop. "Leave it, Panzer. It was probably just some animal, and it's gone now." Despite the worker's attempts to calm the dog, it continued to howl. Suddenly, a beam of light illuminated the area near the boulders where Weber, Luka, and Anna hid. The worker yelled once again, "Look, you stupid mutt. There's nothing down there. You've scared the animal away. Now shut up, stop wasting my time, and come finish your job."

The dog continued to bark, but not as loudly as before. Weber swallowed his fear and waited as the workman and his dog returned to the train. When he could no longer hear the dog barking, he took the rope from Luka, climbed back up the slope, and prepared to scale the embankment.

Luka and Anna followed Weber as he climbed up the slope and joined him at the bottom of the embankment. Luka noticed that Weber was planning to climb the embankment and continue spying on the workman, so he asked him to let him do it instead. "Robert, let me do this. You're taking all the risks. I'll watch the workman and let you know when he's finished his inspection."

Weber thanked Luka for his offer but declined it, saying it would be unwise. "I appreciate that you want to help, Luka, but I don't think it would be prudent. We need to keep your whereabouts a secret from the Nazis and the police. Currently, they have no idea where to search for you. If you are recognized by anyone on that train, such as that railway worker, the Nazis can track you down."

Anna agreed with Weber and insisted that Luka remain with her until it was safe to board the train. "Robert is right, Luka. Wait here with me until he signals it's safe to board the train."

Luka reluctantly agreed to the plan, and Weber handed Anna one end of the rope. "Do you remember the signal?" he asked her.

"Yes, Robert," she replied. "Three yanks, and then Luka and I will scale the embankment and board the train."

Weber nodded his approval but added a warning. "Don't forget about the dog. Silence is critical." Then, he draped the rope over his shoulder and climbed the embankment.

Upon reaching the top of the embankment, Weber quickly spotted the workman and his dog. They were walking on the other side of the boxcars, about fifty meters ahead of him, on the trestle bridge. The workman stopped beside one of the boxcars, opened its door, and climbed inside, followed by his dog. Weber heard the workman whistle, and then the boxcar door slammed shut.

Weber hadn't heard the rail worker whistle during their last encounter, but he assumed the man was signaling the engineer that it was time for the train to leave. There was no time to waste. He quickly grabbed the rope and pulled on it three times. After that, he rushed to the boxcar directly opposite him and tried to open its door, but it was jammed. He then proceeded to the next boxcar and tried its door, which slid open a little. Feeling encouraged, Weber pushed the door with all his might until it slowly rolled open.

Anna and Luka stumbled onto the top of the embankment, spotted Weber, and ran toward the open boxcar. Weber helped them get inside and then rushed to the side of the bridge to retrieve the rope. He'd only run a few steps when the locomotive's engine revved up and strained against the weight of the box cars. There were loud thuds as the train's forward motion eliminated the slack between the boxcars, and then the train began moving across the bridge.

Looking towards the train, Weber saw Anna and Luka waving from an open boxcar as it rolled past. Anna remained true to her promise; she waved frantically but didn't make a sound.

Weber knew he was running out of time as the train picked up speed. He sprinted towards the bridgehead, unhooked the rope, coiled it, and hung it over his shoulder. By then, most of the train had already passed him, and the caboose was fast approaching. He dashed alongside the moving train, and as the caboose rolled by, he reached for the railing beside the staircase leading to the back door of the caboose. As his fingers wrapped around the lowest rung, a bullet whizzed past his head, struck the railing, and split into fragments, one of which tore a furrow in his scalp.

Weber felt as though a hot knife had been drawn across the top of his head, slicing through skin and cutting into his skull. Blood flowed from the wound and ran into his eyes, and the accompanying shock and pain made him lose his grip on the railing. He fell backward onto the tracks alongside the train.

Dazed, bloodied, and gasping for breath, Weber lay in a heap beside the tracks with the rope lying next to him. Even though his addled brain told him to lie there and rest, he knew it was a bad idea. At the moment, he wasn't sure why it was a bad idea, but after thinking about it further, he knew it had something to do with Anna and Luka. Yes, that was it. Anna and Luka had left him behind and were inside a boxcar, traveling on a train he had been chasing. There was something else too. But what was it? Oh, yes--as implausible as it seemed, someone was trying to kill him. Those seemed good reasons not to dawdle, so he struggled to sit upright and got to his feet.

Weber pulled out a handkerchief from his pocket, wiped his eyes, and stanched the bleeding from his head wound. As he looked around, he noticed that the train was slowly making its way up the steep mountain slope on the other side of the bridge. He remembered Luka's earlier comment about trains slowing down on steep mountain grades. Could he still catch the train without getting shot? It was a risky move, but he was determined to try. He didn't want to leave Anna and Luka to fend for themselves.

He slung his rope over his shoulder and ran alongside the tracks until he arrived at the point where the rails left the embankment and crossed onto the trestle bridge. He stopped there because he had noticed during daylight the day before that the ground under the wooden rail ties ended at the entrance to the bridge. On the bridge, the rail ties rested on a ladder of steel I-beams, leaving more than a meter of open space between the ties. Those gaps were wide enough for someone to fall through, making the bridge dangerous for foot traffic. He'd also noticed that the gaps provided a clear and alarming view of what lay hundreds of meters below—a massive bluish-grey glacier.

He thought about using the flashlight attached to his belt to light his way while crossing the bridge. However, he changed his mind when it occurred to him that the illumination would attract attention and make him an easy target. He had no choice but to move forward carefully and rely on his sense of touch to ensure he did not slip and fall through one of the gaps in the darkness.

Standing at the entrance to the bridge, Weber drew a deep breath and extended his right foot, trying to feel the first rail tie while struggling to maintain his balance. When his right foot found the first tie, he used his left foot to discover the next one. He mentally noted how far he had stepped and used it to guide each succeeding step. His feet landed squarely on ties for the next few steps, but suddenly, there was a loud gunshot behind him. The thunderous blast in the otherwise still night startled him, causing him to misstep and fall into the gap between two ties. He reached out and grabbed the tie in front of him and held on tightly as his body tumbled into the gap and slammed against the horizontal I-beam that ran below the tie. He ended up with his face pressed against the side of the rail tie, with the pungent smell of creosote filling his nose.

Weber tenuously clung to the rail tie until he heard another gunshot, this time much closer. The sudden noise startled him, causing his right hand to slip off the tie. His left hand also started to slide towards the edge of the tie, making him realize that he was about to fall. As he hung by one arm, expecting the worst, he imagined himself plunging into the gorge. As frightening as that image was, it gave him an idea. He quickly uncoiled the rope from his shoulder with his free hand, let go of the rail tie, and dropped into the gorge. As he fell, he threw the grappling hook towards the steel crossbeams that formed the lower arch of the bridge in the hope that the prongs would anchor themselves in the latticework. He spiraled downward for what felt like an eternity until the rope suddenly pulled tight and began to slip through his hands. He desperately tried to hold onto the rope, but his hands were not strong enough to overcome the force of his weight. One, two, and then three knots quickly slipped through his grasp. When the fourth knot reached his hands, he clutched it with all his might and wedged his bootheels against another lower knot on the rope. The combined restraints broke his fall.

Air rushed against Weber's face while the rope swung him like a pendulum beneath the bridge. He had presumed that the rope's arc would swing him away from the side of the gorge, but instead, it swung him towards the cliff side, causing him to slam against it. The impact made him lose his grip, and three more knots slipped through his hands as he slid down the rope. He wasn't sure how close he was to the end of his rope, but he suspected he was near it, literally and figuratively. Fear gripped him as he thought about how far he would fall before gravity ended his life on the glacier below.

Weber tried not to panic and focused on Carl, Anna, and Luka. He was determined to survive this mishap or die trying. He climbed up the rope, knot by knot, and his terror gradually subsided with each knot. Soon, he found himself dangling under the bridge next to an I-beam. He tied himself off, hoisted his torso onto the lip of the I-beam, and leaned against a rail tie to rest his aching arms and shoulders.

After regaining some strength, Weber attempted to climb up onto the tracks. However, he stopped midway when he heard what sounded like footsteps. The sounds were coming from the direction where he had previously crossed onto the bridge and were moving towards him.

Weber slid back down onto the I-beam, crouched, and lifted his head above the rail tie to focus his gaze toward the source of a sound. A partial moon had risen in the night sky, so he could now see more of the faintly lit bridge. Despite this, he couldn't detect any sign of movement at first. However, moments later, he spotted the faint glimmer of a flashlight.

Someone was looking for him, and he felt sure that it was the gunman who'd fired on him when he'd tried to cross the bridge to catch the train. He ducked his head and lay flat on the I-beam, below the level of the rail tie, and waited. While he lay there, he pondered the gunman's identity. Who, he wondered, was trying to shoot him? Surely, it wasn't the sniper who'd tracked them through the Alps and triggered the avalanche. That man had to be dead—he was buried at the bottom of the crevasse under a mountain of snow.

A few moments later, the suspected attacker stepped over the rail ties that were just above Weber. Weber quickly got on his knees and grabbed one of the man's legs, pulling it with all his strength. The man yelped, lost his balance, and fell into the gap between the next set of rail ties, just ahead of where Weber was crouching. As the man fell, he dropped something that descended into the gorge and made a clattering noise as it hit the glacier below.

Weber quickly climbed onto the tracks and peered into the gap where the stranger had fallen. In the dim moonlight, he saw a man dangling in the gap, clinging to a rail tie. Aware that someone was watching, the man pleaded with him. "Help me, I beg of you. Pull me up! I can't hang on much longer."

Weber's first impulse was to step on the man's hands. Hadn't this bastard just tried to kill him? What if he tried it again? Was it worth the risk? Just get rid of him! But then his conscience reminded him that he hadn't seen the gunman and couldn't be sure that this was the man who'd shot at him. What if this guy was just another rail worker? In the end, his conscience prevailed. He took a step back and asked the man to identify himself. "Who are you, and what are you doing here?"

The man mumbled something that Weber couldn't hear, so he asked the question again. This time, the man shouted, "Just help me, will you? Pull me up on the tracks, and I'll tell you anything you want to know."

Weber knelt, slipped his hands under the man's armpits, and lifted him until his knees slid onto the I-beam. Then he stood up and offered his hand to help the man onto the tracks.

Once the man climbed onto the tracks, he covered his face and groaned, "I believe my nose is broken from the fall." Weber decided to examine the man's injuries with his flashlight, but he realized it was missing from his belt. He approached the man to inspect his face in the moonlight, but the stranger pulled away and kept his hands over his face. Weber found this reaction strange and asked, “Why are you so jumpy? Do you have something to hide? Who are you, and what are you doing here?”

The man kept his face covered and let out a sigh. “I feel a bit shaky and don't want to fall again. Help me off this bridge, and we can talk.”

Weber hesitated. “Hold on a minute. What did you drop into the gorge?”

The man appeared hesitant and lost in thought as if reluctant to respond. “It was my rifle. I live at a farm nearby, and I was hunting for game. I saw movement on the bridge and thought you were an animal.”

Weber's temper flared. “What kind of hunter are you? Do you stumble around in the dark shooting at anything that moves?”

The man defended himself. “Like I said, I mistook you for an animal. I thought it was a reasonable assumption. No one in their right mind would cross this bridge in the dark.”

Weber's frustration was evident in his voice. “So, I’m the one that’s crazy, eh? Look, whoever you are, I think you’re lying.” Weber grabbed the man by the arm and led him off the bridge.

Chapter 28

Winter 1928: Southwest of Munich, Germany, Near the Austrian Border

When Gunter arrived at the cliffside slope where he'd intended to capture Luka, the boy was nowhere to be found. Weber, whom Gunter believed was mortally wounded, was also missing. All three fugitives had vanished, thwarting his plan to snare Luka, bring him back to the base, and lock him in a cell. The only evidence Weber, Anna, and Luka left behind was their footprints in the snow.

Furious because his plans were foiled, Gunter shook his fists, cursed his bad luck, and kicked loose rocks off the cliff's edge. After that brief outburst, he regained his composure and resolutely set out to track the threesome. He followed their bootprints all the way to the top of the mountain, down the other side, and up another trail that led him toward the peak of a second Alp. As he pressed on, the fear of losing Luka was consuming him. Gunter knew he had to find the boy or suffer the embarrassment of telling Göring that he had been outsmarted by a kid, his mother, and his enemy, Robert Weber. It was never easy for him to admit defeat, and doing so under these circumstances would be especially galling.

To boost his flagging morale, he told himself he'd snare the boy and dispense with Anna and Weber before the day ended. Those three troublemakers had evaded him long enough. He'd soon have them in his sights and end this nightmare.

After several hours of slogging through heavy snow, Gunter sat on a rock, feeling sore and exhausted. He used his telescopic sight to search the trail ahead and noticed some movement near a crevasse. Upon closer inspection, he saw Weber and Anna on one side of the crevasse while Luka was on the other. A rope with knots was tied across the crevasse. Gunter observed Anna as she lowered herself into the crevasse and traversed it using the rope. The rope wavered when she was halfway across, but Luka managed to rescue her. Gunter couldn't help but think it would have been a fitting end for Anna if she had fallen into the crevasse.

Now that his quarry was in sight, Gunter felt a sudden surge of adrenaline. He picked up his rifle and continued trudging along the trail through the deep snow toward the crevasse.

Upon reaching the crevasse, Gunter searched for the knotted rope and eventually found one end coiled around a boulder. The remaining rope portion extended over the edge of the crevasse and down the cliffside where he stood. As he retrieved the rope from the crevasse, Gunter noticed it had been intentionally severed from the other end and left hanging. This discovery led him to suspect that Luka and the others had purposely sabotaged the rope to prevent him from using it. This was a calculated act to buy themselves more time and indicated that they were fearful and desperate.

After extracting the rope from the crevasse, Gunter untied the anchored end and fastened his rifle securely to the other end. He then threw the rifle across the crevasse, causing it to crash against the boulders on the other side. Although the wooden stock broke off, the hardened steel barrel wedged between the rocks. Gunter pulled the rope with all his strength to ensure it was secure and then tied the loose end to a large rock.

Within minutes, Gunter managed to cross the crevasse and retrieve his rifle. He reached into his pack, pulled out some tape he'd scavenged from Gabel's shed, and used it to reattach the stock to the barrel. The stock was not as sturdy as before, which could affect the rifle's accuracy. However, he was relieved that the weapon was still usable. The telescopic sight had some scratches, but it was operational. He used it to scan the trail ahead, which stretched from the crevasse to a snow-covered slope near the summit of the mountain.

As Gunter scanned the slope from the forward side of the crevasse, he spotted three climbers crawling on their bellies alongside a cliff. Seeing the feckless climbers dragging themselves atop the deep snow made him chuckle. They lay prostrate on the snow, wagging their arms and legs as if they were defenseless animals, making submissive gestures toward a predator.

He carefully scanned the group of climbers to identify Luka and then drew a bead on Weber. Shooting Luka was not an option, but Weber was fair game. He pulled the trigger, and when the rifle fired, the damaged stock recoiled and broke off against his shoulder. The shot went wild and ricocheted off the cliff above Weber.

Gunter reattached the stock as best he could, chambered another round, and fired again. The rifle jerked sideways, the stock collapsed, and the shot went wild again. He swore as he watched the climbers crawl toward the cliff, seeking cover. Then, he witnessed something even more disturbing. A sheet of snow as large as an iceberg slid away from the cliff and cascaded down the mountainside. Within seconds, a rogue wave of ice and snow thundered toward him, dislodging boulders and burying everything in its path. Gunter's life flashed before his eyes; he knew he had seconds to live.

He quickly slung his rifle over his shoulder, grasped the rope at the edge of the crevasse, and lowered himself over the side. While suspended alongside the cliff, he withdrew his knife from his coat pocket, extended his arm over the ravine, and sliced through the rope. The portion of the rope he was holding onto went slack and dropped suddenly, causing him to be slammed against the cliff wall. The impact nearly stunned him, but he gripped the rope tightly to keep from falling further into the crevasse.

As Gunter hung inside the crevasse, he felt the walls begin to vibrate. Large chunks of snow began to roll over the edge and fall all around him. Afraid that the snow might hit him and knock him into the gorge, he began to lower himself down the rope knot by knot until he reached the last one. He was now suspended against the cliffside, about two meters from the top of the crevasse. Fortunately, his position on the rope was far enough down to ensure that the force of the avalanche, as it rushed over the rim, projected the snow out and away from where he was positioned. It was as if a giant wave had crested over him, creating a pocket where he was protected from its fury.

The avalanche continued relentlessly, with successive waves of snow thundering into the crevasse, battering against its walls, and plunging into the abyss below. Gunter clung to the rope with all his might but soon began to feel the strain. His back ached, his knuckles turned white, and cramps developed in his arms and shoulders. He knew he couldn't hold on for much longer. If the avalanche continued, he risked losing his grip, falling into the crevasse, and being buried alive under the snow.

As Gunter hung there, dangling over the abyss with only minutes to live, he began to feel sorry for himself. Existential questions arose in his mind. How had he ended up in this situation? Why was he going to die alone in this obscure place where no one would ever find him? Catching Luka didn't seem very important compared to his impending demise.

After what felt like an eternity, the snow and ice stopped falling. Gunter looked up and saw the clear sky through the opening of the crevasse. The avalanche had ended, and he was still alive. He let go of one hand from the rope, reached over his head, and grabbed the knot above him. Slowly, he pulled himself up the rope, knot by knot, until he reached the crevasse's top. After pausing to catch his breath, he cleared the snow from the edge of the crevasse and slowly slid his body onto the rim. Then, he used his legs to push himself onto the snowbank that had formed alongside the edge. Once he had climbed up the snowbank and escaped the crevasse, he felt a sense of relief for having survived the ordeal.

Gunter sat on top of the snowbank and pondered his next move. He pushed aside all the morbid thoughts that had crossed his mind while stuck in the crevasse. He was alive and had a mission to accomplish, and that was all that mattered. He took a deep breath, surveyed the side of the mountain, and tried to imagine where the trail had been before the avalanche. As he contemplated the route, he remembered seeing Luka and his companions crawling in the snow near the top of the mountain. Even though the landscape had changed, he decided it was still the best place to start. With his rifle in hand, he began climbing up the trail.

For the first few hundred meters, Gunter found nothing. The avalanche had erased the trail and removed clues about the trio's whereabouts. However, after he hiked past the cliff near the top of the mountain, he spotted the outlines of a trail and three sets of bootprints in the snow. He followed the prints across the mountainside and, an hour later, just after dark, came to a rail line that ran up an elevated embankment and over a trestle bridge that spanned a deep gorge.

Gunter headed east along the embankment until he came across a two-story building nestled into the mountain beside the tracks. He became suspicious when he noticed lights inside the building and smoke rising from a chimney. He inferred that the place was inhabited, and since the footprints he had been following led directly to the building, he had a good reason to believe that Luka and his companions were inside. However, he wasn't sure if other people were also in the building, so he decided to watch the building from a distance and gather more information before taking action. He continued walking eastward along the tracks until he discovered a ridge beside the mountain where he could observe the building without being detected.

Several hours later, a freight train stopped in front of the building, and Gunter saw a workman and his dog step out of a boxcar. As the workman walked toward the front of the train, the side door to the maintenance building opened, and Luka, Anna, and Weber snuck out and hid behind an outhouse. The train departed, and the workman entered the building and left his dog outside. Shortly after, Luka, Anna, and Weber dashed behind the building, crossed the tracks, and ran westward along the embankment toward the trestle bridge.

Gunter wasn't sure what was happening, so he remained in place and closely watched Luka, Anna, and Weber. While he was watching the trio, another freight train arrived and parked on the bridge. Soon thereafter, the workman and his dog emerged from the building and headed towards the train. They started inspecting the boxcars, but the dog became unruly, and the workman struggled to control it. After disciplining the dog, the workman completed the inspection and climbed into a boxcar with his dog.

Then, the locomotive's engines started running, and Gunter saw Weber standing beside the train. Weber opened a boxcar door and helped Anna and

Luka climb inside. As the train began to move, Weber rushed to the bridge, grabbed a rope, and returned to the train as it sped away from him. He attempted to climb onto the caboose as it rolled past him.

Although Gunter knew he couldn't stop Anna and Luka, he still had a shot at Weber. He aimed his rifle, fired, and watched Weber fall by the side of the tracks. Gunter assumed Weber was dead, but to his surprise, Weber got up, ran towards the bridge, and started crossing it. Not wanting Weber to escape, Gunter fired another round, and this time, Weber fell between some rail ties and disappeared from the bridge.

Gunter walked to the bridge's entrance, stopped, and looked for where Weber had fallen. When he saw what he believed to be the correct location, he raised his rifle, took aim, and pulled the trigger. A sharp ping followed a loud explosion as the bullet ricocheted off one of the steel rails. He waited for Weber to cry out, but when that didn't happen, he decided to investigate.

He cautiously stepped onto the bridge, carefully avoiding the gaps between the rail ties. After a few steps, goosebumps formed on his skin, and something eerie happened. A hand emerged from below, grabbed his right leg, and pulled him off balance. Unable to prevent his fall, Gunter tumbled through the tracks but managed to save himself at the last moment by clutching a rail tie and holding on tightly.

As Gunter hung from the rail tie, he felt his strength ebbing away. Suddenly, Weber stood over him, demanding to know who he was. Despite being vulnerable and needing help, Gunter refused to comply with Weber's request. He knew that if Weber found out who he was, his chances of survival would be slim. However, if he pretended to be someone else or remained anonymous, he would stand a better chance of being rescued. So, he ignored Weber's question and begged him to lift him back onto the tracks. To his relief, Weber took pity on him and helped him up.

As Gunter climbed onto the tracks, he covered his face, claiming he had broken his nose so that Weber wouldn't recognize him. Shaky and weak, Gunter wanted to get off the bridge before confronting Weber. However, Weber continued questioning him, asking what he had dropped into the gorge. Gunter hesitated, scared to admit that he had a rifle in his possession, as Weber would know that he was the one who had been shooting at him. Gunter's mind raced as he struggled to think of a plausible explanation, and then he had an idea. He told Weber that he resided at a nearby farm, had been hunting for game, and had mistaken him for an animal in the darkness. The tactic worked. Even though Weber got angry, accused him of lying, and impugned his competence as a hunter, he didn't suspect that he had just rescued Gunter Meissner.

As Gunter followed Weber off the bridge, he felt relieved, thinking he had fooled Weber. As his fear subsided, he contemplated taking control of the situation and overpowering Weber. While considering his options, he mindlessly toyed with the chain around his neck. At that moment, he realized he had made a mistake—he had blown his cover.

Winter 1928: Southwest of Munich, Germany, Near the Austrian Border

Weber firmly gripped the stranger's arm as he walked toward the maintenance building. He was uncertain whether he could trust the man's story. Although some aspects seemed plausible, something about the stranger made Weber suspicious. Upon further reflection, Weber noticed several inconsistencies in the stranger's story that troubled him.

First, why was the stranger hesitant to introduce himself and explain his actions? He appeared caught off guard and defensive when asked to do so. It felt like the stranger made up his story as he went along. Second, was it realistic that the stranger was a farmer? While it was not impossible, his clothing did not match a typical farmer's. Third, was it plausible that the stranger had mistaken a person for an animal? For this to be true, the stranger would have had to assume that animals crossed the treacherous trestle bridge and could navigate the empty spaces between rail ties in the dark.

After thinking it through, Weber concluded that the stranger's story contained too many inconsistencies. Moreover, the man's voice and gait seemed familiar, as if Weber had met him before. He stopped the stranger to look at his face and noticed that the man was fiddling with something hanging from a chain around his neck. It took Weber a moment to identify the object, but he eventually recognized it as a shell casing.

"Meissner!" Weber shouted, "You merciless assassin!" Weber lunged, drove his shoulder into Gunter's chest, and knocked him to the ground. When Gunter rolled over and started to get up, Weber kicked him in the groin, and Gunter fell backward, writhing in pain.

Weber raised his boot, intending to kick Meissner again, but then he hesitated and tried to control his anger. He took a moment to calm down, drew his pistol, and warned Gunter not to resist. Gunter raised his hands in surrender, so Weber pulled him up, twisted his arm behind his back, and marched him towards the maintenance building.

As they walked towards the maintenance building along the embankment, Weber kept Gunter in front of him and occasionally poked him with the barrel of his gun to prevent him from slowing down. As they approached the building, Gunter suddenly turned and hit Weber's arm with a powerful blow, causing the pistol to fall out of his hand. While Weber stooped down to pick up the gun, Gunter quickly slid down the embankment and fled towards a trail that led down the mountain.

It took Weber several seconds to find his pistol in the snow. When he found it, he stood, took aim, and shouted at Gunter. “Stop Meissner, or I will shoot!” Gunter kept running, so Weber took aim and fired two shots, both high over Gunter's head. “Do not test me, Meissner; I will not miss next time.”

Gunter skidded to a stop and turned to face Weber, attempting to gauge the threat. When he saw Weber's determined expression, he raised his hands and walked back toward the embankment.

Once inside the maintenance building, Weber bound Gunter’s hands behind his back and tied him to a chair. Meissner complained that the ropes were too tight, cutting off his circulation. Weber ignored the complaint and asked Gunter what he had hoped to accomplish by pursuing him and his companions into the mountains. Gunter refused to answer, so Weber spoke for him.

“I know why you're following us, Meissner,” he said. “You believe that Luka is Goring's illegitimate son by a Jewish mother, and neither you nor Hermann can afford to let that information become public. Such news would be damaging to your reputation as Nazis, especially for newly-elected Reichsminister Goring. Isn’t that correct?”

Gunter refused to look Weber in the eye. He squirmed in his chair, stared at the floor, and said nothing.

“Don’t you have anything to say, Meissner? You were quite talkative when you were fabricating stories on the trestle bridge. Why don't you tell me, Farmer Meissner, about the scheme you and Göring plotted?”

Gunter’s face flushed with anger. “Don’t call me ‘farmer,’ he bellowed.

“Oh, so you’re not really a farmer, Meissner? How would you characterize your occupation? Judging from your actions, I’d say you’re an assassin. You've been shooting at us during every step of our journey.”

“Weber, you’ve misconstrued my motives. I don’t intend to harm Luka.”

“Do you expect me to believe that? Your deeds say otherwise. I think you and Göring decided to silence the kid with a bullet. Am I right?”

“Luka will be safe if he surrenders and comes with me to Berlin. He must do so willingly and immediately. His father wishes to meet him and discuss certain matters.”

“What makes you think Luka would go with you? You’ve given him too many reasons to distrust you. Besides, you’re in no position to make demands, Meissner. You’re tied to a chair, your rifle’s at the bottom of the gorge, and my pistol is aimed at your head. I’ll be the one who decides what happens here.”

“This could end peacefully, Weber, without bloodshed. Just tell the boy to surrender."

"Meissner, I have a counterproposal for you. Rather than continue this ill-advised endeavor, return home. Your plotting, stalking, and attempts at assassination have all been for nothing. You see, there's something you don't understand: Göring isn't Luka's biological father."

Gunter attempted to hide his surprise, but his facial expression gave away his emotions. "What are you talking about? That's a lie. Hermann's name is on the birth certificate. I saw it with my own eyes at the Munich Standesamt."

"His name might be on the birth certificate, but he's not Luka's father. Göring has nothing to worry about. Return to Berlin and tell Göring to forget about Luka and leave us alone."

"This ruse won't fool me, Weber. Do you think I am naive? But, for argument's sake, who do you think is Luka's biological father?"

"A man named Rolf Ehrhart," Weber replied.

"You are deluded, Weber. Rolf died in the Great War."

"Perhaps so, but not before fathering a son."

"Do you expect me to believe Rolf sired a child with Anna? That can't be true because I grew up with Rolf, and from an early age, he was engaged to be married to a girl named Maria. He loved her deeply and only had eyes for her. Your allegation that Rolf was Luka's father is preposterous."

"It's true, Meissner. You might as well accept it. I obtained this information from an unimpeachable source."

"I will never believe that, and neither will Hermann. How dare you dishonor the memory of our friend and comrade!"

"Be realistic, Meissner. It's not so hard to believe. Anna's a beautiful woman who no doubt turned heads as an adolescent. Rolf probably found her attractive. You know what adolescent boys are like."

"That's enough, Weber; I can see through your lies! You have no scruples. I refuse to discuss this matter further."

Weber's face contorted with anger as he spoke. "You're disparaging my morals? What about you, Meissner? How many people have you killed? I know you arranged the plane crash that killed my first wife, Anna. And then you tried to shoot Carl and me when you thought we were asleep in our beds. Now, you're trying to kill Luka and his mother. What kind of a man does that, Gunter? Only a ruthless, black-hearted man who's lost his soul!"

Gunter feigned laughter and redirected the dialog. "Where do you get these ideas, Weber? Neither Hermann nor I would ever harm Anna. We have been friends with her since childhood, and we have worked closely with her for years at the Reichswehr."

"That was before you thought she'd concealed Goring's paternity. Your plans for her changed after you saw Goring's name on Luka's birth certificate. Did Göring ask you to add Anna to your hit list, or did you do it alone?"

"I'm not going to discuss anything Hermann might have said to me."

"That's exactly what I'd expect an inveterate sycophant to say. But let's move on from that. What about me? I know your intentions toward me are malicious—that's been obvious since we worked together in Sweden. What I don't understand is why. Was it something I did? What actions of mine led you to target me and my family?"

"You brought this on yourself, Weber. You're blaming Hermann and me for something that you started. All this began when you committed a murder, and now you want to disavow the consequences."

"Me, a murderer? I haven't the slightest idea what you're talking about, Meissner. This is another attempt to shift blame for your despicable actions. By now, I would have thought you'd have exceeded your capacity for treachery and deceitfulness."

"You like to think you occupy the moral high ground, Weber. But all of this—the deaths, suffering, and guilt—is your fault. It's all on your head, not mine!"

"Meissner, what kind of twisted accusation is that?"

"You killed Rolf—the man you claim is Luka's biological father. That's how all this began. You committed a brazen, unscrupulous, violent act that took Rolf's life."

"Have you lost your mind? I never met the man, let alone hurt him."

"Don't deny it, Weber. You've as good as confessed. You said it yourself--Hermann and I heard you admit it.

"When? What did I say?"

"It was the evening we discussed night flights at the Hökens Näbb Pub in Stockholm. We sat around a table with some Svensk-Luft Trafik pilots and ground crew, and Hermann asked your opinion about night flights. You recounted a mission where you descended on a German aerodrome before dawn and fired on the planes and aircrew. Hermann, Rolf, and I were stationed at that aerodrome, and we were asleep at the time of your attack. Hermann and I woke up and ran for cover, but you shot Rolf in the head before he could get out of bed. Rolf was no threat to you—he was asleep—and you murdered him in his bed."

"That's what this is about? Something that happened during the war? If that actually happened—which I doubt—I knew nothing about it. I was a combatant, just as you were, and my sworn duty was to attack and defeat the enemy. If Rolf caught a stray bullet, his death was a casualty of war, not a murder. Shots were fired, but not at Rolf. How could you and Göring possibly think that I murdered him?"

"What would you call shooting defenseless airmen while they're asleep in their bunks? Some people might call it manslaughter, but I see it as premeditated murder."

"Our orders were to photograph the aircraft at your aerodrome. Your men initiated the shooting, and we just returned fire to defend ourselves. Rolf's death was collateral damage."

"That's your excuse? You were just following orders, and doing so resulted in 'collateral damage'? You're hiding behind that euphemism to shirk responsibility for your actions."

"Meissner, you're not hearing me. We were at war. It was a novel surveillance mission that didn't go as planned. Your side, not ours, initiated hostilities. Because of that, there were unintended consequences—unexpected casualties."

"I disagree with you, Weber. Your attack was a deplorable and unprecedented tactic. There were valid reasons why such missions were eschewed in the past, as the tactic violated the ethical codes of civilized countries. By introducing it, you desensitized people to previously objectionable and unethical tactics, making them appear acceptable. Your actions have made it possible for airmen to engage in unspeakable forms of brutality."

"I feel remorse for any contribution I may have made to developing novel combat tactics. However, wars often lead to the creation of new military tactics and technologies, and the Great War inspired a frightening array of them. For instance, that war introduced the use of poison gas and facilitated the use of aircraft for combat. While soldiers and airmen may deplore such changes, they are not in a position to resist or object to their deployment. You know this is true—it's a reality neither of us can deny."

"Weber, that's the kind of argument soldiers use to rationalize war crimes."

"Meissner, there's no reasoning with you. Do you know what your problem is? I think you experienced shell shock during the Great War, and because it went untreated, your thinking became warped, and you developed many self-serving delusions. You reinterpreted your wartime experiences, blaming the Allies for everything you found offensive, real or imagined, and you made them responsible for all your misfortunes after the war. Your anger about the Versailles Treaty and Germany's woes fed into those delusions and strengthened them. Now, you attribute hostile intentions to anyone who isn't German, and especially to people from Allied nations who fought against Germany. Because those threats leave you feeling vulnerable and persecuted, you go to excessive lengths to protect yourself by preemptively attacking or seeking revenge against those you see as threats or blame for your misfortunes. You attacked me and my family because we were convenient scapegoats for your paranoia and rage."

"Weber, spare me your mind games. I know what you did, no matter how you twist the facts or try to characterize me as disturbed. You think you know me, but you've got it all wrong. I have a deep understanding of how the world works. I'm cunning and streetwise and know how to play all the angles. Nothing escapes my notice. I am skilled at manipulating things to my advantage and cannot be easily deceived. I have a keen sense of what motivates people and can read their thoughts and desires. My ability to fix things has been honed since my childhood on the farm, making me a successful fighter pilot during the war. Now, I use my skills to excel as a test pilot, street fighter, hunter, and investigator. You might think I'm disturbed, but my friend Hermann thinks highly of me and values my skills."

"Meissner, you're depraved. I'm repulsed by the depth of your guile, lack of empathy, and inability to feel remorse."

"You find me repulsive? You hypocrite! Imagine how Luka is going to feel about you when he finds out that you killed his father. Your revulsion toward me will seem like nothing compared to his reaction. I'd like to see the expression on the boy's face when you tell him."

Troubled by Gunter's taunt, Weber withdrew from the altercation. He inspected Gunter's trusses to ensure he was still securely bound to the chair and then climbed the stairs to the second floor. He lay down on one of the bunks and covered his face, trying to sort out his feelings. Had he killed Rolf Ehrhart, or was Gunter's story an elaborate, self-serving lie? There was no way to verify or disprove Gunter's claim, but the mere possibility that he might have caused Rolf Ehrhart's death left him uneasy. If his pre-dawn raid were the cause, even if it were an accident in the line of duty, it would have radically changed Luka's life by depriving him of his father. He was hesitant to believe Gunter's accusation because acknowledging it would require him to deal with the consequences and confess to Luka and Anna about what had occurred. He feared that such an admission could irreparably harm his relationships with them. Nevertheless, if Gunter's claim was true, he understood that he had to face that grim reality.

The sound of a distant train whistle snapped Weber out of his daze. He admonished himself for losing focus and reminded himself that he was in a dangerous situation and needed to prioritize finding Anna and Luka to ensure their safety. Realizing that time was of the essence, he quickly gathered his pack, rope, pistol, and other belongings. He knew he had to make crucial decisions before the freight train arrived at the maintenance building.

His main objective was to steal aboard the train and travel along the railway, searching for Anna and Luka. But before he could do that, he needed to find a way to deal with Gunter. The rail worker and his dog would arrive any moment, and he hadn't yet figured out how to keep them from discovering Gunter. He didn't know what Gunter might do in that situation, but he was sure he would do everything he could to ruin his escape plans. The safest option was to keep Gunter close and control his every move.

The screech of the freight train's wheels grinding to a stop signaled Weber that he'd run out of time. He released Gunter from his chair while keeping his hands tied behind his back and hustled him out of the building and behind the outhouse. When he was sure they were hidden from the train, he made Gunter lie on the ground and then put his boot on his neck and aimed his pistol at his head. "Don't move or make a sound, Meissner. If you make the slightest noise, that workman's dog will attack and rip your throat out. And just so you know, I'll let him do it."

A few moments later, the train departed, and Weber noticed the workman and his dog entering the building. Gunter remained silent and still as a statue while Weber watched and waited. He was surprised that the workman had taken his dog inside, which was unusual. However, when nothing out of the ordinary happened, Weber assumed it was safe to proceed. He got Gunter up and guided him across the tracks and along the embankment to the bridge, where they waited for the next freight train to arrive.

The second train arrived promptly and stopped on the bridge. As he had done before, Weber waited for the worker and his dog to inspect the train, and then he and Gunter climbed up the embankment and entered an empty boxcar. After closing the heavy steel door, Weber pulled his flashlight from his pack, turned it on, and watched the beam penetrate the boxcar's dark, cavernous interior.

As Weber shone his flashlight around the boxcar, he noticed that the air inside was dusty and smelled of manure. Upon further inspection, he discovered the reason for the smell—the floor was covered in straw and animal droppings. The walls of the boxcar were lined with stalls, each large enough to hold one or two farm animals. Weber realized that the boxcar was probably used to transport cattle, horses, or both. Although the stalls were empty, it was clear that livestock had recently traveled in them.

The train started moving, gaining momentum as it climbed the steep grade on the mountainside opposite the bridge. As the train picked up speed, Weber used a rope to secure Gunter to a metal shackle inside a stall at one end of the boxcar. It took several attempts before he was successful, as the boxcar was pitching and swaying, often causing both men to fall to the floor.

Weber eventually managed to secure Gunter and then stumbled to the other end of the boxcar. Due to the boxcar's movements, he couldn't stand, so he had no choice but to lie on the straw and hope he wouldn't get covered in manure. He attempted to remain alert to safeguard Gunter but soon found himself unwinding and on the verge of dozing off. He withdrew a narrow-gauge cord from his pack and tied one end to his pistol's trigger guard and the other to his wrist. Then he tested the tether to make sure it had enough slack for him to draw and aim the gun, but not so much that the weapon could be taken without him noticing.

Even though Weber struggled to keep himself awake, he eventually fell into a deep sleep. When he woke up, he realized that Gunter was nowhere to be found. He hurried to the other end of the boxcar, entered the stall where he had tied Gunter, and saw the ropes lying on the floor. Somehow, Gunter had managed to untie himself, but Weber couldn't figure out where he had gone. Upon closer inspection, he saw that the boxcar's door was ajar, and a fragment of Gunter's clothing was caught on a bolt that protruded from the door's latch. Now, Weber understood what had happened. Gunter had jumped from the moving train. He wondered if Gunter had survived the fall but dismissed the thought and told himself he had more important things to worry about, like finding Anna and Luka.

Chapter 29

Winter 1928: Somewhere in the Alps West of Munich

The train journeyed through the night, slowing down while climbing sharp grades and speeding up while descending steep slopes. Weber stood beside the gap in the boxcar door, breathing in the last of the frigid night air. He was eagerly waiting for the sun to illuminate the rugged landscape surrounding the train, hoping that daybreak would arrive soon so that he could start searching for Anna and Luka. Sending them off in a boxcar to unknown locations was never a part of his plan, and now that they were separated, he feared he might not be able to find them.

Rather than dwelling on his fears, Weber devised a plan to help him locate Anna and Luka. He assumed they would have stayed hidden until they found a safe place to disembark from the train. Though he wasn't sure where that might be, he thought he could improve his chances of finding them by conducting a systematic search. He decided to disembark at the first station along the train's route and then thoroughly search all the areas where Anna and Luka could have gone. If he didn't locate them at the first station, he would proceed to each town or village where the train stopped and search them all.

Just after dawn, Weber pushed open the boxcar door, leaned out into the brisk morning breeze, and scanned the tracks ahead to see if he could spot a place where the train might stop. At first, he saw nothing, but then, as the train crested a hill, he spotted a rail station near a mountain village in the distance. He closed the boxcar door and waited to see if the train would stop at the station.

The train gradually reduced speed as it approached the village and eventually stopped. Weber peered through the gap in the door and noticed that the name on the station was Alpenseite. He then cautiously made his way to the other side of the boxcar, opened the door opposite the station's platform, and jumped down onto the tracks. Fearing he might be caught as a stowaway, he crawled under the boxcar and concealed himself behind the rear wheel carriage. From there, he watched people milling about on the platform in front of the station, waiting for an opportunity to escape unnoticed.

After the platform had cleared, Weber emerged from under the boxcar, slipped out of the station, and proceeded down a street leading toward the village's center. As he walked, he passed by several homes and shops, observing people out for a morning stroll or on their way to work. He was about to ask someone if they had seen Anna or Luka when he noticed a police officer directing traffic at an intersection. He approached the officer, and as he was about to mention Anna's name, he suddenly remembered that she was a fugitive. Realizing his mistake, he quickly walked away, wondering how he could have been so absent-minded. Involving the police would have been unwise, especially if they were politically affiliated with the Nazis.

Feeling the gravity of his mistake, Weber paused to reflect on his actions. He realized he had almost helped the police locate Anna, who was smuggling the design portfolio out of Germany. If she were taken into custody, she'd not only be prosecuted for espionage, but Gunter, if he were still alive, would be able to find her. As Weber envisioned those consequences, his mouth went dry, and his heart raced. To compose himself, he crossed the street and entered a nearby café, intending to reconsider his tactics as he ate breakfast. The café was bustling with diners having a meal before heading to work, but, luckily, he found an empty table against the wall at the back of the café. He sat down, and when the waiter arrived, he ordered eggs, toast, and sausages.

As Weber waited for his food, he tried to imagine what Anna and Luka might have done after their freight train had arrived at the village. He assumed they had left their boxcar and entered the town just like he had done, but he found it challenging to imagine what might have occurred afterward. As he considered various possibilities, details from their journey came to mind and gave him ideas about what might have happened. One particular memory troubled him: he had consolidated all their money in his wallet before they left the Gabel's farm. This meant that Anna and Luka were penniless when they arrived at the village. That recollection bothered Weber because it meant that Anna and Luka had gone hungry on the night they arrived and had nowhere to sleep. The thought of what might have happened to an attractive woman and an adolescent boy in those circumstances made him cringe.

While Weber was lost in thought, the waiter arrived and placed his breakfast on the table. Weber picked up his fork, stared at it momentarily, and then tossed it back on the table. He couldn't bring himself to eat; he was too upset. A man sitting alone at the table beside him noticed Weber's unusual reaction and asked if he was okay.

"Say, stranger, the sun's barely up, and you look like you've already had a hard day. Is there anything I can do to help?"

Embarrassed that someone had noticed his distress, Weber sighed and shook his head. "No, I'm OK, but thanks for asking."

The man smiled and extended his hand. "My name is Walter Schultz. What's yours?"

Weber decided to protect his identity; he was alone in an unfamiliar town and unsure who he could trust. He introduced himself as Robert Lorenz.

"Hello Robert, I don't believe we've met before. However, here at Alpenseite, we value helping people, especially visitors. Moreover, it's often said that accepting the kindness of strangers can bring good luck. So, why not let me assist you?"

Weber stood, preparing to leave the café, but then changed his mind and sat back down. Although it was against his better judgment, he needed to confide in someone about his situation with Anna and Luka. "Well, Herr Schultz, I came to this village to meet some friends, but I haven't been able to locate them."

Schultz nodded, moved his chair closer to Weber's, smiled, and spoke reassuringly. "Herr Lorenz, I have lived in Alpenseite all my life, so I'm probably in a better position to help you than anyone else you'll meet. Can you give me a description of your friends? Maybe I've seen them."

Weber was unsure about trusting Schultz but decided to take a leap of faith and confide in him. He told Schultz to call him 'Robert' and then provided him with a description of Anna and Luka.

Schultz smiled and said, "Finish your breakfast, Robert. I want you to meet someone."

Weber settled his bill and followed Schultz out of the café. They made their way toward Alpenseite's center, where the village's medieval origins became evident. The street narrowed and eventually emptied into a maze of alleys that snaked between rows of ancient buildings. In no time, Weber lost all sense of direction. Schultz, however, knew exactly where he was going. He strode through the alleys, making turn after turn without looking back or breaking stride.

Eventually, Schultz and Weber emerged on the other side of the village and found themselves on a road beside grassy slopes that ran along the edge of the mountains. Schultz pointed toward a small church between the road and the mountains and began walking more quickly.

Weber carefully observed the church as they approached it, wondering what Schultz intended. The building was constructed in the shape of a cross, with a bell tower overlooking a rectangular nave covered by a vaulted roof.

Several porticos extended from the nave, each with tall stained-glass windows on either side. Weber was impressed by the beauty of the church and its surroundings; both were picturesque and memorable. However, he was troubled by the fact that he was blindly following Schultz, with little or no knowledge of what awaited him when they arrived at the church.

When they reached the church, Schultz confidently walked up the front steps, opened one of the arched doors that led to the nave, and politely directed Weber inside. Upon entering, Weber stood in the foyer and was immediately struck by the simple elegance of the church's interior. The entire structure was bathed in multicolored light that shone through the stained-glass windows. Straight ahead of him was a central aisle, flanked by rows of pews, that led to the front of the church. An altar stood at the end of the aisle, surrounded on each side by choir lofts. Rows of organ pipes, arranged in ascending lengths, were built into the walls above the choir lofts, and above those was a vaulted arch that extended upward into the church's bell tower.

Weber was admiring the church's interior when Schultz came and stood beside him. As the two men stood there, captivated by the church's ambiance, a voice from behind interrupted Weber's thoughts. “Welcome, gentlemen! I was not expecting visitors this morning.”

Weber turned to see who had spoken. The voice belonged to a tall man in his late sixties with greying hair, a slightly bent posture, and a deeply lined face. Despite his age, the man had clear and observant eyes, complementing his friendly expression.

The tall man recognized Schultz immediately. Oh, it's you, Walter. And who have you brought with you today?” Schultz turned toward Robert and said, “I’d like you to meet Wilhelm Berger, the cleric here at Trinity Church.” Then he looked at Berger and said, “'Wilhelm, this is Robert Lorenz. I met him in the café this morning. He came to our village to meet some friends but couldn't find them. I thought you might be able to help him since you are good at finding lost sheep. Can you help us out?'“

Berger walked over to Weber, shook his hand, and welcomed him to Trinity Church.

Weber told Berger he was pleased to make his acquaintance and then asked whether he should call him “Father,” “Reverend,” or “Pastor.”

“Just call me Wilhelm,” Berger replied. “We are informal here--no need for titles.”

Weber nodded and then asked Wilhelm if he had seen a woman named Anna and her adolescent son Luka. Berger studied Weber's face momentarily before stepping back and looking at him skeptically. He replied, “No one I know is looking for someone who goes by the name 'Lorenz.'“

Berger's reaction made Weber uncomfortable. He sensed something was wrong but couldn't figure out what it was. He wondered if he had said or done something that had upset Berger. Then it occurred to him that Berger might have met Anna and Luka, and if they had told him about their situation, Berger could have been looking for someone named Weber instead of Lorenz.

Weber silently scolded himself for lying to Schultz about his identity. He realized that by not trusting Schultz, he had placed himself in a difficult position with no apparent solution. If he admitted to the lie, he would lose all credibility and prove himself untrustworthy. However, he could see no other option. He had to explain why he had lied and hope that Schultz and Berger would understand and forgive him for his mistake.

With eyes averted, Weber stammered an apology. "Uh, Walter and Wilhelm, I need to confess something. My name is not Lorenz; it's Weber. I had to use a false name because my friends, Anna and Luka, are wanted by the Nazis for political reasons, and their lives are in danger. I am trying to help them escape from Germany so they can seek asylum in Switzerland. The three of us have endured a long and difficult journey across the Alps, but we got separated when I stayed behind to disarm a sniper. I was hoping that Anna and Luka found refuge in this village. I need to find them so we can finish our journey."

Berger listened attentively to Weber's confession and then asked for his identification papers. He clarified that he needed to verify Weber's identity before disclosing any confidential information others might have shared. Once Weber provided the papers, Berger instructed him to wait with Schultz and exited the church.

While waiting for Berger to return, Weber tried his best to manage his expectations. Berger had hinted at having confidential information, but he refused to share further details until he could confirm Weber's identity. This made Weber suspect that Berger might know something about Anna and Luka. He hoped his suspicion was correct and prayed that whatever Berger knew would assist him in locating Anna and Luka.

Twenty minutes later, Berger returned to the church with Anna and Luka. Weber quickly got up from his seat and went to Anna. He embraced her warmly and then hugged Luka, thanking Berger for reuniting him with his family.

"I'm glad I could assist you, Robert," Berger said. "I understand your situation and sympathize with you. Anna and I had a long conversation before you arrived, and she informed me about your reasons for fleeing Germany. In our village, many people, myself included, do not support the Nazis. Although they claim to honor God and respect the church, their actions prove otherwise. I am willing to do everything I can to help you continue your journey, and I am confident that Walter will help me."

Weber was thrilled to have found Anna and Luka. However, he knew they couldn't stay there for long and asked the twosome if they were ready to continue their journey. Both nodded in agreement, and Weber turned to Berger for help. He asked Berger if he knew of a freight train that stopped at Alpenseite that would take them closer to Switzerland.

Berger acknowledged that freight trains traveled east towards Switzerland but advised Weber against taking one. Instead, he suggested that there might be better alternatives and invited Weber to join him and his wife for dinner to discuss those options. "I suggest you take some time today to explore the village and meet us at the parsonage this evening for dinner. You can spend the night with us and depart first thing in the morning."

Weber glanced at Anna to gauge her reaction before accepting Berger's invitation. "Wilhelm, that's very gracious of you, and we're grateful. Please let your wife know we'll be pleased to join you for dinner."

◆◆◆

When Weber, Anna, and Luka arrived at the Berger's for dinner, they were surprised to see that Walter Schultz and his wife, Marlana Schultz, had also been invited. The table was set for seven people, including the hosts, Wilhelm and Hildegard Berger. The Bergers had cooked a delicious meal of pork schnitzel, spätzle, and fresh broccoli harvested from their garden. The food was delicious, and the conversation was lively and engaging, although potentially contentious topics such as politics were avoided. After the meal, Wilhelm invited everyone to his study.

When Weber entered Wilhelm's study, he was surprised to see how large it was. The room had a high arched ceiling with an ornate chandelier hanging from the top. The walls were paneled with mahogany and adorned with religious paintings. The floor was covered in decorative tiles, and two large windows overlooked the street outside the house. A small desk was placed against one wall, and a large table stood in the center of the room.

Wilhelm waited until everyone was seated at the table. He smiled at Weber, Anna, and Luka and said, "I have something important to share with you three. While you were exploring the village, Walter and I met and devised a plan that we believe will ensure your safe passage to Switzerland. We would like to hear your thoughts on it."

Yes, of course," Weber replied, answering for himself, Anna, and Luka. "Please tell us your proposal."

"We strongly advise against traveling by freight train due to the significant risks involved. The Deutsche Reichsbahn does not publicize freight schedules or destinations, and boxcars are often redirected to different cities during transit. This means that once you board a boxcar, you will not know where you will go; you could end up in northern Germany instead of Switzerland. Moreover, the rail police actively search for stowaways and prosecute them, which could land you in prison. We understand that you want to hide your movements, but it's imprudent to choose a method of concealment that could prevent you from reaching your intended destination."

A look of surprise registered on Weber's face. "We decided to hop a freight train because we didn't think we had a choice. Are there other options?"

"Yes, we think there might be. Anna told me that she'd purchased counterfeit Swiss passports for the three of you. "How authentic are those passports? If they can fool the railway and border authorities, you're better off taking a passenger train."

Weber grimaced. "Our papers are high quality, but as a threesome, we'll be conspicuous because the police are looking for a man traveling with a woman and an adolescent boy. Regardless of how good our papers are, we'll be spotted immediately and detained for questioning."

"Walter and I have anticipated that problem and believe we have a solution. We plan to travel with you and divide ourselves into groups that are less likely to draw suspicion from the police. Robert and Anna, you both will travel with Walter. All three of you are engineers; Walter is a civil engineer working on a bridge construction project along a road leading north out of Alpenseite. As part of your disguise, Walter will carry the project's blueprints, and if you're stopped for questioning, he will present the blueprints and say that both of you are Swiss engineering consultants who came to our village for a site visit. Walter will also mention that he is accompanying you to Switzerland for a post-inspection conference at your headquarters. Lastly, there's a printer in our village who mostly makes wedding announcements. We'll ask him to print business cards for you to carry."

Weber gazed at Anna and Luka in shock. He couldn't believe what he was hearing. As he was about to speak, Wilhelm raised his hand and gestured for him to stay quiet. "That's not all, Robert. Hear me out; please don't interrupt until I've finished."

Berger continued with his explanation of the plan. "Now, let's talk about Luka. While Robert, Anna, and Walter pretend to be engineers, Luka and I will travel in a separate coach and avoid interacting with the three of you. If the police stop us for questioning, I will say that Luka is my son, and I am accompanying him back to Switzerland, where he lives with his mother. I will share that my ex-wife and I are divorced, and I'm only able to see Luka when his mother allows him to visit me in Germany. To make my story more believable, Luka will nod in agreement while I am speaking. If the police demand more details, I will tell stories about how Luka and I had fun going to soccer matches and drinking beer, things his mother won't allow him to do in Switzerland."

Weber quickly intervened after Berger finished talking. "Are you saying, Wilhelm and Walter, that you are willing to travel with us?"

Berger and Schultz nodded in agreement. "Yes, that's right," Berger replied.

"That's very generous of you, but it's too much to ask and far too risky."

"We wouldn't have offered if we didn't consider it important."

Weber extracted a wad of Reichsmarks from his wallet and slid them across the table to Berger. "Let me compensate you for the risk you'll be taking."

Berger pushed the Reichsmarks back toward Weber. "That won't be necessary. Don't spoil our charitable gesture by offering us money," Berger said with a frown.

Weber sighed and said, "I apologize. I didn't mean to offend you. We deeply appreciate your kindness and humbly accept your offer. However, at least let me pay for your train tickets. Also, I'd like to donate to Trinity Church. I want to contribute to the 'lost sheep' fund. Will you accept my offering?"

Berger smiled and reluctantly agreed, "All right, Robert, we have a deal. Let's now discuss preparations and decide on a departure time."

Berger and Schultz later headed to the village and purchased rail tickets for their travel companions. They booked passage on a passenger train that departed from the village the following morning. The train would take them to Basel, Switzerland, making stops in Stuttgart and Freiburg, both in Germany, before crossing the border.

During dinner that evening, the two men distributed the tickets and reviewed each person's undercover roles and backstories. They reminded everyone to be ready to leave early the next morning.

When the meal was finished, Weber paid Berger and Schultz for the cost of their rail tickets and expressed gratitude to both men for safeguarding his family and helping them reach Basel. Berger acknowledged the gesture and invited Weber and Schultz to his study. There, he poured them each a snifter of brandy and raised his own in a toast. "As we journey to known and unknown destinations, let us pray that God will be with us." Schultz and Weber responded with a hearty "Amen."

The two men then had another brandy and chatted aimlessly until

Schultz became tired and decided to leave for home. As he was about to depart, Weber asked him a favor.

"Walter, do you know anyone in Alpenseite who has a shortwave radio? I want to communicate with Anna's parents and tell them about our travel arrangements."

Schultz replied, "As a matter of fact, Robert, I have a friend who fixes shortwave radios. I'll introduce you to him if you come with me to the village."

Schultz led Weber into the village and guided him through several alleys until they arrived at an Appliance Repair shop. Schultz knocked on the front door, and a young man holding a baby greeted them. Schultz shook the man's hand and introduced him to Weber.

"Hello, Jonas. I understand it's late, but I have a request. This is Robert Weber, and he urgently needs to contact his family in Switzerland. Might you have a shortwave radio that he could use?"

"You're in luck, Walter," Jonas replied. "I have two shortwaves in my shop for repair, and I managed to fix one today. Although my house is a bit of a mess, you're welcome to come in, and Robert can use the radio to contact his family."

Jonas welcomed Weber into his shop as Schultz bid them farewell and left. After showing Weber the radio, Jonas went to another part of the house. Weber turned on the radio, dialed the agreed-upon frequency, and spent most of the night trying to reach Aaron Gabel. Finally, just before dawn, Gabel responded, and Weber was able to inform him about their travel plans.

Winter 1928: Basel, Switzerland

After briefly stopping in Stuttgart and Freiburg, Germany, the train arrived at the Basel Hauptbahnhof just after sunset. It pulled up alongside a crowded platform, where Aaron and Ruth Gabel eagerly waited to meet the passengers.

Weber, Anna, and Luka were sitting in their coach, looking out the window, searching the crowd for Anna's parents. Anna saw them first and couldn't contain her excitement. She quickly rose from her seat and ran out of the coach to meet them on the platform. Weber and Luka collected the threesome's coats and packs from the overhead bin and joined Anna and her parents.

After an emotional reunion, Aaron Gabel led everyone to a taxi stand outside the station and hailed a cab. Once the taxi was weaving through the evening traffic, Aaron explained that he and Ruth were living in an apartment on the city's south side that a Swiss immigration official had arranged for them. "It's temporary housing and not luxurious, but we have an extra bedroom, and you're welcome to stay with us. There's also a pull-out couch for Luka to sleep on."

Weber and Anna glanced at each other approvingly and then graciously accepted. "You have no idea how good that sounds to us, Aaron," Weber said. "After everything we've been through, we're just glad to be alive and here with you in Switzerland."

Upon reaching the apartment, the three travelers unpacked and then joined Aaron and Ruth in the kitchen for a late-night snack. Aaron was curious to know how the three of them had made it out of Germany and asked for details of their trip.

Weber took a deep breath before saying that he wasn't ready to revisit all the painful experiences that they had endured. Nevertheless, he agreed to provide a brief account of their escape and assured Aaron that he would share the details later. Anna showed her support by placing her hand on top of Weber's and nodding in agreement.

Weber began by talking about the destruction of the aircraft at the Alpine hut and then recounted some of the highlights of their trek across the Alps. This included the sniper's pursuit, their crossing of the crevasse, the avalanche that followed, and their eventual arrival at the rail maintenance building. He then summarized the events that led to his separation from Anna and Luka and how they were finally reunited at Trinity Church in Alpenseite.

Aaron and Ruth listened attentively to Weber's story, amazed by all the twists, turns, and close calls. After Weber described the trio's reunion at Trinity Church, Aaron asked how they had made it from Alpenseite to Switzerland.

Anna interrupted her father, saying, "Dad, can't we talk about that tomorrow? Discussing this right before bedtime may increase the chances of having nightmares tonight." Aaron apologized, but Weber continued and explained the details of how he had met Schultz and Berger and went on to describe the plan they had devised.

Aaron appeared to be in disbelief. "So, let me get this straight. Are you saying that Schultz and Berger accompanied you on the train and pretended to be your companions throughout the journey? What made them do that?"

Weber chuckled. "They were just kind-hearted, religious individuals who despised the Nazis. And they didn't travel with us for the entire journey; they disembarked in Freiburg and caught an express train back to Alpenseite."

Aaron was still curious. He then asked, "Did everything go according to plan? Did you face any difficulties with the railway authorities?"

Weber said the journey was mostly uneventful except for one incident where detectives boarded the train in Stuttgart and asked to see everyone's papers. "The detectives were obviously searching for someone, but they didn't specify who. For all I know, they were trying to find the three of us. Berger was traveling with Luka, pretending to be his father. That man should have been an actor because he played his part perfectly. The police believed every word he said, and Luka nodded while Berger talked, lending credibility to his tall tales. The two of them gave a virtuoso performance."

Luka beamed, and his grandfather patted him on the back. "Well done, Luka. I knew you had talents but didn't realize acting was among them. Maybe you should be in movies or the theater."

"Oh, Grandpa, be serious," Luka said. "It doesn't take talent to nod while someone's talking. Berger did all the acting."

Aaron laughed and then shifted his gaze back to Weber, anticipating more details.

"It's time we all went to bed," Anna announced. "Dad, let Robert finish this story tomorrow."

But Weber had warmed to his topic and kept talking. He explained that things became tense when three detectives entered their coach and questioned Schultz, Anna, and himself. "While the detectives were checking our identification papers, Schultz pulled out his blueprints and began describing his bridge construction project. He introduced Anna and me as consulting engineers from Switzerland who had visited his site. However, the detectives paid little attention to Schultz and instead started scrutinizing Anna. They had doubts that she was an engineer and kept questioning her. As time passed, Anna began to feel frustrated, and the situation finally reached a boiling point when one of the detectives stated that he did not believe that Anna was, in fact, an engineer. Anna stood up, looked the detective in the eye, and asked if he knew how to calculate the maximum shear stress of a stationary beam. The detective smirked and demurred but asked her to explain what she was talking about. Anna called him a fool and elaborated on several esoteric concepts such as statical moments, cross-sectional beam width, and the moment of inertia around a neutral axis. The detective looked astonished and stood there speechless. When the other detectives laughed, he walked away in a huff."

Aaron looked amused and asked his daughter why she had quizzed the detective about that particular engineering principle.

"I knew it was possible they were looking for a female engineer and might be trying to bait me, so I was careful not to bring up anything related to aircraft. That's why I decided to quiz the cop about a basic engineering formula applicable in many contexts, including bridge construction."

"That was smart," Aaron replied. "But given how those detectives responded, I suspect they didn't know they should be looking for a female engineer."

"You're probably right, Dad. But I couldn't foresee that then, so I had to play the odds."

Weber checked the clock and noticed that it was past midnight. He felt exhausted after the long train ride and the evening's storytelling session. His yawn prompted Anna and Luka, who were equally exhausted, to say goodnight and leave the kitchen. Weber stayed momentarily to express his gratitude to Aaron and Ruth for meeting them at the train station. Afterward, he told them he would see them in the morning and went into the living room, where Luka was setting up the pullout couch.

As Weber walked past the couch, he bid Luka a good night's sleep. He hadn't intended to say anything else but paused to look Luka in the eye and was suddenly overwhelmed with emotion. "Luka, there's something I've meant to tell you--something that might upset you. It's a confession of sorts, and I'd like to get it off my chest."

Weber knew in his heart that it was time to tell Luka about his complicity in the war operation that might have killed his birth father. He had wanted to tell Luka for some time but couldn't find the right words. Whenever he thought about telling Luka, he would revise the story to justify his actions and make himself seem less culpable. He knew he had to stop telling himself that the event was one of Meissner's lies and do what needed to be done. As he was mustering his courage to tell Luka what he knew, or at least the facts as he knew them, the boy interrupted his train of thought.

"Robert," Luka said, gesturing toward the couch, "Sit down and let's talk. I think I know what you want to tell me."

Weber was surprised by Luka's invitation, as was reflected in the tone of his reply: "I doubt that very much, Luka. I don't see how you could possibly know."

"Is it about my birth father? Because if it is, Mom has already told me what happened."

Weber was flabbergasted. "What? But I don't understand. What did your mother tell you?"

"She said that, during the Great War, you flew a predawn sortie against a German airbase and surprised some soldiers who opened fire on your plane. Your observer returned fire, and one of his bullets went astray and might have killed my father."

"Uh, well, that's essentially correct."

"Mom also said you were flying the plane, and your observer shot at the Germans. So, you weren't the one who pulled the trigger."

"Well, that's true, too. However, I was still involved in the operation despite not firing any weapons. Therefore, I cannot absolve myself from responsibility for what happened."

"But Robert, how do you know what *really* happened? Mom says Gunter Meissner told you this, and we both know he's a liar. That man is untrustworthy and twists everything he says to suit his advantage."

"I see you're familiar with Meissner and his tactics."

"I heard plenty about him when I worked as an intern for the Aviation Coalition. He's also the sniper who pursued us across the mountains. And Mom says he was responsible for the death of your first wife. I think I know enough about him to understand that you and I will never truly know what happened to my father. And, as I said, I don't blame you even if it did happen the way Meissner said it did."

Weber's eyes welled up with tears. "Luka, I don't know what to say. I'm at a loss for words. I've been dreading this moment for weeks. I've been filled with guilt and shame. And here you are, forgiving me even before I figured out how to tell you."

Luka put his hand on Weber's shoulder and spoke quietly but firmly. "Robert, you're a good man. Good men are sometimes asked to do things they detest, like fighting in wars. Since I've known you, you've tried to do what's best for my mother and me. You've always been there for us, and we have a good relationship. Let's not discuss this matter again."

Weber smiled, dried his eyes, and drew a deep breath to regain his composure. "You're an amazing young man, Luka--wise beyond your years. I think of you as my son, and I hope someday you can think of me as your father. Thank you for understanding."

During breakfast the next morning, Aaron said it was time for the family to leave Switzerland and travel to the United States. He revealed that he had made travel arrangements soon after Weber contacted him via shortwave from Alpenseite.

Upon hearing Aaron's declaration, Weber and Anna exchanged perplexed looks and decided to ignore it. They were exhausted from their travels and were not interested in embarking on another international journey, especially a longer one.

Aaron was annoyed by Weber's and Anna's silence and looked to Anna for clarification. Anna sighed and, to keep the peace, she tried to explain why they were not ready to travel.

However, Aaron wasn't to be dissuaded. He pointed out that Anna had not yet petitioned the Swiss authorities for asylum, which meant that she didn't realize there was a limit on how long they could stay in Switzerland. Aaron said that he and Ruth had reached that limit, and they needed to leave immediately. He thought it safer for them to travel together and hoped that Anna, Weber, and Luka would accompany them.

Anna's expression changed as she listened to her father. She turned to look at Weber again, but this time with a look of defeat. Weber also appeared defeated, realizing that Aaron's arguments had shed an entirely new light on their situation. He had already accepted the inevitable: they would soon be on their way to America.

Weber turned and spoke to Aaron, his tone irritable. “Fine, Aaron. You win. When are we leaving, and what's the itinerary? What route will we take through Europe and which seaport have you chosen?”

Aaron shrugged. “Robert, I'm not trying to take over. I'm just trying to be helpful. We can discuss the travel arrangements and make changes if necessary. So, let's start fresh. I'll tell you what I've arranged, and you and Anna can share your thoughts. Let's work together on this.”

Aaron's counterproposal helped to ease Weber's and Anna's frustration, and they agreed to cooperate. To begin the discussion, Weber asked Aaron about his plane and how it fit into his planned travel arrangements. “Are you intending to transport some of us in your aircraft?”

“I'm sad to say, Robert, that I sold my plane shortly after we arrived in Switzerland. I met a man at the Basel airport looking for a crop duster, and he was impressed with my plane's configuration and made a good offer. Also, it may surprise you that while you were trekking across the Alps, Ruth and I sold our farm. It wasn't an easy decision, but we are trying to move on from the past and invest in our future. We plan to use the money to build a new life in the United States.”

Aaron's news was unexpected, and it surprised Weber and Anna. “I can only imagine how hard it must have been for you, Dad,” Anna said while trying to sound sympathetic. “But I think it was the right decision for you and Mom.” Weber nodded in agreement and then asked Aaron to give a brief overview of the travel plans he had organized.

When Aaron spoke, he did so tentatively and was careful not to sound too definitive. “I made reservations for everyone to travel by train from Basel to Geneva and then to Paris. We were to spend the night in a Paris hotel and then fly to London the next day. From London, I booked us passage on a ship to Boston.

Weber and Anna both nodded in agreement as Aaron outlined his travel plans. The itinerary he had proposed and the modes of transportation he had selected seemed reasonable. They exchanged glances, feeling guilty for their earlier reluctance to accept Aaron's plans due to exhaustion.

“I have one minor change to suggest, but I think we owe you an apology, Aaron,” Weber said sheepishly.

Anna concurred, “Yes, we do, Dad, because it’s a good plan. You seem to have thought of everything.”

Aaron smiled. He didn’t hold grudges, especially toward his loved ones. “I accept your apology. Now, Robert, what change would you like to make?”

“My friend, Curtis Taylor, lives in Paris, and I’d like to see if we can stay with him before our flight to London.”

“Of course,” Aaron replied. “That would reduce our expenses too. Use our phone to call him. Now, can you get packed and be ready to leave tomorrow morning? We have a train to catch.”

Winter 1928: Paris, France

Weber, Anna, Luka, and Anna's parents arrived at the Gare de Lyon station in Paris after 7 in the evening. The journey from Basel took most of the day, even though the train reached speeds of over 180 kilometers per hour in some areas of rural France. Weber hailed a cab outside the station and instructed the driver to take them to 25 Place du Panthéon.

The taxi navigated through Paris's narrow, hilly streets while other drivers swerved into their traffic lane and honked aggressively. Eventually, the cab stopped by a sidewalk across from the Panthéon, and the driver informed them that they had arrived at their destination. Weber glanced at Anna and realized she had dozed off during the drive. He wondered how she had managed to sleep during a trip that reminded him of a rough-and-tumble carnival ride. He gently woke her up, walked to Curtis' apartment, and knocked loudly on the door.

Curtis Taylor opened the door, welcomed everyone warmly, and invited them into his apartment. He offered Aaron and Luka a tour, which they eagerly accepted. However, Anna and Ruth were tired and asked for a bathroom and a place to sleep. Curtis chuckled and said he understood why they were exhausted. He took them to the second floor and showed them separate bedrooms with attached bathrooms.

After the tour, the men gathered in the kitchen while Curtis prepared a light meal. He opened two bottles of wine and filled a goblet for each guest. The men laughed and joked while they enjoyed their wine, and when the food was ready, they sat around a large marble table and ate and talked until the early morning hours.

Aaron and Luka decided to call it a night and left the kitchen. Before Weber could leave, Taylor approached him and suggested they meet in his study. Although Weber was tired and wanted to sleep, he accepted the invitation because he knew Curtis wouldn't have asked unless it was important. He wondered if it had anything to do with the conditions he had stipulated for his return to Washington. When he contacted Curtis to organize their stay in Paris, he presented a list of requests, believing he had some leverage until Anna handed over the design portfolio.

Taylor's study was even more lavish than Weber had remembered. As Curtis lit a fire in the fireplace, Weber walked around the room admiring the original artwork on the walls. Once Taylor was satisfied that the fire had caught, he gestured Weber towards a plush armchair and sat opposite him.

"Robert, I know you are curious about what Furst had to say about your return to the States. I told him about your requirements, and he was amenable to most, but he also imposed some conditions."

"I expected as much," Weber said sarcastically. "So, what are they—what are his conditions?"

You asked Furst to arrange for Carl and Luka to attend an aeronautical engineering program at a first-class university, preferably your alma mater. After some investigation, it appears that both boys would have to pass an early entrance exam and possibly complete some high school equivalency classes. They would also have to demonstrate proficiency in English. However, the Director of Admissions at your alma mater told Furst that the boys' outstanding performance at BTS practically ensured that they would be granted admission."

"That's good news, Curtis. Thanks for sending their application forms and arranging for BTS to transfer their records."

"I'm glad I could help you. Now, let's talk about tuition fees. You asked Furst to cover the educational expenses for both of your boys, and he has agreed. However, he has also set a condition that, in exchange, the boys must work for him or a member of his staff for a period that he deems necessary to serve their country."

Weber shook his head and frowned. "When does Furst want the boys to work for him—while they are in school or after they graduate?"

Taylor laughed derisively. "Either, or both, take your pick."

"Figures," Weber snorted. "And what does he mean by a period he deems necessary?"

"He didn't say, but he's not known for releasing people from their obligations," replied Taylor.

Weber smirked. "Yeah, tell me about it. That's a lesson I've learned firsthand. Okay, so what about flight training?"

"Furst asked me to investigate some flight schools in or near Boston, and I found several good options. The school you attended is likely the best choice. The school administrator there said he would be happy to do a 'legacy admission' for your boys, given that you are a graduate. I shared this information with Furst, who decided that paying for the boys' flight training would be in his best interest."

Weber appeared confused and asked, "What does Furst mean by that? How would Furst benefit from the boys' flight training?"

"I suspect Furst has plans to assign the boys some tasks in the future which would require aeronautical skills," Taylor stated.

Weber did not like the sound of that and asked for clarification. "What kind of tasks? What is Furst planning?"

Curtis replied, "I don't know, Robert. Furst never reveals all his plans; he plays everything close to the vest. But think about it; those skills made Furst interested in you as an agent."

Winter 1928: Southampton, England, On Board the RMS Majestic

Early the next morning, Curtis Taylor drove his visitors to Paris-Le Bourget airport and said farewell before they boarded their flight to London. Two hours later, the five travelers arrived at the docks in Southampton, England, and boarded the RMS Majestic passenger liner, which would soon sail across the North Atlantic on a four-day journey to Boston.

After settling into their respective rooms, Weber and Anna joined her parents on one of the ship's upper decks. They sat outside on lounge chairs, enjoying the view as the liner left port and steamed toward the English Channel. Luka had already gone off to explore other parts of the ship. A waiter approached the foursome and asked if they wanted to order a drink. Weber and Anna placed their orders, and so did Aaron and Ruth. They leaned back on their lounge chairs and gazed out to sea, feeling utterly relaxed for the first time in years. It was a liberating experience they hadn't felt since childhood, a kind of freedom they had forgotten was possible.

After the waiter had served their drinks, Weber raised his glass and proposed a toast. "To our new lives in the United States," he said. Anna, Aaron, and Ruth raised their drinks and repeated Weber's toast before tapping their glasses together. Then, all four of them leaned back in their chairs, drink in hand, and looked out to the sea. For the next several moments, the collective mood became pensive as each of the four individuals thought about their future and what it would take to establish their new lives in the United States.

Aaron was contemplating what he could do in America that would provide him with a sense of purpose and worth. He had devoted a significant part of his life to fighting against the Nazis, and although it had been a vital part of his life, he was relieved that it was over. He had been constantly anxious about Anna and her association with people like Hermann Göring and Gunter Meissner. In addition to that, the espionage activities he and his team carried out in Bavaria had caused him considerable stress. All of this had taken a toll on him.

Glad that this part of his life was behind him, Aaron thought about the changes that lay ahead. He wondered if he and Ruth had enough money to purchase a farm in America and whether he was too old to lead a farmer's life. After selling the family business in Munich, he became a farmer and found it the most rewarding thing he had ever done. It had become his identity, and he wasn't sure what else he could do if he couldn't be a farmer in America. He knew people his age who had retired, lost their sense of purpose, and gone downhill physically and mentally. He couldn't imagine just walking in the park or sitting on the couch reading newspapers and magazines all day. He had always led an active life in Germany and wanted to earn an income sufficient to support his family while doing something that gave him a sense of purpose and satisfaction.

Ruth’s feelings about relocating to the United States were mixed, mainly because she found it hard to imagine a life outside Germany. Having lived near Munich since birth, she cherished her Bavarian roots, even though she was happy to be free of the Nazis. Living on the farm had been a fulfilling experience for her, and now she was mildly anxious about adjusting to a new culture, language, and lifestyle. However, she found solace in the fact that Anna, Luka, and her husband were making the move with her and would be a constant part of her new life. Ruth hoped they would live close to her, on the same street or at least in the same city, so she could see them often and remain a part of their lives.

Anna imagined America as a place where she and her family could start a new life, free from their struggles in Germany. When they boarded the ship, she felt relieved that her parents and brother Luka were finally safe and sound. She had been worried about them for a long time and was glad they were on their way to America. As she thought about the future, she considered the design portfolio she had taken from her Air Coalition colleagues and carried with her across Germany and France, hidden in the bodice of her coat. She had guarded it obsessively and was now unsure about giving it to Furst, someone she had never met before. From Robert's comments about Furst, Anna wasn't sure she would like him. However, she trusted Robert and Curtis Taylor, who had assured her that Furst would use the portfolio to promote peace and prevent another war. Anna loved her country, or at least the Germany she grew up in, and did not want its citizens to suffer another war.

As Weber thought about his return to the United States, he reflected on the changes he had gone through since he and Carl had moved to Berlin. He realized he was a different person now compared to the man he was when he arrived in Berlin. Some things changed him for the better, such as meeting Anna, raising Carl and Luka with her, and having a few meaningful experiences as a church intern. However, he suspected that other things had changed him for the worse, such as pretending to be someone he wasn't, sneaking around in places where he didn't belong, and leading a life where lying and spying came as naturally as breathing. He wondered whether embracing those twisted forms of morality had permanently damaged his psyche. He didn't know if he could ever return to being the man he used to be or if that part of him was gone forever. This realization made him feel empty and resentful, but he knew he had no one to blame but himself.

As Weber's mood darkened, he realized that overthinking his past was making him feel depressed, so he shifted his focus toward the future. He tried instead to think about all the exciting things he had to look forward to. Soon, he would be able to live with his family as an average person without having to hide his identity. He could spend his time doing what he loved and be happy.

Those thoughts began to lift his spirits, but then he remembered what Curtis had said about Furst's desire to see him as soon as he arrived in the States. He wondered why Furst was so eager to meet with him. Was it to obtain the design portfolio, or did he have another assignment in mind? Weber wasn't sure if he would accept another assignment because he had other priorities. He and Anna needed to decide where to live and find a suitable house. Furthermore, he'd hardly ever had time to spend with his sons, especially Carl, and wanted to be a reliable and consistent figure in their lives. He wanted to assist Carl and Luka in their education and support them as they established their identities and careers. He realized that these goals were the most important to him and made a commitment to achieve them.

As the RMS Majestic sailed through the English Channel and rounded the Isle of Wight, Weber and his companions ordered another round of drinks and continued their musings. They had four days before reaching Boston, giving them enough time to plan their new lives in the United States. Weber knew that whatever was on everyone's minds would eventually be discussed during onboard conversations. He took comfort in that--they were his family, and he wanted what was best for them. He looked forward to helping the others figure out their futures, even if it meant negotiating disagreements or changing some of his plans. Until then, he planned to make the most of his downtime by resting, recovering, and preparing for any challenges that Furst had in store for him.

Author Note

The Spy in the Berlin Sky is a work of fiction, meaning that all the events, characters, dialogues, and interactions depicted in this book are fictitious. However, to provide a sense of historical context and authenticity, the story incorporates specific factual dates, events, locations, buildings, characterizations, and references to deceased public figures. It's important to note that any resemblance to actual persons is purely coincidental, as all the activities that occur or are implied in *The Spy in the Berlin Sky* are purely a product of the author's imagination.

The book's historical timeline begins just before World War I, in the spring of 1912, and ends approximately halfway through the interwar period, during the winter of 1928. The events in the prologue (Spring, 1912) occur about two years before WWI was declared in August 1914, when some of the principal German characters were still teenagers. Chapter 1 picks up about six months later after the war has begun, when some of the same German teenagers, along with their French counterparts (and the American, Robert Weber), have joined the air forces of their respective nations--the Fliegertruppen des deutschen Kaiserrreiches (Imperial German Air Service) or the French Air Service (FAS)—and become the first generation of young men to utilize aircraft to do battle in the skies. Here, the story is told from the perspectives of the German and French aircrews, both observers and pilots, and the events and settings are drawn from historical accounts of how the air war was waged during that period. It was during this era of the war (Spring 1915) that Hermann Göring first served as an airborne observer and began hanging precariously outside his cockpit's confines to photograph enemy armaments. Several months later, in October of 1915, Göring became a fighter pilot and went on to establish his reputation as a fighter ace and win the Blue Max or Pour le Mérite (March 1918).

The prospect of piloting combat aircraft at night is introduced in Chapter 1 when Robert Weber and his superior, FAS pilot Francoise Durand, contemplate flying an aerial reconnaissance mission before daybreak. According to historical accounts (e.g., Allaz, 2004), pilots attempted nighttime flights as early as 1910, but these voyages were primarily short experimental or trial flights. However, during World War I, such flights were undertaken more regularly out of necessity. Historical accounts suggest that these flights were arduous and perilous due to the lack of reliable avionics, the inability to visually track unknown terrain and avoid unseen obstacles, and unpredictable weather conditions. By the late 1920s, night flights became more common and were used for air mail and passenger services.

The Nieuport 10, flown by Durand and Weber in Chapter 1, was a French fighter and reconnaissance aircraft used extensively by French military pilots during World War I. The biplane was notable for its unique V-shaped struts and unequal-sized wings (the upper wing was larger). Fighter plane variants often featured Vickers machine guns mounted on the top wing.

Chapter 2 of the book is set in late 1920, more than two years after World War I ended in November 1918. The story revolves around the main character, Robert Weber, who now lives in Stockholm, Sweden, and works as a pilot for Svensk-Luft Trafik Airlines. Svensk-Luft Trafik Airlines was founded in 1919 and sponsored its inaugural flight in 1920. One of the first pilots hired by the airline was Hermann Göring. In the early months of 1920, Göring flew Count Eric von Rosen to his estate, Rockelstad Castle, where he met Baroness Carin von Kantzow. Göring became interested in the Baroness, and after a somewhat tumultuous courtship that endured for many months, he eventually married her in February of 1922 (as described in Chapters 5 and 7).

The Fokker F. VII trimotor is mentioned in Chapter 2 as one of the airplanes Svensk-Luft Trafik Airlines obtained through the fictional character Gunter Meissner, who was depicted as a representative of the Dutch aircraft company Fokker Aircraft. The Fokker Trimotor, also known as the F-7, was one of the largest planes of its time and could carry up to twelve passengers. Although the book's characters and storyline are fictional, the airplane and the company that manufactured it were real (Hegener, 1961).

Tromsø is a town in Norway that lies over 200 miles north of the Arctic Circle. Robert and Anna Weber were trying to reach this location when their F-7 crashed on the tundra, as described in Chapters 3 and 4. Tromsø has a rich history, dating back to 1250, and it became a center for Arctic hunting and trading in the late 1800s and early 1900s. According to some accounts, Tromsø was a common destination for Russian immigrants who crossed the border into Norway illegally.

Chapter 6 takes place in 1921 and follows Robert Weber as he departs from Sweden and lands a job at Martin Aircraft Company in Washington, DC. Although the company is fictional, it is based on the real-life Martin Company, which was active from 1917 to 1961 and produced bombers for WWI and other military and commercial aircraft. In this part of the story, Gunter Meissner and Hermann Göring also leave Sweden and return to

Germany. Historical records suggest that Hermann Göring resigned as a pilot at Svensk-Luft Trafik Airlines in Sweden and returned to Munich during the summer of 1921. He then enrolled in university, where he studied political science.

As referenced in Chapter 7, Hermann Göring had his first encounter with Adolph Hitler in the fall of 1922, after which he assisted Hitler with the development of the Sturm Abteilung (SA), or military arm of the Nazi party. The SA was assembled in Munich by recruiting men from the ranks of post-WWI paramilitary groups (e.g., the Freikorps) and the unemployed. Members, sometimes referred to as brownshirts or stormtroopers, wore brown uniforms modeled after Mussolini's fascist "Blackshirts" and served a variety of purposes, including protecting Nazi officials and party meetings, perpetrating violence against political opponents (e.g., Communists, Social Democrats), and persecuting religious, racial, and cultural groups that Nazi ideology unjustly denigrated or blamed for perceived social, economic, political, or moral woes.

Some of the German characters in this story, such as the fictional character Gunter Meissner, express strong resentment towards the Treaty of Versailles because they regard it as the main reason for Germany's economic and political downfall after the First World War. For Meissner and others in the story (e.g., Hermann Göring, Adolph Hitler), the Treaty of Versailles and the politicians who enforced it during the Weimar era served as a rallying point for political resistance. Over time, the Treaty, along with other grievances, was used to justify their seditious and subversive political activities.

The Treaty of Versailles was signed on June 28, 1919, in the Palace of Versailles near Paris. The treaty held Germany accountable for World War I and imposed several obligations to compensate for their war guilt, including paying reparations to the Allied Powers ($33 billion by some estimates), giving up domestic and foreign territories, significantly reducing their military forces (limiting their army to 100K soldiers), and banning the production of military equipment and munitions (such as tanks, submarines, airplanes, and poison gas). Although some concessions were made in the years after the Treaty was ratified, many historians like John Maynard Keynes viewed the terms of the Treaty of Versailles as unjust and oppressive and as contributing to Germany's economic and political instability during the Weimar era, leading to the rise of militarism and ultimately the establishment of the Nazi Party.

Hitler and the Nazi's 'Beer Hall Putsch' and subsequent march on the Defense Ministry in Munich's Marienplatz, as described in Chapter 7, occurred on November 8th and 9th, 1923. The Marienplatz, or Mary's Square, is the central square of Munich, which includes the old and new city hall and other government buildings. Originally established as a marketplace in 1158, it remains a bustling hub of activity in the city today.

The Nazi party was one of several extreme right-wing political factions that congregated in Bavaria to foment unrest and work against the Weimar government in Berlin. These right-wing, nationalist, and often militaristic groups emerged in response to the instability and turmoil that developed throughout Germany after the implementation of the Versailles Treaty. They also sought to counter the influence of other political factions that sought to reshape German politics and government during this era.

Political assassinations, hyperinflation, national boundary and territorial disputes, and resentment towards the Versailles Treaty and war reparations marked the early years of the Weimar Republic. Moreover, the political environment during this era was divisive and rife with extreme political ideologies. The principal aims of right-wing political groups were to (a) counter or eliminate perceived threats from centrist and leftist factions, such as Social Democrats and Communists, (b) terminate the payment of war reparations to Allied countries, and (c) end (i.e., overthrow, replace) the Weimar government in Berlin.

Hitler's intention in undertaking the 'Beer Hall Putsch' was to initiate an insurrection against the Bavarian government in Munich as a step toward building an insurgency that would eventually unseat the Weimar government in Berlin. He, along with more than 20 Nazi officials (including Hermann Göring and Rudolph Hess) and 600 members of the SA, entered the Bürgerbräukeller, a Munich beer hall, on the evening of November 8th, where the Bavarian Prime Minister, Gustav Ritter von Klar, and two prominent local officials (i.e., Hans Ritter von Seisser, police chief; General Otto von Lossow, local army commander) were addressing an audience of several thousand business people. Hitler had previously sought support from Klar, Seisser, and Lossow for his coup and, as a reward, promised the men prominent political positions in a prospective Nazi-led government. Klar, Seisser's, and Lossow's recalcitrance motivated Hitler to act independently. He, his Nazi associates, and the SA stormed the Bürgerbräukeller, took Klar, Seisser, and Lossow hostage, and demanded that they join his putsch. The three officials agreed to cooperate, but their consent was proffered at gunpoint under duress.

The next day, Klar, Seisser, and Lussow recanted, and the popular support Hitler was expecting from the local Munich community failed to materialize, which caused the putsch to collapse. Rather than admit defeat,

Hitler and his associates enlisted the help of Erich Ludendorff, a well-known WWI general, who, partly on his own initiative, led a march of more than 2,000 armed men (mostly SA or brownshirts) on the Bavarian Defense Ministry in central Munich. As the marchers, including Hitler, Göring, and other prominent Nazis, approached the city center, they were challenged and fired upon by a phalanx of police officers. In the scuffle that ensued, Hitler fell and injured his arm, Göring was shot in the groin, and several police officers were killed. Hitler and Göring fled the scene. Hitler remained in Germany and was arrested two days after the march, tried for sedition, and sentenced to five years in Landsberg prison. He wrote *Mein Kampf* while incarcerated and was released on December 20, 1924, after serving only about nine months. Göring, who was seriously injured, went into hiding and eventually, with the aid of his wife Carin and her friends, entered Austria on a false passport and lived in exile until the fall of 1927. While living outside Germany, the Görings struggled financially, and Hermann suffered physically because his wounds were painful and slow to heal. To manage his pain, he regularly took morphine, and once addicted, his behavior became unstable, leading to violent outbursts.

In Chapter 8 of the book, Troy Furst recruits Robert Weber to work as a spy in Berlin. Furst is characterized as a Colonel in Army Intelligence within the United States War Department. It's important to understand that in the 1920s and 1930s, the United States did not have a centralized intelligence agency like the CIA, which was established in 1947, long after the interwar period. Before the CIA, the Office of Strategic Services (OSS) was the only intelligence agency, and it was active only during World War II from 1942 to 1945. The origins of Army Intelligence have been traced back to the Revolutionary War, and historical accounts indicate that its structures and purposes evolved over the 19th and 20th centuries in response to armed conflicts (e.g., wars) and the changing needs for military intelligence (Bigelow, 2012). During WWI, Army Intelligence rapidly expanded its operations in the War Department and overseas. They gained expertise in cryptology and gathered intelligence on foreign armies and socio-economic and political conditions worldwide. Although its size and purposes were curtailed after WWI, it continued to operate during the interwar period and worked to advance new technologies in aerial photography, radar, and cryptography.

At the end of Chapter 8, in the spring of 1926, Robert Weber accepts Troy Furst's proposal to gather intelligence on Germany's rearmament efforts. The mission requires Weber to implement and carry out a spy operation to uncover whether the Germans are clandestinely designing and building military aircraft in violation of the Treaty of Versailles.

At the end of WWI, the Treaty of Versailles essentially stripped Germany of its armed forces, including its air force. The Treaty and the armistices that preceded it eliminated the Luftstreitkräft by demobilizing its staff and requiring that Germany surrender tens of thousands of planes and aircraft engines. The Treaty's terms also terminated subsequent aircraft production, prohibited the importation of planes and aircraft parts, and restricted Germany's use of its airspace.

Despite the restrictions imposed on Germany in the early postwar period, certain events and activities laid the foundation for a covert rearmament program. After the German Imperial Army was disbanded, the Allies allowed Germany to create a smaller military organization for peacetime purposes. This force was called the Reichswehr, or Reich Defense, and was established in the early 1920s. It remained active throughout the Weimar era and briefly after that. Although the Reichswehr initially consisted of only army and naval forces, early leaders, such as General Hans von Seeckt, ensured that former aviation officers were represented within the Reichswehr. He prioritized the analysis of tactics that had helped Germany during World War I and formed study groups to evaluate the military strengths of other countries, including their air power. This was done to create more effective military doctrines and tactics. Various formal and informal educational opportunities were created and promoted to expand the ranks of trained military personnel beyond those authorized for the Reichswehr. This included encouraging former officers and recruits to attend seminars, acquire engineering degrees, and participate in disguised training exercises. The training activities were promoted as civilian events, such as airplane races and flight contests for pilots.

Subsequent developments in the early to mid-1920s paved the way for aeronautical rearmament and, ultimately, the creation of a "Shadow Luftwaffe," or secret air force. The development of military aviation in Germany was facilitated by the re-emergence of civil aviation, which was allowed under the Versailles Treaty. Aeronautical engineers, production experts, and ex-Luftstreitkräft officers affiliated with the Reichswehr collaborated with their counterparts in universities and the civil aviation industry to develop and test aviation technology with military applications. While civilian aircraft manufacturers produced aircraft primarily for civilian air travel, some of these planes were deliberately designed so they could easily be modified for military purposes. Some aircraft manufacturers even built and operated aircraft factories outside of Germany to avoid Allied oversight.

Even more influential in the creation of a Shadow Luftwaffe was the establishment of a secret air base outside Germany that was used to train pilots, teach military tactics and maneuvers, test experimental aircraft, and develop offensive aviation strategies and technologies. Located at Lipetsk, Russia, this base operated from 1925 to 1933 and, as Corum (1997) notes, employed "…a staff of 300 Germans, who were engaged as instructors, test pilots, aircraft technicians, and airfield staff. All were secret employees of the Reichswehr" (p. 115). Base operations were set up to allow the testing of prototype fighters and bombers and to provide pilots with training in fighter tactics, bombing strategies for various types of targets, and battlefield navigation.

By the late 1920s, officials from the Reichswehr planned to close the Lipetsk base and instead build a secret air base within Germany. In the early to mid-1930s, the German government began funding the design and development of a real air force, with the Reichswehr playing a significant role in these efforts. Consequently, the references in *The Spy in the Berlin Sky* to a secret or "ghost" air base near Munich, as well as a design portfolio for a future German air force — including Hermann Göring's involvement — are fictional creations. These elements likely emerged before any feasible or actual developments of this nature occurred in Germany.

In Chapter 9, Robert Weber moves to Berlin to build a new life and begin his spy mission. Initially, he searches for suitable housing, enrolls Carl in school, explores the city, begins his internship, purchases a car, meets with his handler, and takes delivery of a spy plane. After settling in, Weber tests his spy plane, begins surveillance operations at a local airport, searches for an elusive female aeronautical engineer, and investigates Carl's extracurricular activities. Throughout this storyline, several prominent Berlin landmarks and locations are featured.

The apartment Weber rents is just south of the Tiergarten, a public park that covers 520 acres of land in the inner city of Berlin. Established as a hunting preserve in the early 1500s, it was created for the Electors of Brandenburg, who were responsible for electing the Emperor of the Holy Roman Empire. The preserve was later expanded for Fredrick Wilhelm and his descendants and was eventually transformed into a public garden with walkways, bridges, statues, and a zoo.

When Weber meets with his handler, Curtis Taylor, he walks from his apartment through the Tiergarten and then heads eastward along the Unter den Linden, which means "under the Linden trees." This broad boulevard has two lanes, one running east and the other west, with a center median lined with Linden trees. Once on the Unter den Linden, Weber walks through the Brandenburg Gate and enters the Hotel Adlon. The original Hotel Adlon opened in 1907 and was a favorite of wealthy socialites and celebrities during the interwar era. With its grand lobby and over 300 rooms, the Adlon was a popular gathering place for locals and tourists. Its fame and longevity also made it a favorite among novelists, journalists, and scriptwriters who, over the years, featured the Adlon in their books, articles, and movies. The original structure was destroyed by fire in 1945 and was replaced by a new hotel, the Hotel Adlon Kempinski, during the 1990s.

Weber takes delivery of a Potez 25 aircraft after his handler, Curtis Taylor, flies it from Paris to Johannisthal Air Field. The Potez 25 was designed in the early 1920s by the Aéroplanes Henry Potez aircraft company in Aubervilliers, France, and entered production in 1925. It was considered a sesquiplane, which differed from traditional biplanes because its lower wing was considerably smaller than its upper counterpart. The prototype was powered by a Hispano-Suiza W-12 engine (451 HP), and most production versions utilized Renault, Farman, Salmson, and Lorraine engines that produced between 500 and 600 HP. The Potez 25 became increasingly popular after winning several air races and rallies, and France and several other countries used it as a fighter, bomber, and reconnaissance plane.

Weber utilizes Johannisthal Airfield to store the Potez 25 and monitor the latest planes developed by German aircraft companies. Johannisthal, established in 1909 and located southwest of Berlin, was the first commercial airfield in Germany. It rapidly became a hub for aviation research and testing, housing various facilities such as aircraft manufacturers, hangars, laboratories, and wind tunnels.

After Carl begins school in Berlin, he frequently participates in extracurricular activities but seldom tells his father what he and his classmates do after school. When Weber finally confronts Carl, he is surprised to learn that his son is involved in activities sponsored by the Hitlerjugend (HJ) or the Nazi Party's youth organization. Established in 1922, the HJ was a paramilitary organization for boys between the ages of 14 and 18 whose purpose was to indoctrinate young men in Nazi ideology and prepare them for military service. Sports and challenging outdoor activities such as hiking and climbing were used to promote physical fitness and tactical skills. Youth meetings and rallies were held to spread propaganda and teach Nazi ideology.

In Chapter 11, Weber chases a phantom German fighter he'd seen previously at Johannisthal Air Field and discovers that his Potez 25 is no match for the speed and agility of the new German monoplane. After reporting the incident to his handler, Curtis Taylor provides Weber with a newer, faster plane—an 'experimental' Dewoitine D-500. The Dewoitine D-500 was designed by Ėmile Dewoitine and built in France. Production versions of this monoplane were used as fighters in the French Armée de l'Air. The aircraft had a metal fuselage and low-mounted cantilever wings. Early versions were powered by a V-12 Hispano-Suiza engine that produced 691 horsepower. In this fictional account, Curtis Taylor obtains a modified prototype with a tandem cockpit. However, in reality, production versions of the Dewoitine 500 series (e.g., D-501 to D-511) had a single cockpit and were commissioned and flown somewhat later during the interwar period (i.e., the early 1930s) than characterized in this story.

Later in Chapter 11, Weber travels to Anna's parents' farm and helps her father, Aaron Gabel, repair a broken-down Caspar C32 that Gabel uses to spray crops and monitor his cattle in Alpine pastures. The Caspar C32 was an open-cockpit biplane originally built in Germany for aerial spraying during the late 1920s.

In chapter 13, Hermann Göring leaves Austria and returns to Germany when the newly-elected President von Hindenburg declares a political amnesty in the fall of 1927. Upon his return, one of Göring's top priorities was to meet with Adolph Hitler in Munich and regain his former position within the Nazi Party, which included his leadership of the SA. However, Hitler was not receptive to this idea because he had already appointed Franz Pfeffer as the head of the SA. Additionally, he knew Göring was destitute and would be a financial burden on the Party. Hitler advised Göring to seek employment in Berlin and return when he was in a position to benefit the Party. Göring took Hitler's advice and moved to Berlin, where he worked in the aircraft industry. He eventually established a successful business with a partner named Paul Koerner.

In early 1928, Göring returned to Munich and requested Hitler's permission to run as a Nazi candidate for the Reichstag in the upcoming May 1928 federal elections. Göring convinced Hitler that his connections with influential business and government officials in Berlin would be beneficial for both the Nazi Party and Hitler's political aspirations. After some consideration, Hitler finally agreed to let Göring stand for the election.

During the months leading up to the election, Göring campaigned tirelessly, especially in Berlin, and won a seat in the Reichstag representing Bavaria. Joseph Goebbels was also elected to the Reichstag. However, as detailed in Chapter 16, the Nazi Party received less than 3% of the vote and won only 12 of the Reichstag's 491 seats. This poor performance was a source of frustration and embarrassment for Hitler, who had expected the Party to win more seats (Manvell & Fraenkel, 2011).

Shortly after Weber's aerial battle with German fighters near a secret airbase, as described in Chapter 14, he is approached by the manager of the airport where he stores his Dewoitine D-500. The manager claims that someone pretending to be a government official has pressured him to report the owners of non-German airplanes, particularly Dewoitine aircraft. Fearing that enemy agents are pursuing him, Weber asks his handler, Curtis Taylor, to swap his French-made Dewoitine with a German-made plane to make it harder for the agents to track him. Taylor, ever the resourceful handler, provides Weber with an experimental Junkers JU 49 with a single prop and a Junkers L88a V-12 engine that can produce 800 horsepower. Junkers developed the JU 49 in the late 1920s and early 1930s to explore high-altitude flight. Made entirely from metal alloys, the experimental monoplane had cantilevered wings, an oversized propeller, and a pressurized cabin.

After Hermann Göring was elected to the Reichstag in May 1928, he became a Reichsminister for Bavaria. As described in Chapter 16, his primary role within the Reichstag was to oversee transportation communications, including the aviation industry. During his time in this role, he strongly supported subsidizing civil aviation and the aircraft industry. He believed the German aviation industry needed to fulfill its patriotic duty (Manvell & Fraenkel, 2011), essentially a covert reference to the need to strengthen and rearm Germany's air force. He also advocated for the appointment of an Air Minister.

During a fictional conversation in Chapter 16, Göring refers to two divisions within the Reichswehr, including the Truppenamt and the Waffenamt. The Truppenamt was established as the Troops Office of the Reichswehr but, in reality, it was staffed and operated as a military command unit, the German General Staff, which violated the terms of the Versailles Treaty. The Waffenamt, or weapons office, was responsible for military weapons and ammunition. Behind the scenes, members of this unit conducted covert research and development activities that furthered Germany's rearmament efforts during the interwar period. According to historical records, personnel within the Truppenamt and the Waffenamt facilitated the development of military aviation. However, there was no official group like the "Aviation Coalition" as mentioned in this story. The "Aviation Coalition" is a fictional concept created to enhance the storyline.

In Chapter 16, the story reveals that Hermann Göring owns a Fokker

D.XII fighter. Gunter Meissner uses this aircraft for a spying mission. Although these plot aspects are fictional, the Fokker D.XII was a real aircraft manufactured by the Dutch company Fokker Aircraft. The plane was only used for a limited time in the interwar period. A sesquiplane, this aircraft had one and a half wings, a single-seat cockpit, and a V-strut undercarriage. Initially, it was equipped with a 300-horsepower Hispano-Suiza V8 engine, which was later replaced by a Curtiss D-12 engine.

Towards the end of Chapter 16, Gunter Meissner mentions Gustave Eiffel's use of a wind tunnel to study wind resistance while explaining to Hermann Göring why the engineers of the Aviation Coalition are interested in the young intern, Luka Gabel. Gustave Eiffel was a renowned French engineer known for designing a wide range of structures, including buildings, bridges, and viaducts. He is particularly famous for creating the iconic Eiffel Tower. In 1909, he constructed a 67-horsepower wind tunnel to investigate the effects of wind on different structures. This wind tunnel became an effective tool for aeronautical research, and Eiffel gained recognition for his experimental work in aerodynamics.

Several airports that existed during the interwar period are mentioned in Chapter 18 of the book. In this chapter, Weber flies to England and lands at Croydon Airport to surveil Gunter's spy mission. Croydon Airport was established in 1920 in Surrey near London and was England's only international airport during the interwar period. It was known for its innovative air traffic control procedures and was the first airport to have a terminal and hotel. Weber also traces Gunter to Mousehold Heath, a former World War I aerodrome located near Norwich on England's eastern coast. Mousehold Heath was renamed Royal Air Force Mousehold Heath after the Royal Air Force was established in 1918, and it was used by the RAF until 1933. Weber and Gunter then fly to France and land their planes at Paris-Le Bourget airport. Paris-Le Bourget airport was inaugurated in 1919 and served as the city's primary airport until Orly Airport was established in 1932. Paris-Le Bourget Airport is renowned as the place where Charles Lindbergh landed the Spirit of Saint Louis after his solo flight across the Atlantic Ocean in 1927.

Later in Chapter 18, Weber meets his friend Françoise Durand, a former WWI pilot and current French Armée de l'Air major, at Vélizy-Villacoublay Air Field. The term Armée de l'Air refers to the aeronautical arm of the French Army, which originated before WWI when it was named the Aéronautique Militaire. Vélizy-Villacoublay Air Field was a significant player in the French aviation industry due to its proximity to Paris, the hub of France's technical and manufacturing industries. The airport served multiple purposes throughout the years, including functioning as a military base, hosting aviation research and development, operating a flight school, and sponsoring numerous air shows.

In Chapter 20, Gunter Meissner's quest to complete extended background checks on Luka Gabel takes him to the Munich Standesamt, or civil registration office. Established in 1876, this office kept official records of the city's births, marriages, and deaths. Every child born in Germany had to be registered at the local Standesamt or registry office.

In Chapter 21, Gunter Meissner visits Munich's Nordfriedhof Cemetery to determine whether a youth named Luka Bergmann is buried there. Nordfriedhof Cemetery is located in northern Munich and is one of the city's largest cemeteries, with tens of thousands of burial plots. It dates from the late 1800s and is the final resting place for many of Bavaria's prominent citizens and luminaries.

Meissner also visits Munich's Neues Rathaus, or New Town Hall, which was built in 1874 to replace the iconic old town hall. The ornately decorated building, constructed of brick and limestone, sits in the northern part of Marienplatz. A prominent city landmark, the Neues Rathaus has 400 rooms and serves as the workplace for many local government officials, including the mayor and members of the city council.

In Chapter 22 of the book, Anna Gabel visits Munich Hauptbahnhof, the city's central train station. Built in 1849, the large, covered multiplatform station is near the city center. Other central city rail stations, such as Berlin Hauptbahnhof, Strasbourg Hauptbahnhof, and Basel Hauptbahnhof, are mentioned elsewhere in the book.

After Anna Gabel shoots Gunter Meissner during a rail journey (Chapter 23), Robert Weber searches for Meissner in Berlin's Charité hospital. The Charité is a group of medical centers located in central Berlin. It has a long history, dating back to the early 1700s, and has maintained strong connections with top German universities. It is renowned for being a significant location for medical research and discoveries, and many of Germany's preeminent physicians, including Nobel Laureates, were associated with the Charité.

In Chapter 24, Weber travels to Strasbourg, France, to obtain two shortwave radios from his handler, Curtis Taylor. Radios that used the shortest band of the radio spectrum were developed during the early 1920s. Shortly thereafter, they overcame many of the disadvantages of longwave radios and became one of the first reliable tools for long-distance wireless communication.

References

Allaz, Camille (2004). *The history of cargo and air mail from the 18th century*. London, England, Christopher Foyle Publishing.

Bigelow, Michael, E. (2012). A Short History of Army Intelligence, *Military Intelligence*, 38, July-September.

Corum, J. S. (1997). *The Luftwaffe*. The University Press of Kansas, Lawrence, Kansas.

Hegener, Henri (1961). *Fokker—The Man and the Aircraft*. Harleyford Publications.

Manvell, R. & Fraenkel, H. (2011). *Goering: The rise and fall of the notorious Nazi leader*. Skyhorse Publishing.

About the Author

Gary W. Ladd was born and educated in the United States and lives in Arizona with his wife, Becky. His international experiences, including extensive travel in Europe and personal and professional ties in cities such as Berlin, have enriched both his academic and personal life. Over the past forty years, he has worked as a professor and researcher at American universities, authoring numerous scientific articles and books. His experiences with air travel and flight training sparked a lasting interest in the history of aviation, particularly the introduction and use of aircraft in the First and Second World Wars.